IN SEARCH OF MRS. PEARSON

A Novel

by
Scott B. Shappell, M.D., Ph.D.

Hekaśa Books are available at quantity discounts with bulk purchase for educational, business, or sales promotional use.

For information, please contact:
Hekaśa Publishing
7324 Gaston Ave #124
Suite 316
Dallas, TX 75214
Phone: 214 - 321 – 4158
Fax: 214 - 827 - 5292
Email: info@hekasa.com
www.hekasa.com

Cover photo by Linda Apple
Cover design by Travis Scott Lee Shappell
Book layout by Scott Baber

ISBN: (13 digit) 9780983229322

For Heidi

Previous praise for *I Reach Over*, a collection of poems and correspondence on ALS, death, and living, by Scott B. Shappell, M.D., Ph.D.

"… heart- and spirit-filled collection of poetry…"
  - MDA/ALS NEWSMAGAZINE

"I love everything about this book, from the cover to the way [the author] structured the contents, to the actual context of every fragment, sentence, and even word. The poems, the letters, the bucket list… are so well presented. I sense that we are dealing with a pioneer. It is a spiritual boost beautifully worded by, in my opinion, our newest, great American poet, Scott Shappell."
  - Javier Ramano; Poet, Miami, FL*

"… struggling for words to express about [the] book. I have stopped reading it at night because it is too penetrating and thus disturbing. The one word that keeps coming to mind is 'density'… with reference to the ultra-compactness of thoughts. But then, poetry in particular was always like this: slim volumes for [a] lifetime."
  - Anthony G. Hopkins, Ph.D.
    Walter Prescott Webb Professor of History and Ideas,
    University of Texas; formerly the Smuts Professor of Commonwealth
    History at the University of Cambridge

"… nothing short of amazing…"
  - Jack Groskopf, Ph.D.; Director, Oncology Research and Development, Hologic / Gen-Probe, San Diego, CA

"Thank you for sharing this marvelous work. I am not at all surprised at how well researched and beautiful it is. I would expect nothing less. Thank you for your perspectives on life, love and God. You continue to teach and mentor me as you did a decade ago. I will keep this close by for present and future reference. With love and admiration…"
  - From a reader, Nashville, TN

"… it reflects over the phase between life and death - loving, magnanimous search within one's self as a conduit of spirituality. The past year (or so) has been very difficult for him; yet through the dust shaken up from the realization of his impending departure, a blinding wild light radiates from his entire being. …"
- From a reader, Lubbock, TX*

"It's hard to put down."
- From a reader, Plano, TX

"… I am looking forward to spending some quality time with the poems. I was really glad to see that [the author] included the book list, and [the] correspondence with [his] sister! Love the cover drawing…"
- From a reader, Alpena, MI

"What a powerful book. … it certainly has given me a much better understanding of ALS and [the author's] courageous battle and transformation. Cannot begin to describe my feelings about the book, but it has been therapeutic and my admiration for [the author], always strong, has increased significantly."
- From a reader, Granger, IN

"… you are inspirational… you convey a true feeling that is rarely portrayed…"
- From a reader, Public Library, Key West, FL

"Scott Shappell is a lifelong scholar of remarkable accomplishment. … His brilliant and inquisitive mind… has long inspired those who have encountered him. In this book of poems he relates his experience of loss and impending death. Sometimes dark, but like Scott's life, it is punctuated with moments of surprising joy. It serves well as a guide to others who are enduring a seemingly unendurable trial… [and] as a springboard of self-examination for those who believe their learning from a trial past has ended. One finishes this book with the sense they have shared a glass of wine and an evening of conversation with this exceptional thinker."
- From a reader, Austin, TX*

"… a very inspirational book on many levels. It gives great insight and inspiration to anyone dealing with a catastrophic illness. This is a book that should be read from cover to cover in sequence. This book gives amazing words of wisdom for anyone that has one of these debilitating diseases or a loved one that is stricken. I would give this book an A+."
    - From a reader, Cincinnati, OH*

"I am reading and re-reading your beautiful poems. Thank you for sharing with all of us – the world. Some/most are difficult to read and are so heartbreakingly universal. They are helping me on my human journey."
    - From a reader, Lubbock, TX

"I think the book is great. I loved both the poems and your communications with [your sister] Sally. Thanks for writing it. I look forward to your next efforts. I liked it so much that I ordered two additional copies. One is for my son [---], who is an Episcopal priest, …. He will love it. The other is for the priest at our church, The Rev [---]. She will enjoy it as well."
    - From a reader, Escondido, CA

"I was emotionally drawn by the depth of the writing of *I Reach Over*. It was very real to feel the energy of Dr. Shappell and his given journey. This book would be an excellent read for all Doctors who care for people with this dreaded disease. Thank you Dr. Shappell for bringing me into your life. I highly recommend this book, and hope Dr. Shappell will continue to share his incredible journey."
    - From a reader, Foley, AL*

*On or also on Amazon.com

To the reader: This book contains a substantial amount of medical terminology, regarded as crucial to the establishment of the protagonist's character, the setting, and the plot as revealed within the narrative. There is a glossary of utilized terms at the rear of the book. If the reader encounters a medical or scientific term with which he or she is not familiar, it may be listed in the glossary. Interested readers can quickly look up included terms if desired (as well as by accessing usual on line resources if necessary).

-Editors

BOOK ONE

"Miracles occur in the strangest of places.
Fancy meeting you here."

-Willie Nelson, Yesterday's Wine

I

"I'd better get going. Ms. Valery will be worried about me," Leo said, standing up from the bench and smoothing out his gray wool slacks with the palms of his hands. His pants didn't quite meet the tops of his shoes, with boney ankles protruding out under their covering of his thin, age-worn black dress socks. Although soft from years of laundering, his gray and pink striped oxford shirt still buckled at the waist from being inadequately tucked in. At some point during the hundreds of washings, a light red pasta sauce stain had learned to co-exist with the natural fabric colors, and resided about an inch above and two over, to the left, of the fourth button. It put the finishing touches on a gentle, lived-in look to the man that vaguely expressed a certain degree of peace, likely lacking from at least some of us gathered around him, and certainly lacking from Leo for most of his early life. Leo turned to look at the group as he started to walk away, his age defying, persistent thick, but now just original black-high-lighted gray hair wild in the late afternoon fading sun. He made a mock formal bow and turned to walk across the park, a docile man, with a slight left foot drop I subconsciously noted.

Leo was one of the "regulars" in our increasingly frequent park gatherings. In the almost two plus months that I had been back in Houston and spending some of my "down time" in this manner, I gathered that Ms. Valery was the owner/manager/caregiver at a nearby half-way house that Leo lived at, an apparently competent older woman who cooked hearty meals and provided a degree of stability and constancy in the thankfully more peaceful life of a burnt out schizophrenic. These are the essential identifying parameters that I had deduced about the life of the oldest of my park mates, without spending too much time or mental energy on it or directly questioning Leo or any of the others, all of whom had been around the neighborhood longer than me.

For a while, those of us left behind stared blankly as Leo strolled progressively out of our sight. "Dr. Jeffrey Pearson, Neuro-Immunologist to the Stars, and his Montrose Rejects," as my wife Kim had begun referring to us in passing, a little bit kidding, perhaps, but sometimes with just a hint of condescending tone or resentment that I hadn't really ever noticed in her before. She seemed lately to say such things in an almost tragically objective, not completely condemning, but not particularly affectionate, tone. It also seemed at times to stem more from a slight bewilderment, including as to why someone such as me might engage in this form of socializing with this particular group of companions, and maybe at the same time as reflecting on our own lack of co-habitation…and the various factors, so many…and so many years in the making I suppose…that could have allowed it to happen.

In fact, Kim's designation of my park mates wasn't yet from any first hand encounters with any of the group, but based only on phone conversations in which I had begun, apparently over zealously, recounting conversations between myself and my new friends. I guess despite my enthusiasm, I wasn't painting a too intriguingly glamorous picture of my new acquaintances. But I still thought her label was unfair, if nothing else, because we weren't officially in the Montrose area.

...

I had returned to Houston as the next logical step in a hopefully promising and increasingly brilliant academic medical career. I had moved to Houston towards the end of June to work on the faculty in the Neurology Department at Baylor College of Medicine, in large part to conduct a clinical trial on an experimental drug for the neurological complications of AIDS/HIV infection. As one of my Clinical Psychology colleagues, who had an office down the hall from mine in the Department of Neurology at the Neurosensory Center on Fannin Street, suggested one evening while a group of us were having drinks after a joint clinical conference, I might be returning to a "zone of comfort" or "site of prior glory". I didn't particularly like her, and not just that night. One of her associates, who for reasons alluding me at that moment had also joined us, chimed in that perhaps, instead, I was even running away from something perceived as an increasingly unrewarding or non-energizing relationship, or at least one in which I was scared or unwilling, at this demanding stage of my professional life, to exert the effort it may take to glean its potential true love-coated benefits. I liked him even less, and wondered why, as we hadn't even drank that much by then, they felt entitled to comment on any of this anyway. We hard core science boys didn't think too much of those touchy-feely psychology guys, anyway; with their obtuse psyche-probing questionnaires and fucking ink blots. It didn't seem quite fair that they could practice their trade over pints at The Black Lab, a pub on Montrose, when I wasn't proportionately armed with an MRI machine or at least allowed to do a lumbar puncture on them when they were pissing me off.

The circumstances that collectively over the past decade plus had landed my presently-tired ass on that hard wooden bench in a small park in the middle of a neighborhood a few miles north of my current place of employment in the world's largest medical center may or may not be that worthy of analysis. I had earned my M.D. at Baylor College of Medicine, the anchoring institution of the Texas Medical Center here in Houston, where on top of a rigorous clinical experience, I had been bitten enough by the research bug to then go to the NIH for a three year research-oriented residency in Internal Medicine, one and a half years of which were spent primarily doing basic research in Immunology. My budding clinical interests in Neurology and especially my research endeavors in cell mediated-immunologic attack on neurons, as well as my stellar clinical reviews, publications, and apparently hidden desire for urban intellectual life, then led me to San Francisco. During a four year research oriented Neurology residency at UCSF, I managed to write 14 papers (7 first authored; to be added to my growing list of the 9 I had written, with 5 first authored, while in Bethesda and a supposedly impressive 3, with 1 first authored, as a medical student), an NIH K-23 grant that had been successfully implemented at Baylor, and wedding vows to Kimberly Williamson, the most beautiful woman I had and still have ever seen in my life.

At present, however, I was spending more time trying to meet the Specific Aims of my NIH grant than fulfilling those marriage vows. I believe the official term for what was going on with the latter may be a "leave of absence", although it was never stated as such, but rather masked in the thirty-something lingo of "professional goals". Back in Houston, alone, I had rented a charming little bungalow-style two bedroom house on Portland street, about 5 minutes north of the medical center, a block or so east of Kirby and a block south of Alabama, not to be confused by any of the condescending with the Montrose or nearby Shepherd-Westheimer neighborhoods. From my house, one could, if appropriately demented to seek the company of a group of fellow lost souls, walk down to the next intersection, about seven houses to the east, turn north and go up about three houses, and find there to the right, a small urban park, centered around a children's playground. While my professional life would unfold over the next year in tissue culture dishes in a lab on the seventh floor of the Neurosensory Center, the GCRC (General Clinical Research Center) in the adjacent Methodist Hospital, and the Thomas Street Clinic, my personal life would surprisingly play out or at least be exposed over the same time period in that little park.

...

Currently, those left behind by Leo in the park on a surprisingly not too scorchingly hot and hence beautiful late summer evening included (in alphabetical order; after all, I am a scientist): Carl, Curtis, Frank, and Rick. I was not particularly close to any of these gentlemen, not yet, maybe not ever, but at this stage in my emotional travels, anonymous companionship with the "rejects" was better than the lonelier alternative of sitting alone in my rental house. The fact that my current dwelling had experienced little, if any, of Kim's decorative touches may have said as much as anything about the current or potential current state of things between the two of us. Although I would soon find other ways to fill at least some of the Saturday nights, I would continue to come to the park on weekday evenings, Saturday late mornings, and otherwise tortuously empty Sunday afternoons for the next several months.

It was a toss up on those occasions as to which one was the quietest of the lot, Carl or Rick, although I ascribed fundamentally different explanations for their reservedness. Carl was a tall, thin, and gaunt (in the truest sense of whatever that word means), brown hair and brown eyed man in probably his late forties. He had sunken, tired eyes that either appeared to look at nothing at all, when he seemed to be somewhere far away, or else looked right through you, in a manner that seemed to convey that he knew everything you were thinking, and was judging those thoughts (i.e., negatively) at the same time.

Although patients rarely if ever made me uncomfortable, as after all, they were largely presenting acute issues that had to be dealt with objectively, Carl made me somewhat unpleasantly tense in this more personal setting of "friends". Carl worked at the Bookstar on Shepherd, only a couple of blocks away, a wonderful two-story bookstore made out of a converted old theater. As I would learn in just a matter of weeks, the store also earned its other reputation as a great place to "meet people", especially late at night, although the heterosexual nature of my "hook-up" was probably not the usual circumstance that garnered the reputation of this added shopping benefit. Women apparently just don't seem to be as big of fans of the whole casual sex with strangers thing, although fortunately for me (or unfortunately, depending on your perspective), there are exceptions. Also, fortunately for me, Carl was not on duty that night when I met Maura near the magazine rack at the back of the store.

Carl continually wore the same outfit, or at most imperceptibly slight variations of the same outfit, which I perceived as the uniform of the emotionally burnt out, holier-than-thou "veteran of the human psychic wars". Although I may owe Blue Oyster Cult royalties for the last descriptor (maybe hinting at some of the influences that shaped the fertile but clearly warpable mind of my youth), the basic wardrobe for such an apparently scarred tight-ass included faded, worn-thin-at-the-pressure-points brown corduroy pants, striped Oxford, usually maroon and white, but occasionally blue in the same motif, and a sweater, either gray or dark blue. With a shirt tail or collar ever so minimally stuck out, Carl's simple clothes achieved a look of practicality combined with pseudo or maybe even real scholarly aloofness, yet somehow in the admirable manner of not officially attempting it, as though shelving books and quietly reading in your rooms while avoiding life was the only way to bring this about and with the result that could not be artificially achieved by those prep students and chain-smoking journalists striving everywhere for the "disheveled" look. On Carl's tall and lanky frame, under a still largely full head of thin Jackson Brown kind of hair, and dull alternating with piercing hazel-ish eyes, and a thin neck with bulging Adam's apple, they achieved a battle worn, life-scarred look that was too noble to be compromised by medication. The resultant aura seemed to convey that when he gazed at you disapprovingly for something you said or did, it was because he had said or done the same such things, once, a long time ago, and knew of their terrible consequences. For him, at least, the only way to avoid such

7

little horrors of life was hence to live a quiet existence of solitude, surrounded by books, maybe a cat, a few co-workers (although, only while at work), and occasional casual chats with the other neighborhood guys.

...

In contrast, I always got the impression that Rick's silence was…well…maybe, more… because he likely needed a drink. Talking might require some of the concentration he needed to suppress tremors. This may be unfair; after all, there are more "official" ways to diagnose alcoholism than observing someone being silent around a bunch of other guys that might not be all that much worth talking to anyway, and I am, after all, a physician. Still, Rick struck me as one of those guys whose life was divided into the phases of pre-catastrophe, catastrophe, and post-catastrophe. This daily delicate balance of somehow functioning at a moderately high level despite frequent crisis management may have actually helped him professionally. Rick was, in fact, a personal injury attorney, maybe three to five years out of law school, which he completed here in Houston at the South Texas School of Law after transferring from the University of Texas. His father was a UT Law School alum and a hugely successful Corporate Lawyer in Dallas. After all the proper early life provisions in the Highland Park area of North Dallas, Rick had precariously arrived at UT for law school following obtaining probably only borderline college credentials when still following the proper Dallas plan and attending Southern Methodist University. Being expected to live up to his father's reputation and various other life and ethanol pressures had forced a transfer after his first year of law school and the eventual successful completion in five years of the three year curriculum.

Rick had at least one other member in his current practice, I believe, although I think he was even less steadily functional than Rick. He seemed to always be in Mexico, for reasons that never seemed clearly personal or professional. They had adds on park benches and even on some of the buses, but I don't think they were high scale enough for those inspiring TV commercials with the customers in neck braces counting wads of suit-won cash. Rick was as likely to be the reason for missed appointments as his customers, which from what I had gathered thus far consisted of the likes of Spanish-only-speaking bus boys, Vietnamese women without driver's licenses, and the occasional middle age divorcee stressed to the max because her "no good ex-husband who lives who knows where hadn't made a child support payment in months and now what am I gonna do about getting to work with my car all smashed up."

How did I know all this? Some of it came out in minimal comments during the park conversations. Some larger chunks came all at once during one more personal night when Rick knocked on my door at 2:43 in the morning on a Thursday night, when I had to be at the Thomas Clinic at 7 the next morning, and so I noticed the time with the precision that only a combination of shock and pissed-off can achieve. I didn't even know that he or any of my other Park buds knew exactly where I lived. Neighborhood friends need a certain degree of anonymity or dwelling secretiveness. After all, as boys, we need to subconsciously know that we can masturbate in our own living rooms whenever we want to, whether we actually do or not (that is, whether we do masturbate in the living room vs. bedroom or bathroom), without the fear of being interrupted or even worse, busted, when someone randomly stops by for whatever reason, maybe to borrow a Miller Light or something. This particular night/morning, however, I was actually sleeping (I swear). Rick, with the smell of bar on his work clothes, conveyed to me that his car had been towed, and that he needed a ride to the impound lot. Had I been a little more "awake, alert, and oriented x 3" (to borrow from work talk), I would have asked if he knew for sure that there would be someone there to actually give us the car at this time of the night. Saying that he "really didn't know who else he could hit up" was the closest Rick came to apologizing to me. But, hey, what the hell, I threw some clothes on and drove him to the lot. When we got to the impound lot, we waited for 45 minutes to an hour, while the also rudely awoken attendant (amazingly) came to turn over Rick's car to him. During this time, I learned some of the above work and personal info regarding the gingerly sewn together accomplishments and accidents that constituted my new-found friend's life. Reassuringly to me, for truth even in the context of being a fuck-up is a comforting virtue after all, Rick's car had indeed been towed... because it had been illegally parked while he was at a bar. The latter was certainly not anything I of all people could hold against someone, no matter what time of the day it was. I guess, in some sort of boy code, that's less of a fuck up than having it towed from his own place for not having made payments or some such related reason, which would be the underlying factor for our next such trip, some months from now. Still, the latter such type of circumstance at least could have explained how he may have perhaps rather easily walked around the corner and down the block to my place. Which bar he was at when he supposedly had his car towed I can't remember or if he said the name, I didn't know it, and (sadly, maybe) I probably knew all the ones within even long walking distance of our neighborhood. A question not raised by our sleepy Dr. Pearson that evening, was: If Rick could make it back home or to my place, why didn't he just have whomever drove him take him to get his car? The final touch and I guess the answer to the above was when the attendant came; Rick asked me if he could borrow seventy five dollars to reclaim his car. Fortunately, I had my check book in the pants I had thrown on. I like Rick. Somehow, deep down, subconsciously knowing first hand the little secrets we all have and the occasional emergencies that can occur in any one's daily pursuit of work and pleasure: the various pharmaceutical aids for tests not studied early enough for, and the rare near breakdowns behind what appears to many as perfection, I have a healthy respect, tolerance, and even admiration for what can be revealed at any time of night on any given occasion as the lack of perpetual high competence. The good news is that if I ever need a personal injury lawyer, I now get a "freebie".

...

Frank was our token "gung-ho-American-conservative-with-a-touch-of-mildly-enlightened-good-old-fashioned-southern-bigotry-thrown-in" kind of guy. I guess every boys-in-the-park equivalent of a quilting circle needs one. From what I gathered, he was in his early 50s. A voluntary tour in Vietnam was an inevitable consequence of the patriotism with which he was raised, and neither that nor the daily toil of his subsequent blue collar existence had done anything to dampen his enthusiasm for all things embodied in the life, liberty, and pursuit of happiness program. In the brief time I had known Frank, his comments, his mannerisms, even his clothes and the way he smelt, had conveyed that the high and low points of his recent past and near future, to be celebrated and mourned with the kind of internal joy and pain that extends to the bone marrow, were respectively, the absolutely stunning success of the American military in the Gulf War and Bill Clinton's Satan- or Russia-engineered victory in the last November election over George Bush, a man that ranked only slightly behind Tom Landry, George Washington, Sam Houston, and Ronald Reagan in stature of near-divine greatness.

Additionally, Frank was also our only true native; by that, I don't mean Texas native (all but Leo could apparently lay claim to that), or even Houston native (I think Carl was formed in some dark dungeon on the East side), but the actual damn neighborhood we found ourselves molding our butts to the shape of the park benches in. As far as we could tell, except for basic training and enjoying the hospitality of our "even-though-they-look-different" brothers in anti-Communism in South Vietnam, Frank had lived within a probably five mile radius, maybe even less, of where we now congregated to occasionally aggravate him by "challenging the very principles on which this great land was founded." Frank had gone to Lamar High School, a few blocks up and over on Westheimer, where his father taught mathematics according to the principles and symmetry by which future upstanding citizens should structure their own lives, with a little of the God and Holy Spirit thing thrown in, which, of course, no form of mathematics could come close to understanding or modeling. After graduation, as college was not an option for the true worker bees of that time, Frank had joined the starched collar local work force, as a distributor of some sort in the community, and then as an even stiffer-collared supervisor for a company extinct a few years later; after that point in 1967 or 1968, Frank had volunteered for the Army. Future Mrs. Frank, whom he'd known forever and then courted in the appropriate manner during his distribution and supervision years, understood and supported his decision, with the appropriate tears and expressions of support and Penelope-like commitment, loyalty, and fidelity. It's amazing the kind of details of someone's past life one can gather on lazy Sunday afternoons in varyingly autistic to enthusiastic conversation.

Frank had returned from Vietnam, uninjured physically or mentally, and with the forthrightness and resolution that uniquely accompanies the boy-to-man transition of horrors and fears that are experienced at too young an age and internalized for too long a time, of course married his high school sweetheart. Through a friend of his father's in the neighborhood, he had gotten a job in the Appliance Department at the then relatively new Sears Department Store on South Main, a few blocks east of our Park and just a few blocks away from Frank's house. He had been working there ever since, having been made the head of the Appliance Department in 1978 or so, and now knowing more about refrigerators and washing machines than I could even ever aspire to know about HIV-associated cognitive and motor impairments. He and Mrs. Frank had lived in the same house that they had bought a couple of years before his last official promotion, maybe in 1976 or so, when it was clear that Frank's job and indeed future, appeared stable. During the "glory-years" of the 80s, synonymous with the Reagan-Bush years, a subset during which, according to some figures, as many as 50,000 people were moving to Houston a week, many of which with Satanic or Communist symbols on their cars, such as New York, Pennsylvania, and Michigan license plates, Frank had resisted the temptation of moving out to the 'burbs, places like Sugarland or Missouri City or Pearland, where wholesome family-oriented communities were being established, while his own neighborhood was getting continually more infiltrated by eclectics, homeless, minorities, and homosexuals, maybe sometimes all four in a given individual. This, as it turns out, was part of the Frank life plan, a sacrifice in the great spirit of American dreams, in order to save money (by not buying a bigger house and by being close to work, as to even allow for walking in one of the more traffic plagued metroplexes) for the, appropriately, two great things in Frank's life (in addition to Mrs. Frank); that is, their daughters, Mary and Elizabeth, for whom Frank had been able to fund educations at Texas A & M and U of H, respectively. It was fortunate for us that the Franks had subscribed to this life plan, as it kept him here, nearby us to this day, so that we eclectics (you should see the books Carl reads sometimes…), potentially homeless (i.e., Rick if not careful), minorities (Leo was originally from Italy), and homosexuals had a steady friend and companion to torture and be tortured by in conversation in our little park in the humid corner of the world.

Let's see, which one of the "rejects" am I leaving out? Oh, yes …Curtis.

…

Curtis was, perhaps, the most blue-collar homosexual I had ever met; not that I had thousands of candidates with which to compare him to, and I don't mean in a work-at-a-factory or own-a-K-Mart-wardrobe kind of way. But underneath his frequent subtle and occasional outwardly offensive sexuality and a very mild femininity, manifested mostly by a slightly imperceptible gracefulness of movements, he was still, deep down, but modified a little, a Good 'ol East Texas Boy…in some ways. Hell, he could change the brakes on his car; I can't even change my own oil.

Curtis was thin, but in that natural or youthful and not quite intentionally athletic way, meaning no body fat to speak of and with some lean muscle. From the few times I had seen him with his shirt off, an unavoidable and typically random consequence of living in our particular neighborhood, he was toned, his stomach was flat and firm, but not rock hard, just soft enough perhaps to somehow remind you that whatever shape he was in came totally naturally, that he didn't consciously work at it at all. I suppose, appropriately, that it was the kind of physique that a naturally thin, still quite young and hence metabolically active, guy would have in part from a life style that included long nights of bar hopping, dancing, energetic sex, and eating only for sustenance when standing still long enough to realize that he was starving, having not eaten since…well, not really remembering when.

That kind of naturalness and vitality, being in shape without trying, may make the average gym toiler and Weight-Watcher meal eater a little envious, I suppose. Over the ensuing months, I heard several girls (in addition to more likely to be rewarded guys) make comments to the effect of how cute or dreamy he was. Random older women seemed to always want to take him home and feed him.

The way his thin light brown hair hung over his forehead and eyes, if he wasn't running his hands through it to brush it back out of his face, was as natural and easy as the rest of him. According to a couple of my female colleagues who had seen him, in a few random instances of our being together at various eateries or shopperies in the vicinity, and even my wife, who on one occasion would meet him during the next year, it was particularly his long and beautiful eyelashes that made them "hate him" out of implied jealousy, when commenting on how they would kill for such lashes, and which went along with his twinkling, slightly mischievous and life-filled "puppy-dog" big brown eyes.

Curtis would continue over the next many months to provide a great deal of color to our park encounters, much to mine and Rick's entertainment, Leo's probable oblivion, and Frank's and Carl's consternation.

II

- *Recollections: Houston 1981*

When I started Medical School in 1981, I would not have necessarily predicted that the vast majority of my early "career" would be dedicated to HIV-related research and the care of HIV-infected and AIDS patients. At that time of my maximal medical ignorance, AIDS was a brand new increasingly large blip on the medical and social radar screens, not even known as AIDS at that point. To many, perhaps including me, it had the aura of a mysterious doom that befell individuals, maybe even real people, made so much scarier by the quite realistic potential of becoming a true global plague. With each new statistic on case numbers and death tolls, continually evolving speculations as to how it could be spread (with fear of everything from toilet seats to mosquitoes), there was an increasingly palpable buzz within all societal elements, medicine and science included, that not uncommonly acquired B-horror movie like gut wrenching implications of a civilization-changing disease, but with the bonus shocker that this was real. This so compassionately initially named homosexual plague was quickly emerging as something the likes of which our planetary society had never seen before, a reputation that would only be further substantiated over the next several years.

I remember reading a Newsweek cover story while still a basic science medical student (probably one of the last lay reads I would allow myself for almost a decade with the possible exception of maybe holiday toilet reading) and long before joining the competent medical community, which had the dual journalistic purpose of concretely presenting the dramas of some of the real medical aspects of daily patient care of infected individuals as well as conveying the broader,

14

almost surrealistic doomsday issues, with what I hoped at the time was over-dramatized possible end of the world implications. The next several years would bear out that the latter were not particularly overstated, especially for Africa, but more politically at least, noticeably suffered here at home. With the increasingly "global" economy, however, even if the ridiculously implausible threat of potential direct infection through contaminated toilet seats weren't enough, the shear economic impact of fighting this global menace would make Night of the Living Dead look nostalgically mild.

The tip of the iceberg, now legendary, first reports of unexplained cases of Pneumocystis carinii pneumonia and Kaposi's sarcoma in homosexuals in Los Angeles and New York had appeared in the summer of my greatest content, or incoherence, the one last surge of fun in the sun before the anticipated cracking down in Med School. Once Medical School started, even for those occasionally contacting the outside present, the contemporary, or so-called "real world" and hence a steady surge of panic and judgment-filled commentary on the still being figured out AIDS, the disease necessarily moved to the background of the seemingly millions of things that needed to be learned, or at least memorized, by the frequently paranoid and hopefully sponge-like receptive mind of the typical overachieving medical student. We had no perspective. AIDS was no more a priority in our study at that point than phenylketonuria and galactosemia in Biochemistry or Leptospirosis in Microbiology (none of which I've actually personally encountered as the primary care giver on any Pediatric or Medicine service while in training and outside of an esoteric Grand Rounds conference).

This new epidemic was officially named my second year of medical school, and during the extraordinary work leading to isolation of the candidate causal retrovirus, we were absorbed with the traditional stresses of learning the structures of the brachial plexus, the enzymes of the Kreb's cycle, which bacteria were Gram-positive or Gram-negative, and the histopathology of grand old diseases such as Rheumatic Heart Disease. Of course, the specter of this latest doomsday disease (not every generation of trainees actually gets a legitimate one....) often manifested in the non-curriculum-oriented weekend party geeky med stud conversations, typically in a manner probably confirming our ignorance and frighteningly, even though we didn't realize it at the time, only suggesting some of the clinical challenges ahead.

"My Dad had some homo AIDS patient that he removed two gerbils from his rectum, after he saw 'em through the endoscope," said Mark. R., a future third generation doctor/son of a prominent San Francisco gastroenterologist. Gerbil stories always seemed to be prominent with Mark R.

"How are the endoscopes sterilized between procedures?" asked the concrete thinking, slightly paranoid Roberto L., a highly muscled Puerto Rican, whom most of us thought must have been there on some sort of special program, but who contributed immensely to these early basic science parties by the nature of the extremely hot, hard bodied, non medical student babes he consistently brought with him.

"My roommate knows a guy whose cousin had a friend in medical school that caught AIDS from a needle stick he got drawing blood in the E.R. one night after he'd been up for like a hundred hours in a row," said Billy C., an aloof student, who eventually dropped out of medical school following two semesters spent in Guatemala barely treating more parasitic diseases than he himself suffered while apparently successfully wooing a reportedly nymphomaniac missionary student.

I probably went to get another beer.

III

- Recollections: a personal TX history

Whether it was memorizing the enzymes involved in glycolysis in Biochemistry, deducing the location of lesions within neural pathways to produce specific motor or sensory symptoms in Neuroanatomy, trying to keep straight which part of the renal tubules did which direction of pumping of which ions, or learning the properties of various bacteria and the names and treatments of rare parasitic diseases (which we all struggled with except for Billy C) in Microbiology, I approached all of my first and second year curriculum with the equal intensity of someone who felt fortunate to be there.

Whereas several of my medical school classmates had fathers that were physicians, and a few also had grandfathers that had practiced medicine, and even one or two that I knew had mothers that were physicians, I did not come from a family with doctors, and I had little idea of what to actually expect as I began my medical training. My parents were highly intelligent, hard working people, more formally educated than their parents before them, and in further typical American-dream fashion, wanted even more for their kids, yet without ever consciously imposing any sort of expectation of the accomplishments necessary for achieving it. I grew up in the highly German-American town of New Braunfels, Texas, about halfway between San Antonio and Austin. Amongst the typical childhood and teen activities that tend to homogenously distract American youth from basic facts about our surroundings, I did eventually come to appreciate a few historical and social aspects of my home town and its somewhat unique character within my home state. Although it had to do with things like land grants and probably other political and financial agreements and things involving Mexico and Indians and agriculture and some other stuff I must not have picked up in my mandatory Texas history classes, from my non-sociologist perspective, it seemed so natural to me for these decent, hard working, but beer drinking, and colorful Germans with a deep appreciation of the fundamental to be living in the rugged mesquite and cactus covered lime-stone hills of Southwest Central Texas, the so-called "hill country", that it may just as well have been fate that their ancestors arrived to the area and established towns such as New Braunfels, Fredericksburg and Boerne, where some newspapers continue to be published in German to this day.

As the more easily farmable lands of what would eventually be East (or South East) Texas were being settled by American Anglo-Celt descendants under the guidance of the legendary Stephen F. Austin, those who would become the original Texans and form a large part of the group that would eventually win a surprise victory over Santa Anna under Sam Houston at San Jacinto in 1836, German immigrants were already coming in small numbers in the 1820s and 1830s to San Antonio and the fringes of Anglo Texas, in the region northwest of San Antonio. This became a more official immigration in earnest in the latter part of the ten years of the Texas Republic. In the mid 1840s, Prince Solm-Braunfels headed up a formal German migration to Texas. Although the aspirations may have been somewhat greater than at least the initial efforts or potential, the Germans were apparently interested in providing a new world market for their industrial endeavors, and wanted a colony, so to speak, that increasingly crowded and less than happy agricultural peasants could take their work-ethic to, in a manner potentially helping the fatherland as well as themselves. The Germans had acquired, or so they thought, a massive land grant, way west of where they eventually settled in the hill country, non-farming land, really, even compared to the hill country, and in the middle of scalp-unfriendly Comanche territory. The Prince apparently had bad intelligence, with the early German land scouts assuming that all of Texas had to be like the fertile southeast regions they had already seen. Prince Solm-Braunfels founded a town on the Guadalupe, the same river that I would spend so many sunny afternoons inner-toobing down where only the hot Texas sun and many, many cold beers could eventually take one's mind off the butt-numbing greater coldness of the river on the parts sticking through the tube. He named the town he founded in 1846 New Braunfels, intending it maybe as a weigh station, on the eastern edge of the territory his people would be migrating to, knowing how tired they would be after making the journey from the Gulf Coast. From what I understand, the Prince boogied on out of there back to the homeland shortly thereafter, but some of his people stayed. In a historic journey from where some 5,000-10,000 German immigrants suffered typhoid and starvation on the Gulf Coast, these hardy settlers made it to New Braunfels.

This was not ideal farming land, but they stuck it out, furrowing small plots in valleys amongst the limestone and scrub oaks. They never made it to the original targeted far more barren and Indian controlled region that had been granted further west. They created a staggered series of little townships extending west from New Braunfels, the Boernes and Fredericksburgs that would become the names of the schools I would play against in high school. Although the Germans who settled as merchants and other workers in San Antonio around the same time may have given up their German language and integrated more wholly into a developing society of Anglo Texas at the intersection with Old World Spanish-Mexican influences, the more separated German settled hill country towns retained their German language, German newspapers, and cultural ways for many more generations, with some strong vestiges even to the present.

For reasons that can only be ascribed to blood seeking blood, or pretzel eating, pilsner drinking, hard working genes looking for their genomic soul mates, as military personnel who had commonly been stationed in Deutschland after World War II retired out of the large number of Army and Air Force bases in San Antonio and looked for places to work in garages, bakeries, and hardware stores or to develop business ventures catering to like spirits, the North side of San Antonio and the surrounding Texas Hill Country became natural repositories for these people.

My father was the offspring of one such stout, surprisingly squat, hard working, and decent German-American, and had taken essentially permanent root in the hill country as a young teenager, when my grandfather retired there. The lime-stone laden soil and hot sun, combined with spicy chili, mesquite-seasoned beef brisket barbecue, and reportedly large quantities of Pearl and Lone Star beer had effectively combined to give 6 more inches of height to my father than my little Arian grandfather had, and was progressively loosing by about an inch a year while I was in high school, until he died during my senior year. A good looking (at least according to my mother and a few similarly aged women I occasionally became engaged in conversation with in town during high school and ensuing increasingly less frequent visits over the years in college and med school), easy going fellow, my father apparently was somewhat of a high school football hero, who was smart enough, or lucky enough, to make sure that the beautiful local girl he would eventually marry was also potentially the sweetest human being on the planet. We speak now, without bias, of my wonderful mother. They both attended Southwest Texas State University in nearby San Marcos, with my Dad majoring in business (seemingly more of a minor compared to football and beer from what I hear from the occasional "old college buddies" I have likewise encountered, but in the most unlikely venues, over the years), and my Mom majoring in education. They were married in 1958, in a ceremony that from what I've heard in descriptions and seen in old black and white photos would make Norman Rockwell blush for its wholesomeness. While my father continued to sow his wild mental oats in various ill advised business adventures, my mother provided stability in the form of teaching elementary school in San Marcos. As a consequence of the wild physical oats, I came along in 1960, the product of an admirable very love-filled marriage, from everything that I've gathered retrospectively as well as personally analyzed once I reached an age where human children begin to ponder things besides themselves. Why it took until 1969 to generate a sibling for me was only partly explained by my father's enlisting and volunteering for Vietnam in 1966. He returned a slightly mellower version of the All American Boy, a good and decent man, with loyalty to his fellow soldiers, a surprisingly large number of which ended up within a 50 mile radius of San Antonio, and to my mother. His ability to schmooze with any organism, from a neighbor, to a fellow vet, to strangers in restaurants, to the eventual young professionals beginning to populate Austin and surroundings in the late '70s, to the Yankee infidels migrating in droves to Dallas and Houston in the glory days of Reagan and Bush in the '80s, made my father's eventual settling into real estate the career match of a lifetime.

The dot.comers and Dellionaires of the peri-Austin Texas Hill country would not exist for many more years, but the 70s and 80s saw enough folks coming to the sacred heartland to more than make my parents comfortable and secure on his share of the 3 % commissions (particularly when the broker's license came along in 1978). In part to get closer to the steadily increasing retired military community of San Antonio and its Northern surroundings, we moved from the outskirts of San Marcos (if such a town deserves a designated "outskirts"), to New Braunfels proper in 1973, moving into a beautiful Tudor-style house overlooking Landau Park. I spent 9th through 12th grades there, in a manner that makes white bread look like the building block of the one true American dream and that would bring a tear to Ronnie's eye, albeit with the usual accompanying mishaps that befall, but hopefully don't derail, the American male teen.

...

In the background of my father contributing to the expansion and development of New Braunfels, and indeed the surrounding Hill Country, and my mother serving to set the standard for community service and social good graciousness, I became arguably one of the best, if not the best, students New Braunfels Canyon High School had ever had. In addition to straight As, I excelled in all UIL academic competitive endeavors I participated in, especially those that were mathematics related. Lest this should appear geeky (indeed, an at least subconscious perpetual concern in the pursuit of all things blessed or cursed that constitute female), I made it seem at least a little cooler at the time by being a three year letterer in basketball, being the starting point guard the last two years, and being a starting pitcher on a highly successful baseball team from sophomore to senior year. Throw in dating two of the most beautiful girls in school junior and senior year and you have a pretty gaggy high school experience that may, perhaps, hide a certain burning dangerous tendency or two.

Hints of the latter came in isolated incidences that are probably not outside the realm of the above alluded to usual adolescence behaviors or experiences. I totaled my Mom's LTD on a tragically beautiful old Oak tree (embarrassingly in the middle of town) one Saturday night my Junior Year. I draw some consolation more than a decade later knowing that I out drank one of the legendary locals in a chugging contest out of supposedly greater than a dozen pitchers at a favorite Bar and Grill, thanks in no small part to the encouraging cheers of my non-participating, but still very drunk friends. DUI was still a concept reserved for the bigger, more cultured cities then, and a local boy of decent repute would be escorted home to much bigger punishment by the New Braunfels Police Department, as long as no one had been killed or seriously maimed.

I impregnated my girlfriend Jenny in between our Junior and Senior Year. To this day, I'm not sure that anyone besides her, me, and maybe my employer at the Canyon Putt-Putt from whom I borrowed (and eventually repaid) 300 dollars know of this particular miscue. The stress of the episode apparently precluded carrying on our relationship into the pivotal senior year, and I became "sweethearts" instead with Angie Hicks, an absolutely stunningly beautiful blonde with blue eyes, with whom I shared a wonderful array of traditional high school memories. Stupid youthful passion still raised its ugly interfering head, as when I missed the regional basketball playoffs with a broken hand, due to an angry encounter with the windshield on my '78 Ford F-100 pick-up, prompted by a misperceived relationship issue that seemed trivial several days later, sitting on the bench with a glistening white cast. Incremental wisdom acquisition not withstanding, this would likely not be the last of my potential setbacks at the expense of ethanol molecules and passion.

A successful baseball season, and especially a 4.0 G.P.A. and 1420 SATs meant a range of options for me to take my supposed inherent abilities, occasional and hopefully increasingly often hard work, and occasional and hopefully decreasingly frequent immaturity spells to college. My humble hill country background never gave me reason to really seriously pursue an Ivy League education (all the schools for which were also insurmountably located outside of TX). At the time, prior to postgraduate medical training, and at which point I still would have been fine confining myself to God's country, leaving the state of Texas had as much appeal as a third gastrointestinal orifice. Indeed, after seven years of Northeast and West Coast living/exile in the D.C. area and San Francisco, the need in part to reconstitute myself with the healing ointment of all things south of the Red River would contribute to putting me in the strange social position of being Kim-free in Houston for our intended brief period. Regarding college choices, then, Texas A & M and even The University of Texas at Austin, where my darling Angie went, were too big for me. I think perhaps that I somehow needed to be one of those big fish in a little pond kind of guys, at least for a little while more. I eventually decided to go to Trinity University in San Antonio, a very good small school, which would give me the broad liberal arts education that I somehow surprisingly realized would be particularly desirable to admissions committees for a budding young physician want to be.

As rigorous Presbyterians, my parents were quite pleased with my decision to attend Trinity, although I don't remember spending a single millisecond in church the entire four years. Local St. Mary's Street and downtown bars were, of course, a different story. Initially, I made the hour and a half trip to Austin to see Angie about once a month, and she was the most perfect girlfriend any guy could want. But at 19, who wants that, I suppose. So by Christmas, it was over, and I was "dating" someone else. It lasted long enough to not be worthy of mentioning. School was reasonably hard, and thus I studied reasonably hard, albeit commonly in spurts, but to a level subconsciously discerned as crucial to success. Perfectionism in school was something as deeply ingrained in me as hematopoesis in my taken for granted bone marrow. Partying, baseball, etc. were there, but any of these things, and the far more superfluous daily endeavors, such as laundry and cleaning my dorm and then apartment, would always be sacrificed for the need to understand and remember everything I read in every subject, from Ancient Biblical Text to History to Calculus III to Organic Chemistry. From that need to know, and maybe an unacknowledged need to be the best, grades took care of themselves. I played baseball for the first two years, with mixed success, but in the end, the inability to sacrifice beer while maintaining the highest academic integrity did not allow for any sort of externally imposed rigidity in my life, as practice and game schedules can appear to represent in a life of accidental hangovers and exam crammings. One minor screw up in a Philosophy of Man class my junior year (I forgot to turn in a paper, which I hadn't written anyway due to a bad but actually quite awesome weekend with my then girlfriend Amy and several buds in South Padre Island) led to a not particularly disastrous 3.92 overall. Combined with a 72 on the MCAT and the usual slightly exaggerated extracurricular activities for anyone applying to medical school (e.g., volunteering at an Old Folks home I probably couldn't even find on a map) and presumably adequate performances in interviews, I ended up at the highly prestigious Baylor College of Medicine in the staggeringly large Texas Medical Center on August 3, 1981.

IV

- Houston; August, 1993

One weeknight evening, late in August, when it had cooled to about a tolerable 89 or so degrees, several of us were sitting around in the park. I had been feeling overwhelmed, having had a full day at the Thomas St. clinic, interrupted repeatedly by phone calls and pages from Baylor regarding various administrative aspects of our clinical trial (the basis for the grant which I had come to Baylor with and still in its most infantile stages of execution), several of which I had to address in more paper-work-filling-out detail when I got home. When my frustration and tension had peaked (administrative issues are not among my top thousand passions), I stepped outside for a walk to clear my head. After a few blocks of subconscious strolling and mosquito swatting, during which my head kept revisiting a couple of patients from earlier in the day, wondering if I was proceeding correctly in their management (the inevitable consequence of finally being an attending physician and not just a resident or fellow with attending backup if needed), I ended up in our park and assumed a seat on a bench with a fatigue-laden sigh.

On this occasion, we had a full staff, and although I was yet to appreciate this particular regularity, everyone was largely in their assumed proper places. Frank was sitting on the right sided bench (the patient's right, so to speak, as if you were the benches or sitting on the benches; my sense of explaining right and left handedness had been upended from the start of our physical exam courses second year of medical school; this would, I suppose, be the left sided bench if you were facing the benches and using your own self as a reference....). He was in a generic short sleeve knit polo type shirt within the Sears color spectrum and khaki shorts, no doubt bought by Mrs. Frank, and showing, despite the pulled up high white socks, legs almost as white as said socks, to where contrast between them became increasingly difficult as the light faded. Carl was standing behind Frank's left shoulder (patient's left), leaning slightly forward with hands on the back of the unoccupied center of the bench. Leo was sitting on the right side (his right, a straight facing observer's left) of the left sided (patient's left, observer's right) bench. He was in a button up gray cardigan sweater, the right (his right) sleeve of which he was periodically using to wipe the sweat off his forehead, the same sweat the rest of us were periodically experiencing in less severe forms despite leaving our winter attire at home. He had a shirt underneath it, visible at the top, such that he could have removed his sweater. I would have thought that unbuttoning it could have at least incrementally helped before this potentially drastic step of weather-human realization. The "observer" theoretically causing so much confusion with patient or general person sidedness orientation could have been Rick, who sat on the ground holding his knees up towards his chest and facing the two benches from a position essentially precisely in between them. I sat down on the left side of the left bench (both my lefts), at the far end, spacing myself enough away from Leo so as to not absorb any of his torturous heat through some principle as the Zeroith Law of Thermodynamics or such. Curtis was harder to descriptively localize, being more dissipated, varying from standing in different orientations (regardless of perspective) to walking around the benches in no particular pattern.

After some small talk, with me perhaps trying to convey, without getting into too many specifics, why I was feeling a little more stressed than usual, Carl asked with inquisition-like firmness, "So, what exactly are you doing here?"

I must have paused, uncharacteristically, just briefly enough compared to the typical immediate zeal demonstrated when asked about work, maybe taken aback by the sense of accusation in Carl's crisp tone, to allow Leo to add in either mock support or just slightly off-tune acknowledgement of being an at least peripheral part of the conversation, "Yeah, youngster, Mr. doctor whipper-snapper, what brings you to our domicile?"

I felt like saying something like "I'm trying to figure out how to treat AIDS patients so they don't end up as mentally and psychologically fucked up as you two guys," but civility (maybe some of past Kim influence?) intervened.

I took a deep sigh, and responded with intended lay simplicity, "I'm practicing medicine here, and also, primarily, doing a drug trial to try to figure out how to treat patients with HIV-infection so that they don't get dementia or other neurological problems."

"Dementia, you mean, like acting crazy and stuff," Rick clarified.

"Yeah, exactly," I said, tired and uncharacteristically not going into long detail to really explain what all was involved.

"AIDS patients can get crazy?" Curtis asked, now transitioning from usual aloofness to apparently interested, a state, as I would learn, that could last from seconds to three to five minutes at a time, typically proportionately related to the sexual content of the topic of conversation.

"Yeah, but in your case, you were just crazy to begin with," Rick stabbingly interjected.

"Suck my dick you fuckin' drunk homo," Curtis angrily responded, maybe not liking the implications of a neither anticipated nor confirmed AIDS or crazy status.

"I would, but that's Frank's job," Rick quickly replied, proving he'd spent as much time as any of us on junior high playgrounds.

"Huh..." Frank muttered up when he heard his name, likely from the perspective of ignorance of not really paying attention when the conversation had maybe turned to un-Frankness.

"Boy, that Ms. Valery... she can suck a mean dick," Leo shockingly dropped in from somewhere many orbits beyond left field.

We all sat there dumbfounded...silent. Conventional wisdom silently states that when crazy people, or even ex-crazy people, pronounce such fundamentally profound things in such a profoundly fundamental manner...well, there's really not much room for comment.

I think I excused myself and left at that point, hoping we would have warmer (as in inter-personal....NOT temperature) park moments in the future.

V

- Recollections: Houston 1981 – 1985

Young, eager, intelligent, but equally extraordinarily naïve first year medical students often have strong, or at least strongly expressed, but usually ill founded or basis-less ideas of what kind of a doctor they want to be when they "grow up". With often little real medical exposure up to that point, career aspirations are based on romantic notions derived from TV shows, the occasional novel, familial expectations, and notions of what lines will work best with girls at local bars. Macho guys want to be surgeons, "laser surgeons" if they need to throw in a techno term to show an unexpected intellectual side to potential prey that happen to be undergraduate students at nearby Rice University. Athletic guys who are smart enough to have made some early Honors grades in their Basic Science courses, and hence realistically aspire to it after they hear how difficult it is, want to be Orthopedic Surgeons, or Orthopods. Nurturing women want to be pediatricians. The occasional son or daughter of a pathologist, who grew up looking at tumors with long weird names in their father's microscope have a large predisposition to the same field. The weirdest kids are supposed to go into psychiatry, and many actually do.

One safe bet is that as a member of a family with no prior doctors and without much contact with the authentic medical community while growing up, save the visits prompted by the usual childhood illnesses and annual sports physicals, when asked as a senior college student accepted into medical school or as an early first year medical student, "What kind of a doctor are you going to be?" I didn't answer: "Neuroimmunologist." Later of course, to really freak people out at bars, I would claim to be a "Neuroimmunopharmacologist."

Especially in a supposedly "intellectual" profession, one would like to think that they make well informed, carefully calculated decisions along the way that get them to where they always intended to be twenty or so years later. Maybe it is actually a series of interrelated causes and effects, or positively reinforcing components of an orchestrated vicious cycle, or an inevitable, somehow subconsciously guided chain reaction of life circumstances, or some other cosmically directed serendipity, the equivalent of an educated guess, that unravels our fates during a period when we are far too busy to actually stop and ponder them in a way to allow us to completely rationally impact them for the first ten or so educational, training, and professional years.

In my case, I was a strong basic science student in medical school, actually interested in the things we were learning, not just passing time and getting through something I had to get through, in order to put tubes and things into people in the emergency room. Every single one of us that graduated from medical school would be "doctors", and we could go out and practice medicine to hopefully the best of our abilities, using the things we learned, things that were already known, and hence taught to us by others. Maybe we'd even learn some relatively new things along the way, incorporate them into our "art". That never seemed to be enough for me, even when I hadn't yet learned a substantial fraction of the vast body of current existing knowledge.

It's not clear to me why I had to have more, why deep down I knew I would have to have more, and hence, from a complete state of naivety-bathed medical embryonic juices, I began to slowly, painfully through experience, learn what the "system" required of those who were destined to be physician scientists, or clinical investigators, or academic physicians. Some of my classmates were in the combined M.D./Ph.D. program, most of them real hard core scientists, hard to picture as ever being true doctor-type physicians. As I would realize much later, because of the M.D. component, they would likely have opportunities for biomedical research and salary support, for grant and other funding options, that our straight Ph.D. graduate students, many of which we saw every day the first couple of years, would not have. As much as I loved the basic sciences, and as fundamentally inquisitive as I reportedly was, I did not identify with these folks quite as much as I did with those guys in the E.R. putting the tubes in people. I wanted to be a competent physician first and foremost. I guess deep down I was cocky enough, if never outwardly so, to think I could be both: a great doctor, compassionate, competent, clinically savvy, but always wondering why we were coming up short in particular situations, why we couldn't cure certain diseases, why we couldn't even more effectively ameliorate symptoms in the diseases we couldn't cure, why we were so absolutely clueless in the fundamental, and hence molecular, etiologies of some of the most common ailments fucking with the human race.

But it wasn't enough to be curious. How on earth did one go about actually making progress in reaching answers to these questions? To learn the millions of steps along the complex path takes time, takes skills, takes a lot of time to properly acquire those skills and to use them, a process I only could gradually fathom and be awed by as I partook in some basic research training along the way.

There are several semi-silly axioms often repeated to, and by, early and occasionally disheartened medical students, in part, I suppose, to give them encouragement and in part to maybe give them a little career guidance.

Question: "What do they call the guy (or girl—so maybe, person) that finishes at the bottom of his med school class?"

Answer: "Doctor."

Or, there was the rule/generalism: The top third of the med school class will typically go into academics, the middle third will make the best doctors, and the bottom-third will make the most money.

Well, I was way up high in that top-third, and was beginning to increasingly lean towards that "academic" thing, I guess. When this ability/curiosity/willingness begins exposing itself to professors (who, of course, by definition, are in academics), they will offer up all types of options for furthering this "calling" as early as possible.

So, in addition to the usual required basic science courses, I took a couple of electives (a certain number of elective credits were required throughout the curriculum, especially in the later clinical years) in some pretty basic areas that required some actual wet-bench lab work.

Although I would become more valuably involved in later research endeavors to which I would be dedicating larger percentages of time, I still have mixed memories of an early research "exposure" elective, dominated by a particular dark and sinister and flat out freaky episode. In fact, looking back, it's amazing that I stuck it out, not only for that elective, but that I continued in some sort of masochistic fashion to seek out other research experiences. Basic research may not be as glamorous as clinical medicine, but it sure generates its share of bizarre moments. A lot of mine stemmed from late night or weekend or holiday or some other sort of timing situations that generated the kind of aloneness like that often seen in bad horror movies, as when the bit actor (not that I'd ever agree to that role) goes outside to get the extra beers in a remote cabin only to encounter the hideous mutant beast while the popular kids (where I'd want to be of course) are having sex back in the main cabin kind-of-thing. Particularly tragic in my case (and clearly, I could never have been a veterinarian), is that these hideous encounters were with the likes of mice and rabbits, previously peaceful in their cages, and not some sort of grotesque monster emerging at its most horrific teen-mutilating form, maybe after generations of mutations and quietly living for centuries on rarely noted missing quiet kids never heard from again after going to camp, following its original most unholy spawning from some sort of Carrie meets Freddy in the back seat of Dad's Chrysler kind-of-thing.

In one elective that one of my best friends and I took together in the first year of medical school we were supposedly studying mechanisms of tissue rejection in heart transplants. Dan and I were beer drinking and studying compadres (the two often performed in unison until the former precluded anymore of the latter and necessitated performing the former in a more dedicated and concentrated manner typically in a nearby bar and no longer in one or the other's apartment) and foosball partners. The latter, if you take it seriously, is a very serious matter indeed, much like a marriage or committed business partnership…not to be taken lightly, and which in the middle of a particularly intense Thursday night contest at one of the peri-Med Center bars with locals, nearby Rice graduate students, and the occasional other medical school classmates who should have already known better by then to try to take us on, led us to at least be temporarily crowned as Partners' Champs in an apparently reasonably respected local tournament. In fact, apparently our sporadic yet intense and highly successful foosball partnering (I was the back man/goalie) had been so legendary amongst the first year basic science students who would play in the Student Lounge in between and after classes that when we would occasionally get back together, spontaneously, as second year students to beat the living embarrassing shit out of an aspiring pair of misguided first years, it would often inspire a growing crowd of nostalgic on-looking "fans", something akin (although on an infinitely smaller scale…) to a Simon and Garfunkel reunion in a lucky New York café or Central Park.

Anyway, as Dan and I were learning together, a great advantage of mice in biomedical research is the ability to keep pure genetic strains through careful breeding, and many such strains are well characterized. There is an extraordinarily complex array of genes, fairly homologous between mice and humans, which control a vast number of the interacting components in any given immunologic process. Many immunologic diseases in humans, such as the "auto-immune" diseases lupus and rheumatoid arthritis, are at least in part genetic; that is, some people are predisposed to these diseases due to their specific DNA makeup in a number of particular gene families. Some mouse strains are likewise predisposed to similar immunologic disease processes, and it is hoped that these animal models can provide mechanistic insight into potential etiologies of these conditions and useful information when investigating possible treatment modalities. Organ transplant rejection is, of course, also immunologically mediated. Hence, tissue and organ transplant between specific mouse strains, along with some experimental manipulations and some complex analyses of the tissues following varying degrees of rejection can provide some insight into the basic mechanisms involved in transplant rejection. Similar experiments with or without some anti-rejection treatments can in theory aid our efforts to therapeutically manipulate the transplant rejection process in a clinically desirable way in human patients with appropriate doses of the same immunosuppressant drugs. With a little bit of more highly educated retrospective insight superimposed on my recollections of protocols and study designs of those projects I was really only minimally involved in (i.e., compared to those whose full time focus for funded research it was and to my full time focus on the medical school basic science curriculum we were engaged in), this is about the most I remember of the underlying principles behind the experiments Dan and I were a part of.

In what seemed at the time to me the biomedical equivalent of Dr. Moreau's Island, we or various lab technicians would cut the heads off of new born mice pups (little pink largely hairless dudes that looked like tiny Play Doh dogs) of one strain, cut open their chest (very easy at this developmental stage), and remove their hearts. The precision of this wasn't as crucial as in real human transplantation, as it wasn't like we were going to put it back in the chest of another animal, with proper vascular anastamoses, the end to end connection of those great vessels we studied in Gross Anatomy. Instead, and no shit, really, what we did, was implant it subcutaneously (i.e., under the skin) of the EAR of a different mouse strain (above the ear cartilage from what I remember). And now, the really weird part, these things would vascularize (i.e., little blood vessels in the skin would connect to them and/or vice-versa), and you could actually get some sort of EKG readings off of them days to weeks later; that is, the transplant would "take". What Dan and I would do then (and here's where the willingness of medical students came into play) was to come in at all hours, especially on weekends, and give the various mice injections of certain immunosuppressant drugs. After a certain time, then, these recipient mice would be sacrificed, the grafts harvested, and studied by various standard pathology methods as well as by immunopathology techniques (e.g., to study the cells and surface antigens involved in variously severe rejection processes).

One Saturday afternoon I went in to dose several mice with their scheduled immunosuppressant medicine, cyclosporine I believe, which was still pretty new at the time, or a similar compound. I had intended to go in much earlier, but one thing led to another, as in I didn't really feel like it, or I couldn't get off the sofa, or I couldn't get motivated, and so even though I KNEW I had to do it and my sense of commitment, guilt, or fear of not making an honors grade in a fairly straight-forward elective would eventually make me finally do it, I put it off until I could just barely squeeze it in before whatever alcohol-related school distracting event I had planned that evening. When you don't feel like doing something work wise on the weekend, yet you know you have to, nothing is more dystonic, or without conscious recognition, more interferes with your enjoyment of the attempts at relaxation that you're engaging in instead. In the end, the procrastination precludes both your work and the enjoyment of the procrastination as well. I guess the old proverbs are right, but it's hard to be 100 % motivated all the time.

I hated being in the medical center at times like that; it reminded me of those afternoons where you finally went in to study, after feeling all day like you really should be, but you didn't feel like it, and deep down, your mind, which always somehow knew when it was time to panic and learn intensely, knew in this case that it wasn't REALLY that time; and so, you put off going in, and when you got there you couldn't concentrate, you stayed for a while trying ineffectively to force yourself, and then you created the somewhat panicking sense (not enough to really study, just enough to ruin your evening) that you didn't know anything, because you couldn't even concentrate enough to recognize the things you did know when flipping though your notes or syllabus to get to the area you had intended to study. These little turbulences of the student psyche were probably an auto protective mechanism trying to tell your overachieving ass it was time to take an afternoon off, go to the park, play some hoops, get some exercise, re-set the gauges.

So, that's exactly how I felt when I forced myself to go play super-immunologist-some-day-want-to be, by paying my current dues, humbly contributing my little mindless part, the necessary grunt work of the long term animal intervention project. These particular labs were in an older part of the medical school, one of the original research wings off of the main and oldest building. Newer constructions extended from multiple sides on the old hallways of the central oldest part, a relatively new building for medical school lecture halls, anatomy labs in the basement, and smaller teaching labs above the lecture halls to the North and even newer research buildings, continually being added to the east, like sequential cars on a train, giving rise to hallways that seemed to go on forever, as they passed from the old medical school building, through that housing the labs of my current elective, and then sequentially through the newer research wings, heading towards the parking garage that separated Baylor from the Ben Taub County Hospital, although neither was directly accessible from these long research building hallways. A maze, so to speak, perfect for mice work I suppose.

The labs I was working in were actually not along those long hallways, per se, but in a small hallway like some sort of almost secret passageway, connecting two minor hallways, such that I often had a hard time finding them initially; and even when going directly there, as in the current instance, I felt like I had come to a dead end in one of those very rodent mazes. How appropriate then, that I would come upon cages and cages of my murine colleagues, stacked up against a wall in this seemingly remote site. Being in an older lab can have a couple of quite opposing effects on the casual passerby or temporary student worker. It can impart a sense of prestige, an aura of accomplishment, longevity, past and current greatness, to be respected, admired, making one want to contribute in whatever small way to the legacy softly stated from the old journal volumes from no longer stylish cabinets and shelves; or, it can look like a small collection of some of the lesser desirable lab space within a growing competitive research environment, in which lab space is at a premium, and surely the really good stuff must be going on in those pristine looking modern prefab lab constructs along the infinite hallways further along in the maze. At this stage, in this likely silly oversimplification, I wasn't sure which was the situation in our case, but on this particular occasion, on a late Saturday afternoon, in a quiet, almost hidden, and completely unoccupied (by humans anyway) very interior older lab, I felt a sense of left-behindness and under-fundedness, and hence, possible less than crucialness of the work I was attending to, that made the rather dour task ahead of me all the more acutely dreaded.

In this lonely, feeling sorry for myself for having to be here at the time state, I may have let my mouse guard down. As an aside, I prefer working with tissue culture flasks, the test-tube kind of thing, and real humans. I am not a humongous fan of animal experimentation. Lest you think this is some sort of noble, cosmetics-not-tested-on-animals-sort of touchy, feely, bullshit thing, rest assured, it has nothing to do with that. I definitely do not like to do any biomedical research with dogs, and never have had to be in that situation. Although those employed in research are often mongrels, maybe going to be put to sleep anyway, and dogs are ideally suited for some types of work, particularly surgical and cardiovascular stuff, I just can't do it. I love dogs too much, and it would kill me. That's about where it ends. I have no problem recognizing the hugely important role that animal research has in our quest to conquer disease, and no *in vitro* systems can recapitulate the necessary complexities that good animal models offer (and even then, in manners that still have to be carefully translated to targeted aspects of specific human diseases). I just don't like dealing with rats, mice, rabbits, etc.... because, quite simply, I don't want to get bit! Shit, it's not even the pain or any sort of largely non-existent biological risk. It's that damn anticipation; not knowing if or when it's going to occur...like the silly cranking of the handle on the jack-in-the-box or passing around the hot potato or time bomb games we had as kids.

I especially don't like to handle rats, and have largely avoided any such work. They're good for some pharmacologic and toxicologic stuff, but they are not genetically manipulatable in the same way that their smaller murine cousins are. At the risk of offending the animal rights people, who maybe should skip these sections, it is common place to sacrifice lab rats by grabbing their tails and then swinging them quickly such that they hit their heads on the lab bench. They experience no pain in the process, and this and other sacrificing protocols are approved by experimental lab animal use committees in all major medical centers.

I just don't want to do this….ever. I suspect that if you "miss", they'll bite the living shit out of you, a reflection of the not particularly unjustified rodent revenge principle inherent in the "What the fuck are you doing to me?" survival attitude. Fortunately for me, killing mice is much easier, and in most cases, is not fundamentally different from the very gentle manner in which I have anesthetized them over the years in long term experiments, requiring occasional manipulations not possible in the un-anesthetized state. This commonly involves an intra-peritoneal (IP) injection (i.e., in the abdominal cavity, from whence a drug is effectively absorbed), with sacrifice simply involving a larger dose (essentially an overdose) than that which is involved in manipulations (which is essentially equivalent to human surgical anesthesia) from which you hope your little genetic marvel, and hence expensive, subject will recover post manipulation.

In this case, we gave the immunosuppressant drug by the same IP injection route that we would give an anesthetic by. However, also in this case, the mouse is fully operational, with all of his mouse quickness and potential squirminess intact. Actually, as with humans I suppose, some mouse strains are more docile than others; that is, more tolerant of a giant organism reaching down into his dwelling, snatching him up like King Kong to Fay Wray, and giving him a shot in the belly. Boy, would I learn this strain difference first hand on this day.

I had gotten adequately good at this, although I still approached each mouse grabbing, manipulating, and injection with the kind of apprehension I remember when jumping off the high dive at the end of my first round of swimming lessons as a kid. What one does in this process is: draw up the meds in the syringe to be employed, open the cage, identify the next subject (often standing off on his own, maybe like the gazelle standing off from the herd, so that his tail is visible and reachable), grab him (with few biologically necessary exceptions, research mice are typically males) by the tail, then holding by the tail set him down on the lab bench, grab him on the back of the neck-firmly pinching the skin/soft tissue between thumb and index finger so that the head can't move (and this is the key to the whole anti-bite thing), turn him over, take your other hand and grab the tail and pull it lightly to curl it around under your baby finger and tuck it between your fingers of the neck holding hand to control his lower half. In that position, the belly is ready to be injected with a very small volume of medical fluid. You stick him (very skinny needle), draw back same as the zillions of times you have or will to humans you are sticking to be sure you haven't entered a large vessel (you want it IP not IV) or in this site, a loop of bowel, inject, then turn him over while gently lowering him back in his cage, at which point his cage mates will typically give him a good sniff as maybe to the whole "where-have-you-been-and-what- have-you-been-up-to-and-are-we-gonna-have-to-do-it-too" kind of thing.

For reasons that were not clear to me then (at which point I had no reason to wonder or care) nor now, when I look back on the....horror..., in addition to the usual array of subjects of the one particular mouse strain (little brown guys, I forget the genetics description of the particular strain) that we had always used and which were in multiple cages in our usual room, I was told to include an additional...single...mouse...of another strain...in...another...room...at the end of the hallway. Looking back, I suppose, I should have at least recognized this set up for the impending terror to come, like the four teenagers running out of gas in the middle of bum-fuck nowhere, only to be devoured by a collection of inbred mutants, not quite refined enough to even use a chainsaw.

The room I entered wasn't even a lab really, or at least not set up presently to function as a lab. Instead, it seemed like it was dedicated predominantly to disorganized storage. I recognized this quickly, as I had years of experience of cramming shit into closets, etc. One, maybe two, desk or table tops looked like they may have actually been being currently used, as there were narrow right angle connected paths cutting between boxes and piles of papers and books and miscellaneous highly dated medium sized instruments that led from the door to these outposts, their surfaces were a little less cluttered, and they contained random stacks of scribbled on papers and notes that indicated some recent activities potentially relatable to the overall themes of the laboratory. One even had a phone, an active one. It was on this desk that I encountered the single cage, with a single inhabitant. The strain identification and date of manipulations written in pencil on the 3 x 5 card inserted into its corresponding slot on the metal bars at the front of the cage confirmed that this was the last little mouse I had to give an IP injection of cyclosporine to before I would be on my way to a friend's house where an anticipated large and female-containing party was (including PA and supposedly some UT Houston medical students, who for some reason we presumed would be of less mental and hence moral structure than we prime Baylor Beef medical students). Maybe I should have been more focused.

Even with the overhead lights turned on, the room was fairly dim. Several overhead bulbs were apparently out. A desk lamp that looked as old as some of the probably still being decided if going to be discarded lab equipment scattered on the floor gave uneven, suboptimal lighting to the immediate cage vicinity. My next subject was completely white, a profound difference versus the other experimental animals we'd been using, and a contrast that would pale in comparison to those I was soon to discover. I had my vial of clear liquid drug with me, with its air-tight rubber top that the needle penetrated through, and my 1 ml TB syringe fit with its still sterilely capped very small (and mouse belly appropriate) sized needle on its end. I alcohol swabbed the drug vial top (so conscientious, even under these conditions), drew up the right amount, dispelled the air bubbles from the needle (this was my favorite part, so tangible and dramatic…and dare, I hope, medical…), and set the loaded syringe on the desk.

Did he sense it?

I didn't prepare a little work station or anything. The ambience of the room and its seeming lack of credibility displaced onto anyone who would thus work there allowed me to suppose that I could just do all my business right there, on whatever was available on the desk surface. A largely finished writing tablet, with full scribbled and doodled top sheet, declared itself as appropriate. Hell, a little mouse hair or various orifice derived droplets would only add legitimacy, wouldn't it? After all, whoever the fucker was that used the desk had this little shit mouse in his cage on his desk to begin with, like some sort of warped personal desk photograph out of a bad scene from *Ben* or *Willard*, or something.

"*Ben, the two of us need look no more. Ben, we both found what we're looking for,*" an imitation Michael Jackson voice sang in my head. I thought about singing it out loud, but that would be too weird, even for where I was and what I was doing.

I took the transparent plastic top off the cage. Here came what should have been my first clue. In contrast to just hanging there, completely still, as if nothing unusual had happened, the way the usual little brown mice acted, this bony, shaggy, white, hairy mouse was scurrying all over the bottom of the cage. What the hell, I thought, acutely feeling phylogenically superior, and I lashed out with my right hand to grab his….whoa…very short little tail. I missed. He quickly jammed himself in the corner, and I nailed attempt two. I held him from not as far to the tip of the tail that I would have liked, and began conveying him over to the designated work area. Holy shit, he moved at angles unknown to mouse gymnastics, crawling up his own body to try to make his first counter attack on this large offending intruder. Then he bent at even more extraordinary angles, seemingly pivoting on the point where I pinched his tail, but likely at some sort of aberrant hip joint or some other part of his must be weird body, biting fantastically at the air between that point and my dreading, increasingly bloodless tightly squeezing finger tips.

I set him down on the tablet of paper on the desk. I wouldn't have much time. At the same instant, I brought my left hand over his scruffy neck to pinch his skin and control his evil head. I grabbed and I pinched, just like so many times before, but I briefly noted in amazement the laxity of his skin there compared to that other strain I surely already wished I was still working with. Assuming this was as good as it was going to get, I went ahead and started to turn him over, for the whole tail tuck thing (not that that would be easy with this stub…). Well, clearly he could still move his head and his jaws adequately, 'cause he turned it to one direction or the other, probably almost rotating that satanic attachment 180 degrees, to take a giant mouse-size bite out of glove layer one, glove layer two (I had had enough of a subconscious premonition to double glove-not that two layers of thin latex is much thicker than one layer of thin latex), and into Jeff skin layer…who knows how deep. I felt it, for sure, but I sensed it even more. I was failing to accomplish what I was attempting, what I was supposed to do, and instead had a psychotic, evil, possessed mouse wildly dangling from my frantically moving hand.

It must have been a scene like one of those cartoons, in which the hero is holding off his own attacking hand, or a hand puppet turned enemy, holding it off at the wrist as it lashes at him, twisting him around and around, or maybe it was like the little cave guarding attack rabbit from Monty Python and the Holy Grail, that lunged and jumped, gnashing, devouring, finally succumbing to the Holy hand grenade. The more I flung my arm around, the tighter it held on by its gnawing, primordial, sharp little dagger "teethies", until my own crude version of the Holy hand grenade, one particular violent arm fling out of the old "what-the-fuck-am-I-gonna-do?" desperation fortuitously timed when he must have been re-positioning his jaws (for the kill?) so he had to let go for one millisecond, the millisecond his little mouse body was flung across the room, smartly and with a sickening thud, up against the far wall (concrete? … cinder block?…I suspect these old wings were built of more old fashioned sturdy materials than those newer halls with their pretty labs, and where I wish I was right now....doing an experiment on a flask of cultured cell lines).

Brief pause. Silence. Restoration....of mice and men. Now that the immediate danger was over, the fear of the bite was steadily replaced by that most deep fear, the fear of fucking up, irreversibly, the fear of killing an expensive experiment in this case. I slowly made my way over to that far side of the room, not still completely free of the dreaded anticipation that psycho mouse would come rushing at me, scampering across the floor, screaming, like the fucking Tiki doll in that old Lora Black *Trilogy of Terror* movie, before lunging off the floor for my neck in an act of possessed, super rodent strength. I found the still body of my adversary/subject of our research project lying on its side on the floor, about six inches from the wall, next to a pile of old books and papers. I should have brought something to put him in, I thought, his cage, a box, or at least something to pick him up with. Dare I touch the little Mother Fucker. My finger was pulsating from the attack. No movement on cautious closer inspection. In what seemed like one continuous motion, I scooped him up by his tail, ran across the room, and from about six feet away to minimize the chance of his untimely recovery, lobbed him into his open cage. I put the lid on, and then I watched, maybe for a few minutes, maybe for a half an hour...I don't know...alternating between thinking I was seeing shallow breaths and being convinced I'd slain the beast...but...it was an accident... self-defense? That last one was going to be a hard sale on Monday morning. Well, nothing I could do now. I barely theoretically knew human CPR, much less little mouse CPR. What was done was done. If he wasn't back to his full function mad-mouse state on Monday morning, the list of suspects would be short indeed. Knowing what I would know later about experiment tragedies, the proper scientific thing would have been to alert someone who knew how to harvest the experimental tissues, so they could at least be analyzed (even if not at the originally intended time point), before they decomposed beyond utility over the next day and a half or so. In the end, I made the calculated risk that he was alive, and that everything would be fine, and I gave him his scheduled drug injection. Apparently, I got lucky. No mention of any incident ever, so he must have been good to go for the rest of his experimental life. Me, I drank with true purpose that evening. Hopefully, that would be the worst thing I would ever do to any of my "patients", or at the least, the last time that one would bite me.

Oh well...science. You gotta love it.

...

I apparently did...and, do. After a bit of counseling (career-type, not for the mouse incident), some thinking, soul searching, and meeting with specific faculty over possible projects and available stipend support, I decided to take a year off the medical school curriculum in between Basic Sciences and Clinical Rotations to do a pre-doctoral research fellowship. Although some of my closest classmates thought I was crazy, this proved to be very enlightening, allowing me to realize first hand what was required to conduct hopefully meaningful biomedical research, and see how my own humble, albeit energetic, efforts could fit into a larger "program" and to begin gaining insight as to how that program fit into the national, and indeed, international, endeavors in specific focused research areas. I could even begin to see in some examples how targeted investigation motivated by one area of clinical interest often overlapped with the knowledge base and discovery approaches of completely unexpected areas of research in different fields, with potentially positive synergistic effects.

One unexpected difficulty of that medical school research year wasn't realized until afterwards, when I started experiencing the consequences of being out of curriculum and social sync with my previous classmates, and friends. When medical students progress into their clinical rotations, on the wards in the hospitals, in clinics, in different facilities, they're of course broken up into much smaller groups than when they all sit in the same big lecture hall, taking the same courses, at the same time, in the basic science years. Even if 20 or 30 students may be on the same large core rotation, like Internal Medicine, they're in different hospitals (and Baylor had and has several), and only one or two would be on the same actual team. And you can't of course control scheduling and assignment aspects to pick that other student as necessarily one of your prior friends. Sometimes, it's someone you barely knew the first two years; maybe someone with a life independent (hard as it may be to fathom) from the main school related social circles you hung in, parties you went to; hell, maybe they had a family. So, sometimes you made new friends, but typically, you were at least working with someone you knew to some degree from your prior shared classroom, lab, and social recent past.

For me, the separation from inner circle friends was further accentuated. I wasn't even in the sacred, real doctor type clinical rotations. I still hooked up with some of my closest buds, at some of our regular favorite bars, on random, planned, or special occasions. After all, my schedule was more flexible. I worked hard, but could do it in a manner that would usually allow me to be free for a few key hours or an evening of good-old-times when their rigid clinical schedules allowed. Harder, much harder, still, was the pre-graduation hype, and (argh!) the actual graduation ceremony, when my friends that I was now a year behind in the official pathway of doctor degree awarding, were magically transformed into real M.D.'s. Further, in my own clinical rotations, I was now taking third year clinical core rotations in my true fourth calendar year there with folks that were previously a year behind me, most of whom I didn't know, except for a few from foosball in the student lounge during my second and their first year, or from intramural sports, bars, etc., and even those were only rarely coincidentally on my same rotation. Plus, there's always that potential embarrassment of being an academic year older than the other kids in your "grade" (held back, maybe?), for whom you commonly find yourself explaining how you took a year off to do this really sophisticated research, that you're still working on, giving talks on at meetings, writing a paper on, blah, blah, blah. Most straight up clinically oriented students couldn't give a shit and/or thought you were perhaps a bit misguided. Some of the more academic residents (ex Baylor students or from elsewhere) thought it was a good idea, or impressive; the M.D., Ph.D. clinical residents (usually Medicine, less often Pediatrics, rarely Surgery) were either pleased that you had at least been exposed to research, or "bitten by the research bug", or they either sincerely or maliciously (e.g., if they were now no longer committed to any research future whatsoever and wanted you to endure similar worthless suffering, like being infected with the same virus in a Dawn of the Dead kind of way) felt that it hadn't been enough; "Why didn't you just do a Ph.D.?"

"Just" and "Ph.D." or any formal research training should never be used in the same sentence. Learning research is learning research, and it takes time, regardless of what you call it or yourself when done, and I would certainly be putting a lot more hard time in very shortly in the future. So when it came from an M.D./Ph.D. Family Medicine resident or soon to be wealthy Ophthalmology or Ortho resident who would never step foot in the lab again, there was maybe some hidden bitterness there. When the comments came from one of the more research oriented attendings, they thought it was great, encouraged as much of it as possible in the future, and tended to regard you differently than the other student sheep.

Well, regardless of the potentially variable clinical ward interpersonal experiences it would foster in the next few years, I liked the science. I liked the lab. I liked the people I met and worked with there. I liked most of their minds. I liked the endless openness and opportunity of it, the never-ending challenge of it, the doing things no one had ever done before aspects of it. I liked the prestige and respect that it was greeted with by most folks, all the above issues considered. And so, after two more years of extremely grueling, fascinating, and hopefully informative clinical training medical school years, as I graduated with mostly previous strangers and a few new friends, I was off to the research Mecca, the ultimate geek fest (to some of my old and new clinical friends), the National Institutes of Health (NIH), where in the course of my Internal Medicine residency, I would mix a sprinkling of adequate clinical training with a heavy dose of true, hard-core dedicated basic and applied research.

The sore grew. The wound deepened. The cravings enlarged, got more frequent, and even changed flavors a bit, I suppose, as during my years in Bethesda, not only did I make the large decision to switch from a future career in Internal Medicine to a future career in Neurology, I made the possibly even bigger decision to do this in the context of academia, of research, clinical to perhaps extraordinarily basic, and hence to arm myself with the needed skills, by doing ("Yes, it's true Mom and Dad") four MORE years of training. San Francisco would prove to be, as intended when the plans were made while at the NIH, the proper place where I would acquire the necessary background, skills, and credentials for the successful jump into junior faculty and a burgeoning career in academic medicine. San Francisco would also prove to be (quite unanticipated when those next stage of life plans were being drawn out, but certainly very welcome "after all this time" to the same parents, who would instantly and always love my new life partner), the place where I would meet, fall in love with, and marry Kim, and maybe begin to encounter signs that there might just be more to life, or so they say.

Marriage, after all, is not to be taken lightly.

VI

- Houston; October, 1993

"Tell me about the first time you ever went down on Kim," Curtis said in a truly nonchalant manner while he picked the sprouts off his sandwich.

We were sitting at Butera's, a deli at the corner of Shephard and Alabama, in the same block of shops as the Bookstop, at 1:30 p.m. or so on a lazy Saturday afternoon. Prior to this pornographic interrogation session, I had been quietly sitting on a bench at the park, all by my lonesome, actually somewhat gratefully in the absence of my usual-suspect park-decorating colleagues. I had two or three issues each of the Journal of Immunology and Archives of Neurology, a manuscript draft from one of my recent colleagues at UCSF, and a Houston Chronicle. I was, in theory, determined "to get some shit done today." I felt acutely behind on my journal reading, and I had been promising my colleague that I would polish my parts of our joint manuscript and give it a general read (particularly making sure it addressed the study's clinical relevance) for a few weeks now.

I suppose it may have actually been several weeks by now. Time is probably the most subjectively perceived of our objective parameters. If you're waiting to submit a paper that is on the subject most dear to your life and which is one theoretical piece of the multifactorial component of your tenure promotion, three or four weeks is a lifetime. If you're swamped with your own crap and your colleague's paper is one of a perceived 65 million things you're working on, your contribution was a specialized assay and some theory to a project now only remotely linked to your current main focus, then the six or eight weeks time you've had the paper while making the occasional "I'm working on it" promises seems like only one or two weeks.

Guilt had accumulated to a sufficient degree that despite a hellish, physically and emotionally tiring past clinical week, I had actually awoken early on a Saturday morning, made myself breakfast, and sat down at my desk with three cups of coffee on board and one in hand, when I realized that the only way I was going to get anything done was getting the hell out of there. I took my journals, a brand-spanking new highlighter, my manuscript draft ("Protein expression during terminal neurite differentiation: contact dependent regulation of a novel kinase"), and a red pen down to the park. It was a pleasantly refreshing, maybe even rejuvenating day, not unusual for October in Southeast Texas. Humidity levels (not rarely equal in early fall to their late summer "Mr. Heat Meiser" levels) had at least temporarily faded. Temperatures began to fluctuate a bit more this time of year, the gods toying with the idea of an actual winter on the Texas Gulf coast, but ultimately realizing how silly that idea is to the faithful who congregated at a density of 4-5 million per swamp city to be able to play golf or read outside at least eleven months a year.

It had rained on and off during the generally depressing prior week, but today the sun was out in full force; a crisp, dry, and bright last attempt to claim its usual glory before the brief, relatively cool late fall and often dreary, pseudo-winter. It was, in fact, the kind of day that at the opposite time of year suggested the true arrival of spring, to the point that one couldn't help but smell the warm air, sense the sharp illuminated brightness of everything around them, feel the soothing baking effect of the sun on their skin, and get a whopping dose of spring fever, complete with staring at everything female that walked by. Today, in the spirit of productivity, however, I was consciously suppressing any spontaneous horniness that the sunshine might induce. I suppose one seasonal difference between these two weak opposing borders of summer could have been in the flora thing, with spring ushering in flowers or blooms on trees and what not, whereas things here were now still only green or focally beginning the green-to-brown transition, but I never paid attention to any of that flower-shit and as far as I could tell, Houston really only had two colors, generally speaking, when it came to nature, green and brown. Trees were green, at least to my oblivious rare observations, most of the year, turning brown (either by leaf and/or needle design or by loss of leaf and exposure of branch/twig) for a brief six to eight or maybe ten to twelve weeks (the time perspective thing again) at "winter". In contrast, the grass was green a lot of the year, or so it seemed to me living and especially working in a fairly concrete-rich part of the city, except in July and August, well maybe June through September, when the sun baked it (irradiated may be more precise) to a form of Bermuda straw that no hose could successfully oppose.

Today, to the non-botanist, both components were still largely green, with spotty brown. It felt great to be outside and alive. Apparently not that many others in my neighborhood had noticed or appreciated the outside component of that combo yet (assuming they were alive), as there were only a few small handfuls of other people at the park, a likely grandfather with a toddler boy and a five or six year old girl, alternately playing on the swings and chasing each other around a sand-box. An adolescent Hispanic boy and girl were gently flirting at the slide. He had a black Iron-Maiden T-shirt on, and was trying to act athletic and macho, climbing up the slide to where she sat at the top, casually switching between interested and disinterested, while occasionally holding her hands over her eyes to block the sun while staring off into the distance.

But in general, I was fairly oblivious to my surroundings. I had enjoyed approximately two and a half hours of horny-distraction free work vigor. I had a walk-man on and was listening to a debut CD from a new band out of Atlanta called Collective Soul. I had actually read an article in the October Journal of Immunology on a novel pair of cell adhesion molecules linking macrophages to T4 lymphocytes, supposedly relevant to T-cell activation during antigen presentation, and one in the September Archives of Neurology about a novel class of supposedly anti-oxidant steroid derivative drugs that offered protection in a rodent model of head injury (perhaps this explains in part the lack of horniness at this stage), and I had already edited the methods section for my specific experimental part of my friend's paper when Curtis basically came up and scared the living shit out of me.

"Yo, man, what the fuck's going on?" he shouted, after an obviously successful covert sneaking up maneuver to the back of the bench I was sitting on, and now grabbing for stabilization after dropping my highlighter and raising a couple of inches off the hard wood. He took obvious joy out of this, clearly anticipating this effect while he barely had to be stealthy during his approach upon his extremely concentrating friend. He seemed to be in a good mood, light as the spring-fall day he floated in. His dishevelment and satisfied grin was the look I had come to recognize as one reflecting a particularly gratifying (physically AND emotionally) sexual experience of the night before, one that probably lasted sufficiently long and late that he was likely just arising from the recovery period and needing breakfast, right when my breakfast was fading and I could stand some lunch. I'd been there myself enough times, due to partying and/or hopefully equally passionate nights with those harboring twice as many X-chromosomes as Curtis's new loves, that it would be unthinkably rude not to accept his invitation to grab a laid-back sandwich or something.

...

So now we sat across from each other at the Deli, inside, at a window table rather than outside in the sunny day, which Curtis apparently wasn't completely ready for just yet, and I watched quietly, perplexed and curious, as he systematically pulled the sprouts off his sandwich. Unconsciously cataloging data, I realized this was probably about the third time I had seen him do this to some sort of vegetarian sandwich. Here, they were made with chopped carrots and cucumber and large gobs of avocado, and I began wondering why he didn't just order them without the sprouts. I saw him once before here at Butera's, similarly picking out and piling up on his plate large quantities of sprouts while having an early evening sandwich with a "buddy" while I was picking up a to-go sandwich one week night. I was planning to get some work done at home that night, one of the first few weeks I had been back in Houston, so refused their very polite offer to join them.

Then, one previous Saturday afternoon, Carl, Frank, and I had been sitting in the park, debating, I think, the relative merits of being an only child (Carl) vs. being one of several siblings (Frank), when Curtis strolled by, sat down on the bench, pulled a sandwich out of a brown Butera's take out bag, and proceeded to pluck small handfuls and then individual sprouts out of the middle. He tossed them onto the nearby ground, momentarily intriguing a pigeon or two and some sort of ground-pecking sparrow-like-bird (my lack of avian knowledge rivals my botany ignorance for complete and utter ineptitude), before they realized they could probably do better on their own.

Carl looked on, with only the slightest hint of the disgust he probably was really harboring, while continuing to extol the advantages of having more parental attention, more financial resources, and the joys of a lack of sibling torment and rivalry.

Frank, who over the last several weeks had seemed to consciously attempt to show more restraint and patience when Carl, or any of the rest of the group for that matter, said something so seemingly contrary to his meat-loaf and Budweiser American way of life, pondered these comments while alternately closing his mouth tight and puckering his lips and nodding his head, and then responded.

"I don't know, without my second oldest brother, Pete...Peter, I wouldn't have had my first baseball glove, a lot of the clothes I wore to school, and I never would have ever gotten interested in auto shop. Hell, even my first car had been Pete's for a while, till he wrecked it kind of bad."

He paused and stared off into space, towards the empty swing set, as if considering the complexities of fate that would so kindly combine to yield him a car that he probably had to work his ass off on in order to achieve a moving piece of matter that he probably cherished while it would have embarrassed the shit out of most of us.

"What do you think Jeff?" he asked me, pulling himself up a little from leaning his arms on his knees, pleased to have found a way to broaden the debate from just between the commonly opposing forces.

To that point, I had only been vaguely paying attention the last couple of minutes, watching, to my left, Curtis eagerly devouring his sandwich, his thin brown bangs hanging over his forehead and eyes as he bent his face down into an avocado-colored mess, apparently completely oblivious to all around him, savoring the apparently much needed life-sustaining fuel that would get him through this up-coming evening's adventures.

I had heard enough of the "brother-give-car" thing to hopefully meaningfully contribute, "Without me as an older brother, I suppose it would have been harder for my younger brother to get Playboys and Penthouses and that kind of thing, when he was like in junior high or early high school and found things I'd left around the house, maybe when visiting from school and stuff," I paused, now considering. "Oh, and I helped him with his first fake ID so that he could buy beers later on." I paused briefly, and then thinking back, added, "It was one of my old ID's or expired licenses, basically, and we just changed the expiration date without messing with the picture, which may have been taken when I was just a few years older than he was at the time. Funny, we didn't even look that much alike, but it worked often enough to be useful, I guess."

Carl rolled his eyes, while Frank let out a somewhat cautious smile, as if my comments supported his claim in general, but not necessarily in a way he would completely approve of or that he was hoping for, more like some weird cut of veal he wasn't familiar with, rather than meat loaf.

At this point, although none of us would have even thought the sandwich-scarfing Curtis had been paying attention, he had finished eating and he leaned his head back and took a deep thoughtful breath through his nose, and sighed. He had about a one centimeter glob of thick, moist, and sprout-free avocado at the left corner of his lip, actually more officially on his lower cheek or upper chin, not quite touching, but very near, the corner of his mouth.

"I think I would have liked to have had an older sister," Curtis now pondered out loud, while he curled his mouth to the right and slightly squinted his eyes, as if really giving it some careful consideration. "My Mom was always getting pissed-off when I borrowed her makeup."

This prompted Carl's eye-roll to be accompanied by shaking his head gently back and forth, nothing too athletic. Frank had a perplexed, maybe even sort of confused, look on his face. I was pushing a pile of sprouts around with my foot. We sat there for a few moments, staring, thinking I guess, quiet and comfortable in each other's company. Then, as if one reminded him of the other, Curtis stood up and wiped the creamy avocado off of his mouth with the back of his right hand, and said while standing, "I gotta go. I promised this guy I know that I'd give him a blow job before he goes to work this afternoon."

...

So now I sat opposite Curtis at our table next to the window on the Alabama street side at Butera's, watching him extract the sprouts out of his sandwich, again, first in large clumps, then in smaller groups, and finally single strands, occasionally partially coated in avocado. Again, I momentarily wondered why he didn't just ask for his veggie sandwich without sprouts. Before I could ask, though, I saw as he took his first bite that a few strands of sprouts stuck out of the bread, maybe about 10 % or so of the original sprout volume. Apparently, the perfect Butera's veggie sandwich, in Curtis' opinion, was one with about 90 % of the sprouts removed, a sandwich that was best achieved by removing the bulk of the sprouts, not obtainable, obviously, by asking for such a sandwich without sprouts, and likely more consistently reached by extracting the right amount out of the original sandwich in a personal fashion rather than risking inadequacy by asking potentially variable sandwich makers to put less or only a handful of sprouts on.

I, on the other hand, had my typical ham sandwich, but in this slightly unusual case, on black rye, and I think with provolone instead of Swiss. When not thinking about things like sex or immunologically mediated neurotoxicity, I occasionally ponder the truly great mysteries in life. Over the course of many school and work lunches, I believe I have come to the non-scientifically substantiated belief, not soon to be published in a journal coming to your town, that most of us form our characteristic or favorite sandwiches early in life, with steady reinforcement over the years of inevitable sandwich eating, and despite occasional forays into the exotic... maybe when your spouse says things like "Oh come on, why don't you try something different," when you're standing in the line of a nouveaux sandwich shop in a trendy Seattle neighborhood, one that goes up to 42 on the sandwich list, and you don't even need to scan past the ham and some sort of skunky goat cheese listed at number 3.

I suppose I'd been eating predominantly ham sandwiches for about 25 years. Did I find comfort and uncomplicated sustenance in ham sandwiches because my Mom had made them for me as a child, or did my Mom make ham sandwiches because that's what I'd liked and that's what I would actually eat? Who knows? Maybe a little of both. Who cares? Probably not something that I was going to write an NIH grant on. Or even if I did write one, maybe in one of those Jeff-has-finally-snapped   Jack-Nicolson-"All-work-and-no-play-makes-Johnny-a-dull-boy"-in-The-Shining-movie kind of moment, it likely wouldn't get funded, and in this case, not because it would be "too ambitious" (a recurrently experienced mild to moderately severe criticism I'd seen too many times, even at this relatively early stage of my "career"). Anyway, if Curtis's Mom had made him avocado sandwiches with shredded rabbit food when he was a kid, it would just be one more reason why I would love to meet the woman someday.

And so I now proceeded to share with my gay lunch mate the extremely personal details of my first episode of cunnilingus with the woman I would eventually vow to spend the rest of my life with. Of course, as a typical male, wherein all things sexual have the potential to generate alternating opposite feelings of bravado and insecurity, I would like to think that my skills in this particular and subsequent similar endeavors are part of the complex, interrelated reasons that

Kim also eventually vowed to spend the rest of her life with me. Then again, we certainly didn't know that would be the case when we embarked on a mutual oral exploration a few weeks after we had met at a museum in San Francisco for an AIDS fund raiser. And since my current conversation partner was seemingly unlikely to ever progress from analogous encounters to a lasting relationship, I certainly didn't intentionally emphasize the potential romantic aspects of this particular heated episode.

"I think it was our third or so 'official' date," I began, washing the taste of ham and mustard down with what had accidentally become my third Beck's Light during what I had initially intended to be a quick lunch. The chances of me subsequently resuming my previous productivity of the morning were quickly diminishing.

"We had gone out for dinner once, and met for drinks and munchies once or twice...."

"I hope you didn't actually call them munchies in front of her," Curtis interrupted. "But then again, I guess we wouldn't be having this particular conversation if you had."

"Hah...Hah..." I said sarcastically. "I'm sure I was the epitome of cool, at least early on.... Anyway, we had made out and stuff, a lot the first time we went out, not so much the second time, even though we really wanted to, but I think it was a weeknight, and we both had to work the next morning, and I think I was actually on call the next day."

"Ah ... 'made out and stuff'...so hetero of you," Curtis interjected, not completely jokingly, more with the tone I imagine one assumes when discussing competing religions, acknowledging a fact of yours that one may know from reading or attending services with a friend of such faith, while simultaneously conveying one's preference for his or her own. "And waiting till the third date. How chivalrous of you," he continued, more sarcastically.

"Well, some of us actually get to know the names of those we perform sexual services for, especially those that may turn out to be serious," I said with equal, only moderately defensive, sarcasm.

"Hey, I know the names of a lot of the guys I perform services on," he quickly replied, "or at least, I know the names of what I call them...you know, in the throes of passion and all."

"I'm sure you do," I said in a manner not offering up too much credibility to his claim.

"Plus," I continued, now objectively attempting to provide a few key pieces of dogma of my particular sect, "a lot of us hetero males have that old double standard of wanting to meet slutty or easy chicks, for obvious reasons, but I guess we don't officially want to marry one, so when we encounter a truly worthwhile babe, there may even be a subconscious, although unwelcome, imposed morality, waiting for a day or two, sometimes even longer, just so as to not formally disqualify the individual lust object as a potential "keeper.""

"Fascinating culture," Curtis observed.

"If Kim heard me saying this stuff, or actually, telling you any of this, she would kill me," I appropriately added, sort of like the disclaimers of the financial details at the end of a radio car advertisement or the listing of potential side effects at the end of a prescription drug commercial.

"I won't tell if you won't," Curtis reassured me.

"Actually, I'm not sure that Kim likes you all that much, so you may not have much conversation opportunity to bust me anyway," I said somewhat kiddingly, although knowing somehow that this blatantly sexual and honest confidant would never squeal any of this, or anything else he may know or discover about me in my current life situation.

Curtis wasn't outwardly hurt by this potentially true revelation, and didn't miss a beat when he responded playfully, "It's probably cuz she senses how hot you are for me."

"Something like that, I'm sure," I said with the subtle kind of only mild sarcasm that only a fairly intelligent individual with a matching sense of humor could appropriately detect.

After a brief pause, in which we sat there silently, each taking a couple sips of our beers, I continued with renewed vigor.

"So, for this particular momentous occasion that you crave knowledge on, I guess it was our third date. Kim had actually called me, well actually paged me, but it still seemed like a hint of an ascension in our potential relationship, as it was during the day and I was at work…in the lab, I think," I continued.

"O.K.," Curtis commented as evidence of paying attention, while I took another sip of my beer, "but if you're gonna use words like 'ascension', I'm gonna have to go into the bathroom and masturbate."

"I'll try to keep that in mind. But let me first explain something about our "culture." She had called to invite me to a work party, a casual get together to celebrate the landing of a major ad campaign by her firm. It was going to be mostly just drinks and yes, munchies, at the house of one of the firm's partners, basically her mentor, a middle aged classy executive kind of woman, whom I had heard about in admiring fashion, but of course hadn't met. For "we" people, inviting someone to a work-related thing where all your co-workers that you see and talk with everyday meet your "date" and talk with them, basically get to know them, is sort of a big thing; kind of meaning that this is someone with potential that I'm willing to have meet my friends and have my even more casual associates meet, and hopefully approve of, and ask me about and tease me about at the coffee machine in the office, etc."

"I see," Curtis responded, moderately intrigued. "Again…fascinating."

"Actually, that's not completely true. I mean, it's a little more complicated than that," I began to clarify. "Guys, at least most guys, will bring any babe to an office party, the babier the better, and particularly for holiday parties when there's even more potential for getting dolled up. Hell, it could even be an escort, as long as it will gain the admiration of male colleagues and the potential future sexual interest by female co-workers who may not have paid much attention to them before. Of course, if it happens to be a foxy chick that you are actually interested in and that can speak in complete sentences, at least before she's drank too much, that's not necessarily points off. But, for women, it's usually a bigger deal, they being somewhat more secure, and often being able to engage in conversations at parties without some male eye candy on their arm. For them, bringing a date to a work function is usually a bigger deal."

"Hmm…I see," Curtis responded again, as I began to stand up to go get us two more beers. "That may explain why I like guys more.….That and because they have dicks," he continued when I had stepped far enough away that the necessity of raising his voice turned heads from a two or three table radius.

"So," I began again when I returned and gazed around enough to make a few heads turn back to their lunches, "Kim and I arranged to meet first at a bar we both knew, a few blocks from her associate's house in Pacific Heights. I think it was my suggestion. I was a little nervous I guess, and thought if I could get a couple of pre-drink drinks in me, and see her first, I would then be my usually charming self."

"Did the bar have that many drinks in stock?" my sprout sucking compadre chimed in, clearly starting to enjoy this.

"I'm not sure, smart ass, but it didn't matter. When I saw how hot Kim looked, I only had one organ that needed feeding," I continued, bringing it down to Curtis-level vulgarity, only for a while, as my mind drifted to just how amazing Kim did look when I walked into the bar and saw her sitting on a bar stool. She glanced over to me in the doorway to her left, her hair tossing softly with the movement. It was about shoulder length, auburn-tinted light brown, a blunt cut in touch with the times, medium bangs, combed over to the left. Her eyes seemed to sparkle from the candles on the bar counter, even at that distance. She gave a soft smile. Her mouth was so amazing, all I wanted to do at that moment was kiss it, maybe forever.

"Yo, don't leave me hanging over here," Curtis said, while he threw in my direction a half sprout that had survived on the table after someone from Butera's staff had taken mercy on us and cleared our plates from our table despite the usual policy of clearing one's own place, perhaps sensing we were in one of those personal sexual stories that can take quite a while and require many beers, all more enjoyable on a moderately clean surface.

"Oh, sorry," I resurrected my mind. "So we had a couple of drinks, while I asked her for the synopsis version of who her co-workers were that I would soon meet, what they were like, whom I had to watch out for, whom it would be a bad idea for me to mention to how badly I wanted to bang their co-worker Kim. This got me a flirtatious elbow to the side, followed by a very soft, lingering kiss, with a deep gaze into my eyes as she pulled away."

"God, I love kissing at bars," my beer drinking companion observed. I clearly had an attentive audience at this point. Curtis's face seemed aglow with the anticipation of hearing sex talk.

"She had come straight from work, and was the essence of the hot, well-dressed professional babe. She had on a brown, I guess, brown and black wool suit, you know a very fine plaid; short jacket, pretty short skirt from what I remember, and it conformed to her ass and hips just perfectly, a plain black silk blouse underneath her jacket, black hose, and supple black leather pumps," I must have paused again, picturing her in my mind, watching her while she walked to the restroom and I ignored everything else around me.

"Yo, space boy," Curtis again brought me back to deli reality. "That's a pretty good fashion description. You sure you're not gay?"

"Pretty sure," I understatedly replied. "Especially that day." I took a long swig out of my green bottle of Beck's, finishing it, and continued after I set the empty

53

bottle down. "So after a couple of drinks we walked the few blocks to her friend Edith's house. There were already pretty many people there, including a few of your people," I added to be sure I was keeping the attention of my audience.

"Were they wearing short skirts too?" said audience inquired in typical smart ass fashion.

"I don't think so," I responded, but then added, mercifully, when I saw my companion's pouty frown, "Well, maybe a couple of them."

When his frown changed to an approving nod, I continued.

"We had a blast. I met everybody, and had many alcohol-inspired deep conversations with complete strangers. It was nice to not be talking just medical shit, I guess, and I apparently demonstrated that I had strong opinions on certain advertisement issues, many fairly directly relevant to the impassioned lives of my new friends. Kim and I found dozens of opportunities to get back into immediate physical contact with each other, but I also enjoyed watching her interact with her friends when we were in different conversations, the way she smiled when she spoke or listened, the way she would put her hand on a friend's arm while whispering into her ear, or smack one of her male buddies on the shoulder playfully. I caught her watching me a couple of times, when I came up for air in the middle of some of my zealous debates, smiling in general and then straight at me, as I guess she got a kick out of how I was fitting in."

Again, my mind must have drifted, as I saw Kim's eyes smiling at me from across the room, maybe occasionally squinting playfully as she turned her head to the side, giving me a coy inquisitive look.

"I get the feeling we're getting close to the good part," I was shaken back to Earth again. "I need another beer for the muffy parts. Want another one?"

"Is that one of those gay rhetorical questions?" I replied as Curtis got up to fetch us more boy-talk fuel.

The whole scene unfolded in my mind while Curtis was gone, and with my lonesome-guard dropped under the assault of the first four or so beers, I began to miss Kim, badly, wishing right now that I was between her legs, tasting her again, for the thousandth time, as if for the first time, then holding her tight, so close we could barely breathe, squeezing her so that without a word between us, she knew that I fucked up, that we fucked up, that we should never be apart, not for even a millisecond, much less this absolute crap of living in two different cities.

"You O.K. buddy?" Curtis asked nicely as he sat down while sliding my beer over to me.

"Fine. Thanks, man," I replied, then took a long refreshing, sentiment rinsing, but memory enhancing drink. "It got late," I readily continued, "but things were still going strong at the party, maybe with half the guests still left, maybe 15 or 20 or so, of what I gathered was the largely inner circle. It had mellowed a bit. I walked up behind Kim, as both of our mutually independent conversations had faded, put my arms around her waste, pulled her closely to me, smelled her hair and neck, and got a little light headed, as I whispered into her left ear:

> *"I want to make love to you so badly, I think it would be un-healthy for me to wait much longer."*
>
> *She squeezed my hand, and turned towards me, looking up into my face, while our bodies pressed closely together, my hands switching to find the small of her back, on her silk blouse, under her jacket.*
>
> *"This is bad," she said. "I've been watching you all night, and I think I could be persuaded to fall in love with you," as a slight smile curled at the left corner of her so amazingly sexy mouth.*
>
> *"That is terrible," I said. "And because of that and how incred-ibly beautiful you are, I don't think I can wait till we make it back to one of our places."*
>
> *In the greatest single thing I think I have ever heard still to this day, she squeezed my arm so tightly I think I had a bruise for a week, and she said, "I don't think I can even wait...period."*

"Then, we mutually glanced around the room, together, as a single organism, in conspiracy. We walked over to the hallway, arm in arm, almost sideways, still facing each other, feeling unnoticed, but then again we were pretty oblivious to everything around us. When we made it to the stairs, we walked up the steps, quickly, but mock quietly tip-toeing. The first room to the right was that of Edith's (that is, our host's) daughter, who was away at college. Kim and Edith were close, I guess, the kind of closeness where you can have sex with your new boyfriend in your boss's daughter's room-kind of close, although we weren't really thinking about repercussions or consequences or impressions. I guess, retrospectively, this was a fairly eclectic and open-minded, and fortunately considerate group, the kind of folks that enjoyed seeing their darling Kim so enthralled, and not likely to go snooping around when they hadn't seen the two new lovebirds for awhile."

"We closed the door behind us," I continued, "Kim in front of me, my back to the door. Fortunately, it locked, my last thought possessing any true caution. We kissed deeply, in the same motion that I removed her jacket. I loved the way her firm breasts felt through her blouse. At the same time I pushed her towards the bed, I think she pulled me towards it even more firmly, while my hands had moved under her skirt to feel her amazing ass through her silk panties."

I noted that Curtis was actually now gripping the table with both hands, while pushing his back firmly against his chair, but I was too entranced to pause for long to ponder his apparent growing interest in this heterosexual tale.

"Through some total fucking miracle that only further confirmed that we should be together, I found buttons, hooks, zippers, or whatever, on the back of her skirt, and before her sexy bottom had even found the bed, I had removed her skirt. She had lace thigh-high stockings on, thank God, 'cause after the skirt miracle, I'm not sure I could do the conventional garter thing with the suave smoothness I may still have wanted to convey through my total lust at this stage. In theory, we were pressed for time, despite our apparent oblivion of our surroundings. I pressed my thumb on her black silk panties, gently against her pouting, you know, girl parts, feeling the moistness, before sliding it up to rub against her clit….You can look that one up when you get back home. After pressing and rubbing for a few barely tolerable seconds, I bent my head forward and pressed my nose up against her panties, taking a deep breath of the smell that I would come to crave like fucking oxygen from then on. I pressed soft, then firm kisses against her panties, then pushed the crotch of her panties aside a little, and ran my tongue up through her vagina, tasting her, before flicking it over her clitoris. She let out a soft moan, and squeezed my shoulders with a touch that seemed to impart something not only acutely sexual, but of a level of intimacy and knowing and closeness that we only get to experience every few billion years or so. Well, maybe you get to on a nightly basis in the News Rooms on Richmond, but still…"

"I don't know," Curtis uttered, somewhat breathlessly. "Keep going."

"I took my time, savoring her taste, savoring her response to my tongue on her engorged clit. After some time, I scooted up her body, while she slid to get completely on the bed, and we opened her blouse up, then off her shoulders, and I stopped her from taking her bra off momentarily, so I could feel her breasts through her very sexy sheer black bra. We kissed deeply, then as she took her bra off, I placed soft kisses on her nipples and then sucked on them, and I entered her, for the first time in our lives."

"You had your pants off already?" Curtis inquired, clearly paying attention to details, and proving he was indeed….a scholar.

"I skipped those parts," I responded, "you know, to maintain a certain level of professional-alternative-lifestyles-friendship kind of thing, I guess."

"O.K., O.K., then what?" he quickly encouraged me.

"After a while of feeling so extraordinarily close, making love slowly, consciously restraining ourselves at almost peaked moments and forcing ourselves to slow down, I pulled out, in part to prolong things, if you know what I mean, and I moved back down her smooth, now completely naked body," I continued to my table squeezing bud, whose skinny pale knuckles were whiter than usual.

"What about the hose?" Curtis inquired, again reminding me why he was, after all, the Yoda of sex in the neighborhood.

"You're pretty good at this chick stuff, buddy. You know….it's never too late. Well for those taking notes, I had slid them off, one at a time, while holding up first her right leg, and then her left leg, then after I'd been inside her for a while I held up both her hose-free legs enjoying the resulting extreme depths of penetration."

Curtis nodded, as if acknowledging the legitimacy of this explanation and approving of the deep penetration thing simultaneously.

"As I lowered my face back down between her legs, I slid my hands under her, and gently felt her perfect rear in my hands. As I took my time, flicking my tongue over her clit, I raised my hands up and gently cupped her breasts and tugged very softly on her beautiful nipples. It was clear I was making progress. In part, I guess, I wanted to convey, here, early on, that I was thoughtful, not selfish, and I thought if I could make her orgasm…well that certainly wouldn't argue strongly against a fourth date. Plus, man, I was just so much getting off on it… the whole thing. I kept seeing her face in my mind, from the bar, from across the room at the…Oh my God…still going on party…the way her skin felt…from her feet to her ankles, all up along the length of her legs, her smooth, silky, thighs, to her waist, to her shoulders, where I occasionally dug in, after fondling her beautiful breasts."

My mind drifted…When Kim came, I didn't pause to feel good about myself though. I loved the way she momentarily felt helpless in my arms, I loved the thought of her feeling so close to me that she could let herself go. I wasn't scared, even a little, no, not at all, when I got a flash in my head that this was the first of prayerfully many such nights. At this early stage, I wasn't sure where things should go next, given that there were folks downstairs, etc. Maybe I even thought I would earn future brownie points if I stopped there, as difficult as it may have actually been, at that point, to walk downstairs.

I continued for Curtis:

"As I lifted up and partly away, this sexed up beautiful woman grabbed me by my left wrist and pulled me on top of her and said something like, 'Not so fast, cowboy', and she kissed me deeply, totally getting me off on the idea that I had her taste all over my mouth. There's probably some sort of homo-cum tasting version you can relate to, I guess. Anyway, needless to say, after a few more minutes, I came in a manner in which I thought I may need a stretcher afterwards, and it was all I could do to slide off of my future wife's boss's daughter's bed and put some semblance of my clothes back on to go downstairs and act, you know, like we were just upstairs looking, apparently in some great time consuming detail, at some of the art on the hallway wall."

I paused and took a deep drink from my slightly warming beer.

Curtis's eyes were wide, and fiery in that energetic and eager Curtis way. He took a deep breath, and said, "God, you make it sound so fucking hot, I may want to try it someday."

"Right," I frowned sarcastically.

"Well, probably not…not really…you know…but…you know what I mean, but don't tell anybody…you know…" he floundered.

…

"What about the second date …must have been pretty good to lead to that scrumptious third one?" Curtis asked as we lazily strolled the half block south down Shepherd before cutting over east towards our neighborhood, as if he was now making a casual study of my conquest strategies.

I had lived through enough of these types of afternoons in my semi-adult and adult life to know that I was at that critical juncture of theoretical possible later functionality vs. more likely irreversible lack of constructive accomplishment for the day. I could go home and take a hopefully brief nap, wake up a little later than I had intended, drink enough coffee to get sufficiently temporarily wired to get less done than I wanted to, then go to sleep really late, mad at myself for wasting so much time, get less sleep than I needed, and then be partially worthless the next day or I could drink and hang out for a little bit longer, relax without getting actually shit-faced, go to sleep actually early for me, tired enough to fall asleep without feeling too guilty for not getting the work done that I had aspired to for the day, and then wake up actually a little early for me, get a few hours of stuff done while I drank coffee and felt productive for being up so early, get to work on time, and have a productive day, to the point that I would feel warm, fuzzy, and accomplished the following evening.

I'm not sure that I actually processed these possibilities at the time vs. just deciding that I felt like talking some more, especially about Kim, and drinking some more, enjoying Curtis's easy company. As a biochemistry-oriented hard core Neurology type guy, I ain't no Freud expert, but maybe the sub-conscious controllers of our immediate needs are better judges than the higher rational intellects, or something like that.

Anyway, I can't believe that I subsequently shared some of the evidence of the occasional nightmares of my periodic anxious weirdness the way I did. Maybe revealing aspects of events and behaviors at least partially misperceived at the time of their occurrence is a futile attempt to remind ourselves not to do it again, not to "be that way". Or maybe I enjoyed being able to be so honest about my occasionally-oh-so-human self with someone whom I perceived was so down to earth as to realize, perhaps to have likely experienced, that one could feel not so on top of his game, not so utterly confident at some periods of life, maybe so sexy and in control some moments and yet so utterly and hideously insecure and tarnished or blemished at other times, so as to not even want to go out in public. Or maybe I'd had a beer or two too many to keep the ol' ego guard up effectively (how's that for Freudian?)....

Basically, as I now disclosed to Curtis while we lazily shuffled along the side-walk in that five-beers-down-don't-wait-too-long-to-keep-drinking-some-more mode, was that on the occasion of my second date with Kim I had the biggest zit in the history of my male-hormonally-challenged life...or at least, what I per-ceived as the biggest blemish ever. Clearly, the Complexion Gods, potential ruin-ers of proms, weddings, class pictures, and even repeatedly-shown drivers license photos if one's sins were particularly deserved, were fucking with me at a most inopportune time.

Of course, as I have been reminded several times subsequently by my reassuring partner in the context of a close personal relationship, this may be, at least in part, hopefully in large part, a matter of perception. After all, certain parts of the face don't have a lot of room for growth and also happen to be highly innervated; for example, the tip of the nose, certain parts of the chin, or that part of the forehead right above the bridge of the nose between but a little above the eyes where glasses, sadly, don't quite cover when afflicted by a bright shiny acne gumma. As these sites tragically give rise to even miniscule red bumps, barely visible from more than one or two feet away, especially in a dark bar such as might be used as the setting for a second casual date, hypothetically speaking, one feels them as much more shockingly evident than witnessed by even the interested outside observer.

However, herein lays the problem, probably largely anxiety related, and not necessarily in that deep tragic, inevitable consequence of the self destructive human condition that some of my psych (or is it psycho?) colleagues may point to. That early little tingle, that barely perceptible slight bump appreciated by the extraordinarily sensitive tip of the finger during a casual face rub or a hopefully on schedule face wash, elicits a response ranging from a "not again" frustration to an "Oh My God, not now" panic, say when it is the day before a big event, such as, oh I don't know, maybe a second date with someone you are already overly intrigued and essentially mesmerized by, if your gut feelings are on track or if your inability to eat, concentrate, or not pick a zit is an accurate gauge.

So, despite having told yourself so many times before, "Don't pick it" or "Don't mash," it is impossible to resist. After all, if it would just "pop", you know it could largely go away by tonight even, and certainly be essentially acceptable by tomorrow.

"Fuck, it didn't pop," you say to your progressively unbalanced self, the Mr. Hyde losing all sense of self control in front of the mirror, as you squeeze harder. Nothing. Shit. Fear, maybe even panic, has now overtaken any dermatologically-educated rational self, and your wrists and forearms are maximally taut as you strategically place the sadly too long nails of your recently grooming-ignored index fingers on either side, like a thing possessed. Crap. Now the already made sensitive skin has been raped of its most superficial, and yes anti-bacterial protective, layers. This injury-to-insult borderline psychotic futile attempt to achieve normal faceness for the next day has now led to an erosion, a red, raised-edge defect covering an already throbbing, increasingly purple mass, a hopefully will-stop-weeping-soon catastrophe that was an essentially un-noticeable nothing a few moments before.

What leads to these Job-like attacks on a substrate that can look like the poster child for healthy, tan, care-free and zit-free casual easiness in the middle of a Texas Hill Country summer? I suppose you don't have to be a medical researcher to recognize that one: Stress. Ah, my familiar life-mate; the Satan of the modern overachieving world. Physiologists may point out the accelerated heart rate or moist palms, the familiar physical manifestations of acute stress. And I've studied and experienced, too many times, the autonomic mechanisms of intestinal manifestations that a good old fashioned humongous medical school examination or auditorium sized lecture can induce in the perfectionist. This kind of multiple week long stress, this nagging, recurring and occasionally suppressed, prolonged angst seems to wreak havoc not only on the old bowels, but also those pores, those greasy little barometers of what's going on deep inside the still not precisely localized neurons of the dread-center.

"Must not have been too hideous," Curtis's comment following my account shook me out of my subsequent brief recollection stupor. "She went out with you again, and you guys got down and nasty...and hell, she even married you."

My mind again drifted, to the occasion of Kim's and my "official" second date and how much I enjoyed being with her, once the anxiety of my zit had partially faded, thanks in large part to her apparent not even noticing (I still avoided looking in the mirror when I went to the bathroom at the restaurant, not wanting to acutely remind myself of the less than perfect picture I was perhaps presenting to this amazingly beautiful woman that I was finding otherwise so easy to talk to). From this memory and the feelings still lingering from my lunch reminiscences came spinning off, all at once, in one complete and perfect sensation, a thousand other little memories of the years we spent in San Francisco, a collage of an endless number of daily-life things, special occasions, resolutions of love's occasional crises, quiet simple joys mixed with passionate intensities, leaving me with the mixed sensation of total visceral warmth complicated by the acute emotional agony of Kim's not being there with me, and all which that may or may not mean.

Curtis and I walked along in silence, and I was barely aware of him continuing. "I remember, I had like a pimple or something on my butt once, maybe a couple of years ago, probably summer time, you know how the sweat and stuff can cause that sometimes, even on someone like me. And, well, I had this sort of date planned, and I knew it was gonna lead to … you know…me getting fucked."

In the ongoing battle in my head between fond and sensual Kim- and happy Jeff-Kim-memories and the contrasting darkness of the current uncertainty of things between us, the crassness of my companion's comments were making it harder to stay in the warm fuzzy places.

He relentlessly expanded, with a few sordid details, and then, I thought…. finished.

And I think I was somehow beginning to appreciate that Curtis, and even some of my other unexpected park friends, had a way of putting some of my life symptoms in perspective. In the soul of a true diagnostician, constantly sorting through symptoms and signs (and no group of physicians maybe other than Pathologists spends more time on the diagnostic and non therapeutic side of things than Neurologists), I acknowledged plenty of negative symptoms right now; so maybe….this was a good sign.

"I figured, chances are I'll never see this guy again anyway" Curtis surprisingly persisted "so I may as well have a good time." Brief pause. "And boy, did I." "I'm sure," I added pretty automatically, trying to keep my participation going, but clearly for me at this stage of the afternoon's drinking, talking, and thinking maybe a little too much, the magic was fading.

Apparently still considering his awful (to me at least) analogy, Curtis then thoughtfully concluded, "but, I guess in your case it was a little different…you know… because you did want to see her again."

"Yeah," I absently commented. We had reached the front of my rental house, standing at the sidewalk leading to the front porch. We were paused, facing each other from a few feet away. Knowing damn well that I was unlikely to do anything but inadequately feel sorry for myself the rest of the evening, I politely lied, "Well, I've got some work shit to finish up this evening."

Far from being offended, and maybe even pleased that I must have felt the need to explain why we wouldn't keep hanging out together, as I turned to head up to the house, Curtis started to spin away while happily chirping, "That's cool. I'm gonna take a nap, cuz I'm gonna probably hook up with a couple of buds later on. Thanks for the entertaining sex tales," he added as he started to walk away up the street.

"Yeah," I responded in my last upbeat act of the day, although not sure if he could hear me now as I unlocked my front door. "Thanks for making me feel better with the whole butt pimple story thing."

Inside; safe in my pretending to at least do a little reading and checking over some data related to enrolling patients in my clinical trial, the very little I was accomplishing was increasingly interspersed with more and more memories that were leaving me more and more sad and empty as I continued to drink more and more beers and then rum and cokes. At one or several points, I thought about calling Kim, but maybe I guess I didn't think it was such a good idea given the things I maybe would have said. Fortunately for me, the cumulative effect of a good ten or so hours of drinking finally led me to a very sound, surprisingly dream free sleep, and I woke up feeling somewhat emotionally purged, and ready to attack the biomedical world once more, with renewed vigor.

VII

- Recollections: San Francisco; February, 1993

By February of my last year of Neurology training in San Francisco I knew I would be back in Houston come July. Well actually, I knew that I *could* be back in Houston if I wanted to, that is, if Kim and I wanted to move there for the next phase of our lives together, my first-real-grown-up-job phase, so to speak.

The medical profession, by definition, is associated with or maybe even causes a delay into real adulthood; that is, if one considers measures of personal and professional maturity things like reaching a real job not associated with trainee status, in that more traditional bread-earning, going to bed at regular times to wake up for fairly defined work kind of adulthood sense. Perhaps delaying this professional maturation in part accounts for the accompanying delay or even failure to develop the corresponding emotional maturity that, sadly, one not uncommonly encounters in physicians. When as a medical student, at an age when you're college class mates have real jobs, you don't have to balance a checkbook owing to the ludicrousness of the fact that you're actually paying to work 80-100 hours a week and the money that you do have shows up miraculously by signing forms in the student affairs or financial aid office at the start of the semester, an act that will ultimately haunt you for years of loan repayments to come (when you're still making squat), caring about "real-life" details seems…well….unnecessary, compared to trying to make honors in or just pass Anatomy, Biochemistry, Physiology, Pathology, etc. In fact, it's hard to feel grown up when you're still taking tests at age 22, 23, 24, 25…30…and… even beyond!

Hell, the first two years of medical school Basic Sciences aren't even all that dissimilar from the previous four college years, which can be particularly frustrating, as you've come to Medical School to learn how to be a Doctor…and you, of course, naively have some sort of smashing insight as to how that metamorphosis should transpire. And so….you go to class, you study, you party…you party harder after exams…you cram harder for the exams if you've partied too hard during the semester or term or whatever it's called at your particular institution of Basic Science torture. Only the subject matter is a little different.

If you're lucky, the same parents you hit up in college you hit up for even more bucks in Med School. That formula works particularly well for the financially blessed scholars in those families in which Daddy was a doctor, maybe even his Daddy was a doctor, and so on and so on, back to the colonial period. If you're unlucky, or typical, the student loans you took in college (minor in my case, as I had a tuition scholarship, but that damn beer and fast-food budget…) follow you in deep-dark-hidden, double-secret-probation status to medical school, where now their new versions, unknown to you at the time, are…..quite larger.

So, now, you work for no pay. That isn't that different than college, per se. Except that most psyches have learned to accept just four years of it, the tuition and other related educational costs generally increase at this next level, and in contrast to just reading and taking tests, in the third and fourth clinical years, you're actually providing some very useful and, if it weren't you doing it, very expensive services. It may cost $10-20,000/yr to be there; you need food, rent, caffeine, stress relief, and big books. $25,000-30,000/yr in student loans somehow dilutes to $1000/month or so to live on. Rent can be a relatively minor part of this if a roach-infested dive shared by six to eight similar pop-tart eating, beer drinking crammers is your style. It's a much larger portion of your budget, of course, if quiet is a time you desire other than when it's a group hangover. Subtract food and you wonder why an evening out with your cute classmate has to be carefully weighed against your share of a kegger you may need even more than sex.

Four years later, the last two spent as playing almost a real doctor (the joy of which after all the anticipation must be a major factor in not noting the financially unfavorable circumstances under which it occurs) and having the privilege of staying up days at a time and being able to study when not at work and enjoying all those damn tests, and well…now you're on your way.

So, graduating $100,000-150,000 in debt, to a job with the romantic title of "intern" that paid $28,000/yr when I started, and, I've got two words for ya.... "De Fer."

So you defer the loans, and defer them some more. You occasionally forget to turn in some forms that you may or may not have received in the mail on some, and hence default on a couple. You get them out of default status (after all, you were *eligible* for deferment), and fuck up your credit for the next several years, so that while your old college friend who peaked at $40-60,000/yr is buying a new car, you can't get a Blockbuster Video rental card. No one can feel sorry for us. After all, doctors have the highest average salary of all professions. But, it does come late, and commonly you start out in the hole. That tuition and $1000/month you could barely live on for four years somehow translates to $635.28/month of loan payments for what seems forever. Pity, there is...eventually...an end to deferment strategies.

No matter how you look at it then, by training or by finances either going out or coming in at distinctly increasing increments, there is a well-defined chronology and hierarchy in all of this: college, medical school, internship, residency, maybe a fellowship, depending on one's career goals. You are not only aware of this, but so are the loved ones around you, some of them (long-tortured, patient souls) having been involved in multiple such phases. As such, each next stage of this process often defines major life changes and their corresponding geographical locations. Where to go to medical school? Where to do residency, etc.? Spouses (if already acquired), theoretically, have more potential re-location flexibility.

In my case, four years of medical school had been turned into five by virtue of a one year pre-doctoral fellowship in "Molecular Immunology". (It was within the Department of Immunology, but as we had all taken Immunology as late first year medical students, I added the "Molecular", with the subconscious blessing of my superiors after frequent use to the point where it ended up on my fellowship certificate, not only to reflect the content of the research endeavors, paralleled by the growing role of molecular biology in Immunology in general and even showing up in the names of new Journals, but particularly, to make it sound more sophisticated and appealing to my classmates, my drinking buddies from as early as the first few days in Med School, who wondered what the hell I was doing with my life).

But the good news was that I didn't have to pay tuition during that research year while on leave of absence from the medical school curriculum, and I actually had an $8,000/yr stipend on which to live! I was borderline resentful a year and a half later, towards the last half of my last year in medical school, when I learned that it had increased to $12,000/yr when I met a second year student who would begin the fellowship that July during one of those luncheons where the incomings are supposed to meet and be inspired by the "success stories" of the program.

Of course, that year was influential enough that I decided shortly thereafter that I would do a research oriented Internal Medicine residency at the NIH, with built-in dedicated basic and clinical immunology research training, adding up to almost one and a half years total research time. That fairly rigorous experience, of clinical patient care interspersed with the steady challenges of the lab, led to the subsequent four year combined clinical and research Neurology residency/ Neuroscience research training program at UCSF. Of course, most people who do Neurology training do it right after medical school and don't do a full Board Eligible qualifying training program in Internal Medicine or other specialties first. However, my research endeavors at Bethesda led me irreversibly into the Neuro stuff, and the only way I could see combining my research interest with truly relevant patient care endeavors most related to the science I wanted to do was by being a true clinical Neurologist. Actually, "Neuroimmunopharmacologist" was the term I often employed, easing the pain of all the years it had taken to get to that stage in my life, when many times during the last several years folks like my parents would inquire why I still didn't have a "real job", like some of those "nice boys" they had met in my roach-infested, beer can-lined dive apartment the first two years of medical school.

So, by the time Baylor College of Medicine offered me a job as a tenure-tract Assistant Professor in Neurology, with joint appointments in both Immunology and Neurosciences, I had 12 years of additional school/training post-college. Needless to say, that type of path is usually geared toward a career in Academic Medicine. Fortunately, by the time Kim and I had met along this trajectory, it was already the San Francisco years. But the hierarchy/chronology thing was still in effect, for at least a little while, and the next phase was hence reflected in: "Where am I going to take a faculty job?"

The requirements for such a position, with the highly specialized and relatively narrow focus culminating from a fusion of multiple disciplines (and as further demanded and partly supported by the specific grant I was bringing with me) made matching skills to available faculty needs and positions actually much more limiting than even past residency and fellowship choices. So, by the time I was about to turn thirty-four and had been offered my first "real" job, it appeared that Houston was the place. I would like to think that I never once thought that this was not going to be a joint decision and that I hoped Kim would find a job she liked and that was truly right for her career, and that we would consider all other realistic options and locations based on what she wanted as well.

VIII

- *Houston; October, 1993*

"So, just what kind of doctor are you anyway?" Carl asked me one evening when most of us were gathered in the park. We had enjoyed a few minutes of casual conversation, about the weather, the goings on in the park, Leo's haircut, being glad we were away from work, etc., with perhaps the work thing prompting Carl's question.

As usual, I was sitting on the left side of "our" left bench. Carl was standing off to the rear of the right side of "our" right bench, with Frank in between us, sitting on the far right side of my bench. Carl's tone, a perpetual cause of my general apprehension, seemed to indicate that in my answer would lay the revelation of just whether or not I deserved to be there at that particular moment. Although we had once earlier had that brief conversation about my work on AIDS neurological complications that had terminated in a frustrating display of juvenility, we hadn't gotten that specific about the "doctor" side of my job.

"A Neurologist," I replied, thinking that uncharacteristic brevity was the best course to pursue with the likes of Carl.

"But you do research too, right?" Curtis added. Perhaps that was in part a consequence of politely referring to what I was doing and reading the other day right after he scared the living crap out of me sneaking up on the bench. I wasn't sure if he was just adding to the conversation or if he sensed an oncoming Carlish Inquisition, and maybe somehow thought that the implied self-sacrifice and likely lesser financial rewards of a research associated career would further my chances of official blessing…or maybe I was just being paranoid or self conscious. I think especially after some of Kim's "…and his Montrose rejects" comments regarding my park colleagues, I tried not to bring too much attention to the fact that I was a highly educated physician-scientist, in the presence of two salesmen, a burnt out schizophrenic (or was it a bipolar with some psychotic components), and God-only knows what Curtis did to keep his rent paid and himself occasionally nourished. At least when Rick was there, there was another advanced degreed professional…in theory.

"Yeah, but on AIDS patients, right?" Frank in turn added, proving too that he had also paid attention to related comments made in passing over the last several weeks. One could only assume the underlying sentiments reflected in the "but" of such a statement. However, given the way he squirmed while offering up this knowledge, as if it was something one would normally want to hide, it would seem as if he was almost trying to spice things up a bit, at least in his mind, by bringing out the taboo topics with the arrival of evening, as officially evidenced in the setting sun only still halfway over the roofs of the houses over to our left, between us and Shepherd Avenue.

"Why do AIDS patients need Neurologists, per se?" Carl inquired, again in Carl-like tone.

Maybe it was an innocent question, reflecting a perhaps even sincere curiosity. After all, he was one of those book kind of guys. But I felt like the challenge had been made, the glove thrown, so to speak, and now the door was opened, and the causes for my brevity removed. Maybe it was my irritation at Frank's tone. Maybe it was my irritation at Carl's existence. Either way or for no other reason than that's just the way I am, they were now going to get the full version… at least the attempted lay full version.

"Well, first of all, they don't all have AIDS. They all have HIV-infection, many with AIDS. I assume you have a rough idea of the difference."

A few silent nods, reflecting an actual contemplative response to what I had intended as largely insulting sarcasm to just a subset. Rick had joined us a few minutes before, silently and unobtrusively sitting on the grass a few feet in front of me. Leo had then sat next to him, even attempting a similar position of sitting with his legs crossed in front of him: Indian-style, I guess we called it as kids, but after a little grimacing difficulty, settling for a more age-appropriate approximation. He was resting his right elbow on his leg, and was leaning his chin on his closed right fist, in a contemplative, studious manner, apparently meant to convey to me his focused attention on my anticipated impromptu lecture. Given what I presumed at this stage of our "friendship" was his likely inability to comprehend much of anything, this only accentuated how silly I was acutely feeling. Nevertheless, I continued.

"So, anyway, patients with AIDS can get various infections and even tumors in their brains, as a consequence of their messed-up immune systems. But HIV-infected patients, particularly those with AIDS, can also have impaired neurological function, affecting their cognition, you know, their thinking, as well as their motor systems, the way they walk, for example, all of which can be very debilitating, even fatal as it advances."

I paused, glancing briefly around to see if everyone was still with me. I was losing some of my anger towards Carl, who seemed genuinely interested. Leo, my most astute pupil, had shifted his chin to his left palm now.

"We call this condition AIDS dementia complex, or ADC, since of course in medicine we have to have abbreviations for everything," I added the latter with a little warmer sarcastic smile.

"Yes, you do," Rick commented. "It's one of the things that really piss us lawyers off. I think that's one of the reasons we like to sue you guys so much," he followed with similar sarcasm.

"That…and because you're all scumbags," Curtis toyingly sparred in, from overtop of Rick's head, while playfully pushing it down, as he walked around the front of the bench.

"Dementia? You mean like in Alzheimer's?" Carl asked.

"Yes," I responded, having turned to face him, as I continued. "So patients have impaired thinking and memory, and find it progressively more difficult to do complex and eventually even basic tasks, but unlike the sort of dementia in Alzheimer's, the "complex" in ADC refers to the fact that a broader range of brain functions are affected, especially motor systems, but sometimes, even behavior."

"What causes it?" Curtis asked in an uncharacteristically somber tone.

"Well, it seems to be due to direct infection of the brain by the AIDS virus. But, the neurons, or brain cells, that are damaged and destroyed aren't infected. Other cell types, cells like macrophages, a sort of white blood cell that lives in tissues, including the brain, and cells called astrocytes, which are important for maintaining the health of neurons, seem to be the responsible culprits."

I realized that I had probably gotten a bit too specifically detailed at this point. One of my early research mentors had told me once that there were basically two types of talks one could give (i.e., to a medical and/or scientific audience): the basic type to really attempt to teach (at a level lower than your knowledge on the subject, which was your focus and not necessarily theirs) or one at a really high, complex level, much of which was over the head of many of the audience, at least on the particular topic. Such a talk serves only to show that you know your stuff and could help for job security if the right research administrative folks were in the audience. Maybe this little impromptu blurb to non-medical "rejects" was somewhere in between.

"Lots of us are working on the basic mechanisms by which infected macrophages can then adversely affect their neighboring astrocytes and neurons, such as by secreting, or sort of squirting out, molecules that damage the neurons and lead to the symptoms of ADC. The more we know about these processes, the more targets we may have for effective drugs to treat or prevent ADC," I finished, maybe sounding like some sort of corny research fund raising brochure.

"So, is that what your clinical trial is addressing, are you treating ADC?" Carl asked. Clearly, he'd been paying a little more attention to me these past several weeks than I might be comfortable with.

"Yes, that's exactly what we're doing," I recovered. "We're testing a drug that blocks a receptor…a…um…protein molecule on the surface of nerve cells, that may be able to prevent some of the damage that HIV-infected cells are causing to their neighbors…so to speak."

"So, how do you know if someone has ADC?" Curtis quickly inquired.

"Well, there're guidelines, of course, for making the diagnosis. And our clinical trial has certain rigid inclusion and exclusion criteria. But, we take patients at all stages of the disease, from later, obvious stages, where patients are severely affected, to perhaps the earliest stages, when we're not even 100 % sure that they have it. After all, it may turn out that a treatment may have little effect later on, but with early diagnosis and treatment it could have significant impact," I variously intrigued, confused, or bored my audience.

"Makes sense," Rick politely responded.

Illuminated by the last few photons of dusk and a weird glare from the recently activated street lamp from behind Carl, I noticed that the residue of the human formerly known as Leo had closed his eyes, still leaning his chin on his left palm. I had already gotten the impression from the opposite end of the bench that Frank had pretty much checked out, refusing to participate in a conversation related to a basically inherently evil topic.

We sat there in silence, in the first peaceful moments of near darkness, that time in which the reality of hectic days has passed and before the promise of completely dark night unfolds its mysterious energy; when families are indoors, children in from playing after school, dads home from work, mom and her nest enjoying their evening meals or at least executing the ceremony of the evening meal, when children reported their school day events and upcoming needs for permission slips and special projects, when mothers mentioned to their fatigued spouses little reminders of things, tasks undone that they had little energy or desire left for, or discussed regional or national events that impacted them uncertainly in small theoretical ways, and on which they could exert no meaningful effect; when they noticed little things about the other that repulsed them in their chronicity and their inevitable eternalness, and which they couldn't wait to finish the meal to at least gain some temporary rescue from; that transition time that quieted the day people, wound them down to their respite to do it all over again tomorrow, but awakened and energized the night creatures, alerted them to the coming of the magical darkness, of the potentially limitless promise of night.

Surprisingly, it was Frank that broke the silence, who spoke into the black void the park was quickly becoming, with only isolated pockets of flying-insect spotted light coming down in progressively fainter cones from the surrounding street lights.

"So, folks like Curtis are at risk for ADC, since they're at risk for AIDS," he observed, as if pleased with himself for making this rather straightforward deduction, with its implied condemnation.

"In theory, I suppose," I offered up in casual dismissal.

"So, Curtis could be one of your patients someday," Carl added for no apparent reason other than to provoke, maybe as we had both become uncomfortable with the favorable connection we may have been accidentally generating previously, keeping the topic restlessly alive and even allowing for deterioration. He suddenly seemed to be in a bad mood.

"Let's hope not," I quickly responded, hoping to let it rest now.

"Let's hope he uses protection," Carl snidely added, quickly becoming the night's lowest common denominator for the group's demeanor, for whatever reason.

"Let's hope he's not here," Curtis responded, eyeing Carl's silhouette from across the group from where he stood near my left side of the bench, "so he doesn't get pissed that you're talking about him," he continued, intensifying his stare at Carl, who even in the pale almost non-existent street light and foreshadowing the deterioration ahead, I could sense didn't even look away.

"Well, this wouldn't even be an issue if Curtis didn't lay with other men, and was either celibate or in a healthy monogamous, heterosexual relationship, in accordance with God's law," Frank opined.

Oh, shit, here we go, I thought. In my increasingly fatigued state after a long day, and already having been a little mentally taxed by trying to lay-translate what I usually discuss only with other physician and scientist types, I suspect I had zero reserve of whatever human quality would now apparently be required to prevent the slamming down of a medium mood to a frankly foul one in the presence of the black cloud hovering around Carl and Frank's usually brown aura-side of the bench.

Kim and I have often commented, sadly after the fact of confirming it, that married couples, or maybe even close friends I suppose, can get away with saying things to each other that they never would to new infatuations or merely casual acquaintances. Either the next 20 minutes were going to be a testament to the closeness we had all strangely acquired over the last few months of occasional park sessions, or this would be the last one. A damn broke in my head, and by default of fatigue and/or crankiness, I relied, initially anyway, on profession-related metaphors to viciously respond.

"Jesus, Frank," I turned towards him, "can your neurons even oxygenate in a mind that closed?"

He looked confused.

Rick chimed in, from his still sitting position in front of us. "Dude, just because a bunch of old Jews got together and wrote some colorful Old Testament stories, and some hippy disciples wrote some gospels, and then a bunch of power freaks assembled the Bible and formed the vehicle of greed and domination known as the Catholic Church doesn't mean the rules conveyed as part of the brainwashing known as Christianity apply to the larger group of we ...um, more secular heathens."

Wow, I dig that legal speak, I thought, but adding religion to sex was probably not the way to lessen this growing tension. Maybe, we could just add politics and a few insults to our respective Mothers, and we could really have some unhealthy fun!

"So, Frank, if it's not right to lay with another man," Curtis began to sarcastically inquire, "can I still get fucked while on my hands and knees, you know, doggy style…woof, woof…or while leaning up against the wall in a bathroom stall?"

To his credit, he knew what buttons to push on his conservative rivals, and he wasn't afraid to slam his entire skinny might down on them.

"Actually, I think the missionary position is the only one officially sanctioned by the Church," Rick added with factual tone that partially masked its sarcasm.

"Didn't that change with The Vatican II, or whatever that book was," I said not sure if I was being also sarcastic or actually curious. "I thought the church was relaxing a bit, you know, to keep its younger clientele. I think you're even allowed to have oral sex, like once a year or something" (now the mood congruent acrimony of at least a few of us was quickly re-surfacing). "They give out some sort of coupon book, you know, to keep track," I further deteriorated, clearly opting now for just flat out wise-ass.

"I'm not Catholic," Frank firmly informed us. "But it doesn't matter. The Bible indicates that celibacy and monogamy are the only right choices, monogamy with the opposite sex, that is."

"Actually, I don't remember the celibacy thing in your book. Wasn't that added later, by the Church, like as part of an effort to not dwindle land holdings by not having heirs, or something like that?" Rick the sage counselor added in inquiry.

"I wouldn't know about that," Frank responded, not much to our satisfaction.

"So, Frank," Carl surprisingly volleyed in from behind him, "after thirty plus years of marriage, which one are you: monogamous or celibate?"

"Very funny," Frank answered, blushing slightly, betraying at least a little of the universal male ego, but none the less, not actually answering, at least not directly.

But he did turn towards me, and stated, "Jeff, you're married, you understand monogamy."

I didn't answer.

"Monogamy," Leo pondered out loud, and I didn't even know he was awake again, "it works for me."

We all stopped and stared at him in silence for a couple moments, sitting there in front of us, now with his hands deep in his pockets. Either he had no idea what we were talking about, or we had no idea what he was talking about, or both.

I then tried to bring it all to a close, from the humane and objective medical perspective.

"All I know is that two consenting adults should be able to do whatever they want with each other, and that shouldn't get you killed…by exposing you to one of the most evil diseases in the history of human kind, that just unfortunately happens to be spread via a sexual route, and particularly by routes more likely to be employed by male homosexuals."

But apparently we weren't done, not even close.

"Some say that AIDS is God's way of punishing homosexuals," Frank sunk to an all time, albeit, unoriginal low.

"Yes and those people should be taken out in a field and shot," I replied, clearly joining Frank in the basement of human sentiment and not necessarily rigidly adhering to my Hippocratic Oath. "If HIV happened to be spread by a respiratory route, would God be punishing people for breathing?"

"It's just not normal," Frank continued, all of us knowing what *IT* was.

We all sat there in silence for a few minutes; although I think Rick was somewhat playfully flipping off and making faces at Frank who by virtue of darkness or ignoring couldn't see it, even if I could. I don't know who left first, but within a matter of minutes, it seemed, the park was empty, and I was back in my rented bungalow house, utterly drained.

IX

- Recollections: Houston 1985

The stirring of my emotions by our conversation in the park that evening gave way later to an acute bout of introspection: "what was I doing with my life?" and "how did I get here?" sort of stuff, I suppose. I wasn't quite feeling sorry for myself, but I was certainly a little worn out. I started thinking about some of my early encounters with AIDS patients and my first impressions of the disease in the context of the hopefully more open-mindedness of the caring medical community, set against my own ignorance when I first started clinical training and the more global ignorance we as a shocked society still had in those initial years. Clearly, despite rapid scientific and clinical advances since then (still not rapid enough for those dying a miserable death on a daily basis) Frank's prejudicial attitudes were as good an indication as any that even after all these years, we still had a ways to go to remove some of the cerebral bullshit from some of the non-victims.

Recalling a handful of those first engagements with AIDS patients, almost a decade ago now, had the unexpected effect of unleashing an entire avalanche of early clinical training memories, met with perhaps mixed emotions, and something that had been occurring with unanticipated frequency lately, perhaps facilitated or even precipitated by actually being back in the same physical environment where it all began, I guess.

Although I officially "took care" of several AIDS patients as a clinical medical student (that is, patients I was assigned to work up and/or follow on the wards under the supervision of the residents) and encountered many more in briefer settings, such as in the E.R., I find that I distinctly remember a particular few, for whatever reasons.

AIDS is not completely unique in its hideous capacity to take back lives eons before a just universe could possibly see fit, although it certainly does seem to do so in numbers substantially greater than rare potentially fatal neoplasms or genetic disorders that cruelly strike pediatric and young adult patients. There is, sadly, a large number and broad spectrum of fatal or disabling illnesses that are certainly worthy of great pity and which rightly inspire great empathy. If anything, many HIV-infected patients are of a class of individual that elicit, instead, great disgust. Even conscientious physicians may make condescending comments about certain patients when out of their presence, even though we have no choice (based on personal composition and/or law) but to take care of them as best we can: drug addicts, who in the pre-HIV era occupied hospital beds for up to six weeks while receiving IV antibiotics for their bacterial endocarditis or who put their care givers at risk during invasive procedures due to their chronic hepatitis B state in the pre-vaccine days.

The first AIDS patient that I can distinctly remember at least casually encountering in medical school perhaps stuck in my mind in large part because of a steady display of flat out disgusting hygiene habits that he purposely displayed over the four to six weeks I was exposed to him on the wards of the VA hospital in early 1985, and maybe also because of a potentially life threatening contact of likely virus infected CSF fluid with my unprotected self. On retrospect, particularly given my level of training and experience at the time, the latter event was due primarily to the cavalier attitude of one of the theoretical early shapers of my medical psyche and clinical armamentarium, actions which further solidified how absolutely insane my first medical intern was.

...

Horror stories, or good and juicy, detail-laden descriptions of gore or clinical extremisms encountered, are an important part of Medical School; for example, they give young clinical students ammunition to impress even younger basic science first and second year medical students, who are basically in a feeding frenzy over anything clinical, and especially non-medical old college friends during holiday visits back to the home town, when still under the impression that someday being a doctor and obnoxiously demonstrating it in public (i.e., a bar) entitles one to casual sex with all girls within a five year age range.

Horror stories....

Probably some of the best for me and my classmates came from our Core Surgery Rotations at the Harris County Ben Taub Hospital, which for me was now a good eight years or so ago. Ben Taub was and still is, a major Trauma Center, the "Houston Knife and Gun Club", as we sometimes affectionately referred to it, for self explanatory reasons. Medical students on Core Surgery rotations were valuable members of the "team", actually doing a great deal of things during the day and especially during the night, as the house staff (interns and residents) were pounded on to the degree of infamy in the medical education community. Back then, for the house staff we were trying to help out, it was five years of general surgery residency with every other day call (e.g., as opposed to every fourth night call or even every third night call in some of the more old school surgery training programs, which still paled in comparison on the brutality scale....something to be proud of only in that Marine Boot Camp kind of way, I suppose). I once explained this to a parent of a friend of mine as basically working a 137 hour work week. I shit you not. There are only 168 hours in a week. He didn't believe me, and thought it was preposterous. It is worse than preposterous, especially because it was true. So, out of pride or defensiveness, I outlined it for him in more detail.

For some, sleep is a rare luxury, and one must learn to live and function at a very high level without it. Under these conditions, interaction with spouses or children is essentially impossible. Better to avoid that on the front end; alternatively, somewhere along the way it will likely resolve itself, as no spouse should have to endure the kind of human being or fraction thereof that one must become during such a physical and emotional ordeal. What this meant in reality for the two interns and the two or three residents on my team at that time was that they were basically on 42 of every 48 hours. For example, if you were "off" the previous night, having gotten home in the late evening, also known as night, one started the next day at 5 or 6 a.m., making rounds and getting everything tuned up for the day on the 40 or so patients you were following and taking care of "in house", before the daily O.R. or clinic schedule started. One was swamped during the day, with the chief resident and the fourth year resident operating a lot, with the attending Surgeon occasionally scrubbing in on one of the earlier scheduled bigger cases. The younger residents would occasionally be in on some cases, but more typically would be in clinic, following up on patients returning for check ups, seeing new patients potentially getting scheduled for surgery, or in specialized clinics, such as rectal clinic or tumor clinic.

Medical students would alternate between these various activities, either scrubbed in on OR cases, even at the first assist level on occasions, doing procedures in clinic, or taking care of more time consuming activities (changing dressings, swapping out IVs, etc.) on the ward than were possible during morning "rocket rounds". Then came the evenings.... In our "hypothetical" day, our intern or resident is on in house call tonight, after the already demanding day alluded to above. After late afternoon or early evening rounds, it's back to the O.R., doing cases that had gotten bumped during the day, maybe because of some trauma cases, and especially progressively handling the horrendous trauma cases rolling in that night, the favored time for the various blood letting activities of new and established members of the Houston Knife and Gun Club. Sleep was unheard of, except for maybe an hour or two for the Chief. One had to really be desperate to page the Chief out of this luxury that more junior house staff would some day earn. Between the hopping E.R. and O.R.'s, one was up and doing things all night, needing to wrap up the often hopeless efforts against human body tragedy in time for morning rounds, to start the whole process over again. Under extremely favorable conditions, the fortunate house staff officer that was off that night could finish by 6 p.m., after essentially 36 straight hours of non-stop activity. But usually, it would take till 8 or 9 p.m. to finish all the little, but still necessary, tasks that got postponed during the day or one would have to come back at 3 or 4 a.m. the next morning to do those that could be postponed for a few hours more. Time to get home and sleep a few hours, before coming back...just to be on call the next night.

Medical students rotating on that service had it a lot better, in part because we were just passing through, after all, not necessarily having committed to the honor of having this particular life style. When on call, we certainly stayed up all night doing things with our house staff or on our own in the E.R., which certainly made the next day difficult. I learned early on that it's a lot easier to be sleep deprived and functional when the functions are fairly mundane physical tasks, like holding livers back with retractors in major abdominal surgery as a student, or when they are forced upon you in a manner where not to complete them is not an option, such as seeing more than 60 patients/day at the Thomas St. Clinic in my current clinical situation, than when one is trying to caffeinate even a few highly fatigued neurons in order to design an experiment or analyze data that one could, in theory, put off for a day or two or even longer and get away with it. In general, internal motivation is necessary to get these less structured tasks done, but certainly, when one was crippled by sleep deprivation, they could at least wait for a power nap; not so, for patient care.

In contrast to our heroic house staff, as paying customers, we medical students at the time were on call only every fifth night, regardless of whether we were rotating at the County Hospital, hanging with our team or being in the E.R. when on call, or were assigned at one of the other hospitals during the day, and then spending most of call night in the Ben Taub E.R. Especially if one were in the County Hospital part of their rotation, call night could often see you in the O.R., in one of several major trauma surgery cases going on simultaneously. Because of this, a medical student could easily be the only other scrubbed-in "surgeon" on a case being done by a resident, and a good "stud" was a very useful commodity indeed. Down in the E.R., medical students did essentially all of the suturing. Occasionally, an upper level medical student (such as a psychically misdirected future surgery or E.R. resident) doing an "externship" would be down there, sharing his own horror stories from the glory days of the last couple of years, providing key info for the end of rotation written and oral exams (if another Baylor student) or, even if from the "outside", answers to typical "pimping" questions for rounds.

...

Getting pimped, of course, is one of the great rights of passage of a medical education. There are some classic pimping questions in the various medical specialties, used consistently rotation after rotation with different students, to test for a hoped for or expected strong core fund of knowledge; that 'ol "fund of knowledge", which was of course being exponentially expanded daily as the fog was cleared by rigorous clinical exposure and teaching. However, there is no guarantee that each installment will have fallen securely into place prior to that particular point in which it is examined for by a superior. Sadly, therefore, it wasn't uncommon to be completely humiliated by failing to even remotely approach an approximation of an even barely acceptable answer to an actually fair clinical question only to have a damn lecture on the topic the next day or to reach that part of the text that night in your reading. The opposite situation occurred occasionally, wherein one was getting pimped, almost miraculously, on a topic that you had just read the two brief pages on in the condensed version of one of the pocket texts that morning over a quick breakfast, or a cup of coffee, or a grumper, or a combination of two of the three. These moments were to be capitalized on, much like winning the lottery or riding a wave, and only an idiot would say something such as, "Wow, I was just reading about that this morning." Usually, an unpredictable up and down mixture of humiliation and successful pimpage encounters would occur over the course of a rotation or that portion of it for which a given attending was responsible for you, so that at worst, you came out at least average.

Then there are other types of pimping questions, maybe not universally experienced, but making their way out of the twilight zone and to yours truly, coming from a remote outpost of a small hard-to-get-to suburb of left field, like those I occasionally succumbed to particularly on my Core Surgery rotation. These were more unique to whichever particular manic over achiever was acutely responsible for your tuition dollars at that particular point in your education.

Early on in my clinical rotations, I once asked an upper level Medicine resident, the head of my team at one of the private hospitals, if I could use the restroom real quick during our trek to the beginning of our rounds. I would not have had the audacity to ask *during* rounds, and being still young and athletic, I knew I could probably catch up. I had had enough coffee during the early a.m. hours, just to be there and somewhat functional, that (as all we coffee drinkers know) I had to take a really mean piss, which I'm sure is how I probably phrased it to my all male companions. I would have suspected that this would be excusable, as my upper level had already told me once, likely in advice mode, that he had three cups of coffee in the morning before he did *anything* else. I wasn't sure if this included making coffee, and didn't pursue it any further at the time.

"Sure," my upper level resident responded, without breaking stride, or even turning to me, but likely deriving extreme pleasure from this unanticipated opportunity to torture an eager young colleague, "if you can tell me the three mechanisms by which coffee, that is caffeine, makes you have to go pee."

I suppose "go pee" instead of "urinate" was his showing the friendly nature of the inquisition. Needless to say, this was not one of the things they had instilled in us during Basic Science Physiology in our first year. I derived some sort of not particularly useful pleasure from the fact that I nailed one of the three, and adequately covered a second one, but all-in-all, I still had to take a major, record breaking, massive, belt loosening, pain in groin, lower abdomen, and back, gargantuan fucking piss when rounds were finally over. Recall, Internal Medicine docs like to do a lot of standing around the bedside "mental masturbation" kind of stuff on rounds, dragging things out through contemplative meditation and discussion, sometimes ultimately impacting things to such an insignificant degree through the questionably worth it effort, that it could psychotically infuriate any of the hustle and bustle, impatient, more physical task oriented future surgeon types, who would have moved past such patient rounding events with more lightening speed, so as to get "scrubbed in" in order to "remove something" already a long time ago.

For the record, I think the three mechanisms include: increasing cardiac output (and hence renal blood flow); caffeine acting as an osmotic diuretic (that is by passing through the glomerular filtrate as a solute, it extracts some compensatory water from some part of the nephron; this one I got partially); and, by inhibiting the enzyme cyclic AMP phosphodiesterase inside certain renal tubule cells, it accentuated the action of certain pro-diuretic hormones, the details of which I can no longer remember, but this was the one I actually "nailed". I remembered in part, that the methyl xanthine compound theophylline, closely chemically related to caffeine, and used to treat asthma, supposedly exhibited a bronchial smooth muscle relaxing effect by inhibiting cyclic AMP phosphodiesterase (the kind of thing you are actually taught in the Basic Science part of medical school; although, if I recall correctly, as I got more interested in clinical pharmacology, I think we subsequently learned that it's major mechanism of smooth muscle relaxation in treating asthma was by virtue of being able to activate adenosine receptors). Blah, blah, blah....this is not the major point here, if there is one, although for years, I continued to use theophylline in tissue culture experiments, as was standard at the time, to inhibit cyclic AMP phosphodiesterase and potentiate cyclic AMP signaling inside cells stimulated in various manners. Small world, I guess; but sadly, the bladder is smaller still, and I continue to have un-fond recollections of this particular Internal Medicine resident, but nowhere near as much as for my very first Internal Medicine intern, already alluded to for his strange mental processes, matched only by his complete lack of compassion, consideration, and most other elements adding up to a basic human being.

In the end, I think, renal physiology was second only to pulmonary physiology for facilitating my decision to not continue a career in Internal Medicine after my first residency, and to switch to Neurology instead; that, and I like the brain...and as such, have developed a hate-love relationship with the things that mess it up.

...

The attending physician of my particular surgery team on the county hospital portion of my first surgery rotation as a medical student was particularly notorious for asking pimping questions so peripheral to mainstream medical education as to bring into question his basic sanity (or at least raise the likelihood of a manic component perhaps not that uncommon in a trauma surgeon or surgeon in general), except that, in all fairness, the sphincter modulating torture seemed to be on top of the basic core stuff that would be expected of all the usual medical drones.

Whether you ever officially encountered this individual or not, he was already notorious to every medical student even potentially passing through the Taub. For example, some of us semi-inappropriately, occasionally-to-often, parked in the County Hospital parking lot even for the purpose of just attending medical school classes at Baylor during the pre-clinical years, as they were adjacent buildings connected by a tunnel. (Students were supposed to park in a remote parking lot and take a shuttle into the medical center.) Some of us, barely holding on to a delicately balanced level of overachieving, never seemed that organized to spare the extra thirty minutes in the morning. It could deplete your entire student loan money to pay the parking lot fees for the regular parking garages adjacent to Baylor or some of the private hospitals in the medical center. Whereas parking along the road at the much farther away available streets in adjacent Hermann Park was hit or miss, one could assume they could find or create a spot in the highly crowded Ben Taub Parking garage, which was far cheaper than the other Medical Center garages, subsidized I guess to accommodate the largely indigent hospital population. Pragmatism didn't allow we potentially equally, if only temporarily, indigent students to feel guilty for doing this. Once successfully parked in this pathetically only two-story structure, a quick pass through a brief portion of the hospital into a remote stairway and then into the tunnel connecting the hospital to the medical school, passing the Therapeutic Radiology facilities (so commonly located at basement levels) got one quickly to class. This strategy could even facilitate getting a student to other hospitals within the Medical Center during clinical rotations.

However, the huge, life threatening problem with parking at that same lot during the clinical years, even when working at some of the other Medical Center Hospitals necessitating a slightly longer walk than to just the medical school (but when it may have been even more needed to save as much time as possible) was the following: many of the Baylor affiliated teaching hospitals at the time, essentially all of the private ones, such as The Methodist Hospital, St. Luke's Hospital, and its affiliated Texas Children's Hospital, had light green scrubs. We all collected large quantities of these, hell they were even "interchangeable". No one at St. Luke's cared if you had the right colored scrubs on and they happened to say The Methodist Hospital, and vice versa. No one cared if you went from patient rooms at Methodist into the O.R. in the same scrubs; after all, you would be scrubbed and gowned for the O.R., as per protocol. In striking contrast, Ben Taub allowed you to be in official Harris County scrubs in the hospital; that is, white scrubs that made you look something like Storm Troopers in Star Wars or orderlies on a psych ward, but you switched into light green scrubs (yes, the exact same color as all of our other hospitals' scrubs) when and only when you were in the O.R. suite complex…some sort of infection control or other presumably logic-driven principle which eluded us. Hence, if you were "caught" in the county hospital, to include, of course, the basement tunnel connecting the hospital to the medical school, in scrubs of the color only allowed in the O.R., you were, supposedly, officially, irreversibly, and instantly kicked out of medical school on the spot…by you know who.

Some of us had more direct encounters with said individual, being on his "team" at Ben Taub Hospital on a surgery rotation. Despite the fear with which we were raised, we overcame it to at least resemble functionality in his presence, and far more competence outside of it, because, in the end, patient care takes priority, and we were all there for the same reasons. As an example, though, of some of the strange rules of the regime that we lived under for those few weeks, it was actually more important for the students and residents to attempt to finish afternoon duties, in the O.R.'s, clinics, or on the Ward, in time to get changed out of scrubs (white then light green then white, or sometimes white, then light green for a long time, then white, then light green briefly, then white, then light green, then white, etc.) and into regular clothes, with a tie and white coat, than accomplishing anything particularly medical within those last few crucial minutes.

Also, despite how the rest of the medical community may function, as my new lawyer buddy Rick had already noted, it was absolutely blasphemous to abbreviate any medical terminology, including in manners that had become well engrained in our protoplasmic minds from essentially standard practice elsewhere in the Medical Center (and, apparently, the rest of the world). For example, to present patient labs (i.e., laboratory results) during rounds in a manner such as, "his total billi was ...." (i.e., as opposed to "his total billirubin was...") would cause an interruption in rounds, with a good thorough anal cleansing, followed by a discourse on the problems of education and softness in contemporary American medical training, etc.

Of two attending pimping sessions I remember the most from this time, one had little to do with medicine per se, and involved the whole team, the other singled me out in a way unique to medical education, in that, with each answer I got correct, the further I dug myself into a pre-planned humiliation from which there was eventually no excavation.

Our ward, like others in the old Ben Taub Hospital (subsequently replaced by a brand new still named Ben Taub Hospital, by the time I had returned as an attending), had a wide entry hall, with a couple of private and/or isolation rooms off of it, before you got to a large nursing station directly facing you, on either side of which were large expansions of the room, going way back past the nursing station, and in which were about half the patient beds on either side. The beds were oriented with their feet towards the walking space of three or four aisles or rows perpendicular to the length of the ward, with a narrow back area connecting both sides, for hanging out and smoking for the mobile patients, and located behind the nursing station and contiguous intervening areas of supply storage and some working stations. The walls of the hospital, with their windows facing either the front or back of this large, but always over-stuffed red-brick legend, were to the far right and left in relation to the nursing station, with the windows along the lengths of the walls to which the patient beds were aligned parallel, with some immediately adjacent to the wall. It's probably far clearer in my mind, firmly etched in the form of memories burned eternally deep and almost surreal in a manner perhaps unique to some sort of combination of sleep deprivation, stress, and initial exposures to the scope of human diseases, than I can adequately convey here. One afternoon, as we made our way to the back row of patients on the right hand side of the ward, in a manic frenzy my attending interrupted the usual flow of rounds and the relatively smooth discussions we had been having presenting pertinent patient information and making management decisions, racing ahead of the team to point out a couple of bullet holes in some of the windows at the back of the ward, facing the street in front of the hospital.

"Which way did these bullets go: outside-in or inside-out?" he whirled around and asked the first intern as we caught up to him. After getting a vote from the surprised intern, he then quickly passed his glaring glances and pointing finger around the semi-circle of paranoid trainees: "outside-in or inside-out?" he successfully asked each member of the team.

In that distorted elongation of time waiting to become the focus of query, I remember thinking that either way, it doesn't say a lot for my immediate environment, although somehow having someone with a gun on the ward seemed more likely and fathomable than seemingly more random and hopefully way-off their mark shots from the street or patient drop off circle below.

...

At some slightly later point during this pleasure cruise portion of my education, I was presenting one of my patients on the left side of the same ward. As a bit of background, for alcoholic patients or anyone else not able to speak or to speak comprehensibly to whomever was admitting them and hence representing a potential undernourished abuser who might put himself, because of his habits, in the kind of harm's way that would land him on our ward to begin with, we often applied to the usual intravenous (IV) normal saline or ringer's lactate going into an arm vein a vitamin supplement that came in the form of a clear yellow fluid, which at the VA Hospital in particular we affectionately referred to as "gomer-aid". Presenting my patient to my attending, I of course included what meds he was on (proceeding right to the names of the various drugs, in a well rehearsed sentence without actually using the term "meds" of course).

When I was done with that segment of the history, I was interrupted with, "Is that all of the medications you are administering to your patient?"

"Yes, Sir."

"What's this in the intravenous bag going into his arm, then?"

"It's a multivitamin preparation, Sir." I of course had not included this, as none of us really think of vitamins as medications, do we?

"Which vitamins are in that preparation? Which vitamins are you giving to YOUR patient?"

To not be able to answer would have been, in a sense, an admission that I had not read the product insert, the equivalent as far as any medical student would be concerned, of not knowing what kind of toilet paper was in the ward bathrooms or what was on the breakfast menu. These were vitamins, after all, not beta blockers, antibiotics, or diuretics.

Thinking quickly, since this was going into a vein and we weren't trying to give this guy a lipid embolus into his lungs, or something to that insightful effect, I recalled my biochemistry, a course in which I, of course, had made Honors; and so I named all of the water soluble vitamins. You know, those B-complex things. Very impressive, or at least I had hoped. I could tell my Surgery residents thought I was a geek, probably a future Internist.

"I see," my un-phased attending calmly said, beginning to lead us to the next patient, even though I was only half way through presenting my new admission. "When you know more about how you are treating your patient, one of only four or five on this ward that you are primarily responsible for, we'll hear some more from you."

Of course, had I been further into the beginning of my hopefully some-day brilliant research career, I would have had more insight into this piece of vitamin trivia. I would have known all about ionic and non-ionic detergents, which I would eventually use to break up cells, to dissolve their lipid membranes while I extracted proteins for Western blots, etc. I knew, of course, at the time of this particular torture session that the fat soluble vitamins were A, D, E, and K. Hell, I knew what each one of them did, such as the blood coagulation proteins that require vitamin K and the various steps in which the vitamin D molecule is activated by hydroxylation in various tissue sites to become active. I knew what deficiencies of each one caused. I even knew that you could get hypervitaminosis A from eating polar bear liver. I just didn't know that there were things like Tween-20 (a detergent chemical so to speak) that could let you get these little greasy, oily suckers into the thirsty arm vein of a patient.

These weren't the kinds of things that were written up in concise grumper-reading form in the little surgery pocket paper-back or spiral books we carried around with us, designed for intense on the job ward training and which I read constantly, including when taking a shit (the frequency of which was probably increasing in anticipation of these attending encounters). I knew at least ten causes of pancreatitis; not just the common obvious things like alcohol, gall stones, and trauma (the latter etiology being one which you could pretty much throw in as an answer to anything at this particular hospital), but things like meds (I mean medications), such as glucocorticoids, and hyperchylomicronemia (type I hyperlipidemia in the Friederickson classification of hyperlipidemia for us future Medicine geeks).

I knew everything about the staging of breast cancer. Why couldn't I be asked questions about *these* things? I knew everything about the differences between gastric vs. duodenal ulcers. I knew all the post-gastrectomy complications. (After all, this was in the days before we knew about that little pest bacteria *H. pylori*, which is so causally important in chronic active gastritis and peptic ulcer disease, and even gastric carcinoma and lymphoma; before the days when we treated such gastritis with so-called "triple" antibiotic therapy; hell, this was right around the time when H2-blockers, such as Tagamet and eventually Zantac, were just coming on board to treat peptic-ulcer disease.) Gastrectomies and antrectomies (or partial gastrectomies), in which all or part of the stomach was surgically removed, were common for intractable ulcer disease, or for ulcers complicated by bleeding, perforation, etc. ("What are four indications for surgery for peptic-ulcer disease" was a fairly standard surgery pimp question then...the kind I wanted to be asked...). The stomach and proximal small intestine are linked in a kind of bizarre or maybe ingenious way. Remember, this is all from remote memory by a Neuroimmunologist ("Neuroimmuno-pharmacologist"). The ulcer is typically in the duodenum, the first part of the small intestine, but when it just won't heal, you fix it by taking out the stomach, or in those already partially modern days, the distal stomach, that is, the antrum. That's because cells in the antrum, the one's we tweak with Zantac, etc. control the acid secretion from further up in the stomach, the acid that washes on down and screws up the duodenum, or something like that. Of course, those cells are also controlled by nerves that run from the vagus nerve (if I remember correctly) to the front and back of the stomach.

Two very prominent general surgeons, one an attending at the County and Methodist Hospital and the other at the V.A. Hospital, had different surgical approaches to these ulcer cases in our very prominent neck of the woods. You indicated your enlightened personal preference for one approach over the other depending on which of these highly intimidating individuals you had for your Core Surgery Rotation Oral Exam. As such, I sang the praises of the antrectomy with highly selective vagotomy a couple weeks later as I blew my oral exams away. One (perhaps the only?) advantage of having a particularly brutal attending on your rotation was that that individual could not be your oral examiner (kind of like not being able to judge your own country's figure skater during the Olympics, I guess). Hence, I was blessedly spared questions such as, "What are the nine knobs on a ventilator for?", which I distinctly remember hearing one of my friends complaining about in disbelief, when coming out of his oral exam with... you know who (and essentially decompensating, as he'd never yet adjusted a ventilator in the SICU or anywhere else at that stage of our training, so he was only able to meagerly bullshit a possible function for one or two of them, inferred from our first year basic science physiology course).

Some pimping questions appeared to be even less clinically relevant, and seemingly went right to degrading the recipient, as if that would quickly improve the deteriorating conditions of a particularly troublesome surgery in which these assaults were staged. I remember being scrubbed in on a big case that the attending was doing with my chief on a weekday morning: an esophageal resection and colonic interposition procedure for an esophageal squamous cell carcinoma. The attending looked up from the operative field, and glanced across the curtain separating our sterile area from the very busy Anesthesiology resident, actively minding to his respirator displays, his charts of fluid ins and outs, his series of syringes for tweaking this old, cachectic patient's heart rate and blood pressure.

To this trainee in another department, my surgical attending declared: "There are only two reasons for an Anesthesiologist to be sitting down during a case. Either he's not worth a shit or he's a drug addict. Which one are you?"

These are hard questions to answer.

X

- Recollections: 1982 - 1985

E arly on I knew that I didn't want to be a surgeon, probably even before I went to medical school, actually. Especially for those without physicians in the familial gene pool, surgery was probably one of the more familiar and macho glamorous medical specialties, as perceived by the non-medically educated MASH or soap opera watchers. But as quickly as even just the progression through our basic science courses, even those of us with little prior exposure began to get a feel for the specific kinds of doctors that took care of what kinds of diseases and how they basically went about that. This budding insight into potential specialty compatibility or incompatibility was then progressively confirmed during our clinical years. However, my need for a more research compatible subspecialty and lab time that can't come easily when in the O.R. 8-10 hours a day had likely already started expressing itself to my subconscious long before I concretely solidified my desire for research (or even before I did my Core Psychiatry rotation and even learned that I had a subconscious).

A career as a surgeon, no matter what anyone will tell you, including "Academic Surgeons", is not (with perhaps an exceedingly rare exception) compatible with a career as a basic science oriented medical researcher. For individuals actually practicing medicine and doing research (i.e., as opposed to non-practicing M.D. or Ph.D. biomedical researchers) being truly competitive in acquiring hopefully continual (or at least often) funding support is typically the domain of hard working individuals in Internal Medicine, Pediatrics, Pathology, etc. Surgeons, frankly, spend too much time in the O.R. to be basic science or even "translational" biomedical researchers. Equally frankly, you don't want anyone opening you up in the O.R., operating on you, and putting you back together in a way that you're actually going to function again that spends too much time in the lab and not enough in the O.R.

What I couldn't necessarily anticipate, though, was how much I would really love my surgery rotations, at least on retrospect. Just because you're not going to do something for the rest of your life doesn't mean you can't have a blast while you're doing it for a little while.

However, I wasn't engaged in basic biomedical research for those months on my surgical rotations, such as the two months of Core Surgery, and I love surgical diseases; that is, I love the pathophysiology inherent in traditionally surgical diseases. In addition to taking out the inflamed appendices and the gallstone filled gallbladders underlying bouts of cholecystitis (the pathophysiology of which alone is interesting), surgeons own a large chunk of the clinical cancer domain; and in addition to my apparent passion for all things immunologic, I love cancer biology. Yes, Oncologists treat cancer patients, and yes, so do Therapeutic Radiologists, and all of these folks commonly work together. However, it is the general surgeons, maybe with areas of emphasis within the broad realm of surgery, who arc the guys (and occasionally girls) doing the mastectomies for breast cancer, the colectomies for colon cancer, the pneumonectomies and lobectomies for lung cancer, etc. Similarly, those in the surgical sub-specialties such as Urology and ENT see the prostate and renal cell carcinoma and head and neck squamous cell carcinoma patients, respectively.

So, during the periods I enjoyed scrubbing in on these long cancer resection cases, holding retractors for hours on end and cutting indicated sutures (at hopefully the perfect length above the knot to avoid verbal or worse forms of ridicule) like it was a special treat, I also got to read about the causes of these diseases, often along side seeing their manifestations and current treatments. Understanding the molecular mechanisms for the altered growth and differentiation of cancer cells, their local invasion, and metastatic spread is fundamental to developing rational pharmacologic strategies for treating and maybe even preventing them. And, there's even room for Immunology! Tumor vaccines and other exotic endeavors, such as growing up a cancer patient's tumor infiltrating lymphocytes (the same types of cells infected with HIV in other patients) and juicing them up before squirting them back in to kill tumor cells, are within the realm of optimistic future anti-cancer strategies.

As I always particularly enjoyed the molecular side of things, Surgery wasn't for me. When then, did I realize that Neurology was it (or, hopefully, is it). Obviously, it wasn't before I journeyed north of the Mason-Dixon Line and did an entire Internal Medicine residency. Actually, in all fairness, this isn't fair. After all, every good medical exam includes a neuro exam, just like it does a good cardiology and pulmonary exam. I always particularly enjoyed this neuro aspect. I loved Neuroanatomy in basic sciences, and took to it so well that I found myself giving review and quiz sessions to subsets of my classmates closest to me. But in addition to the clean cut "find the lesion" problems, wherein, for example, a specific part of a specific gray matter area or white matter tract may get whacked by a thrombus in its corresponding supplying vasculature, I found myself intrigued by the more nebulous systemic disease things, things that came or went, or in mysterious sometimes apparently unpredictable patterns, took out parts of multiple areas in ways that took great deciphering combinations of patient physical exam, imaging studies (especially MRI) and other ancillary testing to deduce. Immunologic or theoretically immunologic diseases, including those traditionally in the Neurology realm, such as multiple sclerosis, and those classically belonging especially to the Internal Medicine geeks, and especially the particularly geeky Rheumatology/Immunology subset, such as Systemic Lupus Erythematosus, are particularly hideous in their way of attacking in hard to predict and harder to handle ways. I'd like to think that being a competent Internist has made me a better pharmacologist and a better Neurologist....but the jury's still out I guess.

...

Maybe unexpectedly, then, it was also on my Core Surgery rotation that I encountered my first memorable clear cut case of Organic Brain Syndrome. As an occasionally cynical Neurologist, to me this clinical term refers to the neurological and psychological manifestations of a group of diseases for which we think we know what physical ailments of other non-brain organ systems can cause someone to act majorly messed up. What a non-organic brain syndrome would be, then, is not "inorganic" per se, but those apparently more primary and still ill defined brain-localized causes of being insane, or demented, or just not quite completely there. In parallel to some of the other conventional medical terminology, secondary and primary messed up brain syndrome would be more precise.

That frontier-quality lesson in semantics aside, to the credit of our ancestral brewers, distillers, and vintners, whose descendants function with great success towards mixed societal effects today, the little two carbon cause of many of life's great pleasures and great pains is also the underlying cause of some of these apparently permanent fucked up states (not to mention the non-permanent impairments).

Far from being judgmental in this particular arena, like many passionate youth of my era, I had already survived years of sporadic out-of-my-mind inebriation, in college and early medical school, and during this time had, of course, observed my friends in similar states, both from the perspective of mutual altered consciousness all the way to embarrassed (for them, or maybe even me at the time...) sobriety. However, despite this prolonged repetitive ethanolic insult to my typically overstressed neurons, I had, in theory, no permanent scars.

My first professional experience with the truly clinically chronically altered and profoundly sub-optimally functioning mind, the focus of so much of my eventual career, came on one of my E.R. call nights. I was in the suture room well into the night, having already sutured a large number of scalps, wrists, fingers, and facial tears, including a nose completely bitten through on the under portion between the nostrils of a young black woman who supposedly suffered this unique insult during love making. Ah, that fine line between sex and cannibalism.

What came next was the sort of thing one can only hope to be blessed with in order to provide enough excitement to supplement the caffeine and crappy late night cafeteria food in keeping the adrenaline going until morning rounds. The police brought in a middle-aged to elderly black male whom they had interrupted in the middle of apparently crucifying himself in his living room. He had two large nails, probably three to four inches long, pounded through the middle of his hands, one in each hand, nailed in from the palm side. They still stuck out about two inches to their heads on the palm sides, and the sharp or pointed ends impressively bulged out the thin skin of the dorsum or back side of the hand, without yet having pierced through the highly stretched skin. I smelled a psych consult....

I don't remember what or who had alerted the cops, but they reportedly arrived just when he was beginning to nail his ankles to the floor. Needless to say, this patient was not a lucid medical historian. When asked if he was Jesus, his answers during the night varied from "Yes" to "No, I am a representative of his." I wanted to give him points on the mini Mental Status Exam for just using a word like "representative".

In the grand scheme of a steady flow of trauma cases, of victims of motor vehicle accidents and multiple gun shots to the chest, as entertaining as this guy could potentially be, he was simply a distraction to a trauma surgery or E.R. resident, and thus was clearly medical student material all the way. It was evident to me early on that this was a patient with chronic liver disease. From there, the most likely etiology would be chronic alcoholism, a shocking reminder of what we all, or at least a lot of us, could become, if we weren't so damn effectively distracted by the real world issues of study and work. The first tip was that he had breasts; that is, well developed gynecomastia. As a core surgery student, I knew all the classic clinical sequelae of chronic liver insufficiency. The traditional and probably research-supported teaching (here's just another example of that ol' surgery disease pathophysiology I was so steadily in love with) was that the liver, which normally metabolized or conjugated or otherwise got rid of steroid hormones (surgeons don't necessarily get off on the biochemical pharmacology), could no longer in this end-stage, scarred, cirrhotic condition break down or otherwise remove estrogens, small amounts even we boys were walking around with. The resultant elevated levels of these female hormones caused gynecomastia, or growth of the male breast.

During my quick physical examination, interrupted as it were by entertaining gospel-inspired acts or phrases related to his particular Organic Brain Syndrome, I noted other associated physical abnormalities typical of liver failure, including what we refer to as portal hypertension, when the pressure inside the scarred liver causes build-up back into the portal circulation that normally sort of drains the intestines into the liver. This circulation connects with the more normal heart: to arteries: to organs: to veins: back to the heart circulation at a few key spots, wherein the portal hypertension of liver cirrhosis can either cause life threatening havoc (such as when esophageal varices rupture and cause massive GI bleeding) or give easily noted clinical tale-tale signs of its existence. The "caput medusa" of dilated cutaneous veins around his umbilicus and partially stretching over his ascites-distended belly was one such sign.

But in this case, the best abnormalities to a budding Neurologist side tracked by a bout of Internal Medicine exuded from his toxin riddled cerebral cortex. Another consequence of this screwed up metabolic state is a poorly understood process known as hepatic encephalopathy, a dangerous and often fatal condition related in part to the liver's inability to deal with ammonia and some downstream biochemical consequences of its increase. Although we often measured serum ammonia levels in this setting and tried to prevent things that caused its elevations (e.g., reducing protein in the diet and using antibiotics to get rid of some intestinal bacteria that broke such proteins down into ammonia), ammonia itself probably wasn't the brain culprit. Some weird dopamine metabolites were the in vogue suspects at the time. Regardless of the specific chemistry, a classic physical finding in this state is known as asterixis, a very characteristic type of hand tremor. If you have such a patient hold his arms out in front of him, straight out from his chest, and turn his hands up such that the wrists are sticking outwards towards you and his fingers upward (that is by bending his hands towards his chest), and spread his fingers out, his hands will flap back and forth. Don't ask me - or anyone else - why.

In this case, I didn't have to test for asterixis. Nor did I want to place too much more attention on his distal upper extremities and see his nail-ridden hands flapping around in the E.R. breeze. As impressive as the nails through his hands were to look at from the outside, so to speak, the x-rays were even more impressive. As dense as bones are, and hence as radio-opaque (white) as they are on x-rays, good old fashioned steel nails are even more so. One could clearly see the long straight nails passing right between two of his metacarpals (or "hand bones") on each hand. The lateral views of the X-rays were my favorites, as they were of most everyone else who passed by to "ooh" and "ahh" over them while they were hanging on the suture room light box.

Professionally speaking, there are a shit load of muscles, nerves, arteries, etc. passing in those bone surrounded hand spaces (things we memorized for a few weeks in first year Anatomy), not to mention how bad infections in the very tightly compartmentalized hand space could be. For example, this is why you don't suture human bites on the hand, as you don't want them closed off to allow nasty infectious processes to wreak swollen havoc in a closed space, with all its pressure-sensitive structures. When you think, especially in the Houston Knife and Gun Club where occasional foreplay can involve a good old-fashioned punch, of how many guys are popping people on the mouth, wherein a fist can hit some surprised yet effective teeth, this wasn't an uncommon scenario down in the E.R. Self-inflicted nails through the palmar fascia…well, that's a different story.

This kind of patient required a visit from the "hand docs," that group of orthopods that specialized in hand injuries, and who had actually re-learned the names and functions of all those muscles, nerves, and arteries, and who knew how to detect their injuries and to repair them. A Level I trauma unit like this one had Ortho and Neurosurgery docs, typically upper level residents or fellows, on call in house at all times. While we waited for whoever was covering the Ortho/ Hand service, I did those standard E.R. admission work-up things, such as draw blood for labs and perform whatever physical examination could be done, without messing with the nails or otherwise fucking with his hands.

This proved to be a rather religious experience. First of all, in the spirit of the Lord, my gynecomastic savior want-to-be felt it necessary to re-arrange the three exam tables that were in the suture room, one each normally situated parallel or length wise along each wall besides the one the door was on. Keeping the one opposite the door where it was, he slid the other two to lay end-to-end, perpendicular to the one he didn't move, so as to make the shape of a cross, blessing the process several times along the way. I think this was while I was gathering a vacutainer and needles to draw blood and a urine cup. He actually knew exactly what to do with the urine cup (from the specimen collection point of view), and he dropped his pants right there in the suture room, and began filling it up, holding it in his nail-filled left hand, braced between nail and curling around finger tips and his thumb, while blessing the whole urinating process several times with his nail-filled right hand. This part of the lab ceremony completed, I now drew blood from a very cooperative, almost serenely pleasant patient. When I was done, he would not let me hold pressure on the area over the needle puncture site, but instead held up his arm to allow the dripping vein (the failed liver is not a good supplier of coagulating proteins in this state) to send precious drops of "sacred blood" onto the floor as he systematically blessed them. I suppose to the encephalopathic brain in the middle of a Jesus or Jesus-supporter delusion, the opportunity to actually have the blood of Christ made so readily available from the official doctor community (or whatever we were to him at this point) was good fantasy fuel.

Patience was wearing thin in my upper level house staff officers periodically viewing this fiasco while passing by, and I suspect my own enthusiasm was waning for baby sitting a patient who probably needed some pharmaceutical neuronal massaging along with or instead of my calm questions regarding his specific role in the whole Jesus/crucifixion process....while we waited....and waited....for the hand docs. Finally one of the third year surgery residents on the E.R. service, who was supervising my working up of this guy and whom I remember as actually quite a nice guy, came in, took one last look at the films, and said "I'm sick of this shit," and using hemostats, very quickly but deliberately and methodically, without being swayed in the slightest by the religious objections of the patient, pulled each nail out. While discarding them in the nearest waste basket, he said to me while walking out of the room and without looking back at me: "Clean those out real good."

I was a very conscientious clinical medical student, taking all of my duties seriously, and usually looking for extra ones to perform with equal vigor. In fact, this was pretty much all that my short and sweet Core Surgery rotation evaluations said. Whereas my medicine rotation residents and attendings individually wrote long paragraphs, occasionally even more than a page, expounding my virtues, my intelligence, my work ethic, my compassion, etc., etc., surgeons are busy little task masters, men of few words. "Excellent student in every respect," was the extent of it from my private hospital Core Surgery rotation attending. My county hospital residents' and attending's evaluation was almost verbose in comparison: "A quiet, but eager student, who performed all of his assigned tasks well." This is from memory, more than ten years later. I think I was mildly insulted, and my friends/family members that I shared it with were a little surprised by the "quiet" part. For this quality, I am not usually known. It must have been the sleep deprivation.

Anyway, I now undertook my assigned task with apparently characteristic eagerness, not quite knowing how exactly to proceed, but quickly pleased with how my accidental ingenuity was paying off. I took a 60 cc syringe, one of the big suckers, and filled it with beta dine solution (undiluted). The tip of the syringe (i.e., without a needle attached) fit into his nail holes like they were made for each other, seemingly as well or even better than the hubs on the needles the syringe normally fitted to. With this snug fit, I proceeded to inject sterilizing juices into his impressively swelling palms, fascinating both me and my patient, who now was able to recover from the sadness of having his nails pulled out. I pumped at least two full syringes into each, stopping to express the solution out of the holes, giving an impressive water gun like stream with only minimal pressure. What fun. In the coma of late night/early morning E.R. duty, I probably could have done this for hours, but there were many other things to do. There was no way those hands were going to get infected though. When I came back from some other task, my Jesus/Jesus representative was gone, snatched up by the psych residents who were to haul him off to join likely equally entertaining companions in the locked psych E.R. unit that I would someday get to play doctor in as well.

Clearly, I was forever impressed as to how the biochemically and, as I would some day learn, immunologically deranged body could manifest itself in the form of altered behavior or cognitive capabilities. The human brain clearly doesn't like when the lesser organs living underneath it shed their pollution into its blood and cerebral spinal fluid environment, the air it breaths and the water that it drinks.

XI

- *Houston; October, 1993*

The next day I was covering Neurology consults at the County Hospital. During the course of the day while the residents, a student, and I were seeing various patients on the Wards, we were called on three patients who were being evaluated in the E.R. The first two were in the mid morning, and especially given the relatively straightforward focus of their neurological symptomatology, we decided to "knock them out" as a team, rather than have the student of even just a lower level resident see them first before the upper level or myself, as I'd ultimately have to sign off on whatever we found and recommended from the Neurology team perspective.

In the afternoon, as the various different tasks had begun to disperse us into smaller working units and individuals, we received a consult request on an HIV positive patient with predominantly respiratory related symptoms, but with noted weakness on the initial E.R. exam. The E.R. resident wondered about a myelopathy and decided he'd get a Neuro consult while the respiratory issues were being addressed, either for subsequent discharge or admission.

As the chief resident and I were individually wrapping up a couple things, we decided to send the "stud" down to get things going. If I was correct, this young man, whose name I hadn't bothered to learn yet and/or kept forgetting, was at the start of his 4th year. As such, he'd had a lot of clinical rotations already, core and electives, and this was part of his one month Core Neurology rotation. I believe he was leaning towards a surgical sub-specialty, maybe ENT. The residents thought pretty highly of him, but I had not yet spent as much time working with him as some of the other attendings. As new as I was at this part of my teaching job (but highly familiar with the process from seven years of residency), I decided I wanted to be able to add something meaningful for his evaluation.

We sent him down to the E.R. to work up the patient from the Neuro point of view; i.e., the history of his weakness and especially a thorough Neuro physical exam. I would compare his findings to mine as a clear objective way of evaluating him. I reasoned that this should be straightforward at this point of his clinical training and having been on Neuro for a couple of weeks already. But I also told him to do a good mental status exam (after all, this was a possible candidate for my clinical trial, so I would at least do a quick mental status exam), by which I could also test the student. This part of a work-up may be less familiar to him (perhaps depending on whether he'd had Core Psychiatry or how much time he'd spent in the E.R.). But his little pocket Neuro books would have some brief content on how to proceed. Students can of course take markedly longer to do things than more experienced residents, which is why they only have a partial patient load compared to the house staff. But, this was an E.R. consult, and our responsibility and reputation (at least mine and the residents') couldn't allow for a process drawn out for several hours. So I told the stud (Kevin, I believe) that I'd meet him in the E.R. in about 20-30 minutes.

The stud did a great job evaluating this guy, who did indeed have objective weakness and some possible short term memory impairment. It appeared that the patient was going to be admitted to the Internal Medicine service to get his lungs hopefully more tuned up, so we decided to go ahead and get imaging studies done while he was in house, primarily to address the possible spinal cord/ nerve involving myelopathy. I could follow up with him regarding possible trial enrollment while he was in the hospital, or be sure that a follow up clinic day (at a hospital based clinic or hopefully even Thomas St. Clinic) was a day that I was on, so I could address it then if easier. So, I decided it was justified for me to share the high opinion of the house staff for our student.

It really wasn't that long ago that I was in a similar situation as Kevin Rogers, MS IV, the student whose evaluation I had just briefly written out based on the house staff recommendations and my brief interaction with him, and agreeing with the awarding of an Honors recommendation. Maybe it wasn't that long ago, but so much had changed since then. I had found Kim, and now I didn't know quite what was happening there…or why. I was done with all of my training now, and I was in charge…at least of a few things I'd not ever been before. And yet, I was sort of back where it all started. I found myself thinking not just about my work, the challenges of our clinical trial, my current grant and the need to keep on working for more funding, but this all had me thinking also about medical student education and experiences, and medical training in general. Perhaps especially still simmering somewhat from the conversation in the park the evening before, as I sat at home, my thoughts pretty much picked up right where they had left off then. So I found myself thinking about med school, AIDS, and possible altered brain again. The latter two were common topics for my ruminations these days; the former, again, perhaps reflecting a component of site-specific nostalgia and maybe a bit of wondering where all the time had gone.

XII

- Recollections: Houston 1985

My first encounters with an AIDS patient acting strangely were actually on my Core Medicine rotation, my very first clinical rotation. To be more clinically naïve would have been a cosmic impossibility. I was perhaps even more handicapped than my new classmates also beginning their first clinical rotation, as I had interspersed a year of essentially unrelated basic research between the end of basic sciences, when we had taken introductory courses on performing medical histories and conducting physical examinations, and now, at which point I barely even remembered having been exposed to those fundamentals, which I suppose were intended to be immediately reinforced by actual clinical training.

Regardless of this potential added challenge, I had been advised by several well intentioned upper level students and some clinicians I had worked with during those physical examination courses not to do my Medicine rotation first, as this was the subspecialty I was already most interested in as a career. It is assumed that one cannot "shine" on one's first clinical rotation, during which time one is often just struggling to learn the ropes and how things actually happen on the wards. Hence, especially when one may be compared to past or future students rotating on the same services after having gained experience on other clinical rotations, he or she may not be able to get the kinds of grades and evaluations necessary to facilitate acquiring that highly sought after top-notch residency.

Whatever. I was so anxious to get exposed to things I thought I would really enjoy, I probably presumed that my eagerness and extreme knowledge of things at least remotely related that I had learned the last two and a half years would more than make up for my ignorance in all things practical and pragmatic regarding the day-in and day-out issues of patient care on the wards. I was partially right. The first couple of weeks were particularly painful (in that humiliation kind of pain), and represented about as steep a learning curve as humanly tackle-able.

"Don't proclaim your ignorance," was one particularly relevant piece of advice subtly, but firmly, offered downhill by my upper level resident, made in response to one of my passing inquiries while strolling the halls of the private hospital where I spent the first six weeks of the 12 week rotation. And, after all, these were supposedly the nice guys, the intellectual geeks, who spent a fair amount of their time bad mouthing the surgeons behind their backs (for supposed lack of certain higher cortical functions), and potentially acting a little in fear or misplaced envy of them in their presence (maybe, perhaps for a certain direct approach to problems that their intellectualizing or anal-retentive/constipated nature would not allow). This particular comment came from the same resident who had previously quizzed me on the mechanisms of caffeine's diuretic effect, so obviously I was growing particularly fond of him. Actually, from what I remember from the time and based on what I learned over the ensuing years, I think he was a firmly competent physician and probably taught me a fair amount, even if he wouldn't make my Christmas Card list (that is, if I sent Christmas Cards out, something that probably didn't really occur in any household I was affiliated with between the time I moved out of my parents house and the first Christmas Kim and I spent officially living together. Of course, even then, she filled them out, although, and I want some credit here, I did help pick out the cards we bought, even though she may have occasionally vetoed some of my relatively vulgar first couple of choices, and I did offer a couple of suggestions as to whom to send them in my family).

Anyway, the first time I encountered an AIDS patient in this rookie, future doctor setting, and in this case, an AIDS patient acting *very* strangely, was only hours after the first time I ever saw someone die. I was clearly checking off a lot of the bigger items on my clinical "to do list" or at least getting my tuition dollars' worth those few weeks. These particular events were in the second part of that rotation, served in the old Houston VA Medical Center. Regarding finally seeing death outside of the movies, we were rounding on some patients on a ward one floor above that of our major or "home" ward, where most of our patients were located. The wards, somewhat similar to the old County Hospital, were large rooms, actually two parallel elongated large rooms, with the nursing station located in the middle of the largest room, up against the wall it shared with the other adjoining patient room. Two passage ways or openings in the wall between the rooms were located on either side of the nursing station, so you could make a circle through the ward, starting at the front of the largest room that one entered off the main hallway, passing by beds on opposite sides of the center aisle space, then turn right, through the first opening to the smaller of the two ward rooms, going through its entire length, also with a single row of beds on either side, then passing through the farther of the openings between the rooms, then rounding back through the main room, from the rear back towards the front or entry, passing in front of the nursing station. The bathroom for the ward was at the front end of the second, smaller of the two large ward rooms, the one without the nursing station, and was a common congregating area for smoking and talking for the more mobile patients.

Our home ward was on the first floor, at the front of the hospital. You entered this or the other wards from a long hallway, two of which were parallel to each other, with a center, even wider hallway, but starting further back or more deeply into the building, from the center front drop-off circle, such that it may have resembled something like the starship Enterprise from an aerial view. The center hall continued from the front circle in a non-interrupted fashion for about two city blocks, like some sort of straight brick alligator tail, tapering in medical-student-less-commonly-visited distal aspects, with various progressively smaller halls and buildings branching off, giving rise to the kinds of things found in big VA hospitals: pulmonary function testing labs, Oncology Wards, Physical Therapy, Addiction Rehab Wards, etc. This doesn't include the dozens of out buildings contributing, along with a semi-neglected 9-hole golf course at the southern rear of the complex, to the staggering breadth of the VA campus, which was about a half-mile or so southeast of the Texas Medical Center.

A few years after I graduated from medical school, they replaced the old VA with a more conventional appearing (i.e., taller) 1074 bed VA hospital, that we were told was officially the second largest government building in the United States (the Pentagon being the largest). I would come to spend many hours in this beautiful new facility when interviewing and examining candidate HIV-infected patients for my clinical trial when I returned several years later.

In addition to the two large rooms of the main in-patient wards of that old VA hospital, there were four small individual patient rooms, two on each side immediately off the short entry to the ward off of the main hallways. Hence, you passed these patient rooms before you got to the main part of the ward. These rooms each had their own bathrooms and were commonly used for isolation type patients, such as those with suspected or potentially having TB (prior to confirmation, which took awhile) or AIDS patients, in the early years, when they were relatively novel, more concern existing about potential exposure, and before their numbers grew so large that they had to be included out on the general ward.

Anyway, one typical day, as a still relatively clueless first-clinical-rotation medical student, tailing along at the keep-a-low-profile-so-as-not-to-get-pimped-too-much rear of my team, a position from which one could quickly explode to the front if the topic were one that you happened to know a lot about, or more commonly, had plucked the one key fact that plugged into the suspended answer blank because you read that portion of a study aid just last night or that very morning, we had come out of one of the wards on the second floor and were heading down the hall towards the front of the hospital, towards the ward immediately over our home ward, when a Code Blue announcement came over the hospital intercom. The location, announced through an intricate system of small round non-Bose speakers designed to moderately reach all those needed, from medical teams responding to codes to orderlies and others who would need to remove remains and linens spoiled by ex remains in the event of an unsuccessful code to the one or two hovering family members or Angels who may give a shit, was the ward we happened to be heading to, and the event was located in one of the small private rooms at the front of the ward.

By the time we got in there, the small room was already packed, with one of the other medicine teams running the code, likely having already been there, maybe even rounding on that patient, when he coded. Despite being a "quiet but eager student who performed all of his assigned tasks well" on some future rotations, I would progressively over the years become one of those aggressive clinical types who would always jump in. However, at this embryonic stage of my clinical career, I was lacking even any peripheral grasp of the specifics of what was going on; i.e., what drugs get administered at the progressively more desperate stages of a code, etc. As I stood up against the far wall, I watched the futile efforts of the various residents doing chest compressions and taking vials out of the crash cart drawers and injecting them into existing lines, wondering, without immediate compassion for the thin disappearing black man who was at the center of all this, whether I would actually transform over the next couple of years to one of the major actors, executing the well defined maneuvers of life-saving, and yet at the same time thinking that "atropine" signaled a rather late stage in this process.

One or two of the house staff officers on my team contributed to the code process in various ways, again showing that there was some sort of well orchestrated medical song that almost everyone in the room but me knew the words to. After this particular patient was "pronounced", we exited the room from our various locations within it or in the doorway, and the team re-coalesced like so many drops of mercury coming together after a thermometer is dropped (or like the liquid metal Terminator 2 guy after being temporarily minorly fragmented by an Arnold shot-gun blast for the younger folks) and continued on our rounds like nothing unusual had happened.

...

At that point in time, in early 1985, from what I remember, we had only two AIDS patients on our service when I began my rotation at the VA. One was an older middle aged male (not that there were many female patients on the VA Wards yet), a retired enlisted previous bad ass, whom I was not assigned to take care of per se, and so rarely encountered much even in the setting of patient rounding. He had contracted the virus by a blood transfusion for a non-emergent surgery, maybe a coronary artery bypass, and his wife was always there visiting him. In my recollections, he was still fairly healthy and still a little overweight in fact. I can't remember what had brought him to the hospital for that admission, maybe thrombocytopenia (low platelets).

He had, of course, contracted the infection in the time before there was any antibody-based test for checking the general blood supply or any blood derived products, such as the factor VIII concentrates required by hemophiliacs. This was, in fact, when we were still learning as medical students the risk factors for HIV-infection by using the mnemonic "The 4-Hs"; that is, homosexuality, heroin (i.e., IV-drug abuse), Haitians, and hemophiliacs. This was way before, for example, that we knew the reason being Haitian was a risk factor was the unpublicized or maybe even unappreciated fact that it was because Haitian males were prostituting themselves to visiting tourists, largely American male homosexuals, for obvious economic reasons. Hemophiliacs were at particular risk from blood related products because of the relatively large numbers of donor-derived units required to prepare the concentrated blood components they needed, but the "hemophiliac" category also encompassed the general population of blood transfusion recipients, like this particular patient, whose wife accompanied him like a permanent vigil and whose son occasionally showed up like an angry victim.

It is amazing in medicine how just a decade or so before can sometimes seem like the "Dark Ages" in some specific regards. At this particular time, just about nine years before my clinical trial for ADC was being optimistically undertaken, we were still in that era when blood-borne hepatitis (i.e., that acquired with transfusion in clinical settings), was known as non-A, non-B hepatitis, before the hepatitis C virus had been cloned, blood could be checked by antibody based techniques to detect it, and most cases of such transfusion-related hepatitis would be eventually identifiable as being due to Hepatitis C. We were vaccinated for Hepatitis B while I was a medical student, and the blood supply was essentially safe from Hep B, but at some point I remember hearing while in medical school, that a unit of blood at the County Hospital, for example, carried as much as an 8-12 % risk of "non-A, non-B" hepatitis. So, if you happened to have been in an argument, and you got shot before you could adequately make your point or effectively pull your own gun, or if you were taking advantage of a convenient ATM machine while one of your not as law-abiding Smith and Wesson-wielding super citizens was walking by and thought shooting you in the back was easier than asking for your card and PIN number, and were subsequently bleeding out faster than the old cell saver could suck it up from the pooling sidewells of your own belly-splayed open O.R.-chilled body, filter it, and put it back in you, requiring a not uncommon 8-10 units of blood (I've seen WAY higher, more than 30 units) could give you a pretty good chance of coming out with chronic liver disease. And you didn't have to be in the wrong place at the wrong time. There are some pretty bloody standard major operations: a good old fashioned hysterectomy or a radical prostatectomy, for example. So sometimes being sick or just accidentally getting a not necessarily even aggressive cancer and needing surgery could be a little dangerous. Fortunately, fairly quickly after the satanic AIDS causing retrovirus was identified, antibody-based tests became available to start improving the safety of the blood supply with regard to HIV-infection, the same antibodies whereby death sentences were delivered by screening ELISA and confirmatory Western blots on blood samples of patients being tested for HIV infection.

...

Our other AIDS patient on the ward at the time was perhaps more typical in terms of his risk factors. His behavior, though, at least during the week or two that I observed it from the periphery...well that's another story; and to me at least remains, fortunately, somewhat unique.

"You guys may not want to come in here," our intern said to me and the other student on the service, a fourth year extremely attractive petite girl with curly reddish brown hair and disarmingly big brown eyes, who was doing an Internal Medicine externship and who seemed to me, particularly at that early stage of my training, to know a whole shit load of medicine; not just the text book geeky test stuff, but the useful clinical pearls and tidbits that really helped in managing patients, such as late at night when not only staff, but functioning neurons, were few. She also seemed to be willing to share this in energetic, open, and almost nurturing fashion, such that between her looks, a surprising tendency to feel comfortable with her in close quarters, and this freely shared knowledge, I found myself being very fond of her in a daily manner, maybe like two strangers thrown together in circumstances different from their usual lives, and becoming quite close for a brief period, not to be confused with or even contemplated as something that would be possible in a situation outside of the here and now surrealism that we were submerged in. Although the parameters by which to judge such things are not necessarily objective, well established, or universal, we as a pair formed an effective lower part of a highly functional team, the weakest component of which now continued as he, one of our first year interns, pushed open the door to one of the private rooms on our VA Ward while we made our morning rounds. "He's been getting pretty nasty lately."

The intellectually curious, often a barely disguised form of the morbid, cannot resist an invitation like that, and so Amy and I followed Dr. Adams into the room. Neither she nor I were officially "following" or taking care of this patient, and we hadn't even rounded on him as a team yet in this early part of the rotation, so we knew very little of him, other than, perhaps, that he had been there for quite some time and that he had AIDS. We were only part way through the door and into the room when the invisible fog hit us, that unmistakable "how can humans make this?" barfogenic funk smell of voluminous liquid stool and synergizing equally nasty stench of "dead bowel" that adds up to the unique anti-world aroma of "sick" diarrhea.

Now if you've been on this planet more than a month or two (as infants are particularly guilty of being common offenders in the diarrhea game), you've smelled the usual variety; probably, hopefully, mostly your own; or, maybe that of a loved one; certainly a child if you're a parent; or, maybe that of an aging parent or sibling in a care giver role; maybe, even, that of a partner co-stinking up a less than well-decorated and poorly equipped nasty motel bathroom while sharing a food-poisoning-on-top-of-everything else-bad-night-in-Mexico experience; or, the occasional gagging random brown liquid stool of an unknown stranger when suffering a public restroom at a concert or rest stop, etc. But, where daily world nastiness from personal experience meets enlightenment from Microbiology Course knowledge, these discharged liquid abominations are typically the product of defined viruses and sneaky little toxins fucking with the enterocytes lining your bowels, like the turn-on-the-intestinal-fluid-pumps toxin of the toxigenic E. Coli affectionately known to be responsible for "Montezuma's revenge", and for which we even learned the biochemical mechanism for in the Basic Science portion of our medical school curriculum.

But to this day, I swear, there seems to be something about truly sick-person diarrhea, that process of profuse, but often somewhat viscous, liquid stool generation that so commonly seems to go along with the accelerated stage of peri-terminal decaying human organism in certain fatal conditions. After all the years of training, I don't even know if this is an established fact or just a deeply burned olfactory memory generated by specific encounters. Maybe, at least in part, it's the way the aromatic component of the product itself interacts with other noxious fragrances endemic to the hospital, and especially the intensive care unit, setting. Certainly, it must in some situations incorporate elements of blood and actual dead bowel in conditions of bloody diarrhea or necrotizing conditions, such as ischemic bowel disease. Anyone who's watched and smelled in horror, despite efforts at intervention, someone "bleed out from below" or who has partaken in the at least up to that date futile efforts of diagnosing and treating the sadly increasingly common refractory diarrhea of some AIDS patients can probably appreciate the implications of what we smelled as we entered the room. The meaning of what we saw once we were more completely immersed in it as we ourselves circled the bed for rounds may or may not make a little less sense.

Mr. Evans (as I learned his name from my subsequent quick stealing glances towards his now intriguing chart) had made his room a seemingly random collection of repositories of his diarrhea. The first one I noticed was on his eating cart, the height-adjustable hospital-tray holding table that could be wheeled out of the way, or made to position under one's chin when one had the head of the bed elevated at the same time that the life-sustaining, but not necessarily haute cuisine appreciation-enhancing VA Hospital food arrived. This liquid fecal-decorated government property was currently stationed at the lower left (patient's left) end of his bed, such that we sort of almost ran into it as we came into the room, or at least we all had to deal with it as we assembled around the bed for rounds, during which we were, of course, supposed to discuss the patient's "progress". On the top of this cart was one of the VA-issue sputum cup-like things (they probably had an official name), a kidney bean shaped green plastic object, about six to eight inches wide, where the indentation (or hilum, to use official kidney, or maybe even bean, terminology) was intended to be able to go up to the patient's chin, right under the mouth, allowing for efficient collection of sputum, spit, or occasional smaller volume vomits, and the various interesting things that went along with those. In contrast, today, Mr. Evan's plastic green sputum thing held sick-diarrhea obviously intentionally planted and displayed there, and not completely flawlessly, as drippings on the side of the green sputum thing and the underlying not quite matching or camouflaging brown food cart were obvious. About eight to ten inches away on the same tray was a true sputum cup (a round plastic cup holding about eight ounces of potential contents, the kind we collected true sputum samples in for microbiology cultures) almost completely filled with a similar diarrhea product, although if I remember correctly, it was of a slightly lighter hue, although of course, this could be a perception artifact, given the clear plastic of the sputum culture cup vs. the not nearly as transparent green plastic of the sputum "tray".

Tragically, these were not isolated exhibits. The small four drawer (two on each side) dresser opposite the bed held some of the more obvious additional elements of the collection. On top were at least two similar liquid colon deposits, another sputum tray and a cafeteria coffee-cup, each with some good drippings on the side, and if I'm not mistaken, the vase of a less than thrilled declining flower collection had some sub-optimal human fertilizer in it as well. Amongst the chaos, while Amy of the sexy tight butt and big eyes and pretty good fund of clinical medicine knowledge and I of the … well, who knows what at this stage, were semi-professionally trying to pay attention to the clinical comments the upper level resident was making to the also trying to be cool attending, none of us, the presenting resident included, could help but casually, discreetly, scan around to see what other more covertly hidden dregs there may be. The way one's face may have brightened with the mix of decreasing disgust and horror but increasing, yet hopefully suppressed in the spirit of professionalism, thrill or sense of self fulfillment of detective success when a less obvious muco-bloody-liquid brown remnant was discovered in a corner or amongst a pile of clothes on the floor or papers on the nightstand reminded me of the jubilation a child may have had when finding one of those monkeys or owls or a possible pseudo raccoon in the similarly curvilinear line filled tree in one of those Highlights magazine hidden object pages.

While most of us continued this well-intended effort to remain doctor like, Dr. Adams ventured into the Mother Ship, the room's private bathroom, on the far upper left (patient's left) side of the room.

"Jesus Fucking Christ."

Brief pause. More discovery?

"Holy Fucking Shit!"

With this litany immediately passed us, our fairly conservative attending physician, in pink-striped Polo Oxford, expensive blue blazer, and tasseled loafers, which at this point weren't necessarily as exponentially foreign in this uniquely decorated room compared to our Kelly green VA scrubs as they normally would be, escorted Amy and me out of the room, in some sort of primal, paternal, last grasp of dwindling civilization or normalcy mode, while at the same time quietly delivering some sort of largely non-medical terminology command to the presenting resident intended to translate to either a custodial crew or a psych consult visit to the site of our latest human condition surprise.

Clearly the ongoing consultations with the gastroenterology and infectious disease sub-specialty services had not yet resulted in the identification of a cause, or at least an effective treatment, for this patient's worsening chronic diarrhea hideously complicating his AIDS illness. On my hurried way out of the room, escorted and encouraged as it was by my appalled attending (who was a quite famous researcher over at the main part of the Medical Center and who had to spend one or two months a year at the VA as part of his clinical Internal Medicine duties), while I heard my still under control upper level resident convey to Mr. Evans information regarding the planned further clinical diagnostic invasion of his lower intestinal tract, I did happen to notice some good smears of diarrhea juices on the closed blinds over both windows, with a better identifiable hand swoop over the right one. Later, the stellar Dr. Adams shared with us that based on his quick survey of the private restroom, the toilet seat and especially the walls had a good collection of now dried and crusted, but still stinky, diarrhea painted wall symbols, I guess perhaps analogous to the Charles Manson freaks' blood-painted walls of the whole Helter Skelter thing, although in this case, there were no words, just brown, stinky, once painfully derived liquid expressions of frustration and despair.

XIII

- Houston; October, 1993

I had been conveying a large part of the Mr. Evans story to what had unexpectedly become a full park committee meeting. It had started out with just Frank and me, on a surprisingly early Saturday visit for me. I had gone into the clinic very early to perform a couple of detailed physical examinations, including complete neurological examinations, blood draws and lumbar punctures, for three patients to be newly enrolled in my clinical trial that I had seen briefly during the previous week, and for which there hadn't been adequate time during the usually hectic weekday clinic schedule to complete all of the mandated entry examinations. It had been a productive morning. I had been impressed that all of the scheduled patients had returned for their scheduled appointments, since after all, this was for getting enrolled in a clinical trial during which they may or may not get a drug that may or may not be effective in preventing/delaying/ameliorating disease manifestations that they may or may not become increasingly severely affected by. Their motivation sparked mine, and my increasingly favorite nurse in the universe, Cheryl, and I went to town, getting everything we needed done and spending even more time than usual going over with each patient all the details, expectations, and requirements on their part for their successful participation.

Normally after a really early Saturday morning like this, after not getting quite enough sleep to catch up for the week past, I would likely go back to the rented bungalow hideaway and eat whatever remnants of takeout or delivery leftovers were remaining after hopefully being put adequately away the night before. Or in discovering the contrary, it may prompt a brief contemplation of ambient temperatures and how many hours since I had just been eating their progenitors on my desk from the night before or of similarly questionable, but still possibly viable entities from the last grocery store trip (often dependent on when Kim had last visited) that may be quick and easy, and try to catch an hour or two of still fairly early in the day sleep so as to be able to potentially productively encounter a large percentage of the afternoon and evening, which along with the night comprise to me the best parts of the day anyway.

Feeling remarkably energized and almost silly with optimism and that ridiculous internal glow that comes with the so easily adopted notion that one is doing some good, I instead stopped at the Steak and Egg on Montrose and had two eggs over easy, with four slices of bacon, three should be illegally-thick pancakes, four glasses of orange juice to begin to productively challenge my perpetually dehydrated state, and three cups of coffee to keep it all going. I alternated my readings of some journal articles (on some in vitro studies on novel glutamine receptor antagonists that were chemically related to the compound we were clinically testing, but which may be more potent and hence effective at levels less likely to cause certain side effects, yet which were still years away from any clinical trials) and The Chronicle and The Scene, just for a little reality checking and so as to not push the whole mood thing just too far. With a warm belly buzz and a near cardiac arrhythmic level of caffeine on board, instead of entering the house right away when I got back, I parked, but went for a mildly cool, adequately sun moderated, walk that inevitably led me to the park.

Frank was sitting on the bench when I got there, surprised to see me so early on a weekend day. When he sensed my energy, he wanted to hear all about my morning. After patiently receiving what was probably a too detail-laden account, he found most fascinating the frightening concept of doing "spinal taps" on AIDS patients.

His horrific awe was clearly related to his impression that the fluid removed could be hideously infectious. I sometimes got the idea that the reason why Frank thought I was so crazy to be a Neurologist dealing with HIV-infected patients had to do with his perception that much like the Night of the Dead, Dawn of the Dead, and Day of the Dead Zombies (Frank and Mrs. Frank were BIG video renters), this equally frightening plague must be related to human brains and the viruses that feed on certain key parts of those brains (imparting by default then, the potential future need to kill said zombies by shooting large projectiles through those brains, I guess, although I never really discussed this notion with him in any expanded detail).

"Do you where gloves and stuff?" he asked in appropriate Romero-ic ghastly fashion.

"All but one time," I subconsciously responded while letting my mind drift, thinking, with full correctness, that this is nowhere near as dangerous as a blood draw, but at the same time recalling the cavalier entity known as Dr. Adams, my first public hospital intern, the one in theory more responsible for "showing me the ropes", teaching me procedures and the like, than anyone else I would encounter early on.

So, right about the time that Rick showed up, looking a little less filled up with life-juices than I was apparently still feeling at the moment, I conveyed certain medical practices and instructions passed on to me by Dr. Adams, several of which I had no choice but to incorporate immediately as the only standard I knew, but the vast majority of which I was able to quickly improve on or completely eliminate ("before the malpractice shits like Rick got a hold of me," I kidded with the steadily increasing group, now that Leo had smilingly joined us in a pair of pants that looked like some form of old tuxedo trousers and what I perceived as must have been his pajama top).

"For example," I now proceeded to provide some specifics, "when I had been at the private hospitals, there were lab services that would do the blood draws. At the VA, except for scheduled in advance early a.m. blood draws, we drew the blood. We did arterial sticks to determine blood oxygen in the long time smoking so-called COPD…er…sick lung patients, and any venous sticks for any routine labs. But instead of the typical antecubital fossa, you know, the front of the elbow arm stick we all know, he showed me how to draw blood by femoral vein sticks, you know in the upper leg, groin region. This is great for emergency room, circulatory collapsing patients who've lost a lot of blood, so you need a HUGE vein to stick, but Jesus, can you imagine, a smiling, timid medical student, coming up to your bed, telling you 'we need a little blood', then lifting the sheets, sliding your VA issue hospital PJ bottoms down, then stabbing a huge needle and syringe in. Good thing, for me…and them, I guess, I got to remember my Gross Anatomy Mnemonic "NAVel to the navel", wherein if you start from the outside and move towards the navel…you know…belly button…, you have the femoral nerve first, then the artery, which you identified as the guide to all of this business by feeling for the femoral pulse, and then the targeted vein, which you would then collect blood from, in this case, using a huge 16 or 18 gauge needle on a 30 or 60 cc syringe. Of course, as veterans, as ex-military men used to taking orders, these stoics would assume you knew what you were doing, and go along with anything. Finally, one such instance was witnessed in almost shock horror by my third year resident, who promptly corrected my phlebotomist methods, teaching me the civilized arm approach to routine blood collection, followed I'm sure by a good anal cleansing of the notorious Dr. Adams."

My audience, all of whom I'm sure have had routine blood draws, was looking at me with varying degrees of appall and disgust (Carl had also arrived by now). After a few more moments of silence, I offered up for peace: "But the good news was...when I got to the E.R., I was great at doing femoral sticks in the trauma shock rooms."

After a few not so sure nods, I continued with the whole thing I meant to bring up about Frank's lumbar puncture question. I explained how I was walking into our main VA ward one afternoon when Dr. Adams peeped his bald head out of Mr. Evan's room and asked me to come in and give him a quick hand.

I think this was before the whole diarrhea room decoration thing, but I knew who the patient was and what his medical condition was. When I got into the room, I didn't have much time to think and assess the situation. What I soon gathered was that Dr. Adams was doing a lumbar puncture on Mr. Evans, all by himself, probably for fever or altered mental status...maybe the kind that may lead an AIDS patient to decorate his room with liquid feces in the near future. Anyway, he handed his ungloved, med stud recruit one of the CSF fluid containing polystyrene tubes, saying "Here, take this," and the student, of course, did as he was told, and remembers feeling the liquid also on the outside of the tube, contacting his skin. Several more tubes followed. The procedure completed, the masked, gloved intern took all of the tubes from his forced assistant, gathered the rest of the gear, gave the student a 4 x 4 gauze, telling him to hold pressure over the LP needle site in the lying on his side patient's back, and left the room.

Frank was rigid, his eyes glued to me as I continued, the story teller, the brain doctor, the one who had survived the zombie attack. Of course, as the whole topic of potential altered mental status in HIV-infected patients had arisen in the park a couple days earlier, I was hopefully bringing our review of it to a conclusion; but, I couldn't tell this aspect of the Mr. Evans story without detailing the whole diarrhea deposited and smeared all over the room thing. Remember, I was pancake, coffee, and bacon animated. Curtis's recent arrival not only completed the group, but had given me even more liberty to descend into the gross and disgusting.

So after detailing the whole foul account, I had apparently paused in my story telling. My mind must have drifted to us reconvening in the hallway outside of Mr. Evans's room, and my upper level resident, the competent resident on the service, providing us the necessary background about the patient that had led up to this liquid brown horror and then calmly translating that morning's events into the "where do we go from here" pragmatism necessary for VA Ward survival, including things like augmenting supportive fluid therapy and checking on the status of findings of already ordered GI and Infectious Disease consults.

"So what was the deal with that guy?" Rick asked from his usual position on the turf in front of the benches. "What makes a guy spread his fucking diarrhea all over the room?

"He was just insane. It's the AIDS." Frank responded from the right side of our bench.

"Oh give me a fucking break," Rick quickly responded, implicating his questions were potentially just morally rhetorical, thrown out there to state something which he at least regarded as obvious.

"So what was the cause of his diarrhea?" Carl inserted, rationally.

"We never found out, or at least not by the time I left the Ward," I answered, thinking back.

Then, beginning to space out a bit, as sleep deprivation was beginning to catch up with fading breakfast caffeine, I elaborated.

"From what I remember, and I was still pretty much new to these things at that stage, we had ruled out all the usual suspects. He didn't have Cryptosporidia, Isospora, or even Microsporidia, and certainly none of the mundane causes of diarrhea that even non-immunosuppressed patients can get in the hospital, being on antibiotics and stuff," I semi- subconsciously effused on retrospect. "We'd apparently had the GI docs consulting on this guy for weeks. He'd had upper GI tract endoscopies and colonoscopies, including with biopsies, multiple times. The geeky Infectious Disease Service guys had been consulted as well, and they'd GI scoped him multiple times, like each time they came up with a new bug or other cause as a possible culprit, and that required specialized collection processes, and hence another endoscopy. That guy's bowel mucosa had probably been examined more than any in the history of the VA," I concluded with no sarcasm intended. Curtis, who had been surprisingly quiet the whole time he'd been there, offered up in unaccustomed solemnity, "Some patients with HIV just get diarrhea, and it can kill 'em…no body knows why."

"You're right," I acknowledged as our eyes met in a rare moment of apparently mutual seriousness. "You rule out the things you know about, and then you get desperate. You get the experts to come in, and sometimes…often…they can't do shit either…it's just the way it is," I felt another twinge of the buzz come-down.

"No matter how much you're probed and prodded," Carl for some reason quietly and sadly added.

"That doesn't give you the right to smear your own crap all over the room," Frank angrily responded.

"Doesn't it?" Rick challenged. "Maybe he was just tired of all the probing and prodding," he added, appearing enlivened for the first time that morning, while knowingly looking over at Carl.

"I say he was just fucked up in the head," Frank retaliated, with rare obscenity.

"Being fucked up in the head is no way to go through life," Leo surprisingly contributed.

There was really nothing more that could be added after that, I suppose, and the whole group fell silent.

After a few minutes, his anger and passion apparently abated, Frank asked me, sincerely, "Did that intern ever teach you anything useful?"

"I'm not sure," I seriously paused to ponder. "Although he did ask me once: How do you ever expect to learn any medicine if you don't watch St. Elsewhere?"

Book Two

"There's Heaven, then there's somewhere else
And those that fall between
The cracks and land upon their feet
With the rhythm of the King
Me, I sway from side to side
Just to keep this story lit
And hold your hand across the rooms,
The borders and the lines

I don't need you
Like you don't need me
You don't need me"

-Alejandro Escovedo, Don't Need You

I

-Recollections: San Francisco; Autumn, 1990

The first time I ever met Kim, almost exactly one and a half hours after the first time I ever laid eyes on her, I probably wasn't at my best. I was post-call and in a setting that could only best be considered as foreign. It was certainly not in a setting, such as a hospital or a bar, where I could have welcomed a potential home court advantage. But then again, at the start of that evening, the second one, really, for me that day, as I hadn't had any sleep the night before, I wasn't exactly anticipating meeting someone who would...well....have so much impact.

I was a second year Neurology resident, with a still very limited knowledge of the city of San Francisco, per se. Except for a few visits to some of the more standard tourist sites when my family had visited a couple times, I probably didn't have a good grasp of much beyond the UCSF campus and the very specific streets incorporated into my daily journey to and from there, most of which didn't really require any real paying attention to on my part. I hadn't even very proficiently mastered the few blocks within the area of my very small third floor apartment in an older building in the Mission District, other than those in the specific direction of the walking distance to the San Francisco General (which certainly had some advantages for call coverage) and the possible exception of one or two neighborhood cafes on Valencia that I often had take out or delivery from for evening suppers that I wasn't having in the less than world class cuisine serving Med Center or The General cafeteria. I suppose one or two coffee shops in my still relatively new neighborhood could by now claim me as a local, probably receiving a higher share of my not particularly generous residency stipend than anyone other than my landlord.

I had originally been attracted to this part of town, as it was somewhat conveniently located in between the UCSF campus and The General, had relatively cheaper rents compared to more posh SF neighborhoods, and had a Latino atmosphere that I was comfortable with from my near San Antonio upbringing and my San Antonio and Houston education days, along with the recent trend of a rather Bohemian/artsy Caucasoid invasion that my apartment locator had carefully pointed out, as if that element were somehow more comforting and reassuring to me than the mixture of remaining Italians, influxing Vietnamese, and growing predominantly Hispanic elements that actually reminded me of the mixed neighborhoods north of IH-59 towards downtown from my Houston Med School days and on the fringes of which at least I would be dwelling again in the not too distant future. Even the proximity of parts of the Mission District to the Castro added a certain degree of slightly different flavored gay ornamentation, somewhat like the proximity to the Montrose did for the analogous Houston area. However, the typical single unit dwelling versions of the latter didn't come with the charm of the occasional dead I.V. drug abuser in the entryway of the multiunit buildings in the Mission, a feature clearly under emphasized by the rental location service.

Once again, I had to get used to the idea of not being able to drive to work. A guy I had met on my first visit out there, a tall and burly Englishman doing research within the department (in an area that seemed to be geared toward some hardcore developmental work, like modifying mouse brains or even building models of some portions from scratch) was an ongoing useful source of relocation related information. On a repeat trip to UCSF, during which we made an English ale-focused (to the point of out of focus) tour of one or more too many of San Francisco's many charming drink holes, this murine Frankenstein had made it clear to me that despite my otherwise noble plan to Texanize at least parts of San Francisco, driving to work at the Parnassus campus should be stricken from the official plans of the agenda. In his words you pretty much had to have a Nobel Prize already to get a parking space there, and aside from the obvious timing issues there was the much greater (much, much, much greater) fact that not I nor any of the other far more relevant judges would be that optimistic for the work I had yet to complete in my remaining Bethesda time. Yet, it was actually pretty convenient to get back and forth. Especially when on time as planned, I could have a pleasant walk with a cup of coffee over to the General, and during research rotations might even be able to do a couple things or if on consult service see patients over there first. Regardless, from there I could just catch the shuttle over to the Parnassus campus and come back home just the opposite way. Alternatively, I might catch a bus or the Muni, the N. Judah stopping on Irving, from which in one of the weirder aspects of the commute, based on the combination of campus layout and especially campus density, I could then either take the elevator or a bus up Parnassus street.

Despite my still almost perpetual need for the city map I had received at Residency Orientation more than a year before, things were going quite well workwise, I suppose. I had finished a year of clinical Neurology training, which had been intense and demanding, both physically and mentally, but at the same time had allowed for numerous encounters with patients that translated well to my emerging areas of clinical research focus. In addition to the usual General Neurology rotations, diagnosing and managing stroke victims, honing my physical examination skills along with becoming at least competent with neuro CT's and MRI's, interpreting EMG's and NCV's in myopathy and neuropathy workups, facilitating social placement of dementia patients, etc., covering the E.R. while on call and a few months on the Consultation Service had given me a substantial exposure to the Neurologic complications of HIV infection and AIDS, in a city that had been and still was being particularly ravaged by this uniquely evil plague.

In addition to gaining fairly extensive clinical experience with the more common secondary central nervous system (or CNS) complications of AIDS, such as CNS toxoplasmosis and CNS lymphoma, and even occasional encounters with other more unusual secondary complications, such as progressive multifocal leukoencephalopathy (PML), the emerging clinical biology of the fundamentally more primary CNS complications of HIV infection was well suited to my burgeoning "expertise" (or at least interest) in Neuroimmunology. As with so many areas of HIV infection and AIDS, UCSF had a large number of the world's most preeminent experts in the clinical aspects and possible underlying pathophysiology of AIDS dementia complex. No doubt, decisions regarding my eventual "career" (hopefully no longer to be delayed by yet still further formal training) and the concepts of disease causation underlying the hypotheses I would investigate here and especially in Houston were impacted essentially daily by the conferences and conversations I was being steadily exposed to by some of the most important research leaders in this area. The clinical importance of this work was mercilessly driven home to me that first year, as night after night I saw the human deteriorating consequences of our nasty little retrovirus.

...

My immediate future was fairly clear, with the second and third years of my four year program focused primarily on research. Even during my first year in SF, the planning stages for this period had put me increasingly in contact with one Dr. Hassel, an M.D., Ph.D. board certified Neurologist with primarily research emphasis as Associate Director of Research in the Neuroscience Department. Hassel was clearly gay, if you allow a slightly effeminate demeanor, absence of the usual middle aged guy comments about wife and kids, and energetic support of an organization that would put me square in the dry-mouth, cat-got-your-tongue, dizzying, life-soon-to-be-turned-upside-down first encounter with the young, disturbingly beautiful, intriguingly intelligent, and refreshing sense of humor possessing Ms. Kimberly Williamson.

Hassel was a truly smart guy, and in that diverse and sophisticated manner that you often get in the polished and successful folks at places like UCSF, Harvard, Stanford, Yale, etc., in that they didn't have to spend 24 hours a day on job related stuff to be world leaders in their area. These people typically don't waste time like us average blue collar over achievers, watching football, drinking too late at bars we shouldn't have gone to in the first place, watching movies we've seen several times already, just because we came across it late at night while channel surfing and were feeling sentimental. They tend to spend their non-work time (leisure?) doing things that most of us would probably consider as...well...work. You know, the department chairman who is also a concert pianist; the incredibly busy surgeon who runs marathons (and hence spends the time training for them); the clinically competent but administratively prone dean, who is increasingly active in city politics.

Hassel was not only one of the top Neuroimmunologists in the world, being on the Editorial Board of several relevant top-notch journals and on multiple NIH study sections for reviewing grants, but he could have made a separate living or at least carve out a meager existence as a critic in multiple cultural areas, those kinds that I couldn't even answer more than a rare trivial pursuit question on (you may remember, the pesky brown and pink categories in literature and art and entertainment). He particularly liked 18th and 19th century English literature, which I could occasionally nod my head at comments on in the hallway, as well as all forms of art, during similar casual conversations on which, I would probably have to excuse myself to go down to clinic or the E.R. or the lab or any other more comfortable environs.

It turns out, that in addition to the snootier charity venues in town, and SF has many, he was a vigorous supporter of an association of largely gay artists that gave shows to generate revenues for HIV-related research, including portions of proceeds from sales of specific art pieces. In actuality, and perhaps under Hassel's influence, a substantial portion of this was targeted for neurological complications of HIV. At the time, I didn't know if Hassel or any of our UCSF associates directly received any of these funds, although it couldn't have been better spent than this, I guarantee you. However, as I later learned, Hassel was careful to be sure that none of the raised funds ever actually entered his hands, to avoid potential conflicts of interest, etc. (not that he needed the funding). Fortunately, though, he did have some influence as to how and to whom those funds were distributed, as he was probably even a better judge of quality and/or promising high risk research than he was of 19th century European Impressionists or late 20th century Castro Realists, whose reality had been becoming progressively immersed in a devastating nightmare.

...

So, on a Friday night in late September of my second year out in SF, there was to be a showing of art related to AIDS, mostly by local artists, at the M. H. de Young Memorial Museum in Golden Gate Park. The significance of the associated broader scope and more mainstream venue that this was a part of, and the complex constellation of political and financial events that had combined to take such an edgy showing of potentially controversial work out of the usual smaller galleries in traditional gay neighborhoods, was lost on me at the time. Hassel, as a big supporter of the organization and possibly even a benefactor of some of the artists, would usually be a sort of VIP guest at such a function, but on this particular date, he was scheduled to be at my old stomping grounds in Bethesda in Study Section to review NIH grants. I was flattered when he asked me to attend in his place, assuring me that nothing formal would be expected of me, but that there should be someone there from the "program". I was essentially working full time in Hassel's lab by that time, focusing on my interests in mechanisms of immunologic and inflammatory injury to neurons, which was still primarily basic and theoretically translatable to dozens of diseases, but tragically at that time in 1989 and 1990, probably 95 % of the victims of those diseases shared one common diagnosis, and many of those unfortunate individuals lived in our fair city, my temporary home, and Hassel's since he had commenced his residency at UCSF in 1976 after medical school at Harvard, and even more solidified when he had joined the UCSF Neurology and Neuroscience faculty in 1980.

This is why my work fell so well under the auspices of Hassel's HIV-oriented program. However, I told him (perhaps in more polished speak) that I knew shit about art. He replied that he knew that. (I guess that much had emerged from our hallway conversations that I so quickly tried to escape from). He said he didn't want me to attend because of my appreciation for art, but that he wanted me there because he thought I would probably look O.K. in a suit (the cordial funny part of the compliment, and not meant sexually in any way), and that no one he knew at present had more passion for the need for research endeavors in this area, nor was soon going to learn as much as I would about how hard it is to get relevant funds on a regular basis. Besides, he said, I may learn something about art. I was flattered.

Still, I felt compelled to at least prepare in some fashion, likely a reflection of that still in medical training instinct, that operating mode somehow involving anal sphincter-modulated primal deep brain limbic structures or something along those lines, wherein even something like a 2 to 5% chance to make a favorable impression or a 1 to 4% chance of avoiding the sort of humiliation that puts oneself in the hole of an unfavorable impression prompts prophylactic reading just in case a recently studied item could by the fate of the gods become the even momentarily central focus of the conversation you accidentally stumble into when playing on such unfamiliar ground. For example, when one finds oneself in those few awkward moments standing next to the thick, older woman whose lovely sequined gown seems to be of equal circumference from neck to hem and before learning she's like the richest person there (maybe she's carrying wads of cash within her dress, explaining the obliteration of even the crudest remnants of female form) and someone else within the same circle has already taken the most obvious safest ground with making a complement in the form of praising her brooch right around the same time that you remember that that's the name for the statistically more likely to be worn by older women piece of jewelry not uncommonly represented in the shape of an oval or a giant insect, such that you're left hanging in that precarious moment of choosing between the potential lesser of two evils of appearing as a moron for walking away without saying anything after having officially been within the group perimeter vs. the often alcohol-favored utterance of something ridiculously incorrect within the context of some vague topic you sense as being group addressed, so that not only do you get the blank stares and perplexed grimaces that would result in your spontaneous combustion if evolution had rendered humans with oropharyngeal flame generation and targeted projection corresponding to inter-personal thought content, but you get the persistent stares and hand-covered whisper/snickers later in the evening from people who weren't even in the original circle group to begin with, indicating that your humiliation or at least the originality of its cause is spreading widely.

Given that art knowledge was out of the question in the timeframe and existing schedule complicating preparation period I at least read up within my scattered piles of San Francisco pamphlets, brochures, booklets, and substantial enough to be cut out and saved newspaper articles on the historic event-based birth and architectural aspects of the night's venue. Amongst other details, I had learned that not only had the original building (persisting after some kind of fair from whence the original museum was derived) been destroyed during the great 1906 earthquake, but the very building I would be in actually received damage in that one from just last year that I originally attributed to the shaking of a poorly performing cameraman filming the world series game while watching and studying as a perhaps more logical explanation given my earthquake free background. This way at least I did not pronounce to any far more in the know that I liked the way the museum had fused what would seem like a logical "spanishy" motif ("motif", a word I would already have to approach with the same proper respect for mouthing any other virgin) with the modern fairly uniform, symmetrical, matrix like tubular metal face, due to unforgivable misinterpretation of the fairly straightforward external bracing repairs to achieve stability and augment some sort of principle or property like a "seismic resistance". Nor would I be in the danger now of confusing an overheard reference to Loma Prieta as conversation related to the name of one of the contributing artists. Though none of this precluded me from generating overall relatively mild looks of confusion on the faces of two men and one woman when, within trying to joke about the chances of being killed by an earthquake in a clearly past demonstrated vulnerable building on this very evening, I indicated that it could not be ruled out by a suspected possible pattern of an 83 year frequency, as there was not sufficient data to completely exclude something like an 83 year, one year, 83 year or any other combination of 83 year, one year,... (17, 83, 1,... or many other permutations I gave), regardless of what had anteceded the 1906 quake, in what was likely a left over brain fragment from a conversation I had had recently with my parents that casually brought up the history of two strikes already on the structures of the de Young museum. With that early and minor one under my belt being perceived as the official episode of possible failure, I could proceed as formally belonging-for better or worse.

...

The eventual consequences of that night have bronzed my memories of many of the normally little and trivial events that immediately preceded and followed it. When, after my conversation with Hassel, I looked at my occasionally maintained calendar, I saw that I was on call the night before. Even though I was in the lab theoretically full time then, I still had to take call, not super often, just 3-4 times a month, but it was a real call, as the SF General E.R. had a steady need for Neurology consultation at night. I would likely be up most of the night before, but that was maybe even better regarding going to a social function the following evening, as I would be too tired to get anything else more useful or productive done lab work or reading wise. Plus, being still in underpaid trainee physician status in an expensive city, I remained, somewhat embarrassingly, in that "anything-for-free-food-and-alcohol" stage (does it ever end?), and Hassel had reassured me by saying that there would be food, probably pretty decent food if he remembered correctly, and an open bar ("several actually"). So, I may have gone anyway, even if I didn't just want to please Hassel.

On top of my obvious total lack of familiarity with any of the specific artists whose works were to be presented that evening, which was superimposed on the background of my basically complete lack of any knowledge of art or even more famous artists in general, acute deficiencies which if I put a little effort into it I might get away with hiding, I may have stood out for a couple of other reasons.

First, I may have been one of the few heterosexual males there. That may not have necessarily been obvious by mannerisms per se, as not all the other guys present were, as they say, "flaming", but my attire was probably a better clue, giving away, perhaps, not only my sexual orientation, but some other aspects of my basic composition at that point in my life, or at the very least, my complete ignoring of any aspects of my life outside of work and the indulging in few leisures and occasional evils that allowed me to maintain my intense approach to that work (i.e., which didn't often include clothes shopping). Let's just say that if prizes were going to be given away at the end of the evening for certain categories of "costume", I would have, hands-down, won the male award or maybe even a unisex award, for "most conservative". I pretty much had my standard "preppy doctor" attire on, as outside of scrubs, sweats, shorts (including the save-a-buck cut-off scrub variety), and jeans, my dress clothes for any occasion in which the former were inadequate pretty much were still of the khaki pants, light blue oxford, linen jacket or blue blazer variety, probably with some sort of tie that would make Ronald Reagan and George Bush proud. Now, in all fairness, each component was of relatively moderate or high quality: Ralph Lauren or equivalent, down to whatever Dexter type loafers or Nunn Bush brown oxford shoes were the least muddy in my closet, and which (hopefully) were at most only a couple of years behind fashion....in a different sort of environment.

I actually got to the museum that evening fairly early (this, when shared later with and analyzed in retrospect by my future partner, a mutually acknowledged hideously uncommon event), perhaps in order to earn a couple of brownie points, the all pervasive motivating factor of the perpetual medical trainee. Even this, of course, was largely an accident, it taking much less time to get over to the Park from the Parnassus Heights main UCSF campus, where I had stopped to run a work-related errand (dropping off a research sample I had collected in the early morning hours at the General), than from my apartment. I noticed quickly several guys in drag, one end of the spectrum of male attire, ending at the other extreme of the spectrum (the range of which not including yours truly), with more common and variously straight acting patrons in artsy black shirt and black pants, with or without matching black jacket. So, just to start things off, I had against me not only my lack of general art knowledge and my lack of familiarity with some of the local artists and apparently some even better known artists from LA, New York and elsewhere, including some painters and other visual artists whom had contributed to the national Art against AIDS program initiated the year before and whose works were on display there, but also my potentially self-consciousness generating lack of dark clothing or at the least, eyeliner and bitching stiletto pumps.

Not to be dismayed, not even in the slightest, I took this as an opportunity to learn something new, something perhaps even essential. I suppose a default or comfort mode for me is to learn. I can't stand to not know something, when confronted with aspects of whatever that "something" is; I don't know why. I don't think it's just about competition, blowing away the other humans, or some sort of life sustaining need to be on top, always. I suspect, and hope, that it's much more fundamental...the desire to know... to understand, regardless of whether there's competition or not...but I don't really know....at least, not yet. An acknowledged deficiency of knowledge, of any type, is at the very least... a gaping wound. Fortunately, or at least, hopefully, this guaranteed anxiety-at-the-least, borderline psychosis-or-worse-at-the-most mentality can mature to an energetic openness in which one can actually absorb new things for the purity and beauty of the facts themselves, the things learned, and processed and integrated in increasingly hugely broad, all life encompassing contexts, where they may be...consciously or even subconsciously...appreciated.

But even before issues of such global enlightenment, after all, if I was here as a representative of the local HIV-related CNS or other biomedical research community, and this was an existing or potential source of research revenue (for someone), then my lack of complete mastering of all related aspects of this function, and the community from which it derived, was something that needed to be rectified, beginning immediately. Secondly, there was, after all, an open bar, with accompanying "munchies". So, I immediately attacked my new challenge by two courses of action, at least one of which helped my later interactions with my still-unknown-to-me-at-that-stage future wife: firstly, I grabbed a copy of the catalogue related to the artists and the works on display, some of which were for sale, and began to read it quite attentively, and secondly, I drank....liberally.

Matching approximately one drink per page of the colorful brochure, keeping in mind that there were a fair amount of pictures, navigating through the display rooms to see the actual works described, I was on page five when IT happened.

...

I had made it through the first of the three medium sized rooms with the art displays, which were open along their widths off the back of the large central room where one first entered the event from the outside. This central room was where everyone was gathered, drinking and talking; those individuals who weren't actively looking at the specific pieces being displayed. When one entered that main room, the bar and tables with food were located over to the far right; this consequently had the densest collection of small groups of people. I had become familiar with this area, having made four repeat visits already, the first two hits resulting in a consequent delicately balanced overloaded plate of pretty damn good finger foods. These artsy-fartsy types apparently hadn't often encountered the likes of the underfed medical scientist types, at least one of which they were aggressively feeding that night (on which I hopefully only internally offered commentary to myself the first three trips back to the food/booze section). The last trip, either due to gastric satiety, social politeness, or just bad judgment, I hadn't actually made it over to the food table, perhaps as my growing interest in the art works were actually prompting quicker descents on the bar, before heading back to the displays. I was, apparently, a man on an artistic educational mission. It's possible that none, or few at best, do it better...the whole reading, learning, drinking thing. The population of black shirts and less common blouses tapered off gradually from the bar and food area towards the center of the room, and was thinnest of all towards the opposite end, where in the center of which a portable podium was situated, with a projection screen behind it, and rectangular collapsible tables with two folding chairs each on either side. (I knew conference room settings oh so well by then). A small room, likely something such as a supply closet or storage room, behind the speaker area had some educational materials about HIV and AIDS and some specific San Francisco programs and services scattered on a couple of similar collapsible tables.

A steady flow of quieter patrons, alone or in occasional pairs, made their way through the three interconnected display rooms. A sadly non-trivial percentage of the more serious viewers had the characteristic sunken cheeks and sallow eyes and clothes hanging on bony projections of their wasting skeletons that we were becoming too accustomed to seeing daily in the wards of the General and the streets of the Castro. Soft whispers between friends with moistening eyes accompanied the occasional longer and more reflective pauses at certain works, conveying perhaps even personal messages or painful memories of their creators. On a few such occasions, I couldn't help but feel less deserving to partake of these works, not from my lack of formal art appreciation, as these seemed so different from the usual gallery or museum pieces that I had seen pictures of in my one art history class that I aced by the usual test cramming without apparently remembering too much or had actually encountered in real life on the rare, seemingly tortuous at the time, externally imposed on me visits to actual museums, but more so because of a sense of not belonging, of not having the capacity to truly feel what those around me felt, those that seemed to have gone through some sort of purification process that accompanied the physical destruction of their shunned bodies or at least having witnessed such a process in the local artists being celebrated at that moment.

As I read the small labels accompanying each work, many of which were matched by similar synopses in my now very folded catalogue/brochure, I confirmed my suspicion that many of the artists were themselves HIV positive, many suffering from AIDS, and too many, already dead. Maybe as one who visits somebody else's church or eats at a restaurant of a friend's very different ethnicity can choose to be shy and reserved and not participate in certain foreign customs and practices or instead select to be adventurous and throw self consciousness and embarrassment to the wind, as in the end, the only one who gives a potential shit is you, I chose, at least this time, to feel comfortable, and to learn…and feel. The amazing part, I gradually realized, or maybe didn't even realize until later, was that I liked the stuff I was looking at more than the usual snooty art stuff, and it seemed so much more approachable to me. After that night, mainly through Kim, I would re-visit this issue many times, and come to partly understand, or at least appreciate, the influence that the horrific psychological forces that ones own illness or the deaths of friends and lovers at the evil hand of a world changing disease could have on one's increasingly desperate so-called creativity.

…

The keynote speaker for the evening was a local SF physician, a well recognized AIDS patient care and research advocate, whom I remembered, after his introduction and some of the comments made during his talk, from a long newspaper article published earlier in the year, excerpts of which I had more likely read in one or two UCSF newspapers. Dr. Don Francis had been the head of a SF HIV Task Force that had been appointed by Mayor Art Agnos, and which had made strong recommendations for substantially increasing the city's budget for HIV and AIDS to almost double its existing amount of spending to reach over $300 million dollars a year.

That evening Francis again made a few comments related to a highly impacting comparison his group had made in the Task Force's published report back in January. He made reference to the amount of money made available in aid in relation to the number of involved mortalities raised in response to the October 1989 SF earthquake and that of the current AIDS crisis. Although the earthquake may have been more acutely in the city's collective conscience in the fall of 1989, not quite even a year later, with AIDS looming larger daily, the comparisons were at best a little embarrassing. Billions of dollars had been made available after the October 1989 earthquake, which tragically killed 13 people. In contrast, along with a very admirable system of volunteer programs, the city's past annual AIDS budget was in the $150 to $200 million range, despite the fact that a staggering and staggeringly growing 5,000-10,000 SF citizens had died of AIDS, with 25,000 to 35,000 already infected with HIV.

I remembered the SF earthquake, or at least news images, descriptions, and reports of it. After all, I already lived in SF by then. Like any good American, I was watching the World Series. The occurrence of an earthquake, impinging on something so sacred, was beyond surrealistic. For my family and friends still dwelling in less faulted lands, the irony of the stereotype humor of it, once my safety had been verified, was hard to bypass. I had lived essentially all of my life in regions largely at low risk for natural disasters. The hill country and San Antonio were prone to occasional flash floods, but were rarely ever subjected to a minority of the tornadoes that orbited the mobile homes of our fellow Texans living in the flat landscape of the Texas Panhandle and Prairies. Houston had its hurricanes, the force of which was usually diluted after they'd rearranged the terrain of our Galveston brethren. Bethesda was cursed by proximity to the unnatural world of politics in the nearby D.C. area, but to my knowledge was probably at less than the national average for risks of earthquakes, tidal waves, tornadoes, wild fires, etc. My family joked about my hopefully temporary re-location to the Bay area, cautioning me to watch out for earthquakes, as if there is some sort of way to do that, like avoiding a dark parking lot in a bad neighborhood or something.

I don't really remember accounting for such issues in choosing my training destinations, perhaps more in keeping with what has been described as a certain aloofness regarding my non-educational or non-professional self. Even the love of my life, who at this moment I had still not officially met but only gazed upon from medium distances, has made "affectionate" comments to this effect. Basically, I didn't actually even notice the earthquake right away. I had been in SF for about 4 months, again the irony of "only there for a couple of months before the first damn earthquake" not escaping my family, but those were full clinical rotation months and that afternoon I was post-call, not that tired per se I guess, as I was actually studying a little for my Internal Medicine Boards, which I was scheduled to take that coming spring. I was, of course, board-eligible following my residency at the NIH, and was determined to take them before I forgot everything, potentially facilitated by training in a new specialty. Thus, between my Neurology readings for my new current residency program and related to the patients I was seeing every day, I attempted to squeeze in occasional Internal Medicine Board studying. Even some of my more in depth Neurology reading was intended, when possible, to be in areas of potential overlap; that is, general Neurology topics such as stroke, headache, CNS complications of meds (I'm sorry, medications) and systemic diseases, which were covered in the Medicine boards. That day, I had the TV on with the volume off, and only noticed something strange when I looked up at the World Series game and noticed the televised sections of the stadium collapsing in. Only then did I grasp the fact that my apartment was undergoing a fine to occasionally or even periodic medium-coarse tremor. I have shaken a few times in my life, largely due to the various physiologic consequences of failing to eat, failing to sleep, failing to not control my anger at whatever…and I would shake again in the not too distant future when asking the still unknown Kim to marry me. Earthquakes were not high on my shaking differential diagnosis list. It broke two glasses, one plate (all dirty, on the edge of the counter as opposed to rinsed and in the sink where they may have been safer), and my concentration. I gained further appreciation for what I had failed to adequately marvel at then by reading the newspaper the next day (an unusual event per se, but my post call state and three chapters in

Harrison's Principles of Internal Medicine eventually caught up to me and I zonked before possibly watching the evening news as I had intended).

As I drifted back from recollections of my first, and fortunately unsatisfactorily experienced earthquake, my gaze again found its way across the room to the unnervingly beautiful brunette, tastefully dressed in a black silk blouse and black wool skirt, yet somehow so amazingly different in my perceptions from the other black blouses there, female or otherwise. Her shoulder length hair had reddish highlights and even in the slightly darkened room I felt I could see the sparkling in her big brown eyes that I had caught a glimmer of in an inspiring passing glance when we walked by each other while browsing some of the pieces earlier, and then noted her elegant long lashes in profile, as I admired the apparent intensity with which she paid attention to the works. It made me feel a little guilty, subconsciously or actually consciously, lusting during this rather serious presentation, kind of the way I may have used to feel if I caught myself similarly gazing at a decked out babe in the middle of a sermon when accompanying my parents to church in high school. The serious attention now being paid to our speaker by the future Mrs. Me checked my drifting thoughts and I caught back up to Dr. Francis's comments.

For some reason, even with the potential dilution of the comparison by the growing temporal separation from the actual earthquake event, the impact of our speaker's cited numbers was larger on me this evening than when I had read parts of the HIV Task Group's report and the various impassioned editorial comments it had spurned several months ago. Despite the subtly growing ache in my deeper viscera, I found that one especially impassioned, but largely speculative, argument that Francis made, in particular, struck a medical chord with me. He was proposing that a substantial portion of the newly recommended budget be used to make AZT more widely available to SF patients. AZT, the drug that inhibited the HIV retrovirus enzyme reverse transcriptase, represented the only FDA approved drug used to specifically treat AIDS at the time (i.e., as opposed to agents used to treat the common opportunistic infections afflicting AIDS patients). Further, he was arguing that it be made available substantially earlier in the course of HIV infection, not just for treating patients with full blown AIDS, as was the current practice.

To my knowledge, there was no real data to support the potential benefit of early AZT treatment, but increasingly to me and my even more informed colleagues in Hassel's group, this made some real conceptual sense. Francis, and others, argued that if early treatment could delay, or even prevent, progression to full blown AIDS, not only would this be tremendously beneficial to the disease's unfortunate victims, but the added cost of longer drug treatment with this ridiculously expensive agent (the "ridiculously" being my editorial adverb) would be way more than offset by the savings of less and delayed expensive treatments for the common, inevitable consequences of end-stage disease.

...

In the ongoing universal struggle between idealists and realists, cost-effectiveness is and always will be a major underlying governing principle of medical care in the American societal system. For all I know, it may be even worse elsewhere, and before one criticizes too much, keep in mind that it takes hundreds of millions of dollars to bring any drug to final FDA-approved clinical application. The consequent cost of new prescription drugs isn't just to put large quantities of bucks in drug company CEO pockets. There are chemical reagents, lab equipment, experimental animals, toxicology studies, technician, physician, nursing and even biostatistician costs in clinical trials, all the expenses to cover for the literally hundreds to thousands of interrelated and sequential well orchestrated steps that necessarily occur from the basic chemistry and laboratory science to numerous stages of clinical research for proving true effectiveness and safety of a drug under the massive governmental regulations of the FDA, not to mention the seemingly mundane aspects of packing the specific chemical along with stabilizers, etc., into neat little pills, to the cool looking advertisements to hopefully encourage drug use under narrowly approved specific applications to begin allowing the slow, steady recouping of the vast amount of invested revenue, and allow people to stay employed and begin working on the next, hopefully more effective, and less toxic drug.

For those personally affected or having loved ones affected by a lethal condition, especially a new disease unfairly striking patients much younger than good old-fashioned common cancers and heart disease, medical progress, under sound scientific principles, can be ridiculously slow. It may be a little different in some countries, say in Europe or Japan, explaining in part, of course, the growing American pharmaceutical companies' efforts in these relatively lawless lands, but

American society, at least the legislative variety, has decided that making true, steady progress in this manner is better than wasting zillions of dollars and irrecoverable hope on potions, lotions, and snake charmer powders that are, under the rigors of scientific clinical investigation, shown to be not only ineffective, but potentially toxic, not to mention potentially steering the masses away from the only true promising drugs, even if they cost more per year than one's rent.

As I stood there listening, in my post-call, post five or six drinks, post having read more art-related reviews than I had since cramming for a test in a liberal arts course some nine years before state, and acutely feeling a little tired and as perhaps incompetent as the rest of the frustrated world, I reminded myself that in the year before, despite the realities of research and development, production, and advertising costs, Burroughs Welcome had "generously" lowered the cost of AZT down to a mere $10,000 or so per patient per year. I suppose even healthy working people would prefer not to make this kind of outlay, especially in a city like SF, where your rent could run you up to 30-50 % of your gross income. These things barely merit mention, maybe; however, I seemed to be more attentively noticing them, prompted occasionally by not-necessarily mal intended parental comments as reminders, as someone who could barely pay for rent, food, and a few fairly controlled vices, despite four years of college, four plus years of medical school, and four years of residency under my belt. I acutely felt poor, and made my way back to the bar, with the added intention of passing by the food table, to consume whatever I could to allay the need for breakfast, not to mention, the potential for maybe pocketing something, as I suddenly felt physically and mentally, and maybe even emotionally worn out, perhaps intending to head out soon.

I now stood at the back of the crowd, post one more successful visit to the bar but less than stellar assault on the sadly now largely depleted food table. Dr. Francis was now going into some seriously intense analysis of city fiscal financial policies that exceeded my current citizenship, and my tired mind drifted again. The less tired portions scanned the crowd and satisfyingly spotted again the most beautiful woman I could remember having seen in a really long time.

As I stared intently, almost meditatively, at this gorgeous creature who seemed to be paying more attention than me, the background budget comments, perhaps subconsciously, raised up thoughts of my own financial status that could impact my pursuit of the level of woman I thought I was now gazing upon. Cost of living had occasionally been a major consideration in my own life choices, even up to this relatively early stage of my career. For example, staying in TX for medical school had been much cheaper for me than going to a snooty northeast equivalent. But now, the cost of living in San Francisco was challenging my residency stipend in a manner that probably didn't allow for much flashiness in any pursuit of romance.

Clearly, the ongoing presentation was now lost on my beer, then rum and coke, then red wine, now what was this, oh yes, scotch (I hardly ever drink scotch…who was I trying to impress?). So, as I continued to analyze my own lack of financial health in the humbling context of the AIDS health budget, I shifted my approach to penetrating the crowd over to the left, peri-brunette side.

As I decided to go from Bethesda, not the cheapest site on the planet, to San Francisco, even I pondered the potential cost of living aspects. Obviously, this is not the highest priority for me, or I would have taken a lucrative private practice job after residency (not that I had exactly geared my training for one), rather than pursuing a further academic medicine career in an area requiring a second research oriented residency. Still, costs were a major consideration, I'm sure, when my parents wondered why I couldn't do my Neurology training (if I "had" to do a second residency) in San Antonio, or Dallas, or Houston, or…anywhere but California. I remember seeing "data" to the effect that the average percent of annual income going to housing costs was in the range of 18-20 % for these large Texas cities, and was similarly low in such cities as Kansas City (not high on my differential list) and Denver, but reached a nation leading rate of a whopping 50 % in San Francisco. However, this was THE place I HAD to be for the specific kind of training experience I wanted, and up to this point, I had no regrets. I did not dwell on the fact that I made about $30,000/year, after approximately 13…and steadily increasing… years of post-high school education and training. I didn't even have a roommate (yet), but I won't bore anyone (including myself at that particular moment) with the depressing details regarding the size, location, or general state of disrepair of my current habitat, or the nature of my diet dictated by my post-rent residual resources. Thank God for cost-supplemented hospital cafeteria food. Still, I didn't have to also miraculously find a fucking $10,000 a year for a drug that may or may not do me any good, and yet I suspect that if I were an unemployed drug addict or a young male homosexual that had already lost his medical insurance it would be even harder.

I am not an economist or a fiscally conscientious human being. I do not (did not at the time) even balance my check book. I had learned that ATM cards were a satanic invention designed, by virtue of their convenience and the consequent failure to record transactions and to not incur your bank's machine service charges, to financially destroy me and those like me. I spend if I have it, and then find art shows with free food when I don't. Still, financial issues aside, three loosely defined rows from the back into the crowd, maybe twelve feet from the object of my acute obsession, close enough that I tried to see if I could smell her against the background of the intervening black shirts, on the basis of Francis's ongoing financial arguments and the need for increased use of AZT, I now switched my paranoia from personal budget issues over to more medically relevant fears. Few people in that crowd probably spent as much time as I do thinking about the cellular and molecular aspects of Medicine. Aside from the scary economic aspects being outlined, a major biological consideration arguing against early AZT treatment would be the anticipated potential development of AZT-resistant HIV strains, hence negating the "effectiveness" of the drug at later stages of disease progression, like full blown AIDS, for which it was currently employed. In my own mind, influenced as it was by the daily intense conversations with those like Hassel and our colleagues, this was a bridge we would face when we got there. Delaying the potential CD4 cell devastation during the clinically quiescent phases of HIV infection when the little viral fuckers hung out in lymph nodes covertly killing its citizens had some seriously attractive theoretical medical advantages. For those advocating such early intervention, a seemingly requisite future accompaniment would be the FDA approval of other anti-HIV drugs, which even if they still only targeted reverse transcriptase (as AZT did), were chemically different enough that the same mechanisms of resistance to AZT should not apply. This was why I was in Hassel's lab, this is why I went to the VA and especially over to the General to collect samples late at night. This is why I would eventually go back to Houston. The fantasy of turning AIDS into a chronic illness, one which we could then systematically counter attack all of the other organ and life destroying consequences of, was a dream many of us had in that room that minute (as my thoughts blurred with Francis's comments), except maybe those whose CD4 counts were already less than 200; too many already, who made or bought the art that night.

...

I had moved through a thin resistance at the back of the crowd, over to the far left, towards the main door, where with less than a 30 degree angle head turn to either side, I could see and somewhat listen to Francis, watch with increasing commitment the gorgeous brunette, and glance over to the galleries, with their tales of destruction, frustration, and devastation, still being attended to by a few who had come for other than the shrimp, wine, and financial/medical commentary.

I continued to think through and past the speaker's comments regarding early AZT therapy and pondered further the future treatment pharmacologic implications. Combination therapy to kill potentially mutating microorganisms was a well established medical principle. I took another drink of my scotch. It went down hard. I was more of a beer or bourbon kind of a guy. (Again, who was I trying to impress?) God that woman is so fucking beautiful, I remember thinking. She was paying such careful attention to the presentation. My frustration at not having her glance over at the non-black shirt and my inability at present to do anything about it gave no choice but to be countered by increasingly deep pondering over some of the now largely speculative issues that Dr. Francis and my ethanol tinted and so fatigued brain were raising. Combination therapy, I considered again, borrowing from principles so deeply ingrained in my medical brain that they were like reflexes beat in by a pharmacologic drill sergeant.

For example, using multiple drugs, including with different mechanisms of action, has long been the mainstay for treating tuberculosis (TB). AIDS, in fact, had brought this recently even more to the clinically well-known foreground, with the increased prevalence of Isoniazid-resistant TB. Consider that maybe a group of these ancient bacteria mutated to become resistant to a single drug at a rate of one in a million. However, if the pleasure of having breathed in some derelict alcoholic's TB breath or being a school aged child in a crowded home acutely housing your Mexican immigrant Uncle who seemed to always be coughing up blood into a handkerchief had given you a good old-fashioned dose of acute pulmonary TB, such that you were walking around (coughing up to your co-residents or co-classmates) with an infection with one billion organisms, then it wouldn't take you a whole long time to have a whopping case of Isoniazid-resistant TB (i.e., TB resistant to one drug). However, if you were on three or four drugs, given that any individual little TB bug had a one in million chance to develop resistance to each of these, the chance that one of the uninvited lung and eventually other organ destroying organisms could develop resistance to ALL of the drugs with three (or four) such agents being used would be like (one in a million x one in a million x one in a million) (x one in a million), or one in 1,000,000,000,000,000,000 (or 1,000,000,000,000,000,000, 000,000 if four drugs), which would be hideously unlikely if you were infected with "only" 1,000,000,000 organisms. The same principle could eventually be applied to treating HIV, if more drugs would someday be available.

Was that a glance? An acknowledgement of the intense guy pacing at the periphery? Although not sure, I was optimistic. In an effort to bolster up my still not realized reputation as the guy in the room who potentially took this more seriously than anyone else, I paced the back of the crowd again, before returning for one of the few remaining maybe crab meat on small toast things and a...Jack Daniels.

Still, if AZT could delay the development of AIDS and its complications, I thought as I penetrated the back left of the crowd again with a bit more bravery, up to the point of just a two black shirt separation, and was rewarded by a slight turnaround/imagined smile at the crowd disturbance, I suspect a fair number of HIV-infected individuals, having seen their friends and loved ones suffering at the end stages of AIDS, may choose early treatment. They may willingly sacrifice any potential modest-at-most benefit of treatment at more traditional late stages that developed resistance may preclude. After all, despite statistically significant survival improvement or reduced opportunistic infections that clinical trials may have objectively shown in large groups of patients, this didn't exactly typically translate to any sort of miraculous improvement in individual cases with current AZT use strategies. But maybe now, I was just buzzed, and cynical, and....so....distracted.

Now, in the spirit of tired, ethanol infused optimism, I allowed myself to continue in my partially directed thoughts on what still remains one of the greatest nights in the history of Jeff. Possibly flavored with the substantiation of retrospect, I considered that in the near future, use of other reverse transcriptase inhibitors in combination with AZT would be expected to minimize the chance of development of resistance, such that patients could be treated with combinations of drugs for long periods of time, or be switched to another agent if tests suggested that resistance to AZT had developed. Further, history and confidence in good old-fashioned American ingenuity and work ethic indicated to many of the optimists in the medical world that other agents would come along, and indeed were already in the works, which would target other candidates in the limited number of steps of the highly efficient assault machinery of the HIV virus. (Protease inhibitors would be on the horizon within the next several years. In antimicrobial and even anti-cancer pharmacology, targeting different steps in a process not only helped reduce resistance but also often achieved synergy in effectiveness). Hassel and I had had this optimistic discussion several times. It energized my increasingly HIV-targeted work at the time in his lab, and was the unstated underlying foundation of my future Houston-based clinical trial for which I would leave, all "grown up", in a few years. My new found personal confidence emerging in this current assembly, based in part on my speculated future contributions to the focus of all those present, led me back (yet AGAIN) to the left side edge of the crowd, where my at least subconscious mind and other deep seated organs could better ponder the things it even more acutely craved. The movement this time had been even more noticed by the object of whatever focus I had left, and from this new position I continued steadily on awaiting any chance fate would excrete forth, bolstered up by the two-carbon scaffolding from the one last drink my courage would need to make an actual confrontation, once the excellent presentation had reached its conclusion, which I sensed had nearly arrived.

I enjoyed the last five minutes of Dr. Francis's talk, but enjoyed being there, and feeling so paradoxically comfortable and anxiously excited at the same time, even more. I thought about Dr. Hassel; his excellence, his brilliance, his dedication, his apparent compassion for patients, although he didn't actually see that many directly anymore, and pondered whether I was capable of representing adequately what we all stood for.

Miraculously, maybe even pathetically, then, given my growing focus on the target of my still covert, yet increasingly bold, and strategic crowd penetrations that had almost placed me within smelling distance of this incredibly beautiful woman, my mind, the sleepy ethanol-linked silly neurons that it was, drifted again; drifted to the things that I was so acutely and intimately exposed to that evening, superimposed on a growing sense of belonging and competence that I was perhaps steadily gaining by being part of Hassel's lab and the heretofore almost taken for granted combination of such rigorous clinical and research training. Having these newly-reinforced emotional and mental balls and the hoped for someday bucks to begin thinking about strategies such as early AZT treatment and future combination therapy, my nocturnal day dreams fused with the colors of Dr. Francis's last few slides. These were the optimistic fantasies that were the keys for beginning to turn the corner in order to someday make HIV infection a chronic disease that one could live with, much like diabetes or rheumatoid arthritis, at least conceptually. This was the phoenix that had to rise from the hideous ashes of despair so blatantly conveyed in the art we were encountering that evening. The suffering was known, such a deeply branded component of the lives of so many that were there that evening. We were there to acknowledge it, but not to celebrate it, not any of us, hopefully none to take morbid comfort out of the transient sick security that might come with the recognition that it was happening to others. We were there to be sick of it, appalled by it, not to accept it, but to be motivated by it.

...

And then the lights came on. I realized that my mind had drifted largely to a plane not very concretely represented in my immediate newly illuminated surroundings, bemusing so intently that as I caught myself and shook myself out of it, I wondered how long I had been standing there in the middle of the now clearing room, basically staring straight ahead at Kim. If she had noticed at all, she was now not returning my glance, perhaps unnerved by the freaky trance I may have seemed to be in while perhaps glaring at her in some sort of scary way. But hopefully not, as despite my proximity, maybe nine or ten feet away, we were separated by a portion of the rim of folks who had apparently gathered around her immediately after the presentation had ended.

Knowing later what Kim's role in this function had been, I suppose this was a group of variously affiliated co-workers or others associated in some manner with the event who wanted to congratulate her, or praise her efforts, or maybe point out any minor catastrophes that needed her expert hand to quickly dispel, etc. They ranged from two young females, at least one of which dressed and carried herself like the loyal, but anxiety suffering "assistant", to two men, one middle aged, one much younger, both in versions of the official black artsy attire, and who were either a couple or at least very good friends, with the younger one carrying on quite melodramatically about something to do with the placement of a particular piece of art in relation to another by a once rival, but now dead, artist ("brilliant"... "so insightful"), with Kim's somewhat surprised or questioning look in response perhaps reflecting an unspoken confession that it had actually been an accident, to an older, very professional appearing, silver haired woman, still very attractive, and who occasionally placed her hand on Kim's shoulder, in an almost maternal fashion.

As I was not in any way a part of this group, being either in front, beside, or behind them depending on your perspective while noticing the dork just standing in the middle of the room, after the few moments needed to make my observations and a few speculative interpretations, even the combination of fatigue, alcohol, and lust/infatuation couldn't completely numb my social reflexes, such that I eventually realized that I really was just standing off by myself, staring at a group of people I had nothing to do with, and hence, needed to relocate. Clearly, my well conceived and patiently executed plan to finally make direct contact with this woman was at least going to have to be put on hold. Hopefully she wouldn't leave while I was pretending to find something else to do. Without even really noticing, I had already armed myself with an adequate wine reserve to continue to supplement the at least four or five too many drinks I had on board already, so the usual default comfort zone of lumbering over to the bar was out. I regretfully turned my head away from staring at the woman for which it already seemed to pain me to behold in a manner less than the passionate familiarity with which I already fantasized it, and I headed back over to the art displays, where I would try to appreciate at least some towards the front of each row, such that I could cast an occasional glance back to identify my next opportunity for making a fool of myself or something.

...

This turned out to be quite a different experience than I ever expected. I thought I would just stare at some paintings or sketches with the same "I don't get it" internal blank stare while trying to outwardly convey the "um, yes, interesting" intellectual gaze. After all, this is pretty much how I had experienced every other art-viewing episode I had been tortured with in the past. Pictures of ridiculously pale, at least moderately fat women, with at best B-cup pushing C-minus cup breasts (despite the obesity), laying naked with some sort of gloriously colored blanket or drape or quilt type thing only partially covering a thigh the size of a side of beef that more properly should be conservatively covered, maybe in slimming black, while some sort of winged nympho-cherubs floated around her head and some saint stuck spears in someone in the background; or, maybe some 19th century painting I was supposed to remember as "Impressionistic" where a boat sat in the middle of a pretty ho-hum looking pond, the water of which swirled at the distant shore, blending in with some acid trip induced distorted sunflowers that then blended in with a gray-blue-green sky in a swirlo-smudgy style that looked like the painter just got bored with the work and finished that part quickly. Or there was some bold (I remembered this adjective from Art History, fortunately not called Art Appreciation, class) red chunks admixed with interrupted puke-green strings, with scattered blue balls, in some sort of supposedly brilliant arrangement called "chaos" or some other name for coke-head, martini sipping upper classers to remember while trying to impress secretly similarly underwhelmed social climbers who happened to be in their "flat", the kind of stuff that proved if I just would have kept my finger paintings from kindergarten (or those things we did where we dipped string in paints and then squashed them between two pieces of paper, maybe on rainy days when we couldn't go outside and play), I could have sold them in posh New York galleries, by women either named Biffy or Gladys who wore those Navy uniform kinds of jackets, with the big brass buttons and shoulder pads or men named "Jean" or "Jun" or "Jon" or "Jah" (you're not sure, because it's said with a French accent too thick to be real) paradoxically wearing mother of pearl plastic librarian type glasses low down on their pierced nose and saying things related to the artist that you don't even understand or find uniquely absurd while you ponder the $26,000.00 price tag, such as: "…they say he did this one while staying up for six weeks straight and reading the Koran backwards…in braille" or "you know…there's a rumor that he only eats cat food during the months he paints."

But in contrast to my usual boredom and self-conscious ignorance and frustrated disconnection, I found myself very drawn to these pieces, as if I understood them, at least a little, and certainly was getting something out of them. They seemed more "real" to me, more approachable, maybe more concrete, or if that is potentially insulting, at least "less abstract". A term I appreciated later, as I learned more about HIV-related art at this time, in large part from the brochures Kim did for several more shows while we were in San Francisco and from various discussions on the subject with all types of folks, was "direct". I came to realize that artists suffering from AIDS or watching loved ones die of AIDS and maybe realizing that a similar fate awaited them, shortly, and at a time when little or no hope existed for a cure and only frustration and maybe even panic resulted from the perceived lack of adequate political and scientific attention to this crisis, would approach their art in certain ways, that at least to me, made a whole lot of sense.

I suppose that an artist can be filled with despair, true despair, and this could be conveyed in their work, sometimes horrifically; or perhaps at another stage of dealing with the disease, one could be filled with anger, anger at being sick, anger at the lack of hope, anger at a real or perceived lack of action being taken by others, and this anger could be reflected also, and sometimes in a manner almost appallingly graphic; one could be consumed by grief, the grief that uniquely comes from losing a loved one decades before it should happen, and that grief could be tragically displayed, maybe simply, maybe profoundly, perhaps in a work falling short on artistic merit alone compared to what that same artist could have achieved in a different life, in a different time, on a different time scale, when they weren't panicked by their own impending death, when they weren't progressively distracted by their own deteriorating mental and dexterous skills, when they weren't desperately reaching out for our help, for our attention. And maybe, one could be filled with hope, hope for community, hope for medical science, hope for compassion, hope for humanity.

Even from my naïve perspective, I saw works that I believed expressed the gamut of these fundamental human feelings, these immortal basic elements and values: paintings deep in medieval symbolism or even more concrete images drawing comparisons to the plaque, the only historical global tragedy really approaching legitimate comparison. Funny, how many times from a medical perspective, facilitated perhaps by the media and often prompted by comments from friends and colleagues, I had actually already attempted these analogies in my own mind or been exposed to them by others. As a medical and scientific logic-machine, I typically corrected and at least partially negated such comparisons; after all, one was bacterial, one was viral; we can now treat the plague with simple antibiotics similar to those we use for good old gonorrhea and the same as those we treat pubescent teens with for acne; doom saying the fact that there'd likely never be a vaccine given the mutation rate of HIV and there may never be a cure, given the fact that with antibiotics we could target well defined genetic and biochemical differences between bacteria and our own cellular machinery vs. the fact that viruses, by definition, use that very machinery. We rarely cure viral diseases. We rely heavily on our own inherent immune systems to contain them (not that these processes aren't involved in slightly different mechanisms with these more treatable bacterial processes). Unfortunately, ironically, it was that very immune system so needed for viral containment that was being not so covertly attacked by the HIV virus itself. How incomplete and borderline stupid, of course, was this rigid stance as from the medico-pharmaceutical point of view, there were still unique targets (for drugs) whereby that satanic little shit head retrovirus even gained access to those cells and that cell machinery. In 14th century Europe, they didn't know about either bacteria or viruses, and no one would have predicted we could effectively and safely drug target bacterial vs. human ribosomes or even know what ribosomes were. But as we were being bathed in the pain and anguish so directly exuding from these paintings and sculptures and other art forms I didn't know quite how to describe, I'm sure we collectively hoped that the six hundred or so years between the worst outbreak of the plague and tetracycline of the 20th century would be much shorter between HIV and truly effective antiviral medications.

If we needed a reminder that we just needed to work harder or that we just needed to care more, if we needed augmented realization of the personal apocalypse these young people, mostly men, were facing....we were in the right place. The art that shockingly put AIDS in your face were the pieces I think I liked the best. They were tangible, inescapable. One was actually done using the ashes of the artist's former lover as the canvas. To imagine the anguish that each moment of this work's creation called forth is to know the depths of human loss and despair. One couldn't separate the global statistics from the thousands, hundreds of thousands, of individual lives that were being taken and devastated. To not notice this and give a fuck is beyond inhuman. Others were graphically sexual, but not pornographic so much as loud and blunt, as in a manner saying, "hey, we're not going away"; in a message relating something like "AIDS is inseparable from our sexuality, but sex is basic, sex is human, sex is fundamental, sex is killing us, sex is going to kill all of us… wake up and smell the fucking cum-stain."

My mind was racing with these images, with the thoughts and emotions they provoked. I had already bought two very small painted pieces at a small table at the end of the first row of work (hoping their relatively modest prices wouldn't put my humble credit card over its continually flirted with limit, and come back to embarrass me later, as they had not incorporated ways of checking those fine little details at the time of the actual event), and had made it to the middle part of the center row of the displays, when I heard a voice that I would come to know to the alternating points of craving it as if I'd only ever heard it once, like a divine siren, and recognizing that it was the key to all happiness to sadly taking it for granted, and I looked up to see the most beautiful woman I had ever seen.

"I'm not sure if I've lost a stalker or gained an AIDS art enthusiast," she said with a warm smile.

After I recovered it off the floor, it still took several moments more for my jaw to regain any sort of communication skill, during which time Kim graciously didn't dismiss me as a complete neurotic and pityingly continued until I snapped back to some partial version of eager, if not completely competent, predator form.

"This painting was done by a well known artist, who just died himself of AIDS, about six weeks ago," she more seriously continued, referring to the work we simultaneously stood in front of.

"I know," I finally managed in some sort of default overachieving student mode. "I learned that in this excellent and beautiful little brochure," I continued with a minuscule more confidence, while whipping my folded, miscellaneous page corner bent, and focally red wine stained "Coldest Autumn: An AIDS Memorial Art Show" catalogue out of my back left pocket.

"Glad to see that thing works," my stunningly beautiful conversation partner smiled, as if kindling a growing connection, her beautiful light brown eyes sparkling, just from the distant overhead lights, high above in the loft-like ceiling, and the small white, plastic encased bulb specifically placed on the display to enhance the specific piece, and illuminating the scattered subtle red highlights in her beautiful light brown hair. She gave off an admirable, almost worshipable air of that acutely relaxed manner that comes with working hard, and having succeeded, and now subsequently relaxing a little bit, still winding down from the pre and during event stress and exhilaration of a job largely perceived as well done, persisting now in more after event praise, a smaller but still appreciated unexpected reminder of one's acute success, like the fourth or fifth, lesser, still special because perceptually temporally separate, climax of a tumultuous and eventually fatiguing multi-orgasm. "I wrote it," she continued, in what I would recognize later as justifiable pride and satisfaction that gains added sincerity when set against a usual only quietly confident modesty.

"I know," I replied, not missing a beat, despite being potentially handicapped by the combination of light headedness and total body warmth manifested by a peripheral flush radiating from a stomach knot with a mild touch of fortunately alcohol-lessened nausea, accentuated with a little tingling in the pelvic region, distinctly different from just needing to pee from drinking too much, that I felt in her presence, that I would continue to feel on the next several occasions we were together, to the point that I would ponder going to the student/resident health clinic to be sure that I didn't have mono or a hormone-secreting occult tumor or something and the exact opposite and worse version of which I would soon feel whenever I was not around her, when I couldn't smell her. "I realized that early on this evening when I saw your picture and bio at the back of the brochure, while I was studying the various pieces I may want to purchase…or at least analyze in more detail," I now continued in a hopefully not too obviously bovine feces laden manner. "You don't think I'm just talking to you because you're beautiful, intelligent, and interesting, do you? I'm not that complex."

"Something warns me that you're fairly complex," she said cautiously.

"Yeah, but in a good way, right?" I tried to offer up in quick recovery.

"I was thinking more in a dangerous kind of way," she said while tilting her head back slightly, and giving me a quick but deep stare, that made my nausea extend down even below my pelvis, into my upper inner thighs, in a highly unusual manner and the degree and distribution of which made me actually instinctively run through the gamut of known neurological diseases, particularly the demyelinating variety, to make sure that I wasn't actually, in a case of really bad timing, coming down with a likely viral-induced autoimmune thing that would lead to an embarrassing ending to this emerging fantasy by requiring a very public ambulance trip to the E.R., which combining with a slightly different and somewhat dizzying sensation moving in the opposite direction and which was now completely neurologically unexplainable, was giving me a really weird feeling, one that I either needed to run away from, or enjoy like opium.

"Yeah, but maybe in a good kind of danger, right?" I persisted and semi-beggingly smiled back, before accidentally returning her intense stare.

She looked down after holding my glance for a scary brief second, and grabbed lightly at my wrapped paintings. The moment, indeed, needed lightening.

"You bought some pieces," she said. "Which ones?"

"Rosary Ashes" by an artist named Castillo, who lost a lover to AIDS, and "Thunder Penetration" by an artist, who I believe preferred to be called Princess Tiffany…who's dead himself now" I replied, beaming that I remembered the names of the works and the artists. Then, confessing, in an effort to win points, "I learned about them in my catalogue."

"That's very generous of you," she said matter-of-factly, "although I suppose, in theory, a small fraction of a small fraction may get back to you in the lab somehow."

Ooh….I not so subconsciously acknowledged to my analytical self: someone else has been doing some investigating, as to who's who and what do they do. I may have or at least should have had a new found security or confidence, but I was unable to recognize it or use it the way I would perhaps have liked to when submerged in whatever magical field I was floating in, harness it to apply against the numbing effect of being so completely sleep deprived while in the presence of an object of desire transforming before my eyes into something so frighteningly much more.

"I think they're actually pretty cool," I now continued in some sort of out of body and out of mind fugue state, instantly regretting the use of the uber teen word "cool". "I especially like Thunder Penetration, but I also like the Rosary one. I was going to give one to a friend. She needs some things to decorate her new condo back in Houston. But, I may actually sell it to her, at cost of course, mainly just so I can pay my rent next month. She'll particularly like the intertwining of the graphic fatalism with the medieval and religious themes in the Castillo piece." I was likely spilling third or fourth date openness and detail on pre-first date domains. Then just to lay out everything a little more, I added, "Her mind's almost as weird as mine."

"I'm sure it's nowhere near as weird as yours. But actually, you both have good taste. Those are very interesting and expressive pieces," Kim responded, while leaning ever so lightly up against the brick wall we had gradually slid over to, and then taking a small sip of her wine. I'm sure, by this point, she must have been very tired, as well as emotionally drained from all the effort she must have put into this show and its advertisement and promotion.

"Well, to be honest, initially I was just trying to impress you, hoping I'd get a chance to discuss my new acquisitions, but now they're growing on me. I think they're an excellent way to start my collection," I said, while re-filling her glass with the bottle I had sweet-talked the bar tender out of about 20 minutes or so ago and now had on the little side table beside me.

"Well, it's a good start," she coyly smiled, not indicating whether she was referring to my collection or to my attempt at impressing her. "But, I would have been more impressed if you had bought Wërner's Dying Venus Sculpture," which I remember noting that at $275,000.00 was by far the most expensive of the pieces being shown that was actually available for sale.

"Well, I was going to buy that one," I said, and then paused, and took a medium sized gulp out of my glass, still needing an extra bolus of courage despite the loading dose (overloading dose?) I had been building for the last six hours, "but I was afraid that... I...then wouldn't have enough left over to ask you out," I said, letting it hang for a millisecond, then realizing it sounded pathetic, and tried to add in noble clarification, alluding to my future likely to be improved status and desirability, "You know, they don't pay us residents that much yet...not like we'll make eventually."

Not evidently disturbed by this potentially too direct or at least moderately awkward assault, other than straightening up from the wall, as if this next phase needed a little less fatigue, Kim, whom at that very moment I wanted to grab and kiss, but had an even stronger unfamiliar desire to especially hold, deeply, strongly smiled, the smile that I would come to love like chocolate ice cream, ham, and Dallas Cowboys football, said, "You're pretty funny. Is that just an alcohol-related thing, or can I count on that all the time?"

Whoa...who's turning it up now....Holy shit, I thought, or at least somewhat perceived in a deep limbic area. Not to come across as too intimidated, I tried to keep the hopefully vaguely recognizable charm going, despite the weird loss of sensation in my left foot that had apparently been catatonically leaning up against the wall in some sort of ankle-joint defying and ischemia inducing strange orientation while I stood there gawking the last few minutes or so. I had largely successfully dismissed all weird and unanticipated neurological phenomena earlier, so was O.K. with the "fell asleep thing" (which actually has simple neurological explanations). "I think I've always been that way... I guess. Some sort of childhood injury or genetic thing. My

Mom used to actually rent me out … for parties…and stuff, you know, when I was a kid."

"Hmm…I'll have to keep that in mind for my next function," Kim flirtingly responded, while subconsciously placing the fingers of her left hand on my package (my paintings…come on). "Maybe you should give me her number."

"Actually, I'm handling all of her west coast accounts now, so I should probably just give you mine…and, of course, strictly for professional reasons, you should give me yours, just so, you know, there's no confusion…in terms of the time or place." I was stumbling, verbally, mentally, and emotionally. I thought about whether I could actually sleep for the couple of days I think I probably needed, and my mind even bizarrely drifted to whether or not I even knew what kind of mattress I had at my apartment. Then I wondered if I had a mattress pad, like my Mom used to use, and then I began to ponder the origins of intrusive thoughts.

Reality check time for the young professional, hopefully always responsible, woman living in the big city by herself, with just the right amount of cautious "escape" mechanism in case, well, who knows.

"I've got an idea," she said, while finishing the last swallow of her wine, and then in some sort of patented Kim simultaneous-straightening-of-her-clothes-fixing-her-hair-gathering-of-herself-and-collecting-her-wits fashion. "Meet me in the bar at the Cypress Club. Six o'clock, this Friday. Happy hour. We'll see in the daytime if this magic is real."

This last comment, which soon carried me home on a layer above any fog that could make it all the way to the mission district, came with a warm smile that put a proper frame on everything and molded everything I had felt up to then into a global sensation best described, in simplicity, as a "happy buzz". I suppose if one or both of us didn't show, after some interposed non-emotion, non-alcohol filled pondering, that would be it. I knew her name and employer from the catalogue. She knew my name and employer from somewhere, but this was either going to be real, at least for a while, or non-existent. Neither one of us was likely to hunt the other down, although I couldn't promise that at that moment, necessarily. Then…enough to keep me going for the next 136 hours, she leaned forward, grabbed my left hand (the one not on my package) in her soft, yet strong, and so perfectly constructed right hand, and slightly up on her tip toes, she kissed me quickly on the left cheek, and turned and walked away.

I stood there for a while, in a daze, in a state somewhere between enlightenment and coma, created by the impact of the entire evening, the sum total of my realizations or near realizations on all fronts, the gut-wrenching, viscerally experienced, near consciously felt, but not yet cerebrally processed sensation of potentially life changing events, of soul turning catastrophes and miracles. I watched her walk away. The gentle slope of her toned shoulders, tapering to her back in her tailored jacket, her narrow waist, her perfect hips and rear (I was too formally unfamiliar or intimidated to think "ass" at this stage), the way her hair gently fell on her shoulders, alternating more to the right and left as she walked, the confidence, hope, and optimism of youth, beauty, and cleverness, mixed with what I wanted so badly to be vulnerability, that only I could melt away, while my right hand squeezed my brown paper wrapped frames, unknowingly. Then, as she pushed open the right-sided door of the paired glass doors at one of the side exits, she turned, and smiled at me, and the smile quickly turned to the inquisitive, head tilting, eye squinting, penetrating, essence opening glance that I would come to worship, to need, and eventually to miss, so despairingly.

II

- Houston; October, 1993

On Oct. 14, a pleasantly fresh and crisp Thursday, as I had noticed on the few times I had sneaked outside to clear my head and on which fleeting occasions I had probably wished I was able to be somewhere else-maybe even just sitting outside and doing nothing, I had by the end of my "shift" at the Thomas Street Clinic officially enrolled our seventh patient in my clinical trial.

Given the fact that our targeted number of patients randomized to either drug or placebo was about 350 over an 18 month time period in order to hopefully achieve statistical significance for drug vs. placebo effect given a conservative estimated improvement with treatment in the various primary and secondary end-points analyzed as part of the many clinical and laboratory parameters we would be measuring with a follow up of at least two years for those that lived, this wasn't exactly a mile-stone worth celebrating.

As I stepped outside for the last time that day, and watched a few homeless guys trudging down the opposite side of the street in a fading orange hue of urban concrete modulated sunset, I still felt an acute sense of satisfaction, and a very brief sense of security, and perhaps even a quiet, confident determination. From when I had officially started at Baylor, on the actual payroll so to speak, in addition to likely generating much larger amounts of revenue from my clinic duties than reflected in my relatively humble academic paycheck, it had taken essentially two plus months of staggeringly diverse efforts just to get everything in place and ready to actually begin enrolling any ADC patients for the clinical trial. For a myriad constellation of scientific/data collection, administrative, and dare-I-say, political reasons, we really couldn't get going until a bewildering and naiveté-purging array of infrastructure and paper work, laboratory readiness, and medico-legal and other administrative aspects of the trial had been adequately addressed.

In the months prior to my departure from San Francisco, we had prepared as best as possible to really hit the ground running, so to speak, with dozens of phone calls, faxes, and fed-ex'd documents between me at UCSF and various labs, clinics, hospitals, participating faculty, and particularly regulatory offices within Baylor and The Harris County Hospital System. Over those several months following the awarding of my grant, the final decision to join the faculty in Houston, and the subsequent arrangements necessary to proceed with the clinical trial in the context of my clinical and research duties there, and the time where I actually arrived on site, I and a few of my increasingly intimate colleagues spent a tremendous amount of effort, perhaps only marginally reflected in the steadily growing piles, stacks, and eventual columns of relevant paper work, to get to a stage where I could actually get things done "within the system".

The detailed protocol for the clinical trial, including all the specifics of the drug administration and safety monitoring and reporting, had gotten through the Institutional Review Board (IRB), but there were additional administrative issues to be addressed within the actual Clinical Trials offices of Baylor, the Department of Neurology, and particularly Harris County facilities, such as The Thomas Street Clinic and The Ben Taub Hospital. For the number of correspondences I had made to the latter, alone, it eventually became the understatement of ironic anti-climaticism that, when finally in Houston, I had to minorly adjust and sign one trivial document, after a twenty minute expedition in the various bowels of the hospital basement finally led me to an essentially closet-sized office that seven of eight inquired upon individuals along the way had never heard of, at least six of which I'm convinced actually worked for the hospital.

In all fairness, when I finally did achieve the necessary connection at the end of that particular quest, the very large African-American woman who helped me address my final paper work needs was refreshingly competent, and compared to the trivial remaining paper work issues spent much more time grilling me on a personal level as to what my trial was expected to accomplish. She had had a cousin who had already died of AIDS, and a neighbor she helped take care of who sounded pretty end stage. She gave me the "you got that right, sugar" thumbs up on the need to address the CNS aspects of this "um...um...terrible disease," and told me if I ever needed anything in the actual Medical Records section of the hospital, where she spent three days a week, to let her know, and also gave me the name of an apparently similarly exemplary functional individual in the Harris County Dept of Public Health Office, who had sadly had a brother die of AIDS and whom she'd met in a support group and now enjoyed both personal and professional interactions with. I passed on my thanks, walked away assuming that all of the personally alluded to victims had been IV drug addicts, without specifically inquiring, and hyper-vigilantly looked for the stairway that would take me up to ground level, and the more familiar territory of the E.R., etc.

...

The Department of Neurology at Baylor College of Medicine, with its official affiliations with The Neurosensory Center and The Methodist Hospital, had a wonderful Clinical Trials Coordinator, an RN with over twenty years of clinical experience, who also had a highly capable staff. Several of those staff I had almost gotten to know through the many phone conversations and other communications we had had in the months prior to my physical arrival. Two of them actually turned out to vaguely physically and personality-wise resemble the way I had come to picture them in my mind during our long distance non-visual interactions, but most turned out to be completely different than I had imagined them. They were truly fantastic in getting everything going, efficiently making up for my complete lack of experience in the formal clinical trial arena.

That being said, I still spent in the first few months what seemed or could actually have been almost a hundred hours in up to thirty to forty variously sized meetings regarding the actual execution of the many little to large tasks necessary to finally execute the trial on a daily basis. The scheduling and coordination of these meetings alone was an accomplishment in-and-of-itself, not to mention the heretofore unanticipated need for occasionally conquering surprising personality-driven pissing contests unearthed amongst even the most trivial of project components.

From the laboratory perspective, once the various administrative and medicolegal aspects of collecting and transporting the "wet-bench" or more basic laboratory research related fluids (i.e., blood and CSF) were tackled, the actual experimental or assay development and performance tasks were at least approachable under more of my complete control. That doesn't mean there weren't a lot of headaches and frustrations along the way. Some of the assays which we were to apply to blood and other fluids collected during the trial were fairly straightforward; they were either already established as commercially available kits or were at least based on technology and strategies routinely applied to usual target molecules (e.g., proteins, antibodies, small molecules, etc.). Others, such as some *in vitro* bioassays that involved cell culture and cell toxicity experiments, which had been included in the grant, were a little less certain. But, wisely, the trial and hence its funding had at least been presented and apparently reviewed so as to not depend on the successful establishment of any of these potentially new methodologies, and we certainly didn't wait to actually enroll patients and collect clinical trial specimens before we established any of these still relatively new techniques in the laboratory, generous space and equipment for which I was provided from existing resources or very easily acquired from the start up money that was part of my recruitment package.

There were new techs to hire and train, or partial efforts of existing techs in other labs to arrange, instruction manuals of new equipment to read, bits and pieces to clean or bang on of old equipment we tried to rescue from other dwindling labs in the ever necessary financially conservative process inherent in funded biomedical research. There were literally dozens of assay protocols to fine tune; buffer compositions to tweak, things as mundane as determining blocking strategies and specific antibody concentrations to optimize for ELISA assays for various cytokines we intended to measure in CSF, and especially working out culture and treatment conditions for some of the more functional mediator-cell interactions in *in vitro* experiments we would hopefully soon include patient specimens in or at least match experimental conditions and results to levels of such mediators as determined in patient samples. Some of the more uncertain experiments of the basic science components of the grant had worried a few reviewers, but intrigued others enough that the net-effect was that those parts were perceived as a beneficial high-risk high-gain component of an "ambitious grant". The more likely to be successfully accomplished largely clinical parts led more unequivocally to support for funding even in the more conservative reviewers' eyes.

With the vast majority of the clinical, administrative, specimen storage, and laboratory aspects supposedly in place, we got started. I've always told graduate students, residents, fellows, etc., those that even at my stage may be in even more junior phases of training in the labs I've worked, or anyone else who would listen or at least pretend to: "You can sit around and plan forever. You design the experiments as best you can, but at some point you gotta just take the plunge (or "fucking plunge," depending on who was listening or pretending to) and get going. You can always refine things as needed early on." There are always little things to sort out in the beginning after you actually get started; from where you store the ice bucket with specimens that you'll take back to the lab that night, while you're seeing other patients, and hoping your precious samples don't get thrown out, to who's going to be sure patients actually make their follow-up clinic appointments for all the additional testing and sample collection related to the trial along with the more usual indicated medical care aspects.

T. Scruggs was the first patient officially enrolled in the drug trial, a 36 year old black male I saw at the clinic for the first time on Sept 2, a disoriented IV drug abuser with moderate to severe motor weakness, a surprisingly messed up gate, and a ridiculously low score on the expanded mini-mental status exam we were using for the trial, in addition to other AIDS-associated complications (PCP for which he wasn't always good about taking his Bactrim and Pentamidine, which of course didn't necessarily bode well for his rigidly taking his clinical trial meds; likely disseminated histoplasmosis +/- some not rigorously documented vague history of possible TB combining to give his chest X-ray some definitively positive findings), which along with his CD4 count of 56 would likely not allow him to reach 37. This guy was towards the bad side (low or far end) of our ADC-related clinical trial scale, which we used at enrollment, all through monitoring, and as the major primary end point for the trial and determining if our drug was having any possible benefit.

We had decided to enroll patients across the entire anticipated spectrum of this scale, which assessed primarily cognitive and motor status, as an index of the severity of ADC. After all, we had no idea at which, if any, level of disease progression we may see some beneficial therapeutic effect with our drug, whether it be clinical, as detected by this scale, or biochemical, as detected in the lab (and at least offering some future hope, maybe with better therapy refinement). Effect at the early stages, more likely perhaps biologically and pharmacologically, may be hard to detect, given the difficulty documenting ADC at these early stages and where other processes could be causing deterioration as reflected in still difficult to objectively assess parameters. For such patients, we were probably also less likely to reliably detect subtle or small ADC score changes given possible slow or variable progression in controls, and by high enough patients we may be able to detect a small but statistically significant benefit, including also the possible subjectivity in scoring some parameters in these early stages, with less certain reproducibility in the assessments, etc. But on the other side of the spectrum, the late stages may be too far gone, so to speak, in terms of achieving a progression retarding or even improvement benefit, from the pathophysiologic standpoint. Alternatively, if even small in terms of the quality of life improvement or if only achieved in some treated patients, an effect may be detectable at these stages as progression at the late stages was more dramatic and more readily objectively assessed. Of course, we hoped for dramatic effects at all stages. We made rational, intelligent hypotheses about the kinds of drugs that could have benefit based on the pathophysiologic mechanisms of neuronal injury as we felt that we understood them at the time, based on hundreds of papers and our own studies, and we knew what doses of the drug reached concentrations in the CSF that were effective in ameliorating these presumed injurious processes in our models *in vitro*. We had hope, we had optimism. It's not just the paycheck that keeps us coming to work every day.

III

- Recollections: San Francisco; Autumn, 1990

Meeting Kim changed every aspect of my life. Perhaps that's melodramatic. It was either Einstein or me, at a party for my mentor at the NIH, that said: "Scientists are, after all, closet romantics." A more realistic assessment may be that falling in love with Kim disrupted, or perhaps shattered, every aspect of my daily existence.

I wasn't naïve. I knew that there were more than just rumors of other things besides studying and work. I had experienced them, lived them passionately, but only in those short bursts that allowed for the appropriate extremes of both; work hard, play hard, in the truest unrecognized self-serving over-achieving spirit.

But...from the first time I forced myself out of Kim's bed to go over to the lab to treat some cells that, if I hadn't would have fucked up an extremely expensive, and time consuming, potentially important experiment, I started to do every non-Kim thing a little bit more quickly.

I'd hurried to get laid before; hurried to get back to a new infatuation. This was somehow different. Always the biological philosopher, I suppose it must have been like the first aerobic organism, I guess some sort of bacteria maybe, needing oxygen to sustain itself, to take it to another level in that slow evolutionary process. I wasn't sloppy at work, per se; that's not really ever been an option. But, whether it was in the lab, in the E.R., or on the Hospital Wards, if Kim and I had plans, or if I even thought there was a chance to see her if I finished unexpectedly early, I just didn't dally. I didn't invent things to do. For the first time in my life, I was able to survive the maybe partially subconscious inflicted, but century's old,

Presbyterian work ethic-induced guilt for not acting constructively and achieving every moment in one's calling, all the time.

So, quickly, this must have become not just a getting back into bed, not just touching, sexing each other up thing. That part stayed, and still stays, amazingly. It was, increasingly though, all the little things, every micro-act and every thought, big, little, expressed or acted on without expressing, that filled an evening or a lazy afternoon, as our minds, our habits, our moods, our smiles nurtured and reflected a mutual respect and friendship that made even tired sex so erotic and every *just a good-bye kiss* so amazingly psyche-probing.

...

One Friday afternoon, about three and a half weeks after we'd met that second time for happy hour and two and a half weeks after her work party when we'd spent some interesting time in her boss's daughter's bedroom, Kim paged me to see "what are you up to?"

It was a gloomy, drizzle-off-and-on-afternoon-after-a-heavy-rain-morning kind of a day, as I had repeatedly noted consciously and probably more subconsciously while gazing out the lab window on the fourth floor of the Health Sciences East or HSE tower, in that part in which I mostly worked of the multifocal Hassel laboratory empire (due in large part to the often noncontiguous way in which lab space expands according to the grants up and down fate of various investigators in a usually filled to the max lab occupancy status of competitive centers). I had never worked in a setting where the viewed outside world and hence any influence it could have on the inside spirits of the inside worker were so astonishingly variable at even quickly reached different foci of the same University system. The Health Science towers were located immediately behind the Moffit hospital building, in which there was even some residual island of neurology/Hassel lab space, to which I occasionally flocked for tissue related things including when working at the hospital. Moffit itself was about thirteen stories high and the research towers went up another three floors behind. I sometimes wondered, or joked out loud to poorly receiving individuals as based on the expressions of their likely urban-gene controlled faces, if you might even be able to do altitude-related or differential elevation effects on various systems research here within the same building. If you had the right windows you

163

could be blessed with great views out to the Pacific to the west and north across Golden Gate Park, even across the Golden Gate Bridge itself and to the Marin headlands. But in the summer, which somehow seemed particularly strange to me, the fog would come rolling in like some bad horror movie, during which those on the outside might be only able to see the tops of our towers. And on an especially bad day, you couldn't even see the ground from the top floors, a particularly freaky effect for which I might occasionally specifically visit higher outposts of the Empire or its Allies. In another seemingly counterintuitive seasonal associated phenomenon, in February (often regarded as a winter month by advanced primates of the northern hemisphere) there were incredible views from the VA hospital from which one could even see out to the Farallon Islands, such that if I were not rotating or covering consults there, I might volunteer to help pathology collect neurological research specimens or find some other excuse to take the shuttle across the park to and from the VA for a little mental cleansing time. But even without officially sampling from each of those spots, today was one of those days that looked shitty from every vantage point and instilled shittiness into each one holding any of those particular perspectives, and I was challenging the maximum tolerated human dose of caffeine to keep the internal drive/personal mission going in the lab.

"Just looking over some recent data," I responded, not quite shaken back to wakefulness even at hearing my new lover's voice, looking out of the lab windows over the sodden landscape stretching, if I could have seen it, over a hazy city towards a hazy bay.

After, perhaps, waiting for something more, maybe a little quintessential Jeff smart-ass comment or some other earth shattering event, she responded, "Sounds…important…but maybe… not quite thrilling?" with a tone that was mixed with respect, maybe still cautiously at this early stage, but with a slight, almost hidden, sensual impish undertone, as if she were going to shortly offer up a more attractive alternative.

Perhaps reflective of the stage to which our relationship had already accelerated to, the alternative of even "just want to be with you" no matter the setting could likely beat the living shit out of what I was currently ineffectively not quite immersed in.

"Well, it's nothing special," she continued with unnecessary cautious qualification, "but, there's this show coming up over in The Embarcadero that I'm supposed to write a blurb for, expanding on the artist who has a couple of pieces there now, maybe even as a prelude to his part in a bigger show in LA in the spring," she continued with nervous energy. There was a pause, which took me a while to notice. I was divided between flipping pages of my lab book, staring out at the gloom, and the slowly alerting senses that Kim's voice was stirring.

"Problem is," she continued, maybe a little more uncertainly without my chiming in as of yet, but then, surprisingly, after another pause, "I just don't get him."

There was a sense of frustration here, as if this shouldn't have happened, objectively, not to one who approached her projects the way she did. Then a little more relaxed, as if she had resolved herself to be O.K. with this, as long as....

"I thought that maybe you'd come with me, you know, to give me that fresh perspective of complete irreverence you seem to be able to bring."

I noted this, and was processing information better now. Funny thing is, she didn't seem to mean this condescendingly, or even more shockingly, she seemed to give my "art approach" a certain degree of specific case-by-maybe-rare-case relevant credibility that far exceeded the absolute extremum of ignorance from which it barely ascended.

My lab book closed. As I stood up, the caffeine that hadn't seemed capable of crawling up against the gravity of weather gloom and cross the blood brain barrier to energize my cerebrum, quickly spread to this and all the other thought centers, and I felt newly mission-assigned. While trying not to show this obvious redirection on my face or in my voice, I announced to my fellow lab mates, "I'm going over to the library," and with my back-pack slung over my shoulder, I headed out for the weekend.

...

We had a blast. One would be hard pressed to find a better 12 hours of shared human experience than that which stretched from my meeting Kim at the gallery at about 5 p.m. to the point that we mutually, at a last grasp towards responsibility (I still had, by this time unreasonable, plans to work in the lab the next day), agreed to get a couple hours of sleep at about 5 the next morning. My previously somber mood that had been harmoniously underachieving with inactive neurons as cloudy as the misty day outside the conspiringly contributing dirty lab windows seemed to quickly and steadily explode to the opposite end of the emotional spectrum, either due to my return to a previously unrecognized comfort zone of viewing art I still didn't understand in a new small gallery on Capp Street (probably even within the orbit of the radius between my crappy apartment and San Francisco General, but which I probably still couldn't find myself with a map), the peri-toxic doses of coffee finally hitting in, or seeing my baby in a red silk blouse and black leather skirt and the biggest smile anyone's ever greeted me with. Kim seemed to take more pleasure out of stealing me supposedly uncharacteristically away from my work than she did out of officially hosting a small but important showing to an audience largely if not completely there as a consequence of marketing endeavors she had directed as part of her growing duties at her firm.

Our mutually sky-rocketing moods conspired to elevate her away from the frustration I knew she had been feeling with this particular project over the last week and a half. Even with her growing status within the group, clearly, this particular relatively minor project wasn't crucial to her career, and was a relatively low priority at Kim's firm. But still, I was recognizing in Kim as I was getting to know her even at this stage, a deep sort of caring about things, things that affected real people, no matter the relative size of the project on the usual material world scale. And like everything else I was seeing and learning about her, it made my dick hard. Hence, as I apparently let myself progressively go that night, I could see that even if it reached embarrassing levels on the usual human scale, it would cost her absolutely nothing at the professional level no matter what her "partner" did, and yet it seemed to be just what the occasion needed, somehow even eventuating in some weird ass cosmic collision kind of way to augmented sales and gain to the studio and the upcoming larger show project, and consequently, to my beautiful, artist-marketing, hot partner in "crime".

It turned out that my so called irreverence, my cynicism, the "you're so full of shit" approach to our featured artist was exactly what his creative combo of art/politics/shocking fashion/social commentary self was looking for, was perhaps even hoping for. Part of Kim's project included ongoing coverage of the show and the studio, and I seemed to awaken some passion in our artist host that even the drippings of which made for a great interview, and hence, story. I was having fun. I was relaxed, not thinking about curing the whole world one molecule at a time, and was with Kim.

We started out with conservative gallery finger food and Napa Cabs provided by a couple of the sponsors. People came and went; we stayed; we drank…a lot. Jeff (only by going third person can I begin to deal with and/or escape the embarrassment I'm sure the grand total of subsequent acts warrants) began to query our host over certain aspects of canvases that were beyond his (i.e., Jeff's, not the artist's) current level of appreciation. By 9:30, one of the server chicks who had sort of bonded with us was grabbing bottles to open just for the three of us. By 10:45, we had gone upstairs to see a couple of works in progress (he presented here frequently enough that he shared use of an empty storage-like room upstairs that he often worked at when the gallery atmosphere provided a specific type of inspiration), accompanied by some really bizarre story I unwittingly quit listening attentively to…that somehow involved his mother, and a junior college art professor he was working with, a local art supplier, and (am I remembering this correctly?),…a kazoo?

Anyway, around midnight, Kim, me, the featured artist, the server girl, two Japanese "collectors" still somehow seriously pursuing some work that wasn't supposed to be on sale or who knows what, and a flaming gay guy who professed passion for art and the need to be around those who felt similarly, and whom we have no idea at which point of the night he had joined us, were at a nearby bar gingerly alternating between refined glasses of wine and increasingly painful shots of bourbon then tequila, the latter some sort of intended tribute to my own Texas heritage.

From what I was reminded (not that it made sense even then), I made some sort of complex financial, female quality, and STD-risk comparison between a very rewarding low profile "place" and the "official" Boys Town over the Mexican border and two bars respectively in Piedras Negras and Nuevo Laredo, that corresponded with (isn't it always) the Tequila period of the enlarging night.

Between then and 2:30 a.m., when we were having eggs and waffles at Lori's Diner on Mason, we had lost the Japanese guys and the gay guy (although I don't think at the same time?), and it was down to just my emerging art hero, Kim, our lovely but looking pretty tired drink server girl (Kristi?), and an apparently still pretty caffeinated (or just excited?) if alcohol moderated me. With this much-needed infusion of ethanol absorbing calories, we dropped our co-passengers off from our jovial cab, and Kim and I fell into her bed around 3:30 a.m. or so.

"Thanks. I have a great story," she said, naked and looking down from on top of me. Our eyes met, briefly, intensely. She stared at me. "Oh, and by the way," she continued, "I'm in love with you." At this, she proceeded to go down on me, not giving me a chance to respond I guess, not that one was needed, as if this was the official proclamation for the both of us.

I am competitive, if nothing else. After I came, and she had come back up to where I could hold her close in my arms, I softly touched her cheek and kissed her, and looked at her the way I don't think I've ever looked at anyone or anything ever before, nor ever since, and staked my ascending participation. "By the way, I'm pretty in love with you, too."

...

One of the most impressive things of that night, I suppose, besides that I'd met a Japanese guy that could do Tequila shots to a level that would make any Mexican proud, was that Kim had actually extracted information and perspective to write a truly informative, fair, and insightful art review and artist bio summary that did our charismatic artist friend justice in a fashion that even his cynical ass could approve, celebrate, and endorse as they would gear up for a larger future show. Few of his composition could ask for much more.

As for me, with the two rounds of sex that Kim and I squeezed in from 3:30 to 5:00 a.m. and the 2 and a half hours of sleep we got in each other's arms, I never felt more alive and alert than I did the next day. The data and ideas I had been struggling with and the complexities of where they would take me from there that had tortured me the previous dull day actually inspired me the next morning. In retrospect, what I had been working on, even if occurring within a fairly narrowly defined *in vitro* experimental world, now seemed more meaningful; the emerging conclusions were cohesive, it was definitive, and it was motivating. Or was that some sort of alchemical mind altering effect of the woman that now smelled so damn warm and delicious next to me? Either way, it's never a good idea to tempt fate and screw-up this sort of upswing…especially on a weekend. So, we both took the day "off", although I'm not sure the subsequent hung over hours qualifies as a "day".

We woke up. We ate some bowls of some healthy kind of cereal with dried fruit in it and a skinny chick on the box, drank enough coffee to be awake to eat the cereal, had sleepy sex, "napped" till 2 p.m., called out for Chinese food while we watched some old black and white movie with Barbara Stanwyck, "napped" while nakedly intertwined until about 9 that night, woke up briefly to eat left-over Chinese food (I think I had another bowl of the colon-blow cereal that was kind of growing on me with my moo shoo pork) and talk about life, and then went back to bed until 10 a.m. Sunday.

IV

- Houston; October, 1993

I walked into the Thomas Street clinic at 6:45 a.m. on a Monday morning in the third week of October, a slight space-time continuum aberration perhaps, as I usually had a hard time getting there by the 7:30 or so I typically aimed for in order to at least roughly figure my day out before I had to see my first patients at 8:00. By 7:30, Cheryl usually had all the charts for the morning's patients organized in my rack at a small station outside of the two exam rooms I had assigned for my utilization. Most of these charts typically had few if any entries outside of patient identification information on a generic front sheet. Occasionally a copy of a note from a recent E.R. visit that prompted the clinic appointment may have miraculously made it over via fax by a particularly conscientious resident or nurse or a still paranoid-to-do-all-the-right-things intern, or some other administrative mechanism I was still unfamiliar with and would be leery of given info I would often elucidate during my workups. Of course, despite the HIV emphasis of the clinic, we also had a fair number of "frequent fliers", some patients additionally cursed with the more usual ailments of the typically chronically ill, including neighborhood indigents and near indigents whose hypertensions, diabetes or renal insufficiencies we attempted to manage according to all of the latest American Heart Association, American Diabetic Association, and National Kidney Foundation guidelines, despite fairly common medication non-compliance, even more frequent diet non-compliance, and a limited county budget that would not always allow us to prescribe the more expensive, more effective, lower side effect so more tolerated, newest drugs to patients who could ill afford even the cheaper older formulary Name Brand or Generic even older agents on their own.

And of course, there were numerous AIDS patients, whom we routinely saw for monitoring their CD4 counts, searched as needed for new opportunistic infections based on elicited complaints, physical exam findings, and the frequently indicated chest X-rays, which along with limited basic labs we had at our handy disposal there in the clinic.

Chart entries on even the most complicated of such patient visits were necessarily kept to a minimum as the number of patients to see was most often staggering. Physicians who could see the forest despite the trees and get to the crucial issues on each patient could commonly handle it within a fast-paced, no real breaks, eat on the go kind of 8-10 hour shift, with interspersed or subsequent periods of administrative paperwork to be sure that anyone who required was channeled into appropriate follow-up including ancillary facilities, as indicated. Those concrete thinking, compulsive for compulsive's sake, pathophysiological-practically challenged morons we occasionally had, who not only focused on trees, but on individual pieces of bark and leaves, could easily be two hours into the day, on their third or fourth of more than 50 scheduled patients. As you can imagine, these residents and junior faculty were the favorites of the nursing staff.

Allowing for patient type variation and hence sometimes corresponding chart thickness heterogeneity, I had quickly, after three or four shifts, subconsciously figured out an average chart thickness, so that a quick glance at my rack at 7:30 would tell me how many patients I had that day, or at least that morning, with the occasional walk in that had to be seen or other unexpected events usually adding a handful. A full rack typically meant about 60 patients. When it spilled over, so that the charts for the first couple patients were stacked on top of the desk, that was a bad sign. When an additional chart rack was hauled out of some unknown storage location, that was a really bad sign. Ninety-two was my personal record, which meant an aerobic switching out of patients between my two rooms, utilization of two other less equipped smaller rooms, an occasional visit only in the hallway, and staying until 10 p.m. or so, as late as I could talk needed staff in remaining (on the down-low to avoid county employment policy violation, etc.).

Needless to say, in this general medicine/general neurology emphasis scheduling situation, I could usually only spend adequate time necessary to just discover a potential patient for my clinical trial or very quickly do the appropriate entry evaluations or, if I'd already seen such a patient previously, do appropriate follow up exams and lab draws as the trial required, and even then on just a few such patients a day. Fortunately, I had more time for such specific clinical research endeavors over in the Methodist Hospital General Clinical Research Center (GCRC) on essentially any other non clinic days of the week and, before long, my colleagues at the Thomas Street Clinic, who knew I would more than eagerly do all aspects of necessary care even unrelated to the nervous system aspects of the trial on candidate patients, became very good at referring patients, the majority of which I could actually enroll. Friends and co-workers in the E.R., on various services within The Methodist and within Ben Taub, were similarly conscientious or utilitarian, such that we started gathering a little momentum for patient enrollment quickly. It's always pleasantly surprising when things, especially complicated things, work as planned.

As I explained to Cheryl, the Chief Nurse, thank God, on most of my shifts at the clinic, and to a couple of the other more friendly nurses, what exactly it was I was trying to do, in typical over-inclusive detail, and what it was I hoped the drug could do, not only now, but in the future when HIV-infected patients may hopefully live longer, for the people they saw suffering right in front of them day in and day out, they became at least subtle allies, despite common under the breath stoic to sarcastic complaints about having to do extra work, maybe in part because they appreciated how quick I was, and how I made their shifts much more tolerable than some of my bark and leaf analyzing colleagues.

All told, within a short time frame, my co-workers and I were officially enrolling > 20 patients/month, which would quickly put us quite ahead of the proposed 100 scheduled for that first fiscal year that had begun the previous July, especially when one considers that the first couple of months were mostly organizational. When you consider that it was intended that in addition to monthly specialized neurological examinations to assess cognitive and motor function, there would be for each patient monthly blood draws and quarterly lumbar punctures for CSF fluid collection during the first year, then quarterly blood draws and CSF collection every six months thereafter for those that lived long enough, I was collecting a fair amount of samples to be stored in a -80 °F freezer back in the lab before being processed and subjected to various research lab tests, as well as having the residual samples maintained theoretically indefinitely. The GCRC was used to collecting specialized research samples. But Cheryl and her staff were getting to the point of not only tolerating, but actually facilitating, collecting and storing on ice the requisite samples for each new study entry or each appropriate follow-up visit. I swear to God, there were times when I might be in an exam room with one of the other type patients, whose malady was totally unrelated to the realm of my trial, that Cheryl or one of her staff might have already, and completely appropriately, collected blood on one of my trial patients.

"It's already done honey child," Cheryl might say with coy satisfaction, as I frantically scrambled with my blood sample collection kit to the next exam room, where one of my study patients may be waiting. CSF collection was, of course, a different story, requiring as it were a lumbar puncture, affectionately known in the lay community as a spinal tap. This more specialized procedure requires laying patients on their side, sterilizing the region, then using a long needle to penetrate through two adjacent lumbar vertebrae, through the protective tough dura, and into the cavity where the CSF fluid dwells, the same fluid that bathes the brain and that goes down to similarly nurture the spinal cord, and is steadily re-absorbed up on top (in channels above the brain) and generated again in a specialized collection of cells deep inside of the brain (where it is released into spaces, the ventricles, that communicate with all of the above). To say it could offer molecular hints to the cellular wars going on inside the gray and white matter of one's deteriorating brain is the potential understatement of the Neuroimmunology universe. But, again in credit to her growing (if pseudo-begrudgingly acknowledged) commitment to our work, Cheryl would often have the appropriate patients already prepped for the procedure to coincide with my exam room entrance. I even started to wonder about her ESP or mystical capabilities aside from her obvious chart reviewing and organizational skills.

Subsequently, the techs back in my lab, along with me on days where I was there for long enough periods, were continually running various tests on both the blood and CSF. The sterile kits standardly used for such lumbar punctures included a series of tubes to collect successive fractions dripping out of the hollow bore needle now effectively dwelling in the CSF space, like a keg tap, basically. In usual clinical situations, these tubes would be preferentially dedicated to the lab analyses most appropriate for what one thought was going on with that patient, such as for cell counts to determine potential bacterial or viral infection, culture or other ancillary studies to detect specific causative infectious organisms, cytology to detect possible involvement by certain tumors, etc. Of course, for our specialized tests, we had certain ancillary tubes with special buffers and media, in which to collect CSF for our research purposes, in addition to more standard tests, such as cell counts. These were kept separately, so as to supplement the convenient use of already packaged commercially available (and also paid for out of the grant) standard lumbar puncture kits. Boy did I get good and quick at lumbar punctures. This is an important procedure for most internists, pediatricians, and neurologists to be able to perform. As such, it is not uncommon for programs to have house staff officially document the number of times they have done this specific procedure, as well as other fairly standard clinical procedures, such as thoracentesis for taking fluid out of the pleural space surrounding the lungs, or bone marrow aspirations, wherein bone marrow was sucked out of the back of the hip, using an even thicker needle. In Bethesda, during my Internal Medicine residency for example, I had documented having done 11 lumbar punctures while a resident, not bad. Being on the Neurology service in San Francisco, I had easily done more than 50, including the 37 officially documented. By the end of this early started day, I would have done my 114th of the still not half way through medical fiscal year, most of which were for research, several others late at night on call in the Ben Taub E.R.. They weren't all smooth of course, especially in older patients with a little dose of degenerative joint disease, affecting the lumbar vertebral column, but there were times I remember, when intrusive, unwelcome thoughts (those little buried cortical demons that are more likely to complicate sleep deprivation) would come, wherein I literally wondered if by now I couldn't actually stand across the room and throw the lumbar puncture needle, like a dart in a good game of Cricket over at the Gingerman in the Village, and hit the perfect 1 x 1 mm space on the betadine-scrubbed region I glared at. Of course, I never really tried it…..

V

- Recollections: Early November, 1990

On the first weekend of November, Kim and I took our first official trip together.

If there's any potential interest in continuing an evolving relationship, one should probably be at least moderately careful about where and what the first "get away" as a new couple is. Certainly, romance should be expected. But maybe too much totally-alone-as-a-twosome time can generate unnecessary anxiety regarding that component? Maybe better is a situation that allows some excitement and adventure, and maybe even physical exertion in a more public format, only further fuelling the sexual energy that exists at a potential maximum at this early stage of a relationship, and that is then free to manifest when it's the right alone time?

Dancing at the sex-charged nightclubs and sunning and swimming at the beaches of the stereotypical honeymoon and resort sites, like Waikiki or Cancun, or Miami Beach, still allows for ample intimacy at night back at the hotels photographically represented in the back of Bride's magazine and travel brochures maybe a little more luxuriously than physically appreciated in actuality, and maybe sneaking in a passion and rum-filled quickie on a patch of sand or out in the warm waves on a seemed-pretty-deserted-at-the-time beach, while hoping the jelly fish are minding their own business.

No matter how many nights you've spent at each other's apartments already, and even if a woman has a couple of outfits stored in a designated spot in the closet or a spare toothbrush and a few essential cosmetic items in a specifically cleared out drawer in the bathroom at the guy's place (the kinds of things which when viewed alone the day or two after the latest in home visit generate alternating pangs of butterfly-like excitement and flushing, light-headed confusion), that first true vacation trip together with publicly witnessed and blessed equal cohabitation of a mutual dwelling, even if just a small hotel room, is a milestone in a new relationship, a potential unanticipated turning point or decision branch in the life tree, with one branch leading to years and years of dozens to hundreds of increasingly comfortable and routine trips, and the other either gently or God forbid, precipitously, spiraling, with either sadness or relief, down the "maybe we're not really right for each other" cliff.

More couple philosophy from a non-expert: If a first trip away as a couple centers on a specific activity, say cycling or horse back riding or sailing or even hang gliding, I should think most males would prefer it be something they're good at, or at least competent in, or at the very least, familiar with, regardless of the corresponding skill level of the new mate. Otherwise, one possessing less than the complete pair of X chromosomes necessary for the faintest hint of security could be afraid of the eventuality of one or more of several potentially damaging outcomes, including: coming across as geeky or uncoordinated; appearing un-masculine or un-athletic, potentially worsened by the presence of highly skilled male partners in other participating couples or even more worsened by the demonstrated easy mastery of the task at the highest imaginable skill level by the handsome, but aloof and only subtly flirtatious trainer or guide; and finally, death or severe injury to yourself or your new love, neither of which is particularly nurturing for a burgeoning relationship.

However, lest one Romeo wanna-be draws potentially false comfort and confidence from the anticipated studly demonstration of past mastered masculine sporting skills, the opposite danger in choosing a weekend get-away centered on an area of expertise is that of appearing elitist, arrogant, snooty or even mean. Female libido killers in this setting might include lover-boy's comments, which however indirectly and covertly made, convey how woeful, uncoordinated, stupid, silly, or inept some other less experienced individual comes across while trying to perform the same activity that you are clearly a star in. Now, if you make such comments directly to and about your new love interest, who agreed to this particular trip despite little or no experience in the particular sporting-like activity the trip is focused on, well, let's just say you don't deserve any more romantic getaways-with this or any other person naïve enough to initially regard you as decent. We dig our own cold showers.

On the plus side, for those who can't get enough of this Zen-like guide to early love, this latter sort of trip could be an opportunity for one to actually, and hopefully sincerely, demonstrate their possession of some of the more female-desired attributes a candidate mate may be at least dusted with: patience, gentleness/tenderness, concern, tolerance, and that underestimated relationship paste...communication skills. Let's hope that they're genuine, but all of these could come across in some fun sun-filled days of teaching your new girlfriend how to do something that you're experienced with. The added bonuses include often having to touch her while positioning various extremities and even the pelvis in some kind of athletic activity or holding her close and tight, her potentially scantily clad backside to your hopefully somewhat more supportive clothing-covered front, while perhaps demonstrating the proper position or motion from anything as harmless as a perfect golf swing to getting on a horse for a beach ride, to properly casting a fishing pole or rowing a canoe.

Depending on the composition of your new partner, the demonstration of these high-end attributes not only shows what type of father you would be (for the more serious and long-term relationship thinkers), but at least helps guarantee you the same courteous treatment when you really score big points the next time, by exposing your humility and openness in allowing yourself to be in an environment more in her realm of experience.

For Kim's and my first get-away, then, I would have likely preferred something within the realm of human endeavors that I was at least vaguely familiar with; if not something involving tasks during which I could display my knowledge, skills, and manliness, or even those other things, like sensitivity and good-heartedness, then at least something more along neutral grounds, something akin to a sexist demilitarized zone...maybe like hiking; after all, everyone, boys and girls both, can at least walk. We were both in good shape, and Kim could acquire the perfect outfits, gear, and accessories, and I could admire them, whether from the front, from the vantage of turning back while being ahead on the trail in a manly manner and pausing for her to catch up, or more strategically, from the protective-male-at-the-back-of-the-group, staring at her ass point of view.

Instead...................at this SO crucial phase in a heating up, strongly charged and passion filled developing relationship, I found myself right in the middle of girl-camp: a SPA.

...

Neither of us was in a position to take too much time off from work at that particular time, so on Friday afternoon we drove up to stay three nights at a Spa in Calistoga. The only potential saving factor was that it was, after all, in Napa Valley. In addition to the background ambience of good food and wine, both within the spa and at the several nearby restaurants, we would be visiting wineries and doing wine tasting/drinking as an official trip task.

If there's one arena in which I feel at home, and did even back then, even sooner than then, even much sooner, it's drinking. Wine, beer, familiar brands, new and strange products, it's all good.

As my mom used to say, probably with more sarcasm than pride, "If drinking were an Olympic Sport, Jeff would have never gone to medical school....or at least, would have waited for a few years of maximal competitiveness and eligibility before going." Or if she didn't actually ever say that, I think I gave her a few too many nights in which she could have at least thought it (amongst other things).

The various atmospheres in which consumption of fermented and/or distilled beverages occur seem to share at least 98 of the 100 pigments of my aura.

Aura.....sounds like spa talk.

...

The drive up from San Francisco was a strange combination of alternating thrilling nervous anticipation and gut-tangling something else. The thought of spending a weekend away with Kim, checking into a hotel and functioning there amongst grown-up strangers as a couple, was essentially intoxicating. Even better than these outward signs would be the opportunity to be with Kim in that fascinatingly intimate manner of finally spending all day and all night together; not just going over to her place at night, after being in the lab or clinic all day, and both of us having to get up early in the morning, tired already from a long day to the point where even dinner or watching a video ("normal couple stuff") turned the opportunity for relatively prolonged love making into that for just a quickie prior to having to get an already diminished number of sleep hours, just barely sufficient to be operational the next day.

"I'm warning you. I can be a real bitch when I'm tired," I was cautioned on one such occasion, when I suggested a second round, when it was already just five hours prior to wake up time for one of us. When I began to weakly counter by suggesting that she could take a nap when she got home from work, I was advised in an appropriate moment of maturity and responsibility, "and I'm sure your patients would prefer to have you well rested."

Actually, I realized early on, even back in medical school, that I could generally function quite fine in a clinical situation when I was tired from inadequate sleep the night before. Parts of the day, you'd consciously realize you were moving a little slower than usual, and would force yourself to "snap to", maybe with a fifth or sixth or seventh cup of coffee, but then there would even be occasional bursts of energy, seemingly physiologically unexplainable spurts of clear-headed productivity, that you rode till the crash later on that evening. However, this often came at the expense of either a nap in the early evening, which kept one from going over to one's new girlfriend's place, or in lieu of the nap, came at the expense of being a less than stellar companion during that evening's eating, movie watching, or love-making activities.

But, in stark contrast to the above, if I was really tired, I was largely worthless in the lab, not commonly able to motivate myself to do an experiment, to look at data, to read, to write, or anything that required at least a 75 % competent neuron set. As addicted as I was getting to Kim, I needed to avoid these kinds of days in my current environment. Sleeping in, working in the afternoon and at night, and generating a vicious cycle of nocturnal mania was romantic during the Basic Science portions of medical school and during my early years of research, but it was less than the desired degree of professionalism for an M.D. researcher, who also had clinical responsibilities, and if for no other than political and appearance reasons, had to spend more time interacting with the other long white coats in the department than what had been necessary in the past as the unshaven, black t-shirt laden, scruffy hair, nicotine tinted free thinking naïve research "stud" (student).

Hence, a few weeks into our romance, we had evolved into a self- and couple-preserving mode in which we gave our jobs the necessary, if not slightly distracted effort, and concentrated all other time units on what came more naturally... falling in love with each other.

But now, on a trip like this, we got to brush our teeth together in the morning, without being "late already". We got to have a leisurely breakfast, before spending entire days at the same physical location. We got to "meet up" back at the room, in between "sessions". And, aided by virtue of being in a room with less than the usual home accessories, we were almost forced to lay in bed together early in the evening, maybe while watching a movie, but not necessarily one we really wanted to watch, and that plus the added liberating influence of the foreign surroundings and vacation atmosphere could only mean starting making love earlier. We could hold each other close, we could talk into the wee hours, my favorite part of the day when so much of me functions at its best, and we could make love again, maybe even again. We could sleep in, certainly relative to the usual work day craziness, even if a relatively early morning "activity" was scheduled. And, now, really, who cares if one's a little tired for a yoga class; after all, that should only facilitate relaxation. And being tired for a facial or a massage, at least to my XY-mode of thinking, would only promote a little snoozing lapse every now and then, only helping to minimize the perceived duration of the particular skin or posture torture session.

Ah, there in lies perhaps one aspect of the sense of what I now recognized as one of the forms of dread. As we cruised ever so successfully up highway 12 to 29 in Kim's small, older BMW with what seemed like an at least partially supportive Northern tailwind bolstering us, a warm-natured and apparently Atlas competent albatross overhead guiding us, and even all the right songs coming on at the right moments on the radio, as I looked over at Kim, acutely twinged in some unidentifiable intercostal space by her incredible beauty, that highest form I've noted when her eyes sparkle when she's happy, I kept getting periodic even deeper and harder to localize stabs, that sadly demanded mood squelching analysis.

Why, at this moment, was I not just frankly orgasmic?

Quite simply... I didn't play spa.

I didn't grow up playing spa. I didn't watch spa played on T.V. As I wiped the sleep from my eyes and poured a bowl of sugary cereal in the morning before school, I didn't skip the comics and go right to the spa pages in the paper on our kitchen table to look up how my heroes had performed in spa the day before, in late night west coast spa sessions I hadn't been able to catch on the radio while I laid in bed supposedly asleep. My Dad didn't come home from work and put his spa gear on, so we could go in the back yard and play spa, so he could see how I was progressing in my spa skills, as he didn't know my spa coach this year as well as he knew my spa coach last year. My school didn't have a spa program. No one even pushed for them to introduce one.

I had heard that some other places spent a lot of time playing spa. Compared to us Texas Hill Country folks, who thought a facial was something you got if you wiped out in the forward direction on your dirt bike or something from the porno world if you were really wise, a cleansing was something the hard core Baptists did down at the river when they should be toobing and drinking beers, sprouts were something related to hops the Germans used to make beers, maybe only for the special Oktoberfest brews, and that yoga was the way that really dumb guys pronounced the name of that old baseball guy who said funny things and who we were always surprised when we learned that he had actually played (or that cartoon bear if you were REALLY dumb), those Dallas snoots reportedly had spa programs, but even then it was just for girls. And they weren't official school programs, with UIL sponsorship or anything. They were apparently expected extracurricular activities for some types of folks. During the last couple of years I was in high school, and when resurfacing periodically during occasional forays into the real world during college and med school, I had appreciated rumors that "spas" were hot tubs. I could do hot tubs, no problem. But this was, of course…different.

The spa I was heading to was not just a hot tub. I felt that maybe I was going to a knitting contest, without even any exposure to the basic yarn manipulating moves that I would want to be prepared with. I was perhaps going to an Emily Dickinson reading session. I was going to an entirely female Coliseum, competing with Amazon women while wearing only a condom. O.K., that last part doesn't seem that bad, but still, as I shook myself out of my latest trepidation laden day dream and smiled over at Kim, I caught her giving me an inquisitive eye-brow crunched, lip corner slightly raised on the same side look that over the years I learned to decipher even various subtle variations of, as running the spectrum from "Are you O.K.?" to "What the fuck is wrong with you?".

...

As we drove into Calistoga it was just late afternoon, and the quaintness of the town and the feeling of being somewhere so undeniably dedicated to leisure, food, and wine recharged the excitement of being alone together on a mission of relaxation and mutual exploration. After we checked in at the Spa and our luggage was taken away to a room we hadn't seen yet, we met, as a couple, with some sort of Spa Consultant, I suppose to finalize our schedules and to be sure that all of our Spa Objectives were going to be met. I felt a little silly, but certainly didn't express that out loud, and Kim was as happy and eager as I'd seen her, and I sensed that by participating so formally that I was somehow contributing to that. And I liked that.

When an available opening was revealed for a cooking demonstration later that evening, a session which allowed ample tasting along the way to an eventual complete gourmet, if albeit healthy, meal along with perfectly matched local wines, my apparent exudation of sincere zeal to sign up was met not only by a warm smile and hand-squeeze from Kim but some sort of brow raise/subtle smile combination from our Spa liaison that was perhaps some sort of female-to-female code thing, barely discernible to me as a male and hence used to the more overt boy head nod thing in our code system, and perhaps implying something akin to "girl, you've got a good one there," which only seemed to add to the tally of brownie points that I was gradually becoming aware of.

We loved our room. It was quaint and easy to feel comfortable and relaxed in as individual humans, enough to help me ease instead into the state of being truly nervous about being there as a couple, I suppose, and so we both quickly unpacked to get a little "spa time" in before dinner. The tinglings related to the intimacy of being there together like that I subsequently partially channeled into an intense short workout while Kim was participating in some sort of demonstration of a new sunless browning skin product, which I later learned that I kind of liked the taste of.

Afterwards, we joined two other young women and a mother-daughter pair in a brief stretching /yoga exercise, which made me realize that despite being in pretty good shape that I had male flexibility, or lack thereof. Still, I seemed to hear several comments from the participants and the instructor, a woman in amazing shape that was perhaps in her mid forties, alluding to what a great sport I was, as if reaping the benefits of this exercise alone was not enough motivation for the usual Cro-Magnon male to participate. But truth was, that on top of everything else, a certain pain/stiffness in my neck/right upper back region that had been pestering me a bit the day before and on the ride up had already seemed to disappear, and I was secretly beginning to think that there could be something to this Spa stuff, even if it was potentially largely mental, as I'd be one of the last people in the world to dismiss this as a legitimate mechanism.

The cooking class for dinner that evening was actually quite fun and the food, at least to us, was beyond great. We made a very simple (as in the royal we, and simple according to our instructor, or maybe you call them chefs) salmon dish, with some sort of red wine and balsamic vinegar sauce (or "reduction", which prior to this episode I thought was a term for weight loss or specific chemical reaction related to electron transfer or some such process). A major point apparently was to emphasize the taste and nutritional and health superiority of wild salmon vs. the blander farm raised variety. Another point of emphasis was the excellent pairing that salmon and Pinot Noir represent, which I sincerely appreciated and partook of liberally, enjoying both the Carneros and Russian River Valley Pinots we were tasting and comparing. I participated eagerly in all of the preparatory and tasting aspects of the event, and apparently excelled notably in a few, including: adding just the right amount of olive oil to the pan in a motion polished off with a flick of the wrist maneuver that would make even the most accomplished alchemist jealous; slicing a rustic bread loaf at just the right thickness, slice after slice, with a regularity that would make one think I was using illegal instrumentation; getting the eight or so other participants to progressively let loose and drink up the Sauvignon Blanc we had with our salad and multiple bottles of the two Pinots we had with dinner to the level (or maybe a little more...) that our Chef probably wanted but was not achieving on his own accord and who noticeably appreciated and commented on my imbibing recruiting efforts; and, getting the full and spirited participation of an initially highly reserved Japanese tourist couple who spoke essentially no English, by virtue of some sort of progressively evolved/discovered hand and hand to mouth sign language and acting out pantomime that proved so effective in American-to-Japanese and Japanese-to-American kitchen athletics that evening that the Spa is formally considering adding illustrations of such to one of the versions of their published Cook Book.

Kim, who was noticeably tanner than when she picked me up early that afternoon, and in an almost so natural appearing way that I was pondering the chemistry of melanin stimulation and wondering if I should be doing dermatology research instead, and looking as lovely as ever and smiling and joking to a level that I thought I should try to sustain regularly, seemed to be having a good time, and was kissing me so often I thought we may be violating even some fairly liberal spa public display of affection policy (not that I was complaining…), and I was beginning to appreciate subtle differences in the way she tasted depending on what stage we were in the meal preparation. For example, even before I knew anything about terroir and Dijon clones, I appreciated that I liked the way she tasted when she kissed me after drinking the Russian River Valley vs. the Carneros Pinot. I was beginning to feel that wine tasting that weekend was going to be a lot of fun.

For dessert, it was kept simple. Some cheeses, including some from a local Sonoma producer, with some hearty Cabs….after all, we were in Napa Valley. Exhausted, and determined to get a good Friday night's sleep in order to get an early start and put in a full Saturday, we hit the hot tub briefly, and without any formal proclamations attesting to our first bout of official cohabitation, we crawled into bed naked and warm. As I alluded to, I decided I liked the taste of the apparently at least partially water proof non-UV bronzer, and as I enjoyed some sort of combination of Yoga, Salmon, Pinot, Cab, hot-tub, skin buzz, Kim made love to me as if I were the honorable mayor of Spa town.

…

I think we must have been exhausted, and I'm pretty sure we woke up the next morning in the exact same position we had fallen asleep holding each other in. I lifted my head up a little bit over Kim's, where her hair tickled underneath my nose, and saw a faint trickle of cruel sunlight coming in through the curtains. I felt like I'd been through some sort of soul cleansing or at least disorienting process. The lab, the hospital E.R.'s, the clinics of SF overflowing with AIDS patients seemed so far away. I noticed about a one-inch diameter partially dried drool spot on my pillow as I braced myself up on my left elbow. Kim's right leg was partially out of the covers, and I stared at the smooth skin of her lateral calf and the fine shape of her knee, while subconsciously my right hand glided over her right thigh, up over her hip, pressing my thumb lightly on her posterior superior iliac crest, my morning rock-hard cock sliding to attention up over her left inner thigh and left buttock, beginning to nestle into the peri-home base area.

Kim stirred and raised her head slightly, "What time is it?"

I felt foreignness; new concepts into the film of early morning pastiness. But always the helpful citizen, I focused on the alarm clock on the night stand on her side.

"8:17," I said with scientific precision, as if that was the time most suited to pressing my cock between her sexy, smooth ass cheeks, looking for any accommodating orifice it could find.

"Whoa, cowboy," she said, grabbing me with a downward stroke before rolling over on top of me in impressive gymnastic like fashion, kissing me sweetly, and then sadly rolling over and then heading off into the bathroom in one concerted motion, calling to me while peeing with the door open, "I've got a hair appointment in thirteen minutes."

The astuteness with which she subtracted 8:17 from 8:30 for such concrete detail without any coffee was astounding, but it didn't stop me from standing naked in the doorway, holding my boner in my hand and saying with full juvenile enthusiasm, "I got your appointment right here, baby,"

Responding the way only a truly perfect woman can, and leaning her rear up towards me, rather than away, to wipe, she said, "I've got a feeling that's gonna take a lot more time and attention than my hair…or anything else around here," while simultaneously standing up, kissing me firmly on the lips, pressing her hands on my chest and pushing me out of the room, closing the door, and turning on the shower. Temporarily defeated, but ridiculously happy, I lunged from across the room back into the bed, pulled the covers over me completely, and breathed everything in deeply.

At an amazing 8:31 (essentially prompt for a weekend on a vacation, as it was less than one minute from the room to the Spa proper, where I suspected the hair salon was also located) Kim emerged from the bathroom looking Spa-ready and was heading out the door. She came over to the bed, where I had now at least come to a sitting up position on the edge, and took my hands in hers. I felt the texture of the dorsal side of her fingers and thumb under my finger tips.

"I'm getting my hair then nails done this morning. What are you going to do?"

I wasn't sure how to respond. I knew I wasn't going to get my hair and nails done. I must have sat there a little blankly for a second or two, as my helpful spa companion offered up, "You could get a massage…or a man-facial," as she poked me playfully.

Although the massage sounded potentially nice, the man-facial crossed a line my testicles would not permit, so in a not quite awake act remotely analogous to self preservation, I responded without plan or forethought, "I'm going to go play a round or two of golf."

"Excellent idea," she beamed. "Can you meet me back here for a late lunch?"

"I don't know," I now more objectively responded, thinking about the practical specifics. "It depends what time I start, whether I play 9 or 18, I guess" (and where the hell I can go to play, if anywhere, around here, I thought to myself. Wine tasting, even just at the Spa bar, started to seem like a good and practical alternative, and I wondered if they had any kind of breakfast special).

"Well, I'll look for you around 1 or 2:00. Otherwise, I'll go ahead and get another treatment this afternoon. Just leave a message at the front desk," said super Spa chick as she pecked me on sleep-tinged mouth with those great moist lips of hers, and then she hurried out the door.

…

Years from then, when I might be more polished in these arts and more fitted to the role of physician husband of a spa goddess, I would have realized, or at least presumed, that a spa of the character or level that we were staying at would have likely had relationships and arrangements with nearby private or semi-private golf courses and/or resorts, such that I probably could have squeezed in a round at a more nearby and spa guest-appropriate facility. Instead, I followed my still ingrained blue collar roots and asked the concierge, at an impressive 9:13 a.m., if there was a public golf course around, assuming, logically, that as I wasn't from around there and wasn't a member anywhere nearby, that that would be the only recourse for an outing of embarrassing stroking of the little round white ego-punisher, which although potentially humiliating at my level of rustiness would at least allow me to keep my word to my "woman". Taking her guest's request literally, and respectfully, as likely so often instructed or reminded, rather than potentially informing me of any other possible options, if indeed they did even exist, my lovely service person resorted to the phone book to indulge me and heroically attempt to satisfy my request, no different than if I had wanted to order a pizza or book a trip on a space ship.

Much to our mutual glee (or at least relief), there was indeed a public course in Napa...yes, all the way back to Napa, as in the town, as in not the winery-oriented more Northern towns of the similarly named "valley". Oh well, distance is all relative, and 25 or so miles to hopefully physically and almost certainly emotionally exert myself and fulfill my statement to Kim was still likely less than the equivalent male human units of life currency than sitting in a chair during the endurance of a man facial. So, instead, I grabbed one of the pamphlets with the best Napa Valley map off the small rack on Tiffany's desk (I guess, just in case our Atlas had disappeared out of the car the previous night), and hopped into Kim's car, with almost a little too much purpose and perhaps slightly dislodging the valet from his assumed state of tranquility that "spa" mandated, and began heading down the St. Helena Highway to Napa (the town) and my ultimate destination of the Napa Golf Course at Kennedy Park.

Ironically, or maybe even tragically, as I seemed on a laser guided path back towards San Francisco, we had seen a sign for an exit to that very golf course off of 29/128 at a point that had still seemed an early phase of the journey north, away from work life and towards our get-away destination. Now, about ten minutes into my non-rigorously planned and buddingly perceived potentially to be unsuccessful expedition, I started to think that I might as well be heading back to play a round of golf in San Francisco, itself. if so, I wondered, why hadn't I been doing that exact thing more often, and so I strengthened my resolve to play some golf, of some who knows what quality, in Napa (town, valley, winery, road side or parking lot if needed...whatever) no matter what.

On the way up, in fact, with its almost palpable lesson on autonomic innervation of the gastrointestinal tract and not necessarily mutually exclusive pelvic region, I remember that, at a somewhat relaxed interlude, we had even commented on certain aspects of that black art known as golf when we had passed the exit sign to the very course that I now stormed towards. Later, revisiting the same theme when passing some more exclusive private courses closer to and even in Wine Country (a few of which I had just passed in the reverse direction and wondered why I couldn't be playing at those instead and hence already be where I needed to go, and maybe I needed to work more outside the box with the Spa

Tiffanies in the future), we had mutually expressed that we couldn't believe that "they" would actually allow such large chunks of land, even on the southern valley floor, to go to non-vineyard purposes. I responded by speculating that such land allocation was likely compensated for in the green fees, which likely rivaled the price of a case of the finest local Cab. Plus, I also speculated, not subsequently confirmed (thanks, Tiffany), and probably fortunately given my oft zigzagging slice alternating with hook approach from tee to green, that the fairways on those fancy Napa Valley courses were likely lined by rows of primo vines, such that hitting a ball into a row of old vine Zin grapes was probably much more severe than a water hazard.

At that point, I was probably trying to impress Kim with my knowledge of distinct varietals (or at least that distinct varietals existed, some of which I knew the names of), but that "primo" was not an officially sanctioned vine description allowed just enough of my already obvious naiveté to show through, such that it was clear that the wine tasting part of our trip could be just as educational as the carrot-juice and exfoliating Spa portions.

Kim even asked, appropriately casually as we drove by these various courses, if I played golf, and I got that acute pang from the cusp of budding familiarity again; that reminder that we still knew so little about each other and that we were in the midst of processes potentially revealing and serious, spreading into opportunities for exposure beyond what our heretofore shared urban and work-compromised interactions had allowed. However, I did know already that Kim's dad ("Daddy" in some affectionate contexts; "Father" when alluding to certain business and other personal successes) was a big golfer. Thinking of him acutely more in the "Father" sense (as in "Sir, may I have your permission to bang your daughter out of wedlock in a Calistoga Spa" than in the "Daddy" sense, as in a group of us hugging affectionately and drinking arm in arm in a bar or opening up Christmas presents in our PJ's), I felt that my answer could almost be part of an interview or audition, albeit hopefully unintentional.

"I used to play a fair amount with my Dad over the years, a bit still when I lived in Houston, but especially when I was in high school and then in college in San Antonio....maybe a weekend a month, maybe a little less. A couple of my buddies and I would go every now and then in Med School....but, not too much lately," I paused, and maybe foreshadowing some of my life perspective contemplations to occur later that weekend, started to wonder why I hadn't been playing much golf lately and whether I missed it, when Kim responded.

"I bet you look cute in those little plaid golf pants," she impishly jabbed with a slightly upward curl of those sexy, soft lips.

Although I'm sure I appreciated the fact that she was already picturing me in semi-fantasy imaginary scenes (although I hoped she had a few better ones than the golf-pants thing going....), lest I begin to acquiesce to a woman who had likely had her fair share of time in Daddy's country club and could be dressing me in green and pink and yellow and blue checkered golf pants, assuring matching to a spectrum of similarly colored Izod polo shirts and sweaters, I offered up in blue collar beer swilling defense: "I think we usually played in cut-off scrubs."

Not missing a beat, something I would increasingly appreciate at alternating penile inflating and neck strangling (mine and hers, respectively) urges, Kim playfully responded, "I hear that's a growing fashion statement."

Cupid's now bionic arrows were sinking so deep that they'd already need the bypass machine to fix me....even if I'd let them.

...

Once I had settled down a bit after driving for fifteen or twenty minutes or so, I remembered that I felt rejuvenated that morning by the mix of passionate love making and maybe even more by having had the most deep sleep I had probably experienced in a long time. Now, I added a bit of pride and anticipation for actually taking the initiative to get some likely much needed physical activity and some fresh air. On top of those things, already enough to almost ensure an adequate day, now that I had succeeded in my get-away, I think I felt a borderline illegal rush from the combination of getting away from exfoliating and/or rejuvenating lotions and the rapid consumption of a six pack of mini powdered sugar donuts I impulsively purchased from a rack of other evils on the counter at the cash register of the gas station I had just stopped at to finally ask for directions to the golf course after apparently (again) blowing by the exit that we had so easily noticed on the way up.

But now that I finally pulled into the parking lot of the golf course, I felt that old familiar surge of competitive adrenaline (epinephrine, to be more biochemically precise) kick in; that surge of mentally gearing up a hopefully physically ready self; a notion a little distant, perhaps, but so ingrained from the past;

a feeling that always surfaced at various, but usually pretty high, intensity levels, whether accompanying me to the pitcher's mound in my youth, or even in a slightly more hung over form, to a lazy weekend morning intramural basketball game in Medical School. It was always there. I couldn't kill it, even if wanted to. And so: I am, or have been, a great golfer…about 25 % of the time. I play golf the way you might expect a coordinated, athletic guy who never really took formal golf lessons and who hasn't really been playing sports anywhere near as often the last couple of years as he used to might play golf.

Of course, as any fellow hacker knows, that doesn't mean that I go out and play scratch or par golf one out of every four infrequent times that I go out and play on unfamiliar courses in strange and foreign places. That means, as all my inconsistent little white ball stroker compadres know, that every so often when I'm out playing this silly game, I hit a perfect, I mean truly perfect, golf shot. In mathematical terms, I hit the shot I want, a shot I can easily play…the shot needed with the appropriately chosen club…maybe one out of every four strokes. The problem is, of course…all those other shots.

…

The course was busy, as one might expect for non-vineyard land and especially back towards the over-humanized bay area, but not as busy as I would have expected for non-vineyard land in this part of the country during post-harvest and pre-too cold for old farts not to play golf time of the year. I base this rather empiric observation on the facts that one, I could get on without a reservation, and two, the group that I got put in with was not even a complete foursome. At an 11:45 tee off, I was put together with a rigid, perfectly clad, golf courteous but not overly warm and fuzzy sweet swinger and regular player of the game, who had his own cart and was a local gent, one of the few non-viticulturally affiliated valley dwellers, and a fellow pull cart swinger/hacker, whom I instantly recognized as my more natural partner of the day when I saw that his wood head covers were made of leopard print velvet.

We had a civil game, despite my occasional to frequent topographical deviations off the appropriate fairway, compensated by my occasional to less frequent beautiful hole-salvaging shots off the parallel fairways (quickly stroked in the face of players coming in the correct opposite direction properly on their own fairways) and those sporadic "holy shit, where did that come from" master strokes, my ability to make at least civil conversation with mister stiffy in his nearly fluorescent stereotypical golf pants and custom-made clubs. Cart guy…Carl Sneed or Kirk Smart or Cal Smirk or Ken Weener or Dick Head, had been playing there for almost twenty years, since he had moved up from the city during peri-retirement from one of those ill defined money management jobs for several ill defined West Coast corporations. To me, he hit the ball straight (a trait particularly admirable compared to my hooks hopefully compensated by slices mixed in with hopefully equal doses of surprising straight shots), but it seemed to be for the same length, whether a three wood, five iron, or even nine iron.

Whereas I really only encountered Cart Stiffie on our tee shots, the greens, and one awkward moment in the can in between the front nine and back nine, I spent a lot of mutual moments with velvet leopard club covers, particularly in the rough, and I enjoyed our pleasant and pragmatically informative interactions. This was the kind of guy, in his tight burgundy polyester pants whom I could easily picture his furniture and even his wife being covered the same way as he and his golf clubs. This was the kind of guy that had never met a stranger. This was the kind of guy that, even if he hit a ball right down the middle of the fairway, would walk with you, dragging his pull cart through the overgrowth without acknowledging the extra effort, to help you reach your ball in the ultra rough, the stuff you didn't think could grow and engulf a golf ball in temperate zones, just to keep a conversation growing. This was the kind of guy that you didn't really remember ever seeing in prison, but would talk your ear off on the gallows the day of your mutual execution, pleasantly distracting you for a few brief moments before you didn't really have time to notice that you swung from a noose, only to be continuing the exact same conversation the next day in heaven, him not missing a beat of the exchange, while you were still glancing about trying to figure out what was the deal with all the fluffy clouds and white robes.

Fortunately for me, at this particular time and especially location of my insecure romantic life, at which I could use some wooing ammo, Mr. Soave was also a self professed wine expert; and I mean, at apparently all levels, from soil analysis and turnover, vine trimming and management, to harvesting, to fermenting (I believe I was exposed to three or four different strategies of "pressing down" alone), to cork taint prevention, to marketing (boy, it got really grandiose there), to pouring, tasting, even how to use wine sexually to optimal advantage. Turns out, my even passive absorption of even a fraction of potentially/likely only partially factual information in these areas would prove useful the next day during winery visits. A spirited drinker could perhaps identify at least some of the more obviously present and still interesting aspects of a wine (against the non-perceived and seemingly imagined provided descriptions, resembling to me, at least, something more equivalent to oenophilic bovine feces, a quality not included in the concept of terroir as I so far appreciated it) that may still turn into warm conversation pieces in the joyful arena known as tasting room.

...

I got back to our spa in Calistoga around 5:30 that afternoon. After the valet took Kim's car from me, I walked into the small lobby feeling a little bit more like me than when we'd arrived, although I again felt that strangeness of unfamiliarity descending upon me, but this time I was at least more comfortable.

My sense of belonging was surprisingly reinforced when the young woman who had replaced Tiffany at the front desk, and whom I'd not seen before, greeted me by name (Dr. Pearson), which I still thought was a little spa-freaky, and then handed me a message from "Ms. Williamson". Uh oh, I thought, the truth of the different last names was officially out. Desk girl didn't seem disturbed by this reality – as if it was not so uncommon in secret spa world. Whether we were married and my strong willed wife (whom, after all, had dragged her "husband" to a spa) had kept her last name, whether we were married to other people and had snuck off to spa land for a clandestine affair, whether we were mysterious international spies, or whether we were simply boyfriend and girlfriend (or some version thereof) and sharing a room out of wedlock (which apparently didn't violate any sort of heretofore unstated spa morality code in which use of the proper moisturizer on the appropriate body part was perhaps more crucial) did not seem to matter to her.

After she handed me the note and loitered for a brief moment, as if to see if I may need anything else or wished to respond in some return handwritten form as if that was how Kim and I routinely communicated, she added to the impression of perhaps this spa etiquette of official generic and non-judging, non-presuming approach to "couples", with "Ms. Williams is certainly a lovely young lady."

"Yeah," I nonchalantly responded while unfolding Kim's note, "she's starting to grow on me."

Kim informed me that she had gotten some sort of nail treatment in the mid afternoon and since I'd not gotten back yet, was going to get some sort of "wrap" that would last until about 6.

I glanced up and noted that my response had not been quite what my pleasant hostess had expected in the zone of polite spa communication and she had a slightly perplexed look on her face, as if dealing with alien forms had not been covered in her orientations or handbook.

I rescued her briefly by adding, "...I mean...she drives me crazy." This reassured her temporarily, and her expression changed to a polite smile, but then the confused face returned in less severe form, maybe when she processed the actual content of my comment and considered that it could have been in the literal, psychiatric sense and not necessarily the more spa-friendly romantic sense.

Enjoying my perceived advantage in this transient disturbia and maybe still in the playful mood that had inspired at least half of my common recovery shots in my recent golf outing, I plainly and matter-of-factly addressed this polite young woman with, "If you see Ms. Williamson, will you let her know that her lover is over in the bar," and I walked away feeling that my latest task in counter spa had been successfully accomplished. While I walked towards the bar, and noted the scattered beautifully maintained and up-scaled comfortably to luxuriously dressed predominantly women in the environment, I knew that my victory was at best short lived and futile. But observing them and knowing how Kim looked in this environment, I wasn't so sure that defeat was a bad thing in this setting.

It wasn't officially a bar, but more some sort of off lobby café with a spa-compatible comfort-inspiring name that served juices derived from various roughage, light healthy meals, and a wide variety of wines by the glass. I subconsciously reached into my left front and rear right pockets to see if I had cash and/or wallet respectively, and while safely noting the latter, tore up and threw away my removed recent golf outing score card, lest Kim or anyone else should discover the concrete evidence of how I played overall, despite some stellar shots that came despite the long time since I'd actually played, and discarded the fragments discreetly into a waste can as I entered the "bar." I was on my second of a three glass Pinot Noir flight when Kim entered. Without saying anything, she kissed me firmly. She smelled...interesting, like an appetizer or something similar so that I wanted to keep running my finger on the plate and licking and tasting after all the more substantive named parts were gone. She took a sip of my current glass, and kissed me again. I liked this game. We still hadn't spoken.

Then she cracked first, and said, "Order me a glass of that," alluding to the middle of my flight, a good choice I had decided even without having tasted the third wine yet. Then she sat next to me and while taking a bite out of some sort of mixture of dried fruit and nuts that I'd been nibbling on even though I didn't recognize any of the components (the spa bar equivalent, I guess, of the more usual bar nuts), asked me, "How was your golf game dear?"

After a brief conversation in which I likely exaggerated my good strokes and down-played the likely equally frequent dehumanizing miss-hits and explained my interactions with my playmates in a way that made Kim smile and occasionally burst out laughing to a degree that she once or twice had to turn around to see if anyone's reaction may indicate we were violating spa tone, we went out for dinner. We (I, all by myself upon recommendation from one of the Spa Girls) had made reservations at what turned out to be a wonderful little place in St. Helena. Dinner success, perhaps facilitated by several glasses of outstanding wine, seemed to add to the high level of passion and even stronger emotions with which I was being welcomingly treated by Kim, and which any hesitancy towards responding similarly on my part had disappeared as completely as my "short game" earlier in the day.

When we returned to the Spa in Calistoga, we had just a few minutes before we were scheduled for a "couple's massage". Contrary to the sort of amateur couples' massages I may have been fortunate enough to experience in the past, this one involved two other people (i.e., the masseuses) who weren't actually naked (at least to my largely closed eyes' perspective). Not being accustomed to such professional massages, and hence not knowing what to expect or how to "respond", it was all I could do to agree to the Deep Tissue Massage, which was fantastic, and in the course of an hour essentially turned all my previously not adequately noted tense fibers into some sort of myoglobin jello. In contrast, my Spa connoisseur mate got some sort of massage that involved a plethora of blended oils, herbs, emollients, and other classes of natural organics the vast majority of which I'd never heard of and as many as a quarter of I'm not sure I could even pronounce when reading the little pamphlet "menu" of massages available. I only got one soft jab when I noted to Kim that I didn't think that most of these were FDA approved.

Needless to say, after full days, dinner and wine, and our massages, we were exhausted. After the post-massage bottles of water we were ordered to drink and maybe one more glass of wine, we went to bed.

For maximum detoxification and other touted effects of her treatment, Kim was not supposed to shower all those juices off that night. So as she laid with her back towards me as we were falling asleep, and I ran my right hand over her shoulders, back, hips, and legs, I noted that some parts were slipperier than others. Housekeeping would now have even more reason to change our sheets in the morning. I smelled her skin as I placed soft kisses on the more accessible sites. I could detect the lavender and maybe some sort of spicier or herbalish fragrance from what I remembered from the list of ingredients I had read in sarcasm earlier…maybe, sage?

Although I couldn't be sure, as I don't think I'd ever really had an official whiff of sage before as some sort of reference standard. But, maybe, this was good practice for wine tasting tomorrow, I thought. As I lay there for just a few more conscious moments, I took in what I was able to perceive of Kim's total presence to me. The way her naked body felt against mine in a way that words can't really adequately describe; only those who've had the experience of holding someone they loved deeply and were also deeply physically attracted to may know this intoxicating and disjointing feeling. In the background of all the strange new fragrances from her massage, I could still smell the essence of my lover that I had been growing accustomed to. And yet, despite any hint of potential familiarity, at least at this stage, one could not underestimate the seemingly narcotizing effects of that sense of erotic mind numbing and spirit exploding pleasure.

…

Sunday morning we woke up early enough that we weren't rushed for anything. To be rested and still have that luxury was absolutely exhilarating. We had coffee and breakfast with the most leisurely morning conversation we'd had to date. In fact, to that point, I'm not sure I realized that one could have truly meaningful personal interactions in the morning. Back in our room, we had the sort of nasty sex, with me initially entering Kim from behind while she leaned her hands on the bathroom counter and we both could see everything in the bathroom mirrors, that actually makes two people feel closer just because you can do it and still feel comfortable after, as well as great during, and then showered together before tackling the rest of the day's fun filled agenda, already off to a great start.

Kim had an early make up consultation appointment, which seemed somewhat ludicrous to me given how perfect her skin is and how super model perfectly she already seemed to do her makeup. It made me think of something like an Olympic Gymnast stopping into a local gym to work out, but why not, as I guess even the greatest athletes keep practicing, regardless of where they temporarily are. I suspect the make-up chicks at the Spa must have had a blast working with that protoplasm, and selling - to a credit card that I hadn't yet started sharing the burden of - an apparently large stuffed shopping bag of mostly organic products. Kim had politely offered to have me join her, claiming, with likely full Spa authority at this point, that they could probably squeeze in a simultaneous "Man-Facial". The term alone sent estrogens through my entire being....

Kim had, and still has, one of if not the best complexions I've ever seen. Her skin, facial and all other wise, is like magic, like perfectly textured and colored silk. Although it seems like such blessed female humans would not need any specialized products or procedures, I'm willing to allow that they are part of an elite sorority of skin goddesses that are always eager to explore and experience novel products, supplements, emollients, and other exotics that at least allow them to celebrate their dermal blessings or feel like they're actively participating in the maintenance of likely natural beauty. If this is even only a small percentage of females, it's a safe bet that we male types, the far other half which, by definition, have things like facial hair and androgens that add up to pore chaos, could more than theoretically benefit from cutaneous advice from chemically armed professionals. However, despite our mutual acknowledgement that I had already complained about my male complexion on a couple of specific occasions (even Kim, though cordially, had expressed that she didn't agree with me and didn't see what I was talking about...bless her), I felt that getting a man facial was crossing a line I just didn't feel comfortable crossing at that point...or ever. There are some lines that just can't or at least shouldn't be crossed. We know some or most of these, even if not oft expressed. Life's little daily rules. You can occasionally smoke pot if you want to, you can rarely snort coke...hopefully not much more than a curious experimentation, but you should NEVER do IV drugs; you should never cheat on your spouse; you can eat quiche, but you should not have a man facial, etc.

So, instead, I did manly things...maybe with a sensitive twist or two. I put in a brief work- out and even purposefully met up with our yoga instructor from the afternoon before to address some back stretching activities, which were quickly becoming an intended part of my regular routine back in the real world. Kim and I were going to visit some wineries that afternoon and early evening, in Rutherford and along the Silverado Trail, so I decided it might be a good idea to do some related reading before hand. Although typically far more used to playing catch-up and being behind in studying for the massive amounts of medical training related reading paralleling whatever lectures I've received at various stages, on rare occasions I have admittedly read ahead to be particularly prepared and receptive on specific topics of extreme interest, and this one seemed like one of those indicated times. But, perhaps in part to make it seem a little less nerdy, I did do this brief session in the hot tub I was starting to get quite accustomed to, and which felt particularly nice after the work out and stretch. We then had some sort of session during which we received instructions in couple's massage therapy, which I enjoyed not only for the magic Kim seemed to easily work on that same targeted upper back/interscapular region, but because we were addressed and interacted with in a manner identical to the three other couples there, at least two of which were for sure married and seemed long established.

In the afternoon, we made our escape and hit the wine tasting rooms of several of the many great wineries within Napa Valley. We hit a couple on the main drag, such as Sterling, where it was less formal and we could take a self-guided sort of tour, and Mondavi, where we took a guided tour. Tasting at both wineries, although we may have been able to note what we especially liked, we were ripe for educational comments from our pouring hosts, the degree of which seemed to grow at each stop as we kept putting more and more bottles (sometimes multiple of a particular wine) on that credit card of Kim's, accompanied by my obliged comments each time that I would pay my share to her later. After about the third time of essentially blowing such comments off, she finally said something like, "Whatever. You just have to promise to drink all of them with me."

No problem, I thought, responding with "absolutely," but thinking to myself that as good as these wines were which we were acquiring, I would promise that even to someone I didn't even necessarily strongly care for, such as a particular co-worker or such. But to have the added bonus of being able to drink them with Kim was an offer I was incapable of refusing, to the point that I didn't necessarily make any distinction between the purchase of wines that folks told us were drinkable now or in short term vs. some of the more monster Cabs that could benefit from 5 or even 7 or even 10 years in the "cellar". Optimism was the theme for the day, and our trunk was almost full of bottles after making a couple stops along the Silverado Trail, such as at Sinksey and the legendary Stag's Leap, before heading over to Silver Oak towards the valley floor, by which point we had begun incorporating the back seat for the storage of our acquisitions. Some were, of course, targeted as presents, such as to Kim's father, maybe a bottle for Hassel from me for an appropriate occasion, etc. Somehow, this made us look less like oenologically camouflaged alcoholics vs. just taking advantage of being at the right place for personal and unselfish gift shopping. Whatever.

That evening back at Spa-Land, before our now ritual nightly couple's massage, we drank a few wines by the glass at the lobby bar kind of thing, semi- to largely-joking about the noses, bodies, and subtle flavors we pretended to note (or maybe in Kim's case, that she did actually taste, as a committed eater of the various mysterious fruits and vegetables for which I may have only been able to make a very short list of at that time in my life). "Hint" and "nuance" became the preferred words of the hour or so. "There's a hint of boysenberry on the edge of the predominant currant flavors," said a trying not to smile Kim. "Yes, but can you appreciate the subtle nuances of railroad track amongst the other mineral characters on the frame," said Jeff while letting the wine impinge on various parts of his tongue in histrionic fashion, feebly imitating the skilled maneuvers of a little old lady we met on our tour at Mondavi, a few drops of which came out in a fortunately finely atomized and not very distantly projected mist of laughter, when Kim responded with, "I got your frame right here, buddy." And I formally announced that after this hopefully final residency, I may just take off from medicine for a couple of years and dedicate my life to Tannin research, as I was intrigued by the speculated "polyglycanization" chemistry of the whole process. "I just like it when you say 'polyglycanization'," Kim said, and then maybe not quite softly enough for the older couple at the table next to us, "It makes me want to take you on my mid-pallet." We had clearly been wine tasting for a while. It was a good thing we weren't planning on going back to San Francisco, or anywhere else, that night, and with the level of affectionate flirting and comments that had been transpiring the last 8 or so hours, I almost wanted to skip the massage, but….

I was just getting Spa-adventurous. That night, I added hot stones to the joy of my para-vertebral muscles, while Kim got another exotic cocktail, this time involving mud, to which I couldn't help adding a few mild smart ass comments despite the apparently widely known etiquette of relative silence during massages, but surely those had to be a little relaxed for the couples thing...or what was the point...not to mention possibly depending upon the personality of the masseuse or the massage recipient. Fortunately, the mud was wiped off (prior to some other goo application), as there must surely be a limit also to the tolerance level of the sheet washing housekeeping staff as well.

As we lay there falling asleep that night, I tried not to think about what was facing me when I got back, especially compounded (essentially 20 % of a week's worth of required or self-imposed duties) by taking probably all of tomorrow off as well. The end of a vacation, however brief, always seems to be accompanied by the dread of what you return to by virtue of being gone to begin with, something I would increasingly realize as I took more vacations of the longer variety in the future. The insanity you seem to return to almost negates the benefits of the trip to begin with. But not this time, I thought, as I held Kim close to me and thought about the apparent steps our relationship had taken that weekend, and what that may mean to us when we got back. I forced my mind to quit punishing myself by over-thinking the implications of the latter. There was nothing wrong with taking it an enjoyable day at a time.

The next morning we left Calistoga at about 11 and had a leisurely lunch and overall trip on the way back home, including stopping at a couple more wineries: the tasting room of BV in Rutherford and maybe one other, possibly Cakebread or St. Supery or both from what I remember. Yet we were able to get back into SF before maximum rush hour. We ate some take out at Kim's place and went to sleep very early, without any potentially unnecessary discussion of the trip's consequences, only mutually acknowledging what a great time we had.

Relationships, no matter the stage, are probably not supposed to be competitive, some sort of a contest. But, considering the trepidation I had when I entered the foreign atmosphere of The Land of Spa, I sort of felt like I'd squeaked out a win on a long road stretch. Maybe next trip, I'd have a little more home field advantage. "Next trip"...I thought to myself, and yet I didn't think I was at all getting a head of myself. As I held Kim while I was falling asleep, she was holding my hand while already asleep. I thought, as I drifted off, she sure does smell good, her skin sure is soft, my back sure does feel good, and we sure have some bitchin' wines to drink. Yum, yum, yum....

VI

- Houston; November, 1993

A n E.R. resident, a friend of mine, just a friend, an extremely attractive and remarkably sassy third year resident with slightly longer than shoulder length red hair and a fair complexion with scattered freckles that seemed to be decreasing in the autumnal months compared to when we first met during the late summer and a hard body from her essential addiction to running, biking, and swimming as her on-when-you're-on-off-when-you're-off E.R. schedule allowed, paged me at about 1:30 in the morning on a Thursday night in early November, knowing that I was on call, and in house.

"I've got one of your kinds of guys down here in the E.R.," she said, when I answered her page just a few minutes later. I didn't typically sleep but an hour or two, three at the most, maybe from 4 to 7 in the morning or so, when I was on call. I suppose I knew that I was going to be tired the next day regardless, such that I might as well get some work done, particularly in the late hours of the night and early morning, as a commonly decreased intensity of seeing patients allowed. This seemed a pragmatic way to be sure that I was making progress on all fronts: the clinical responsibilities; the potential patient enrollment, even there, directly in the E.R., or by seeing consults while in house, or just by snooping around; and on the research side of things, some data analysis and review, maybe in the cafeteria, a quiet lounge, or one of the on-call rooms, which was what I was in the middle of doing when Kathy paged me. After all, I was increasingly in the lab by then, allowing for a fairly flexible schedule, including sleeping as needed the next day, waking in time for at least touching base with my research techs in the afternoon. This sort of thing wasn't too disruptive to the overall schedule, since it was only a couple of days a month, and handling it this way, I could usually be well rested enough the next evening to get a few more hours of productive data analysis and/or writing in, before falling asleep at a reasonable, regular hour like midnight or 1 a.m., allowing for a rapid return to a more normal schedule. Plus, sometimes the late hour, the environment, and sporadic interesting patient encounters could give me a manic-like infusion of energy, such that I found I got a fair amount of shit done some nights.

"What does that mean?" I sarcastically responded to Kathy, "Is he cute?"

"I suppose to some he could be," she said without pause, showing her typically understated, but quick sense of humor, or at least her immunity to mine. "But he's rip-roaringly HIV-positive, and he's fucked up in the head."

Knowing Kathy, "rip-roaringly HIV-positive" could either indicate advanced disease, i.e. AIDS, or refer to his being flamingly gay, but I was especially going to need a little more detail on the "fucked up in the head" part. Presumably, this was in reference to some sort of obvious behavioral issue disrupting or at least entertaining the E.R. staff and probably not some sort of subtle abnormality on a not likely to have been administered yet detailed neurologic exam. Maybe because I have a tendency toward a passionate love for molecular minutia, I was drawn toward the kind of no b.s. direct approach that folks like Kathy necessarily exhibited in their daily work. She was the kind of physician (and person) that wanted the huge gaping wounds, the flagrant life-threatening defects that she could recognize and dramatically make an impact on by doing something: a tension pneumothorax that required not only brains and experience to appropriately recognize in a chaotic setting, but the balls (or ovary equivalents) to immediately intervene, with no regard for the potential negative consequences of action, only the far more likely and disastrous consequences of not acting; a belly stab wound that required a gloved finger poking into the skin defect, feeling deep for either the barrier of only partially penetrated musculature and an intact peritoneum that indicated that the situation was no big rush and that the patient could hang around awhile and maybe even occupy a compulsive rotating medical student vs. the soft gushy feel of bowels and blood and other tissue juices that meant an immediate trip to the O.R., without stopping at go and collecting your insurance papers; or in the gray areas between, the immediate acquisition of a peritoneal lavage kit, which I had seen her begin using to tap someone's belly to see if there was blood in it by subsequent lab tests (thus also earning an essentially immediate trip up to the O.R.) before it was even completely unwrapped by the assisting personnel. Then there were, I suppose, the outside of work life equivalents: a rock that needed to be climbed; a ski slope with the highest concentration of warning signs on the mountain that needed to be down-hilled; and in my one or two urban equivalent encounters, a row of shot glasses that needed to be consumed to prove her abilities, right along side mine, until out of mercy (for both of us, as I don't tend to loose these particular athletic events, but I knew she wouldn't stop until she had either died or made us both wish we had), I acknowledged her potential greater skill because of a lower body mass index. These were the particular attributes, along with her healthy, wholesome, and functional beauty, that made me want to make passionate love to her every time I saw her if I allowed myself to think too much. It was out of extreme respect for her abilities, and maybe even more so because despite our differences in approach and the scope and focus of our work, she truly respected mine as well, and that she had the intelligence (verified by a highly successful academic record that obviously covered a lot more in the past than just belly probing) to understand everything we talked about related to what I was doing professionally, that I never made my non-professional feelings socially evident. Although, I suppose it did almost come out, but if it did we didn't remember, when we were so dangerously scraping away the surface and potentially allowing things to explode from the alcohol-exposed deep, on the inhibition-nullifying shot contest night, as words of mutual praise came out easily from close mouths on close faces of physically and emotionally tired work-committed and acutely undersexed, for different reasons, adults, who could smell and almost taste their mutual tequila-tainted breath and came within lip surface scraping micrometers of kissing, before they both realized that the aftermath wasn't worth it, that it could somehow ruin things. I might agree with Billy Crystal's character in *When Harry Met Sally* that men and women that are attracted to each other can't be friends, but if they avoid late night drinking sessions together, they can at least be productive, professional colleagues.

"I don't know, Kathy. Sounds more like a psych thing. Maybe you need a psych consult from the boys and girls down the hall in One-South," I said teasingly. Even if that were true, I would go down to the E.R., even if she just needed someone to draw blood....or empty the trash. One-South was the locked-in Psychiatry Ward for psych E.R. admissions and short term observations, before more permanent disposition, ideally suited for the kind of extreme screwed-up-ness that not infrequently accompanied visits to this kind of hospital in the wee hours.

"Maybe," she said, unfortunately taking my comment seriously, "but I just have a hunch about this guy. He seems psychotic, for sure. I remember that much from medical school; but other than that, he doesn't seem crazy, you know, like he hasn't been crazy for a long time, so maybe it's an AIDSy thing, you're kind of thing. I don't know. That probably doesn't make any sense. Plus, I just don't like those psych guys, they're kind of weird." And then, after a brief pause, and exposing a more personal connection, she added. "Plus, we have cookies down here. Alicia brought them in. They're homemade chocolate chip."

"I'll be right there," I enthusiastically responded, as if it were the cookies that pushed me over the edge. Truth is, like I said, Kathy was the kind of person I would do just about anything for, for lots of reasons. Plus, if she had a hunch about a patient, and she thought I could help, that's worth more than all the cookies in the world (or at least Houston). She was the kind of physician that if she paged me in the middle of the night and said she thought she had an alien down in the E.R., I would come running, with my special alien sample collection kit.

When I got down to the E.R. and went into the long observation room, with two opposing rows of beds, most with their surrounding curtains open, where I assumed my new consult would be, I saw Kathy at the nurse's station located towards the far end of the room. For the few seconds before she noticed me, I admired her concentration on her current task, and the way her soft hair fell partially over the right side of her face while she was leaning her head slightly forward, and the way it laid on her right shoulder and upper back, the way she bit her lower lip, which she did sometimes when she was thinking (or trying not to barf up tequila). In a moment, she might take her right hand and push her hair back behind her ear, really getting down to business. As if she sensed me, or maybe as I might wish she did, she looked up and over to me, gave a soft, fatigue diluted smile, quickly grabbed a chart off the top of the counter at the nurse's station, where she had specially placed it, and began walking towards me.

"He's all yours," she said, handing me the chart and simultaneously pointing with a slight head nod to a young male patient, who was in restraints in one of the eight parallel beds on one side of the room, one of only three patients on that side, and with no one in either of the immediately adjacent beds. "The cookies are in the lounge next to the supply room."

With that, she turned and immediately went back to the nurse's station, then after giving a few authoritative but polite commands, headed back over to the hopping trauma rooms. A visit would be nice, but she was busy, and by now, she knew that I didn't like to be messed with while I was working.

...

My new patient was a young white male, maybe in his late twenties or early thirties, with thick, wavy light brown hair and dazed blue eyes. As I gathered by quickly reading his brief admit note while standing a few feet from the foot of his bed, he had been picked up by H.P.D., as he apparently was wandering aimlessly in a residential neighborhood a few blocks east of Montrose, actually not too far from my own neighborhood. He was apparently confused when encountered, and had become slightly agitated with the police (never a good idea). Insightfully, they did not perceive him as intoxicated, but more likely mentally disturbed, and brought him down to the Ben Taub E.R. He was readily identified as he had his wallet on his person, and in a surprising demonstration of not usually expected efficiency or conscientiousness, his medical records had actually been pulled from the basement, and so I had them with me along with the results of the vital signs at admission.

Timothy W. was 28, and was known to have advanced AIDS. His last CD4 count, from approximately two months prior, was only 87. He had had past admissions for Pneumocystis carinii pneumonia (PCP) and some other suspected complications. He had had a few other clinic visits for miscellaneous complaints, including diarrhea, but there was no apparent record of past CNS or behavior abnormalities, at least on my quick scan through his records.

When I approached him, he was in 4 point restraints, with his wrists and ankles secured tightly to the bed rails via soft leather straps. He was quiet, but behind his stillness there was a confused and frightful look in his haunted eyes.

"I'm Dr. Pearson," I introduced myself, standing at the side of his bed, on his left. "Your doctors asked me to come see you, to help you feel better," I continued, politically acknowledging my current consult status, and not having anything more insightful or reassuring to say.

He looked over at me, seemingly lucid and calm, although a little groggy, perhaps, and said, initially softly and gently, and then barking out the second part, "I'm thirsty…I want to drink your piss."

Interesting, I thought, maybe a little loss of inhibition?

"Let me get you some ice water," I matter-of-factly responded, not overtly acknowledging the slightly weird and socially inappropriate nature of his statement, but beginning, hopefully, to incorporate it into what I thought could be going on with him.

I returned just a few moments later, with a Styrofoam cup of ice water, which I got from the break room, and quickly chewing the last bite of the cookie I had grabbed at the same time and then wiping the crumbs from my mouth.

I got closer to him and slowly bent forward to hold the cup to his lips, assuming he would raise up to take it in mutual human endeavor, given his expressed thirst, and his obvious hospital-imposed physical impairment. Horrifically, he lunged forward and took a big bite out of the Styrofoam cup, the edge of his subsequent bite imprint millimeters from where my thumb held it. I pulled back in shock and subsequent panic, quickly noting all that had just transpired while simultaneously processing the near miss exposure and my slim avoidance of potentially irreversible danger. He said, eyes glaring at me, "I want to suck your cock. I want to drink your piss."

I was instantaneously much more awake than I had been two minutes previously, and at the same time, had unavoidably developed a profound dislike for this mortal fragment who had the appalling nerve to put me, of all people, at risk for the same malady that he had willfully put himself at risk for. Clearly, this evaluation and workup wasn't going to get very far with him in his current agitated, disoriented state, not that I deeply gave a shit at the moment. I looked at the cup, with its likely saliva-coated tooth indentations compared to where my hand still was, like a pathologist noting the margins on a recent surgically excised tumor for prognosticating whether it had all been removed or increased danger of tumor and clinical recurrence remained. I threw it in the nearest biohazard bag on the way to the nurse's station, from which Kathy, back with another patient for observation in that room, looked up at me inquisitively, implying an unspoken "done already?" I suppose being a few moments away from my recent panic, and seeing this person that I was so fond of, brought me back to some semblance of caring physician-hood, and I replied, "He needs some of that Hound-dog medicine."

"Hound-dog" was the affectionate nickname I had acquired, for use in settings such as the current one, from my chief Surgery resident way back in my medical school core surgery rotation, for the antipsychotic drug with the trade name of Haldol. Vitamin H is another similarly respectful occasionally used designation. My Chief was undeniably a redneck, in most senses of the word, originally from Arkansas I believe, allowing as one might for the application of redneck designation to someone who actually had an M.D. and was in his fifth year of post graduate residency training. He approached many frustrating issues with the irreverence and pragmatism that his life situation at the time justified. Haldol was commonly administered in combination with the benzodiazepine Ativan, in proportions more familiar to those of us spending any time in E.R.'s than rum and coke or scotch and soda, to agitated patients who were either psychotic, manic with psychosis, or just acting fucking weird and scary, to calm them down while we figured out which of the above they were.

I wrote for the order and walked away, not bothering to meet Kathy's glance, as she would essentially figure it out if she saw my quick note before the nurse drew up the meds and gave my foul-mouthed patient the shot, and I strolled back down the hall to the break room. There I sat, gathering myself, while I ate six more of Sherrie's very satisfying home made chocolate chip cookies, and drank a cup of strong coffee, wishing I had something more resembling milk than the plastic jar of generic powdered synthetic lard cream substitute that I poured into my coffee, which I normally drank black, until it formed an inch thick sediment at the bottom of my...unbitten...Styrofoam cup. I was having one of those surrealistic moments, wondering what the fuck I was doing, sitting on this lovely orange vinyl chair, surrounded by a couple of keeping-their-distance, nomad-like 11-7 shift African-native male nurses, at almost two in the morning instead of being in bed with my wife, in a real house, in a city that we mutually dwelled in.

"Oh well," I thought, as my sugar, fat, and caffeine kicked in while Timothy's Haldol and Ativan were having hopefully largely opposite effects, and I stood up, pressing down my scrubs where they had climbed up my legs, along with my hopefully transient self doubt, and I went back out into the main E.R. observation area. "This guy needs my help, God-damn-it," I said to my secret self, "and I may be the only guy here that may know what to do for him."

In an act of perhaps less than stellar professional maturity, I took advantage of my status as an attending to have my consult transferred to the locked E.R. Psych Ward. I probably could have worked him up there in the E.R., after the anti-psychotic/anxiolytic juice kicked in, but I probably thought that a little time in la-la land would be appropriate pay back for his less than cordial behavior towards me up to that point. Without directly passing Mr. Timothy W., I went around the observation area and proceeded through a more or less back entry to the same nurse's station where just a short while before I had harmlessly been lusting after my colleague. While subconsciously noting that the observation beds had more than half filled just in my brief absence, I wrote the orders for his Psych Ward temporary admission, actually not really that outside the realm of what was objectively best anyway, given his mental condition, not worrying about whether one of the only eight 24 hr. observation psych beds was available, knowing from extensive past experience, both as a student and E.R. consulting staff physician, that multiple similar patients could be kept strapped to their gurneys in the hallways surrounding the physician work stations and separating them from both a handful of exam rooms on one side and the official observation area, with its eight beds, on the other side of the E.R. Psych Ward.

This would allow not only a likely to be needed E.R. bed to be available for some minor trauma or still-blossoming-emergency surgery patient, but would also put Timothy's baby sitting and probably soon to be needed social placement in the hands of the more appropriately qualified and staffed Psychiatry personnel. As I had not yet completed (or actually, begun) my official consultation evaluation, I would appropriately be by to see him from the Neuro perspective fairly shortly.

In fact, I went immediately, if not hurriedly, to the E.R. psych ward, pushed the code on the door to enter, and then took a few more minutes to ensure maximum Hound-dog medicine effectiveness by briefly pausing in the TV room area at the front end of the ward. In there, the rows of non-dangerous vinyl padded chairs against the three walls without the TV held a scattered array of the more well behaved and docile but not quite all there "visitors". A few other, perhaps even more functional, patients stood near the entry of the room to which the main door of the ward opened towards, furthest from the TV, and where one young, slightly disheveled white male, exhibiting classic symptoms of the manic, was gaining increasing attention from patients and particularly staff, for his progressively loud and perhaps perceived as potentially emerging threatening comments and behavior. I stood about five feet behind him, towards the main door, generally surveying the whole room, in that brief fatigued pause of the middle of the night/early morning time zone, wherein one simultaneously recognizes feeling acutely tired, being hungry, but too tired to reach ravenous (and which I was probably protected from by the recent cookies anyway), and having a funny taste in your crusty mouth while wondering whether that smell is from you or the surrounding medical funk, but can yet still gather oneself, to muster up just adequate energy and competence for whatever task is yet required and for which his training and especially interests has prepared him for. *The Terminator* was on the TV, a movie, of course, we all love and admire, but which I distinctly remember pondering, in my state of borderline exhaustion-induced insight, whether was truly appropriate given the high percentage of paranoid schizophrenics and other synaptically-challenged humans in the audience.

After the scene where Arnold, as the still more respected bad terminator, guns down an entire police station, gaining at least the attention if not the belief of the psychiatrist, and acutely hoping that none of the watching patients were planning on taking a similar approach with our resident psych docs, I walked down the hallway on that side. After passing two other gurneys, one harboring a large black woman who made a very sexual comment to me as I passed, to the point, that along with Timothy's earlier lewd advances, I acutely found myself wondering if I was wearing some new irresistible after shave, I found a very quiet and frightened young man, remotely resembling the belligerent fetishist I had so recently encountered on the other side of the E.R. He was lined up in the same head to foot arrangement as the other four or five beds lining the wall and containing the overflow patients I had so generously contributed to, and he was facing out towards the hall, not just looking at the wall like some of the others. He still seemed to want to avoid or at least not acknowledge the confusion and chaos passing by him at a steady stream, but even before I came completely up to him, I could see a more perceptive fear and uncertainty, and what almost seemed like shame, in his face. His dopaminergic neurons having been effectively massaged by the non-phenothiazine neuroleptic, he was likely now, at best, only a blunted version of his past self, but a more officially allowed version of him than that which we had previously encountered, and which I now suspected, and maybe hoped, was a manifestation of ADC with psychosis, a not particularly common combination of symptoms brought about by molecular processes that I and others like me hopefully were at least beginning to have some sort of future manipulatable emerging handle on.

I came along beside him, and paused, waiting until he had registered me, so as not to startle him when I greeted him. It was pointless, and potentially counterproductive, to imply that we had encountered each other previously, when he was maybe anti-Tim.

"Hi," I said, looking hopefully calmly into his cautious face, "I'm Dr. Pearson," I left off the "I'm here to help you" part.

He didn't say anything right away, just staring up at me, not quite ready to be hopeful, I guess, with moistening eyes, still reflecting what must have seemed like a bad dream state he found himself unwillingly in.

"Are you Mr. W.?" I asked next, in a tone hinting at not really knowing, and needing some participation from him in the form of an answer.

I sensed the slightest up and down micro trimmer of his chin, a still reserved acknowledging gesture that one would have missed if not clinically scrutinizing his face. I guess I was starting to see the Timothy W. more like the one his Mom loved and raised than the evil piss-drinking ogre I resented previously, and I not only didn't feel threatened, but I felt sorry for him being there, being there in the locked psych ward and in the E.R. to begin with.

I didn't look for any other clues of who or what he was or what he was capable of, as I reached down to un-strap his left wrist closest to me, and then his right wrist, farthest away, up against the wall, leaning over him, my lab coat rubbing against the sheet covering him in his skimpy gown, while saying, "Let's get you into a room where we can talk, and get you away from all this crazy crap." I think I intended crazy as in the lay chaos sense, not as the slang adjective for the diagnoses matching half or more of our ward mates.

Either because he felt reassured or had no better options, he took my offered right arm for support, sat up, then slipped down to his feet, while still holding my arm, and walked with me the five or ten feet further down the hall, before we entered together one of the small empty exam rooms, with always-everything-inside-visible safety glass windows and two vinyl chairs as ugly as those of the TV room on opposite sides of a harmless desk, composed of some sort of synthetic wood grain appearing product, likely having been shown in careful industry studies to not be destructible or break-down-able into dangerous smaller parts.

VII

- Houston; Early November, 1993

The bulk of my subsequent patient interview with Timothy W. I shared the next evening with my park crew, as part of my fatigue-compromised minimal contribution to the cool autumn night's conversation, on one of those increasingly rare occasions that we were all present, even Curtis. Talking about patients in this manner is commonplace among physicians, and is in no way some sort of violation of any kind of patient confidentiality thing. We don't use names, and the recipients of any information revealed in this manner have no way of knowing the particular patient, nor are they in any way capable of doing anything that would positively or negatively impact the essentially theoretical person as a consequence of having participated in the conversation. We probably do it mostly for our own psyches. I usually shared this kind of thing with Kim.

I had spent longer with this patient than I had ever intended and probably longer than would be typically necessary for the level of consultation, in part, because I did indeed, after all, enroll him in my clinical trial, after judging that he was adequately competent to decide on such, and getting a confirming opinion to that effect from the Psych attending on call. Although we already had many patients with similarly low or even worse CD4 counts, there certainly weren't but a handful, at best, of patients who had even close to the psychotic symptoms at presentation. ADC is actually only uncommonly accompanied by such prominent behavioral abnormalities essentially constituting psychosis. After addressing the more immediate clinical and personal/social concerns in my roll as admitting physician, as a pragmatic matter for trial enrollment, I completed essentially all of the necessary first visit type information collection, a detailed neurologic physical examination, including the "Pearson scoring system" for muscle strength, and even collected three tubes of blood, two of which went back with me to my lab. I stopped short of doing a baseline lumbar puncture, as it was four in the morning by then, but I did go back to see Tim on the ward around 10 a.m. or so, later on that morning, to retrieve a few basic pieces of information I had forgotten when working from sleepy memory the night before and without the aid of the official specific clinical trial enrollment forms to guide my history and physical examination. At that point, I did indeed do a lumbar puncture, and even ordered a head CT, with contrast, to further rule out any brain organic lesions, such as toxoplasmosis or lymphoma, which would exclude him from the trial, and which were pretty unlikely, based on absence of focal signs, confirmed on a shorter repeat Neuro exam, which agreed with my impressions from the "night" before.

"I think after the meds had kicked in, he was glad to have someone to talk to," I reflected to the group.

"I imagine he was pretty frightened," Carl observed. "I know I would be if I were in the same position."

"I hear ya. I know I'd be pretty scared to be in the same small room with Jeff," Curtis sarcastically commented while beginning a slow steady orbit around our bench.

"Oh come on, you know you'd love to be trapped in the same room with me," I sarcastically responded. "It's every gay guy's fantasy." Then after a brief pause, I continued, turning my head over my right shoulder towards Carl. "But you're right. He was scared. He's scared in general. He started crying when he told me that he sometimes can't remember the code to get into his apartment complex's gate, where he's apparently been living for years, and that things like that are happening more and more often. He had no idea how he got to where the police picked him up, or what he was doing before then, but I got the impression, he had simply been trying to get home or had even made it home, but then panicked and got confused when he couldn't even get in."

"Is that because of the ... AIDS?" Frank asked, speaking the last word with the aghast tone of B horror movie drama, as if just saying it put one at risk of exposure.

"Duh," Curtis said, loudly, while poking his head in over Frank's shoulder, immediately to the side of his left cheek, as he buzzed behind the bench, between where Carl was standing in back and where Frank had been calmly sitting, but suddenly lurched forward when startled. Then, as Curtis continued around the group, "Haven't you listened to any of the shit we've talked about, like the last six fucking months or so, about what it is that Jeff even does here?"

"Well...I thought so...gosh, I just was trying to understand..." Frank responded somewhat timidly, as if feeling he was a step or two behind the other kids in the class.

"Turns out he had been living in that apartment with his partner...for a long time, and they had both been ill for awhile. His partner died about three or four months ago," I continued, slowly.

"Of AI..." Frank began to inquire, and then caught himself.

"My patient had actually been diagnosed with AIDS first, and his partner had apparently been wonderful. Then when his partner got sick, he deteriorated much more quickly, and my patient had to take care of him, even as it got more challenging because of his not yet recognized mental deterioration, right as it was getting to be so demanding. Since his partner died, he's apparently had no one."

"Could it be grief as well, then?" Carl asked sincerely, alluding to the mental compromise of my patient.

"That part certainly can't help, but it's clearly more, and it sounds like it's been going on for some time, you know, before his partner died," I answered.

"What about family?" Rick asked, which was interesting, given what I perceived as the issues with his father.

"That's the worst fucking part," I blurted out, apparently re-igniting the anger or at least the frustration that I had felt the night before, or actually, that morning. "He told me that he hasn't seen his parents since he told them he was gay."

"How long ago was that?" Carl asked, while slightly turning to his left to notice Curtis passing him again in his steady circular motion, and offering up an expression of amused but not irritated bewilderment at this steady pacing around, head mostly down to the ground.

"I'm not certain, but I think it's been quite awhile, maybe almost ten years or so. He spoke tenderly of his mother, and clearly misses her, but it seems out of the question for him to even think about contacting them," I responded.

"So they don't even know he's sick?" Carl continued.

"Or going to fucking die soon," Curtis ejected as he rotated around us.

"Probably not," I answered Carl, as Curtis's comments seemed off limits to the rest of us for now.

We sat there in silence for a few minutes, the only noise that of Curtis's dance-like stomping around us.

"So how's he doing now," Carl thankfully asked, breaking the quiet.

After a potentially maybe unnecessarily long pause, during which my mind had been elsewhere and back, in multiple poorly defined cycles, I essentially sub-consciously finally responded, "Better...better, for now."

VIII

- Recollections: San Francisco; Autumn, 1990

Returning to San Francisco after our spa trip, it was as if an unspoken barrier had been crossed. Despite resuming the demanding tasks of our current professions and doing them with the same dedication and high level of accomplishment as usual, we had become a couple, in that sense that it was essentially unnatural to do anything alone that could be done together, even if somewhat less efficiently.

Saturday errands were particularly exemplary. A far cry from the usual haste I'd begrudgingly apply to no longer procrastinatable duties, such as doing laundry, writing checks for the few bills I was burdened with like utilities or the minimum payment on the never decreasing credit card balance, these and similar sundry activities became sessions of shared real-world encounters of such implied closeness, intimacy, and burgeoning commitment that they may as well have been officially foreplay.

Groceries were purchased together, even if initially they were separated into Kim piles (fresh fruit, yogurt, vegetables I hadn't known existed) and Jeff piles (reduced for quick sale meats mutually agreed still safe for consumption, hamburger helper, whichever decent domestic beer was on sale and/or most cost effective per can or bottle) in the cart or basket and purchased separately at the register. Picking out such items for those increasingly uncommon meals eaten individually at corresponding apartments prompted affectionate comments of gentle agastness (on Kim's part) and, on my part, alternating sarcasm with sexual innuendo ("Oh, you mean you can cut that up and put it in a salad, too?") to true gastronomic curiosity ("How in the hell do you eat that little armor-coated thing?" in reference to the newly introduced concept of an arti-choke, for example).

Increasingly, there became purchases of obvious partner influence, such as the bananas and/or whole wheat bread that Kim may have placed in my pile as a suggested alternative to a quick breakfast of Pop-Tarts on clinic days and…maybe not so many examples of impact in the other direction. Also, there was a steady growth in both pre-made list-targeted and spontaneously assembled collections of items for our mutually consumed meals, more formally consisting of skilled (on Kim's part) assemblages of members of the various food groups. Our Napa trip had ignited a sincere and academically-approached interest in wine on my part, and I at least contributed to these joint dinners by choosing what I deemed as appropriately matched good but not overly expensive wines, with acknowl-edged growingly consistent success (or else Kim was her usually polite self and/or we weren't all that picky or discriminating in those days).

These joint meal grocery acquisitions were initially placed on Kim's side of the cart, as without exception they were prepared and enjoyed in her nicer apartment near Lower Pacific Heights. However, as a chivalrous Texas boy, I felt obliged to pay for them. As they increased in frequency and sophistication and as they were in the piles that included Kim's other needs, including non-grocery items, this quickly exceeded my relatively finite grocery funds, such that eventu-ally I just put in what I could, and Kim filled in the rest, regardless of whether that may be less than or more than 50 % of the total.

I still ate a lot of lunches at the UCSF cafeteria, which no one would ever even accidentally confuse with world class cuisine, or some nearby quick-serving places, mostly along Irving Street and 9th Ave within just a ten minute or so walk of the medical center. Most of these were the likes we in South Texas might col-lectively and thus potentially inappropriately label as "Chinese Restaurants" (or at least as serving "Chinese food" if not granting full restaurant status), not having been afforded opportunities to discern differential Asian origins, at least at the strange sounding (and sometimes tasting) food appreciating or at least consum-ing level. Minh Tri on Irving between 5th and 6th, as a source for really cheap Vietnamese lunches, got me borderline addicted to rice and noodle plates, such that I would seek them out specifically when I eventually returned to Houston and this time around realized and took advantage of the rather substantial Viet-namese section not too far from me between 59 and downtown. And if more lubrication was needed or enough time had passed for me to have forgotten that it wasn't, I might go to the Empress of China on 9th Ave, between Irving and Judah, popularly known as "oil changers" and which in the debate as to why, I would certainly favor the greasy nature of its food rather than the topographical fact of its backing onto a mechanics shop, although excluding that the two may be related would have required a bit more detailed chemical analyses. Despite the fairly unavoidable occasional late night meal at the Hospital cafeteria when on call, I was increasingly spending the night at Kim's and thus grabbing (healthier) breakfasts there, and high quality leftovers were gradually replacing burgers and such for lunch and even call meals. Hence, the grocery boundary was blurring, to the point where within several weeks there were no longer distinctions at the register and a progressively smaller "To Jeff's Apt" aliquot of miscellaneous food and supply items were separated out post-purchase in Kim's kitchen, typically placed, then, in only one of the newly emptied multiple grocery bags. Without any formal discussions of what our relationship was evolving toward, even casual conversations were initiated in a different manner those first few post-Calistoga weeks. "Do you want to rent a video?" on a usual Friday night had become "What do you want to see tonight?"

Over the next two months I spent progressively less time back at my own apartment. Despite being perhaps 5-10 minutes further away from UCSF and essentially equally further away from The General, I found it just as fast and maybe even faster to make it to both places from Kim's apartment, when using the bus or Muni, as it seemed that her snootier part of town was serviced by lines that ran more frequently, or at least more reliably. I seldom used my car that much anymore, maybe occasionally to go from my apartment over to Kim's.

I stayed over at my place on some days when I was post-call, knowing that I may not be on my social or physical-appearing best, or on nights when I was pre-call, knowing that nights filled with at least one or two rounds of love making and my habit of post-sex touching, and smelling, and holding of Kim and purposely fighting off falling asleep so as to not deny myself of as many minutes and occasionally hours of these pleasures, these growing addictions, as possible were not conducive to remotely optimal function the next day. Under either of these circumstances I was especially more likely to stay at my place, which I was increasingly appreciating as less attractive, certainly less decorated, and less fitted with objects of comfort than Kim's apartment, if she were also possibly in a situation in which she may need to do a little work at home in the evening or if she may have a big day the next day and hence in need of a little bit more sleep herself than our usual nights at that point in time, and especially on those relatively rare occasions when she may be travelling, such as to LA or San Diego, as I still didn't see myself as feeling comfortable staying at "her" place without her being there.

IX

- Recollections: San Francisco; November, 1990

From the time I met Kim and we started going out, I always had the sense that she came from a well to do family. She had gone to an expensive school (Pomona/Claremont Colleges) and she had nicer things, even just clothes and jewelry, than one might expect for a single young professional working in a city as expensive as San Francisco. In our early conversations that seemingly covered infinite ground and always opened unpredictable topics, it always came across (without any sense of snobbery or bragging) that she and her brother had always had the kinds of opportunities that such kids have in a manner where they don't realize that other children may not have had similar backgrounds and without necessarily appreciating that it made them somehow privileged. Maybe all the other kids of similarly affluent families in the same schools and neighborhoods did many of all the same activities, so that they would never really notice any differences significant enough to promote an even remote sense of entitlement.

Since open space, beer, the opportunity for at least pursuit of an attractive classmate or even a stranger, a vehicle to accomplish those three things, and team sports were all I really had ever wanted in the past and I could largely care less about money at present, other than being able to pay my rent, eat, and occasionally have some fun (and now afford a decent date for Kim and I every now and then when we weren't just hanging out), I never flat out asked Kim if she was rich, as I could care less. She was already all of the things one could ever hope for, and we both had promising careers and futures; surely the rest was just trivial detail.

Instead, in that proper kind of male behavior regarding other males, and in the Texas polite and non-agenda way, I asked Kim (probably not until after a few weeks and many conversations) what her father did. She explained it, almost as if using a rehearsed, concise but adequately detailed blurb (as one might expect from an informed marketing/PR type person) and I've discussed it with him personally on many occasions subsequently. And, I'm still not sure I've ever quite understood it completely. It certainly is basically related to import/export endeavors, but in some kind of indirect, largely legal and administrative fashion. It particularly seemed somehow amazing to me that our production/export and import and merchandising operations had become so complex that there was a specific need for these functions outside of capabilities of individual companies themselves, and that, clearly, someone could make a really nice living doing these sorts of services. I suspect it had to do with aspects of incredible business and legal specialization combined with operations that our Government had in conjunction with long standing tradition made so extraordinarily complex that most companies, especially relatively small ones, just didn't even want to mess with some of these operational details for fear of fines, or worse. I think Robert (Kim's Dad, or "daddy") had particularly been involved early on in trade dealings with China (including at that time in some more direct importing and subsequent retailing), that this had especially positioned him for success in his broader endeavors as well as particularly helping other companies involved in our massive and likely to grow trade with China. He had a tremendous background now in international business, superimposed on a law degree with paralleling legal career focus on trade and business. He and Kim's mom (or "mom") had lived in San Diego, pretty much, I gathered, since right after he graduated from law school. Kim's mom, Patricia, also had a good business background, having variously participated in her husband's firm as properly raising babies and later administering family and social matters allowed, the latter often not readily separable from development and maintenance aspects of her husband's business.

...

The first time I met Kim's parents was when they came up to San Francisco for social and personal reasons and of course, squeezed in a visit with their daughter, maybe a couple of weeks before Thanksgiving. Kim's father ("Call me Bob") and

I seemed to get along quite well from the very beginning. He appreciated my education, admired my work ethic, and respected my family background and its manifestations he occasionally specifically noted in my apparent "upbringing". He didn't appear to mind how much his daughter and I were beginning to care about each other.

Bob was tall, maybe 6'2" or 6'3", and was built solidly, thin in the middle aged professional, largely well maintained sense, with just a bit of the gut of the successful and content American Dream life. It didn't really show unless he was wearing something like a moderately tight polo shirt, and he seemed at peace or content with it, like another checked off item on a long list of successfully checked off life boxes. He was an avid sailor. His complexion would probably be pretty light and fair if he didn't spend so much time outside, and his face had that ruddy look of a fair skinned man who spent time in the sun and getting wind blown. His cheeks often appeared just lightly flushed, like he'd recently exerted himself or had a scotch before you saw him. He had thick, wavy, light reddish brown hair, with just a hint of gray at the sideburns and very front. He was straightforward, spoke his mind, and had a good heart, despite a likely tendency to be firm and aggressive in his business endeavors.

Kim's mother was an elegant and beautiful middle aged woman. If the old sayings are true, I guess that boded well for me in the future if things should turn out to be serious and I should ever find myself with Kim at a similar age. Patricia was maybe an inch or two taller than Kim actually. She had perhaps slightly coarser features than Kim, but lovely cheek bones and the same full lips and perfect mouth that Kim had. Her hair was darker than Kim's, a very dark brown, and her natural skin color seemed to be darker than Kim's. In fact, in consideration of only skin and hair color, Kim was quite the lovely hybrid of her parents, a pairing that had seemed to generate as near to human perfection as I'd ever set eyes on at least. Patti was in tremendous shape. Health club addiction was only beginning to emerge in our society over the last decade, but I gathered that Patti's was more from an essentially lifetime's passion for multiple rigorous tennis outings a week. This and a fondness for gardening were largely responsible for what I gradually noted as an essentially year-round tan.

Kim and her mom were very close. Bob may have considered Kim "Daddy's little girl" and Kim may have allowed this and felt it, but she and her mom spoke on the phone often, and they seemed to get along almost like sisters when they were together, whether in San Francisco or San Diego. There's probably something quite unique about Mother-Daughter relationships. But, Kim was clearly close to both her parents. And after all, you don't have to choose one over the other, at least over the long haul. Kim's mom was so sweet and caring towards me, and we got along splendidly, again, from the very beginning.

...

Bob and Patti enjoyed San Francisco, and would quite commonly come to see their daughter coinciding with some event, such as a favorite opera being performed at The War Memorial. On this particular occasion, it was fall, and probably a little cooler than in the usual dwellings of these sun worshippers. I think they were more or less just visiting for the fun of it and maybe for some early Christmas shopping and, of course, restauranting (which was world class- so I heard- in SF, and still just primitively burgeoning in a more sleepy laid back San Diego). Of course, checking up on their daughter was always intentionally or subconsciously on their list. We had been dating about two months, I believe, and based on conversations that came up that weekend, I was no particular secret.

Kim's parents usually stayed at one of the luxury hotels in the downtown/ financial district area. Kim's place was too small to absorb them, even temporarily, in the sort of fashion they may prefer, especially when they were essentially on vacation and wanted to be spoiled. Plus, I think they recognized her adult stature and respected her privacy.

Given Kim's parents' fondness for site-seeing in San Francisco and submerging themselves in some of the unique aspects of the city's various neighborhoods, it was a good opportunity for Kim to further my civic educational level, which she had already proclaimed her lovely self dedicated to, as I was still pretty much at the Introductory Tourist level.

...

On this trip (and many afterwards as it had evolved into a favorite), Kim and Patti made reservations for high tea at the Compass Rose lounge in the St. Francis Hotel at Union Square.

I wondered if this could be some kind of a "test".

I wasn't really a sit and drink tea kind of guy. And, I'm pretty certain that I wasn't a sit in some sort of snooty ceremonial fashion and drink high tea kind of a guy. Had I been TOO good of a sport at the spa?

But walking around the Union Square area, with all the great shops, on a beautiful clear autumn day and having initially casual conversation with Kim's parents, with Kim there, was very pleasant. Watching Kim and her mother shop was something like watching an informative TV episode on a series like Animal Kingdom or such, and featuring an in-depth analysis on the female of the most sophisticated species discovered so far on another planet. Noting Bob's general demeanor during some of these specific moments, I realized that he had witnessed this ritual on many other occasions.

In particular shops one of the females would select an item of male clothing, and after brief comments inaudible to those of us observing, would hold it up against the appropriate mate, for style, size, or other mysterious reasons, at which point the male would try to receive the gesture in an enthusiastic manner while at the same time not appear to lose some of his maleness in the eyes and other senses of the remaining males in the small tribe subset.

With approximately six bags in various hands, we continued to stroll along and take in the various sites until "tea time". We passed and spent some time admiring the glorious old Curran Theatre, noting some of the upcoming shows that were scheduled. I made some mental notes on ones that Kim seemed to be particularly enthused about. We noted apparent progress or lack thereof, depending on one's perspective of how long things should take, on the Geary Theater, which had been closed for repairs since the earthquake.

At one point, essentially in Union Square proper, maybe in an effort to keep myself a bit grounded, I began counting the number of homeless or other people that approached us and asked for a handout. If I noted that the same individual asked more than one of us, on those occasions where the group had maybe spread out a bit, they only counted once. I think I remember specifically wondering if weekends like this may be better yielding for these beggars than a typical weekday. I supposed it could spin off a hypothesis related to who may be more generous: weekend shoppers and relaxers vs. weekday brown-baggers from all the nearby offices. Maybe I'd have to come back sometime during the week. Of course, this would be very difficult to control for all the admixed, complicating variables: the number of shoppers on weekdays vs. the staff that worked at the shops on weekends as well as weekdays, the number of tourists, and especially, the potentially variable numbers of the needy (hopefully needy) actually asking for money. After all, surely you're more likely to get something if you're one in 50 vs. one in 500, etc.

This must have been occupying more of my concentration than I realized, as at one point Kim caught my attention and asked, "Are you O.K.?"

"I'm great," I instantly responded, which gained me a quick but sincere kiss, which also made me look around for where Kim's parents may be...and I think I lost my count or purposely moved on to other things.

X

- Recollections: including Bethesda (NIH); 1988-1989

I used to think that I was good at being alone. Or actually, now that I thought about it, being alone again after having had something so different for a while, I felt, truly, that I used to be good at being alone, maybe even thrived on it. It is, after all, a key ingredient to the most productive life one can have. One can work whenever one wants to. Maybe even more importantly, one can think whenever one needs to. This is not only crucial to those who are plagued with overachieving, but especially to those who may have irregular schedules. One needs to be able to make substantial progress when the mental cylinders are clicking best. For complex reasons we still don't understand, perhaps related to yet to be identified motivation genes being transcribed in deep neuronal recesses at variable times, the synaptic equivalent of astrology or biorhythms, these hyper-productive episodes are not always predictable, or even worse, not able to be regimented amongst components of a "normal" life.

According to some, there may be sacrifices to be made in order to achieve this state of freedom of thought and task. Hence, while intellectually romantic and even admirable to some, the uninterruptable potentially maximally productive isolated state could come across as quasi-tragic to others, the "touchy-feely" sort I suppose. Those sentimentalists should keep in mind, however, that if a hyper-productive loner is afflicted with an acute sense of sad solitude and craves the need for social interaction or the challenge of convincing someone that he or she is worth spending time with, one could always take a field trip out to the real world, for sexual, ego-massaging, or psychic impaction relief reasons.

But now I wasn't so sure.

That was certainly the life I think I lived in Bethesda, though Bethesda may have been particularly suited to such, at least at my stage of training. Compared to close by areas around the medical center in Houston where there were quaint neighborhoods - some pretty nice ones - having an abundant supply of garage apartments, home or converted partial-home rentals and not only admixed smaller apartment complexes, but also bars and little eateries, the corresponding area in Bethesda made getting to and from the med center at the NIH neither particularly quaint nor conducive to spur of the moment companion searching on the way home. Parking at the Texas Medical Center had been a huge pain in the ass for students, who were supposed to park in a remote lot south of the medical center and take a shuttle, which took a particularly disciplined approach to morning scheduling that I tended to dislike and which was particularly hard to maintain on the likes of those surgery rotations mandating the often peri-dawn arrivals, but which at least gave a student the option of parking in one of many patient parking lots at a mere student-budget "you don't want to do this every day" impacting 6 or $7.00 a day. Arguably in any contest that would have many nationwide entries for worst, a strong contender NIH campus was probably even worse than Baylor and the Texas Medical Center, more so because it wasn't just the med center it was the entire area, which has northeast disease. Many know some of the most classic symptoms, such as very little room to drive around in, very little room to build individual housing or even small complexes thereof within a complexly determined radius involving formulas of commute tolerance/avoid bankruptcy, not enough space for parking (corollary of way too much to pay for whatever space could even be accessed legally), the obviously associated need to use typically southern scorned public transportation, which then exposes you to the worst of the process-the fact that most people with this regional-associated ailment just simply aren't the kind to say hi or be nice to similarly suffering strangers.

For the NIH, there was a big parking lot at the main clinical building 10, which shockingly was not intended for first year Internal Medicine interns, and parking then at various peripheral lots of a still competitive nature and the parking in which had to make one get out the map or pedometer to see if one were really saving any distance or time, certainly compared to walking from the train station, but maybe even from one's apartment building in my case. For like so many others, a slow tough swallow here, I actually lived in a… ugh… um… high-rise.

Though this cluster at Grosvenor where so many of us made our trails and small holes in the anthill were not of the New York skyscraper height, anything even in the 10 or 12 floor variety could make someone from my background feel like they had moved to another country or even planet. There were not even any sidewalks for crazies like me who might want to occasionally walk. So, I along with many other slightly variant droids (most without the "say hi "program installed) took the metro, which after all was only then one stop to the NIH, from whence I would stroll to wherever I needed to go such as the hospital or our laboratory in building 41, conveniently (finally something…) located next to the national library. Yes, if not already married, time at the NIH was certainly conducive to "alone" time.

This was certainly the type of life that I intended, at least, to relocate to San Francisco, a city which I had anticipated particularly facilitative of the ultimate "work-while-I-work-play-when-I-need-to-play-so-that-I-can-crank-it-out-when-back- in-work-mode" lifestyle. Or maybe I just never really took the time to notice whether I liked to be alone or not, as there was always so much shit to do, so much to learn, so much to read, so many tests to study for, so much data to analyze, so much writing to do. So, as I spent a lot of time alone, to apparently great effect, I guess I somehow insightfully realized or blindly rationalized that it was something I liked, for its consequences particularly and maybe for the thing itself. I don't know. Maybe I only had time to notice I was horny or lonely when I wasn't working.

Oh, sure, I had lots of relationships along the way. I'm not a freak. In addition to college romances, Medical School had its usual share of 3 to 9 month boyfriend-girlfriend things. Three worthy of noting, two for their apparent mutual satisfaction to both parties and amicable dissolutions, one for the consequent avoidance behavior, at least on my part, towards the very uncomfortable encounters the vestiges prompted in either social circumstances (e.g., class party) or professional settings (e.g., torrential moments in morning report or small, dark radiology reading rooms).

Residency at the NIH was more gracious for its potential diversity. For starters, the majority of my relationship-potential acquaintances were no longer in the exact same educational or professional stage category. Though this may be true for most residency programs compared to the usual medical school class scenario, I should think the diversity among other parameters is particularly pronounced for the NIH campus given the greater range from which it seems to draw not only it's trainees and even faculty, but especially visiting investigators - possibly made more liberal by being away and with a theoretical advantage (at least to some) of a pretty much guarantee of always leaving to go back home after a finite period. Such variety proved to be a particularly effective work distraction, when needed, and whether directly responsible or not, it or something else at least generated a couple of hit or miss one night stands via some of the more popular bars/cafes in the peri-NIH campus region.

One night in particular suddenly popped into my head, not because it specifically involved a successful effort at such a "romantic" distraction, but rather for an interesting guy that I actually met, whom I thought for a while might prove a reasonable channel to an apparently attractive woman who had potentially multiple reasons to engage in calorie burning and mind numbing physical entanglements, including out of possible spiteful revenge for the very individual who I now recall possibly trying to make this connection through. There were a bunch of bars in Bethesda, particularly along the Old Georgetown Road and surrounding area in which you might run into any of your various colleagues on a given night, including a Thai restaurant that served alcohol that a lot of us working in the lab I was associated with seemed to like to go to, where it was that I think I met and began to annoy this person while one night eating there alone.

He had just finished his training in pathology, which is an excellent field with which to combine research interests. He had come from, if I recall, one of those places like Albuquerque or Denver or Salt Lake City, wherein dwell a high percentage of wholesome people who like to ski and have families-sometimes, at least in the case of the first two places, multiple families (but not at the same time). So this guy had fairly recently gotten divorced and had a child who lived mostly with his ex, and although I don't think they got along all that great, that in itself was being regarded at least by me as not sufficient on its own to guarantee my striking out if the introduction were indeed to come through my temporary co-inebriating scholar cum matchmaker. Why one might ask if one were paying attention, as I apparently must have partially been doing that night, would the ex be available here in Bethesda where this guy had come to do some sort of biotech-nology fellowship and brought his current girlfriend with him , who had actually managed to get promoted to fiancé in the process? The only reason I could think of, and which apparently I kept telling him in that alcohol loosened conversation mode that lowers the threshold for frequent repetition, is something like he must be some stud to have brought two women with him. I'm pretty sure he told me the real reason that evening, but he more soberly reminded a more sober me on a couple subsequent encounters during which I believe I was still increasingly perplexing or frankly irritating him, as I apparently never seemed to be able to get the two women's names straight. He seemed to believe that I wanted to sleep either with both women or specifically his fiancée (and then new bride), as if I somehow had regarded him liberal enough to share partners by misinterpreting the reason why his ex had come along. In the end, it was simple enough but impressively noble. It was basically, and selflessly, so that their son would not be without his father for however many years of the fellowship.

Now tonight I even found myself contrasting his 2X (as in two times, not two ex's) situation of basically "bringing along the woman" vs. my currently being shut out self.

Finally though at the NIH, I did have a quite pleasant 3 or 4 month mostly physical relationship with an Asian-American woman. She had exquisite skin, small perfectly shaped breasts, and what I assume is non-traditional sexual energy and aggression, perhaps as a consequence of a general over-achieving demeanor that landed her in a desirable post-doc position in a lab in the same building as ours, related to how we met to begin with. To this day, my occasional oral cravings for certain Asian female anatomic parts are probably an ingrained subconscious consequence derived from certain performances that became essentially habitual and mandated by my partner during this relationship. One who gave a shit about the deeper driving centers of the human gray matter could probably wonder if this taste, so to speak, at least in part helped drive me to San Francisco, and its well deserved reputation for a large population of beautiful Asian-American women.

This particular relationship eventually ended in quite a mature adult fashion, as she finished her post-doc and took a staff scientist position with a biotech company in the Boston area. It was never one of those things that would dictate life decisions. We stayed in touch periodically for a while (intensely one week when I attended a meeting in Boston), and sporadically thereafter, sometimes prompted by genial issues such as when she had a medical question about a relative or when I had a question about appropriate gene cloning approaches, as, at least in my eyes (or collective memory of other facial parts), her molecular biology skills rivaled her far less published hip-grinding skills.

Oh well....

Now as I wandered aimlessly down the streets of our Houston neighborhood in the fading early evening sun, I for some reason began to mentally scroll through those few relatively long-lived relationships I had during my Internal Medicine residency years at the NIH. However, I suspect, now, in the retrospect of my presumably growing maturity and with the insight acquired from finally falling deeply, irreversibly, in love, that the closest I came to being truly in love during that time of my training was probably with a woman that I actually never had a romantic or physical relationship with…just some sort of alternatively frustrating and perhaps subconsciously refreshing combination of lust, admiration, friendship, and especially a productive working relationship, such that anything past polite compliments and superficial inquiries and then increasingly frequent, hopefully mutual sexual tension prompted kidding would have potentially destroyed something that I needed even more at the time; that is, expertise in two dimensional gel electrophoresis.

...

Diana was the prototypic Swedish "could-have-been-a-supermodel-but-I-became-a-scientist-instead" goddess. She was tall (by definition), 5'9 or 5'10", always in flat comfortable shoes in the lab, and only once witnessed in pumps with any heel of note, at a work-related affair, adding even a few more intimidating inches and the final touch of emphasized perfect calf-shapeliness; blond hair (duh…), typically pulled back in a pony-tail in pragmatic lab- or painfully witnessed jogging around campus-mode, a radiant skin tone shade of "health emphasis" lightly enhanced in the barely perceptible increased warmth of the Maryland summer; blue eyes (shockingly…) that gave off a spark of intensity that one inferred would transfer to every undertaken endeavor; a perfect body, a consequence of not only gifted genetics, but years and years of being a competitive swimmer and volley ball player in those phases of the Swedish education system that parallel age-wise our high school and college and continuing those things for exercise in graduate school, where in one tangible manifestation of her capabilities that probably scared away the majority of her already intimidated suitors, she earned a Ph.D. in Cellular Immunology. The consequent physical attributes of her toned shoulders and chest gave her likely B to almost C cup breasts the most imaginably perfect shape under T-shirts, blouses, and sweaters, under her rarely removed, but typically open lab coat. All of these magical ingredients combined with a perfect mouth that gave rise to the healthiest most heart felt smiles, and a sense of humor, that despite a few degrees of cultural difference reflected to me a humble but highly capable intelligence, made this lovely creature essentially a lab-based manifestation of the divine woman.

...

I began working with Diana Stossl in March of my second year in Bethesda, during a six month primarily research block of my training. Research is, of course, strongly encouraged as a component of a residency at the NIH. In fact, if one wasn't interested in at least some kind of research training or at least rigorous exposure to some form of investigational medicine, from phenomenally basic to very clinical, even epidemiologic, one likely wouldn't end up in Bethesda for a residency to begin with. For one thing, the highly referred nature of a large percentage of the patient population facilitated studies not possible in many other centers. Then there were the vast accomplished faculty, the unique mechanisms of federal funding, and the incredible facilities, all the way down to the highly convenient (again a term used sparsely in those parts) reagent commissary in building 10 (the main hospital building) where instead of buying bread, eggs and milk one could essentially instantly pick up any item from a wide range of fairly commonly campus-wide used standard or common lab reagents, such as molecular biology kits and Western blot detection kits-such as when running gels. A large and complicated looking volume of such sundries was actually in Diana's hands when first I spotted her there, perhaps not truly realistically hoping at the time that I might ever work or do other things with her. Come to think of it, I believe it was there that I once again ran into my so-called friend, apparently during another foot in mouth disease episode on my part and during which his non-verbal response seemed to reflect being unhappy at my regarding him as something like a polygamist pimp rather than a likely highly skilled investigative pathologist.

However, a clinical residency is a clinical residency; there are established, even if occasionally somewhat stretched or loosely interpreted, requirements for the composition of clinical training time if one is to become Board eligible. The potential career fuck-up Catch-22 here is, I suppose, that time spent doing research ate into clinical training, and the amount of research training allowed in a standard length residency may still not be adequate. One could emerge without sufficient clinical skills to be a competent physician-type doctor or without having acquired the necessary research skills and experience and other intangibles necessary to translate to even the next phase on the way to independent investigator. As such, many folks, even M.D./Ph.D.'s with rigorous research training and experience from combined degree training during medical school, ended up spending longer in their residencies, typically taking an additional year or two and sometimes even longer. I once met a PGY 7 (post-graduate year seven), which although not unusual in a General Surgery/Plastic Surgery residency program is perhaps borderline pathologic in the Internal Medicine training scheme, especially without a subspecialty fellowship, such as gastroenterology or endocrinology, thrown in.

Spending an extra year in residency was designed to increase the amount of research time to that which may be sufficient (or intended to be sufficient) to obtain certain skills, to complete certain projects, or to acquire certain credentials, even if just the right numbers of the right types of papers in the right types of journals. Having already done this exact sort of thing in Medical School, I was not inclined to do it again, not at this particular time, even if I didn't know that I would indeed do it and more, again, in the form of a research oriented even longer Neurology residency very shortly. Hence, while at the NIH I was determined to make the most of at least 12 months of primarily research time, in a manner and in a lab that may even allow productive research endeavors when back in full time clinical rotations as well.

With these somewhat pre-conceived objectives in mind, I chose a lab, which in retrospect, was a perfect match. Dr. Matheson's lab in the Department of Immunology was a bit of a fringe lab. On the periphery of the glory of a massive collection of more mainstream investigators involved in areas of antigen presentation and processing, mechanisms of T-cell activation, T and B-cell interactions, cytokine modulation of lymphocyte activation, lymphocyte homing, mechanisms of immune tolerance and potential autoimmunity, and every aspect of Immunology related to transplantation biology and AIDS, John Matheson's laboratory was focused on mechanisms of Immunologic injury to neurons and related cells of the nervous system.

There were several established, older laboratories over in Neurosciences that were focused on immunologic injury in the nervous system, many of which utilized well-known rodent and rabbit models of conditions such as allergic encephalitis intended to be relevant to human diseases such as multiple sclerosis (MS). I typically got the sense that John thought that at least some of these models lacked in some key aspects of potential relevance to human neuroimmunologic diseases, somewhat insightful given that he was a Ph.D., most of whom have little pathophysiologic and essentially no real clinical training. Further, and even more ironic given the location of those labs in Neurosciences and his in Immunology, he felt that the emphasis in some of the investigations in these neuronal injury areas was "too immunologic".

John Matheson was already a highly accomplished young investigator, clearly progressing from junior to intermediate level, and despite the small size of his soon to be growing lab and its potential uniqueness in the department based on subject matter, there was no arguing with the track record of publications and the already successful acquisition of grants. I was still coming to grips with the whole intramural funding program at the NIH compared to what I had at least been exposed to at Baylor as a typical institution with faculty applying for so-called extramural NIH type grants along with the diverse array of other overall lesser grant types. So regardless of dollar amounts, I and others whom I related it to could appreciate the translated version I occasionally heard for the level of grant money as being essentially equivalent to three R-01 grants, impressive indeed and proving that he wasn't that fringe, at least politically and financially, after all. Despite this level of initial success, I got the impressions from my early interactions with John, reinforced by the progressively generous support he gave me, that he was craving M.D.-type pathophysiologic insight and input. It was an added bonus, although likely far less uncommon at the NIH than in other medical centers, that this came from a clinician that actually had a wholesome respect for the mechanisms and slow, steady grind of scientific investigation; from aspects of literature tackling, hypothesis generation, experimental design, down to every little detail of buffer preparation and reagent acquisition, dilutions, utensils to be utilized, to details of execution, data collection and analysis, to cautious interpretation, and the most crucial aspects of "future directions". When these attributes were variously demonstrated in apparently energetic fashion by yours truly, not only was the brilliance of an increasingly traveling John Matheson made readily available, but also was the more acutely needed technical expertise and experience and actual hands on laboratory effort, essentially under my direction, of a substantial chunk of time of three highly skilled lab technicians. As I quickly came to understand the purpose and scope of other projects in John's lab and how each related to my subsequently appropriately expanded focus, two of his techs would actually spend a fair amount of time working on projects under my immediate direction, not only on a daily level side-by-side with my own direct wet-bench activities, but also during intervals in which I would be away from the lab, playing doctor, much of which would lead to papers that I would first author, even after I left for San Francisco.

The lab was working in particular on ways in which different types of cells located in the brain and the soluble products of those cells could lead to neuron injury, potentially relevant to a spectrum of acute and chronic diseases, from MS to toxic injuries such as alcoholism, maybe even dementias, particularly Alzheimer's. When one works in areas so competitive, a major reason for repetitive success in terms of acceptance of papers to major, high impact journals, and especially funded grant applications, is the productive utilization of novel experimental approaches and techniques. Original ideas, even if relatively high risk in that they aren't guaranteed to be correct when borne out by time or those that employ novel experimental approaches not necessarily even certain to yield results, are key to substantial progress in biomedical science, the kind that comes in large chunks, and which can then spin off the slow, steady incremental increases by other followers...until the next such big chunks come along.

John had developed and perfected techniques for short term culture of highly pure populations of neurons, the actual "brain cells", those mysterious guys that do all the fundamental things from controlling movement, to storing memory, to deciding what you were going to have on your pizza that night. Although the lab utilized virally transformed nerve cell lines and those that had become immortalized through other ill-defined mechanisms during years of culture propagation, these cells only mimicked their real counterparts in a few basic, general ways, and certainly had altered expression of genes and proteins that would drastically change their susceptibility to pathophysiologically-relevant injurious mechanisms. As such, it was a bit of a leap of faith (not well recognized by hundreds of labs employing them routinely and presenting the latest potential "cures" for a variety of neurological diseases each year at the various meetings, but increasingly recognized by the true experts comprising the study sections of the NIH and other funding bodies) that any experimental observations made with these cell lines would actually translate into anything meaningful in a complete organism type of environment, with real neurons in real surrounding human brain environments. In fact, not only was it difficult to test potential conclusions made by such experiments in real world situations, but the few that had been carried through to intact organism models seemed to reinforce the already growing skepticism towards these simple experimental models. Hence, however elegant some of the other manipulations may have been in the use of such older cellular investigational tools, their incorporation was increasingly perceived as a potential waste of time and money, both of which always seem to be in such short supply in the slowly progressing, expensive world of biomedical research.

Not only had John and his colleagues developed cell culture models likely much more relevant to the *in situ* (intact human brain) situation, but he had developed elegant ways to study their injury, from subtle and potentially sub-lethal, to acute and quickly lethal, that so far, had stood up under close scrutiny, both internal and external. He hadn't stopped here. It wasn't as simple as growing brain cells and throwing some Jack Daniels on them or depriving them of oxygen or the removal of metabolic wastes, as may be simplistically translated to alcohol neurotoxicity and stroke, respectively. John was, after all, an Immunologist, the organisms of which family typically grow up using isolated hematopoietic cells and cytokines in their daily laboratory lives. John had developed and already successfully applied techniques for identifying, purifying, and characterizing novel cytokines and other mediators derived from cells, such as astrocytes and macrophages, that were stimulated in manners likely highly relevant to the diseases being studied, and which were also highly likely key players in deserting and withdrawing support from or frankly attacking their peaceful neuron neighbors. Astrocytes were a normal population of brain cells, responsible for a complex array of tasks necessary for keeping the brain functioning smoothly, such as maintaining extracellular substances and the integrity of blood vessels. They respond to a variety of insults and injuries, becoming "reactive" astrocytes, and doing things like squirting out molecules that may have reparative or restorative function, the absence of which could be deleterious, but the excess of which, like so many things in life, could be damaging. These cells can even become neoplastic, giving rise to some of the more common primary brain tumors. Macrophages were tissue (in this case brain) localized versions of cells derived from the peripheral blood monocytes, which come from the bone marrow, and that participate in a variety of crucial processes, such as presenting antigens to immune cells, making and providing factors necessary for the activation of such cells, and also for killing things and cleaning up after the battle, from destroying microbial organisms (bacteria) by phagocytosing or ingesting them and similarly disposing of dead tissue and helping to replace it with, sadly, less functional scar tissue. This is, of course, a humongous oversimplification, but from our point of view, it was emerging that such cells played a key role in contributing to the damage of neurons in a variety of processes. As neurons do not regenerate, and cannot be replaced, preventing and minimizing their injury is an obvious approach to ameliorating the occurrence and morbidity of a variety of diseases in the brain.

...

When I came to the Matheson lab, there was increasing attention being paid to the hot topic of the actual mechanisms whereby these different cell types might actually physically interact, how they may stick to each other basically; that is, the specific adhesion protein molecules that could be involved in cell to cell interactions that could allow toxic mediators to be directly passed from one cell to another or allow for their concentration to reach toxic levels in the small amount of space achieved by virtue of close cell to cell proximity. As these adhesion proteins were being identified in our lab and others, monoclonal antibodies could be made against these proteins which might block or prevent these cell interactions or which may bind to their targets on cells in a different manner, actually simulating the cell to cell interactions mediated by their target surface proteins. These antibodies could be produced and characterized in the lab using cultured cells and mouse tissues with increasingly wide spread technology and which bound to specific proteins just like the mixed population of polyclonal antibodies one's own body made against specific antigens such as those of a bacterium during an infection. In addition to potentially preventing or reducing cell mediated neuron injury by blocking adhesive interactions between astrocytes and macrophages and our neuron heroes, we hypothesized that the adhesion proteins on the cell surfaces themselves were sending signals into the noxious cells that were activating them to be injurious to begin with. Characterizing the mechanisms of this adhesion mediated cell activation is what brought me into the unnerving daily contact with Diana to begin with, and we would work closely for the six or so months, leading eventually to three co-written abstracts and two co-written manuscripts that still give me a little visceral twinge when I see them listed on my C.V.

The time course of this cell to cell mediated neuron injury and some chemical inhibitor experiments we had done indicated that new protein synthesis was involved in these injurious processes, likely by the culprit offending toxic astrocytes and/or macrophages, although that remained to be established. The best way to "discover" new proteins was by 2D (two dimensional) gel electrophoresis. Electrophoresis is the method, by which proteins (negatively charged overall) are separated, basically by size, in an electric field applied to a suitable matrix (a gel, such as made of polyacrylamide). Gel-electrophoresis, in which proteins are partially separated out in a single direction, is a straightforward technique routinely employed by any lab needing it. This does not allow adequate spatial separation of all proteins, with lots of different similarly sized proteins migrating at the same distance in the gel lane. Typically, one knew what protein they were interested in, and was quantitating its level under some experimental condition, and after partially separating out proteins of different sizes, the protein of interest could be indentified using an anti-body (such as a monoclonal antibody like those mentioned above), including in a technique called a Western Blot. This, in fact, is the method used to confirm an HIV-positive result on a screening test (detecting multiple HIV proteins). The screening test, an ELISA, is an antibody based technique, in which the proteins aren't physically separated at all, but the target protein is just identified in a well, relying on the specificity of the antibody reagents employed. With some modifications to the detection steps, Western blots following gel electrophoresis can be quantitative as well, allowing for detection of increased or decreased levels of proteins of known interest.

However, for the discovery of unknown proteins, separating thousands in a single dimension was not adequate resolution. Two dimensional (2D) gels were needed, with proteins detected on the gels with chemicals that reacted non-specifically to all proteins. Diana was a true artist in the performance and interpretation of 2D gel electrophoresis. She began passing on some of those skills to me during our work together. Knowing what we needed, Matheson had arranged a meeting for he and myself, with the Director of Diana's lab, given their reputation and publication record involving 2D gels, to which Diana came along as the most likely actual collaborator if things worked out for mutual benefit to the two labs. Their laboratory was certainly interested in seeing broader application of their technical skills, and our laboratory was capable of performing a wide range of other techniques, particularly related to molecular biology and gene cloning. After this meeting, Diana and I just sort of took charge of getting things going and the obvious productivity and progress of our mutual experiments continued to justify the ongoing support of this collaboration from the two laboratories' PIs.

I loved watching Diana work; she was so precise and confident, although I had to often force/remind myself to concentrate on what she was doing technically and to focus more on listening than accidentally staring at her mouth and face when she was explaining things to me. Initially she ran the gels, teaching me as we went. Then I gradually began doing more and more of them, as the number of analyses grew reflecting the number of *in vitro* cell stimulation and injury experiments (including different incubation times) we were extracting and analyzing the proteins from. For example, one could take resting cell cultures as a control and stimulate these cells with an appropriate level of a biologically relevant cytokine to achieve cells that could in theory be injurious to their neighboring cells and compare the patterns of all the proteins in the stimulated vs. control cells.

After appropriate staining of the 2D-gels, new "spots" (indicating individual proteins) may show up in the protein lysates of the stimulated cells, or proteins that were normally present may be reduced or absent after experimental manipulation. These individual proteins could be excised and eluted and studied/characterized in different fashions. Diana was also proficient in a variety of these techniques. Essentially all of her graduate and current post-doctoral work involved some aspect of protein chemistry. The lab in Stockholm where she did her Ph.D. was internationally well regarded in Cellular Immunology, including application of protein chemistry. Her post-doctoral work expanded on this, altering the main focus of the specific Immunology processes she was investigating. But she and her lab were very excited about the complex models in other areas that we were now helping them collaboratively engage in. John felt that this more sophisticated approach to proteins involved in cell injury models would soon have enough data to justify a new grant application, and the potential involvement of Diana's mentor's lab, based on their easily defendable expertise in 2D gels and other protein chemistry, would add strength to the Program Project Grant's intended renewal submission.

Diana had a boyfriend, or a near boyfriend kind of friend, back in Sweden. I didn't want it to come up in our conversations, so I never brought it up, and if it did come up, I routinely tried to change the subject or at least not encourage any real expansion on the topic. Curiously, Diana hardly ever mentioned him when we were working together, or on those few occasions when we were out together. We never had any official dates. Things were going way too well in the lab areas crucial to who we were and where we were going. But we may sometimes have ended up as the last two people when a small group from one or the other or both labs had gone out for a happy hour or such.

We kissed just once. The night she was in pumps, and a very form fitting and hence flattering dress, the only time I ever saw her dressed up. I was relatively dressed up as well. It was a semi-formal departmental affair. She looked amazing. Our kiss was amazing. We were in a very deep and sincere conversation, having had a few drinks and being off on our own somewhere. It was appropriate. It was very nice. But as we pulled away from each other, without saying a word, we both knew it couldn't/shouldn't go any further.

We never even brought it up again during the rest of the time we worked together. I became very proficient in running and analyzing 2D gels and competent in extracting, purifying proteins appropriate for other applications, such as for digesting, partial sequence analysis, and for making appropriate preparations for generating monoclonal antibodies (the latter things like sequencing, antibody preparation, and eventually immuno-precipitation of antibody targeted proteins for purification, etc. would be done with appropriate experienced technical personnel, of course).

I would bring my 2D gel experience and expand on it, especially in my early days in Hassel's lab (before greater focus on molecular biology and gene cloning to supplement cell based experiments). Throughout my time in San Francisco, in fact, I would even collaborate occasionally with investigators in other labs, to provide some 2D gel experiments/analyses, much like I had sought out from Diana initially...but likely performed by me with at least slightly less beauty and elegance.

...

I must have been rambling through our nearby neighborhood Houston streets, apparently aimlessly, my thoughts falling softly but painfully on the likes of Diana, and I think at that moment I was more concretely and perversely pondering, once again, although it had been a while, on whether the perfectly pert breasts of such a fair but tan-able blonde, blue-eyed Swede were capped by pink vs. pink tan vs. less likely tan nipples when Leo suddenly approached me, walking steadily and slowly out of the previously masking dark and into the strange bask of the street light we were now commonly submerged in. Either he saw me, or someone, coming or the decades of Thorazine and related neuron numbing pills had ameliorated the ability to have the shit startled out of him that I had just experienced.

"What brings a young man like yourself out on a night like this, when you should be home with your sweetheart?" he asked, striking me as a little less disheveled than usual. His appearance and the coherent use of a term like "sweetheart" made me wonder if he was ever schizophrenic, at the same time that his forgetfulness of my situation with Kim made me realize that he could indeed be the scarred remnants of an approximated human being, likely perpetually fucked up in part because he couldn't deal with the usual bullshit we all traipse through every day of our less than fucking orgasmically perfect lives. And why had his halfway house or whatever it was he lived in let him out so late...or out at all, at night, unsupervised, as on all those evenings (albeit typically a little earlier than this) we saw him at the park.

I got over my startle quickly, as regardless of shelter considerations, I had come to appreciate if not yet adore this man/partial-man/more-than-a-man guy, and the ever so subtle curl of his right upper lip gave me the sign of a friend that at that point of the night I guess I may have needed, and I was suddenly happy to see him there, showing up like some sort of emotional guardian angel, sensing when you were in a mental danger zone.

"Ah, Leo," I said, reflecting at the same time both my optimistic hope and my cautious acknowledgement regarding the way things were. "You know my wife is in Seattle."

"Ah," he responded, "herein lies the problem. Why are you here in Houston and she is in some other city?" he continued, his lack of specific mention of "Kim" as "she" and "Seattle" as "some other city" giving me the confidence I needed, at a time of possibly vulnerable insecurity, to deal in intellectual and emotional battle with a fried old-fart with faulty dopaminergic neuron wiring.

As I had been border-line pleasantly in deep thoughts, and was potentially in the mood to return to that direction, I quickly dismissed my buddy by concretely responding: "I've told you before, Leo, that it was for professional reasons." And then feeling that some umph or at least substantial detail was necessary to completely destroy my schizo-incapacitated victim, "We had really good jobs in different cities, so that didn't allow us to move down here together, at least for awhile."

This was followed by a moderately long silence, during which I believe my mind may have actually been completely blank, and then I noticed Leo just shaking his head, a gentle, but emphatic "no" or maybe just some form of tardive dyskinesia, and then as he walked away from me, continuing in his original direction, he said, with no avarice at all, and with no perceptible intention to prove a point, "Well, that don't make no sense…if you're truly in love."

XI

- *Houston; November, 1993*

By November 17th, 10:20 a.m. (as officially designated on my daily in house note entry in a Mr. Becker's patient chart), I was in the middle of my second affair since Kim and I had separately departed San Francisco in the summer. At the present time, as I pondered my current circumstances, I was somewhat fatalistically recognizing that it was probably more towards the tail end of this particular ill advised, and soon to be ill-fated, "relationship". I was feeling maybe even a little guilty, as I was multi-tasking by charting Mr. Becker's disappointing motor skill evaluation results at the same time as talking to Kim on the phone about our Thanksgiving and Christmas holiday plans and the specifics about travel and which families to spend what time with, while I was unavoidably staring at the professionally dressed, but very shapely figure of my current lover Sandy, also entering notes in a small work room off of the Nursing station of the 7th floor of the Neurosensory Center.

Sandra, as she was professionally introduced to colleagues or patients, was an amazingly vivacious, All-American type, blue-eyed blond Neuropsych P.A. that I was essentially having an aerobic sexual relationship with. I entered into this likely no-happy ending situation with no more forethought than some of my patients did when having unprotected anal receptive intercourse with total strangers in video booths of Adult Bookstores in parts of town not too far from where the lovely Sandy and I first let our mutual attraction and physical needs pass the theoretically sacred, but too frequently penetrated, professional boundary line.

I finished Mr. Becker's note and walked by the side room where Sandy was, with an acute nauseating panic of "what the hell am I doing" mixed with several centimeter lower abdominal or pelvic twinge of horniness, as I noticed the curve of her hips and the firm gorgeous form of her butt in a tasteful light gray wool skirt. Although she had a fairly simple and straightforward approach to life, work, and sex, I knew she would not overtly say or do anything to alert our colleagues to our potentially reproachable on-goings. Still, there's a way that two people who spend a fair amount of time exploring each other's genitals interact with each other, when not doing said activities, even when supposedly making a conscious effort not to allow their intimacy be known to their co-workers. Especially in the early, infatuation, highly sexually charged phases of a relationship (basically as far as one like this could possibly ever go), the desire to be away from work and having that energizing physical interaction can, I suppose, show up in a glance, a not intended to be observed passing touch or overheard provocative comment.

There are probably many figures in medicine and science whose lack of personal credibility brought on by repetitive real and/or rumored indiscretions has unavoidably damaged their professional reputation as well. The Department Chairs (hopefully, or at least at the really good places), the Editors of the best journals, the guys with 3 NIH R-01 grants and a hallway of labs with the best post-docs and grad students, the hard working, dedicated, brilliant physician scientists actually helping make progress against the perplexing complex mechanisms of disease attacks on the human condition are not typically the clowns who get caught fucking their secretaries or who are perpetually hitting on young female medical students. Of course, not being completely naïve, there certainly are exceptions. If you're good enough at the money making science and/or clinical aspects, the University community will brush an incident or two under the Ivory tower wall-to-wall carpet. But you still pay a price, being the subject of unheard student jokes or in that barely perceptible way that junior colleagues may look at you when recognizing a mere mortal rather than a god.

Sandy was beautiful and maybe especially in that really cute kind of way, and reasonably smart, conscientiously hard working, and completely professionally competent; but I think there must be a certain gradual tension that develops in such a woman, a woman who is inevitably different in the early phases of catching the right man than she will eventually be in the later days of living with that individual in the long-term chronic "for better or worse" and "in sickness and health" phases. Sandy's upbringing in a wholesome family environment in nearby Katy, Texas, had somehow subconsciously programmed her to believe that the thing to eventually do was make meatloaf that would be ready just in time for when you've picked up the kids at baseball practice and your husband walks in the door after parking the family sedan in the 2-car garage, pausing only briefly to pet the family dog on the head, before bending down to give you a respectful, obligatory brief kiss on the cheek. She was the temporary cheerleader, party girl that would someday make the perfect corporate wife, who would likely give up her career, with who knows what buried future resentment. Don't get me wrong, there may be nothing inherently deficient in this wholesome fate, but sleeping with a highly unlikely candidate for the future Mr. Cleaver, an almost by definition unobtainable married man, may represent a last ditch effort to delay the ascent into this evolution toward suburban bliss. And even if this assessment of my current lover was slightly off target, she was certainly different in so many aspects from the other involved party of my first Houston miscue.

...

I met Maura at 4:32 p.m. (I pretended to be looking at a clock on the wall behind her, while trying to catch her glance) on a lazy Sunday afternoon at the Bookstop, Carl's bookstore, which was located in an old theater on Shepherd, in the small strip complex that included Butera's deli at the corner of Alabama and Shepherd, about two and a half blocks from our park. That we weren't making love until 8:15 p.m. at my place was essentially the consequence of an unacknowledged co-conspiracy to delay the inevitable for as long as humanly possible to heighten what was already such extreme anticipation that when it finally happened I found myself medically thinking that we may need a crash cart next to the bed. She was, and still is, so incredibly sexy, in an almost diabolical, quiet, seemingly self assured way that the mere unintentional thought of the way her skin felt and smelled can send me almost irreversibly into a moment of weakness in which I give in and call her, despite the progressive disgust I felt as our short but heated affair deteriorated before it reached what I dreaded as a Glen Close kind of moment out of Fatal Attraction.

Maura was English, but had lived in the States for more than ten years. She had been working in a small editorial office in London in her early twenties, when her boss had moved to a large firm in New York and taken her with him. She had been in Houston for the last two or three years, working as a publicist/editor, having left New York for an apparently complex series of professional and likely more important personal reasons, including getting away from what I sensed as a painful but seemingly addictive relationship with her married boss. These were, of course, things I learned much later, during soft conversations between rounds of love making into hours that were so late it occasionally added sleep deprivation to all the other daily challenges, something that I hadn't experienced for these reasons in quite a while. She had been shaped and flavored by seven plus years in New York, but actually appreciated the many unique aspects of Houston, especially the inner city/River Oaks/Med Center social scene, with its air of Texas confidence but bright eyed and smiling openness contrasting with the stereotypes of the New York publishing scene, which one may tire of with the acquisition of that thirty-something wisdom some hopefully get. In addition, she had evidently come to love the heat of Texas, even in its least desirable humid Southeast Texas manifestation, a girl then after my own heart, although clearly that was not the part of my anatomy she was most interested in. As our love making and friendship or whatever it was grew over the late summer and still scorching hot September and early October, my perpetual response to her skin was proof that the sun did her good. She had red hair, but a soft, almost reddish-brown vs. the glaring orange variety, the kind that accompanies a head to toe and all parts in between complexion more like that of a light brunette's skin than that of a fair skinned, pale red head type girl that only populates skin with sparse freckles when exposed to those soul cleansing UV rays we Texans worship. Maura had light skin, but with imperceptibly small freckles, that either gave way to a real tan or else a confluent monolayer of freckles, such that she took on a beautiful light bronze, with sun exposure that only served to heighten her already piercing pale blue eyes, blue in the light, a soft hazel as we lay in my bed that first Monday morning, when thank God, I was scheduled to be in the lab, rather than in the clinic.

Our initial small talk at the Bookstop, intended solely to get to the next transition level between stranger and lover, may have almost been embarrassing to anyone overhearing it. We had ended up in the same aisle due to shelving issues (which I never actually asked Carl about) that placed self help books about codependence and defining oneself through sexual interactions, Maura's topic for the evening, adjacent with those rapidly generated, typically crappy short books on self remedies for AIDS, which I was perusing in order to gain further insight into some of the things that many of my patients seemed to be ingesting in often large quantities, and which were likely strange enough in chemical composition that I began at least wondering if any of them could actually potentially interfere with the compound we were testing in my clinical trial, in some manner or another, to the point that I had also began considering that we should be collecting more systematic data on this as a potential confounding variable in any emerging trial data. Fortunately for me, Maura either did not notice what I was reading or never assumed I was interested for my own sake. Maybe I didn't look like I could have AIDS, and by the way I was already ocularly devouring her absolutely exquisite face and a likely amazing body under a pair of jeans and light blue t-shirt, she probably assumed I wasn't gay. Also, fortunately for us, the intervening section on sexual enhancement through foods and aromas and interesting related topics was rather scant, so that as we browsed the extremes of our respective subjects, me on the far right of mine and her, on the far left of hers, we were only about 7 feet apart. Such a distance allowed some casual passing comments about the store in general, such as the reputed use of the store for homosexuals to meet late at night in a manner potentially far more promising for lasting relationships than some of the adult bookstores located within a few blocks, etc. That the same purpose could actually be accomplished on a late afternoon Sunday visit for hopefully well adjusted heterosexuals was apparently intriguing or at least entertaining enough for the both of us that we now turned to partially face each other. I was enchanted, maybe mesmerized, maybe just horny, without pausing to think why at this stage in my life or relationship that I should or should not be (enchanted, not horny), and quickly followed with a comment that I was just grabbing some stuff to read while eating and drinking outside, as the sun set and I sat on the upper deck of nearby Café Adobe. Maura replied that that sounded great, that it was a perfect evening for Margaritas, and when I simply said "let's go," it didn't seem premature, dangerous, or anything, just the next inevitable step in what was at that instant in my life apparently no more of a choice for me than when by randomization I put one of my patients on our investigational drug or placebo.

...

With Maura, the sex was physically fantastic. Often, frightfully too often, it was emotionally fantastic as well, in some sort of almost imaginary consciously obscuring way as if life were being experienced or witnessed through an only vaguely transparent or mystical fog. I believe, at least now, that there is an emotionally dangerous sort of creature, often perhaps scarred, who is either so psychically in need of others and maybe so far removed from a complete and confident soul, that by conveying the utter abandonment of their entity, a distance more easily traversed by them than almost all others, that when making love they can make you feel that you alone can reach zones of such exquisite intimacy, which despite your occasional sense that they have shared that proximate place with many others, that this is the time it may, with just a few more of the right touches and phrases, be truly blissfully reached, in a way that garnishes you infinite love, admiration, devotion, and desirable awe that no matter what becomes of you as a couple, you have reached a special place with them for all eternity. By definition, Maura was physically responsive. When holding her from behind, a soft touch to her lower back would make her pelvis squirm. She was vocal. Soft kisses on her ears, a touch to her inner thigh, or placing a warm palm over one of her firm ass cheeks, with their creamy, tasty skin, would make her utter little whimpers, conveying a certain vulnerability or need for you that had that mixed effect of making me rock hard through some sort of deep sense of sexual power or control or special gifts or the fact that one was about to engage in an act of submersion with a special mystical recipient in a way that proved sex to be what it truly could be versus imparting a hopefully quickly gotten over slight twinge of reserve from uninvited intrusive thoughts of an inevitable act, motivated by deep unexpressed psychological holes and needs, that had been delivered in many similar past performances, and then wondering what sort of dark places were in possible danger of being opened up.

Fortunately or unfortunately, depending on your perspective; that is, your relative valuing of great sex vs. marital fidelity, this relatively infrequent scary thought provoking aspect was not enough to counter the absolute engorging effect of Maura's hypnotic blue eyes, perfectly freckled chest with divinely shaped full breasts, flat belly, and light reddish-brown sparsely haired flawless pussy. She gave herself so deeply and inspirationally, that as long as I didn't think too much, the sex was passionate, stress cleansing, and deeply satisfying. But on nights where I might be unfortunately missing or subconsciously hoping for more, there was some sort of indescribable tragic aspect to it. Maybe I was as much to blame, then, for the increasingly frequent post-coital and pre-going to work dystonic moods and terse, just-falling-short-of-accusation conversations, but to me sex should, at least eventually, be an act that brings two people closer together, however inappropriate it may be.

Not to plead total ignorant virtue and blamelessness, as after all, I was engaged in a heated extra-marital affair, the passionate sex of which had even led to separate and occasionally simultaneous episodes of broken furniture, cramps, bruises, healthy and occasionally more severe soreness leading even to a slight limp the next day, extreme dehydration, but too often, tears. Maura progressively became morose after our love making, especially when I left her place or she left my much more humble dwelling in the early a.m., to allow us to maintain some sort of distance assurance or semblance of desire to maintain some professionalism. Although, in theory, this could be perceived as a normal response by one who was actually falling for one who was, most likely, not "available", the things she said, the way she acted, and her natural sinking into this mode seemed to convey a certain zone of comfort or at least familiarity for her, a projection that this is exactly where she perceived that this endeavor, like so many others previously, would evolve to: a hopeless fork in the relationship, where one non-permitted branch would lead to a state of supposedly normally desired but psychically avoided bliss and eternal love and happiness, and the other path, always chosen almost of an inevitable consequence of the men she inhabited by potentially subconscious desire, a black-hole gravity empowered, inevitability that would lead to termination and a return to the beginning of the cycle. Hence, despite the absolutely divine physical aspects of our encounters, the increasingly frequent gloomy despair of the aftermaths began to have a negatively reinforcing impact, and as she predicted, at some point, I stopped calling Maura.

...

However, one late Saturday night in early December, after a few too many drinks with largely male co-workers and about a week after Sandy and I officially agreed to call it quits after a two or three week peri-Thanksgiving quiescent period during which some of us were either visiting family or having spouses come into town, and almost two months after my last Maura episode, I found myself missing that vulnerability, that sense of needy fragility or whatever the hell it is that leads to total abandonment. It makes for intense sex, and maybe without thinking about it, people like me have the desired attributes provoking it and taking advantage of it, the intentionally or subconsciously perfectly shaped pegs fitting into the matching shaped holes (speaking from a psychological perspective, of course). Certainly, sex with Sandy was not of the same potentially soul blightening nature. Sandy was a "keeper", a Homecoming Queen kind of perfect mate for the perfect banker or accountant and future co-raiser of 2.2 children.

So, when my balls quivered with a dangerous recklessness lately, two permeating images passed through my evil mind. Maura, laying on her bed, in the wee hours, just around sunrise, with a pale light coming through the windows of her balcony, laying with her left arm under her head, towards the center of the bed, with her left breast flattening somewhat to a perfectly shaped and deliciously broadened outline, her fiery blue sexed eyes looking at me, as if one more round would fuse our beings into an irreversible perfect darkness. The other was of Kim. Kim in any position; Kim at any time of day; Kim with a few freckles on her tan cheeks after a few days on Coronado together, or an even more scrumptious week at St. Thomas. Kim laying on our hotel bed, her skin tan and warm but cooled by the evening breeze blowing in through the open balcony door, along with the moonlight enlightening her firm, tan belly, where I placed soft kisses before moving down and tonguing her slowly, in a manner in perfect harmony with our smooth sun, delicious dinner, and rum buzzes, where after we made love, we held each other so close that we weren't just one person, but one person with the perfect sun-delicious dinner-rum-yummy-sex buzz. Kim stepping gingerly off the curb in a great fitting blue suit, in the middle of a down pour, the sight of her perfect legs taking away my gastric hunger and replacing it with some sense of complete happiness and pride, as I picked her up one March day, before we went to a show and then had dinner at Grand Café. Kim with a baseball cap over her beautiful light brown hair with its reddish sun-infused highlights, sunglasses covering her eyes, suffering a hangover rivaling mine, as we sat along Maiden Lane and progressed through a series of lattes, coffees, and cappuccinos to recover the motivation for a major apartment furnishing shopping spree that got sidetracked by the side effects of a drinking episode induced by a one-on-one game of truth or dare, played largely naked, and with more just flat out life and future talk more than anything else, in front of the big window in our first mutually rented apartment as husband and wife. The way the streetlight played off her sparkling eyes as she expressed out her not quite true anger at her father for something subsequently trivial, but fortunately for us at that moment, had led to her grabbing two handfuls from a case of 1982 Lafites from the front hallway of her parents' house, destined for the wine cellar of course, but now four bottles depleted, as we each took another sip from our non-appropriate stemware and she playfully ground her ski sock covered right foot into my boner laden crotch. Kim, as she wept so tenderly for Luis Gonzales's death from AIDS, a manic painter of strange apocalyptic images on plush black velvet whom we had first encountered at our now legendary art show in Golden Gate Park. Kim squeezing my hand SO tightly, when I boarded that 7:40 a.m. flight to Houston, just three days before she drove our only mildly beaten up "puke" pale yellow Volvo sedan up to Seattle to officially put both of us in our current situation.

XII

- *Recollections: San Francisco; Autumn, 1990*

In the early days of our relationship in SF, driving my car over to Kim's place was complicated by the fact that it was usually hard enough to find one parking space for her car, which she used for work many days and which we essentially always used for mutual errands requiring this often inconvenient form of transportation, much less two spots within a distance justifying driving to begin with.

It is a Texan's birthright, of course, to drive his vehicle wherever he goes and for whatever he's doing. With long distances between just about everything in most parts of the state, abundant land for most parking situations, and against a historical backdrop of locally drilled and refined petroleum products, one's pickup truck was essentially the same as one's horse in prior generations; a steady companion and functional accessory, condemning public transportation to isolated pockets within places like inner city Dallas or Houston, reserved primarily for the less fortunate.

However, I had gradually learned the advantages of public transportation over futile parking space searches in situations of high human density during my years at the NIH and surrounding areas of Bethesda. This was even more apparent in SF. I could more easily take the bus from Kim's to work in the lab, then take the bus either home to my neighborhood, or back to UCSF or over to SF General and then finally back to Kim's, than find a parking space and deal with the embarrassment of my piece of shit being parked in her neighborhood.

My innate sense of God-given right to accomplish all tasks by aid of personal vehicle had also diminished over the last several years as a series of increasingly nice pick-up trucks, a common parallel to progress in life's stages for many men in Texas, had been interrupted by a turd-brown 1978 Toyota Corolla currently with 106,000 and some odd miles on it. It still ran reliably, despite no consistent attention to anything remotely resembling preventive maintenance (at least during my tenure of ownership), the bare minimum of repair outlay to any acute crisis as when it may have left me stranded at various inopportune times, and two or three orangeish rust spots located largely over wheel wells and that appeared to be slowly spreading in largely contiguous patches that to me resembled some sort of cutaneous fungus or macular rash, but had yet to be accompanied by full thickness body perforation.

Hence, as we neared the holidays and the end of the year, both my apartment and my car were becoming somewhat superfluous, if not quite vestigial, like organs or tissues vital to a previous stage of development, now in need of something akin to molting, the shedding of past phases…as I emerged into an exciting but unknown world, ready to try my new romance wings.

…

I had bought the Toyota from a fellow in Allergy/Immunology at the NIH in the spring of 1987, towards the end of my first year there. My truck had become too big for Yankee-sized driving scales, was harder to find parking for, and as embarrassingly noted, I was essentially forced to take the particularly convenient train for going the short distance from my apartment to campus. As I was getting further and further from the fraternity of fellow students, its regular services in moving furniture for friends and even casual acquaintances and picking up kegs were becoming less needed. Plus, I could use the extra money that I would get from its sale minus the cost of whatever little, lesser vehicle I might purchase for miscellaneous short outings, such as the grocery or liquor store. It was still a painful goodbye and a somewhat formal declaration of an increasingly felt exile from Texas.

My first pick-up had been a white 1960 Ford that I had formally "inherited" from my father when I got my license as a junior in high school, although I had driven it many times before then. It was an appropriate vehicle for the time, distinct, with character, allowing for friends and classmates to know who it was when pulling up at a party, and seemingly made out of scrap tank metal given how un-scathingly it survived through various ill-founded excursions and accidents.

In what can only be ascribed to beer-related sub-optimal judgment, I once drove it through a friend's Mom's greenhouse while supposedly doing some healthy off-road type driving on their property not too far outside of New Braunfels. How that occurrence got rectified without me depleting my meager saving's account or at least temporarily losing driving privileges I don't quite remember in full detail, but a heavy Dad component was likely involved. Gradually, dependable performance out of that almost twenty year old truck exceeded my lack of auto-mechanic skills and as the need for a more steadfast vehicle for going away to college was reached, I got, as an essentially early graduation present, a near new 1978 Ford F-100 short bed pick-up. This wasn't as elaborate or as much a manifestation of being spoiled as it may seem, as the price of pick-ups varies tremendously, depending on heftiness of the frame, size of the engine, and options. Other than air-conditioning, this one had essentially none of the latter. It had the standard 300 cubic inch straight six engine and a 3-speed shifter on the steering column. With after market addition of a name brand AM/FM stereo cassette player, amplifier, roof mounted 3-way speakers, and the typical white spoke wheels and mud tires, though, it was a pretty sweet rig, which I had until near the end of my junior year at Trinity, at one point of which, when parked somewhere downtown while actually on a date, a group of never identified lowlifes decided it was better suited to be in their hands and likely driven to and sold in Mexico. A not particularly great date from what I remember having gotten even worse and heartbroken by this theft, I replaced that truck using the surprisingly generous insurance settlement with a low mileage 1979 long bed Ford F-100, which I eventually similarly equipped. I was content with this vehicle essentially all through medical school, but decided I needed a slightly more "professional" appearing pick-up for my relocation to one of the bastions of Northern medical education. So, I traded it in on a very clean dark blue 1984 Ford F-150 before leaving Texas for what I then thought would only be three or four years. And, so, shortly thereafter, I sold it for right about what I had paid for it to a nice older gentleman who had a small farm somewhere between Bethesda and Hagerstown, and I bought the little Corolla that I would hopefully never be spotted in back home.

The car reportedly had a long record of ownership by various young physicians and doctors and scientists in training, the lineage of which was passed on to each successive owner in some sort of Homeresque oral history tradition. It had originally been purchased in D.C. by a young man completing his Internal Medicine residency at Georgetown. It was then transported to the Bethesda area when he came to do a two-year GI fellowship. Towards the end of this period, as he had secured a reasonably lucrative private practice job somewhere on the East Coast (the exact location was, of course, conveyed accurately to me upon my acquisition, and the omission of detail here is clearly a shortcoming on my part), he sold it to a third year surgery resident, who approximately two years later, sold it to an anesthesiology resident, who was also doing a substantial amount of more bench-type research, which facilitated its transition from the pure clinical to more basic science domains. It was sold to a practical Japanese post-doc in 1984, who regrettably had little choice but to sell it upon his return to Japan, in 1986, at which point it was purchased by a young German Ophthalmologist, who was doing a one-year sabbatical within the Division of Neurosciences, on whose bulletin board I noted it and the torch was passed to me in 1987, with 92,834 miles on it.

In a major defining event in the little brown turd's history, I relocated it to the West Coast, with a large bulk of the miles that I added to its odometric legacy coming on the relatively unadventurous cross-country drive, with all my various possessions crammed in its trunk, back- and passenger- seats, and miscellaneous compartments and spaces. It had continued to perform admirably, if not stylishly, for me along the steep terrains of San Francisco, and now, over the Thanksgiving Holiday of 1990, I sold it to a Chinese post-doc doing research on growth factor receptor tyrosine kinase associated proteins in the Department of Biochemistry. A young lab assistant from Southern California who worked in a lab a few down from ours and that I loosely knew from seeing in the hallway and making casual lab- and life-related conversation had expressed some interest after seeing in our hallway one of the many ads I had spread all over campus. Fortunately, it didn't work out with her, as it's always potentially awkward to sell a used car to someone you know or who knows where to find you if you're still going to be around afterward. There's always that chance that if anything goes wrong, even up to many months afterward, they try to hold you responsible, at least morally if not financially, as if you actually knew whatever problem occurred was likely or at least potentially to happen and you intentionally kept this undisclosed.

This was unlikely to be a problem with Dr. Wang, who in typically quiet Asian manner, appeared to take me at my word that the car ran very well indeed, as I assured him when we met in the main UCSF cafeteria to exchange money and keys and hopefully adequately filled out paperwork for legal title transfer.

He did seem a little perplexed as I went through, in detail, the car's physician and scientist ownership history, two or three times, even making him repeat it to me, which he successfully did with utmost concentration and requiring only minimal prompting from me.

This task accomplished, I returned with renewed vigor to the lab work schedule I had set for myself over the Thanksgiving Holiday.

Kim had naturally invited me to spend Thanksgiving with her and her family at their house in San Diego. But I had agreed to take call over Thanksgiving long before I had even met Kim, largely as I had no personal issues that conflicted compared to other candidates for clinical coverage, all of whom had families there. It was too expensive and too brief a time to justify going back home to Texas. Besides, I always found this a good time to get a lot of work done, with everyone gone and things largely quiet, and even clinical demands typically reduced as routine patient scheduling was largely suspended, at least for Thursday and often for Friday as well, depending on what sort of facility one was working at.

So, other than the Cowboy's game on Thursday I had nothing officially scheduled, and other than the occasional emergency or consultation for the Neurology service I was covering on an essentially in-house call basis at The University Hospital, I was free to get a great deal of research-related work done in the laboratory, hoping only that a true emergency wouldn't occur in a manner possibly botching a critically timed experiment component, and going back to my apartment a couple of times for some sleep and a shower.

When Kim happily returned, we resumed our accelerating relationship and by mid December we had mutually agreed that it was pointless for me to renew my apartment lease the first of January, at which point we would officially be living together.

XIII

- Houston; December, 1993

"You O.K., honey child?"

I startled awake from my apparent spaced-out state to see Cheryl's large concerned face in the doorway to the little clinic office I often used for research related activities or just for patient care issues when I was having a particularly difficult time concentrating amongst the chaos in the hallways. I must have had my head in my hands, while theoretically finishing my last unexpectedly challenging clinic note. Today had been a particularly grueling one, I guess. Such things are probably worse when you're not all that on top of things to begin with.

It started out fairly routinely, drawing some bloods for CD4 counts, renal function tests, refilling meds, follow-ups; the usual. Around ten o'clock, my fledgling medical Spanish was challenged when I saw a large Hispanic woman, about three weeks post-op for a right sided partial colectomy. She was in her mid 50's; big family, some grand kids, the usual. Apparently she had developed symptoms compatible with large bowel obstruction over the Thanksgiving Holidays. I even remember briefly pondering the slight irony of Hispanic-"American" families potentially celebrating Thanksgiving, a manifestation of either cultural disorientation or more likely fusion. With inconclusive films, bad symptoms, and poor response to conservative treatment (so I gathered from her records), they took her to the O.R. and took out a 20-30 cm segment of very edematous right colon, with cecum, and small portion of terminal ileum. They probably wondered about cancer, as they noted some enlarged lymph nodes. At the time of frozen sections performed during the surgery, the pathologist (likely pathology resident, given the nature of county hospital call and the emergency peri-holiday surgery) noted "necrotizing granulomatous inflammation" in her bowel and nodes, possibly Crohn's disease or infectious. Turned out on further studies it was TB.

Ileocecal tuberculosis was something from the "old days". Shit you saw in ancient textbooks, back before pasteurized milk, when you could drink *Mycobacterium bovis*. Or the kind of intestinal TB that less than otherwise completely "with-it" and society-banned folks could get with uncontrolled TB in the sanitarium, before drugs to treat TB – when you coughed up a big glob of TB lung crap and swallowed it and it infected your bowels. Oh, in addition to its new and unique weapons of holocaust, all the wonderful old evils AIDS has brought back, I thought.

This woman was 56 years old; a monogamous, catholic, non-drug using, no-English speaking mother of 5. Not only did she turn out to be HIV positive on subsequent testing, but her CD4 count was 56 (AIDS by definition, and on its way to progressing to end stage). Postoperative recovery turned out to be complicated by her having to figure out how she could have possibly gotten a disease she'd only heard of on TV and in passing conversations, a disease for homosexuals and drug abusers. She'd never been with another man besides her husband, almost 40 years of fidelity. Turned out, he didn't share her virtuous life; ran the streets, machismo shit, occasionally used drugs, mostly in the past. Today, we were continuing the AZT they had begun when she was discharged from The Ben Taub Hospital, and starting her Bactrim prophylaxis. As I filled out her note and a prescription for her anti-PCP meds, I felt like adding "Get a gun, blow his fucking brains out."

"Yeah...I'm fine, Cheryl...thanks," I slowly replied, looking over towards her and picking up my pen to resume a few scribbles against human biologic entropy.

This conscientious, albeit occasionally annoying, but progressively accurate gauge of my professional, affected by personal, performance self must have briefly taken me in, registering all necessary information, before she turned to go while depositing a look that probably indicated that she hadn't been completely convinced by my offered up re-assuring somewhat forced pseudo-smile.

Cheryl had already been so amazing in our enrolling of patients into "my" clinical trial. Clinical trials hadn't made it from the Medical Center out to the trenches of the "front" very often, and I think she liked the idea of the "smart" people doing something a little more than just passing time and gaining experience at the expense of "her" people. If I thought deeply about it, while sometimes watching her with patients, so gentle and patient, but so maternally firm when she needed to be, I sometimes sensed in this very caring, yet pragmatic woman, a certain hidden realism/fatalism regarding medical care in general, and especially in the less than fully reached ideal of it here at the Thomas St. Clinic.

Although designed primarily (maybe even exclusively) as a clinic facility dedicated to medical service for HIV-positive patients, one of, if not the first, such "neighborhood" AIDS-Clinics in the U.S., the Thomas St. Clinic could address a broad range of medical needs. No one who could be treated was turned away or referred per se, as they would basically just be referred or eventually show up at another County funded facility anyway. Continuity of Care was an emphasis, although with the growing burden of HIV-infection on the inner city regions of Houston, its main focus on AIDS diagnosis, prevention, and treatment, including of AIDS associated secondary illnesses would quickly consume more than 100 % worth of similar sized and staffed medical clinics. How many superiority-complex laden Internal Medicine or other residents had she seen pass through these stinky rooms. Feeling good about themselves for tweaking Mr. Smith's anti-hypertensive and anti-diabetic meds, working irritatedly within the occasional confining barriers of the county budget limiting drug formulary, and occasionally bending the rules a little to get the meds they really wanted, maybe from some hot drug company rep-derived free samples, to practice the way they really wanted to, according to the latest "green journal" article/editorial/review. Feeling pleased about not only putting a nice dressing on Mr. Jones' recent BKA amputation stump, while being able to prescribe from memory the correct dose of the precisely called for latest cephalosporin, based on results from some recently obtained microbiological cultures (retrieved by the "help"), maybe even showing some fly by the seat of your pants social management skills in bucking the system to get some home health care for future dressing changes.

But...you weren't there when an earlier version of you was tweaking Mr. Jones' anti-hypertensive and anti-diabetic drugs. Did we collectively buy his legs a few more years? And you won't be there in five or ten years when Mr. Smith needs attention to his stumps, when his peripheral vascular disease, from his high blood pressure and diabetes, necessitates his amputations; or maybe when he goes on dialysis from the attack of the same slow but relentless tissue destroyers on his kidneys.

What is the biggest enemy of helping these people? Is it the inherent short-comings of current 1993 medicine, even against the common and long time recognized ravages of diabetes, hypertension, and even cancer, and now even AIDS? Or, is it also and especially that despite good standard of care within these clinic walls, that these efforts so perfectly and objectively delivered, at least against the "curable" things like high blood pressure, are then hindered, belittled, and rendered less effective by the underachievement of the self care aspects from these "lesser" individuals when faced with trying or at least caring to overcome the pragmatic issues of daily life, the little social and financial and familial pressures, so commonly ineffectively resisted, leading to the hindrances of unfilled prescriptions, continuing to eat an unhealthy diet, failing to exercise, failing to break the chain of tolerated pre-mature morbidity?

Well...maybe, to those cursed with these intrusive sorts of thoughts in the middle of anything, the Thomas St. Clinic and its non-HIV focused analogues scattered all over urban areas in Third World America is the kind of place where one SHOULD be conducting clinical trials, not just on anti-HIV and AIDS treatments, but maybe even on things as exotically mundane as recombinant growth factors and wound healing in refractory, chronic diabetic foot ulcers. I don't know. Maybe there's more to it than considerations of numbers of patients, expected outcomes, and potential statistical significance. It certainly was appearing to be a good place to find HIV-infected patients who already did or maybe soon would have cognitive and motor or other neurologic problems from their disease, on top of everything else.

We had, in fact, enrolled two patients and potentially two others, just that day.

One had to practice medicine the best they could, to the best of their ability, and with the collective diagnostic and treatment knowledge arsenals available within the medical community as a whole, and available to them at that moment in time. If one were lucky enough, or cursed, to want more, one pushed the envelope in one area, say, maybe, developing effective strategies to make chronic HIV infection more tolerable, a more human condition, to allow one to experience, enjoy, and suffer, for as long as possible all the little and not so little daily things that human existence delivers, once, or at the same time, someone else (maybe thousands of someone else's, really) figures out how to stop the virus from replicating: shutting it down and putting it in its place in a few well behaving infected, but dormant, lymphocytes within some deep-down buried and finally relatively harmless lymph nodes.

Cheryl certainly seemed to think that that's where my heart and soul and energies should lie, and that support was further reflected in her own extra efforts to facilitate, indeed, ensure, our little clinic's effort in this one particular battle. I'm sure she appreciated my care for and skilled and committed delivery of medicine to non-directly AIDS related issues as well, for which my Medicine training and Boards were often more utilized and which had helped secure this clinical position facilitating my Neurology-related research endeavors to begin with; from the swollen arms of a lymphedema-suffering breast cancer survivor who had received adjuvant radiation treatment, an old before his time multi-infarct dementia-suffering confused skinny little old man whose hundreds of little strokes had collectively knocked off all the key areas responsible for memory and integrated human social function, to the almost welcome non-HIV infected children of known moms with good old-fashioned rip-roaring strep throat, who had a curable ailment, whose prompt antibiotic treatment would prevent the rare but dreaded complications of rheumatic heart disease and post-streptococcal glomerulonephritis and possible renal failure, and who had their whole lives ahead of them, as if we were in the snootiest Pediatric office in River Oaks.

"You care too much," Cheryl once softly admonished me at the small work station outside of our two most used patient rooms, where I had spent more time with a chronic lower back pain-suffering middle-aged woman than needed simply to get a physical therapy and/or ortho-clinic appointment, only to discover that I thought she may have been really, or at least additionally, depressed, having recently lost a dear sister and a friend, and now faced the daunting task of taking care of an elderly mother, with the added financial insult of recent abandonment by a likely neglectful, but at least employed, husband. I had, additionally, arranged for a psych consult (after all, I knew some of these guys), and investigation by/consultation with a social worker service, within the ever perplexing operations of the Hospital District.

"Can you really ever care too much?" I responded, in a somewhat sarcastic, not-take-ourselves-too-seriously-tone.

"You can in this place," Cheryl replied right back, with more meaning than a few words can quickly convey.

261

"It's never stopped you," I fired right back, mutually turning up the seriousness level, as I collected my pink referral forms and headed back into an exam room.

"That's different," Cheryl began to summate, as she went back into another exam room, with iced collection tubes and syringes and consent forms for a patient I had seen previously, whom we were enrolling into our clinical trial. "That's all I have to offer."

...

Tonight I had taken all my angst from the grueling day and a little aliquot of Cheryl's from the last 13 years back home to my little rented bungalow.

As I had pondered the open and largely barren refrigerator earlier, I was momentarily ecstatic to discover the leftover Star Pizza, which despite fresh and real ingredients and air-permeable boxing, was well within the medically, smelled O.K.-ish, and especially really hungrily-time limit of acceptableness, and subsequently went through two rounds of one piece at a time of delicious Star Burst Pizza with matching cold lager, not even bothering to fuck with the microwave phase for the less important pizza aspect.

Only about an hour later, I couldn't remove my ass from the sofa to get the beer I really wanted. Instead, I flipped through TV channels, unaware of what I was watching... Home Shopping Channel or some clone, a real estate infomercial, ESPN?...didn't even pause. Some music video came on, some thin chick, with great shaped small to medium tits, in a tube top, leather pants....I, in the boy default mode, placed my hand on my dick, cupping my balls. I can masturbate, I must have subconsciously thought, acutely perking up, as then I would at least temporarily have a purpose, and task orientation can be therapeutic when flirting with bottoming out. But, after a few moments without any sign of welcoming reception, I realized that even that wouldn't do it. I felt dead inside.

Maybe I needed company, the "real" thing. Should I go out? I've had "good" luck lately (depending, I guess, on whether you had my or Kim's, fortunately unknowing, perspective), but I didn't feel like going through the hassle of selling myself.

I need someone who knows me, understands me, is sympathetic to the black hole my heart is in at this very moment. Kim. What the fuck is going on with me and Kim? What the fuck is wrong with me? Oh you poor baby, you're married to a beautiful, sophisticated, intelligent, sensual woman. Yes, but she's 2000 miles away, I reasoned with myself, as if that were the problem. Christ, I'm dying. What am I doing here? Do I really give a shit about HIV-related neuroimmunologic bullshit? Fuck, I'm famous to like 12 really smart people who remember my grant or a paper. I go to non-exotic science meetings in New Orleans (which I usually DO enjoy), Washington, D.C., and Orange County, occasionally to even more interesting places for the annual AIDS conventions. I get weird, semi-respectful looks at bars when I describe what I do in "lay" terms.

The panic of self-doubt provided the acute energy I needed to make it all the way to the refrigerator for that beer (the matching Star Pizza pieces having sadly expired after the second round), but I grabbed two, before I returned to my fading residual butt imprint of stupid introspection on the sofa. I didn't get all this education for nothing. Only a real genius would plan ahead to not have to get up for the next beer.

Some old Clint Eastwood movie moved to the screen, one of the Dirty Harry flicks. The sudden compulsion to name them all: "Dirty Harry", "The Enforcer" (is that this one?), "Magnum Force" (David Soul's true triumph or was it that Steven King movie he was in, shit, man, Starsky's wife and kid died of AIDS, I hate this fucking disease; is that Hal Holbrook? O.K. then, this is Magnum Force; remember that movie he made with Adrian what's her name from Maude? ... huge fucking tits), where was I ..., "Sudden Impact", "The Dead Pool"?, the later, "forgotten" one. All right, you're a fucking worthless trivia genius. Next channel....

Maybe I should eat...some more. Go up Montrose, get a killer burrito at "the burrito place"... or whatever it's really called, do you good to get out, walk, see some young at risk boys in leather, or at least dirty jeans, even more aimless and despaired than your pathetic ass, help you forget about your own problems. I looked through the fridge again, no hidden one more piece of pizza or anything else even remotely approaching edible had appeared, but, ooh... up and about, clearly on my way to emotional recovery. You should call Kim....

...

Is there anything worse than a near perfect relationship? Maybe couples that are so fucking miserable are much better off. They know what they have…or don't have. It's pointless to wish for anything better in the current situation, you can't have it. Accept it. Move on. Have some fun. Don't be scared. Maybe having a beautiful, successful, well raised spouse that you get along with on 95 % of the stuff is a curse. Having someone like that who loves 95 % of you is even more of a curse. Maybe that 5 % is the crucial thing defining you, making you what you are, and making you the 100 % you need to be to fit into you. Maybe taking the other 95 % of you and adding the 10 % of something else that she seems to want or you seem to want in her, doesn't add up to 105 %, but brings it all down. I'm me, God-damn it. It's too late to change. Love me for what I am, accept the 5 % bullshit, the socks on the floor, the fact that I feel as comfortable with blue collar racing fans as I do with stock brokers, the fact that I just feel like being lazy today, the fact that I burn somehow lifelong for something, the fact that I have weird friends I hang out with at a park in the middle of a mixed inner city neighborhood…. Ah fuck it. Go get a burrito…maybe some reflux and gas later on can only help with this despairing self-analysis.

XIV

- Recollections: San Francisco 1989-1990

It was really the *in vitro* experiments, the investigations on mechanisms of cell injury and cell death using cultured neuronal cell lines with emphasis on immunologic mediators increasingly implicated in HIV infection and ADC that became my major focus at UCSF. This area of increasingly acknowledged and rewarded supposed expertise (as much "expertise" as someone at that stage of research experience can have) along with the intensive clinical training with a large AIDS population and the ability to extract from the UCSF faculty the large bits of relevant basic and clinical research excellence is ultimately what combined to allow for me to write a successful grant application for translating the work to my eventual faculty position in Houston.

Culturing neuronal cell lines and treating them with various agents, growth factors and small peptide mediators presumably relevant *in vivo* during brain development and injury, was an area I had worked on extensively when at the NIH. This background, of course, was what led me directly to Hassel's lab to begin with. It has to be kept in mind that these cultured brain cells were not really derived from actual normal neurons, the thinking and movement-controlling brain cells of the human mind and that we most wanted to study. After all, these particular cells once formed and differentiated into their functioning versions inside your head don't divide; i.e., they can't grow and replace themselves or their neighbors. We couldn't even really keep them alive in any semblance of their normal *in vivo* forms in a way to properly study them for prolonged periods even if we had an efficient way to isolate them from a fresh human brain to begin with, such as at an autopsy performed with intentional quickness for research purposes.

As anyone who's ever been a teenager and been lectured to by their parents after a careless, accidentally excessive drinking binge, "all those brain cells we just killed" can't grow back. Fortunately, the equally stereotypical "only use 10 % of our brains" or some other explanation I haven't yet encountered kept us from deteriorating to the zombie morons we were clearly on pace to drink ourselves into. However, the true non-dividing, terminally differentiated nature of these brain neuron cells does mean that those of us trying to study them on little plastic culture dishes had to come up with something a little different than the real thing.

A common mechanism for this sort of thing is to use cells that are derived from actual tumors of the cells of interest. Tumors have developed ways to escape the normal molecular mechanisms regulating cell growth, proliferation, and death. Often, these cells can be propagated *in vitro*, and sometimes, if they don't already have them, while living and thriving in the lab, they develop some additional genetic alterations that allow them to propagate indefinitely; i.e., they become immortalized.

In the 1980s (or maybe earlier, but that's when I studied it), we learned how to use some viruses (oncogenic viruses, or viruses that have been implicated in causing some cancers, especially in animals) to immortalize cultured cells of non-tumor origin. Needless to say (although I and others find we have to point it out to some concrete thinking investigators all the time), such cells that can grow and divide indefinitely, all by themselves when cultured on plastic and fed media with a calculated variety of hormones and vitamins, do NOT 100 % accurately reflect the status of their "real" counterparts that live in the intact human organism, touching their neighbors of the same or other cell types and deriving their sustenance from the complex milieu of cheeseburgers passing through the gut, to the proteins and lipids occupying digested and absorbed juices, making their way through lymphatics to the liver, to the systemic blood, to the protected portions of which are allowed into the brain, and which along with the CSF, variously nurture the magical little cells that make us "us". That's where I wanted to come in to this big complicated picture, I guess.

My aspired to forte when I went from the peri-DC to the even more expensive SF area and which I was finally making some headway on when I moved in with Kim was to try to make immortalized neuron cell cultures into cells that more faithfully recapitulated their "real world" *in vivo* state, including (in theory) when they became altered in various ways during the progression of ADC. It was one thing to try to make immortalized neural cells into cells that looked like and expressed the genes and proteins of normal brain cells, which we had spent decades studying. It was another thing to take these or similar cells and to try and make them act and look like and especially express the same genes and proteins as their counterparts in deteriorating AIDS brains, which we were still actively characterizing in AIDS brain tissue sections, so we could figure out what was killing them and how to keep them alive and functioning.

The idea of making a concerted effort to expose cultured neuronal cell lines to lymphocyte and/or monocyte/macrophage/microglial derived mediators to make them look like the targets in an ADC-affected brain did not spontaneously emerge the day I walked onto the UCSF main campus like some sort of ray of brilliant heavenly anal squirted sunshine emerging through a pre-dawn fog lifting off of the bay one morning. It was, in fact, a large part of a Hassel suggested participation in a collaboration between his lab and myself and a couple of Neuropathology junior faculty and fellows during my first year there, when I was first affiliating with Hassel's lab during a primarily clinical year. This steadily reinforced direction helped provide me with the focus that the rest of my work in Hassel's lab would take over the next few years. These specific early collaborations also led to my first official AIDS-related research abstracts, and my largely still peripheral participation at that point in the somewhat infamous Sixth International Conference on AIDS, held, coincidentally, in San Francisco in June of 1990.

...

I was a co-author on two abstracts for the San Francisco International AIDS conference, a generous reflection not so much of my minimal input to that point, but especially an anticipation of the birth of collaborations that would turn these into more complete study submitted manuscripts and which along with my own primary research effort would be manifested in a total of five such abstracts for next year's version of the same meeting in Florence, Italy (intended in part to hopefully gain me a paid trip there!) and nine the following year (to be held in Amsterdam...and ditto on the trip thing...as I hadn't been quite successful in securing my European voyage the year before).

I was largely oblivious for that SF meeting, although some tweaking of my clinical schedule did allow me to attend one full and another half day of the sessions. The abstracts on which I was an author were based on work that I would increasingly participate in though, so I was eager to be involved with or aware of any discussions and/or criticisms that arose during their presentation by the first author. I was a full time Neurology intern then, so any time I could put in the lab was limited. However, my experience with neuronal cell culture from Matheson's lab at the NIH helped a couple of techs in Hassel's lab support those early collaborative efforts with our Neuropathology colleagues. The latter group had collected a large amount of predominantly post-mortem material wherein they could characterize the expression of certain proteins on neurons in the brains of AIDS patients who had suffered with varying severity of ADC and other AIDS-terminal CNS predicaments. Using a combination of immunohistochemistry and in situ hybridization (using specifically targeted antibodies or nucleic acid probes to "stain" certain proteins and RNA molecules on the cells in tissue slides) in formalin fixed paraffin embedded and even some freshly obtained frozen sections and ELISAs on peri- and post-terminal collected CSF specimens (using antibodies to detect proteins in solution with colorimetric tests), these investigators had begun to characterize the patterns of expression of certain molecules on the surface of neurons in centers of the brains most severely affected in ADC and the mediators that made it into the CSF that may be responsible for affecting neurons to alter their surface antigens or other genes. This logical approach would tremendously influence much of my future work in this area.

My contribution at this early stage and in much of the next year when I'd spend more time in the lab was to try to translate the messages in the CSF analyses to the expression patterns on the brain cells in tissue sections in a manner that may best allow us to manipulate culture conditions and added stimulants to make our test tube imposters best recapitulate the CNS pathophysiology of the too-rapidly dying AIDS victims. Early on, I was pretty swamped with the day-in and day-out aspects of trying to be a good first year Neurology resident. The month the abstract submissions were due I was on a General Neurology Service at San Francisco General ("The General"), up to my hippocampus in evaluating stroke victims and consulting on patients admitted to other services with weird Neuro exam findings and the like.

But by the month of the meeting, June 1990, I had a full year of Neuro under my belt, and maybe was feeling a little cockier, especially considering that this was superimposed on a full Internal Medicine residency at the NIH. I was no medical fetus. That month, I was acting as an upper level resident, heading up the Neuro Consult service at the VA Hospital, which allowed a little more scheduling flexibility. At this stage, almost ten years post-college, I felt I was pretty medically and scientifically savvy. What this still semi-naïve TX hill country boy didn't expect was potential interference in this crucial area of medicine from good ol' fashioned moronic bullshit politics. (Not that we didn't occasionally have our own versions on different subject matter down in the heartland. I guess, shockingly, no place is yet perfect).

The Sixth International Conference on AIDS was held on June 20-24 at the Moscone Convention Center and the nearby Marriot Hotel. I've been to dozens of similar medical science meetings, but this would turn out to be the only one I'd been to up to that point that seemed to have controversy more related to legal and social than medical and science aspects.

We often say in medicine that "hind sight is 20-20," so I try to remain objective.

At the time, US Law actually barred HIV-positive persons from entering the United States, a consequence of a panicky moment of Congressional insight back in 1987. This law, along with that requiring large bright "A"s on designer cashmere sweaters for fucking out of wedlock, had recently come to heightened international awareness.

About a year before the meeting, the US law had actually accomplished the jailing of the Dutch AIDS educator Hans Verhoef in Minnesota, that hot bed of political controversy, and even that happened, ironically, while he was changing planes to attend an AIDS conference in San Francisco...California...USA...land of the "free" (I guess that was intended to mean "retrovirally-free"), home (not to be confused with "homo") of the "brave", a nation that had made a reputation for justice by fighting fascism and communism, with the vigor that it was now apparently unleashing on consenting adults. But I digress. I look back with knowledge that none of us, including page-boy fucking congressmen, had at the time.... Hind sight is 20-20.

In laudable insight, INS had indeed allowed even a year before a 30 day waiver to permit HIV-positive persons to enter the US for purposes that would include non-Fascist activities such as obtaining medical treatment or attending silly little conferences. To obtain such a waiver, however, involved a process far more complicated than that which would have been involved to allow Mussolini or Hitler, or even Stalin, to lead a parade (driving a Chevy) down Main Street in

Apple Pie, USA. Further, any justified exception to the ban would allow the successful applicant to proudly display such on his passport. I guess this was more cost effective than tattooing a "666" on their forehead.

Not surprisingly, then, more than fifty international organizations advocated boycotting the Sixth International Conference on AIDS in SF in 1990. Looking back now, this wasn't entities like BFCLNPLWIS (or, "Butt fucking on the congressional lawn by nipple pierced leather wearing infected studs"-I made that up…I think), but pretty damn respectable organizations like the British Medical Association. The rising criticism of US policy for HIV-infected individuals led to several fairly rapid policy changes, including a 10-day waiver for travel for AIDS conferences. The Sixth International Conference even had a five page letter available to all participants registered from outside the U.S. explaining VISA situations and how these translated to HIV-infected persons planning to come to the meeting. Hinting at what may perhaps be the most important issue, after all, the 30-day waiver applicants had to show that they could pay for emergency medical treatment, whereas the 10-day waiver candidates (clearly at just one third the risk of breaking the country's medical piggy bank during their visit) had to prove they were just planning on attending a conference such as ours. I'm surprised there was no clause stating that they wouldn't do any bungee jumping while on (or above) US soil.

These were tough times. A seemingly constipated government was in highly conservative theory trying to protect its citizens including by being sure that we wouldn't all go broke absorbing the world-wide cost of this spreading plague. A perhaps more educated, or maybe more enlightened, or maybe just more liberal, scientific community may have felt that this was not the best way to support and maybe even accelerate development of cures and prevention policies.

This sort of stuff was all very new to me. Up to that point, issues about research had largely been restricted to issues of the quality of your work, what you chose to work on and whether or not anyone gave a shit (complete absence of any funding over many years might eventually indicate the latter), how smart you were, how hard you worked, and at worst, how well you played the "grant-game".

The local AIDS activist groups were thrown into a fit about all of this, and as I increasingly became involved with Hassel's lab, I couldn't help but hear about it. In fact, although ACT UP/New York was attending the Sixth International Conference, ACT UP/SF was boycotting. In highly locally publicized actions, the

San Francisco AIDS Foundation was attending, but Shanti was also boycotting. Regarding names I more readily recognized, The American Red Cross, an entity I had grown up with, from my Mom's spirited blood donation drives to my own laboratory medicine training encounters, was coming to town for the meeting despite expressed opposition to the HIV-entry restrictions, whereas the more tea and biscuit flavored International League of Red Cross and Red Crescent Societies were boycotting.

Several other smaller, largely local groups and organizations variously criticized but still attended or very vocally boycotted the meeting. A few of these were just unfamiliar names to me at the time, but I would come to know them better over the next year or two in large part due to Kim's work in marketing for some of the more artist affiliated groups.

As for me, I don't think I'd ever had two more stimulating days in my life. I met more people from all different clinical backgrounds and research perspectives, had more conversations, from signal transduction cascades to national funding politics, and sensed the largest gamut of human emotions, from utter depressing despair to stoic bolstered optimism, and I think I bought into the latter. I couldn't wait to finish my currently scheduled clinical rotations, even though I think I loved every moment of every day and each miniscule component of every patient encounter, to get into the lab, and I would take that energy with me, only to be eventually reinforced and challenged by my next substantial life encounter of note, my love for and increasing commitment to Kim.

XV

- *Recollections: San Francisco and San Diego 1991*

I was initially amazed at how much work I still got done when I had officially moved in with Kim. I was regimented, and so the things that could have been impeded by a lack of singularity were actually maximally efficient instead. We woke up together. I would have felt a little guilty otherwise, as it was usually my minimally-resisted fault that we may have stayed up just a little bit later than we had actually intended. "Round Two" syndrome is what Kim came to affectionately call it, that slightly tired, less than 100 % optimally work-tuned mode suffered through the next day, but endured with typically surprising ability to overcome it, being not so tired as to suffer a total waste, and easily spurned on in part by the buzz of the events that caused the feeling to begin with, and sleeping particularly well the next night.

We ate breakfast together, and I was getting to work in the lab much earlier than I had usually been in the recent past months. Of course, I was also leaving MUCH earlier than typical, which only uncommonly threatened to screw things up, like a late started experiment that I had to put off or work through as quickly as allowed by the experimental protocol employed and get home a little later (or a lot later) that I had indicated to Kim earlier in the afternoon, and such. But the latter scenario was, fortunately, quite rare, as I was usually energized enough in the morning that I manically got right to it. No procrastination, as I needed to get things done in order to be finished and do the whole evening, night, and morning social and love dance thing again with my new partner. By the time work hours were over for the majority, I had almost uniformly accomplished a rather satisfying amount of experimental work that had to be done at the lab. With this temporary almost blue collar-like work ethic in place that ensured routine production if not regularly allowing for the temporally demanding extraordinary without some potential relationship deviation or drama, I was indeed making tangible steady progress in my laboratory endeavors as well as satisfactorily fulfilling my diminished clinical responsibilities.

But, truthfully, I was so ecstatic to be with Kim in the manner that living together allowed that I'm sure I wasn't spending too much time at that point analyzing whether I was getting 85 %, 100 %, or 115 % or whatever percent of what I might theoretically aspire to get done in a vacuum. And if I did actually objectively ponder such things fleetingly against the background of thinking about Kim what seemed like almost all of the time, I would have likely thanked my new life for its unexpected benefit of regular hours. At this stage of my lab experience, steady effort in doing a steady number of experiments for steady generation of anticipated useful data was more important than late-night manic big idea ponderings.

And the nights were going so well in the non-science and non-medicine arena, all of our big ideas were centered on our feelings for each other. Kim and I were falling more deeply in love with other with each passing day, each passing moment. We spoke, especially lying in bed, as if we would always be together. Without what could have seemed premature specifics, though, the only formal plan hatched at this stage was for my first visit with her to the parents in San Diego. Without what could have seemed like unnecessary further open analysis as a couple, this seemed at least to me like a potentially serious landmark and hence crucial event with all the usual precarious implications.

...

Hence, the second time I saw the Parents Williamson, the much tanned Bob and Patti genetic contributors to the entity I was unconsciously becoming addicted to, was down in San Diego in the spring of 1991. Kim and I went down for a quick weekend visit, leaving on a Friday afternoon via the non-glamorous mode of mass but convenient transport known as Southwest Airlines. The potentially most ominous part is I don't remember us separately paying for individual tickets. I think we just bought them out of already fusing funds. I had actually arranged to go in to the lab early enough to be productive and still hopefully finish in time to catch a flight around 4:30, which put us into San Diego at a time of traffic not nearly as bad as what we had already gone through to barely catch our flight in San Francisco. An advantage of our spatial as well as our temporal arrival, though, included the proximity of our landing to that of all our unfolding destinations and plans. The San Diego Airport is actually on the harbor in downtown San Diego, unlike those sprawling metropolises that out of some sort of civic-demon delivered vision to inhumane city council members decide to put their airports conveniently an hour or two away in the middle of nowhere, such that you have to leave so early to catch your plane you might as well have driven to your destination if it's not on a different continent.

Or, there's even that situation, where to go somewhere that requires a big plane from the inconveniently located newer, big airport located somewhere outside what at least seemed like the city proper, one would actually catch a smaller plane from the more easily vehicular-reachable older inner city airport, the transit glory of bygone simpler times of poodle skirts, olive colored kitchen appliances, and vinyl forms of music. In my not too distant future, I would do enough of these, seemingly conceptually silly, flights from the old Houston Hobby Airport south of the Medical Center to Houston Intercontinental WAY north of the city and especially in the other direction of landing at Intercontinental and flying to Hobby to get me aerially closer to where I wanted to be, which depending on how many drinks I'd had (mostly on the longer arrival flights…) in transit, I would begin to ludicrously speculate on the potential pseudo physics of it all. If the airports were that close (those particular flights took seemingly longer to taxi/take off and land/taxi than to actually fly in the air) and we were flying at jet speeds, I'd perhaps even wonder if we could possibly be moving backwards in time; you know, the whole space-time continuum thing. But of course, not only was that not the case, as we weren't actually approaching the speed of light (I'll be a much bigger fan of air travel then!), but I realized that airport locations likely had little to do with convenience per se. It was all about land: land availability, land legalities, and especially land purchasing costs. I'm sure there were other issues. I could barely keep up in my field, so civic politics, urban design, and construction costs were not anything I was likely to give impromptu seminars on. I suspect that with essentially all male-dominated or even just male-participated decisions since the beginning of time, most activities contributing to the scrolls of history, however mundane, come down to some aspect and/or combination of land, money, and prized women. I suppose in the modern era, where much of the land is owned and new channels for frenzy and civic pride are needed (and considering only the U.S., for example), one could throw in professional sport fandom as well, for the last of the great motivating factors for all acts of thoughtless and aggressive passion. Although this didn't make it so far as to practically co-localize airports and sports stadiums, at least in the case of Houston. Maybe the airport and/or team owners had an interest in the automobile fuel industry as well, or at least a shared interest in perpetuating pollution.

I was going to learn more about San Diego shortly and, to me at least, in this particular case, we were blessed by an apparent lack of city-state airport relocation progress. Over the weekend, in a visiting tourist-based total lack of historical perspective, I came to the simple conclusion that in this setting of sun-drenched blessedness, they sent rich people up to the potentially even more glorious coast of La Jolla (of course, that Pacific ocean water front thing has a whole lot to do with distribution in the North-South vs. West-East direction for all aspects of California people dispersion) and let us land in a near water front location only ~5-10 minutes from our destination for drinks and a dinner reservation at Morton's on J Street, a Bob-favorite old and up-scale type joint in the Gaslamp Quarter. It wasn't quite Bob and Patti's style to pick us up directly, so Kim's folks had arranged for a limo to pick us up and take us to dinner.

From what I gathered in the usual frenzied conversations of normally apart loved ones put together instantaneously in numbers greater than 2 and with a "new-comer" necessitating at least a component of polite small talk and accompanying orientation, this part of San Diego had been experiencing quite a rejuvenation the last many years. I think the particular restaurant we were at had actually been around a long time, had survived a period of probably outdated décor and loyal long time customers only while maintaining an impeccable reputation and famous wine list, and had survived, to now be enjoying a deserved boon period facilitated by being located within a few square blocks of all the proper cafes and "eateries" to be seen at in the proper attire, with the proper people, in the beautiful San Diego evenings. Looking around as we made it from the bar where we met and rapid-fire talked to our table while less efficiently heard similar talk continued in variously paused single file fashion, it was quite possible that the décor was probably considered esoteric in some sort of nouveau retro style only realized as authentic by the potentially few long-time local diners who along with a few insightful critics probably gave the joint credit for staying true the whole time to the fundamental aspects of good restauranting: great food, great wine, and attentive but not overbearing service. Maybe they'd added an emphasis to martinis and other non-Bordeaux-derived beverages at the bar, and in keeping with the times had added some non coronary-clogging meals to the menu, with a supposedly city-acclaimed emphasis on fresh seafood according to one blurt of the Piranha-paced initial conversation I caught a part of when we had entered and hooked up with Kim's parents.

It seemed to me, it was the kind of weird combo of old guard steak house, where the city's established elders could still go out dressed up for a nice dinner like in the "glory days," where the emerging next generation of tragically not to ever be as genteel power players could stop by in their more casual work clothes or even post golf clothes (if a weekday, mostly for the martini and bar appetizer part, and they would at least change their shoes), where the same may take their families out when a crowd of out of town relatives had descended, and where fresh seafood was being served in a setting accidentally just off beat enough compared to the pick up bar dime a dozen haut cuisine places all around it to give it eclectic appeal to the younger crowd out on actual romantic dates. All this combined in some sort of culinary surrealism to put me at gustatory and social ease.

Adding to the above, Bob was in some sort of 90s for mature man pants that I myself couldn't distinguish as to causal new man work, gardening, boating, or golfing attire, with a bright red polo shirt that was probably the most luminous item in the room. In temporal or constitutional contrast, I, of course, was in some permutation of the usual. A striped blue oxford (but this time it was actually a Ralph Lauren, purchased for me by Kim), a nicer than usual version of khakis (dress by at least my standards; also purchased by Kim, but that time I was at least there), brown dress shoes made in Italy by someone I couldn't pronounce (but it made me feel sexy when I read the shoe box; guess who bought those?), and a blue blazer (this one, I think I brought with me, but it maintained approval). I looked like I should be giving a lecture, maybe on Milton or Dante or The Federalist Papers at a Liberal Arts college, but at least a really high tuition one. Kim, who also had worked part of the day, was the essence of professional sexiness in an off white silk blouse and a form fitting black skirt with leather pumps made by an Italian designer with a name even sexier than on my shoe box, and a set of pearls that came from like her mother's, mother's, mother's etc. mother...like they'd been in the Captain's safe on the Mayflower or something. She was so fucking beautiful, and we kept passing those knowing glances at each other, that at one point I thought I was going to have to go outside in that glorious San Diego fading spring sun, just to get out of the mesmerizing/quasi-hallucinating effect of the dark room, the self-imposed parent pressure, the burgeoning wine, and the combining bonergenic smells of old wood, garlic from the kitchen, the candles, and the lofting essence of that increasingly known combination of Kim's skin and her perfume, even from almost three and a half feet away.

Kim's mom was wearing a black spaghetti-strapped surprisingly short, silky black dress that showed off her shoulders and her tan and made me feel a little weird when I stopped, took stock, and objectively realized that she was probably the second hottest chick in the entire restaurant. Rather than taking the time to feel guilty, I suddenly wondered if Kim had told her parents that we were actually living together. But, I'd had too much sensual infusion of the positive kind, two beers on the plane, two Martinis with Bob (on his recommendation/insistence) at the bar while we were waiting for our table, was now about a quarter through my delicious steak, and on my third sip of something essentially miraculous called Mouton Rothschild that Bob had ordered with a grin to go with the steaks that only he and I had ordered, to worry too much about...well, just about anything. In one of those moments that I probably didn't process per se in too deep an analytical state, but only appreciated subconsciously for the contra-normal calmness they embedded, I would let each moment take care of itself. Each bite of delicious steak, each glorious taste of wine, each glance and smell of Kim, each breath; I would relax, and gluttonize myself for now.

Kim and her Mom ate fish, which by the bite Kim gave me during the meal, and the three bites I ate to finish it when she couldn't was really good, and they drank some sort of white burgundy to go along with it, the name of which I couldn't begin to pronounce even if I had a test the next morning, and which Bob had suggested and ordered with Patti's knowledgeable approval. That also meant that all of the Mouton divine juice went to Bob and me for our medium rare T-bones, as well as a second bottle of a slightly lesser ranked, but almost as delicious, Bordeaux. After Chocolate Mousse and a couple other deserts shared amongst the table with some tawny ports, we drove to the Homestead Williamson in Bob's

Cadillac. Statistically, he'd had too much of various two-carbon molecule beverages, but as someone who had had at least as many or more and was in more of a position of ass kissing than safety criticism mode, I eagerly sat in the back seat with my hands on Kim's thigh and a few sneaked kisses, while Bob made a likely familiar drive through mostly back streets into their comfortable, established large-house neighborhood only about ten minutes away.

When we got "home", we had a night cap (wine for Kim, me and her Mom; scotch for her dad, which despite all the pressures for male bonding that weekend, I wisely resisted), and then Patti was tired, and so she excused herself and Bob quickly followed. The "kids" were up alone, but rather than celebrating it, going out to the back yard or making out on the sofa, as we may not see each other for eight hours, Kim simply said that she was very tired and asked if I was tired too.

I didn't know how to respond as I think I was on an emotional scale somewhat distinct from awake or tired, but taking my lack of response as an affirmative or feeling something even different that made my response irrelevant, she took me by the hand and led me upstairs, into what I astutely realized was her "old" bedroom.

"Where am I supposed to sleep?" I inquired in some instinctive self-imposed sense of girlfriend's parents nearby state.

"With me, you big dork," she provocatively responded while unbuttoning my shirt, and I then noticed she had already slipped her blouse off. "But only after you make passionate love to me," she continued in a part speak and part irresistible kiss that seemed like one harmonious motion with unzipping and lowering my pants.

Participating willingly in the current physical activities, but in a weird almost outside of self-psyche state moderated by a nag in the back of my brain that if one had to put a concrete visual pattern on it would surely involve Kim's Dad and a shotgun, I hesitantly inquired: "What about your parents?" and then in some sort of unfamiliar but yet wise puritanical and self-protective qualifier, "Won't they want us to sleep in separate rooms?"

"They already know we're living together," she effectively argued while slipping her tongue in my mouth. In between alternating states of seeing my guts 12-gauge blasted all over Kim's well decorated and memorabilia filled room and trying to concentrate on the legitimacy of her relationship claims, I noticed that she had largely achieved by herself a state wherein we were now both completely naked and she had my rock hard penis in her warm hands.

As if I now needed still more convincing, she added, "so…I'm pretty sure they realize that we're likely sleeping together….Hence, they felt…whatever, what's the point…we might as well sleep together here, too….plus…they seem to like you."

O.K. I wasn't going to enter into any kind of already lost debate with someone who could still use "hence" after all the drinking we'd been through. I also figured that I could always sneak out to another bed room after we'd made love, not that I had any idea of where anything was up in this grand upstairs area; I would be sure that my clothes were all nearby, so that I could quickly dress, and either present myself as just having fallen asleep on the floor or come in for an early morning, but outfit appropriate visit to my girlfriend. Whatever, these thoughts were for the next phase. Phase 1 was well under way. In the midst of being where I now felt best, I did acutely pass oh so momentarily from mystical to conscientious phase and comforted myself one last time in the knowledge that Bob and Patti's bedroom was essentially in another area code down a very long hallway. Still, I tried to be quiet. I tried to be at least sonically controlled…and I think, in the effort of self-imposed intended respectful silence, I must have bit like 40 % of my lower lip off when I came.

…

The next morning found me not in as quite a presentable mode appropriate for a male guest of families with young desirable daughters as I had intended. When I finally awoke, I was still completely naked, sprawled out on my front in the form of one who'd slept very well, with a bit of sheet strategically covering my butt. As I turned over to more of the unexpected, I kept the sheet in place as needed and mentally encouraged my morning erection to subside while I tried to take in the evidence around me that might at least hint at what had transpired between Kim waking up and the current moment.

Despite my well hatched (or at least well intended) plan of having last night's clothes on the floor beside my side of the bed for immediate action, if needed, and at the very least being able to don them for stepping out into more common areas of the house this morning, of course, being seen in the same clothes as last night before locating my suitcase for a quick change could have implicated me in some acts of going to sleep where maybe I shouldn't have. But it would certainly be better than strolling around naked, an act with similar implications but even less feigned courtesy, or it could even imply that I was up, had already gotten dressed, and just happened to be a light and practical packer. I could even wear the same thing all this next day just to prove it.

However, on a quick and then more visually focused swing of my arm down to the floor by the bed, said outfit was not evident according to prior strategy. Before panicking completely, I allowed myself a near 270 degree scan of the room, taking in essentially everything but the wall behind me that the head of the bed was up against, with the intention of finding a chair that Kim, in an also recognized need to retrospectively add some civilization to our (mostly her) barbaric manner of disrobing the night before, would have neatly folded and stacked my conservative, "nice young man" outfit on….But, nothing.

Then, on a second visual pass, in one of those recognitions that one can at least briefly ponder as perhaps some form of minor miracle, those potentially classified in the mundane or domestic category, I noted my suitcase sitting quietly on a bench like thing at the foot of the bed.

But then, miracle status was negated by emerging implications. Hopefully (*surely*) Kim had brought it up, maybe it had even been there all night? No, I would have insisted on bringing it upstairs, which would have prompted a much earlier discussion of sleeping arrangements. No, this was a relatively new placement. I didn't see Kim's. Maybe closet? Hopefully, her mother or father had not brought it up (*Oh my God, was that even possible? Maybe they were up first, maybe they didn't like seeing the luggage still in the entry way---did we at least get them in from the trunk of Bob's car last night?)*---before Kim even got up; after all, given the drink, the time of night, etc., our pleasure in sleeping in together when neither of us had to go to work…that would have been terrible! They (*would they have really brought it up together?)*….No, he or SHE would have seen us in bed together….A good view, given the suitcase's location. That's ridiculous. And, I don't remember any "staff". Instead, Kim would have gotten up earlier than she should have physiologically, as she was at home, visiting her parents. So, now, in an increasingly clear-headed reconstruction of events I'd obviously slept soundly through: Kim woke up, dressed, went down stairs, at some point, brought hers and my suitcases up, put hers in her closet, had picked my clothes off the floor and put them in my suitcase, and in one apparent last and clearly at the time unsuccessful gesture to maybe at least gently wake me up, had opened the blinds. Hopefully, this was all relatively recent, so when I went down, it wouldn't appear that I was a complete bum for sleeping in late compared to Kim and her likely awake parents. After all, older people never sleep in, do they?

But, at least now, I could go down stairs, confidently, in fresh clean clothes of what I perceived, at least the other day when packing, as appropriate for a Saturday in San Diego. In my first naked step of the four it would comfortably take for me to reach my suitcase, facing fully frontal to the door, the door flew open, without a knock, without any warning of any sort, stopping me dead in the tracks of my humility, and a male creature I'd never seen before was standing loudly in the doorway.

"Dude," it began, "if you want any breakfast, better get your ass downstairs."

It had almost shoulder length, wavy reddish brown hair, portions of what might be regarded as bangs, hanging over his eyes. It was the kind of hair that Bob or maybe even I would have worn in the late seventies. It also had on a primarily lime green tie died shirt that in my quick glance said something about "Monterey". Fortunately, it didn't want to be involved in this stand off much longer than I did. Before he closed the door, he gave me a quick glance, and then in that one eye scrunched, lip pursed type face of classic male nodding, he added, acknowledging my nakedness, "Nice." Fortunately, but again reminding me of the full spectrum and implications of the current situation, I don't think he was offering a critique on me anatomically, but was appreciating the fact that I was there, with Kim, in the house he grew up in, and the house where his parents lived, in a manner comfortable and confident enough to be naked.

After the door closed, I quickly threw on the what I had calculated as an appropriately casual pair of light pants and polo shirt, things that Kim had bought for me in my presence with our fused funds, just a few weeks ago, and I tried to nonchalantly make my way downstairs. I calmly and quietly strolled into the kitchen area, trying to give off a non-guilty air, as if maybe I'd been awake for a while, and had just chosen to remain upstairs, perhaps reading (plausible), or meditating (less plausible), or admiring furnishings (somewhere in the middle). I'm sure I was completely unconvincing. Kim's mother, already looking effortlessly elegant this morning in a light blue short sleeved top (blouse?) and tan pants of some specialized sort (Capri perhaps? based on my still rudimentary but inevitably growing "fashion", at least, "noticing", if not yet "sense") was in the large kitchen surrounded on various counter surfaces by a moderate stack of used plates, and serving bowls and platters, the latter still mildly filled with a surprisingly wide spectrum of breakfast menu items. Residual omelet portions and bacon caught my attention. The cleaning of plates and gearing up for packaging of leftovers (still no staff noted as yet) must have been what prompted my visitation by the 1970's entity in the green tie die who now sat on a stool in a completely visible form, like a badly groomed avatar of a hippie divinity for a cult I hadn't heard about yet. It was eating what looked like a sinfully rich pastry with a generous shoveling of confectioner's sugar on it, which (as if in some sort of celebration of the triumvirate for whatever sect the zeal of eating in such fashion was a ritual of) appeared to be amazingly equally distributed between his shirt, his who-knows-how-long-in-progress beard want-to-be, and his plate.

As if right on cue (like in some sort of amateur community theater or one of those 30 minute sitcoms with the fake laughter tracks, which to my perception we hadn't yet had any moments to trigger as of yet), *enter kitchen/breakfast area left,* Kim appeared, and to add to the surreal disorientation of reluctant protagonist, had a handful of mixed flowers in her hand, which she handed to her mother. While out of the corner of my eye I sensed the female act of vase acquisition and vase filling with water and flowers, Kim had already assessed the situation with all the domestic charm of the true star of our episode, and brightly asked me, "Have you met Barkley yet?"

And then without waiting for any answers from the others in the scene, as if any introduction other than by her didn't count to her level of approval, she continued, "Jeff, this is my brother Barkley…Barkley, this is Jeff"

"No shit…really…," Barkley offered up first, and then barely looking up from the newspaper he was reading while dispersing the sweet white grains of devotion, he reached up to shake my hand, saying "Nice to meet you."

"You too," I responded with all the appropriate brevity my current confidence mandated, and we shook hands firmly, and then he returned to his paper. I had miscalculated on first quick glance the distribution of the powdered sugar. It must have been more like a 30% split on each area as a good healthy 10% now dwelled on my right hand. Anticipating the potential disasters of such a loaded appendage while walking around the house, and inevitably touching something, probably something very non-white and likely expensive, I casually wiped my hand on my mentally noted fairly similar if not perfectly matched off-white pants.

Without looking up again, Brother Barkley added dryly, "I almost didn't recognize you with your clothes on."

I was a bit taken aback, given real grown up company being present, and indeed Kim's mom did glance up from the kitchen with a slight quizzical expression; but in a display of likely being fairly accustomed to her son and smart-ass comments in general, she restored some semblance of order, with, "Jeff, would you like some breakfast?"

"Yes ma'am, please," I responded.

"What can I get you? But you'll have to quit calling me ma'am…," she politely continued.

"Sorry ma'am…I mean, sorry. Some of those eggs and bacon and a piece of that toast would be great, m…," I dribbled.

"Let me make some fresh toast for you, this is a bit cold," she began moving about.

"Oh, that's not necessary, m…," catching myself again. When she looked up with mock (I hoped) sinisterness, I chided myself out loud, with "Sorry… (pause to contain the ma'am that would normally follow), I guess it's a habit…one of those Texas things"

"It's very nice and respectful. It's a good habit, we like those Texas things," Kim now offered up in defense of her new beau.

"Yeah, you know, like castrating bulls," Barkley spoke through powdered lips without looking up, spraying the appropriate sacrificial amount onto the plate below.

Or hippie time warped freaks with scruffy pubic hair on their face, I thought, but refrained (for now) from saying.

Kim's mom looked up at her son, with gentle motherly disapproval reflected on her lovely face, and then to further emphasize the acute trouble state he was not really in and my hopefully acute favored state, she said to the whole room, "We're just not used to such politeness around here," at which point she re-fixed her mock glare on the Barkley organism. Then, turning to resume her assembly of my breakfast, she added, sweetly and with a well appreciated brownie point towards me, "If you keep it up…we may just have to adopt you."

Not missing a beat, and with his mouth partly full, Barkley now offered in commentary on this latest social twist, "If you adopted him, he and Kim couldn't have sex."

"Yes, we could, you dickhead," Kim surprised me, and while grabbing the newspaper away from her brother as if in some alpha-sibling relationship act, she clarified, "It wouldn't be like we were officially related."

I remember noting several things, either in succession or simultaneously. Firstly, my confidence in Barkley's apparently precise ritualistic spreading of his powdered sugar was reinstated, as despite how he'd hovered over both plate and paper simultaneously, there didn't appear to be a single sucrose molecule on the paper as Kim tore it away from him in a fashion that would have unleashed a dustbowl full if this hadn't been so; secondly, I was in the middle of a typical family, a true family, situation, where likely most topics and deliveries were not off limits. From whatever section Barkley had been reading, Kim immediately turned to the weather pages.

"Daddy's offered to take us sailing this afternoon, if you're up for it. The weather should be great," Kim said as she turned to me with a loving and anticipating smile.

"Absolutely," I responded with enthusiasm that made her smile bigger. "Can we take Barkley...or is it Dickhead?" I directed towards Barkley and then back to Kim and her Mother, "so we can...like...drown him...or feed him to the sharks?"

"Nice," he gave an approving grin for the whole room to see, as he had finally finished his last bite and gave me a similarly acknowledging firm pat or two on the shoulder as he walked out to apparently go upstairs.

I didn't realize until later, when Kim was brushing white confection sugar off of the back of my bright some form of light bluish-green colored polo, that'd he'd powder indoctrinated me...one last time.

...

Kim's father kept the family's sailboat at one of the most ideally situated marinas in the main San Diego Harbor. It was one of those that seemed just a bit of what I may have disorientedly perceived as south from where the Star of India was "kept", or whatever the official word is that Bob used when he reported it to be the world's oldest active sailing ship and to have apparently been serving as a museum since long before Bob and Patti arrived in San Diego, or even before Bob and Patti had arrived anywhere period. Apparently amongst the sailors, that was something like a bragging right, as the ship had actually been put in service in something like the 1860s; whereas amongst the scientist, it only seemed to make me glad that we were going out on Bob's far more recent boat than that boat or ship or museum or whatever, especially when I learned that it was made of iron-as I would have suspected that boats back then would have been made of something that floats even in its unaltered state, maybe something like wood as ivory soap bars would not have been practical even if they had existed back then. Though I must admit while some comments from Bob about different riggings went over my low head of ignorance, I did think it was cool that there was a mutiny on its very first mission (or voyage?) and I suppose I was impressed that it had made it around the world something like twenty times, as probably not too many things left over from the 19th century can make that claim.

Bob's wasn't the biggest boat in the harbor, but it certainly wasn't the smallest. If anything, it was more towards the upper half. I was from central TX. I played land sports in my past life, and spent more of whatever leisure time I allowed myself in the arena of bars, which was more of a nighttime sport. What the hell did I know about boats? And I tried to convey this potentially momentarily embarrassing and hopefully not relationship precluding void in that subtle manly fashion, in which one doesn't want to appear too naïve and clueless, so you exaggerate your meaningless past "boating" experience in a hopefully adequately vague and non-descript fashion, so as equally importantly, your vastly exaggerated and maybe even blatantly lied about aquatic past doesn't commit you to too much unsupervised sail-boating tasks on that actual day (say, before you can get back to San Francisco and discreetly take lessons) to the point of putting yourself and particularly your girlfriend's and her exquisitely boat-dressed father's life at danger.

So, taking a jon boat out on Canyon Lake with your buddies for largely ineffective fishing and more efficient beer drinking (especially afterwards, as we WERE safety conscious), and going out once with one of said high school buddies on his dad's REALLY small sailboat and talking about going down to Baytown to go sailing with a med school buddy becomes in early romance, trying to impress girl-friend's dad, white (pushing gray) lie speak: "I had a buddy in high school who had a sail boat and I used to go out with him every now and then, and I had a friend in med school, who's parents had a pretty big boat....but, I'm far from experienced."

That and maybe the early more overt signs of cluelessness as we set foot on board and set sail and made "boat talk", spared me from frank nautical embarrassment and manslaughter that day. Kim, not an avid enthusiast per se, but exposed in the past in no-choice offspring style, stayed by my side that day, in girlfriend, rather than self preservation style, which gave me more cover. And, indeed, we had a great day. The weather was what I imagined God must sprinkle on his own front lawn every morning. Kim acted towards me as if her father wasn't there. And Bob acted as if being on his boat with people who appreciated it was his greatest calling.

We met Kim's mom for dinner at a fairly new big tourist-like seafood place on the harbor that juts out on the water (the Fish Market, which I had to subsequently go to every time in San Diego), eating upstairs in an area more fancy than the downstairs "tourists in tee shirts and jean shorts" part. I ate fish I couldn't pronounce and drank more white wine than beer. Bob and Patti drove home in Bob's Cadillac. Kim drove me home in Patti's Saab. We had night caps…several. Patti excused herself again as tired, and Bob followed as per protocol, but not before giving me a firm hand shake and Kim a kiss on her cheek that I interpreted as approval.

We sat there in silence for a few moments, sunned from the day, buzzed from the day, and I think, mutually, even more buzzed from some sort of sense of proper placement; in a world in which we had only been minimally as yet exposed to its frequent and widespread crapness, we were properly placed in love, in place, and in time. Those moments, the true ones, are not to be taken lightly, as the world that derives from the outside and especially from the inside will shit them out of you faster than a bad menu choice in a Mexican border town or HIV-enteropathy.

Kim grabbed the bottle off the bar we had communally been night capping from, again some sort of obscenely delicious old ranked Bordeaux out of Bob's cellar, poured one more very full glass into each of our likely extremely expensive stemware specimens, grabbed her glass, placed my glass in my hand, and grabbing my free hand, stood me up and started to lead me out to the back yard through the kitchen, saying in tones directly connecting to erectile tissue, "Come with me if you want to live."

She let go of my hand, moved a few steps ahead of me, took a big gulp out of her wine glass, stripped as if she were an ex-Olympic Gold Medalist casual yet exotic de-clother, while I did nothing but sit there and sip my wine while watching her naked silhouette from behind as if I were a two-time ex-Olympic Gold Medalist voyeur, and I followed the outline of perfection as it closed on and then dove into the pool, my last vision a faint moon and remote outside light illumination of her barely spread legs going into the pool viewed from behind. I non-graciously stumbled and tripped out of hopefully all my clothes and suavely set my empty wine glass on the table next to Kim's remnants and, hopefully non-viewed, dove into the pool after her.

We swam and mostly held each other while treading water in the deep end and kissed and fondled in every part of the pool for what must have been at least an hour or two, time that went by in residual wakefulness and barely sobriety that I would trade a thousand subsequent reality particles for one milli-fantasy remembrance of. Kim tasted so good; it was pure unadulterated feasting to kiss her until our pruned bodies demanded more ambient air. Despite the perfect situation I found myself in, including noticing that all upstairs lights were off and which supported parent deep coma status (as we had already let out some pretty shrill cries and loud teasing screams to no perceived awakenings), and how Kim's wet smooth body with the help of the warm pool water was making me appreciate myself like an at least amateur porn star from the purely anatomical perspective, I had the occasional uninvited thought that it was about time for Barkley to show up. In the deep recesses of my cerebrum, those gyri devoted most to bizarre surrealistic intrusive but vivid images, my day long sun, beer, white wine, and most acutely Bordeaux and girlfriend lubricated mind saw an entourage of his no sense of personal space associates, standing at the edge of the pool; a bunch of scrawny, non-athletic guys with slight beer bellies and similar laughable belly button fuzz on their chins, girls of non-identifiable ethnicity-fair but dark, in part because of their unshaven legs, their unshaven armpits revealed as they lifted their arms up to pull their hair back to put up before jumping into the global pool where two inappropriately physically romantic worldly indulgents were linked on my rock hard penis. Fortunately, Barkley and the imagined "Barkletts" did not show up, and I did not inquire where it and they were. Fortunately they were only fleetingly in my mind, in such a transient manner that the glory at hand was not really affected, and Kim and I began to make love in the water, where we could both barely stand with our heads above water, continued at the edge of the pool, and briefly continued on the cool/coarse grass before we mutually and simultaneously realized it was time to take this budding ritual indoors.

As I lay on the grass, looking upward into a ridiculously full moon, and had just started to wonder about what I felt on my left lower inner thigh and what could be crawling on me, Kim threw a towel on me and was standing over me, with her towel already wrapped around her in that from just above the breasts to below the muff and butt manner that they must teach at girl camp, as they can run around in those things with the confidence of a tied up (albeit less comfortable) corset, while the average guy can't tie a fucking towel around his waist in a manner that will even allow him to shave or brush his teeth without having to re-tie it at least a dozen times.

"Let's move this show inside," she seductively said, while squeezing the last water molecule out of her hair in another unique female action.

"Right behind you," I said, hopelessly following behind, adjusting my towel, while staring at the shape of Kim's ass in the moon and the kitchen outside door light, wishing I had come up with something to say a bit more appropriate to my mood.

We entered the kitchen/breakfast room from the same (now revealed to me) door that Kim had surprised me through with flowers in hand earlier in the day. The house was almost completely dark in most foci, with pockets of eerie faint light coming from various appliances, as exotic as the fridge in the wet bar of the family room area. I pulled myself away from Kim's hand, and said, as if I was a complete master of the blackened floor plan, and while giving her a quick reassuring peck, "Go on up, I'll be right there."

"What?" she implied in the appropriate combination of "how could you give up what we have going" and "what are you going to do/where are you going to go."

I nodded my head toward the fridge, which Kim could apparently appreciate in the minimal available light, and with female insight related to male needs modulated by already known Kim/Jeff things and maybe even appreciating my acute effort to increase my energy which she may shortly benefit from. Maybe she knew from our life already and maybe took some couple warmth from supposing that I would be quick and not leave her unattended in her towel removed self for more than a breath or two. She emphasized the latter and unnecessarily demonstrated such power over me, by sliding her tongue into my mouth one more time, then squeezing the contents of my crotch through my still slipping towel, she uttered the parallel and hence unnecessary words, "Don't take long." She turned and seemingly dematerialized for only faint residual glimpses as she moved through the dimly illumed darkness up to our room.

I had only vague plans. But if I could execute them within that dictated time frame, I would. One, I was, despite the earlier food orgy, a bit hungry, and as noted, in the spirit of appreciated physiology, any largely simple glucose source would soon be put to quick use.

And, two....

I miraculously found the box with as many as four left over pastries of the kind that Barkley had partly imbibed and partly baptized me with that morning. I ate one as fast as was primate possible, if not digestively sound. Then I gathered my other senses. I used my chlorine flavored towel (since it needed readjustment/ re-cinching anyway) to wipe my mouth, the refrigerator door, and especially the floor between me and the refrigerator. Then, having, strategically (and probably hopelessly) rewrapped it's moistness around me, I glanced around, possessed by the spirit of the pastry and full moon. Reflecting the reason why paper towels were white rather than black (regardless of those silly little barely recognizable patterns that some manufacturers put on in the spirit of white trash kitchen decoration), the roll on the perfect counter tops declared itself to me. I put one more pastry, very securely, inside four pieces of paper towel, in a manner that not even a quark's worth of sugar particle could escape from. I returned the vestiges of the likely non accountant level maintained content count pastry box (not that my Karloffian state allowed for such rational thought), removed my towel one more time for that one last brilliant psychopath's crime scene broader wipage, and made my way upstairs.

Illuminated by a bizarrely fortunate hallway's worth of oh so subtle moderately high art and/or family photograph illuminated dim lighting, I stealthily made my way into what I intuitively hoped was Barkley's ashramic lair. (I knew which door was Mr. and Mrs. Kim's; any other opening could be mortally endured in my current Bordeaux, Kim, pool, and sugar saturated state of harmlessly intended criminality).

His room revealed itself to me. It wasn't anything like divine or spiritual communication from something at least partially residing inside it or anything like that. It was more of an architectural hunch of upper class suburban child bedroom arrangements, and maybe some sort of boy smell thing I only vaguely perceived, as I disturbingly more prominently noted a mild sugar particle appearance from the paper towel mass onto the front of my still slightly moist towel. Brief panic nocturnis ensued, but I reassured myself by looking down the hallway and comfortably noted the absence of at least obvious Hansel and Gretel like confection sugar crumbs. Even in the only eerie light of those likely expensive subtle and dim bulbs from the fairway length hallway and the moonlight coming in from the partially opened curtains in the room where I stood in the doorway, probably like an intentionally dimly lit scene in a B-movie (at best) slasher film in which a boy/young man in only a towel (so, maybe one of the gym locker room type scenes) gets his head cut off (maybe with Psycho-stealing glimpses of the fake blood going down one of the shower drains…amongst chunks of brain that won't fit through the drain holes), or scared by a teammate depending on how long his character is in the script and how far into the movie we are, I could see the signs of Barkley in my emerging non-imaginary surroundings: a Hendrix at Monterey festival (nice), a photograph of George Harrison with the Maharishi on his dresser (I thought about stealing that, but that would be too obvious), and a stack of dirty jeans, black (by absence of visibility or actuality) T-shirts, and more discreetly scattered items, such as socks and underwear (yuck) at some point further into the room. Moving slowly inward, at the point of noticing a Dead concert poster on the wall opposite the bed but close to the trickle of moonlight coming in from the windows at the far side, I realized I had reached my destination and my plan became disclosed to me.

Obviously, I had encountered no evidence of Barkley's presence in the house that night. I assumed he was out late or for, who knows, a period of days, however long it takes to transmit or receive the proper aliquot of bullshit for whatever he was most recently into. But, in order to make double sure (as if I'd have some sort of excuse if I'd encountered the opposite of what I expected), I roughly pounded my right hand along the full length and width of the bed. Satisfied that nothing was in place, the same right hand lifted the pillows and my left hand strategically placed its sarcastic sacrament of overly-powdered pastry under the pillows. As I imagined the floury, lipidy, saturated fatty, doughy, and especially powdery sugary consequences of the smushing of such goodies under the curly haired, pseudo bearded little shit, I made my way back to our room, in a manner as if I'd lived there all my life.

Kim and I made love with no regard on mine or anyone else's part for any noise that could even theoretically upset this perfect universe. We slept naked. We slept soundly. Sometime during the night, with only the Gods to see, a small white piece of confection sugar that had miraculously survived our kisses, made its way from my lower inner lip to her immaculately soft shoulder, fusing us as securely as the surroundings we found ourselves in.

...

The next morning (barely), Kim and I took Patti's car up the coast to La Jolla. We drove around the town with the top down, admiring the ocean view- and especially ocean-front houses and the general ambience of a town filled with high end boutiques and the people that could afford to live and/or shop there. We parked and had a nice time walking around, window shopping, and entering some custom jewelry shops and especially small art galleries. We had a wonderful late lunch and a bottle of wine at a nice little café overlooking the ocean, and walked some more. At one point, we ended up at a segment of beach that appeared to be protected as a sanctuary or such for seals, as dozens of them appeared to be just hanging out lazily, maybe not quite realizing the value of the real estate that had been allotted to them. A few of these interesting looking distant cousins occasionally exhibited what I (without being a seal expert per se) would rate as at most moderately intense seal physical activity of play and swim, while we, the self professed sole species with free-will, stood along the sidewalk or the deck flanking the seal paradise watching them display the good taste of living at least part of the year on a gorgeous southern California beach.

Leaning up against the rail of the beach front sidewalk and looking down at the harbor seals in the gradually descending sun, it made me think of the sea lions that had been steadily making their home at Pier 39 on Fisherman's Wharf. In some ways, I felt a little perhaps non-biologic kinship with these other essentially foreigners. Like me, they had basically just come to San Francisco in 1989 though they had the good judgment to wait until after the October earthquake. Who knows why? These things can have broad ranging ecological effects I suppose, or maybe with a disturbing to me at least amount of marina-side city falling into the water, real estate prices or their water equivalents were lowered in a sea lion favoring way while certainly not favorably affecting my rent or my landlord's amenability to conversations about such. Even with numbers just growing gradually, there were enough to keep me temporarily partially intrigued, such that even before meeting Kim and eagerly submitting to her San Francisco Awareness and Appreciation course, I had at least made it down to Fisherman's Wharf, on multiple occasions, initially as a new resident/tourist, either by myself or with some co-workers, and then as a slightly less new resident, when serving inadequately as a tour guide when my parents first visited me in San Francisco. The waterfront ambience, with its spectrum of fishy smells, its weathered decks and piers, and tour-providing shops and souvenir kiosks made Fisherman's Wharf an experience easily appreciated as different from Central Texas even without me providing any smashingly insightful bits of tourist info beyond what we could read even while walking with guidebooks in hand. I did point out the sea lions on Pier 39, of course. The first time I had been there, gazing at these creatures in the proximity of an urban human population as large and especially as dense as the bay area only seemed to add to the eclectic nature I was already effortlessly noting and absorbing by just being in San Francisco.

Now, with Kim likely admiring our gracious aquatic mammalian hosts, the general ambience from the beautiful day, and my hand in hers, I found myself wondering if seals and/or their genetically close relatives were pretty much just scattered all over California, as I seemed to be encountering them with some regularity here. If I went to Sacramento, for example, maybe for some sort of official state business, would I encounter seals on the lawn of the Capital or in the lobby of whatever building housed the Medical Board offices? No, probably not, in fact, these could very well be two of the more celebrated peri-urban seal hangouts in the state. So, instead, I began wondering which of the two locations I would most likely prefer to live in if I were one of these California seals or sea lions.

Would I choose the backdrop of a seemingly decadent city rich with a colorful history of pirates, sailors, tattoos, Height-Ashbury inspired hippies, and boats going by along a waterway into which my pier home jutted out into and along which sidelines tourists came to see me as just one of many attractions? Or would I chose the perhaps more laid-back but upscale lifestyle of a luxurious beach in a wealthy town, which although a possible shopper and eater's haven, I had less competition for overt specific points of tourist voyeurism? Pros of the former could certainly include cast offs from kitchens of waterfront restaurants along the wharf. Pros of the latter could include a generally quieter swimming and hunting environment. Not sure that sea lions and harbor seals necessarily get along in real life, but for the purposes of this already ridiculous speculation; who knows, maybe I'd like to live in both places during different parts of the year: summer in San Francisco to gluttonize on the left over and reject carcasses from fish markets. Winters in the San Diego area, to mate and lounge around making sounds and awkward movements of brief appeal to art collectors and diners pausing from their shopping and eating duties to admire what their species perceived as the weirdness of nature.

I'm sure that none of these perhaps uniquely human perspective considerations at least consciously entered into seal dwelling "decisions". If I even made it through one book on the topic, I'd probably learn that it had to do with strictly biologic and ecologic issues that Zoologists specializing in aquatic mammals and related topics could easily make seem as natural and objective as the rising of the sun, tides, and all those other events blessed with the absence of free will choices. Maybe dwelling places for seals, as with most or all wild animals and fishes, had to do with time of the year, eating, and mating habits, etc.

If only when it came time for we supposedly advanced and civilized humans to make such pivotal decisions as to where we would live, who we would live with, and how we would pass our time, these could be controlled by similar choiceless and "ogic" factors. We wouldn't have to weigh pros and cons, anticipate the future, consider the opinions and wishes of others, and make what should be natural hunting and mating behaviors into such anxiety provoking gesticulations of "free will".

Kim finally brought me out of my state of amateur comparative psychobiology, having either begun to think that I was prone to absence seizures or apparently appreciating the zeal with which I was currently undertaking our shared activities.

Yet she added another level of complexity to my seal real estate ponderings when in response to my passing admiration for possible human citizen concern for another species she began to gently inform me that this area was in reality not set up specifically for seals at all. She had just started to tell me that it was actually supposed to be a protected beach for children, that is of the *Homo sapien* variety, when a female adult version of such slashed into our conversation as if she had just been lying in wait to spring at the appropriate opportunity and cue, like we had tripped a Claymore mine wire or the switch for some other type of unpleasantry. This wiry haired earth mother like creature buzzed in and out of us while proclaiming, it seemed mostly in my face, as if I were the final person on earth that needed converting, more specific information about this apparently highly contested bit of beach. Apparently this site had been donated by one of the Scripps family, which I assumed linked somehow to what I knew as the some-where nearby Scripps Clinic of legendary research reputation, "blah…blah… Children's Park…blah…blah…" …thankfully light earth mother spittle in my face… "blah…blah…seals had no right…(really?)…blah…blah…animal rights quacks…blah…we…multiple suits…blah…optimistic…new countersuit…bl-." Feeling the threat of erosion of the relaxed mood I'd seemingly accidentally slid into and sensing something like an impending request to sign something or show some other sign of another unit of human endorsement, I rotated partially out of my recently assumed anti-saliva-spray mode and offered up calmly, "Seals are people too."

Probably only her perplexed struggle with the actual content of my statement prevented her partially pinking face from going full red. But finally coming to take me as at least a possible supporter of the seals in this battle, she assumed a stone-like determinism as if I were threatening to take all of her silver and tur-quoise jewelry, and stepping back to finally more fully take Kim and I in as a couple and perhaps noting that we were not in similar uniform, she logically con-cluded, "I take it that you don't enjoy children."

Not wanting at present to get even superficially into a topic with a stranger that had actually arisen more appropriately within personal and intimate set-tings recently, I responded with apparent recall of some old school Jonathan Swift exposure that was likewise apparently not recognized or at least not ap-preciated by our sunset inquisitor, "Actually, I think they can be quite delicious if prepared properly."

With Kim squeezing my hand as if in recognition of something, we turned and began to walk away at the same time as our attacker, perhaps either giving up or going to get some sort of local authority … or mental health representative. Case in point I thought to myself as we continued. No matter the ecology, physi-ology, you-name-it-ology, as soon as you get modern humans involved there have to be official designations, boundaries and limits, and the inevitable legal paper-work telling you how it all is to be and how it is to become when it no longer is.

But I suppose that if one wants the prime possessions, that's the price one has to pay, the risk one has to take.

"I didn't know you were such an animal enthusiast," she squeezed my hand more firmly and turned me towards her. "If you stare at me even half that hard later on tonight, we'll play seal games that would make these guys blush," she nodded towards the beach below.

"Maybe we should go, then," I grabbed her other hand and pulled her into me so our bodies were pressed firmly together, "so that we can get an early start."

*Seal games...*I said to myself. *I wonder if they really do those things...or is it just so much "ogic" working... with no games, no complex considerations involved.*

...

Several mostly non-ominous foreshadowings had been seeded on that first trip to the future in-laws.

Kim's mom and I would continue to get along from then until indefinitely, certainly past the point in time when she was forced to wonder why her daughter and beloved son-in-law were moving to different cities, pursuing careers the significance of which she refused to accept as greater than that of being together, always. It wouldn't matter what we both together and independently reassured her of our plans to find a way to be back together...soon.

Bob and I would spend several more episodes on his sail boat together. Most of these would be without Kim; just me and her Father in some semblance of male bonding I suppose. Kim would typically be shopping with her Mom on these occasions, and I think she especially liked that her Dad and I were spending time alone. Sometimes we would go as early as the morning, but more often thankfully, perhaps due to drinking and socializing and staying up late the night before (such as when we'd arrived on a Friday evening for a quick weekend visit), these would usually be afternoon excursions. I loved the sun, the usually warm breezes that somehow seem unique when experienced on water, and the motion of the sailboat.

Bob would patiently teach me or at least show me various aspects of the art of sailing, and I was at least a moderately attentive student/audience. He seemed to hold that acts of leisure requiring acquired toys and skill were the sacred right of the man of means and accomplishment. Sailing was the clearest and highest example, perhaps, given the obvious cost of a boat and the obvious time demanded to master the skills necessary to be a good sailor. As I was a promising young man well on his way to accomplishment and likely means, given my chosen profession, and was wooing his daughter (that part was never explicitly addressed during these various discussions over things like knot tying lessons), it was appropriate for me to learn to sail or at least appreciate sailing at this phase of my life/career journey.

I suspect I was there, on the boat with Bob to begin with, exactly because I was wooing his daughter. Spending time with the target's parents, during which they hopefully come to like you or at least appreciate you and at least appreciate how you treat and regard the target, is commonly an important part of the drawn out mating process in our society, particularly when the target has parents with which she is still actively involved. Whereas, maybe at least partly subconsciously, it seemed to me unlikely that I would ever take a day off to do something as frivolous as spend that day on a boat, my own boat and by my own choice. More consciously, I pondered the logistics and time commitment aspect a bit more, and it seemed to me, that if someone is really going to chip into their productivity as a man of means and accomplishment (and ongoing demands and challenges) by spending time on their own boat away from the setting of those accomplishments and challenges, then it might as well be a motor boat, so one doesn't have to spend the even extra non-productive time learning how to sail, which appeared to me more skill demanding than driving a car, the latter being more akin to motor-boating. Perhaps the ability to relax and to commit to learning demanding things unrelated to one's profession was also something that one acquired along the way as well.

I suppose the only true mishap from that first visit to Kim's parents in San Diego had to do with that buttery, sugary pastry I had covertly shoved under Barkley's pillow that last night we were there. I didn't tell Kim about it. I didn't want her to make any inquiries as to the hopefully humorous experience of its discovery. I wanted Barkley's hopefully messy adventure to unfold itself to our awareness more naturally.

I had no idea, certainly at the time, and perhaps for several weeks afterward, that Barkley had not spent the night in his room that first night after the pastry placement. He had indeed left to go out of town shortly after we had left to go sailing, that day he had discovered me naked in Kim's room and then harmlessly tormented me at breakfast. By the time I learned all this, it was too far along into the unknown history of sugary pastry evolution (or de-evolution) in the dark, oxygen poor under pillow recesses, so I refrained from EVER confessing to this still presumably unknown act.

In fact, it would be over a year before Barkley would sleep again in his old bedroom at his parent's house. It would not be until the night before Kim's and my wedding in San Diego, a event of such magnitude in the lives Williamson that even the wandering quasi-misfit younger brother would temporarily return home.

Right after Bob, Kim, and I had left to begin my sailing appreciation initiation, Barkley had left to go visit (or live with depending upon one's temporal definitions of the subtle difference) some friends in, I believe, Santa Cruz, a group that included a couple of ex-classmates from his college days, who had just started becoming engaged in some sort of fledgling business activities that had little or nothing to do with any of their educational trainings. From what I gathered from Kim, based on information she had apparently gained in conversations with her mother, the trade Barkley was currently involved in was largely related to the selling of T-shirts, jewelry, and other items based on Hinduism, Buddhism, and other Eastern philosophies and religions.

They say that things go in cycles in popular culture, especially in the United States. The clothing and hairstyles of one classic decade can resurface twenty-thirty-or forty years later, in various partial or full manifestations. There's no rigidly defined frequency, and surely it's modified by other factors, as complicated as the economy, the collective psyche of a variously post-war, post-depression, or post-boredom nation, etc. Pubescent high schoolers will support mall-derived fashions, which they believe make them as unique and cool as any organism since the first primordial fish stepped with his flipper/paws onto land, only for their parents to see them with déjà vu eyes and wish they'd kept their clothes from 25 years before (not that any such child would accept hand-me-downs from life forms as alien as their parents), if for no other reason but to save some money, as one consistent thing in this series of repetitive cycles is the perpetual increase in even relative (allowing for inflation, etc) prices for similar clothes and haircuts. Much less motivation for parents remarking on the similarity to bygone trends would be the unfathomable attempt to demonstrate to their offspring that they were once as with it as the kids currently think they are. Regarding the more mysterious mathematical aspects of the higher costs of these otherwise already complex fashion and attitude cycles, the clothes, perhaps, have indeed become higher end garments, with better materials, more big-name fashion designer input, etc., but marketers probably also recognize that most parents are a little better off today than were their parents. Whereas Grandpa and Grandma may have been a little tight with wardrobe support, out of budgetary necessity, Mom and Dad are more likely to cough it up these days, if for no other reason than just to get their kids, who have acquired the widely disseminating sense of self-entitlement, to shut up. It also seems that the reasons for wearing said clothing items may change, as well; from comfort, communal anti-establishment statements, and facilitating free-sex by easy on and off apparel (as for past hippy clothes) to being "cool" and "fashionable" for the current generation. But, this could, like so many things in life, be a simple matter of perspective.

Whatever, I'm neither a sociologist nor an economist, and clearly, not a fashionista per se, but more of an appreciative innocent bystander, regarding what I'm increasingly encouraged to wear. However, I do think, at least at this time of revival of prior decades, there were many of us out there, vestiges of the Hendrix, Cream, bell bottom, and long hair phase transitioning smoothly into the Zeppelin, Rush, maybe slightly less long hair days, where standard wear of jeans and concert T-shirts reflected a society in which bands could actually play their instruments and hair didn't require weird layered cutting and gel (or much of anything at all) who were hoping that we'd be long gone from this planet before the cycling back of Members Only jackets, parachute pants, Boy George, and Haircut 100 infused darkness of the 80s, where snorted cocaine and BMWs became the accessories of superficial MBAs in the urban areas and greed and flamboyant bad taste seemed as rampant as one-hit wonders on MTV. But, it's possible that I am old fashioned.

As stated previously, Barkley (whom at some point might want to consider changing his name, as Barkley makes me think of bright green Izod pants on the Golf Courses of the Rich and Famous or Privileged) seemed to be one of those pushing the edge of the flannel shirt, grunge and alt-country music brilliance that ended hair bands (a bastardized succubus breeding of new wave styling with untalented hard rock compared to the 70s glory days) towards a softer, kinder, more introspective era paralleled by apparel and hair more keeping with traditional hippy attitudes.

I've never been to Santa Cruz and only know of it by reputation, and so, it's possible that unlike most supposedly civilized areas in the U.S., it may have been relatively spared of the 80s and stuck, like a hemp-drizzled monastery trapped in an ecstatic THC time warp, to its true soul. Maybe it was something like one of those medieval cities that during the most horrendous plague episodes that claimed as many as one-third of Europe's population in the 14th century surreptitiously lost only a few of its less desirable citizens, and never quite noticed what all the fuss was about when out-of-towners (maybe with only a few covered buboes) passed through for a pint. Santa Cruz was, after all, an eclectic University town that gave rise to the brilliance of the likes of Camper Van Beethoven. And, I'd seen "Lost Boys". Even if there was no particularly high density of vampires, the background population of the non un-dead seemed eclectic enough that, with a steady infusion of tourists supplementing it, the kind of endeavor Barkley (how about Swami Barklamana for God's or Shiva's sake) and his friends supposedly were engaged in seemed like it could probably find a worse place to fester on the wallets of mankind.

Swami Barklamana's job within this business enterprise, given his formal training in anthropology and his ability to multi-culturally bullshit in complete sentences, was to write the little blurbs that went on the small organic cardboard tags that attached by organic strings to the T-shirts and jewelry made in India, or in finer print on some items, Taiwan or China (not that such Asian countries were not of relevant religion and/or philosophy, it just had the possibility as coming off as a little bit more stereotypically cheap merchandize purchased in the entrepreneurial spirit of taking advantage of foreign workers/assemblers). Although unclear to at least family members where and how they had acquired their initial stock of merchandize goods, there didn't appear to be a vast arsenal of daily life sustaining private venture capital, such that 6 young men of supposed similar composition and patience, lived together in a large gutted out room in a decaying prior house structure on whose first floor slightly more hospitable surroundings contained the incense and boy-odor infused shop.

One month into this financial black hole of apparent non-personal enhancement, in which the squalor of their living conditions could have been modulated by at least being able to afford food (and other substances) in a manner allowing what they'd hoped was going to be at least a spiritual journey to near financial happiness, the inability to pay bills, eat, etc. drove Barkley away from this T-shirt and jewelry selling supplement to his further awakening, and he came back closer to San Diego, and he entered rehab for two months.

And so…the under pillow pastry remained undiscovered, the budding anti-lotus blossom smell not yet creeping under the closed door of his bedroom in mustard gas fashion out into the hallway that his supportive mother passed by multiple times a day.

As far as I knew, via Kim, and as far as Kim's parents knew, and as I eventually would confirm in subsequent conversations with Barkley, he had absolutely no problem with drugs whatsoever. He drank socially like any of us did, and probably less than Kim or I did, and hardly ever used drugs, with rare sharing of a joint toke under particularly unusual celebratory circumstances. The true bottom line was that he just wanted a place to relax and read and hang out for a while, which wouldn't cost him any money, and he wouldn't have to really work, other than a few hours a day of attending some sessions and performing some mundane tasks around the ward which for someone not really recovering from drug withdrawal were quite simple to perform, quickly.

In a true testament to brilliant pragmatism, this gave Barkley plenty of time to read, think, etc. He had once been stopped by the cops with a small amount of pot (supposedly belonging to a friend), although he had not been charged with anything, but which along with parent support (thinking that this was now the identified cause of his apparent drifting, most recently manifested as the business/communal dwelling failure of the Santa Cruz Ashramette) and parent financial contribution, was enough to get the insurance company to kick in a major chunk of support for at least the first six weeks of his confined eight week vacation.

Immediately following his "release", Barkley decided to go on a six month trip to India, Thailand, and Cambodia. It was loosely affiliated with some long named Eastern Mysticism society that wasn't recognized by anyone, and the major benefit of which appeared to allow you to informally acquire a verbal/quickly scribbled list of hostels, cheap hotels, and people's shacks in which to stay for free or nearly free. Barkley's intent wasn't clear, maybe more spiritual searching, maybe to make contacts for cheap merchandise purchasing if he decided to re-visit his gift-shop days again, but I suspect procrastination towards real life was a major conscious or sub-conscious motivation. In support of his spiritual and site-seeing expedition to at least some places of high moral standards and despite the fact that some other destinations included where locally abundant drugs were probably safer than drinking the water and as a potential deterrent for a relapse to a problem that they didn't realize their son never had, and only supported by his stellar "report card" regarding drug related behavior while in rehab, Bob and Patti were only too eager to underwrite this, after all relatively inexpensive, prolonged travel adventure.

As a clear sign of the benefit of all these endeavors to outside witnesses, when Barkley returned to the States, through some sort of a friend of a friend of a friend arrangement, he took a summer job in Orlando, teaching a course at a junior college on comparative religions. So by the time Professor Barkley returned to San Diego for our wedding, it had been 12 months, 1 week, and three days since he had been home.

XVI

- *Houston; December, 1993*

On a Monday night in mid December, I was missing Kim so bad it hurt in a way that can't be translated by poets or physicians into visceral symptoms or lab values, even if the latter seemed to be the only way I was thinking lately. She had been there, in my place, in "our" place, just two and a half weeks before, and as I looked around, there was still physical evidence of her little touches in my ill developed, largely work-oriented "accidental-bachelor" pad. She had given me large quantities of shit for having no Thanksgiving decorations, which was in reality more rhetorical sort of grief, as we both knew that any seasonal or holiday oriented decorations in our past co-dwellings were largely (i.e., exclusively) a consequence of her actions. This doesn't mean that I wasn't physically with her on at least some shopping endeavors that resulted in the acquisition of decorations or that I didn't offer eager and actually sincere opinions as to specific wreaths or napkins or wrapping paper, etc. Let's be honest, it's just that such shopping trips would never have occurred if it wasn't for Kim's commitment to making holidays special, as they should be.

Now my eyes settled on a little "Rock-and-Roll Turkey", some promotion thing from a local radio station, taped, appropriately, over my clinical schedule on the wall post between my small kitchen and my small dining room. Time limitations had not allowed for more formal and complete correction of my Thanksgiving-decoration deficiencies, as Kim had not gotten in until Wednesday evening. With her guidance and consultation, though, I had appropriately secured all of the key food supplies, including the right size and kind of turkey, and all the "fixin's", largely from a single outing to Whole

Foods on Shepherd, which I could walk to, including on a late Tuesday night, as I needed to leave straight from work to pick Kim up at the airport for her holiday visit on the Wednesday on which I would normally have done such shopping tasks. My little guitar wielding turkey, which was surviving heartily into the next month, was a promo sticker on a cardboard display at the cash register at Cactus Records, where Kim had insisted we stop on the way home from the airport, as she wanted to get a CD from a Seattle band she wanted me to hear. Shockingly, I hadn't gotten around to taking him down yet; plus, I thought he was kind of cool, even if he had originated as a holiday oriented advertisement for a local band that probably spent more time eating the heads off live birds than cooking them during wholesome nostalgic holidays, and had the obligatory radio station call letters and radio dial numbers at the bottom. Kim hadn't even been to my place yet on this particular trip, to appreciate the decorationopenia, but with a handful of CDs in her arms and under the eye-sparkling influence of a few drinks on the plane ride down and the excitement of the holidays, she thought he was "cute" and put him on the register to be included in the bag of our music purchases, while casting me a sideways flirtatious glance, and stating that she expected I probably hadn't spent much time decorating for Thanksgiving.

While becoming a little more aware of the pelvic stirring of my growing horniness for this absolutely beautiful women that despite our physical separation was officially my wife, I stated in affectionate mock defense, "Actually, my place is so scary right now that you'll quickly realize that I just haven't gotten around to eliminating the Halloween feel."

Knowing that I was likely alluding to dirty socks on the floor and scattered shoes in a virtual obstacle course from the front door to the bed, her response was only one notch of forgiving below the maximally arousing, as she said, while casually slipping a goofy radio station turkey into our bag, "It'll be even scarier when I rip your fucking clothes off and throw you in the sack and make smokin' sex with you."

Smokin' sex was the kind of term we steadily and playfully had replaced things like "passionate love-making" with so many moons ago, probably beginning right around the time we had become comfortable farting in front of each other. ("Only in the bathroom or kitchen, and only in the morning," and probably more me than her, but who's keeping track).

My response to this holiday and vodka sassiness was, "Check please," which our nasally-pierced cash register attendant wasn't sure was a comment on the timeliness of our transaction or an internal couple thing. Seven minutes later, the amount of clothing debris in my hallway had indeed increased, although most of it wasn't mine, and I was underneath the sexiest, best smelling, best tasting woman in the whole fucking universe. I don't think I slept very much that night, even though after round two Kim had zonked soundly, and I laid there while we lay on our sides, with her back to me, and I softly touched her shoulder and back, smelling her skin, and placing soft kisses on her shoulder, devouring the taste without moving any other part of my body.

When uninvited little brain sparks, intrusive little demon fuckers my psych "colleagues" could spend hours debating the origins of, but more likely emissions from the still to be defined by us more objective neuro types as "guilt cortex", arose as we lay there, I tried not to think about the fact that just less than a week before I had been in the same bed with Sandy. But when I did, and thought more like a scientist, I confidently realized that there was no comparison. Maybe it was the holiday spirit, that kind of wholesomeness that family gatherings, several servings of turkey, and too many glasses of Chardonnay or Pinot can induce, that jubilee infused disembodiment that leads one to sincerely hug aunts and cousins that one hasn't seen in years and even in the act of hugging can't remember the names of. Maybe it was because I was so deeply in love that I resented the fact that we were apart, that we let real world bullshit get in the way of us being together and that despite finally meeting the person that could not only make us feel wonderful, but that could make us feel so pissed and hurt that we finally missed what wonderful was when it wasn't there, we let pride in the guise of careers interfere with a more steady life sustaining dose of the very thing I was experiencing at that moment. As I lay there in a room of now wonderful smells, pressed tightly up against "until death do us part", it was perhaps out of the mature couple respect for how soundly Kim was sleeping or some different form of respect for the mental swirl I was feeling that I righteously decided not to do anything more about it, other than to just enjoy the warm glow and pressure of its existence and the goddess-like entity lying next to me from which it derived, taking it in internally, at the risk of exploding all over the room.

Of course, a perpetual state of horniness is what makes us single X-chromosome organisms most boy-like. That night, as I lay there savoring Kim next to me, buzzed in our post-sex state and sustaining that buzz by her smell and the warmth of her familiar skin, I made another vow (this time to just myself) to forevermore be faithful, something akin to that moment when one promises to go to church if the cop will just let you off for a potential DUI or I imagine, to survive a heavy night of artillery while shitting bricks in a foxhole.

However, now two plus weeks of reality removed from this hopefully sustaining experience, on this early night in December, as I stared at my guitar wielding fowl buddy on the wall and as my mind drifted from data analysis to sex, I had some unwelcome thoughts about maybe out-of-the-blue calling Maura. But on this particular night, a conflicting subconscious (I was clearly spending too much time with my psych dweeb colleagues) or barely conscious sensation was also present, indicating that what I missed was more than just sex, the millions of little things that add up to make sex and everything else with the right person so much more. As I contemplated, in an almost trance of surrealistic displacement, the tragedy of the lack of a name for my calendar-covering strata-caster wielding butterball became exaggerated as another sign of regretted infidelity. My mind fluttered to random and absolutely meaningless flashbacks of the daily life I had shared with Kim in San Francisco, and which now after having had a recent few days fix of, I missed like fucking oxygen.

...

The only real sense I had of an impending Christmas holiday was a pile of newly acquired Christmas decorations sitting on the far side of my dining room table. We had bought them the Friday after Thanksgiving, not officially participating in the busiest shopping day of the year, but picking up a couple of things, just at a Target down by the Medical Center, while out running a couple of more mundane errands. In our years of co-habitation in San Francisco, briefly while living in sin and then for two years living in our larger space of most of the second floor of a converted Pacific Heights Victorian after getting married, we had actually accumulated very little of the essential domestic possessions of couples. This was for a combination of reasons I suppose. First, it was so expensive to live there, that for two young people basically still on trainee/junior staff salaries and who liked to eat out and partake relatively infrequently of some of the finer things of life, money that could be spent on Christmas tree stands and ornaments was better spent on dinner out or a bottle of Napa Cab. Secondly, we knew even then that that phase was, essentially by definition, temporary. We would finish this stage of career development and find the perfect city for both our jobs and the next stages of our lives together, which would include the right house on which to bombard our share of key annual holiday supplies. Thirdly, with Kim's folks in San Diego, we spent many of our holidays and special occasions with the future/subsequent real in-laws, traveling back to Texas to visit with my folks as time and limited funds would allow.

When Kim would eventually move to Houston, we certainly didn't expect to live in my rented partially run down bungalow, which lately was progressively metamorphisizing into a black hole of landlord-resisted repairs. However, as this was the city we theoretically expected to jointly call home, my rental was currently unofficially the place we would collect the small official "household" possessions, until that time when we would have our real place. Hence, the small pile of new Christmas ornaments sat neatly stacked in their firm cardboard boxes on the dining room table at which I now sat. I suppose other, more anally-inspired, individuals would have stored them away in some of the rather ample, and largely unused, closet space. But I had plenty of room to eat at the near end of the dining room table, and, I suppose, I liked seeing them there. It seems to me, in one of those moments of rather shocking clarity perhaps perceived as origins of convenient excuses by others, that each human has a finite number of individual expended efforts in this life, dictated perhaps in part by some complex motivation-to-laziness ratio, and a lot of mine right now were being spent in daily tasks at the Thomas Street Clinic, the Neurosensory Center, and the Methodist General Clinical Research Center, as well as by performing data analysis right here on the part of the dining room table not occupied by ornaments. Just like it never made much real and truly defendable sense to me to make a bed that one was going to be sleeping in later on during that very same day. If one were to critically analyze the relative merits of all performed tasks in such manner, one could also easily see the meaninglessness of taking down my meager individual residual Thanksgiving decoration. After all, by this time, I clearly knew my own personal clinic schedule that it so tastefully covered. Further, removing one set of past holiday decorations, simply for the sake of room or holiday appropriateness, for the placement of decorations for the next round of festivities had steadily emerged as one of Kim's official tasks, not because of laziness per se on my part, but because my parallel role had similarly developed into providing the appropriate supportive praises for decorating success or smart ass comments as I supplied the necessary accompanying holiday alcoholic beverages and made lewd, but affectionate comments as to how great her ass looked as she stood on step ladders to place decorations or bent over to remove them from their storage boxes. Plus…there'd be a Thanksgiving next year, I was pretty sure, and this way, we'd already be partially ready or if we were to take it down, it would be at the same time as moving…no difference, really.

XVII

- *Houston; December, 1993*

"When do you get to see Kim again?" Carl asked politely, a few minutes after we had all assumed our proper positions and were sitting quietly in the park one slightly chilly Sunday afternoon in mid-December.

Of the two adjacent benches we occupied, I sat on the right side of the left bench, being somewhat then in the middle of the group. Leo sat on the left side of the same bench, where he would alternately stand up, facing us, and occasionally intrigue the group by standing on either just his left or just his right foot, as if proving to himself and others that he could still do it. In conversation lulls, I sometimes wondered if this was just some sort of posturing that medicated, largely burnt-out schizophrenics sometimes did, and made mental notes to try and notice it in other such patients that I might, though rarely, encounter in my daily activities.

Frank sat on the left side of the right-sided bench, closest to me. Carl stood behind that same bench, leaning his hands against the back of the right side, a couple of feet away from Frank. Rick typically sat on the ground if front of both benches, even when in his work clothes, about eight or so feet in front of us, as if slight removal from the human element and more direct contact with Mother Earth, even if in the middle of a city of three to four million, was partially curative, or at least soothing, for whatever metabolic imprecision that he was currently in, and which various empiric combinations of aspirin or Tylenol, Rolaids, coffee, and Pepto Bismol hadn't quite rectified, and now a dose of fresh air out and about might effectively synergize with.

In contrast, Curtis didn't sit, perpetually buzzing around the group in varying radius circles, depending on how interested he was in the current topic, occasionally stopping at the correct orientations to respective members to hear, or more usually, comment on, a particular statement.

"Is she coming here for Christmas?" Carl continued, from my right and slightly to the rear.

"Yeah," I casually responded, barely turning towards him, "she gets here a couple of days before Christmas."

"Ah...holiday boom-boom," Curtis offered up in commentary as his orbit brought him around to my front left. "Is there anything better?"

"I don't think it's called "boom-boom" when you're actually married and in love," Frank said with a slightly condescending tone, as Curtis' resumed trajectories took him square in front of Frank to receive the innocuous jab.

"Why not?" I inquired, without glancing at anyone or anything in particular, except maintaining my somewhat comatose stare at the swing set in front of me off in the distance. I was more tired and emotionally fried than I would have normally hoped for on a Sunday afternoon, when I typically wanted to feel more rested and restored prior to the next weekly onslaught.

"Seems to me, the closer you are to someone, the more comfortable you should be with doing things behind closed doors...like boom-boom," I continued in a more analytical tone, perking up a little having apparently decided to take out my irritation on someone unsuspecting.

"Yeah...exactly," Curtis proclaimed in support while placing a comrade-supportive hand on my left shoulder as he continued his ceaseless rotation around the group, apparently acknowledging my long awaited enrollment in the Anti-Frank Constipation and Conservatism Coalition, which I really never tried to officially participate in or sanction, as I quite liked and admired many aspects of The Frank.

"What are you talking about Curtis? I thought you would do anything...with anybody...any time...even strangers," Rick's dyspepsia finally allowed him to chime in, after Curtis had completed another rotation past him, such that it was said largely to his back.

As Curtis then passed behind Frank and Carl's bench, to where he was essentially opposite Rick, he said without pausing his pacing, holding his hand to his chest and facing slightly skyward in mock dramatic fashion, "This isn't about me."

As he continued, rounding my bench, placing him at his farthest point from Carl, at the opposite end of our little galaxy, Carl commented, in typical Carl judgmental fashion and tone, "I thought *everything* was about you."

Curtis paused and faced Carl directly, and opened his eyes and mouth widely, as if hurt or insulted, raising his hand theatrically to his chest again. Standing there, right in front of Rick, his butt basically in Rick's too-wiped-out-to-move face, he then nonchalantly responded, "It is. I just thought I'd say that to fuck with you guys."

After a brief pause for emphasis, he then playfully shook his ass in Rick's face, and then continued his circular course.

XVIII

- Recollections: San Francisco; Early summer, 1991

Kim continued her personal mission of showing me parts of San Francisco I had not yet been exposed to or adequately absorbed. Sometimes these were elaborately planned excursions, which I initially greeted with extreme couple pleasure. Other times, they were more spontaneous extensions of casual outings that would accidentally lead us near somewhere that I then confessed to never having been to, etc.

Kim's firm's involvement in advertising art shows, both small and large, flavored some of our endeavors, from trips to museums for general and affordable education, to specific small galleries to see certain works, to wandering along particular streets for exploration missions. SOMA and its steadily expanding art scene amongst the leather bars and piercing shops was a frequent favorite casual destination.

One Saturday afternoon, on an absolutely beautiful day, as part of the mission for Jeff Civic Awareness and perhaps more "concrete art" viewing by my request after a few really weird galleries over the previous few weeks, we made our way to the Rincon Center. Again, Kim was shocked that I had not yet been there. I tried to ineffectively make up for it by telling her that I'd been to Candlestick Park at least six times already. As a prelude to our journey, Kim had pointed out the famous murals of the Rincon Annex lobby, as well as their intended purpose to "bring art to the people." Buzz words to bring points home to her intended audience were easily plucked from potentially far more complex lexicons given Kim's role in the PR of the SF Art World to begin with, and I typically appreciated the "Cliff Note" versions while occasionally pleasing her by sincerely probing her for lots of details when a certain topic would particularly grab me.

The murals were located in the lobby of the Rincon Annex, which had been the main downtown post office. They had been done by a Russian artist named Anton Refregier, commissioned by the WPA to depict the history of California and San Francisco from the period covering as far back as the native Indians up through essentially World War I. The old post office was going to be torn town when the huge new Rincon Center was being built, but citizens from all over cried out passions for their preservation, and so the maintenance of the murals was incorporated into the new center's design.

The city had plenty of monuments to the early settlers (some of which I think I had even seen, such as in Pioneer Park), those that had come before the Gold Rush and the periods of San Francisco that at least I found racier and a little more interesting. In the construction of his beautiful murals, Refregier took a more realistic and accurate view of the great diversity contained within California's history. Not only did über conservatives consider the consequent results potentially "left wing" and even "pro-communist", it didn't help that the painting style was a little "modern" for the time. We all know how that modern art can rub even some of the liberal bubbas the wrong way.

As I noted in my guidebook and one of the pamphlets I had picked up on a lobby tour of the murals, apparently poor Refregier was attacked by numerous offended organizations even during the painting process, which had been briefly interrupted during World War II, and he even made some changes to get folks off his back.

For example, in the "Transcontinental Railroad" mural, most of the workers are depicted as Chinese, which of course, is accurate, but which over the early years appeared to offend especially the non-local critics. You would have thought they'd have been adequately appeased by the mural of the Irish agitator "Sand-Lotters" beating up Chinese men, which supposedly to downplay any implied racism had ultimately just been called "Beating the Chinese", to reduce any more explicit portrayal of the Irish lads apparently. I guess the point here was that if you don't depict history it doesn't negate it, but it prevents the consequences of its awareness. Maybe we can get rid of Holocaust museums. Surely these are far more unpleasant.

Lotta Crabtree's buxom demonstrating pink outfit was, of course, considered far too risqué at the time, but fortunately for those of us admirers viewing her with appreciation in the early 1990s had been permitted and of course preserved. God forbid that any art, whether murals, music, or poetry could contribute to even just heterosexual horniness or romance. After all, what impact would sexual reproduction have upon the preservation of the species? Best just not to think about that stuff. Keep it behind closed doors, so no one will realize that sexual urges and sex occur. Man, if those hooters bothered sex afraid portions of the populace in the old days, what would they think if they could see some of the "explicit" (and likely far more "controversial" from at least the sexual orientation side of things) public art that had shown up a couple of years ago and a few remnants of which were still persisting around town from the Art for AIDS and even earlier city of San Francisco initiated public awareness posters, etc.? If the sticks up their skeleton asses would allow it physically, they'd really turn over in their graves.

Even the Catholic Church got involved in some of the objection processes... shocking.

I was having fun learning details regarding some of the more absurd criticisms to Refregier's wonderful murals. The Mexican government had protested about the Mexican flag being on the ground in the mural entitled "California Becomes a Republic". I'm sorry, but as a native South Texan who has visited the Alamo many times, I believe accurate history does indeed support victories over Mexico to generate official possession of land that would become two of the most populated states in our Union. Instead, I suppose under irresistible pressure (after all, this was a government funded project...one must respect the patron....), Refregier painted over the original flag. I particularly liked, though, that on very close scrutiny one could still see the outline and faint details of the previous flag on the ground. I mean, come on, I love Mexico and I love the Mexican heritage so well represented in San Antonio and in my soon to be wife's own home town of San Diego, but at the time these works were being done, we were putting together one of the largest and certainly most sophisticated military machines in the history of the world (you know, for that little thing called World War II). What, were we afraid that Mexico was going to invade us and try to reclaim California?

Oh, and speaking of WWII, if I remember correctly, didn't we (albeit maybe out of a bit of necessity) have to ally with Russia in order to successfully combat the mighty German Army? Wasn't the artist of these murals himself

Russian? Couldn't we extend a little break here? But, of course, in the years after WWII, the artist, progressively completing the murals, was accused of using too much red paint, clearly a not so cleverly disguised leftist and communist propaganda maneuver.

So, in the background setting of cold war politics, in 1953, some b.s. committee in Congress began a debate to consider removing the works. Richard Milhous Nixon, then a Republican Representative from California, and whom we all know as one of the fathers of 20th century enlightened thinking, was surprisingly involved. Can you imagine what these constipated, paranoid, upholders of their version of the Constitution would have done if they'd seen the Art for AIDS demonstrations or even more graphic sexual references contained with San Francisco's own prior and subsequent public awareness campaigns? Could a penis or even just a condom be conceived as a Soviet missile somehow?

Fortunately, the Directors of all three major San Francisco Art Museums spoke up to these Congressional misguideds. They voiced their support of artistic freedom and they argued the historical accuracy of the murals, and they opposed the destruction of them. Hmm… "freedom" … "historical accuracy"…. Weren't these the sorts of things we'd been fighting for just less than a decade before? Five weeks after these hearings, the California Senate itself urged Congress to act in favor of the destruction of the murals, but by that time, the effort against the murals had begun to lose momentum. Maybe Congress had found an even greater threat to the Red, White, and Blue. (Hey, what's that red doing in there?).

I guess it was a time when Americans were supposedly a bit more close minded. Art was supposed to be pleasant, just like all the good and hence protected things presumably around us, things we all knew existed somewhere, deeply ingrained in the "Dream". Art, especially modern art, wasn't supposed to convey things realistically…especially not in a way that could be offensive to some. (I mean, come on, what would be the purpose of that.)

Hmm…maybe some shit never does really change, maybe not completely, at least not for everyone….

These murals were intended to bring art and history to the people. Thanks to the efforts of enlightened citizens, they survived their first attack, from the political side. And thanks to the efforts of concerned San Franciscans, more than two decades later (beginning in 1979), the Historic Murals of Rincon Center as well as the entire "Art Deco Moderne" post office lobby were restored as the entryway to the new retail and residential complex Kim and I were now spending the afternoon exploring. This civic and local art friendly, indeed art passionate, attitude boded well for the Upcoming Center for Arts, then under construction at Yerba Buena Gardens.

...

The facts regarding Refregier's murals I learned on our tour and from the pamphlets and guide books, but their mixed reception as at least partially public educational art some 40 years ago couldn't help remind me of current local and national art programs to provide education about AIDS, certainly most notably in the Art for AIDS project that had just opened its tour in San Francisco in 1989. Perhaps there may be some similar red-necked, conservative, or homophobic (or some combination of some or all of those traits) political and non-political critics, scattered this time even more ineffectively, against such campaigns. The same people, I suppose, who think that handing out free condoms encourages sex and handing out sterile needles will promote IV drug abuse, regardless of whether or not it could slow the accelerating spread of HIV. Kim and I had had numerous conversations relating to ART and AIDS, this being one area that portions of our work partially overlapped. Interestingly to us, at least, and similar to numerous opinions shared within the media, the art composing the Art for AIDS project, whether graphic/realistic or symbolic, was actually quite mild in its literal sexual content compared to what already had been produced and widely distributed in San Francisco, a city whose citizens and politicians had already become all too aware of HIV and AIDS and which had already done so much to take care of its so disastrously stricken people as well as to encourage prevention, including in posters and other "public" information forms that were certainly more graphic than Lotta Crabtree's emphasized lovely breasts painted in a post office lobby. There was nothing that could anymore shock anyone who had seen the scourge of this viral nightmare up close. Art and just about everything else was being seen through eyes a bit different than those congressional committees of the 1950s. Thank God for the enlightened ones, not afraid to speak up for the good of EVERY human being.

Of course, enlightenment can be retrospectively awarded, even if the recipient of such honors demonstrated it accidentally (we can apply *'s as needed....).

So, after this latest SOMA trip and while I was pondering Public Art, including for AIDS education, and Richard Nixon (from his involvement in the anti-mural affair), it reminded me of a bit of irony I had recently noted in an essay on AIDS that a Swedish post-doc in Hassel's lab (this one male and not quite as captivating as my previous encounter with the species) had recently given to me, and amidst a stack of more directly relevant clinical and science literature, I had actually read. It was written by a very established senior level Swedish Tumor Biologist after attending The World Congress on AIDS in Stockholm in 1988.

Given the decades of experience this author had with basic tumor biology, he was well versed in the concept of viral oncogenes and past hypotheses regarding possible viral causes of tumors. This work had largely occurred before my "time" in medicine and science, although the subsequent relationship of these viral oncogenes to genes within our own cells (so-called proto-oncogenes) that coded for various growth factors, growth factor receptors, and other signal transduction molecules, which contributed to normal cell growth and which could have altered expression, function, and even mutation in actual tumors was a familiar component of Medical School and Biomedical Graduate School Cell Biology and Pathology and other courses. I believe in the 1950s, researchers discovered viruses contained within the DNA of certain animal tumors, including sarcomas, and subsequently leukemias and malignancies of other types of tissues. This became a huge area of biomedical research in the 1960s and early 1970s. I'm far from an expert in these areas, especially the more historical aspects, prior to the later focus on the human genes delineated as possibly relevant to cancer emerging from the earlier viral and viral tumor inducing studies. These viruses could also "transform" relevant cell types in culture. For example, a virus that had been found in soft tissue tumors (so-called sarcomas) could cause cultured soft tissue type cells (such as fibroblasts) to become "immortal" when cultured in the laboratory. Similarly, viruses implicated in certain animal (such as chicken) leukemias could immortalize these analogous blood cell types in culture in the laboratory. This immortalization, meaning that cells can propagate forever in a manner ignoring the normal cellular control mechanisms for growth, division, and death, is regarded as highly relevant to tumorigenesis in intact organisms. The viruses that were implicated in these highly studied animal tumors were retroviruses; that is, the same general virus type as HIV. These viruses are made up of RNA (the molecule between the DNA in our genes and the proteins they are turned

316

into after being made into RNA), unlike more familiar DNA viruses, such as the Herpes virus, etc. When these RNA based retroviruses infect a cell (which is typically viral specific) they use an enzyme they carry and encode themselves, called reverse transcriptase (the very enzyme that would become the target for treating HIV infection in the future) to turn the RNA into DNA. That subsequent DNA becomes integrated into the host cell DNA; that is, it basically "sneaks into" the chromosomes of the host animal's genome. It can either lay dormant, and just get duplicated along with all the rest of the "native" DNA during natural cell division, or under appropriate signals/circumstances, the viral DNA could be turned into viral specific RNA and viral specific proteins (using the cell's natural biochemical machinery) and all of this viral RNA and viral proteins could be turned into new viruses (many new viruses) and be released (at the expense of the death of the host cell) to go find a new, happier home, to maybe lay quiescent in the peace and quiet of the host DNA genome again.

Well, it turns out, I think, that during some of these retroviral journeys into the host genome, they integrated in a manner that they "picked up" one of various native host genes. The ones that picked up genes for controlling cell growth and cell division emerged as strikingly interesting as the function of those "oncogenes" (genes that can cause tumors) were implicated in the tumors the viruses were discovered in and were causative in the cell immortalizations they caused in the laboratory. Can you imagine what a breakthrough this was naturally perceived as? Perhaps all tumors were caused by viruses! The implications were staggering. This means that there could eventually be possible tumor vaccines (such as cancer vaccines to prevent or help treat such common human destroyers as breast, colon, pancreatic, prostate, etc. cancer). It could also help identify drugs targeting crucial viral related genes for treatment of cancers already developed.

Hence, in the early 1970s, the Nixon Administration (yes...that Nixon) created and supported programs to provide huge amounts of funding for research into these cancer viruses. Well, as it turns out, almost all human (and animal) tumors (cancers, sarcomas, leukemias/lymphomas) are NOT caused by viruses. This was simply a laboratory and research focus artifact, so to speak, in regards to possible translation to real diseases. There are a few exceptions. For example, a virus similar to HIV causes leukemia in a relatively small percentage of infected cats ("feline leukemia") and a virus similar to HIV, called

HTLV-I (remember the early days of AIDS when one proposed name for HIV was HTLV-III) can cause a leukemia of T-lymphocytes (the cell types infected by the virus), an uncommon form of adult leukemia, most prevalent in the Caribbean and Japan. There is, I believe, even a chicken tumor that is caused by a virus, and for which a vaccine does exist. However, the vast majority of human malignancies, including all the various carcinomas responsible for most cancer-related deaths in humans have nothing to do with viruses. Oh well, it was a good idea for an expensive while. HIV also does not directly cause any tumors. The secondary neoplasms (such as lymphoma) that occur with markedly increased frequency in AIDS patients, just like the common secondary infections caused by organisms not normally dangerous to humans, are actually due to the severe immunosuppression caused by HIV's destructive infection of immune cells (specifically CD4-positive T-helper lymphocytes) crucial to fighting off infections through an intact immune system. Tumors associated with AIDS are caused by cellular reproduction driven by other viruses (such as B-lymphocyte activation and reproduction caused by the Epstein Barr Virus that causes at most mono in immunocompetent people). Such cell division is accompanied by increased chance for mutations (during DNA replication) that can help lead to uncontrolled growth ("transformation", "immortalization"), simply because the host's immune system cannot control the viral infection the way it should naturally. Such tumors were known, and continue to occur, in the setting of mutations that led to primary immunodeficiencies in children with certain rare genetic defects and especially in patients receiving organ (such as kidney) transplants that must receive immunosuppressive medications so as not to reject their transplant.

However, and herein (at least to me) lies the irony: If it weren't for the humongous research into viruses and possible cancer causation supported by the Nixon team, we would have never, as a medical science community, known so much about retroviruses. Without this knowledge under the biomedical research belt, we may not have (likely would not have) discovered the etiology of AIDS as a retrovirus so quickly (labs involved in characterizing the cause of AIDS and discovering HIV had backgrounds in retroviral biology from prior tumor research) and been able to so rapidly identify possible targets for hopefully progressively effective anti-HIV therapy.

Kudos to you…Mr. Nixon.

Now if we can just recast the history of The Vietnam War and Watergate, we could move him off that most-hated list, and allow more focus on Hitler and Stalin, I suppose.

Regardless of these possibly quirky mental digressions and tangential thought journeys, I certainly enjoyed my sight-seeing outings with my exploration partner. Another repeat favorite around this time was just strolling (that's what you call walking when you're in love) along Maiden Lane and eating at various little sidewalk front places, mostly without any pre-determined targets.

The amazing chemistry, which grew like a reaction almost out of control, of even our cost-conscious daily life with the sprinkling of these more exotic outings (based on our shared budget of the time) was leading to something more fundamentally a part of me that I had ever imagined possible. No surprise then, even with the relatively short duration of the relationship to date, that I proposed to Kim at the end of the summer that year (1991). She was so excited, and I guess apparently felt the same, that not only did she say yes but she wanted a Christmas wedding. It would obviously be a relatively short engagement, but she said she wanted to be Mrs. Pearson as quickly as possible. A proper Williamson wedding meant no quick weekend elopement to Vegas, that's for sure. The plans began to unfold. Watching Kim and Patti work was, again, like another and particularly fascinating episode of that "Appreciation of the Female of the Species" documentary we had started back in the early spring.

XIX

- Houston; February, 1994

On a Saturday afternoon in the middle of February, I took a break from studying for my upcoming Neurology Boards and took a journal and a novel out to the park. It was probably just about two in the afternoon. It was strikingly sunny, and unseasonably warm. Days like this at this time of the year were probably why so many people put up with April through September here. The outdoors beckoned to us, as if we were arising out of hibernation, shaking the imaginary ice off of our bodies and making it out of the caves to see what food or curiosities may be lying around in the thawing grass. We had survived what we peri-gulf coast and peri-swamp dwellers affectionately refer to as winter. The warmth sent subconscious reminders that the Cult of Humidity and Mosquitoes would soon be reconstituted. We had made it, to begin another cycle of complaining about the weather of the upcoming months.

I sat down in the middle of our unoccupied bench, appreciably noting the warmth from its several prior hours of being bathed in sacred sunlight. I flipped through the journal, paused on an article of moderate relevance to my work and began to try to read it. Nothing. My brain was saturated with Neurology facts I'd been feeding it with for about the last three to four hours, things I hoped I'd remember come the time of Boards in a few months. I opened the novel to where my bookmark was, on page 37. As I had started this book as many as four weeks ago, and re-visited it only once or twice since then, it took me a while to remember what had been set up and going on in the prior pages.

I had made it about another six pages when this story, too, had failed to grab me under these circumstances. As I moved into a more attention congruent daydream state, I glanced up and then from across the park a young Hispanic mother and her toddler son caught my attention. They were playing together in a mode where all of their lives centered around the other that moment. The mother was absolutely stunningly gorgeous. She was slim, with jet black, slightly wavy hair that danced around her face and caressed and bounced off her shoulders as she playfully ran around her child, who was mesmerized in innocent glee. Her face had the structure and skin of flawless nobility. In profile, I could see the shape of her breasts in a pale thin cotton top. Her jeans were faded and snug enough to show her slender legs, her thin but shapely rear, and had enough room at the front of the waist as she moved around to emphasize the perfect accompanying slender waist. In another set of circumstances, she could have been a trophy wife of any man fortunate enough to land her and hopefully appreciate how committed she was to their son; she could have been a model, gracing the covers of magazines; she could have been professionally and personally decorated with the designer clothing only too lucky to be able to grace this beautiful outline. Instead, I imagined that her clothes probably came from the likes of K-mart or Fiesta or such. Amazing, how we so often see in our social circles many maybe just above average or even average women who achieve just a bit or maybe a lot more by having the expensive clothes, the hairstyles, the make up that their life within the upper crust allows them. Young beaus pursue them when they are displayed this way, and they are perpetually shown to their shared outer world in this manner. One wonders if such lads ever wake up one day, when the make-up's off and when the financially bolstered smile is temporarily non-displayed and recognize that they'd married physically sub-optimally. In these settings, such women could also sometimes be not all that sweet. This is the fertile ground for bitches. The likely humble upbringing and current circumstances of my park vision would likely also foster kindness and loyal commitment. On a more just Earth, she would be the proud wife of an Aristocrat, growing into her natural role of matriarch of a strong and decent growing family, all the biological and even married boys and girls of which were strikingly beautiful...inside and out.

But then, again, even moderate distances can be deceiving. We've all had those experiences where we picture a stunningly beautiful girl when we are approaching from behind, walking or driving, seeing her hair, maybe the outlines of her body, only to see something frightfully off from what we'd been imagining when we catch up or drive past, and finally get to a stage to blatantly or more nonchalantly turn and take in the completion of our fantasy vision, only to be so disappointed. Why do we turn around? Why do we ruin it? Of course, by analogy, this young, elegant Latin-American beauty I was admiring could be similar. Maybe if I went over to say hi to her and her son, I'd be grotesquely turned off by…something; crooked teeth, a nose bigger than I could appreciate from her, old acne scars. But somehow, I doubted that. She was the picture of grace interacting with her beloved child. She bent over again to pick him up within their play, and I added the gorgeous shape of her consequently tightened jeans embracing her perfect ass…and, then, as if sensing my inappropriateness for carnally viewing a Mother, no less, and coming just in time to protect me from myself, Carl showed up right behind me and scared the lust so far out of me I felt like I might need to apologize to the entire Cosmos.

In the more modified version of the Inquisition that the Carl's of the world represented, though, he said nothing directly about my glancing at the hot, likely married or partnered chick across the park. His mere presence was adequately rectifying, and to formalize it, he instead commented on the book that I was "reading", as I had apparently covered it and had it now placed front-cover up on my lap.

"That one's pretty good," he said, "but I like the other two he's written better" (and he added the titles of two novels apparently by the same author; I had pretty much stopped or hadn't started to listen, as despite the mood squelch, I cast one last covert un-Carl-detectable glance towards the glorious mother, as they were actually heading out of the park, child on hip, emphasizing the curves of her hips against a perfect slender waist in heart-gnawing fashion).

I had absorbed enough of Carl's suspended comments to respond, "I don't know. I haven't read either of those other two yet." I added yet, out of some sort of politeness to Carl's mention of them, as at this stage, it was growing unlikely that I would even ever finish this one. Not everyone gets to sit in a bookstore all day, with a seemingly infinite library at their disposal when not inconveniencing themselves to check out a customer, and then go home and trap themselves in a virtual dungeon of self-persecution and likely surrounding classic texts and other literary masterpieces. Despite this, the weather and my already productive morning and early afternoon refused to allow me to be irritated, and I actually found myself welcoming Carl's subsequent conversation. It had been too long since any of the Park Boys had gathered.

Hence, as if on cue, Frank came wobbling towards us with a big grin on his face, a perhaps stupid but yet admirable statement of his contentedness with the World of Frank. After he had eagerly shook both our hands and patted me firmly on the shoulder multiple times, I scooted over to the left side of the bench, Frank sat down on the right side, and Carl stood behind us, casually smoking a cigarette and blowing the smoke away from us, as if smoking had been invented to make him look intellectual and elitist, despite the grief of life his clothes and demeanor always seemed to convey, like a poem I was equally unlikely to read.

He and I both sat and stood, respectively, for a good 15-20 minutes listening to the not particularly fascinating domestic accounts of Frank's and Mrs. Frank's recent visit to their daughter's house in Beaumont. Frank described seemingly mundane and expected age-appropriate activities of his grandchildren with the zeal of a child who'd just discovered ice cream or bubble gum. For reasons I didn't care to analyze, I found them strangely adding to the glow of the warmth from the unexpected intensity of the late winter sun. And then speaking of warmth and sun, as I again cast my glaze upwards toward the side of the park where Mrs. Latin America had recently been, the ray-accentuated figure of what we increasingly recognized as Leo approached us from the North. We watched him awkwardly ascend the curb after crossing the street, and then as he entered the park, the sun glowing down upon him from the West, extending disproportionately long shadows of this rustic creature over the grass, distorting amongst the poles of the swing set, and then coming into more discreet view as his orange right-sidedness and the unlit left side came closer giving the first hint of a grin as warm as immortal friendship. With the slight limp I'd grown accustomed to and often tried to detect any progression of, his whole demeanor appeared like something out of a ---directed Western (I may not read as much, for "leisure" as Carl, but I know the true classics). I was almost surprised when he finally reached us and I noted that he didn't have six-guns wrapped around his borderline cachectic waste.

In a greeting that could only reinforce an at least partial collective consciousness, regardless of any opinions on the collective consciousness, Leo came to a non-perfect landing stop, gathered himself while pulling up his slightly slipping pants, and said: "Greetings Partners. What brings a group of fellas like you out here today?"

My brightening mood had just received a luminous boost. As I looked up at Leo, holding my left hand up to partially shade the sun coming in from the West,

I responded, in a sassy mood anticipating lack of congruity with Carl and Frank, "The weather was making us all a bit horny, and we decided to get outside, I guess, to celebrate it…or something."

Before Carl or Frank could interject their disagreement, Leo contributed to my spirits with his enthusiastic support of these borderline poetic sentiments by responding, "I understand. Spring and its attendant pollination are in the air. I won strip poker with Miss Valery last night."

Rather than dismantling our shared emotions with silly concrete facts of the likes that his landlady would likely not play strip poker with him (or that Leo could effectively manage cards so productively), I admired, again, his life zest. I don't think I had too many M.D. or Ph.D. colleagues who would ever say "attendant pollination." There was just something about this man's connection to reality, or lack or only partial version thereof, that seemed…soothing.

We collectively engaged in bolstering small talk. Although potentially boring in other settings, this was communal medicine. We smiled, we laughed, and we absorbed the presence of our friends in a carrying substance of the warm sun. We were content, maybe all of us, for the moment. But, we were only a couple of partial misfits short of a full quorum. Without any of us even noting it, as it was appropriate and natural, and essentially demanded by the circumstances, Rick appeared, and took his usual place on the thankfully not too cool grass in front of the bench, in front of Frank and me and sitting to the shadow side of where Leo had been steadily standing.

We conversed on a wide spectrum of topics. Rick complained about a lack of love (or uncomplicated sex) life, some practical issues about some business loans, an argument he'd had with his father, etc., but was otherwise quite happy, as how could one feel otherwise today. Leo commented in a fashion that none of us could quite grasp, related to presumably advice on the business loan and father relationship aspects.

All was largely well in Park World.

And then, a cloud temporarily passed before the sun, briefly reminding us of the still lurking cold of the under season. While the sun was still hidden, the slow-walking, head down in unmistakably dejected fashion, Curtis appeared. He carried the gloom of the Middle-Ages upon his slumping shoulders. He stood amongst us for a few minutes, with no one saying anything. It was as if God himself, who had been teasing and flirting with us all day with the premature sun, now covered us with a blanket or a giant garbage bag. When the sun reappeared, it lit up Curtis' center park stage, and as all of us had been rendered mood lowered, we glanced upon him collectively, as if demanding an explanation for this uninvited infusion of somberness.

After a brief pause, as if for dramatic effect, actor collection of thoughts prior to a climactic soliloquy, or sincere grief, this thin grimace of evident despair, spoke, initially quite fragilely.

"Ramone and I broke up," he finally said, softly and dejectedly, but in a matter-of-fact manner as he stared sadly out into the space of the park, as if especially today he too agreed that he owed us an explanation for his gray mood.
No one said anything in response.

I suppose most or all of us didn't realize that Curtis had been in a serious "relationship" or what sort of bond constituted the level of "partnership" in his view warranting the term "broke up", so perhaps we didn't know what degree of condolences we should feel and potentially offer up.

I had at least actually met Ramone once, in passing, at Butera's, of course. He was an extremely tall, maybe 6'3" or 6'4", well built, light-skinned black man, who spoke with a slight French-type accent derived from his origins on one of those Caribbean islands so exotically portrayed in those travel magazines. It was a Sunday, I think, right around noon, and the place was packed, as usual, at that time. As introductions and small talk were being made, I suspected that Curtis had brought Ramone there to show off his new piece of prime beef, as the audience likely included some of his gay competitors within a several mile radius.

That had been at least three or four weeks prior to this current park visit, in which Curtis had appeared with his dark aura that so profoundly contrasted with the sunshine and our consequent collective mood, like a slowly rolling shadow ball, reinforcing a new-found silence among the group. After our initial greetings and small talk, most of us had become quiet as we were content to let the warm sun wash over our brief winter costumes of paleness. But Curtis brought a mood incongruent gloominess that was raising slight tones and postures of dystonia to the formerly peaceful group.

As no one responded to his initial pronouncement of abject despair, he continued his tragic account on The Death of Ramone Romance.

"It wasn't just that his cock was so damn big," he said, his face suggesting an already developing sense of longing nostalgia while prompting other faces to assume a usual spectrum of responses; Rick, a mock grimace conveying an "ooooooooooooh gross" expression; Frank, a wide eyed shock complete with jaw drop and looking around to the others as if seeking confirmation to an unspoken "Did he really just say what I thought I heard him say?"; and me, likely a slight squint of concentration as I tried not to picture the graphic display of the stallion Ramone impaling Curtis from behind, a hedonistic grin of near religious bliss on his face.

"He made my soul orgasm," he continued, in a tone of utter sincere sharing. A pause of complete group silence and reflection ensued.

"I've never had a soul orgasm," Leo said contemplatively, his objective tone reflecting his perception that this was, indeed, something that could be had, like a type of ice cream or a destination of travel, and he'd not yet checked it off his things to do list.

Leo's sometimes surprising comments could often be left alone, perhaps out of respect for his long suffered mental illness and its treatment. But in the spirit of the weather, Rick played along by adding, "Me either," slapping his hands on his knees and making a nod, conveying the accompanying unsaid notion of damn it and it's about time I did get me one of those.

"You should try it," I now chimed in, "No refractory period."

Curtis glared at me, acute anger showing through gray eyes with the slightest beginning of possible tears.

"You bastard," he said, softly, and then he turned and walked away from us, his participation in today's park session clearly brief and over.

XX

- Recollections: San Francisco 1992-1993

In the fall of 1992, Kim's firm in San Francisco landed a client located primarily in the Seattle area. GeoDyne Industries was a multi-faceted corporation, originally founded as a Geology and Energy exploration company, but having quickly added a significant engineering and manufacturing component supporting its own discovery and drilling operation and with increased production, expanding into highly lucrative commercial manufacturing, eventually selling tens of millions of dollars of heavy equipment targeted to the petroleum and construction industries. It was at this stage, maybe in the early 80's, in which both arms had been consolidated within the incorporated name of GeoDyne, and the company had gone public.

A brilliant, creative, and energetic CEO and a technology-based competitive edge, facilitated in part by an available highly educated and technically competent work force in Seattle and surrounding areas, had synergistically led expansion into areas eventually far from its rock and soil origins. EquiMed Instruments extended its cost-effective and reliable manufacturing into the world of medical instrumentation, including an early focus on radiology devices, from improved CAT scan systems to MRI instruments, both with heavy emphasis on state of the art software systems leading to image composition and analysis that quickly became the gold standard to radiologists who had been exposed to these vs. other, still more widely available systems.

Increasing comfort in the highly competitive medical field led to a largely internally generated effort into the pharmaceutical industry, primarily chemical synthesis of high volume drugs, a move accompanied by superior personnel acquisition, including some heavy hitters in the medicinal chemistry field from such giants as Merck.

Synthesizing and mass producing already approved and established prescription and over the counter drugs, including generics, is a relatively safe endeavor, but the profits are obviously strictly limited to the contract price for manufactured pill or caplet minus the cost of the ingredients, production, etc. The potential big money (and inevitably accompanying bigger risk) is in development of new drugs and other medical reagents, for which, depending at what stage a particular company gets involved, one can benefit from various percentages of patents and hence received royalty payments. This is pushing the extent of my understanding of the legal and financial aspects underlying the discovery, development, characterization, validation, manufacture, and promotion of medical pharmaceuticals, to which I far prefer the science and medical aspects of clinical pharmacology.

However, I would gradually learn a great deal about GeoDyne and its biomedical endeavors.

Paralleling the location of the largely West-Coast based biotech industry exploding out of recombinant DNA and related technologies, GeoDyne likely appropriately saw its future in the medical field in the emerging cutting edge areas of molecular medicine rather than just the classic and traditional medicinal chemistry that had given us the likes of non-steroidal anti-inflammatory drugs (NSAID's), b-blockers and angiotensin converting enzyme (ACE) inhibitors for hypertension, and H2-blockers for treatment of ulcers and gastritis.

Through its PharmCon Division responsible for the manufacture of pharmaceuticals, the company had grown a still relatively small biotech research program, operating both internally and through support of collaborative investigators in academics, including in the Seattle area, as well as Medical Centers in California. PharmCon had rapidly grown its production ability of monoclonal antibodies, and with its first patent for a diagnostic application in hematology, it was decided to create a separate arm concentrating on development, manufacture, and promotion of commercially available molecular diagnostic and especially future therapeutic agents. The name Immugen Pharmaceuticals reflected its emphasis on genetically engineered products targeted to clinical applications for immunologic disorders, including HIV.

Having one monoclonal antibody approved for diagnostic use, dozens of others available for sale for research applications, one humanized antibody planned for clinical trials, and the rights for commercial development for several promising recombinant proteins primarily targeting immunologic disorders, the executives in charge of the commercial expansion of Immugen had decided that it was time for a dedicated marketing, PR, and advertisement program.

...

GeoDyne had a long standing relationship with one of the older, established advertising firms in Seattle, a good ol' boy (if such a term can be applied to long term residents, but most of whom had moved to the Northwest from all over elsewhere) network which had handled essentially all of the marketing and advertising needs for GeoDyne going back to the early days of initial selling of just oil discovery-related machinery and instrumentation. They had transitioned fairly effectively and smoothly in their efforts to support all of GeoDyne's marketing and sales operations, including more than adequately tapping into the market place for EquiMed's Diagnostic Imaging hardware and software. As Kim informed me, up to their coming on board with Immugen, this had largely always been a fairly straightforward endeavor: no frills marketing pieces objectively representing well made and reliable products from a reputable manufacturer at competitive prices. As she also indicated to me, there was also basically nothing wrong with this approach, one that they wouldn't deviate from substantially, just adding some "bells and whistles" for selling modern and futuristic products to a modern and increasingly futuristic world.

Medicine was changing. This business arrangement gave Kim and me things to talk about more in direct line with my daily life than weird art. The cloning of genes and the production of pharmaceutical quantities of genetically engineered bioactive peptides and the modification of *in vitro* produced monoclonal antibodies to make them safe for therapeutic administration to patients were just two examples. The explosion of biotech companies was making for a competitive market place, despite the potential for the typical patenting on specific products, and even while the jury was still out amongst the medical community regarding the clinical effectiveness and especially the cost-effectiveness of any given genetically engineered therapeutic agent, much less the whole new molecular approach.

For its small but expensive high-end biotech operation, GeoDyne wanted a similar boutique advertising program, something a little more edgy, more artsy... so to speak, something hot and vital to reflect the energetic and revolutionary approach to challenging diseases such as AIDS and other rapidly evolving medical needs such as fighting organ transplant rejection. With its location in San Francisco, time-zone and spatially convenient not only to Seattle but especially the head started competition in adjacent areas such as South San Francisco, Palo Alto, La Jolla, and other parts of California, the involvement of Edith's firm in the Art and especially Modern Art world also gave access to potential design and even potential artists. The prior involvement with the HIV/AIDS community only helped cinch the deal. Keep in mind that this was strictly for marketing/advertising for Immugen, a still relatively small endeavor in the grand scheme of things such as the scope and size of GeoDyne. A large GeoDyne marketing account would have likely surpassed Edith's firm's capabilities. But at this stage, Immugen, with some participation from within the company itself, likely only required one full time person and some partial effort from a few members within the largely more technical and production staff. If you wanted young, energetic, and sassy, even without any bias on my part whatsoever, it goes without saying that Mrs. Kim Pearson was your girl. Her presence in various interviews and meetings had quite helped in the negotiations to land the advertising account to begin with. The fact that she was more medically fluent than anyone they'd encountered to date within various candidate advertising firms certainly didn't hurt as she indicated to me on at least a couple occasions. I was proud and eager to learn about Immugen's R & D and GeoDyne in general. I commonly if not always offered comments and opinions on various art and poster, etc. designs that accompanied Kim's advertising efforts, whether solicited or not, and typically welcome, if for nothing else than the natural rules of relationships to begin with, as in one should be interested in what one's spouse does and should be supportive. I'm not sure if my comments up to that point had necessarily ever been useful, although Kim did (perhaps politely) acknowledge that she had edited some specific pieces based on my "insight".

As with my own emerging Houston magnetism evolving over the next 6 or so months, similar driving forces in a quite opposite direction would pose a Seattle and GeoDyne obstacle to what might otherwise be the typical, or at least an easier, evolution of our marriage.

XXI

- Houston; March, 1994

O n the last Tuesday morning in March, I headed over to the Thomas Street Clinic with an almost glowing sense of professional accomplishment and optimism, bordering on cockiness. I was tapping my fingers rhythmically on the steering wheel with an occasional bang on the dashboard while moderately mis-singing the words to a Soundgarden song I had blaring on the CD player I had recently put into my otherwise uninspiring latest car. I was well rested. I had woken up in time to make my own breakfast at home, and had enough coffee on board to imagine myself as a pretty competent drummer accompanist to the real "Spoonman" shaking my entire car. I was enjoying my job and was looking forward to another round of it.

A consult at Ben Taub the evening before had generated the 142nd patient to be enrolled in our clinical trial. We were still ahead of schedule on that aspect, and we were becoming an increasingly efficient team regarding all aspects of patient identification, information and sample collection, and follow-up.

The lab aspects were going as good as or better than could be expected. One always faithfully anticipates successful experiment after successful experiment, ready establishment of new assays, and data that is abundant and upon analysis of which, supports one's hypothesis with easy to demonstrate statistical significance. But then there's the real world, and in that place we have to spend so much of our time, it is usually a slower and far more frustrating process, more like one step forward and two (or two dozen) steps back.

However, we had actually already successfully established and validated numerous ELISA's (antibody based colorimetric assays), with adequate sensitivity to accurately analyze levels of target molecules noted in patient biological fluids, and we were steadily quantitating various cytokines and other possible disease mediators in the blood and CSF of enrolled patients.

The in vitro cultured neuron toxicity assays were working consistently, and we had successfully validated them with addition of physiologic and presumed (and increasingly validated by the ELISA's described above) in vivo disease-related levels of implicated biological mediators of toxicity and even shown protection against such cell injury and death by levels of our investigational drug compound that we believed we would be achieving, at least in the CSF, with doses being administered in our trial.

Things were coming together SO well. I was nearly done with a first proof of principle manuscript, which I hoped to have submitted for possible publication within the next couple of weeks. Writing my progress report for the first year of our funding would be easy; and the results would be impressive. We expected a large number of abstracts to be submitted in the summer and fall to various relevant meetings at which we would proudly present our work. The Department Chairman had reportedly told my senior colleague, my supporting sponsor on my K-23 grant, that I was "certainly a good hire."

...

My first patient that morning was a black woman in her 60s with a long history of type II diabetes. She would perhaps have been better or at least more routinely served by going to a specific clinic for chronic diabetic patients over at the county hospital. But, we were certainly capable of giving outstanding general medical care for ailments regardless of specific association to HIV-infection and AIDS and making referrals to other clinics and sub-specialty treatment as needed. For some reason she seemed to prefer me and had a habit of missing her appointments made elsewhere. She had a grandson who had AIDS and whom she accompanied to all his appointments at the Thomas Street Clinic, and this was the mechanism by which I had originally encountered her. When asking about her own health in passing, it was clear to me that it was not being attended to as rigidly as that of the far grimmer prognosis of her grandson. She made a request to see only me (and hence, mandating this particular clinic venue), and in a system where county money and salaried physicians are as inadequately stretched in one setting as another, flattery will often get you health care one doesn't seem to be taking advantage of elsewhere. I spent an extra long amount of time with her this morning, patiently discussing how we were going to work together to more optimally achieve better glucose control, and I diligently mapped out the extent of her sensory peripheral neuropathy and carefully performed a robust optical examination, noting some hypertensive and diabetic type retinal changes, in part to convince her that I too cared about the possible consequences of her disease in the various organs commonly affected by diabetes, supporting my emphasis that she should especially care. She agreed to a mildly modified anti-hypertensive regimen and more careful urine and even blood glucose monitoring, with potential subsequent tweaking of her diabetes medications, and gave me a brief warm hug after I stood up and before I left her.

When I opened the door to the adjacent exam room to see my next patient, I was surprised to see Curtis in there, sitting up on the examining table to my left and staring at the opposite wall.

It took me a second to recognize him. He was so thin…shrunken really. Then when I did, I acutely figured he was here to see me for some sort of personal reason, something akin to Rick wanting to borrow money from me in the past. But surely he couldn't have absorbed my schedule so well through casual conversations over all these months to the point of knowing I'd be at this clinic on this morning….

As he turned to face me after a few seconds, perhaps finally registering that someone had entered, he gave me a wry smile, something along the lines of someone getting caught doing only a minor offence they shouldn't be in the process of committing, and I noticed two small slightly raised reddish-purple nodules on his left cheek and chin, foci of Kaposi's sarcoma most likely, each only about 3-4 mm in size, and in an instant I realized that he wasn't there just for personal reasons.

Sensing my recognition of the circumstances, he said with a forced casualness in a squeaky high pitched voice that he quickly corrected with a throat clearing, but which I think had hinted at his underlying fear, "I heard that the best of the best was back here at the Thomas Street Clinic, so…here I am."

While subconsciously thinking it strange that a guy like Curtis would make a reference to a line I think I remembered from the movie *Top Gun*, with all its Hollywood machismo, I stuck out my hand to firmly shake his in reassurance.

...

My friendship with Curtis was casual enough that I wouldn't have considered it inappropriate to see him as a patient, had I even stopped to really ponder it, especially for an initial screening type visit. I sensed no awkwardness on either of our parts, including during the physical examination portions, and I knew based on the extreme intimacy of some of our past personal conversations that Curtis would not be a shy historian.

He had been confirmed HIV-positive only a couple of months ago, although he had suspected he had HIV for a long time, opting apparently for the "I don't really want to know" approach that we often encountered but which didn't exactly optimize chances for any AZT treatment benefits. He'd noted a pretty marked and accelerating weight loss, which he also felt had made it easier to increasingly notice some pretty prominently enlarged lymph nodes, and the emergence of the KS lesions on his face. He had also noticed a few spots elsewhere over the last several weeks which had all added up to a finally undeniable truth, the scariness of which may not be best dealt with alone.

But what appeared to be causing him the greatest concern (and I don't know how much some of our past conversations regarding my work may have fertilized this), and what most prompted him making an appointment and specifically requesting to see me, was a frightening sense of increasingly frequent and possibly worsening severe confusion, which he only seemed to gradually emerge from, sometimes after sleeping. He realized during lucid moments that these periods of confusion were also causing trouble at work regarding his job performance, reflected in acts and especially deficiencies he wasn't even aware of, until pointed out afterwards. He had finally been fired last week.

He also felt weak, especially when walking, and wondered if this could reflect more than just the weight loss he was experiencing. He said he remembered from some of our conversations that HIV could cause some of these things, and that I was the "expert", and probably the one best able to help him.

After I completed the history and physical exam, as I left and re-entered Curtis's room, drawing blood, filling out forms to order lab tests, even a chest X-ray despite the lack of any respiratory symptoms at present, and which we could do on site, some more casual comments between my patient and myself, perhaps to relieve some of the justifiable perceived seriousness, must have conveyed a pre-existing familiarity to some of the staff within the vicinity and helping me with various paperwork and lab-related activities.

"Friend of yours?" Naomi asked, with her head cocked slightly back and a brow raised, which along with the not so subtle judgmental tone, seemed to constitute an inquisition as to my own life style or at least an implied pronouncement that it may be O.K. to take care of "them", but we shouldn't necessarily "associate" with them.

Naomi was one of the nurses on Cheryl's staff, an attractive middle-aged black woman with whom I'd only occasionally worked with thus far. We were standing next to each other at the Nurse's station, outside of ear-shot from the exam rooms. Cheryl walked up at that point, a stack of paperwork in her hands, but as always, with a more global sense of everything and everyone that was in her clinic. And as she handed me a thankfully much thinner sub-stack of forms for my signature, said, with only clear medical objectivity, "Probably not a good idea to try and enroll him for your trial then."

XXII

- Recollections: San Francisco; December, 1992

"Why can't you work on the Immugen marketing stuff from Houston?" I childishly inquired, knowing some of the more obvious reasons but hoping that my question at least conveyed my true awareness of how important this growing opportunity was to Kim personally and to her career at this moment.

I had just found out that my NIH grant for the clinical trial was funded.

I had already had a formal interview trip and two subsequent visits to Baylor regarding a faculty position and then, even the planning of the resources and mechanisms necessary for conducting the studies involved, especially if the initial grant were funded. This whole process (e.g., correspondences about possible future job positions, research areas of interest, etc.) had started so far back, critically before Kim's and her firm's involvement with Immugen and GeoDyne, that the whole grant had been written with the idea of conducting the studies at Baylor with some ongoing collaborations with key folks at UCSF. We had even attached a letter of support from Baylor's Chairman of Neurology attesting to my position there if the grant were awarded and pledging necessary resources and support. A faculty appointment may still have been possible even if the grant wasn't funded, with a higher burden of clinical duties and the use of other lesser funds, such as start-up money and intramural awards, to generate more preliminary data to make for a stronger subsequent grant proposal. Now, with the grant awarded, it was essentially a done deal. My ticket to Houston would be enthusiastically stamped and I'd be on my way, if I wanted it (if we wanted it).

If I wanted it? I had no idea, at present, what else I would do, as I had worked this option almost exclusively, as it was clearly the best fit for that current combination of everything I'd been working towards for the last 12 or so years.

"There's just no way that's possible," Kim responded, fairly objectively, but firmly. "It's hard enough, nowadays, to even do it from here in San Francisco, where I'm working at a firm that actually has these guys as a client and thus commits appropriate staff and resources."

I hated when she used "thus" in our arguments/discussions, but this time the word "appropriate" also resonated in my head. It reminded me of the carefully calculated and financially justified technician efforts and materials budgeted into grant applications, such as my recent successful one, where the right amount of people and tools were discerned to just barely get a specific task accomplished, completed well, and without spending unnecessary time and money that could usefully go elsewhere. (For example, 30% of a particular technician's effort on the project if funded supposedly translated to 12 hours/week of their work, and which thus mandated that exactly 30% of their salary plus fringe benefits calculated at standard NIH rates went into the budget. In the budget justification, in addition to descriptions of that technician's role and appropriate skill/experience level, it certainly wouldn't hurt to describe where the other 70% of their salary would or especially did come from; after all, no collection of gray hairs controlling the limited national research budget likes to put money into a sinking ship or a fantasy person that one couldn't really afford to hire).

In other words, Kim was where she needed to be, with the right help and focus, not that different than what I'd been steadily orchestrating for Houston. In fact, she'd been spending increasing amounts of time in Seattle to more effectively work on site with critical ("appropriate") people at Immugen. There had even been rumors of creating a full time position for her in Seattle, still essentially through her current firm, and with generation of an appropriate staff, and maybe even extending some of the recently developed marketing strategies and products for Immugen to some other areas of GeoDyne's large empire. It seemed more inevitable that this was the direction Kim's efforts and success were progressing towards. Another occasionally considered option was for GeoDyne to finally establish its own full service marketing division, and it would be difficult to overestimate Kim's potential role in any such operation.

"It's not like I can just join a firm in Houston and expect to transfer a major client to the detriment of Edith's firm, when there's already contracts in place, etc. and/or that the new firm would commit adequate resources for me to get anything done if I tried to continue on some ad hoc basis," she unnecessarily continued as I'd more or less at least conceded the logical general issues.

The use of the word "detriment" and the "and/or" made me almost wonder if this speech had been rehearsed, something I might do perhaps, although the "etc." argued otherwise. I wasn't sure how to interpret the "ad hoc", although I don't think I'd ever been in a personal (i.e., non-work related) conversation in which it had been used. Kim did have a highly sophisticated vocabulary, almost equally displayed in both pre-prepared material and spontaneous discourse. I hadn't thought about the idea of a possible ad hoc arrangement: Kim continuing to work on the Immugen project in some kind of free-lance way; either arranged directly through Edith's firm or in some sort of GeoDyne supported arrangement that could be set up in a way financially attractive to and hence supported by Edith and her colleagues. I might need some more time to ponder this and fool myself with some argument points in its favor, but there's no way this sort of arrangement could be optimal and adequately meet the growing needs of a group as sophisticated as the one developing at Immugen.

I was processing a lot of thoughts in response to Kim's comments, and she must have sensed that, giving me time to digest some of the implications of each subsequent fateful remark. Her reference to "transfer" made me wonder if she were rendering opinion on her possibilities vs my own.

As if reading my mind, she now continued with, "Why can't you transfer your grant to Seattle?"

This was the first concrete or official reference to the notion that living in Seattle could be in the differential for our mutual life.

It didn't take me long to respond, perhaps too vehemently.

...

We gave each other a break. Kim went into the kitchen, maybe to make a cup of tea (or get a drink). I went off into the small space in our second bedroom where we kept a weight bench and a few free weights. I sat on the bench and started to do some curls. I had to do something active. I had that angst that comes from everything not being right, not all fitting together, not being solved, and I had to start taking steps to make it perfect; like that feeling when a test was coming up, there was one section of the book you hadn't studied yet, and so you couldn't wait another psychically-uncomfortable moment to start reading it…no matter what else was going on with you or anyone involved with you. This mental unrest was accompanied by or quickly followed by a slight nausea, when I even vaguely allowed the thought of somehow not going to Houston creep into my mind. How in the hell could I ever pull all this off again, especially at this late stage. All the planning, down to every last detail to successfully accomplish the ambitious aims of my grant, all the resources worked out through potentially dozens or more of collaborators scattered all over the world's largest medical center and even off site clinics, all the worked out aspects negotiated through numerous higher ups in various departments of my clinical assignments and various other aspects of my professional obligations.

No…this was untenable, incompatible with my life without suicide. And yet, I was at possible odds with the one I loved. I felt like vomiting up the dinner we hadn't had yet.

After who knows how long, maybe minutes in the usual world, but what seemed like an eternity in the space-time warp of distorted perceptions in couple-dom, Kim came over and got on her knees in front of where I was sitting and took my hands in hers: "There's no way I could ask you to give up your research. It's important to you, and it could help a lot of people someday. And I can't ask you to give up your grant and your position at Baylor."

She looked up into my face and our eyes met, and I can't say that I'd ever seen before what I saw there, as she continued, "But I also know what's most important to you."

At that moment, she must have been waiting for me to say something…to make that look go away.

But I didn't know how to respond. So, I didn't.

After a pause, after enough time, she got up saying, a little too matter-of-factly, "We'll figure something out," and walked away.

My heart sank and my guts tightened. I don't think I liked the broadening of possible choices somehow transmitted in her tone.

Book Three

"Someday, the Saturday sun will shine
Another chance to get it right
Another chance to get it right
You give me something to look forward to
All we want is something to look forward to
Everybody needs something to look forward to"

-Jon Dee Graham, Something to Look Forward To

I

- Houston; March, 1994

"How was your day, dear?" Rick asked me, in the right combination of sarcasm and sincerity that suggested it appropriate to actually respond, as I fatiguely plopped down on the bench next to him. Apparently, he actually sat on the benches when he was at the park alone. Proving that no conversation was off limits for whatever reason, including a maximum score on the "Who gives a shit scale," this had actually been the non-earth shattering subject of occasional debates when a few of us had been in the park when Rick wasn't there.

"Not so bad, I guess." I answered, realizing I was happy to have someone to just hang out and make small talk with, feeling a little worn both physically and emotionally. "Saw a bunch of patients in clinic," I continued, "actually enrolled two in my clinical trial, and even managed to get over to the lab to check on things and pick some data up...the usual stuff that's not going to land me on the cover of People magazine any time soon." I then reciprocally inquired, "How was your big day in court?"

Rick usually spent at least part of Wednesdays in court, seeking small fortunes for society's picked on, under-represented huddled masses, but I remember him making some comments this past weekend that he had a couple of particularly big (for him) cases during the upcoming week.

One, if I remembered correctly, involved a young man who had walked out of a "Stop and Rob" (either a Circle K or Stop and Go I think) and broken his leg ("woefully shattered his tibia, the major weight bearing bone of the lower leg" was the terminology we eventually settled on after a few beers in the park that previous Sunday) when he stepped into a "clearly negligently unmarked, and maliciously dangerous" pothole in the parking lot. Normally, this in itself would be sufficient for a few hundred bucks to help with medical costs, or maybe even a life time's supply of Slurpee equivalents. However, in this case, the "victim" was a professional soccer player, using the term professional in the literal sense, as one who gets paid for a service rendered or some such legal speak. I didn't even know Houston had a professional indoor soccer team. This Nigerian citizen, here completely legally (fortunately), may or may not have been (in Rick's rehearsed presentation) a "tragic victim of an increasingly cavalier and self-centered materialistic society, more concerned with selling over-cooked, non-nutritious hot dogs and unnecessary and environmental damaging additive-laden gasoline to its own mislead citizens, already caught up in the rat race, than protecting and sustaining its law abiding visitors, the very people our nation was founded on, who so commonly must resort to such neighborhood establishments in order to purchase the (overpriced) staples of their daily existence;" but he was an athlete that used his right leg, now internally pinned and stabilized externally in an orthopedic instrument that seemed to be right out of a Middle Ages Torture Device Catalogue (fortunately, from the jury perspective), to earn his livelihood, in a manner now obviously more severely compromised than for anyone else who might have a harder time getting to and from work.

This was good stuff I remembered thinking. I believe Rick had pictures of his client's very thin children, still living back in Nigeria and depending on Dad's income for their daily rations of camel's milk or whatever they ate to show during the trial, much like those pictures of malnourished (Kwashiorkor is the proper medical term if I remember correctly from first year medical school biochemistry) starving kids with the big bellies you see on the late night commercials where just 28 cents a month will feed, clothe, and provide medical care for a child just like the one shown, maybe next to Sally Struthers and probably wishing he could have had just one of the seventeen cheeseburgers she apparently has been having for breakfast for some time. In fact, I'm not sure that this wasn't the kind of source from which Rick had actually gotten his pictures. Not being quite the organization level of, say, the Houston Oilers, apparently the indoor soccer team didn't have a standing law firm for this or any other reason, or if they did, Rick's client wasn't aware. Instead, while lying in agony at the edge of the "crater that had just denied him, as a finely tuned athlete and provider, of the very essence of his existence," he glanced over and saw one of Rick's tasteful ads on the back of a bus stop bench bordering the parking lot.

I do remember cautioning Rick about the potentially non-substantiable claims of the gas additives, not from any legal or gasoline composition expertise, per se; but after all, I had watched enough of L.A. Law in the past (apparently at the expense of rounding out my medical education by not watching St. Elsewhere instead) to have some legal opinions. Probably like a lot of folks around that time, watching that show was part of an official Thursday night TV ritual, plus I was continually pleased and intrigued to see how hot Susan Dey had become from her pubescent stages on The Partridge Family. I don't remember much of the details of Rick's other planned "big" case, but it apparently didn't matter, given his response to my genuine curiosity.

"I had to cancel all my cases today," he said rather nonchalantly. I began to wonder if he had been drinking…a lot.

"You're kidding! Why?" I asked, hoping that alcohol was not causally involved.

"You know my new legal secretary?"

"The one with the really full, usually red lips, the very round titties often protruding slightly above her blouse, and the shapely ass, stretching the seams of her short skirts," I answered based on past descriptions from Rick himself rather than direct visual contact, although I did of course have fairly vivid images in my mind. They were images of a slightly overweight, but hence voluptuous, beautiful Hispanic woman, hired by Rick as part of his assuming more direct managerial responsibilities at his "practice." My resulting suspicions of a relative lack of legal or secretarial skills were soon to gain some merit. However, I do distinctly re-member having the impression that Rick hired her at least partly out of kindness and a "good feel" regarding her character, motivation, and potential, rather than just out of any sort of lust, although it seems the latter had grown exponentially since the date of hire.

"Yeah, that's her, Maria," he acknowledged, apparently not finding any sig-nificant faults with my description.

He continued, gazing off into space, with a desolation I sensed was actually more situational than ethanol based.

"Well, apparently, while she was typing up all my dictated statements and hand scribbled notes related to today's cases, she decided she didn't like some of the specific phraseology...never mind that some of it was in direct concordance with our state's sacred statutes," his tone sharpened a little bit.

"Hey, I can relate. I can never understand all that legal mumbo jumbo, fancy lawyer talk," I added, trying to lighten the mood reflected in his non-specifically directed glare.

"So...she changed it. Apparently she took some composition classes at San Jacinto Community College and fancies herself a rather aspiring maker of prose."

"I see," I offered up sympathetically.

"Of course such modifications did, unfortunately, drastically alter some of the factual and legal elements of the intended documents," Rick said, not so much glaring now, as more dully staring in some sort of professional disappointed or mild shock state.

"Ouch," I impotently offered up for condolence.

"Anyway," he continued, seeming to shake himself out of whatever funk this latest setback should have inflicted, "I had to cancel my cases, for obvious reasons, and I spent all day re-typing the documents as I intended them. I just finished before I came out here."

"Wow, I'm sorry buddy," I said with cautious relief at his apparently easing tension. "What did you do with Maria?"

"Well, I think I jumped and stomped around the room that she works in for maybe a half hour or so, explaining the consequences of her thoughtless actions, the reasons why we go to law school, the reasons why we state things certain ways, alluding to the sacredness of the law, and a bunch of other spirited b.s. Then I asked her out," Rick explained calmly.

I was beginning to be glad I came out to the park this evening. This was indeed good stuff, easing my mind off of some of my own looming concerns. Apparently, the shock of his compromised briefs and other papers and the consequences of having to postpone two of his bigger recent endeavors had alleviated the inertia he had been toiling around the office with every day and lowered his inhibitions toward his lovely assistant.

"What did she say?" I was now extremely sucked into this little law office soap opera.

"She said that she couldn't go out with anyone that doesn't respect her work," Rick answered, less dejected than I would have expected.

"Bummer," I consoled. "What then?"

"I spent another thirty minutes or so explaining to her how much I did respect her, and her efforts, and how I actually liked the *style* of the new documents better than the ones I had originally constructed, gently including that it was only for legal reasons that some things were stated the way they had been," Rick continued. "Then I asked her out again, hoping I had convinced her."

"And…?" I inflected, having totally bought into the drama.

"She said that she didn't date co-workers, especially bosses."

"I'm sorry, man," I offered, truly disappointed for my sometimes life-challenged and probably lonely legal compadre.

"So, I fired her," he continued, without losing a beat.

"That's one approach," I cautiously observed. "But maybe not the one that's most likely going to land you, or at least certain parts of you, in her panties."

"Actually, we're going out on Saturday night," he finished, without even modifying his tone to the jubilant victorious one that he could have justified. Maybe he was just too beat after nine straight hours of typing.

"You rule," I responded. What else could I say?

II

- Houston; March, 1994

That evening after the lesson in practical romance from Rick, restaurants (especially if eating just by myself) held no grandeur. I went home and made myself a very uninspiring dinner; something like a grilled ham and cheese sandwich, based on what acceptable ingredients were surprisingly available, with a side of chips. The bag of chips was actually virginal, and I briefly pondered having them exclusively, after a whiff of chip appeal was liberated and much appreciated upon popping open the bag and eating a few heaping handfuls, before the discovery of a forgotten half container of deli ham and a few viable slices of cheddar cheese noted while pulling a beer out of the fridge to go with the chips.

I sat down on the sofa with my short-order museum selection of a dinner, complete with a big blob of ketchup in the center of one of the moderately tacky plates that came with my rental; ketchup, one of the true bachelor-style non-perishable entities on this planet. It was as red and pseudo-fresh as the day its mother tomatoes were invented (or at least sacrificed). In at least temporary human droid fashion, I flipped on the TV, masterfully using from almost 12 feet the remote that hadn't worked in probably almost two weeks...or was it nearly two months? Hey, I didn't watch much TV, and getting up to change channels was consciously noted as exercise during whatever period of nostalgia-inducing primitivity this had been. It was, of course, the diagnostically most likely lesion of dead batteries. In an insight bordering on Edison, I realized that the typical remote batteries were the same size as those painful energizers of our doctor beepers. So, in an act of self-perceived cunning and charm, I got two double A's from our transcriptionist at work, the efficient XX responsible for making sure we were always available when we were on call. Now, as I sat there, literally flipping channels without getting up and eating a warm sandwich made in my own kitchen, I paused in celebration of my own accomplishments, and realized, maybe half-heartedly, that my life was, at least acutely, a testament to essentially meaningless efficiency and empty competency.

While in my non-sustainable state of potential anti-self-glory, I powerfully and authoritatively switched through all of the relatively limited number of channels, with a seemingly small but difficult string of cheese hanging off my left lip and steadily wiping the salt and artificial powders of the chips on my left pant leg, given my fear that exposing the remote (in my right hand) to more than a minimal dose of these mysterious chemicals could counter the still appreciated miracle of the free batteries. Although I had noted some Spanish soap opera with some chicks with well displayed big titties on my second round through, for reasons that only spaced out tube viewers could debate upon, I paused momentarily on some sort of PBS kind of informative show on probability theory impacting rare events and human nature. Examples included gamblers putting large sums on single roulette numbers, despite well appreciated poor odds compared say to more logical approaches to realistic higher expectations of making lesser increments of money. Another one had to do with purchasing slender pole supported luxury houses on the beach in way higher than usual earthquake frequency zones. In my brief viewing per channel on this round of flipping, there was nothing to do with titties (indicating perhaps that the Spanish channel had gone to commercial).

But for some reason, despite the lack of prior beers, wine, or any other reason to focus on mathematics, I became momentarily intrigued by the whole concept of odds and impact on decision making, with no real formulas to take into account the highly impacting human individual component. For no likely reasons other than recentness and absurdity, my mind drifted towards Rick and his voluptuous ex-secretary/future date. As an indication of the seeming meaningless directions this thought experiment was taking me, I began to ponder the chances of them getting married. As one of likely thousands of possible contributing variables, for example, there was likely little way to rigidly incorporate, say, the tequila factor. Much less likely so on any particular individual and even initial date basis. All one could hope to do, maybe, was incorporate a tequila moderating factor, something like electron position wave probability theory in quantum physics I guess, and apply it hopefully effectively over, say, a thousand Rick-Maria interactions.

Human behavior: so complex, so unpredictable.

Then, strictly for the purpose of playing along while stuck on the informative/educational channel, as my fingers were now so chipped up that even my pants legs couldn't protect the remote and allow me to change channels without the currently insurmountable burden of walking across the living room to grab a paper towel (there were only official napkins during and immediately after Kim visits), I kept on the math theme and allowed for speculation on a potential secondary event. If, say, a Rick and a Maria were to get married, what were the chances of divorce? Here, albeit hypothetically assuming a statistically unlikely marriage at this point, the parameters become a bit more defined. One could use more widely available empirically derived data in the probability modeling. However, in addition to the standard divorce rate, it would be more precise if one could also account for contributions such as the mental/financial/emotional, etc. state of the parties involved. I suspect some behaviorologists (or whatever they're called) had looked into these sorts of factors, but it certainly was normally outside of my reading topic range. I would suspect, however, that this pairing would likely come associated with a little higher than the usual national divorce rate, given the not precisely defined but likely statistically supported modulating negative impacting probability factors such as alcohol use (by at least one of the two), Irish-American vs. Hispanic heritage of the two parties, this despite a possible anti-divorce factor of a likely Catholic affiliation of at least one and probably both of the parties, based on ethnic derivation alone.

Whatever; I was effectively boring the living shit out of myself, so when this became past the state of transitory mental indulgence originating out of nowhere vs. moving on to the next *a priori* non precisely predictable action on my part, in sequential motions so coordinated as to be almost simultaneous to a hypothetical less than rigidly paying attention external observer, while grabbing a paper towel, getting more chips for my plate, and flipping to the Spanish soap opera titty-displaying channel, I caught a glimpse of Kim's and my wedding picture on the end table.

As I sat back down and maybe out of quasi lust guilt switched the channel yet again, and wiped my hands on my pants, I began to ponder more personal mathematical issues. First, there were two 100% certainties that manifested on that particular day, events and phenomena that you could enthusiastically and confidently bet the farm, the chip bag, or the whole chip factory on. One: Kim was without a doubt the most beautiful and majestic entity in the history of organisms. Two: I was the most fucking nervous I've ever been in my life.

III

- Recollections: 1991-1992

K im and I were married in San Diego on Saturday, December 7th, 1991. From the time we had become engaged (and I suppose even a while before then), we basically wanted to be married, as we were essentially already functioning that way and there could be no doubts as to our feelings for each other. Kim and I both wanted a "regular" type wedding, with family, friends, a great reception, and particularly, an outstanding honeymoon. Neither of us was especially conventionally religious at the time, so the church aspects that commonly accompany matrimonial ceremonies were not that much of an issue, including for her or my parents. We would be married by the Preacher from Bob's and Patti's church (primarily if not exclusively because that was the most convenient and saved us from having to find someone else), but likely at a non-church location.

In what I'm sure is a common, almost ritualistic, process, as soon as the engagement was announced, Kim and her mother became locked into some form of communication by which plans can be discussed, options researched, analyzed, and decided upon, and novel ideas and unexpected complications dealt with in a blaze of conversations, often without even completing full sentences, in a manner as mysterious to the listening male as the realm of the female mind and spirit from which such abilities likely arise from to begin with.

There is some overlap, of course, between the mental and emotional functions of the two sexes within our species. In theory, we share basic structure and similar genes on 45 of our 46 chromosomes. Clearly, that single Y vs. X and all the downstream developmental effects and the potential consequent altered reception to environmental and societal factors account for those wonderful differences we celebrate on a daily basis. But even at the extreme of wedding planning, there is a spot or two in which the male can insert an opinion or even take on a (likely non-crucial) relatively major task with primary responsibility. I would hypothesize that the more the male inputs, the more he receives in lusciously delivered female rewards all along the planning and execution phase. This should not be the sole motivating factor, of course, just a welcomely received bonus. And so, I responded when inquired of for an opinion on a range of topics, from the date, time, and site of the wedding, to the composition of the invitation list, to the menu for the reception, and especially the details of the honeymoon. In fact, it was the working out the details of the latter that evolved to one of those aspects which became my primary responsibility (maybe the only one, unless you count co-planning or co-directing two different bachelor parties with various combinations of old and new buddies), as Kim was very busy with the wedding and reception details.

San Diego, as may be expected, had many nice options for a wedding location. Had we been married in the spring, we may have chosen The Japanese Friendship Garden. I had come to really like Balboa Park, in general, through my various visits to San Diego, and obviously Kim and Patti were even more familiar with its various contents, including possible wedding facilities. However, some traditional event sites (of adequate size) such as the House of Hospitality and the Balboa Park Club were at the time somewhat deteriorated compared to their past glory. In fact, that year the city of San Diego was apparently exploring financial options for restoration projects to target these specific sites as well as other parts of the Park. So, we ended up getting married and having the reception on Coronado Island, at the grand, historic Hotel del Coronado, where we also stayed for a couple more nights before heading off to Fiji for a whole week!

Thinking back, now, the whole wedding and reception were like a whirlwind. Good thing someone took pictures! In fact, I had those pictures, beautifully displayed in highly tasteful photo albums, here, right here in my ("our") little bungalow-like house in the middle of Houston. I wondered what that meant. That had to be a good sign.

Suddenly, in a sense of precipitated panic, I began to wonder where the china was. Why that, specifically, of the many of our shared possessions and some of the particularly nice things we'd received as wedding presents, I'm not sure. After a brief broadly sweeping analysis of our collective existences, I logically remembered that it was well-packed in a couple of the many brown card-board boxes piled well and tightly within the smallest of the theoretically three bed rooms in my own dwelling (or at least, I'm almost certain that's where it was; where else would it be?). That room was indeed almost completely filled with boxes of unpacked mutual "household" items, things for our future life together that weren't intended to be unearthed this far into the future and which I could clearly temporarily live without.

After moving and getting a bit settled in, I had rearranged the piles of boxes to leave just enough functional width between the door and the opposite wall to allow regulation throwing length from barely into the hallway to a dart board I had hung on the wall. With the music turned up loud enough to hear rigorously throughout the house, I would only occasionally stand just outside the doorway and toss darts at the board, especially when trying to concentrate on a just missing idea regarding the design of an experiment or such. My dart throwing skills were at least adequate, which was perhaps appropriate, as I was living within a few square mile radius of a pub-laden part of town in which darts were almost a religion. But, within my den of mentality, I think I threw worse when mentally struggling the most, leaving more than a few small dart-gauge holes in the wall surrounding the board, with arguably a reassuring greater density immediately around the board (those damn intended double shots…when playing myself in cricket I suppose) than those randomly scattered more distant sparser holes. It struck me as something like a population density map, with fewer and fewer small towns the further away from the board metropolis area. But that probably wouldn't be much of a defense when I had to settle with my landlord.

Yes, that certainly is where the china and much of everything else is I confidently thought and consoled myself. From hence forth, I would no longer refer to that little unused room as "The Dart Board Room" (not that I often did), but instead, as the grander and far less bachelor, "The China Room". Something like the White House maybe has, and in proper proportionate dwelling analogy, I was perhaps now akin to the President; "El Presidente" of a small fledgling nation, somewhere swampy and steamy…and without enough rules.

…

I didn't know quite how to act when we got back from Fiji to our "new" lives in San Francisco, or if we even really were supposed to act any differently. Immediately, we were that unique combination of emotionally rested and a bit still relaxed from being away at a beautiful place and yet tired from the travel and a bit disoriented from being gone awhile and now back in that place where the chaos and stress of the wedding and planning had just recently been. Fortunately, in our travel plans, we had given ourselves a weekend back home before having to both go back to work. Surely, there was stuff that we should be doing, but we didn't want to kill the Fiji/honeymoon spirit all at once.

There was a bit of mail to sort through. We didn't get so much that we needed to have the post office hold it while we were gone or if we did, I had forgotten to arrange it. Either way, it took Kim only a very short time to triage the junk mail that could be thrown away immediately without further exploration, the bills and other items that would indeed require attention at the appropriate reunion with reality when it couldn't be put off any longer, and a more situational third stack of cards from well wishers and a few RSVPs that hadn't made it to us before the wedding. I think that stack was intended for us to mutually go through as "husband and wife" as one of our first official acts as a married couple during the residual relaxation of the weekend.

In the mean time, I watched Kim's female mail sorting prowess with some kind of fusion of admiration, curiosity, and enough bewilderment and "holy shit, we're married" to prompt the occasional upward glance from my lovely bride's concentration to convey a mixture of love and "what's wrong with you, dork?" that only a partner can do in a manner that is somehow affectionate. When she was done with sorting the mail stack, we both let out a collective sigh (as if I had somehow participated), and we mutually glanced over at the large stacks of presents that were almost filling our small living room, simultaneously blocking access to the balcony, the TV/stereo cabinet, and the sofa that I was acutely tempted to, but effectively prevented from, plant my ass on (in a manner horizontally accompanied by the whole body in pre-nap comfort perhaps?).

There was a relatively small stack of variously gift wrapped and brown-paper ship wrapped boxes that must have come to the apartment by hand and mail delivery, respectively, and which the super had been stacking between the door and the entertainment stand. Opening these would give us another easily defined mutual task in our new life together before going back to work. There was a much larger stack of items that we had received at the reception and most of which we had already opened during the two days before we left for our honeymoon. They had made the relatively short distance from the reception to our suite in The Hotel del Coronado, where we as young people with only mild possessions at present and in substantial relative need of a wide array of gadgets, gizmos, and decorations had eagerly opened them. Some were even out of the original boxes; either we had destroyed them effectively during opening or our transporters who'd brought everything from the San Diego area up to San Francisco hadn't been able to figure out how to get them back into the miscellaneous Styrofoam and cardboard original packaging in the timeframe of the patience level allocated to the level of favor they were already doing us. A blender, a juicer, and some sort of vase-like thing were moderately precariously stacked alongside and atop a set of closed boxes that I presumed were various parts of place settings and those other types of getting married things.

That these items, now piled between the entertainment stand and the balcony door all the way in front of two-thirds of the sofa, had made it here (and clearly even before the super had started adding the others to the outer aspects of the mound) was a testimony to the well intended harmony and occasionally matching effectiveness of what sometimes seem like even the most casual of human interactions.

I vaguely remember some passing conversation, probably one of several going on around and/or involving the bride and groom simultaneously at a rather ethanolic later stage of the reception, in which Kim's brother, Barkley, whom of course, I didn't know all that well to begin with, had proposed a plan for getting all the presents to us in San Francisco that must have sounded adequate at the time for enthusiastic approval by yours truly and his bride. In retrospect now, as we glanced around the living room and I somehow felt that every single place setting and candlestick and God knows what else had made it to our home, I remember it was vaguely something like: Barkley had a former roommate at college who was back in San Diego as well, and whom he had seen a few nights before, who had a friend/co-worker (whom Barkley had met that same night and/or maybe had drank with a few times before) that was moving up to L.A. in a few days. He had (not unusual so far) arranged to rent a U-haul to move all his stuff up, and there would be plenty of leftover room for our presents. Barkley's moving friend of a friend's new roommate had a van (like a real van, not a mini-van, apparently a throw back to their Berkley days and attitude and not reflective of the proper youth that at least Barkley's father and probably the other boys' fathers had been hoping to nurture with their well intended past educational funds and likely ongoing support). Well, here was the missing link: Barkley's friend of a friend's roommate had a friend, who I think normally lived...I can't remember where... who was going to be in the San Francisco area for a couple of weeks, "like, wow," right around a couple days before we got back from our honeymoon. He was coming in for some Dead shows in Oakland the last week of December or something like that and he and two other buddies had arranged to borrow his friend's van...and this would save them a trip down to L.A. to pick it up. I think I recall needing that last part explained to me again, indicating if nothing else, that I wasn't quite done drinking that night, and such residual coherence was thus minimally displayed. Simple: Barkley would drive the van up to SF with all the presents, and then he could just eventually fly back to San Diego, if his Father, who had by then joined in the conversation, could spring for a flight back (and, thinking through it later, perhaps an original flight to L.A.?). "Of course," his father, my FATHER-IN-LAW, had loudly endorsed, while patting me on my back. And with whatever male gesture of approval I must have given at the time and Kim's likely look of "whatever," this covenant of wedding present delivery was solidified.

And now I stood, momentarily staring, in humble awe and appreciation, at the piles of goodies before me. I slowly walked over and picked up the blender and examined it as if an artifact from a time capsule or an unknown object contained within the center of a meteor that had disintegrated and spilled all its other worldly contents within our living room. I set the blender down, and picked up the juicer. I pressed the inactive "make juice" button of the unplugged juicer, subconsciously imagining fresh squeezed orange juice, real lime juice for margaritas, maybe some liquefied carrot concoction I may someday be forced to drink... because it was good for me. I put it back down where I think it had gingerly stood in its unboxed state and picked up the vase-like object. I held the open end up to my ear to see if I could hear the ocean or something else.

That less than sixteen hours ago Kim and I were alone in our own little Tiki hut almost 50 yards out in the ocean and removed by only a narrow wooden plank from a remote beach and now were in a major metropolitan area in the

U.S. (a cab of questionably maintained state negotiated across language barriers, a small plane ride, a big jet ride, and another albeit better maintained cab ride still negotiated across language barriers) was almost enough to restore or establish one's confidence in the system of mankind. That all these presents were now in our living room, our mutual married living room, not only strengthened my convictions towards the finer elements of people in general, but made me momentarily tired…for their journey, our journey, everything we had lived through the past several weeks, and maybe a bit for the future.

Kim, apparently watching me for the last several minutes, must have been stirred by my appreciation of our newly acquired matrimonial bounty.

"We should do our thank you cards…while it's fresh…while, you know… we're in that mode," she said spiritedly despite our spreading journey fatigue.

Out of one last gesture of my appreciation for life's beauty and magic, I was already in the middle of barely being able to reach in through the gift rubble to barely being able to open a drawer of the entertainment stand to find and pull out a tape, which through some sort of cosmic connectedness system turned out to be one that Barkley had sent to me on a single such occasion, a Dead bootleg, and getting it into the tape player, and turning and walking towards Kim as a version of "Dark Star" came on (which a note accompanying the tape had informed me that by a consensus of Barkley and some of friends once achieved in a bar somewhere in Thailand was within the top ten versions ever…whatever that meant to my still Dead-ignorant self). I defended myself, pathetically, thinking that Kim meant doing the thank you cards right then, by responding, "Can't we just wait to see which ones we like the best…or which ones we use the most…and then just send thank you cards for those?"

"You suck," she said, smiling affectionately, and then she put her arms around my neck and kissed me firmly, then deeply, her tongue sliding into my mouth, where I tasted my Kim, but under a travel fatigue taste that for some reason made me momentarily realize that even Kim wasn't perfect, even Kim couldn't taste like her usual self after a long day's weird journey. It turned me on so much, I thought I could die, right there, right then, in a moment so shared, so mutual, that nothing could ever take it away.

"Yes I do," I replied in mock sexual professional seriousness, as we made our way to the bedroom. "And I'll do whatever else you request…ma'am…always."

And we made love. For the 22nd time as a married couple (I tried to keep track for a while, but gladly gave up…), the fourth time on American soil, and the first time as husband and wife in our own home.

After a couple hours' nap, we rose in a mental fog just as it was beginning to turn dark outside, reminding ourselves where we were and stumbled collectively into the living room. After standing around for a few moments unproductively, we followed each other into the kitchen, debated coffee briefly, and decided on wine. We took our glasses back out into the living room, and being careful not to spill the powerful red staining juice, we started with the stack closest to the sofa (so I could eventually sit beside Kim during the process), and began to open presents.

Kim had a small scrap of paper that we eventually upgraded to a spiral notebook from the desk in the bedroom so she could note what came from whom as a starter for the anticipated thank you note project. Place settings for our "routine" dishes, flatware (I still wasn't sure I understood this term, as the curved up active portions of the forks and spoons and even the handles of the knives weren't truly or even closely flat) were featured items. Less common versions of our china and crystal were emerging as well, which I liked as some of the glasses looked like they'd be very satisfying to drink from. There was the occasional unpredicted gift, maybe from a more distant relative or friend who had somehow avoided access to the registry lists: three sets of candlesticks, two of which we really liked; some photograph albums, some pans that didn't quite match those on the registry list (but which were quite nice), a gorgeous set of high end cutlery from Edith (Kim's boss; who had also sent two sets of our china), and a set of somehow not completely tacky "couples" massage oils from an old friend of mine from medical school. I was stunned when we opened Dr. Hassel's gift and it was a beautiful sculpture (modern appearing to me) of an intertwined couple. It came with a description, but I'm sure I would receive or could ask for some embellishment as well, when I shocked my system upon returning to work. Kim absolutely loved it, and was touched at his generosity, as she commented that it was likely unique and very expensive.

I added sarcastically (as I, and hence we, didn't deserve this yet if ever), "Hey, I'm making that guy famous."

Sleepy, cute, warm PJ-clad Kim responded, "I'll make YOU famous in a couple hours if you go get the wine in the kitchen."

Leaving the bottle out there was less suave than I'd like to see myself on post-honeymoon, post-sex, post-nap, present-opening, drinking marital bliss occasions. When I came back, I enjoyed the view of Kim's ass as she was bending over the stack still remaining, and moving some things around.

"Hey," I said, "you're not going out of order are you?"

Without turning around, she replied, "Something smells funny over here."

Out of social instinct, I reached my right arm up and smelled my right armpit, and then did the same thing to the left. Convinced, I added, "It's not me."

"Duh," she said, the only organism I'd ever encountered that could make "duh" sound sexy.

I tried to contribute to the growing detective work. I picked up the box with the massage oils and gave it a dedicated sniff. Even with bottles unopened, there was a detectable, but not, at least to me, unpleasant scent. (I think fragrance is the official word for such products). I tapped Kim on the shoulder, needing a more expert opinion, and when she turned I offered up the box towards her nose.

"No, that's not it," she said after legitimately considering my offered up solution even before I had experienced what she was talking about.

And then, as I stood next to her, despite admiring how absolutely adorable this routinely sexy vixen was in her "comfy PJ's", I began to notice and then lock in on what she must have been referring to. It was a rotten, sort of moldy smell. I knew these things. I'm a male that had lived alone. We re-checked ourselves as we'd been traveling. The mystery grew.

I offered up to keep the flow of wine consumption going, "let's just keep opening presents. I'm sure whatever's under there (as if it could be a big stain on the carpet or a dead rat) will declare itself shortly."

"Will declare itself shortly?" she looked at me with that eyebrow thing I wish I had on a pocket video (they'll have those someday) I could watch whenever needed. "What, are you giving a law school lecture or something soon?"

"I was just trying to impress you."

"It's too late for that," she responded with newlywed sass, and we hugged, then hugged even more firmly, then kissed sweetly and resumed our seats on the sofa, and proceeded through the dwindling residual presents. At the very bottom of the stack there was a plain white unlabeled box, which on uplifting and holding at a bit of a distance, seemed to have grease stains or something like them on the sides and on the inspected-before-opening bottom. That last gesture, the combination of moving and bringing closer for inspection, revealed beyond doubt that this mystery small carton was the source of the now growing stinky funk. Liberated from its pile of niceties, it was able to unleash the full assault of its olfactory insult. It was, indeed, as if a small animal had died in a box, but had barfed and/or had diarrhea before it expired, and both animal and excrement had been enclosed for weeks.

I had a sudden, unrealistic notion that maybe some under-enlightened wedding guest had sent us a small pet as a wedding present, maybe a hamster based on box size, and had forgotten to poke air holes in the box as well as appreciate how long we'd be gone. In an act of shear sexism, which I pointed out as such, Kim handed it to me (she had taken it from me to confirm my appall upon looking at the bottom of the box), and said, "You open it."

Do I dare, I may have only momentarily thought. But, I am a scientist, and I have seen many dead humans. I wanted to appear "brave". And so, rather than slowly sliding open the top, such that whatever lurked inside and could still attack me may be better controlled in this fashion, I flung it completely open in one full gesture of potentially dramatic revelation. There inside, after a few moments to allow recognition under dense layers of likely mold and God knows what other types of microorganism cultures, was a rotten pastry, of the exact shape, if shape was still an appreciable property of this experiment in decay, and apparently type that I had put under Barkley's pillow slightly over a year ago. The un-metabolized remaining granules of powdered sugar, carefully confined with wax or similar paper at the bottom and extending up half the sides, confirmed what I already had realized; of course it was the same pastry.

Kim stared at our last wedding present in utter disbelief and dark wonderment.

I just said, "Son of a Bitch."

After a few moments, I explained the whole Barkley pastry thing in extreme detail. Kim looked at me, somehow still affectionately, with an expression that implied, I think, "What have I gotten myself into?"

IV

- Houston; April, 1994

"Well, this is certainly a quiet bunch," Carl observed after a few moments of unintentional group silence.

It was a brisk and clear Saturday morning in April, about 10 o'clock or so, which had found all of us in the park except for Curtis, and Frank, who was visiting his daughter in Beaumont according to Carl's recount of a similarly stimulating park conversation the week before.

Either none of us were quite awake yet or we were enjoying the bright and warm sunshine after a run of unwelcome damp, crappy and unseasonably cool days, increasingly comfortable in each others' company without need for conversation. The benches had been warmed and dried by the morning sun, but the ground was still quite damp, which apparently didn't concern Rick or he was unaware of it, as he assumed his usual seat in front of us bench dwellers. He was in pleated gray dress slacks and a white oxford, which I assume he had worn to work the day before and hence, probably slept in.

"What should we talk about?" Rick managed to reflux out after a few more peaceful moments.

Still silence. A few moments later, as if moved by the delayed synaptic firing of a long quiescent neuron or two, Leo brightly chimed up, "I think we should discuss the great and important things in life."

While no one jumped for joy, per se, Carl responded, respectfully, "Well, that seems a little ambitious for an apparently lazy weekend morning, but hey... okay...what are the important things in life?"

No one responded. I was afraid Carl would start calling on people. Clearly, if we were inspired at all by this generously classified lucid comment from Leo, it was only moderately so, and apparently not too seriously, as after a few more intervening moments, Rick gutterly responded, with a suppressed belch between the two syllables, "Pussy."

"Pussy is one of the truly huge important things in life?" Carl scornfully questioned in retaliation.

"Absolutely," I said in a firm and definitive manner. "Plus, I believe Leo said the great and important things," I continued (Hah! I was paying attention). "To me, at least, pussy is great and hence, certainly important…especially if you drop the word…'huge.'"

"Good points," Rick managed to utter in recognition of the support, while reaching up under his right rib cage and wincing a bit.

"Music. What about music?" Leo offered up with uncertainty.

"Absolutely," I stated in firm support of Leo's excellent contribution. Clearly, 'absolutely' was emerging as my preferred word for the day.

Carl gave a nod in Leo's direction. I had the image of Carl making a list on a blackboard at the front of the classroom.

"One point for Leo, for music," Carl declared, reinforcing my perception, and after walking the two or three steps over to where Leo was, he patted Leo firmly on the back, knocking him forward from where he had been balancing on his right foot, such that he barely caught his balance before falling on Rick, who didn't even flinch.

"How about Literature?" Carl enthusiastically smiled out, as he walked back to his former position behind the bench, like a lecturer pulling out hoped for interactive responses from his oft dullard students, but now glowing in subdued academic zeal as he saw the conversation was turning more serious, as maybe hoped for initially, while the whole scene was spreading some of Rick's apparent gastric distress my way.

"Absolutely," I responded. "But you don't get a point, cuz you work in a bookstore."

"But, after all, isn't all music and literature really intended to help one get pussy?" Rick sarcastically offered up, for our team, to get the conversation back down to the level we seemed to need today.

"Absolutely," I offered up in support of this hence crucial observation.

"That was one of the points Robin Williams made as the teacher in that Dead Poets' Club or whatever the name of that movie I just saw," Frank added from a little behind Carl.

Whoa!! Frank, where did you come from? Apparently he wasn't in Beaumont, and apparently none of us had noticed his arrival; that being a good indication of our collective comatose state, unless Leo's having shifted over to his left leg could have been deemed an acknowledgment. Frank was an avid renter of videos, although I suspect this was one that Mrs. Frank had made him watch.

"That was a pretty good movie," he added, "but it was no Bloodsport."

"Absolutely."

"Ah the cumate," Carl calmly observed, to Frank's and my and potentially Rick's shock, and maybe finally conceding defeat to any loftier aspirations of the day's conversation. "There's nothing quite like it, although I think it was pretty crappy when that guy threw sand in Van Damme's eyes."

I smiled, an almost content smile, hopefully in a manner not allowing Carl to notice from the side. Then, as we sat and stood again in silence, the silence that sometimes comes from inside or a lack of something coming to us from the outside and not necessarily appreciation of kickboxing movies, I found myself wondering if I was the only one there who had a suspicion of why Curtis wasn't there with us.

...

That fascinating conversation on movies was the last time I would see any of my Park companions for quite some time, or at least at the Park. The comforting humor of that last conversation was quickly superseded by an all too more familiar tension: the acute work stress of being faced with an insurmountable combination of tasks that even under more favorable conditions would only just suck. These particular constitution-testing scenarios always seem to grow out of a likely inadequately buried, only viscerally unpleasant when vaguely thought of background, when a pressing event is still weeks to months away, to an exploding anxiety that seems like some sort of horrible flashback…maybe to an exam one had not properly studied for or some other sort of cardio-accelerating tragedy that emits from the dysphoria resulting from the situation in which no matter what one's good intentions were or how soon one thought they were going to begin the assault "this time," it always comes down to the gastrointestinal smooth muscle contracting physiology best described in a phrase such as, "holy shit, I'm never going to get all of this done in time." My colleagues working in even grayer areas of the brain have many theories for the cause of anxiety, from Freudian concepts maybe related to suppressed childhood events recognized somehow as sexual no matter how asexual they could be and unresolved conflicts, to hypothesized imbalances in certain neurotransmitters in certain regions of the brain, based in large part on improvement with drugs thought to "selectively" tweak levels of such neurotransmitters. Of course, what caused those imbalances to begin with is subject to all sorts of debates; from hypothesized genetic contributions back to those suppressed sexual shames and other unresolved conflicts. I have another theory, not necessarily exclusive of the above contributions offered up by much larger experts than my only passing casual interests in psych issues. Anxiety can at least sometimes be caused by the not officially recognized Eighth Cardinal Sin: Procrastination.

Although the chuckling voice of an old school master in an unnamed cavern of the subconscious may now be waiting to explode with a hearty dose of bile-coated "I told you so," erupting up to the level of terror perception in the conscious portions of my cerebral tangles, I can consistently keep him in check (at least in my non-dream states), in part because I recognize that "yes, I may have put some things off too long." Sue me, shoot me, spank me and call me Susie, or whatever the fuck is in order (back to the Freudian aspects perhaps?). I was, in theory, my theory, doing the best I could, all things considered, and balancing a lot of fecal matter. In this case, a heavy recent clinical load, a major surge in enrolling patients in the clinical trial with the resulting extra burden of specimen collection, handling, and baseline lab evaluations and particularly some expanding *in vitro* studies, synergized with the writing of a progress report, and - far more time consuming and stress generating - the need to quickly write up two talks and two posters for a very quickly upcoming Neuroscience meeting for which, along with Hassel and some UCSF colleagues, I had submitted abstracts last fall after coming to Houston. Not only would the talks and posters take some actual prep time, but they were also largely unrelated to the work that I was currently more focused on (which was, of course, more pressingly crucial to my current career). I didn't really want to spend that time; but I also in theory/reality needed to do a couple of experiments to clear up a potentially controversial area for one of the talks. Since the subject of this talk was a little closer to my current work and the results and convincing reporting of which could more significantly impact my future funding status than some of the other presentations, this one may be moved higher up on the procrastination-anxiety-penance "to do" list.

I had never done these specific types of experiments in my current lab in Houston, so there was no guarantee that I could set them up successfully, or more relevantly, quickly. More likely, if after all of the head scratching and wall pounding their true crucialness was confirmed, I would need to go to San Francisco to "crank them out" in hopefully just a couple of days in Hassel's lab. On top of all of this, I was pledged to spend a week with Kim at the beginning of May, in Seattle, away from the lab, away from notebooks, away from data-containing computers, and from technical help to partially bale my ass out for some of this rapidly approaching stuff. To convey the suboptimal-ness of this situation and cancel my time with Kim at this point was likely relationship suicide of a far more lethal magnitude than the potential career assault of not getting "everything" done.

Truth was, stress aside, I couldn't wait to be with Kim. I think that if I forced myself into one of those rare "take a step back and analyze" situations, I probably felt that I was increasingly falling into a phase of borderline unreality or at least suboptimal reality, maybe something we could call "disperspective". Holding Kim close, smelling her, and watching her do all of those Kim-things was the reality checking kick in the ass I needed more than time to get work shit done…that never seems to quite get all the way done anyway, as it seemingly feeds on itself. The more you do, the more there seems to be to do. Each series of experiments, with all the data analysis and interpretation, suggest several more, with all their data and analysis, and implications for future experiments, different approaches, and so on. And that was just the science side. There never seemed to be a shortage of sick patients either. HIV was increasingly seeing to that, in addition to all its older dark angel cousins. It was, of course, not in my interest to convey to my lovely, loyal, still up-spirited and cautiously relationship-optimistic wife that I was "really busy" and during the week we would spend together in Seattle, I would by necessity, at most, "sneak" a little work in, get a few papers read, a few drafts of posters/talks written during the at most rare morning I might wake up earlier than her…maybe on purpose…or maybe when staying up after she fell asleep before making love because we drank too much…although one can only hope for at best mild productivity from the residual self on those occasions.

Bottom line, though, I was exactly where I needed to be, where I was best, at least at getting a LOT done, regardless of how uncomfortable it may seem. It was one and a half weeks before I left for Seattle, almost five weeks before I would leave for the meeting; time to crank. Work: lab, clinic, etc. would all get done with extreme efficiency, while the late nights and early mornings were mine; free time I bought at willing sacrifice to be maximally utilized and during which I would insure I would be only minimally fucked with. Maybe no one did it better. I would read more and analyze more data and compile and integrate more thoughts than any six fucking amateur post-docs could do in a life time. I would travel to San Francisco. I would do the experiments. I would resist the invitations to get together with casual old acquaintances. I would stay in a hotel nearby, and spend a pathologic percent of my time in the lab with a few trusted old colleagues. I would spend the rest of my time: breakfast, grumps, standing in airport lines, etc., looking at protocols, analyzing data, coordinating all of my prior brain contents with newly learned pieces from my Hassel visits, maximizing my oxygen consumption, even making major if not even total and complete progress on the presentations while I was just in SF alone.

However, if during this period of heightened physical and brain intensity over slightly more than a month, my heart had to occasionally be distracted from Kim unintentionally, and if I were to be spuriously visited by uninvited little anxiety missiles even during our one week together, you can easily see why I couldn't give a rat's (or experimental mouse's) ass about hanging out with the "Montrose rejects" in the meantime. I think I saw Carl in passing, one time, maybe at Wild Oats buying groceries or maybe herbs and spices for various concoctions, for curses he put on sinners like me in his non-reading time, and I saw Curtis twice in my clinic.

...

Curtis's name stuck out prominently on a list of patients that otherwise contained only a few vaguely familiar likely follow ups on my worker list for my clinic one Monday morning in late April. I was a little surprised and pleased that he actually showed up for his appointment. If he was keeping to his usual lifestyle, 10:15 must have been a particular challenge, demanding some actual will and determination. But he was sitting patiently in the exam room, offering me a brief and unconfident smile, when I entered relatively on schedule for the day so far at 10:17.

He had become, if possible, thinner, and he had a few more Kaposi's lesions readily evident on his face. On exam, his chest seemed clear and his eyes were still free of any CMV findings, but he was certainly weak, especially in his legs, and likely not just from the weight loss. I made him walk the few steps allowed within the confines of the exam room, and his gait was slightly abnormal. We drew his blood for his CD4 counts, I reminded him how important it was to take his AZT and Bactrim, and I scribbled some comments on the pink note sheets of his growing chart.

He wasn't working. We made some passing comments about not seeing each other around much these days. He briefly admitted to being a little scared about "losing his mind"…and about dying…and I offered useless words of reassurance. What more could I do? What more could I offer? He had an incurable disease. He was already on the indicated drugs, and I was managing and following him according to CDC and other guidelines. I would get his labs back, see what his CD4 counts were, appropriately enter them in his chart, and we'd go from there. We'd "see how you're doing," and "how you're responding to your treatment." I offered some more equally hollow words of encouragement, some likely subconscious clichés I'd uttered thousands of times before. I patted him on the back, and left to go to the adjacent exam room, to see my next patient.

I felt like a putz; a pathetic, inept masquerader, with the weight of the universe on my shoulders. And I was the lucky one.

…

Fortunately, all my other work, the huge numbers of baby steps that I was one of maybe tens of thousands taking similar baby steps, could someday actually be able to help people like Curtis. Seeing incurable patients sometimes had a very humbling way of putting things in perspective. But, I mustn't let such currently unavoidable realities shake me from my defined course that I and all the others like me needed to keep speeding along. At most, you may get that sudden inquisition when fatiguely staring into the mirror, attempting to reassure yourself that you were at least doing all this hopefully at least partially for some of the right reasons.

And so, six weeks after it unofficially began, I was officially stress-free. I had survived the complex combination of routine clinical and ongoing laboratory activities, intense data generation, and personal demands, all the way up to stellar meeting presentations (based on the feedback I got, not necessarily just my own perceptions). And so, I sighed, briefly felt that I had done a good job, wondered in an acute twinge of hard to localize pain if I had given enough of myself to Kim during our fairly nice week together.....and waited for the next round to begin.

V

- Seattle; Early May, 1994

On the first weekend in May I flew out to Seattle to be with Kim, from where I left the following weekend to go straight to San Francisco, giving me most of the subsequent week to work in Hassel's lab. It was absolutely gorgeous in Houston when I flew out mid-morning to Seattle, always enjoying the anti-progressive nature of the time change when flying to the West Coast. In striking contrast, when we landed in Seattle, a city to which I was already predisposed towards resentment, it was substantially less gorgeous.

Further, as if in an effort of meteorological paradox to show a visitor how regions gain their reputations, but at the same time gently reminding us that stereotypes are indeed just stereotypes, four of our six days together in Seattle were as gray and dreary as liquid depression dripping over a Sylvia Plath poem read by candlelight with a glass of hemlock. The rain was so consistently steady that by shear lack of variation in velocity, intensity, or any other potential objective parameter of precipitation that we non-weather experts may characterize rain by, it seemed to be adding to the brain numbing I was already fighting from the fear that some sort of nature accomplice city policy had actually put the sun in some great storage facility, like the dome the pseudo-NFL team played in during even more gloomy parts of the year. Maybe it was just me. I wondered how others there, the "natives" or "locals," took it on an even more prolonged basis. Maybe they really didn't. Everyone was so pale, I thought I might have unknowingly been translocated into another one of those zombie movies, except these were normal intelligence and fairly interactive zombies (maybe it was a mutated viral form that only affected skin color and demeanor), and they didn't seem inclined to bite me so far as I had noticed.

No wonder they drank so much fucking coffee.

Then, on the fourth day, the sun came out. It came out brilliantly, radiantly; a sun of a grand luminosity albeit of apparently less warmth generation per unit sun than that turbo version I was used to in Texas. All about the greater Seattle area, I supposed that Arks were docking and letting off their confused pairs of animals, and Kim and I were finally able to venture out for prolonged periods to explore and run errands, enjoying each other's company in what seemed sometimes an unfamiliar or awkward way.

...

I had finally visited Kim in Seattle in late September or early October last year. This ostensible delay did not really seem, at least to me, to be inappropriate. After all, it was apparent at the time when we had only theoretically physically distanced ourselves from that common San Francisco departure point that my job/future position in Houston was guaranteed longer term, by career intents and even contracts, such that Houston was our "shared" household or should evolve to such over the mid to long run. Kim had naturally already been to Houston a few times by then. But, even at that first visit, her small apartment already had a much more "homey" ambience. I remember feeling a little irritated, perhaps, as it seemed she was getting too comfortable there. But, that was probably a little stupid, or silly, or overly sensitive; at least that's what my rational self said. After all, it was undoubtedly, if anything, a girl vs. boy thing; either the enhancing effect of the second X chromosome or the absence of some sort of negative decorating aspect of the Y.

Regardless, I think I had subconsciously or more regrettably, even consciously, decided that I wasn't going to bother to learn too much about Seattle. After all, this was a brief passing phase. Kim would certainly be bringing her combined efforts with Edith's firm and GeoDyne to the anticipated target level of accomplishment within an approximate six month period, as initially intended.

I would do the stereotypical tourist things. After all, I tried to do some of those in most places I visited, even for work-related meetings. There's a reason why some attractions and historical sites are famous. So, I would approach Seattle in the same manner as I had routinely done with some of the cities that medicine and science conferences were more commonly held in, like Washington, D.C., New Orleans, Chicago, and even San Diego and San Antonio; cities with big convention center facilities and ample hotels to host large meetings. Crowds aside, tackling popular tourist sites is often worth it, and one can sometimes find sites of interest a little more off the mainstream, things a bit more unique in character and/or appealing to more limited "tastes." New Orleans was always good for that in my recollection. So, I would do the Space Needle and whatever else Kim decided for us. I would get exposed to places and people that were part of Kim's daily life. Little cafes and shops closer to "home" and work, several of which I had heard about in passing or even in detail in our near daily phone conversations. This was a bit harder. I suppose I resented or was saddened that she had such a complex and full existence largely independent of me. That was surely some sort of double standard, as I hadn't exactly placed myself in a Houston monastery while we were living alone. But, I suspect for much of the human race that each of our mental histories has shown us that what we sometimes realize rationally and how we feel emotionally are not always identical.

Kim had rented a small apartment in Bellevue, across Lake Washington from Seattle proper. The size of the place was impacted in part by our need to split the finances into two "households". The location was further justified in part by the multiple different offices where Kim's work would variously take her. GeoDyne, including some subdivisions, had nice office facilities in Bellevue itself, basically right along Interstate 405. Some of the newer offices for well paid suits within the expanding medical/pharmaceutical/biotech aspects were in downtown Seattle, essentially right along the Waterfront on Alaskan Way (99). Some older offices accompanying early and still quite active chemical manufacturing facilities were south towards the airport, and some (which she didn't go to, fortunately) were further south towards Tacoma.

Kim's ('our' non-Houston) apartment was in a small, older building with only eight units, in a quiet neighborhood a few blocks east of 405 and a few miles north of 90. Downtown Bellevue was only about 3 miles away, and downtown Seattle was probably less than 10 miles away. It was thus pretty easy for her to not only get to their offices up near 8th street in town, but also to make the tolerable drive across the bridge (East channel bridge of I-90) over Mercer Island to the downtown Seattle offices and made it bearable to go south on 405 on those rarer circumstances she had to go down to the increasingly dated offices near the airport.

As I had at least vaguely dreaded and was soon to learn after our initial separation, Kim's amazing skills in the marketing tasks that had initially focused on Immugen and been largely funded by Edith's SF firm as part of their arrangements with GeoDyne, were being increasingly recognized by the progressively higher ups in Seattle. With Edith's (likely more than adequately compensated) blessing, her efforts were trickling over to several other somewhat related biotech endeavors that GeoDyne was rapidly expanding into in these early days of anticipated glory for biotechnology. These would manifest in our own lives in bonuses and steady raises I was proud of, and which we were somewhat relieved by given the relative expenses of Seattle and Houston dwellings.

As early as right before last Thanksgiving, Edith and her GeoDyne contractors had begun encouraging Kim to strongly consider a six month extension to the initial six month agreed upon collaborating period. Despite our outwardly expressed hesitancy to this, the combination of the increasingly lucrative nature of her deal, which would further grow with another six month commitment, and how hard I was working anyway, led us to consider this option to the point that it was agreed upon before Christmas. The added income could be used towards savings now, which could only help down the line during any transition phase of Kim's eventual moving and job searching. This latter part wasn't discussed as much as it probably should have been over the subsequent Christmas holiday.

Kim's apartment manager was eager to extend her lease another six months. She liked living across the lake from the city. On my prior visits in the fall and again this past February, the enthusiasm and attitude with which I would approach each outing, whether tourist oriented or more local, would greatly impact the way Kim and I seemed to get along that day, and especially that night.

...

On this trip in May, Kim looked different to me. I sensed it, and if I had a chance to stare at her for a while without her noticing, I could attempt to put some potentially descriptive terms on it. She was just as beautiful, maybe more beautiful...if that were possible, but in a different way. Maybe it was a Seattle kind of way. I don't know.

Her hair was shorter, a very professional looking short cut. The subtle auburn or reddish highlights I was used to and that she would get from the sun (that California sun which Texas got a harsh version of but Washington State apparently hadn't read about) were gone. Her hair was as dark as I could ever remember. The short cut allowed her beautiful face to show its glorious bone structure, and soft smooth skin, but the little freckles on her cheek of which she carried at least a few during all the warm months were not evident. She looked like an elegant but fragile goddess, somehow more mature though, and more serious. But the soft lips were still there, as were the sparkling eyes, revealed to me when she looked up and smiled, maybe when she caught me staring at her in that manner.

She was indeed strikingly sexy. And when we made love, there was something dangerously unfamiliar about it. Yet, at the same time there was enough of "us" remaining and it was still deeply comfortable and safe enough to allow me to take advantage of the erotic surreal strangeness. That rainy first part of the week encouraged a lot of indoor time, which facilitated such physical encounters. The dreariness supported sleeping in and some afternoon naps, from which love making was more easily initiated than the spontaneous or even intimate conversation requiring starting from the fully clothed state, episodes that this new strangeness complicated somehow.

The external wet gloom had been imposing enough that when the weather changed towards the end of the week, we seemed to approach the sun-filled days with a cautious skepticism. It was as if we subconsciously felt that if we received it with too much joy and eagerness, falling with full force into the receipt of its temptation, then the cloud Gods who apparently headquartered in Seattle would quickly punish us, soaking us to near drowning before we could even make it to appropriate stable shelter. So our outings were less ambitious and closer to "home" than on my past visits, when we had gone to such destinations as downtown Seattle and the waterfront.

We went over to Bellevue Square one afternoon, a shopping area that had apparently undergone some major expansion in the 1980's, and browsed through some unremarkable national chain shops without much enthusiasm. But we enjoyed the outdoor portions of our strolls, as if undergoing a slow thaw or dry out period that could infuse us with a little more zip for an upcoming dinner.

The next day, again cautiously sunny, we were more peppy and interactive as a couple. We spent time going through Beaux Arts Village, enjoying its tree lined narrow streets and the eclectic mix of architecture of its homes. We stopped for a late lunch at a quaint little café where we shared a bottle of white wine and some healthy sandwiches. I think I even tried to show my evolution by having some sort of fish sandwich. However, I tainted the atmosphere by bringing up, within a background of lighter conversation, whether Kim had started looking for possible jobs in Houston or possible interactions with Edith while based in Houston. In a tone that seemed more possessed of impatience or emotional fatigue rather than frank irritability and certainly not outright anger, Kim responded that she was working her ass off and it was all she could do to possibly train some of her junior associates to adequately take over what she was doing.

I wisely picked up my cue and attempted to change the subject, back to items of the less serious nature that had framed our day with more pleasant interactions up to that point. But, it was out there. And now it lurked underneath; the difficulties of satisfactorily resolving our current living situation, like the subliminal threat that the nice weather allowing even this level of marital enjoyment could be viciously withdrawn at any moment.

And yet, despite the topic that I had brought up perhaps with suboptimal timing and in less than an ideal environment, there seemed to be something deeper still. Something like an ancient city, yet to be uncovered and explored, lying beneath an already discovered prior civilization that itself had been previously found under a modern urban area. Who knows what killed off those prior people, whose lives we would gain very biased fragmentary glimpses of, perhaps a plague of some sort, a disease universally fatal to all involved. Something that had to be forgotten and moved on from, as the descendants moved on, building on past experiences. Or maybe like another Canto or deeper level of Hell, unimaginably worse than what Dante and Virgil had already witnessed as they spiraled on downwards. Whatever this was, or even if it existed at all, at least the thought of it alone subjectively prevented me from eating the rest of my fish sandwich and a significant portion of the sides, and instead encouraged another wine by the glass after the shared bottle was finished.

I particularly don't think I liked the use of the term "possibly." I don't know if it had intended implications. But from an objective analytical approach, there were few other options for interpreting it other than: if it was only possible that Kim's associates could take over what she was doing, work of extreme importance to Immugen (and hence GeoDyne), Edith's firm, and Kim personally, then that meant it was also possible that such associates (individuals largely unknown to me except for passing inclusions of names in phone conversations) may NOT be able to acquire the abilities to the perceived level of necessity...and that's where the sickening implications and dark crossroads loomed.

We recovered from scratching the surface of that next layer down (the hidden depths of the mystery disease-destroyed lovers, children, and prospects for growing families, on which subsequent lives were built upon, without knowing if they'd been aware of their prior nature or had even an opportunity to mourn what had been lost) in time to have a pretty good evening. One thing that was certain: when the darker uncertainties could be adequately, if only temporarily, buried or forgotten, we were two people who still really enjoyed being together; talking, laughing, debating other big life issues (not directly related to us – things like religion, philosophy, best flavor of ice-cream, etc.). We did make love that last night, and I held Kim close to me afterwards, and she took my hand in hers, and we fell asleep soundly.

As Kim drove and dropped me off at the airport, a somewhat somber silence had again descended upon us as a couple despite the third consecutive day of pretty un-obscured sunshine. I had, of course, explained to her upon arrival and during the first evening the approaching intimidating mound of unavoidable work I had facing me the next four or so weeks. She was typically sympathetic, and approached the couple of times I tried to sneak in a couple hours of work while in Seattle with what seemed like respectful and understanding silence. In actuality, I hadn't really attempted to get much done while I was visiting in Seattle. My focus was appropriately on Kim, and this delay in getting started on at least some of the things may have begun causing some minor dread, which could have contributed to some unstated anxiety I may have been otherwise displaying towards the end of the week as well as the mutual quiet now. I felt I had done a pretty good job of giving my undivided attention to Kim, but it was as if my having to go straight to San Francisco under such frantic and stressed conditions (instead of what would have been a stronger reflection of vague normalcy by going home to Houston) was a symptom of that deeper underlying disease that had killed the lowest layer of ancient city and what was causing us our still largely unspoken and deepest troubles.

I certainly felt weird when I got to San Francisco; like somehow, despite the relatively good time we had just had together, something was left hanging, incomplete. That feeling, regardless of the source or conditions, bothered me. I wanted it fixed right away. So, originating under these circumstances, in the context of my marriage, I particularly felt that it should be addressed as soon as possible. But, I wasn't left with much time to be tortured by it. An old colleague of mine picked me up, and we went straight to the lab, without even stopping for me to check into my hotel (which was as close by to the lab as possible anyway). The other realities quickly took over, once relevant science discussions re-surfaced the stress and pressing nature of the work that had to be done, and mandated the exclusive focus that would be required to be sufficiently productive to get it done in time.

That afternoon and the next three days were pretty insane, but the mental intensity and resultant pace ultimately paid off in the form of efficiency and success that even all of us directly involved couldn't have optimistically expected. So, I headed back to Houston with one major chunk of my "To Do" list checked off. I had only spoken to Kim once during those four days, after just letting her know that I had made it safely. In a sudden, regrettably allowed resurgence of the unsettling thoughts that I'd had right before I left Seattle, my thoughts turned to Kim and the nature of things, as I settled into my seat on the plane after they served me my first drink.

VI

- Recollections: San Francisco; 1991 onward

K im was probably the perfect wife from the get-go. After our marriage, I think I was still in the twilight-zone for a while, or maybe longer, or maybe I was just the way I was supposed to be…I don't know. I didn't read as much about marriage as I did clinical Neurology or articles in research journals. I don't think there really is an appropriate guide, other than the reflection of your actions and experiences in your spouse. Kim seemed to be able to adjust to the "H" word very smoothly, introducing me with pride as her husband to anyone we encountered deeming such, from a casual co-worker I hadn't met before to her dry cleaner the first time I had apparently ever stopped in with her to pick up some finished items, which included some of my own clothes (for not the first time, since we'd been living and apparently having clothes dry cleaned together for a while). I don't remember necessarily acquiring a new wardrobe, although Kim had been presenting me with new clothes for quite a while then, not just on official present occasions. But apparently, I had along the way obtained a new approach to cleaning at least some of them. I really don't ever remember dry cleaning anything myself in all those years I had lived alone since I'd left home. Women are fascinating creatures. The specialized manner in which many of their outfits need to be laundered is really just the beginning….

I also seemed to be adjusting acceptably well myself to the use of the "W" word, with the typical gradually moderated anxiety of any major life change. When I referred to Kim as my wife, whether when introducing her to a colleague or referring to her in a conversation at work when she wasn't around, I noted for quite some time that it had an interesting effect of either causing that sort of initial twinge of an incipient erection, a faint dyspepsia of nervous type nausea, or some sort of synergizing combination of both. I found it sexy, in that kind of obsessive way that if I didn't deal with it, it could linger, in a most distracting fashion, and if she wasn't around I commonly found myself calling Kim shortly thereafter.

But at night, when the work for both Kim and I was put aside, it was beyond description. We couldn't seem to get enough; enough of anything together, silly, little things, the kinds of things we could afford...the only kinds of things we seemed to need. Casual and short walks around the neighborhood, discussing our mutual concept of kids again, or the kind of dog we may want in the interval, when we were in a position to have more room, whether we should suggest to one of our neighbors that she really should get a nose job..., what the highest form of art was (she leaned towards Modern Paintings, some of which she would show me photos of when we returned home, opening up books I still didn't realize "we" owned, whereas I consistently defended *Revolver* and *Sgt. Pepper's*, and if I really wanted the loving rib jab, Black Velvet Elvis Paintings). Longer walks, if time allowed, may include Little Italy, where depending on the time of the month, we'd either get a slice or two of pizza at a favorite walk-up place, or actually sit down and eat a meal with a carafe of house Chianti and frequently generate enough leftovers (on Kim's part) to give me lunch the next day. Or, just sitting on the floor, up against the sofa, we'd watch movies that we rented from a newly opened video store a couple of blocks away and that we usually walked to together (as running candidate available films past each other for curiosity and hopeful approval on the other's part was half the fun) and typically paralleling a "theme" for the month, such as old horror flicks, crime thrillers, or old classics, particularly ones that one of us had seen and which we wanted the other to be exposed to...how else would I have ever seen *Metropolis* or would Kim have seen *Cool Hand Luke* for example.

...

I think what seemed strangest to me was the idea of waking up on weekends and planning a day just for leisure. I'm not sure why this was fundamentally any different than all the months, essentially a year, that we'd been living together. I had certainly worked in the lab or occasionally taken clinical call on weekends during the time we'd been living together. Kim had no problem using our time apart, either by doing some work of her own, shopping or otherwise visiting with a girlfriend, or even just hanging out at home and doing something to enhance our apartment. But, as new husband and wife, I must have felt that it was inappropriate somehow for me to go into the lab on a Saturday or Sunday, regardless of how much work I sensed I needed to get done or had piling up, things that I should be doing if I was to be maximally productive in Hassel's lab. I could make up for this though, initially, by doing some things at home briefly, such as reading or some data analysis, which Kim didn't seem to resent, especially if we were able to carefully budget this kind of time and still have "couple time". She would even sometimes try to get things done on her own projects for her firm at the same time.

In addition to the luxury of hanging out alone on weekends, the taking in of targeted local San Francisco sites to visit and enjoy, and the occasional not particularly exotic and not too distant weekend destinations, we would of course occasionally have visitors. Given the regional geography, the means, and the desire to see their only daughter as well as enjoy some of the city's offerings, Kim's parents were certainly more common accompaniments to our Newlywed life than my folks. Of course, when Bob and Patti came they would stay at a hotel, picked more typically on how highly it was currently regarded or for past satisfactions, regardless of how near or far to us within the city it actually was. We would get together, typically for dinner, and they would occasionally come by our apartment particularly if the hotel was coincidentally convenient for such, maybe before or after a dinner outing. Kim and I visited my parents more often in TX than my folks made it out to the Bay Area. On the one time they did come out those first two years of Kim and I being together, they stayed at a more practical hotel, one as close to us as possible based on price considerations and a more practical threshold for acceptable quality.

On most (maybe even all, at least it seemed like all) of those visits by Kim's parents, Kim and Patti would have their customary high tea at the St. Francis, and Bob and I would calculate some sort of believable task to not have to join them for what we considered equivalent to emasculation even though we never outwardly stated it as such (not to each other that I recall, and certainly not to our respective high tea spouses). Depending on the time of year and hence divinely delivered coincidence, these "alternate plans" could be as legitimate as a Giants game (twice that I recall just in the first summer after we were married and which took more time than High Tea, allowing the girls some other female bonding on either side of the tea ritual) or something more spatially and temporally matched to the known Tea Time and anticipated duration of the tea festivities. This could be as mundane as "we really wanted to try this new Micro Brewery," at which the other male would chime in some woefully likely made up support such as, "oh yeah, I read something good about that one" to "craving a crab sandwich…down at that…you know…that little hole in the wall place down by the Wharf." I don't think we were getting away with as much as we hoped that our little clever ploys were priding us with. Once, when neither of us could come up with an excuse, even meeting our low standards of offering up as avoidance behavior (maybe we should have been calling each other ahead of time), we had no choice but to enter the hotel with the ladies. I could feel the collar tightening on Bob's shirt; he could sense my impending shortness of breath. At the last minute, I think he showed the bravery our failing sex required right before the crisis, a lifeboat showing up in the form of a lobby bar, "You know, I think right now…I'm just more in the mood for a laid back beer" (said with requisite male head nodding towards me and then to the bar, as if indicating to the group that said bar really existed); so, on cue, my line became something like "Yeah…you know Bob…if it's O.K. with the ladies, I'm just not really in a High Tea mood for some reason…right now…." In seemingly mutual comments and gestures from our outing mates, we were spared. As Bob and I vehemently drank to our cleverness, I suspect The Tea Drinkers were not particularly surprised, and certainly didn't seem upset afterwards.

Women are fascinating creatures. Knowing when their spouses are full of shit isn't even Chapter 2.

Barkley also made occasional, usually unexpected visits. Showing up at our place typically coincided with some sort of local event of Barkleyesque nature, and in contrast to his parents, our sofa was more than acceptable to him, as was even an adjacent segment of floor for either himself or an accompanying buddy, the decision for who got the sofa and who got the floor not always following predictable logic. We did, however, on some such occasions find ourselves spending time with Kim's brother, typically outside the event that had prompted the trip but within the confines of the time he had allowed himself to be in the city. One such outing I remember included a trip to the original building housing the

Vedanta Society of San Francisco, established by one of those Swami guys at the beginning of the century, as the first (as I learned at the time) Hindu temple on the West Coast. I gathered this was some sort of important pilgrimage for Barkley, one that he had made several times before, and as it was incorporated with an outing that included some other sightseeing, drinks and dinner, Kim and I were eager to go along. The building, some sort of weird ass combination of architectural styles, evident even to those of us with no formal or even casual architectural knowledge, was on the corner of Webster and Filbert in Japantown, which seemed appropriate to me, as one of those American science heads who probably couldn't tell you any difference between Hinduism and Buddhism or any of those other isms of Oriental origin.

I had had numerous Indian friends and even more Indian colleagues over the course of my medical education and training up to that point. Most were probably Hindu. In the various occasional religious and/or philosophy discussions (with or without ethanol lubrication), I had with such friends over the years, and without putting more effort into it by much reading, I always found the complexities of Hindu mythology-infused religion rather...complex. On this particular outing, Barkley confirmed my past impressions, with a brief overview of various key Gods amongst the many Devas, but also enlightened me, in the knowledge, not necessarily in a spiritual sense, that at least in modern Hinduism, these were not separate "real" Gods but merely symbols or incarnations and objects facilitating worship...or something like that. Our timing of visiting the building overlapped that of public access, so my casual instructions on Vedantic philosophy were accompanied by brief entry into the Center, like some kind of divinely delivered Barkley visual aid.

I picked up enough of the key Brahman/Atman aspects on this particular occasion to essentially drive both Kim and even the seemingly infinitely tolerant Barkley crazy by singing during various parts of the rest of the evening, "I am the Atman, I am the Atman, Goo goo g' joob, Goo goo g' joob" to the obvious tune of the Beatles "I Am the Walrus." Pushing it to the point of the affectionate rib jab (I seemed to get more of these than might be expected, although I didn't know what the national average was) when we went to a coffee shop afterwards (for pre-Bar and pre-Dinner energy I guess), I confused the waitress when I ordered and asked if I could have a "moksha". When she asked me if I meant"mocha," I responded, appropriately (and again illustrating my grasping of at least the definition of certain terms...), "Well, if you don't sell liberation here, then I guess that will do," and she walked off just as confused.

VII

- *Houston; May, 1994*

I saw Curtis one more time in my Clinic before I left for my meeting that I had recently worked frantically in SF to generate data for. It was just a day or two before I was to leave, and my presentations were largely done. I wasn't that anxious about the actual preparation at this stage, mostly just about the talks I had to give.

In contrast, I wasn't able to pinpoint any specific medical cause of Curtis's apparent increased restlessness evident that morning. He wasn't febrile. But, I'd seen enough AIDS patients by then and thought about the disease and its victims enough to at least attempt trying to realize how disturbing it must be to face a terminal illness at a relatively young age. After all the usual medical aspects of monitoring his condition were addressed, we continued to talk. I tried further to identify what was most bothering him, and he stressed his almost paranoid level of fear that he had largely lost or was going to lose his mind. I assured him that he clearly hadn't completely lost his mind (although I couldn't be certain of the absence of impairment that could qualify as partial "loss", but I kept this to myself). He did seem confused, as reflected in various aspects of our conversation. I wasn't sure if any of this could be secondary to his anxiety.

I suppose being aware of partial and maybe increasing mental deficiencies could be worse (e.g., to one's sense of self or intactness) than a complete loss of all reality and orientation, for which no residual frame of reference could be there to indicate abnormality to one's "mind" to begin with. It might be something like the early onset of vs. the late end stage of Alzheimer's Disease, for example. I'd thought about this before, on psychological grounds, and now I found myself non-deliberately pondering it as Curtis continued, shaking me back into paying attention with a statement more concrete than some of those over the previous few moments.

"You could give me some of your drug. The drug you made…you know… for AIDS brains that are fucked up…you know…like mine. You could make me better." Curtis proclaimed.

"That drug isn't FDA approved yet.…I mean, we don't even know if it really works."

"But you think that it's going to work…that it helps, right…or you wouldn't even be doing all this work. I mean…you like work all the fucking time on this thing. You must believe in it. I trust you. If you think it would help me. You could just give it to me…as like my Doctor."

"It doesn't work that way…not for drugs that we haven't shown proven benefit for in appropriate ways. You have to do clinical trials, like the one we're doing. You'd have to be enrolled in a trial. Then some patients get the drug, and some get a placebo, or a sugar pill, it's all randomized, blinded… you know, so none of us know who's on the real drug or not, so that we're not biased. Then after awhile we can compare the outcome for the people who were on the drug vs. … the control patients…those who got the placebo. You know all this. We've talked about this before in the park…what I'm doing here, work-wise…here."

"Yeah I remember…sort of."

"Would you like to consider enrolling in the trial, it's not too late?"

"But, then, I may not get the real drug, the drug that helps. I could get the fucking fake drug.…I mean like a fucking 50% chance. Right?"

I was pleased that he was still able to grasp the 50% aspect of the "randomization" thing, from now or previous conversations.

"That's correct. That's how these drug trials work," I responded.

"That's bullshit, man. I'm fucking dying…I think. And…I mean, I can hardly remember stuff and I can barely fucking walk. You know the drug can help me. What the fuck kind of doctor are you?"

"I don't know that the drug works. I hope it does. I hope that's what we'll find. But only by comparing a treated group to a proper control group in rigid clinical scientific fashion can we know for sure. It may not work. Only in this manner can we make true scientific progress, to make sure we're treating future patients in the correct way…vs. just giving them drugs that may not help and could just cause unnecessary toxicity," I continued like a droid.

"I'm willing to take that chance. It can't really hurt….I mean, shit, how much worse could I get…than this…" he indicated himself by spreading his arms over his body, from his head, then over his chest and abdomen, like some sort of dark yoga, before resting them at his side, palms up, on the exam table and letting his head fall downward, his chin resting on his chest, in apparent resignation. I could see several large, almost serpiginous Kaposi's lesions on his scalp, through his thinning hair.

"I mean…you're my friend," he offered up in one last feeble effort, without lifting his head. "Give me something…anything…to help. I don't think the fucking AZT is doing shit for whatever's going on in my head, in my…brain. Give me some of your drug. I bet it will help," he finished with a weak upward glance.

I put my hand on the door to leave. I had to get out of there. This was getting past uncomfortable.

"I can't. It doesn't work that way. Not with this or any other drugs not yet… studied and validated. I'm a scientist."

"You're my doctor. You're a *physician*," he pronounced with mock reverence.

"I'm a physician scientist." I offered in rigid, persistent defense of my medically ethical stance on this matter. (This is all I've ever wanted to be, this is what I've worked my entire fucking life for, I thought, in almost subconscious defense, coming from an inner reminding voice somewhere).

Lifting his head and looking up more completely and over towards me at the door and with a bit of that old Curtis wry smile, almost suggesting the early signs of forgiveness, maybe even understanding, but most likely, that we weren't done with this subject, he uttered: "You're an asshole."

"I'm an asshole *scientist*," I cautiously smiled back, hoping we had reached some sort of temporary truce; but then continued, to reclaim the medical higher ground, as I opened the door and began walking out. "Cheryl will make your next appointment for you when you're leaving." Then after a brief pause and defiantly looking back into the room: "Let her know if you want to enroll in a clinical trial."

VIII

- *Houston; May, 1994*

There were times, fleeting moments, when seeing a trial enrolled patient for follow-up in the clinic, or maybe as my mind optimistically drifted when I was on the elevator or walking down the hall to go see a consult patient in the hospital, or maybe mostly when home alone late at night, when I might let myself think that the drug we were testing was "working." I allowed myself to envision that we would show a statistically significant benefit in at least some of the clinical or laboratory parameters that we were following, following "blindly" to whether any given patient was on drug or not. It could perhaps be in only a subset of patients, as we had objectively classified them at enrollment as to severity of initial symptoms and signs using slight modifications of scoring systems we had adopted from San Francisco. Yes, we would ultimately make some striking observations. We would write up these important findings for eagerly accepted publications in the best journals. We would have something on which to build our own efforts and expand our own funding. We would proudly throw our contribution out there to be interpreted and utilized by others in the context of the work being done by dozens of other laboratories. We would learn from each other, work more and more closely together, and push on…steadily.

Despite the greater complexity and uncertainty of the clinical aspects, we would at least have definitive results for the *in vitro* experiments; the laboratory tests looking at the potential mechanisms of neuronal cell injury, the possible protective effect of our compound on cell injury and death from the various potentially involved mediators. In fact, we would have these results on an ongoing basis, in publishable increments, years before we might have definitive outcome on various aspects of the clinical trial. Hopefully we would find encouraging re-sults; clear cut answers to very compartmentalized aspects of what we thought may be going on in the zillion-fold more complex and likely heterogeneous set-ting of intact humans. We might find brain cell injury induced by levels of various immunologic and other cell derived mediators that realistically matched levels that we were measuring in the CSF of trial enrolled patients; or we might not. We might find that cell injury, induced in at least some fashions, is prevented or ameliorated by levels of the experimental drug that we also detected in the CSF of trial enrolled patients (encoded by sample numbers not matchable to specific patients by testing personnel); or we might not. Even negative results can some-times be informative, especially if the hypothesis being tested is an important one that needs to be proven or disproven in convincing fashion.

Sometimes the most interesting findings and those that turn out to be most important to build on are the ones that get results the complete opposite of what one was expecting. That's why it's always important to design one's ex-periments well, to be able to accept the results objectively regardless of what one obtains, and try not to bias oneself when accumulating and interpreting data. Maybe one day you get an exciting result in a tissue culture experi-ment, and then during a repeat to further support and confirm the results, the data just don't look quite the same. Maybe you're tempted to just "throw that experiment out." After all, maybe the cell cultures were a little older, or passed (split and grown in culture) too many times, or the reagent solu-tions were a little older as you'd been too lazy to make fresh ones, etc. There's a lot of room for rationalization and justification in the hopeful scientific mind. It's not even that uncommon for different labs to get different results when theoretically testing the same thing. There are just so many variables. It's crucial to precisely describe exactly how you do things and to understand subtle differences in your approach vs. someone else's approach. Again, that's why you have to design and execute your experiments well, being prepared for whatever results are obtained. It's all progress. It's just more exciting, and certainly more publishable, when one gets "positive" results, when you get the effect you hoped for, the ones that fit in with the anticipated drama that you could easily set up so well in your potential paper introduction, and that you've thought about to the point that you knew where (experiment-wise) you would go next in that hoped for and expected scenario.

But then…there's the too often experienced laboratory real world; a realm of discovery (or anti-discovery) common to all true and objective investigators, and yet not shared publically anywhere near enough to have the potential scientific utility that it could. In the science world, negative just isn't quite sexy. In my experience in various lab conversations, and hence likely reflecting more widespread sentiment than just my past and present domains, we often kidded around that there should be a reasonably well respected "*Journal of Negative Results*". A place for graduate students, fellows, all the way up to tenured full professors to report the less glamorous results of still well designed and conducted experiments that didn't find the hoped for results. As stated, sometimes negative findings addressing crucial hypotheses are still quite publishable, but there's a lot of work that gets done that never makes it to the scientific literature. Who knows, it could probably save a lot of time. After all, it's likely that given the way we make hypotheses (i.e., reading the literature, discussing ideas, etc.) that many of the things you've thought about have already been thought about by others. You could spend months or years doing experiments that just don't work out, and someone else may have done the same thing months to years ago…and they could have saved us a great deal of time. If we believed their studies, we could have moved on to something else; a slightly different twist on the same hypothesis or use of a very different experimental approach, for example. There's never a shortage of things to investigate, and each of these endeavors just takes so much time and effort. Cumulatively, a "*Journal of Negative Results*" along with maybe even a few other like publications, such as an "*Annals of Laboratory Disappointments*" or "*Proceedings of Post-Doctoral Failures*", could save the scientific community a lot of time and resources.

We weren't expecting a lot of such "negative" findings from the many permutations of the *in vitro* experiments. Showing dose-dependent toxicity to cultured neurons for various mediators that we thought were likely involved in ADC would be a very nice and "neat" or "clean" finding. Detecting and measuring some of those mediators in the CSF of patients with ADC would be a bonus. Correlating the levels in patients of any of those mediators with disease severity or more likely with toxicity *in vitro* would be an extreme pleasure, given the complexities involved in translating the actual biology of the disease to *in vitro* experiments. But, regardless, at least we would have all those well catalogued patient samples, the blood and CSF specimens banked from patients at various stages of their disease.

The accumulation of this patient sample repository would be a valuable research resource, not only for us, but for potential collaborators; investigators at other labs who might have other theories and want to test some of these samples. If we could demonstrate neuronal toxicity *in vitro* with aliquots of these actual patient samples and correlate that with various levels of mediators in such samples, that would also be of parallel major interest, but may be asking too much (e.g., given the possible presence of potentially heterogeneous levels of modulating mediators or substances we haven't even considered yet).

Based on the progress we were already making, we would have some results on our test drug compound effects on the bioassays of neuron toxicity by the end of the academic year. The data would go to the biostatistician for analysis. I had of course taken some biostatistics courses and could do some statistical analyses, and there were lots of software programs available to do most of the standard and even really complex analyses. But, I always preferred to have data separately analyzed (or also analyzed) by a biostatistician, in part to avoid any potential bias on my part in the analysis, but also to make sure it was being done right. After all, this was not my area of expertise. There are biostatistician geeks who understand the proper approach or approaches to data analysis depending upon the design of the experiments, the nature of the data, etc. For example, in just comparing multiple doses of a drug to a control (e.g., cultured cells getting no drug) or in looking at the effects of different mediators compared to a control (e.g., cultured cells getting a small amount of buffer or solvent that the mediators were also dissolved in, but with no active mediators) there could be biases toward showing protective or injurious effects, respectively, if one inappropriately employed techniques like the student's t-test that most people knew how to do. By having a biostatistician involved, the proper data testing techniques would be employed and with their input, I could write these up so those parts of the study would not be an obvious potential area of criticism by outside expert reviewers, which could often include statistician input.

In contrast, it would be years before we would have any definitive results for the patient outcomes for the clinical trial regarding any possible helpful effect for retarding the progression of ADC. Oh sure, we had provisions for periodically examining ongoing data, at the end of year one, and at the end of year two, etc., in a way that I and other key investigators were still protected from knowing which if any still enrolled patients were on drug or placebo. There are times in drug trials where the benefits of the drug vs. placebo are so striking and so easily demonstrated by clinical scientific methods even relatively early on in a longer designed trial that basically the study is done, the support unequivocal, and to not give actual patients the real drug (i.e., vs. nothing at all for the specific conditions the drug now has PROVEN benefit for) is basically medically unsound. We certainly weren't expecting anything quite so earth shattering as this. Given the heterogeneity of patients' disease states at enrollment, the uncertain time course of progression, and the possible mild benefit of a drug that could also be affected on a case by case basis by so many other confounding secondary conditions so common in AIDS patients, we figured we'd be lucky if we could demonstrate any statistically significant beneficial effect in any of the laboratory and especially clinical parameters we were so carefully monitoring. But, of course, that didn't stop me from occasional day dreams for earth shattering effects and further; we were in for the long haul. Despite all of our careful calculations on the front end in terms of how many patients we'd need to detect something, maybe even just some statistically significant benefit in even a minority of well-defined patients, the trial might turn out to not even be big enough, not have enough patients. We might see some hints of results ("trends" on statistical analysis) that didn't quite meet statistical significance. Such results or other observations may support the need for another, even bigger trial, which of course would require even more support, larger grant funding. Or by then, there could have emerged from the pharmaceutical industry some more active (more potent) compounds and/or data from the scientific community to suggest combinations of agents for similar patients.

But, proving statistically that there were no benefits from the drug…in any type of patient with ADC or for any clinically meaningful variable that would be worthwhile trying to treat…well, that would be disappointing. Oh, of course, it would be publishable. It would even be an important "negative" finding. After all, attempting this type of compound for the treatment of this aspect of AIDS was a well thought out "rational" therapy. Knowing that this particular drug didn't offer significant benefit in the manner utilized is still medical "progress."

Then we would know we shouldn't give this drug to these types of patients for the intent of ameliorating their mental and motor disabilities somehow resulting from HIV infection. Unfortunately, especially after all that work, it's just not as exciting, news-worthy, and career enhancing. Worse, still, is that we wouldn't have learned how to really help anyone. After as many as three to five years (depending on how the data analysis went), we wouldn't have come up with any new specific way to treat this debilitating component of a disease with so many debilitating and devastating aspects. At the end of all this we couldn't say, "Hey, take this drug. It will make you feel stronger. It will help you think better." Too bad, also, as there could be emerging anti-retrovirals such as new reverse transcriptase inhibitors and even other virus protein targeted drugs that could potentially prolong life. As patients may live longer with HIV infection, who knows how their modified, more prolonged disease course could or could not be complicated by potentially less prominent or still severe CNS complications. A drug to prevent neuronal injury during a longer course of (albeit potentially milder) viral infection allowed by more effective anti-viral therapy could in strong theory be highly useful. It would be back to the drawing board, at least for me. But, nothing is absolute and no clinical science work exists in a social vacuum over a given period of time. Other skilled investigators were working on this very topic, including in many clinical trials. We may get new ideas over the next many months or few years. We could already be working on many other things by the time our disappointing clinical data rolled in.

...

But still...that irregularly recurrent optimism. The muse of every physician scientist with even a hint of ego. I'd see those patients that I knew were on my trial...I wouldn't, of course, know whether they were on the drug or placebo, but some seemed to be getting better, or at least not getting worse, or much worse, and I'd of course suspect/wish/expect/hope that they were indeed on the drug.

I guess we'd see.

I saw a woman for the 4th time on May 23rd. I had first seen her at the end of November, in the hospital. She was almost medically indescribable. Psychosis could have been her presenting complaint, especially for an investigator interested in ADC. But she was so sick I spent most of my morning working her up, helping the young Internal Medicine resident who had admitted her, just trying to get her to resemble a living human. She was a young African American female, 28 years old at the time, but looking as if she'd already spent 28 too many years on the planet. From the history we could gather from her grandmother who had brought her in, no medically sound poster child herself, she had likely contracted HIV from her IV drug abusing boyfriend, although we couldn't rule out IV drug use on her own (which her grandmother vehemently denied but at least suggested by barely detectable scars). I guess after a while it becomes largely semantic.

She was apparently living with her boyfriend, with whom she had had at least two children already, living there along with two other children she couldn't possibly care for adequately, and it didn't sound like he was around very much. God only knows how they were surviving; maybe the good will of neighbors and/ or that basic aspect of primal survival that appears in all humans, in all places, in all situations; unfortunately, too often in childhood. Her sister had stopped by, apparently for the first time in several weeks despite her own budding concern (which I learned of later) and witnessed the now intolerable circumstances and the striking decline of her sister's health. She had taken the patient to the E.R., leaving her there with their grandmother in order to return to the miscellaneous group of children currently being attended by the patient's (and the sister's) Mother, whose position in this whole family/social situation we weren't sure of at this stage. A much earlier hospital visit would have been beyond justified. It's amazing the different thresholds that American citizens (or their families) of different past and current blessings have for imposing on the health care system. The patient's sister apparently worked multiple jobs, covering essentially two full time shifts, and may have largely been physically unable to do anything much earlier.

After we worked her up as best we could in the E.R., we admitted her to the Hospital for further evaluation and basically to get her stable. I saw her later that evening and each day for many days after until she was well enough to go home. In addition to ADC with essentially complete disconnection to reality and almost complete inability to walk, she had *Pneumocystis carinii* pneumonia and CMV retinitis…for likely starters. I'm sure I must have mentioned the trial at some point, maybe to her sister. After all, we took patients at all stages and it could help with some of the financial aspects of her follow-up visits. It was the latter that prompted a phone call three days later from her boyfriend, who when I returned the call, actually identified himself as her husband. Despite my desire to have advanced patients with psychological symptoms on the trial, I was on shaky ground as to informed consent and permission, with just him on board. To my surprise, two days later, the day before we discharged her, he showed up with a power of attorney (apparently he had lawyer contacts from past misendeavors in society), and after more carefully discussing things with her sister as well, we enrolled her under conditions which we felt were justified and legally correct. Despite his apparent interest, she did not go back to the apartment she had shared with her boyfriend/husband, who had more pressing tasks to attend to on a withdrawal-preventing steady basis. Instead, thankfully, she went home with her sister.

She appeared to have more strength when her sister brought her in for a follow-up appointment right before Christmas, and she could answer some questions about her children, with accuracy confirmed by her sister. In February, she was substantially stronger on neuro exam, particularly in her legs, and she could walk a bit without assistance. I even had a resident working with me confirm my exam regardless of his lower status and lesser experience. When I saw her several weeks ago in early April, she knew where she was, what she was doing there, and what was wrong with her. She was mostly concerned about her children. Of course, I'd like to think that some or all of the improvement was due to her being on the actual drug (vs. placebo) in our clinical trial. But who knows? Certainly it wouldn't be me for a long time, if ever, as I would most likely never go back and look at the records of individual patients after all the codes were broken and the data analyzed. She had so much going on. Who knows how much of her improvement could have been due to being on AZT alone, or even partially due to drugs for her pneumonia, even anti-viral drugs for her near blindness from the CMV, and especially due to better care, better nutrition, and more attention she was now receiving in her sister's care. These were all the factors you hoped to account for by having a big enough trial for these other variables, many of which (like the PCP and CMV drugs in addition to AZT dose/duration, etc.) we tried to record as best as possible.

Recently, I'd seen a middle aged HIV-positive male for maybe also the third or fourth time in my clinic since enrolling him on our trial. He had initially presented with weakness, along with weight loss, as a major complaint, and his CD4 counts had been declining slowly but steadily since starting on AZT but they were still above 500 and he'd had no AIDS-defining illness. According to my notes, portions of which had made it more concisely onto the official clinical trial paper work, I felt that it was fairly easy to document muscle weakness on his initial neuro exam; say, for example, compared to what I might expect for a man of his age and size, and with a faint hint of asymmetry allowing some reinforcement of these impressions (still somewhat subjective evaluations, no matter how many you do). I had struggled with the possibility that he may be improving over the time course we'd been following him on the trial.

In typical clinical notes or admission history and physical examination notes, results of muscle strength, along with separately tested reflexes, are commonly represented in little stick figures, with flexion at the arms and knees and hands and feet indicated by little lines at near right angles coming off the longer sticks, with numerical values from your evaluation written in on both right and left sides, on a scale of 0-4. As if there were possible negative values, we commonly wrote in plus signs after the assigned numbers. For example, 2+ at every indicated tested site may commonly signify normal. But, what was normal for a 22 year old college linebacker and a 78 year old female could naturally be expected to be quite different. However, we seemed to compare tested muscle to tested muscle and matched it to some conception of what we may expect for that individual. We didn't necessarily give the young weight lifting stud a 3 or 4+ for every muscle tested and the little old lady uniformly distributed 1+'s. But the most important thing was to be able to detect asymmetries. So, if you were impressed by the kid's strength, it could be fine to give every tested muscle the same 3+, and if you recognized how generally weak some old lady was, a 1+ throughout certainly wouldn't suggest a possible stroke. It was generally easy and important to detect obvious asymmetries, such as if the right arm was markedly weaker than the left, etc. For example, a stroke victim with a large lesion in the left brain may show marked weakness in the extremities on the right due to the contra-lateral nature of motor and sensory innervation, maybe even both upper and lower. So, he or she may have 2+ strength on the left and clearly 1+ on the right. But if one wasn't quite so sure about more subtle forms of weakness, not to mention trying to account for natural strength asymmetries of "handedness", one may write so as to suggest without committing…a 1-2+. After all, it's amazing how many discreet numerical scales become much more graduated in application. A theoretical five point scale of 0, 1+, 2+, 3+, or 4+ in practice becomes something like a nine point scale, with degrees of subjective imprecision reflected in scores of 0, 0-1+, 1+, 1-2+, 2+, 2-3+, 3+, 3-4+, or 4+.

Noting increased compared to decreased muscle strength may not be common, but hyper-reflexia is a symptom of many neurological diseases, so the same scale was employed for this testing and the human tendencies to the same graduated modifications worked there as well. We strive to make medicine more objective all the time, but in the case of these aspects of the humanly performed physical examination, this is where we were at. We didn't exactly make patients do maximum weight curls or squats, even on subsequent visits. In the typical quick neuro exam of a patient with GI manifestations, for example, this type of evaluation was likely more than adequate. But in the world of clinical neuro diagnostics, these types of things were progressively being supplemented by more objective brain and other CNS imaging. In parallel, I'm not sure if the occasional lack of definitiveness incorporated into the hyphenated scores are a reflection of human weakness and/or limitations or, increasingly, a manifestation of the ever present and growing "cover your ass medicine," the constant defensive posture (maybe even gradually subconsciously ingrained) one must assume in the progressively legal-infested universal ether. For example, if you thought that just maybe you detected a "hint" of weakness in one arm vs. the other, you could do the 1-2+ on the potentially weak side and 2+ on the perceived more normal side. If a subsequent CT or MRI scan, ordered depending on major complaint, other aspects of the history and physical, etc., showed a small lesion anatomically corresponding to the detected weak arm, you'd look like a physical examination genius. After all, you clearly noted it as different from the other normal side. If all the imaging studies were normal, no big deal. After all, you basically called it normal, 1-2+ essentially being the same as 2+, within the realm of normal human variation, examiner subjectivity, etc. No harm, no foul sort of thing. In contrast, if you called it a flat out, and more definitive 1+, and in the proper context, a CT or other testing was ordered, you could look incompetent or wasteful in the mind of the insurance companies, not to mention that they'd likely even burden the patient with some significant share of the expenses. In a perhaps less likely but potentially more damaging scenario, if you thought there could be weakness but weren't convinced and didn't want to deal with some or all of the above, you could reasonably blow it off as 2+ and "get away with it" 99% of the time. But, in that one case, where in heroic fashion you could have cost-ineffectively picked up some subtle weakness early on but still called it a 2+, and that patient showed up later with evidence of a possible brain lesion, maybe a re-bleed in a previous hemorrhagic stroke, or even a separate, "second" event (for which there may not have truly been a first), affecting even a different part of the brain, but activating the over populated lawyer mechanism regarding a general disease process that likely "should have been picked up earlier," say maybe when you examined them a few weeks or months before, oh well, you know…there goes a part of your reputation and maybe your malpractice rates (or the rates of your institution), with all the potential trickling down effects, as shit, even bullshit, seems to run downhill.

And so, as humans, we do the best we can and are forced by our limitations, inherent or imposed, to sometimes stay in the gray zones.

Looking back at this patient's first clinic visit and my evaluation of him, I had initially entered 1-2+ for his right and left upper extremity muscle strength. He appeared to have objective weakness on my exam that matched some of his complaints. I decided that waffling, including for the purposes of the trial, maybe especially for the trial, was not a good idea. I would never know who was or was not on drug, so there couldn't be any real bias there; so I figured I should always try to be as definitive as possible, hopefully consistent enough in my evaluations and upward or downward trends in those tough decision gray areas, such that as much objectivity would be present as could be for this one clinical parameter we would be following, and if there was a real effect, we'd have enough patients to hopefully detect it.

Of course, as a small single representation of my anal tendencies (when it comes to work), prospectively recognizing the potential complicating factors of subjectivity for faint weakness and more minor degrees of possible improvement or deterioration, we had made provisions in the study for scoring these types of 0-1+, or 1-2+, or 2-3+ entries for strength and reflexes in two different manners. We would enter them both as the average of the two scores (that is a true intermediate value) as well as enter the higher of the two scores, and both would be used in separate statistical analyses. (For example, a 1-2+ would be considered both as a 1.5 and a 2 in separate analyses).

But, in this particular patient at the initial evaluation, I recommitted to my sense of striving for definitive objectivity and, feeling the presence of true weakness, I scratched out the 2+ in the 1-2+ entries (making them hence, 1+), with proper initial and date notations at the side of the mark-outs, for the medicolegal aspects of making such changes in your own entries in the medical record. According to our inclusion criteria (again, in part reflecting the desire to enter patients at various levels of motor and mental impairment to see at what, if any, stages of the disease our proposed treatment may prove more effective), we were offering trial entry even to those HIV-positive patients with ≤ 1.5 or a 1-2+ score (i.e., even with just barely perceived possible weakness, without any other obvious cause).

We did indeed consent this patient for trial enrollment and scheduled the rest of his more detailed entry evaluation and sample collection for his next follow-up clinic appointment, at which point he would begin on his "experimental" pills. In his subsequent visit, maybe 3-4 weeks after going on either "active" test compound or placebo, I basically thought his neuro exam was unchanged from that which I'd entered at the prior two visits. About 3 months later, at this most recent visit though, I thought he had more leg and arm strength than I recalled from past visits and what I saw charted in my notes. He also wasn't that prominently compromised in his daily life compared to the complaints he had had of still relatively mild problems when he first came to us. Herein, that same dilemma - his arms weren't quite as strong as one might EXPECT for a man of his age, but then they could be close, and they could even be regarded as normal. Were they 1-2+ (and of course, at this point, even a 1.5 or a rounded up 2 would have been a move in the positive direction from a data point of view); or were they just a 2+? Boy, if he was on the actual drug, wouldn't that be great! If he wasn't, maybe that would make a tiny contribution to only further complicate demonstrating a statistically significant improvement in the total group of all the treated patients vs. those control patients on placebo. Perhaps, there was enough heterogeneity in the way the neurological symptoms may progress or even wax and wane a bit, especially early on, that this minor degree of only mildly perceived improvement could be due to nothing at all, as in, could occur within the natural history of the disease in the placebo controlled group.

We're all human. I really wanted our drug to work…of course. So, if I wasn't blinded to whether this man was on drug vs. placebo, I may not be able to avoid bias no matter how pure one tries to be. It is amazing how even our physical perceptions, especially in potentially relatively subjective areas, can be even just subconsciously (vs. God forbid, consciously) affected by context and other information, even if you were convinced that at the conscious level you were pure. If this guy were on drug, it could have been tempting to go with 2+ in the 1-2+ dilemma. If he were on placebo, that weakness could come across as still pretty prominent, still pretty readily detectable (after all, there's no real gold standard to compare it to…), and you may go with the 1+. This of course, is why those of us collecting clinical data were blinded from whether a patient was randomized to drug vs. placebo.

I thought, firstly, that I do this sort of thing A LOT, and secondly, that he was indeed stronger than when I first saw him. I thought he was doing pretty well. I scored those muscle groups 2+. We'd see how he was doing next time we saw him. Importantly, we also supplemented these kinds of clinic visit evaluations with patient questionnaires that they periodically filled out during the trial. Many of the questions regarding, for example, degree of difficulty of doing certain tasks (with numerical scores matching various categories, such as: no difficulty; mild difficulty compared to past; moderate difficultly compared to past, potentially requiring assistance; extreme difficulty, requiring others to perform) could reflect some of the things we also tested, such as walking related to leg strength, certain tasks related to arm and hand strength, etc. The "placebo effect" as a subjective perception of improvement for patients on a trial is well known and documented, as patients naturally want to improve. They may also want the treasured medical community and their doctors to facilitate that improvement, and they may even want to believe they are doing something themselves to participate in their improvement, say, by going on a drug trial. So, the potential bias may be even larger here than in blinded physician assessments. But, those wishful feelings could be expected to equally influence both the group on "active" compound (test drug) and placebo, roughly equally; and in addition to this hopefully relatively mild effect there could be detected a more easily discernible improvement in these patient survey parameters in the true treated group. As we recognized and discussed these potential weaknesses and potential added benefits of including patient surveys in our original grant submission, this came across as another aspect of our "thoroughness," rather than a sign of unforgivable naïveté; and the reviewers further liked (as we, of course, also pointed out) that we were including these variables more directly related to "quality of life" aspects. After all, how one functions in daily tasks is more important to one's daily life than, say, how your muscles performed on examination every couple of months. A patient's perception of evolving symptoms over time could be useful, allowing for comparisons to their own well known past that could supplement a physician's far less frequent attention to these specific matters.

Bottom line: I thought this particular patient was a little stronger than he had been. I sure hoped he was on the real drug; but, only time would tell. And so, the scientific safety net of logic returned. It would take years and hundreds of patients to know anything for sure. In the mean time, we'll stick to scientific method and rigidity, as much as possible and according to the trial design. The results will be what they are. My career would be fine, regardless.

I just sure wished that the drug would work, would at least help a percentage of patients within an at least definable stage of the disease, and at the same time, that we would learn more about the cause of ADC. At the worst, then, all this could at least possibly contribute to the other work being done and hence towards maybe future improved treatments. Someday we may be able to control the virus better, slow down the progression to AIDS more effectively, make HIV infection something people could live with much longer. This in itself could improve the potentially devastating neuromuscular aspects, or maybe drugs like the one we were testing would help longer-living patients.

And, just maybe whatever we were learning in the lab about death of neurons could also translate to other diseases as well, and give some folks working more directly in those fields some ideas about experimental approaches that could translate to those diseases, just as we looked at related basic research literature in closely related areas of research to see if there was something that may translate to our HIV-focused neurologic injury. I was in a Neurology department where some of the best clinical and basic investigators on neuron injury in the world were working, including and maybe especially in diseases such as ALS. A possible immunologic component there had long been being investigated by some of the most gifted and dedicated local gurus. But, for now, in my somewhat separate HIV world, there certainly seemed to be something much more complex than just virus infection, some sort of interaction of one's body and infection under-lying the brain complications, and it sure would be nice to be able to make the quality of that hopefully someday longer life as good as possible, not to mention alleviate a little suffering during the currently short life expectancy, as well.

...

So, all in all, yes, I did sometimes allow myself to even strongly feel (however briefly) that this drug could help patients like Curtis. It certainly couldn't hurt. I also thought that if he were taking the drug, he would feel better emotionally. De-spite all the theoretical considerations and the need for Scientific Purity, if I didn't think this, if I didn't feel it, how could I be working so hard, or at least how could I be working so hard on THIS? Was this just part of the job, what I was designed to do, and had protected my already fortressed psyche by the knowledge that the *in vitro* work would yield definitive publishable results? Was I bolstered, even when tired, to keep pressing on, collecting all the right types of samples in all the right fashions no matter how busy with other stuff, because I knew that this huge trial, even if negative, would lead to a major or several major papers with me as first author; that my career would be taking the next, necessary moderate to giant step it was always destined to take at this stage in my career?

I felt the drug might work, in some detectable subset of patients for some symptoms of potentially documentable pathophysiology, or we wouldn't have written the grant. The whole thing was based on sound available and growing mechanistic considerations. The Gray-Hairs wouldn't have funded it if more experienced physician scientists besides me didn't think there were substantial gains to be made. Why not give Curtis some of the drug, on the side, so that he and I could be sure that he was getting the drug and not the placebo?

Obviously, I couldn't get pills from the actual trial. These vials with the actual trial tablets were carefully labeled, recorded, and tracked. The pills themselves looked essentially identical for test drug and placebo. The vials were coded that matched information regarding whether test drug or placebo, knowledge held by only those who had no access to the actual medicines or patients receiving them. But, I had similar dosage tablets of the same drug in my lab from past research purposes, formulations that would never enter into this trial. Most (really, nearly all) of the *in vitro* experiments we were doing with cultured cells with the drug utilized powdered formulations of the active compound, which we would put into solution to achieve precise concentrations in our experiments. This was adequate for these purposes, but not for oral administration; not with all the stabilizers and other non-active ingredients as in a proper pill for human consumption. It would be very difficult to make solutions that could be drank (or injected!) in any manner that would allow accurate comparison to the blood levels of the active drug determined in earlier clinical trials using pharmaceutical tablet preparations. But, I had these older tablet preparations from past research projects and to occasionally test in our *in vitro* systems to be sure observed effects (that could, in theory, be translated to observed *in vivo* effects in patients) were not due to the highly unlikely interfering effects of other chemicals in the potential commercial clinical application tablets. I had lots of these in the lab, either in doses identical to that which the unknown half of patients in the clinical trial were getting or in lower doses or higher doses that would simply require taking multiple tablets or cutting certain tablets, respectively. I certainly had enough to give to Curtis or anyone else without making a detectable dent in the Research "stash", of which pretty much I alone knew the details anyway.

But, there are some lines that can't be crossed; some principles that if violated, there is no turning back, or certainly no easy turning back. Even if one never committed such transgressions ever again, this one blemish would be there; if never publicly known, burned forever in one's own memory, imprinted on the psychic consciousness. Could one really anticipate that never in one's life would the combination of events that led to one's moral compromise arise again? Perhaps, once tainted, the threshold for performing such acts against one's principles would lower. Does one's daily function, in every minute detail, depend so crucially on that sense of self that a direct violation of that zillion-component construction could bring it to a forever less effective form? I am a scientist, the first and last club or religion of the purely objective thinkers and actors. There may be some leeway in the touchy-feely fields: the priests, even social justice systems, but there was no room for compromise in the pursuit of scientific truth. Surely, I needed no other considerations but the purity of science (and hopefully scientific medicine) to exclude even the remote possibility that I would cave in and give some of the drug tablets to Curtis. This wasn't like finally submitting to a man facial or a man pedicure. This wasn't even like finding oneself stupidly trying intravenous drugs, just that once, and hopefully not getting caught up in that downward spiral of habitual poisoning. Compromising in this manner would perhaps be even worse than marital infidelity. Holding things in to only one's inner self comes at a price. I was vaguely aware, and likely paying a price for not forcing myself to be more aware, of the self-loathing that can simmer when one goes against certain highly held principles. But humans are humans, I could tell myself. We act, we learn, we move on. If one slips and commits an act of weakness that supposedly 75% or more of males commit, it is essentially "normal," at least according to the science of behavior. Of course, that is paralleled by the equally shocking essentially 50% divorce rate. I would suppose that most of that 50% is coming out of the 75% of cheaters and not the 25% of the faithful. I would have to live with that guilt, and at this stage, I wasn't even sure what the hell was going on in my own marriage.

But Science is bigger than any individual human. I had been raised to believe this. Was medicine outside this? Maybe not for physician-scientists? Compassion is one thing; and this is not even the same as potentially more black and white ethical considerations such as euthanasia and humanely facilitating quality deaths. Science must be kept pure, or what hope have we as a race for moving forward?

IX

- Houston; June, 1994

One afternoon in the beginning of June, I had finished clinic a little earlier than usual. The weather outside was beautiful, and I did not feel like going over to the lab in the Medical Center. It was as if I sensed that I needed a break, however brief it might be; a bit of solar and fresh air recharge. I stopped by the house briefly, just to call the lab and talk to my chief lab tech, to see what was going on and be sure that everything was fine, and to let her know that I wouldn't be over there again until tomorrow morning.

No problems. No crises, no nothing that needed my immediate attention... also not anything even in the steady progress of research category that in the grand scheme of things couldn't wait for 14 hours. I grabbed a can of beer, a lesser quality choice than what existed in bottle form in the fridge, anticipating that Leo may be around. Reminding any of us and even strangers of the "No glass rule" was an obsession of his of a magnitude far past normal safety concerns. I grabbed a book (yes, non-work related leisure reading), and headed over to the park. There were a good few hours of nice sun left, and it wasn't unpleasantly hot. I needed to defervesce, and my Curtis dilemma was still on my mind. Some more mental self-torturing could suffice if I bored of my book.

Rick and Leo were already there, so the plan for reading quickly faded, which was fine with me, as I was more in the mood for conversation than the somewhat difficult nature of the book I had dragged along.

Leo was sitting on the right hand side of the bench I normally sat on. Rick was lying on his back, in what appeared to be his work clothes, on the grass in front, parallel to the bench and with his arms under his head, the crown of which was facing me so that he couldn't possibly see me as I walked over towards them. Leo gave me a big smile, and Rick greeted me by name, "What's up, Jeff?" without ever looking towards me, as if the specific nature of Leo's smile (which he could see from his position) gave him some sort of code for which of their park mates was arriving. Maybe they worked on signals when the rest of us weren't around.

As I walked by, Rick reached his hand up to shake mine, his held in place compatible with not moving otherwise, dictating that I awkwardly bend a bit forward over him. Clearly he was comfortable. When I sat down next to Leo on the bench facing Rick's head, Leo turned towards me and gave me a hug, mostly with his left arm, such that he didn't actually have to lift himself off the bench. Clearly he was comfortable as well.

They were apparently having a conversation on classical music, which I didn't want to interrupt and which they clearly felt like continuing. I was comfortable with placing my book on my lap, turning slightly to my left to absorb rays from the gradually setting sun, and listening. I was surprised that Rick had opinions on classical music, although they seemed to be on more general topics. And I was surprised at how lucid Leo was.

"Mozart was so *pop* compared to Beethoven," Rick opinionated strongly, something which I myself believed I'd heard stated before.

"Yes," Leo appeared to patiently respond, "but it was the music his generation needed. He brought musical melodies to the masses that struck cords matching their personal and social needs."

I was beginning to wonder if this was a well orchestrated crock of shit or if Leo had been abducted and his body occupied by a coherent alien life form, something with a passion for 19th century composers. He continued, in something less than his usual monotone.

"It is much like that...English...bug band that was so popular here in the states."

"The Beatles?" I added in clarification.

"Yes, Yes!" Leo exuberantly responded, turning towards me and patting me on my right shoulder with his left hand, as if rewarding me for my participation. Rick and I were able to absorb the efficiently delivered analogy.

Then Rick, as if continuing on a topic broached before my arrival, asked the wavy haired little guru, "But what is the music of romance? What do I want to put on if I am trying to...you know...impress a woman?"

"Ah," said Leo, closing his eyes gently and taking in a light sun-drenched sigh, "Brahms is the Music of Love."

"What about Wagner?" Rick offered up, as if looking for a bitch slap based on Leo's quick eye opening and change in facial expression.

"Wagner is for rape and pillage," he rectified his young protégé. "Glorious, yes, but it is the music of mythology and grandiosity. Wagnerian opera can stir you to act against all odds. I assume that your romantic endeavors are not THAT bleak. Brahms is the music to loosen the corset strings."

We all sat (or laid) there for a few still moments.

Then Rick got up, dusted off the front of his pants, which I don't think had even been in contact with anything other than air, neglecting the back side, and announced, "I've gotta go. Got a date."

Rick's car, as I'd noted when I'd entered, was parked on the side street parallel to the east side of the park. Apparently he was going to go straight from the park, in likely work clothes, to his date. Maybe he'd even driven by and seen Leo here and stopped for this bit of potentially useful romantic advice. Apparently, Maria was not the kind of woman who minded grass stains or other debris on her boyfriend's ass. Which was a good thing, as Rick was the kind of guy to put them there, as well as do other sorts of Rick things.

I regretted his departure, in large part, as I didn't think I had the necessary background with which to continue the conversation that seemed to have Leo in such good spirits and operation mode.

We sat there in presumed mutual contemplative silence for a few moments, with Leo thinking whatever kinds of thoughts Leo thinks, and maybe more clear now than usual, and me thinking that I might be better off reading my book or going home and trying to do a little work. But out of perhaps some sort of respect for Leo's state and/or some manifestation of inertia, I stayed, and as the sun rays began their refractory progression from yellow to various magically intermingling rays of orange and pink and burnt orange and some shade of light red as it kissed through the low lying clouds, it was eventually me that broke the silence in what I perceived would be a pointless attempt to return to the most recent topic. "I don't really know anything about Beethoven," I finally muttered. I wasn't sure if Leo had stayed where he had been before or drifted back into the suburbs of la-la land. So, in his initial silence, I pathetically continued. "I mean, I know parts of the 9th symphony, I guess, because the main melody, or whatever it is, was the mu-

sic for one of our commonly sung hymns, when I was growing up…in church…
Joyful, Joyful We Adore Thee, I think it was."

Leo responded without specifically changing his expression, "The Ninth Symphony is indeed essentially magical, but you, you in particular, need to experience the 7th Symphony."

I didn't feel like getting into why that may be, as I'm not sure that even a relatively lucid Leo would have any sort of insight into what types of music I may or may not need to be exposed to…for whatever presumed enlightening or other purposes. So, I made a mental note, and remained silent.

"Of course," he began to warm up again, "if you listen to the Piano Concertos, such as The Piano Sonata #14 in C Sharp Minor…The Moonlight Sonata (he apparently added for my lay benefit), you should be aware that despite what most people may believe, Rubinstein's playings are not necessarily the best or even the most approachable."

I thought Rubinstein's name sounded familiar, but that may have been because I had an Internal Medicine attending at the NIH named Rubinstein and a Neurology attending at UCSF named Rubinstein. So, instead, I commented that The Moonlight Sonata sounded familiar to me. At which point, Leo closed his eyes to the fading light and with a face conveying the intensity of a thousand challenging lifetimes hummed in surprisingly complex character the tune of which I did indeed recognize portions. Coming back to at least the park version of reality, stopping his humming, and placing both hands on his knees, he then went on to explain to me that the single greatest player of all Beethoven Concertos, for the perfect combination of technical craft and interpretive emotion, was a young Russian Pianist that he had befriended while a young man in Milan.

Of course, there was no way for me to know this person's name, maybe even if I were a classical music enthusiast rather than a tweaker of neurons. But, this latest recollection seemed to awaken in Leo hints of an underlying majesty beneath the scars of a lifetime apparently largely lost to the ravages of a disorienting disease that we still didn't know the exact contributory effects of genetics, environment, and/or viral infection towards. I was intensely and hauntingly exposed to an impromptu, impassioned lecture on some of the finest subtleties on symphonic and operatic music that I would likely never be able to fully absorb even if I had been taking notes.

Leo went on to tell me such things as why La Scala is the finest opera house in the world, including several examples as to why it could be specifically preferred even over the Met. He vehemently defended Italian opera as the most passionate, particularly with regard to musical orchestration, regardless of Libretto concerns. As I'd never been to either Milan or specifically to the Met those times I'd been in New York, I certainly couldn't comment on the former; and as I wasn't sure about even the difference between orchestration and libretto (in parallel with my general complete ignorance of all things operatic), I couldn't offer much comment as to any kind of comparison between Italian, German, Austrian, or Martian opera for that matter. So, I just listened, apparently in a manner that allowed him to continue. But, this was not schizophrenic rambling; nor was it manic flight of ideas. It was enthusiastically rendered information delivered in appropriate speed and tone of speech that probably, truly, for the first time gave me at least some insight into what Leo's lifetime interests may have included during those hopefully long lucid and peaceful years of a "recovered" or "reclaimed" schizophrenic.

I, of course, had no way of knowing if anything Leo said would be an opinion held by anyone else, as these topics were way outside my expertise, but it sounded rather authoritative or at least reflective of strongly held preferences. I even made some notes when I got home later that evening, as any source could likely enhance my non-existent appreciation of classical music and opera at this stage of my life. Some of the finer details were even more lost on me than the general themes; for example, why he had come to prefer Renata Tebaldi for most Puccini operas, but still preferred Maria Callas in her prime for Tosca (regardless of what some people say about Joan Sutherland), and how Giuseppe di Stefano paired perfectly with both of them in certain recorded versions in Turnadot and Tosca.

He started into Verdi, but sensing that he was losing his audience, Leo shifted the instruction back to classical music and symphony. I don't know if it was for my specific account given my profession and even current emphasis on an infectious disease that was out there claiming the lives of some pretty brilliant and/or creative persons or maybe I just happened to focus in on these aspects given my perspective, as I'm not sure that Leo even in this state could have such didactic intentions, but I was specifically intrigued by a couple of the causes of death for the composers he began to discuss.

For some reason, he began with Schubert, perhaps because this was arguably the most tragic. Did I know, for example, that a young Schubert had been a Vienna Choirboy and had actually been a student of Salieri's?

Without answering (I don't think it was indicated or required), I did note that I HAD at least heard of the Vienna Choirboys, a bunch of sweet singing prepubescent lads that I think my mother had an album of when I was growing up, maybe a Christmas album. I had no idea who Salieri was. But something told me this wasn't the key point, and I didn't bring up this one of many exposed ignorances, so whatever this intended didactic was had a slightly increased chance of staying on focus.

Leo continued, "He hadn't been a good student…Schubert that is…" (as if I might think that he was now going into the academic history of Salieri maybe)… "as he spent all his time composing. When his voice…um, you know, changed, he was released from school. You know, he lived most of his life in…severe poverty. He died of typhus when he was just 31."

I perked up a bit. I probably hadn't thought about typhus, the signs/ symptoms, causative organism, standard treatment, etc. since the first year of medical school.

Leo respected my apparent interest with a brief pause, and then re-involved me, with, "Typhus. I bet you can cure that one now."

"Yep," I replied, "we got that one covered. We don't see it much anymore, not here in the U.S. anyway. But if we made the diagnosis, we have the proper antibiotics…um, drugs…to achieve an effective cure."

"But you Doctors couldn't cure it back then, could you?"

"No." (I certainly didn't know exactly which of those prior centuries Schubert had lived; I would guess 1800's I suppose, but I knew it was pre-antibiotic era). "We didn't have the specific drugs that we have now. We could just treat patients supportively…you know, give them fluids…although they may have tried other non-effective remedies…and hope for recovery…and certainly try to prevent its further spread."

"And now, you can't cure AIDS yet, can you?" Leo switched centuries on me again. I wasn't sure if he was clarifying or attempting to make a point.

"No," I kept it brief, which was hard for me to do in general, but not necessarily in this audience setting.

Leo continued his lecture.

"You know, hardly any of Schubert's music was known during his brief lifetime. His attempts at Opera were not recognized, and his symphonies and his great piano and orchestral compositions, which we know so well now, were completely undiscovered until several decades after he had died."

I assumed by the "we" who know Schubert so well referred to the large classical music appreciating population that I was still on the fringe of. But, his name is a household name, and clearly for his music, so there was something not just remotely sad about the description of this life and the time course of his fame and recognition.

I wasn't sure how to respond, so keeping my contribution somewhat juvenile, I made the observations, "So, I guess I should be listening to some Schubert, and maybe being grateful that we don't lose too many geniuses to typhus anymore."

"There will always be something that takes away our geniuses at a young age," Leo surprised me by focusing on this part of my reply for comment. Maybe he was making a point, but he did follow-up with, "But, yes, you should be listening to Schubert...Ständchen, Rosamunde, and piano pieces like Impromptu in E flat major will only help your writing, which you seem to spend so much time on. The Budapest Strings and The Budapest Philharmonic and the extraordinary pianist Jenö Jando do an exemplary job, and should suit your purposes."

Even if accurate, and it sounded like it certainly could be ("exemplary job" and "suit your purposes" in context appropriate usage are not the typical signs of an acutely scattered mind), this was too much detail on topics that weren't necessarily high priority; but I had enjoyed classical music in the background in our house growing up, and had decided I would indeed pick up some CDs. However, this may have been a little too many specifics given how much neuronal function I could allocate to this purpose at this point. I was trying to remember a few key things to facilitate my subsequent shopping: Schubert and Budapest seemed like good key phrases for this topic, which I could scribble down when back at home, and the rest could come back to me while browsing CDs, like recognizing an answer on a multiple choice test vs. the more dreaded fill in the blanks.

It was dark now, and trying to get this to some sort of wrap up stage, so we could both continue on our more usual paths, I remembered what he had said to Rick before he left, and who was probably at least nose deep in Maria's amble bosom by now.

"What about Brahms? Should I be listening to Brahms?" I thus naturally inquired.

"No....I mean...I would never discourage anyone from listening to any great music. But for you...for you, I would prescribe Tchaikovsky."

The seeming irony that a "burnt-out" (O.K., more respectably, perhaps somewhat "recovered") schizophrenic was "prescribing" anything to me, a physician, was...well, interesting, and worthy of further pursuit.

"Why is that?" I thus naturally inquired.

"Tchaikovsky is the music of struggle. His music was the very illness of his passion," Leo the sage professed.

"Well, I've listened to and even seen The Nutcracker...you know, the Christmas Time thing, and I'm at least familiar with the existence of Swan Lake," I pathetically offered up as to try getting at least a couple of points, feeling somewhat like I was having one of those nightmares in which I had a test in a class I forgot I was even taking, had not been to, or had never studied for. At least Leo had a moderating gentleness that I hadn't yet encountered in those recurring dreams.

"Not the ballets. You need the process of the Symphonies, especially the Sixth Symphony, and maybe for your romantic woes, which will hopefully end very differently than his, you need the Serenade of Strings...and yes... perhaps as an entry even before those, the Concerto for Violin and Orchestra in D major and, of course, the well known Concerto for Piano Number 1."

Feeling a bit information overloaded, as memory works better in the areas of one's major interests and less efficiently in the realm of the unfamiliar, yet wanting to be a good student, even for a possibly warped guide, in the absence of note taking and hoping to keep things simple and maybe overlapping in key terms perhaps, I inquired, "Do those Budapest guys do a good Tchaikovsky?"

"Yes, actually, they do," Leo fortunately responded, and making me not feel as stupid as I actually did. "The very same Jenö Jando does an excellent job on the Piano Concerto with the Budapest Philharmonic, and the Budapest Symphony Orchestra is quite outstanding, with Emmy Verhey on violin."

At the mention of violin, a change came over Leo's face, one of almost sad nostalgia if I had to try and characterize it, in a combination of medicine and humanity perspective.

He returned quickly to add, "You know...it's amazing...again, that these works were also poorly received initially...at the time he composed them...and now they are...immortal...so to speak."

Recognizing the potential similarity, I somewhat sarcastically offered up (in open acknowledgment that I hadn't read Tchaikovsky's Bio in the "Cliff Notes" prior to class), "Let me guess...he died young...maybe of T.B.?"

Leo, giving my inquiry respectful consideration, added "Well...young depends on your perspective. He died in his early fifties...of cholera, I believe."

"Cholera; no shit!" I responded, not recognizing the pun until Leo followed with:

"Actually, lots of shit, I suspect." Then after a brief pause as if in mutual respect to the voluminous death inducing diarrhea suffered by such victims in the past, he continued, "But, I think you guys can cure that one too, now...is that so?"

"Yeah...we can cover that one with meds as well, but we don't see it much, not here in the U.S. The key is prevention. Good hygiene, and be sure to get vaccinated...you know...for prevention...if you are going to travel someplace where it still exists...endemically or in circumstances causing it to increase...natural disasters and such."

"Ah...an ounce of prevention...funny...some things change so much, especially with us humans and technology, but some things stay the same. Wisdom is the key."

No one even without a history of mental illness was going to top that, so I stood up, and said, "It's getting late, can I walk you home?"

"Yes, that would be a pleasure," he replied, and took my arm to help stand up from the bench, and we began our slow walk across the grass of the park.

Schubert, Tchaikovsky, and Budapest" I said to myself a couple of times, for reinforcement. "*S. T.B...T.B.S*"...as we might make an acronym to remember a fact in Medical School Basic Sciences or Clinical Pearls for tests and quizzing and the like. Not a natural one, although B.S. is easy...hmm. *"Total Bull Shit"*...that'll work to remember TBS, from there it was a piece of cake to Tchaikovsky, Budapest, Schubert...and the specific pieces would come to me as I looked at "song" lists on the back of candidate CD's...or I'd overbuy to be sure I had the specific compositions covered...and I could be so purposeful that I wouldn't even have to be bothered with interacting with those

Carl types that seemed to be more prevalent in the Classical Music Section of the "Record" Stores than the Pop/Rock sections, other than saying *"No thanks"* when they inevitably pronounced their superior knowledge just by seemingly politely asking *"Can I help you find something?"* I could even find myself tempted to actually respond with hopefully off-guarding statements, such as, *"Yes...a piece of pussy...or world peace."*

It would be a long time before I realized that such music could probably help a bit on both counts.

...

"Are you Ms. Valery?" I needlessly inquired (as whom else could it be) when an elderly, distinguished appearing woman answered the door. She had the appropriate stern, if somewhat unexpectedly softened, demeanor of the kind of no non-sense woman who would run the sort of half way house that would appropriately shelter the likes of a Leo.

She was probably quite attractive when she was younger. She must have been in her mid to late 60's, probably close to Leo's own age. I momentarily wondered if that somehow could make him her favorite, amongst the likely younger miscellaneous recovering drug addicts and slight misfits that usually inhabited such places, not typically making it for whatever complex reasons to the gentle maturity they could probably share as in Leo's case.

"What?...um...oh...yes," she gathered herself, as she then saw Leo, extending on her tip toes to glance over my left shoulder where he stood behind me on the sidewalk before the steps to the door. "That's what he often calls me...," her mind drifted.

Leo then walked up the stairs matter-of-factly, scraping by me on the top step while unintentionally brushing me towards a shrub of some sort to the right of the door. He paused in the doorway, and "Ms. Valery" gave him a peck on the cheek before he turned down a hallway to the right and disappeared, as if hospitality on his part wasn't an issue.

I stood there for a moment, wondering what to do next, when she said to me, "You must be the doctor."

"I beg your pardon?"

"He talks about you, all of you, his park friends...all of the time."

413

"Really?" I somewhat blustered, sincerely perplexed, given what I would have perceived as unlikely concrete subject matter for someone like Leo to convey to a third party.

"Oh, of course…oh, goodness," she caught herself. "Won't you come in," she continued. "My, I would never let him be out so long if he wasn't with others… that he seems to do really well with."

I entered past her into a small front room, with a sofa opposite the door, a recliner type chair to the right, and a small TV on a cabinet on the wall with the doorway. I turned to face her, still puzzled.

"What makes you think I'm the 'doctor'?" I brought myself to objectively inquire, as if we all played some role at the park like in a soap opera, while still feeling a bit like Alice at just the start of her journey.

"Oh," she said, graciously sitting down on the sofa while beckoning me to sit on the chair. "You're the only one that would ever actually walk him home…I suspect."

"Humm…," I offered in stellar commentary.

"He worries about you…the most," she gently continued.

I was miffed.

"He worries about ME?" I finally uttered, probably too defensively, as in why the fuck would a burned out schizophrenic or at best a burnt out manic with psychotic features worry about someone like me.

"Oh, it's O.K.," she said in a voice as comforting as warm milk. "He just thinks you're…hmm, let's see…unsettled, or restless, or troubled….those are some of his words… I think…undifferentiated, he even said once, although I'm not sure what he meant by that, in particular."

That was already quite a short list. I wondered how many times they'd had such conversations.

I began to need some substantiation, some legitimacy. Maybe it was Rick's influence, but I surely needed to discredit some witness here.

"How long have you known Leo…I mean, how long has he lived here…or under your supervision?" I began my challenge.

"What?" she looked at me a bit confused or maybe like you look at someone else who's confused. "My God…we've been married…38 plus years."

Alice was officially tumbling.

...

Leo's wife looked at me with a smile of cautious perplexity quickly followed with subtle sympathy as she appeared to further process my possible ignorance (at least towards this one fact).

"It's a long story," she then politely continued. "Would you like a cup of coffee...or, a glass of red wine?" She must have taken in my expression and kindly expanded the beverage option.

I didn't REALLY have to work that much tonight, not if something potentially even more informative was in the offering.

"A glass of red wine would be wonderful," I brought myself back to functionality sufficient to answer.

She got up and I watched her gracefully disappear into what I presumed was the kitchen, from which she spoke sufficiently loudly for me to here: "Is Chianti Classico alright? I'm afraid you can take the Italians out of Italy, but not necessarily the Italian out of Italians," she offered as she handed me the generously poured glass. My taking it must have been sufficient evidence of my affirmative response.

"From what I understand about wine, that's not necessarily a bad thing."

"You seem kind," she flattered me. "Do you like opera?" she followed with, as if opera enjoyment was either going to be a confirmation or negation of my kindness.

"I don't really know enough about opera to appreciate it, I would have to say."

"You're young, there's hope yet," she politely responded, rather than just simply throwing me out right then and there. I thought I detected a hint of the same sense of humor that Leo often surprised me with.

She took a substantial sip of her wine, and sat back comfortably into the sofa, and continued, "That's where his nickname for me...Ms. Valery...comes from...from *La Traviata*. I'm not sure if it's flattering or not, but I think he intends it that way. Although, if he's angry or upset with me, he may even call me Violetta or Violetta Valery, as when you scold a child using his or her full name, I suppose."

She must have seen the tell-tale signs of opera confusion on my face, and offered in support of her explanation, "Verdi is his favorite. If you asked him 10 times who his favorite is, he would probably answer Verdi seven times and Puccini only 3."

Wow, a woman who converses in data. I could probably get comfortable here, I mused.

She paused for awhile, apparently in deep thought.

"Leo…was…a tremendous violin player. 'World-class' as they say," she started again. I suspect we were past whatever details of nickname explanation I was going to get, and the story of Leo…and "Mrs. Leo" was about to unfold. I was acutely stunned that I had never learned his last name. She leaned forward a little, and continued to enlighten me.

I stayed there about an hour (maybe longer), mostly listening, and for two more large glasses of red wine that seemed to gently glow inside me along with the details of the interesting life and romance of Leonardo and Angelica Capressi.

She had casually known Leo when they were both general University Students in Milan, shortly after the war. They were both focusing on musical studies and music history. Even then, she noted, Leo seemed different than other young men she had met before, both Italian men she knew within and without the University and the American men she had encountered during the end of and immediately after the war. "He seemed to be so serious," she said, "…quiet, strangely aloof in social settings, and with an apparent intensity." She got to know him, and his family, much better when after University they were both studying music at a highly regarded Conservatory in Milan. Leonardo was 24 and she 22 when they began to encounter each other more frequently in that setting. Leonardo was a highly touted violinist, with frequently discussed unlimited potential. She was studying ballet, as well as piano, but she stated that even then she recognized that she did not have the natural talent of many of those around her. She worked particularly hard in order to try keeping up, but she did not expect a successful career in the Arts. However, to this day, she certainly felt that the level of her training was more than required for many of the various subsequent roles she has had in musical teaching and other endeavors.

She and Leo began spending a fair amount of time together then, and her initial impressions from two or so years before were confirmed. He was more intense and more obsessed with music than anyone she'd ever known. He was a perfectionist. He could play a recital that others raved about and confirming the impressions of his ascending mastership, only to later reveal to her that he thought he had misplayed perhaps a single chord or had not expressed it, stretched the strings to the precise level and timing that the spirit of the piece on that performance demanded. He would sometimes cancel their plans to perhaps meet for coffee afterwards, only to spend essentially the entire night at the Conservatory playing and replaying that piece, modifying his approach, and even experimenting if such modified technique could be extended to analogous segments of scores that he alone seemingly saw analogies or similarities in. His passion for music and the impact of music on the "soul" and the "spirit" were intoxicating to her. She explained it was as if he and others at his level of ability, and they alone, were cleansing the world of the subhuman experience in which it had just been submerged. After meeting and spending a little time with Leo's family, she could see where at least some of that perfectionism came from.

She told me in blunt but somehow not quite condemning words how Leo's father had been seemingly overbearing. He was as much driven for Leo to achieve recognition and success in his musical career as Leo was, a singularly focused man who didn't seem to allow for any outwardly recognizable joy in his life. In contrast, Leo's mother was a gentle and demure woman who doted over her son, her only child, comforting him after particularly severe encounters between father and son, but never confronting the child's father about the nature of their relationship (or anything else apparently), always bolstering Leo back up to listen to his father and to pursue what God had given him. Given the commitment his parents seemed to expect from him, even after he was essentially, chronologically, a grown man, they did not approve of Leo and Angelica's growing relationship and their spending "distracting time" together.

"Courting" back then was different, she reminded me, even noting the datedness of the very term. They had relatively few formal dates, initially, as in prolonged episodes of unsupervised time together. Whether during these occasions or more random conversations centered around the Conservatory, and which seemed to stretch past the time when one or the other of them should have long been somewhere else, he was different, strange but romantically appealing compared to all of the other local boys she knew, including some who had survived very major involvement in the war. She did not go into much detail regarding Leo's involvement in the Nazi resistance efforts, especially during the last two years of the war. She indicated that Leo never spoke much about it and seemed to feel that, at least compared to music, it didn't reflect much of what was worth talking about.

Her eyes warmed when she remembered and described in some detail the first time they went to the opera together, their first "really big" date. It was Maria Callas's debut at La Scala, in *I Vespri Siciliani*, December 1951. Leo had a particular intensity about him that night and during that time in general. It was anticipated that he would actually be auditioning for the Orchestra del Teatro alla Scala before the next season. They were both deeply moved, both deeply impressed by Callas's unique voice and dramatic ability; but for Leo, the very setting and occasion seemed to cause as much anxiety as pleasure. Leo was 26 years old then. She blushed slightly when she shared that perhaps they could have already been considered old for not being married, but recollected herself when she suggested that the war had delayed so many things for so many people. And, they had both been studying so hard up to that point. Over the preceding weeks or maybe even months, they had even occasionally talked about possibly being married, how they would live regardless of their job positions, or depending on what their jobs would be; how happy they would be regardless, as they could teach and still make ends meet while they played their music in whatever way they pleased.

Leo was practicing constantly after that. Angelica was no longer studying music formally, and so she saw him much less. His father effectively prevented her "interfering" with his playing, especially at home. He hardly slept or ate, and he put himself under tremendous pressure. It was during that time, maybe three or so months later, that he had his first…break. Mrs. Capressi looked at me at that point in her narrative, as if seeking validation for use of the proper medical term: "That is what you call it, right, a break, a schizophrenic break? We used to say 'breakdown' or 'nervous breakdown.' I guess it's all the same. I don't think anyone has a break…upwards…do they," she stated as she displayed an unavoidable discomfort, and then continued on.

Leo was in a Mental Hospital about six months that first time. It was difficult for Angelica to see him, as he wasn't allowed much visitation, particularly in the beginning, but she did visit him there, despite his parents' objection. It was almost as if they blamed her…for everything that had gone awry in Leo's life. After that, when he was made by whatever barbaric treatment forms were available then into a calmer, typically quiet fragment of his former self and no longer regarded as a threat to others and especially himself, he was allowed to leave in his parents' care. Then, of course, it was even harder, nearly impossible, for Angelica to see Leo. Their romance and certainly their fantasized-about marriage was seemingly put on permanent hold. As natural for a young woman under such circumstances, after a while Angelica began to date other men. One man in particular (she didn't bother with a name from what I remember) she saw for over a year, under increasing pressure from her own parents to "finally" marry; after all, this suitor was at least sane and had some stable, boring job. But, as she blushingly declared to me, she was already in love and couldn't stop thinking about Leo.

After about a year and a half since his leaving the hospital, she started to hear that Leo had begun making some appearances "around the neighborhood." (I thought about my own seemingly random encounters with the wandering Leo, here, now, in our own neighborhood, even separate from the park conversations). She made herself available extensively at the various cafes and shops where the past local prodigy may show up. It wasn't long before the two of them re-kindled their precious conversations over coffee or even wine. I suspect that these were more therapeutic than anything offered in the hospital, and certainly more than in Leo's own home. Leo was and yet was not the "same person." Despite the lack of encouragement from her family and probably ignorance on the part of Leo's parents, they saw more of each other over the next two years. Both of them were giving private music lessons in their respective family homes and Angelica worked other odd jobs. Leo had missed his window of opportunity for violin fame and glory and was not capable of playing as before. I suspect this was in large part a consequence of his disease and treatment numbed mind. Angelica's family was putting more pressure on her to marry (someone besides Leo) or maybe even (in possible surrender to her apparent independence) move to America, to possibly continue her music studies (and not too subtly hinting at also finding a husband THERE).

Angelica couldn't help but love Leo, even more so in his new fragile state, and certainly thought that she could take care of him, the real him, a lot better than his parents were. Ironically, or maybe naturally, their first "real date" after his prolonged recovery up to whatever state he was in at the time, was at La Scala, again with Maria Callas, in Tosca in 1955. I had no idea of what the operas were or who the performers were, and I got particularly lost when she made some analogy between the profound weight loss that Callas had undergone since they'd seen her last and what Leo had lost, compounded by a brief discourse on their shared opinion on the change in quality of her voice. However, I tried to add a few key names to my already threatened mental notes that I had made during

Leo's similarly detailed lecture in the park in what seemed like days ago already. I suppose the most important detail was that right after the opera, Leo proposed, and Angelica accepted. Neither family was particularly thrilled to say the least, but even in Italy, adults can usually do what they want. They were married, and shortly thereafter, did indeed move to the states, thinking they could have a better life with just teaching music…or doing whatever.

It clearly hadn't always been easy. Leo's mental health had undergone some ups and downs, with a few return hospitalizations and lots of medications. His last hospitalization had been more than ten years ago. In some sort of summary, Mrs. Capressi conveyed that he is a slower, more gentle man (implying not necessarily due to age alone), but that he is still sometimes the young passionate man she fell in love with, and they still share a love for music, and they had saved enough over the years to get by now.

And, no, she had never run a halfway house.

Finally, my gracious hostess recognized the passing of time, announced that she had to wake Leo from an apparent nap and feed him some dinner. I turned down her polite offer to join them, as I felt I had already sufficiently engaged her generous hospitality.

I had a lot of thoughts on my walk home. I had one more glass of wine in my own empty rental house, and went to sleep without doing any work. And then, I had many weird dreams, until I woke back to the harsh world of hopefully more tangible reality.

X

- *Houston; June, 1994*

The next day, on the way home from work, I stopped in at Cactus Records on Shepherd and bought 9 CDs: two Schubert CDs that I think included some or all of the works Leo mentioned, and at least one which included performances by The Budapest Strings and that Jando guy on piano; three Tchaikovsky CDs, which I'm pretty certain included enough symphonies to encompass the one Leo stressed; and two full opera recordings with Maria Callas in La Traviata and Tosca. I then walked next door to the Bookstop and, once I finally found the appropriate Music Section, bought a moderately thick paperback that included plot summaries of the major operas, maybe 3-4 pages each, and which I specifically noted included the two operas which I'd purchased. Fortunately, Carl wasn't working, or at least wasn't at the register when I checked out, so he couldn't give me the understated inquisition that may hide direct accusations but would still seem to subtly imply that I was just acquiring one more tool to try getting superficially and Hell-directed laid outside of marriage. Maybe I was being sensitive. Carl had once seen me at Café Noche on Montrose, north of Westheimer, when I was eating on the outside deck with Maura, so many months ago. He was exiting from the inside, with a couple of male companions, possibly co-workers, as I couldn't imagine Carl having any kind of social life. His eyes caught mine, in a sort of "I know what you're up to" glance. I could have also been "just having dinner" with a colleague, who happened to look like a British movie-star. Does that necessarily mean that she didn't have a Ph.D. in Neurosciences? Or could we have been exhibiting some kind of body language to the contrary during the few moments Carl could have noticed us before I noticed him? However, at least in this not even actualized current case, Carl's imagined judgment would have been unfounded, as I was reading opera for my own sake or for some undefined quest for something even larger that I could still further gain on top of last night's twilight-zone experience. On top of that, if I was to try to impress anyone with my new found awareness, if not yet appreciation, of some classical music, it would be my own shockingly beautiful wife. I suddenly caught myself wondering if it was a bad sign that I may have even subconsciously thought that I needed such at this time.

What a remarkable love story Leo and Angelica had, I suppose. I lay there on my sofa later that evening drinking and thinking about them, after eating the third or so piece of Star Pizza that I had picked up, as it was so conveniently located between my two educational shopping spots and my bland rental house. I was enjoying a second glass of Chianti (N.O.S., not Classico) that the convenience store even closer to my house carried in the borderline nostalgic wicker wrapped bottles. Even this humble but dry Italian wine was surely one step up (at least four dollars) above the Boone's Farm types in the cooler sections. I may be listening to Austrian and Russian Classical music at some point this evening, but I was going to start with Italian opera while I ate my pizza, drank my cheap but very pizza compatible wine, and flipped channels with the volume off on TV while I read a synopsis of La Traviata at the same time as hearing some pretty incredible voices singing words that I had no clue as to their specific meaning. But I could appreciate the context of them when I moderately, painstakingly matched certain named segments on the back of the CD package to what I was reading in my Opera synopsis book.

As I encountered the familiar name of Violetta Valery, I gave brief pause while I grabbed another piece of pizza out of the box on the coffee table, poured another glass of wine, and then focused increasing attention as I finished both and the corresponding synopsis in my already tomato sauce stained new book. I wondered, of course, why Leo chose this name for the beloved woman that had nurtured him through almost forty years of a mental illness challenged relationship. I decided that if there were indeed a meaningful underlying rationale and not just random association, there were two possibilities. Leo may have been angry or resentful of the fact that Angelica had dated other men and especially even pursued another relationship during the interval between their initial dating and their eventual betrothal. Alternatively, although the sexual orientation of the analogy would be reversed, the name assignment could have symbolically evolved as a testament to true undying love in spite of interfering illness; illness that could take one's lover away, physically or mentally. (In Ms. Valery's case, it was TB, common of course in 19th century Europe; not uncommonly fatal, but fortunately in The Arts, it didn't interfere with boisterous Opera singing). Maybe it was the synergistic combination of Chianti and Callas, but I decided there was no way it could be anything but the latter.

More wine (I insightfully or stupidly bought two bottles) led to more thinking, the fertile soil of all late night agony. Surely Kim and I could not feel guilty for just being temporarily, albeit seemingly increasingly not so temporarily, apart. Leo and Angelica never really had true meaningful careers to compete against their perpetual co-habitation. Or was it something different? Had Kim and I drifted to a state where we lost focus, a focus that even a crazy man and a hopelessly romantic woman could recognize, whereas two intelligent and driven participants could force a divergence? Where along the relatively short journey did we cumulatively reach that fork at which we should have recognized that staying together was more important than any individual efforts, that the sum of the two singular efforts was not as effective in at least some realms as the potentially less efficient but synergizing human couple offerings to the great gig on the earth? When should we have sung our "Parigi, o cara," and then blessedly recognized that there was actually nothing, nothing but misguided pride that could interfere with our mutual happiness? Neither of us was sick. Neither of us was a young over-achiever struck with tuberculosis, struck with typhus (wherever the hell you get that?), struck with accidental cholera from a single misguided glass of water, struck with incurable HIV infection, or struck with psychosis.

Was it the gradual emergence of weekends that I said I had to go into the lab instead of going with her and her parents to some recently opened showing, or just hanging out with her on Taft street after a brief visit to a gallery to make sure everything was O.K., or just relaxing in our own neighborhood and our comfortable apartment? Couldn't I have timed some trips into the lab to allow for my inescapable addiction and still allow for my other passion, my trips into the earthly pleasures of time with Kim? When did it happen that somehow Kim sensed that I was irreversibly torn?

At about 3:30 a.m., I woke up briefly, still on the sofa, to recognize that I'd added a little sleep drool to my already pizza haunted book. I closed it, set it on the coffee table, and closed my eyes. I tried my hardest to guide my wise subconscious back to the dreams I was having of Kim. Kim and I were in a cabin in the woods that, when we opened the door, was weirdly then the beach. The CD player had been on repeat mode, and Maria Callas sang my psyche into the tortured caves of everything wrong with the world in which you couldn't have everything, at least not at a hundred percent of everything.

XI

- Houston; June, 1994

On a Thursday evening, in mid June, it was particularly pleasant out-side. This was still, barely, the time of year one was glad to live in Houston. Even if it may have seemed to be a little hot out during the day, especially for some of the non-locals, it was incredibly nice to be outside in the evening, much more suited to sitting outside on the decks of restaurants and cafes than in late Spring in most of the places where a lot of those non-local folks may have come from: the Chicago's, Milwaukee's, New York's, and Fargo's of the world. The humidity hadn't yet come in a distractible fraction of its full force yet, and the mosquitoes were mostly advance scouts, not the Chinese in-fantry of August.

I had been out earlier with a few colleagues. We had stopped by Café Adobe after work and had been glad to get a table outside on the roof-top deck, big enough for the five of us that met initially, and to be able to squeeze in chairs for three more that joined us about an hour and three margaritas later. We had watched an adequate and relaxing, if not awe-inspiring, sunset over the roof of the school across the street. We had already drank and continued to drink enough marg's to prompt what we at least perceived as significant conversation: some work related stuff initially, including not too cruel of comments about co-workers and the usual philosophy of life stuff that only bars and the outdoors can foster. We had eaten that quantity of tortilla chips and salsa that was enough to maintain your basal metabolic rate for about a week but still somehow made you hungry enough to order substantial appetizers (mostly in various nacho forms) that could probably carry a village or two another couple of weeks, but stopped short of ordering any real dinner. This particular right after work situation always seems to leave at least me wondering later if one is supposed to eat again or not, probably by convention more than anything else, as in theory I should have been full till Tuesday. We drank and conversed to that point where some of us, mostly me I suppose, wanted to continue, but the more practical, like the married ones with waiting wives and kids at home and/or those wanting some semblance of functionality at work tomorrow, wanted to go on home.

I was restless. Thursday night always seemed to me like the best night to go out….late…and do things at potential extremes. After all, the next day was Friday. Anyone could get through one day of work feeling tired, or feeling like shit, or both. Plus, a lot of people left work early on Friday. It seemed moderately tolerated if one really had to do it. And if you really were feeling so bad that you had not been that productive, you could always go to sleep early Friday night, and work to catch up on Saturday. Plus, if you had a REALLY good Thursday night, you might even feel energized by the aftermath to burn especially brightly for the hours you would be at work on Friday. There was also the fact that wherever you may be having such a night, not uncommonly a series of such places, would not have the crowds one typically had to bludgeon through on a Friday or Saturday night to have even a fraction of the same experience, assuming especially if you brought at least some of your own company.

Clearly, I didn't adhere to this or recommend this calendar-based debauch policy on a regular basis. But, I'm pretty sure I had advocated it with what my ethanol bathed neurons perceived as eloquent logic to my colleagues earlier this evening, to no avail. I wasn't anywhere near that stage of 'I'll find some fun (or trouble) no matter what and all by myself,' mostly just disappointed, I guess, that I wasn't going to have any further cooperation in getting there. And so, I too, went home, or thought about it. I had intended to call Kim later in the evening, but as I passed my house, I didn't feel up to it just yet. I felt like walking, and so naturally I went to the park. I would have to be content with my own company, at least for awhile, sitting on the bench and staring into space hidden by the light pollution of 5 million people.

However, as if sensing a kindred spirit, Carl stopped by, maybe shortly after nine. He was on his way home from work, apparently working the late shift. We made some small talk, commenting on the pleasantness of the weather. I told him I had been just wasting time drinking with some friends the last few hours, maybe to throw out the triggering protoplasm for some subtly stated criticism for the wasting of time and/or health, or maybe to indicate to him that I indeed had friends other than he and the other weirdoes of the park. Instead, he just briefly acknowledged that it seemed like a good night for that sort of thing, and I silently found myself wondering when was the last time that I had actually drank with just friends, true-friends, and not just convenient co-workers whom, after all, you didn't often want to share too much personal stuff with anyway.

While we sat there for a few more moments in comfortable silence, maybe letting our days go into some sort of natural buffer that existed here despite the surrounding close by density of so many other humans, humans with needs; physical needs, medical needs, emotional needs, some obvious, some never stated, Curtis began to slowly appear against the blended urban darkness and the pale lights from various sources which never let the former grow to completeness. It was as if he were a ghost, and I only gradually recognized him in his increasingly crisp silhouette by the sheer thinness of his apparition and the faint residual hint of his characteristic light-hearted walk framing the slow gait and limp of a fading man ravaged by a horrible disease.

"Good evening ladies," he smilingly greeted us when he finally made it to the bench. "What brings you two out this evening?"

"Carl heard it was a good place to get laid," I responded trying to keep the mood elevated above what Curtis's appearance might otherwise support.

"You mean it's not!" Carl cooperated.

"No," Curtis pondered out-loud, with already what seemed like reduced energy, "sadly, that's the one thing it's never become."

Despite the borderline tragic tone, obviously he was still kidding, which I thought was a good sign.

He sat between us, now all three of us closely beside each other on the same bench, a strange formation for even a partial representation of the group to take.

We were like three little earthly primates, sitting in a row: "See No Evil, Hear No Evil, Speak No Evil," trying to live up to our proverbial pledges in the cesspool of humanity, except I was indeed about to commit evil that very night. In a world where free choice may indeed divine us, I was about to be a bad little monkey. With full knowledge of the virtues that I should be living by, the full ethics that I had heretofore been and always should be working by, with having pondered the line I was about to cross and knowing the irreversibility of my decision and the Raskolnikovian state it may put me in, I had within my bulging pocket the likely underlying summons for why I had needed the calming effects of colleagues and alcohol earlier and the real reason why I had come to the park, just on a hunch that I would see Curtis on the one night I had resolved myself towards actions still impending, actions I would likely not take, maybe even in the same exact circumstances, as many as ninety-nine times out of a hundred.

As if sensing the upcoming darkness, the blackness descending on a city and greater urban area whose skyscraper and refinery lights would never let wholly sleep, whose bedside lamps occasionally arising in the middle of the night to variably forestall sickness and death and nursing station work lights were warmly bulwarking against human entropy in the world's largest medical center just a few miles away, Carl excused himself, claiming the need to get home to have some dinner and to feed his cat.

Barely noticing that I didn't realize until then that Carl had a cat and registering how appropriate that was, as soon as he was out of sonar reach, Curtis and I began a conversation more personal, something I essentially heard as participating in outside of myself; something perhaps more analogous to medieval alchemic chanting.

"How have you been feeling lately?" I began, as if we were having clinic out in the park, at night.

"Same…maybe worse…I don't know, really. I mean, I have some bad days and some good days, it seems. But I don't really know how many of which… it's like, only when I'm having a somewhat good day, like now, do I come to realize that I've just had a series of apparently really bad days…like I'd forgotten to do some important things…or doing stupid things I didn't remember doing. I keep forgetting to pay some bills, and I had my power turned off. And then, my neighbor will ask me if I'm alright, 'cause he'd like seen and talked to me a couple days before and I'd guess I'd been…or seemed…like really confused to him…and I don't remember ever having met up with him…and, I think I'm having, like, a harder time walking…and stuff…and, it seems to me that I have a lot of diarrhea…sorry, but you are a doctor…and hey, you're my doctor, right? I'm breathing O.K. though, I'm pretty sure. I don't even want to talk about my skin though…Oh my God!"

"Are you working?" I continued to address some of the more practical matters.

"No, not for many weeks now...since I got fired from...," he tapered off, as if failing to recall the name of his former employer, but as if comprehending my implied concern for how he was getting by he added, "My Mom sends me a check every two weeks." Brief pause, as if more pondering the impact rather than searching for words, "She won't talk to me, won't forgive me for being gay, but still sends me money...like I'm still her baby...her kid, I guess."

We had been over this ground before, too familiar and too tragic a story for me to address, at least tonight. I was on a different, potentially tragic mission.

As if our brief conversation had confirmed my diagnosis and the proper prescription, I stood up and reached into my pocket, handing Curtis an unlabelled pill bottle, filled with about 120 tablets of the same drug we were properly testing in a trial of which he was not and never would be a formal part.

"Here," I said. "here's the drug, the drug you've been pestering me for...the one that COULD help with some of your mental and motor...you know, muscular weakness issues. It's the real thing, not a sugar pill. Don't expect miracles. We don't know that it works, like I've told you before. And, even if it does, it may just...stabilize you somewhat...you know, maybe help you from getting worse than you would otherwise. Like I said, don't expect miracles."

"You've just given me one...kind of...," he responded, looking up with a recognizable version of the old Curtis grin, supporting that this was indeed one of those "good days."

And for the completion of my rehearsed speech to accompany this transgression, like the pivotal scene in one of Leo's operas, I added, firmly, "And if you tell anyone about this, about the drug you're taking, and where you got it, I'll kill you much faster than AIDS...you hear me?"

He knew I was serious, without being completely literal.

"Yes Sir...Doctor, Sir."

I didn't sit back down. I couldn't remain in the scene where I had crossed myself. I told him I needed to get home, to call Kim, and to get some work done... the always available excuse, whether I actually intended to or not.

"Have a good night then," he called to my back, "...as good as you've given me," I heard him more softly add, against the barely audible rhythmic background of his gently shaking the bottle of pills.

Heavy thoughts on the brief walk home, heavy thoughts as I grabbed a beer out of the fridge, too heavy to call Kim just yet. Thank God for the two hour time zone difference. Again, I felt like I should break into one of those passionate soul searching Tenor "solos" or whatever they're called. Wasn't there an opera based on *Faust*, I seemed to recall from somewhere? Since I couldn't really sing, and certainly not in any language or tone worthy of my emotional state, I collapsed onto the sofa instead.

Can you ever cross the line just once? Can you ever just get one man facial, just one pedicure? Can you ever just do IV drugs, shoot heroin, just once? Can you ever cheat on your spouse just once or maybe just twice, by number of other individuals involved, not specific sexual episodes? Can you ever act potentially appropriately even if outside your nature, but maybe still within that wide spectrum of human just once, under a very unique set of circumstances, and not forever dwell in the bottoms in which you briefly immersed yourself?...not forever after calling up the demons that you were only briefly trotting amongst in the setting of a very specific, defendably virtuous quest, a type in which you maybe naively didn't want to ever involve yourself again during your daily life, which would hopefully never require your journey into the gray nether regions again?

XII

- Houston; June, 1994

About an hour after I got home from the park and my encounter with Curtis, I finally called Kim. Even with the two hour time difference, it was still late, and she had already gone to sleep. She had apparently tried to call me a couple of times earlier in the evening. Had I bothered to check my messages when I'd gotten in, I would have been in a better position to possibly deal with her resultant mood, or I would have not called until the next day, with a prepared excuse and a legitimate claim of not wanting to wake her.

The intended topic was a potentially sore enough spot already. We had been planning for a week or so to finally address some of the pragmatic aspects of yet another extension to her Seattle stay. My dark musings synergized with her frustrations with me and these grew upon the already underlying tension of our overall situation to make this particular conversation even more unpleasant than most of these seemingly increasingly familiar bad encounters to which I'd likely responded primarily with an unhealthy denial, or at best, procrastination.

My life over the last 12 or so years had become firmly regimented into the "Medical" fiscal year. We started everything in July and the year ended in June. Medical school starts in the summer, and each July (assuming passing grades) you instantly moved the next stage up in the progression; an MS-I became an MS-II, and so on, up to the MS-IV, in which case you may actually graduate in the end of May. You started your internship (first year of residency in either your final field, or as a prelude to a later specialty residency) on July 1, as a PGY-1 (first year post-graduate status). The next year you became a PGY-2, etc., either finishing in three years, such as in Internal Medicine or Pediatrics, or becoming a PGY-5 in Surgery, Pathology, etc. Fellowships, if engaged in after residency, started in July and ended in June with potential multiple years. We weren't on the same schedule as the regular January to December folks, and "summer vacations" disappeared back in college.

It was even common to start your first post-training real job, whether in academics or in private practice, in July. After all, that's when you finished training, so it was natural to start a job then. I started my job at Baylor in July. This was the natural order of things. Of course, for individuals further out of training and moving from one job to another, alternate start and finish months could in theory occur; although since a lot of initial jobs started in July, contracts in various multiples of years also tended to run until June.

It is also a natural human tendency to compartmentalize things into convenient fractions, even if they have no real practical value. For example, six months into one of the above periods, one may say something such as, "I'm halfway through my third year of medical school," or, "I'm halfway through my second year of Internal Medicine residency," in which case one could even extrapolate to "I'm half way through my residency." Years...beginning in July; then if necessary, six month fractions; under extreme conditions, perhaps, three month fractions, or "quarters," so to speak.

And so, I guess I naturally envisioned Kim's temporary status in Seattle in these engrained calendric terms. Kim's initial agreement with GeoDyne and Edith's firm was for her to spend six months in Seattle. We would visit frequently, and when she moved to Houston, I'd be half-way through my first year as an attending. Then when things weren't quite ready for her to pass the full load of her efforts to other associates, she agreed, with my "blessing" of course, as we were still married, to a three month extension, a quarter, which would hopefully be adequate. In part, I suspected, because she was so valuable regardless of the pace of skill acquisition by her intended replacements, she was strongly encouraged and well compensated to extend her on-site work another three months. With the service she was providing to Immugen and the value of some of those approaches spreading to other parts of the Geo-Dyne corporation, I'm sure whomever was responsible for interaction with her in these matters probably cared more about his or her job and his or her relationship to those above him or her than the potential impact of three more months of separation on a marriage that had already survived or suffered nine months of physical separation. I suppose we all get a bit of tunnel vision and have a tendency to look out for ourselves and do what's best for us, even to the point of presenting things to colleagues, such as theoretically temporary job extensions, in a manner in which they are most likely to see things our way and agree, even to the point of forcing relative value assessments and decisions with personal implications.

But the April, May, June quarter had seemed to finally make a nice stopping point; one medical fiscal year. I would be a second year attending, having survived, well, the critical first year, for which most initial contracts have some kind of satisfactory renewal clause. But now, another proposed one month extension, and hence opening the door for a possible series of further at least monthly extensions, was fucking up more than my fiscal universe. Problem was, and I always worried about this, that Kim was just too damn good at her job, just like she was at everything she did.

So, tonight's conversation was supposed to address the financial and other aspects related to this latest modification of plans. The most recent and scary twist was even potentially abandoning her current apartment, the manager of which had again eagerly agreed to a month by month rental arrangement, to potentially moving into part of the house of a female (at least it was a female) co-worker, located out on Bainbridge Island. It seemed this wasn't like occupying a bedroom, sharing the kitchen arrangement, but more officially using a finished off separate living apartment within a large house in, of course, a very charming area of the world. This, to me, also smacked of a potentially more than 4 week arrangement, and seemed part of a web further ensnaring Kim into a larger role with GeoDyne, one which I'm sure they would be eager to commit to a permanent arrangement from their end. This particular residence consideration was far from resolved, as Kim was also, and probably even more strongly, feeling the strain of our separation. This was just one of the "issues" we were going to begin to address in tonight's call, with the plan to "finalize" the latest round of life modifications on my upcoming planned trip to see Kim in Seattle.

With the weird mood I was already in after the Curtis "episode" and the foul mood that I had inflicted on Kim by missing her calls and calling her then so late, the timing may not have been best to begin hashing out such things in much detail. It may have been a mixture of feelings from my strange night, but after our consequently brief and foul-toned conversation, I had an ill-defined underlying dread that I hoped would somehow disappear during the night, or at least in time for my trip to Seattle in a couple of weeks.

XIII

- Houston; June, 1994

One of the Neurology residents paged me in the early afternoon the last Tuesday of the month. One of the patients from my clinic had been admitted to the County Hospital. Our resident had been contacted from the Internal Medicine service, the house staff of which must have noted that the admit was being followed by me in clinic and thought either through courtesy or avoidance of having to address any accompanying neuro issues in detail or in the spirit of a teaching hospital, they would get Neuro involved. I wasn't the Neurology attending covering consults that day, but our resident knew me well enough to know that I'd want to see any patient I was normally following, and the Neurologist faculty who was on that week was of the nature that he wouldn't care or be insulted. No doubt, he had plenty of other work to do. It was during the day. I was over in the lab. I was just a block, three hallways, and a long tunnel from the hospital.

I finished setting up an experiment that I was working on with one of our most senior lab techs, and headed over to Ben Taub about 45 minutes later, grabbing a pre-made sandwich from the little deli in the lobby of the Neurosensory Center and scarfing it down with some sort of tea-like beverage on the way over.

It was Curtis. I hadn't seen or heard anything of him in about two and a half weeks, since that last night in the park, when he seemed to be doing a little better. He had been found apparently delirious in his apartment by a friend whom he was supposed to meet that morning, who knows what for, as traditionally morning and Curtis didn't mix. He was suffering from diarrhea (based on the description of his clothes, sofa, and surroundings according to his friend), was very weak, and dehydration had been a major acute culprit given his improved lucidity after a few bags of IV fluids that had made it in O.K. by the time I saw him.

After talking with him a bit about how he'd been feeling recently, I did a consult level neuro exam, about the depth of a follow-up visit, as I'd seen him in clinic several times relatively recently. He gave me a little shit during something like a mini-mental status exam, which was actually a good sign, indicating at least some orientation if nothing else. For the first time, I thought I noticed a little bit of asymmetry in his extremity weakness, more so in his arms, with his left upper arm and wrist flexion weaker than his right. Parallel relative deficits in sensation weren't as obvious, but I still ordered a CT scan, in theory to rule out any focal lesions, such as CNS toxoplasmosis or brain lymphoma, conditions common in AIDS patients. I hadn't been tempted to do this before during any of his work-up or follow-up visits, as I hadn't noted any focal signs on his neuro exams. I had never seen any indications for a lumbar puncture either. He wasn't in our clinical trial, so there hadn't been any trial driven need to obtain a CSF sample, and hence no need even from that perspective to get brain imaging before lumbar puncture (which we weren't doing routinely even in our trial patients, and only if there was a suggestion of focality on their entry or any later neuro exam).

I think I had an appropriately low threshold for ruling out mass lesions of the brain in the patients we worked up according to the trial protocol. Our trial called for obtaining CSF fluid whenever possible. In more than theory, if someone had a mass lesion in the brain that increased pressure inside the very tight confines of the cranium and one did a lumbar puncture, acutely lowering the pressure below the brain, one could cause brain herniation through the foramen magnum of the skull and essentially instant death, not looked upon favorably by family, lawyers, and grant funders alike. Careful neuro exams, especially, and certain aspects of the history of a patient could suggest increased likelihood of these other more focal brain complications of AIDS. We didn't routinely do CT scans, or especially more expensive and newer technology based MRIs, on patients we were enrolling in the trial. ADC could certainly be associated with some imaging detectable brain atrophy, but there was no provision in the trial for doing initial or follow-up brain imaging, as this would be prohibitively expensive and there was as yet no clear relationship between imaging findings and those on more likely clinically relevant neurology examination and neuropsychiatric testing, and we wouldn't have necessarily expected correlation with imaging studies and the novel parameters we were following on a research basis.

If I had any reason to suspect a low (more like, even remote) chance of a focal brain lesion in a patient I was considering enrolling on our trial, I had every legitimate basis for ordering brain imaging on a sound clinical basis. Insurance or the county could choose to pay for it or not based on all those policy aspects that continue to baffle me on a daily basis. If I had to guess, I bet it was for way less than 15 % of the patients we ended up enrolling in our trial. I, or my residents with my blessing and supervision, had done lumbar punctures on more than 200 patients for the trial as of this time without any major side effects, so I guess we knew what we were doing.

Since the Neurology services' consultation on Curtis's in-house admission was an official consult, my evaluation was entered on a proper consult note in his chart. This would miraculously translate to someone in some office somewhere issuing a bill for my time and expertise to an entity somewhere that would receive it with typical insurance company enthusiasm, if indeed Curtis still had or ever did have insurance, or some bookkeeping office that would generate paperwork that would plug into the great county budget machine and fit into a human mind defying formula that would somehow translate, along with input from a maze of other state and private factors related to the Baylor empire, into things as complex as how many residents we could support year in and year out or how much office and lab space we may be allocated vs. a dozen or more other departments.

Without necessarily elucidating all the mysteries of the health care cost universe, I figured while I had Curtis in the hospital and with his current findings, I may as well get a CT scan of his brain. When I explained the procedure to Curtis, he wryly responded that he'd be O.K. with any test that he got to stick his head into a hole of any sort. I then explained to him that I didn't know how many days he'd have to be in the hospital, that we weren't sure what was going on, especially regarding his GI tract, but that I had to go to Seattle for a few days, and I asked if he'd be all right.

"I'll be fine…if you'll just get the fuck out of here and leave me alone," he bravely responded, again increasing my sense that he was indeed O.K. with it.

"You sure?"

"You need to see Kim, you dumb ass…speaking of holes and heads and all that romantic medical stuff."

I must have drifted a bit, staring out the window, past Curtis's bed, thinking about Kim, my future, a million little things and maybe another million that seemed not so little.

"Plus," he continued, shaking me out of my brief coma, "there's this really cute nurse on the floor. He's been in here a couple of times. Dark, but not Hispanic, I think he may be Italian or from the Middle East. Maybe you can use your influence, and get him to give me a sponge bath or something."

"I'll see what I can do," I weakly smiled. Then in more professional doctor speak, I got momentarily more serious and offered up, "You're going to get better in here. You have a good team of doctors taking care of you."

I'm not sure he was convinced, or should have been, but he consoled me with, "At least my brain is better…thanks to your drug."

I glanced around the room, noting we were still alone.

"What makes you think it's working?" I allowed myself to respond.

"Just think how much worse I'd be if I wasn't taking it," he said with sincere authority.

What could I say?

We sat there in silence for a few minutes.

"How's the food?" I tried to brightly offer up, despite having suffered through probably the better versions of that which made it to the hospital cafeteria, changing the subject to something else I equally had little control over.

"I don't know. I think it's mostly been ice chips and a little crappy jello so far."

"How about a veggie sandwich with precisely 17 sprouts?" I asked.

"Ah," he smiled weakly. "You please the gonads of my soul."

XIV

- Houston; June, 1994

On a relatively humid night in late June, the night after Curtis had been admitted to Ben Taub, Kim and I had had a bit of a fight on the phone when I called her after work. She wanted me to move my trip up a week and come up to Seattle the upcoming weekend, on a bit of a last minute notice. She would have "gladly" come down to Houston, but had something early Saturday morning that she supposedly couldn't get out of and that wouldn't take that long, whereas my apparent work desires for the upcoming weekend were less rigidly scheduled.

She seemed to really want to see me sooner than already planned, expressing a sense of urgency in her voice more than the words conveyed. It somehow reminded me of that fatal conversation, that fateful turning point at which without concretely stating it, we had decided we would go our presumably temporary separate ways, out of acute pragmatism of two professionals faced with early branching points of their careers, presuming, without stating overtly, that it was nothing that could interfere with our "relationship," a phrase that seemed simultaneously to capture the sense of new romance lost but still potentially available and the recognition of a status that real world issues filtered through the ego superimposed on maybe more basic human cravings.

On the phone, during those minutes, those fleeting minusculely small percentages of the overall experience of breathing while on this planet, I passed through an agonizing sense of despair, of some sort of promise losable, and after announcing that my travel and other plans were already set, entered an immensely awkward sense of awareness perceived as something monstrously won, something familiar, yet putrid. Out of panic of almost recognition of the latter, I caved, and promised Kim that I would make flight reservations in the morning, feeling her relief on the other side as some sort of black confrontation to the confusion that was swelling inside me like a boil, ready to rupture out of my lungs and unleash an epidemic on the greater urban area of Houston and who knows where from there. At the same time, lancing myself seemed like it may provide the catharsis for what I wanted more than anything: to give up, for just a minute, for just a second, for just a millisecond, and leave myself completely up to the forces that I couldn't control; that I didn't have to study for, that I didn't have to organize, that I didn't have to learn about, that I could somehow immerse myself in...and who knows how I would re-surface. But, we reach a near breaking point, those of us who cannot break, who will not break by nature, and it is the fear of how we will re-surface or whether we'll resurface at all, that held me back just enough.

I carried the residue of these emotions around that evening, some sort of premature hangover way more than enzymatically and historically justified than the two bottles of wine with which I had numbed my after phone conversation feelings, while listening to two of the other three Leo CDs I'd not yet opened. These sentiments were brewing a major internal funk, lurking under the surface like a mythical giant serpent monster in the fog-covered lake separated by a peat moss soured bog from the nearby frightened village. This after seeing Curtis, a pathetic fragment of his former self, closer to dying than anyone his age should be, no matter when the inevitable exact time would come. I was tired of time; trying to fit everything within time. Despite my moderately civil and professional interactions with lab staff, hospital staff, patients and even Curtis that day, the underlying issues were metamorphosizing into an otherworldly funk. It grew, silently, and without approaching myself in any healthy manner, instead, I let it simmer. The fog over the ancient lake was thickening, and the water holding the virally mutated dragon-serpent- hybrid was beginning to boil. What a pleasant human being I must have been, pacing around my living room.

Of the three actions I pondered, I chose the likely least dangerous and regrettable one and walked over to the park. It was still not that late, and despite the unexpected sauna like conditions, Carl was already there, my likely lowest threshold for increased irritability, sitting on our bench and reading in the fading light what looked like probably some sort of classic given the old leather binding. I didn't want to disturb him, as anything I would say at that moment would likely be below juvenile, and despite everything else broiling in my marrow, I, in a clutching definition of myself, respected the fact that he could be such a serious reader. But then again, there's a limit even to how much unrelieved angst I can absorb, even though now I was in a somehow more tangible raunchy mood. Thus, I went over and sat down on the bench, and let out a big sigh that likely few could read through.

With a somewhat frustrating unexpected lack of any signs of annoyance, he quietly placed his bookmark where he was and softly shut his book.

"How are you this evening Doctor Sir?" he then further frustratingly politely inquired.

"I've had better days, I suppose. How about you?" And to additionally indicate that I could probably care less at the moment, I quickly added, "Sorry to interrupt your reading."

"It's no problem at all," he continued in a soft tone that I probably inappropriately judged as martyrdom and that made me want to rip his bulging Adams Apple out of his skinny chicken neck. "I was at a good stopping point."

Too bad, I thought, as I sat there on the far left hand side of the bench (the left one) from his already comfortably entrenched seat on the far right side. We sat there in mutual silence for a few moments. I had already decided that I wasn't going to speak first, unless Carl tried to start reading again.

And now as if a meeting had been called, we both looked up from our bench and saw Leo slowly walking towards us. His broad grinning smile, that we could detect from what must have been fifty feet away, added to background peevish vexation. I thought for a minute, *what the fuck are you smiling about you frizzled-up crazy old sack of schizo dung?*

But then as he reached out and shook my hand and sat on the bench between Carl and myself, putting him in the middle of perhaps a little too much man closeness given the essentially empty park, I felt a softening. Maybe the company of moderately unquestioning friends, as weird as they were, had already brought me down to just drowning kittens from the earlier enter the Post Office with an Uzi mode. But I was far from safe company at this point.

In appropriate caution for the darkness I must have been radiating to even those with old model emotion sensors, we started out with small talk.

"It's pretty steamy out here tonight," I pathetically proffered up to my companions, alluding in part to the weather.

"Yeah, hot as a witch's titty," Leo responded thoughtfully.

I couldn't help but smile and chuckle inside. Carl was about to correct him, but I stopped him with a quick glance to my right and a faster draw on the response.

"Hot as two witches' titties for this time of year, my astute friend," I seriously replied.

While Leo shook his head in support of my slight weather observation modification, Carl said with almost appreciably mock chagrin, "Well, you two must know different types of witches than the rest of us."

"Oh, I've know some witches in my time, I believe. What about you Leo?" I quickly decided to continue on with.

"Six of them," Leo said without pausing, and I celebrated the definitiveness of his answer with a restrained and respectful laugh, as whether accurately founded or not, few of us, especially with decades of Phenothiazine mind numbing on top of whatever mysterious combinations of nature and nurture mingled to produce his initial disease, could have been so strong in our coven recollections.

We switched back to even smaller small talk, until a few moments later when we collectively noted Rick's car parallel parking on the side street to the right of us, foretelling his momentarily joining us.

Carl made some comment to the effect that he didn't know it was a holiday and that all of the skank bars must be closed.

Before I could think of the appropriate response, something slightly less than fatal to ongoing interactions, Rick had already begun to make his way over, carting a six pack of bottled beers, one of which was already in his hand, supporting that he had just picked them up on his way home, which must have been interrupted by driving by and seeing an essential caucus.

As Rick got to within a couple of feet of us, Leo, as if studying him in the last few moments, announced, "You're not supposed to have bottles in the park."

Without pausing, with the quickness of cheap courtroom drama, he blurted out the logical reply of, "You're not supposed to masturbate, either, but I bet you three choke your chicken every night."

Not one of us could come up with an adequate reply quicker than a moderate pondering delay, at which point Leo diligently replied, "We had chicken last night."

"See, my case supported," Rick brought this phase of Mental Olympics to completion, as he sat down on the ground in front of us, with typical lack of regard for any eventuated effects on his work clothes, and began to open and distribute beers.

I wasn't sure I wanted to be in a non bad mood yet, and at the same time wanted to move on past small talk. In order to provoke at least more serious conversation, I decided I would bring up the fact that Leo and 'Ms Valery' were married. I felt that such major personal facts of one another were appropriate for the nature of our apparent relationships, and certainly didn't think I would be betraying Leo in any way for disclosing this tidbit that maybe his condition had otherwise allowed escape from the usual social norms of fundamental information sharing as appropriate to the nature of friendships.

"Did you guys know that Leo and this 'Ms. Valery' were actually married?" I uttered out loud to no one in particular.

"No shit!" Rick screamed to the group, and then turning more directly to Leo, "You go man," as if parallel to the newness of the news, this was an acute or recent development, implying, as it were, that Leo was joining the ranks of the currently getting laid on a steady basis, a fundamental aim (The fundamental Aim) of all male directed activities, activities like even agreeing to marry your landlady under conditions that mattered little compared to the actualized sexual benefit.

As if being called into the scene to support all things related to family, Frank entered the park from behind us (the natural direction from his house location but still presupposing a small fence climb, which he was probably relieved that none of us had witnessed). To bring Frank up to speed (in reference to this particular point at least), Rick repeated the announcement informing of Leo's marital status. Frank appeared to be startled, as evidenced by the surprised look he often gave us when either confused, offended, or both, and which could have in this case been prompted by the pondering of whether Rick was being serious or not. He offered no verbal response to further clarify his take on this unexpected factual information.

"Yes," Carl acknowledged. "The Capressi's were married even before they came to America," implying not only that he had known (for who knows how long) that Leo and Mrs. Leo were husband and wife, but that he knew their last name and a bit of their past (at least residential) history.

For some reason, I was increasingly distempered by Carl's then subsequent brief account of the somewhat tragic tale of Leo's romance. Maybe I was equally or more pissed that he knew some or maybe even all of the details that Leo's wife had communicated to me that night. After all, hadn't we been having conversations in this park for almost a year? Hadn't there been times (I would have thought there may have been times) that we were out here without Leo, in which this could have been brought up somehow? Or, hell, even if Leo were here, how could discussions been had so many times during which this little detail might have been introduced by Carl somehow? Did not even passing comments regarding "*Ms.* Valery" ever get made in which an opportunity could have been taken to clarify the true nature of their relationship? How long had Carl known even just this LITTLE fact, of which I assume that none of the rest of us was aware? It is as if, parallel with my general impression that he was one of those haughty folks who continually judged others, Carl had analyzed me and felt me unworthy of such knowledge. Or maybe, just maybe, I thought we were friends, and I somehow felt hurt…or confused.

And so, whether consciously or sub-consciously, Carl further transformed into the target of my proximate, potentially long suppressed ire against all things not pleasing me to 100% of my expectations, my wishes, my desires, 100% of the time, especially over the last several months. And so, as a first emotionally juvenile salvo, I turned to directly face Carl, and I sternly asked him if he'd ever been in love.

"Define love," he replied, quickly and firmly that it was as if he had been anticipating the question or had the response planned for years, in an immediately retrievable memory bank, should the input prompting it ever arise.

There was a subsequent longer silence amongst the group.

Then, more softly than I would have predicted given the usual strength of his conviction, at least on a matter such as this, Frank finally offered up: "How about spending most of your adult life with another person, raising children together?"

"That could be just habit," Carl quickly noted, flicking it aside like King Kong swatting at a swarm of tiny ineffective airplanes.

"So, now, you mock loyalty?" I stabbed out.

"Are you saying that my wife and I are not...or have not been...in love?" Frank quipped, even as Carl had already been opening his mouth to respond to me, since I had hit my buzzer first.

Without even changing the motion of his mouth or the emotion in his face, he modified his next lightning bolt to address both merely mortal inquiries.

"I admire loyalty," he uttered, facing me. "And," as he turned towards Frank, "I'm not saying that you and your wife are not in love. I'm just simply stating that, to me, that is not an acceptable definition of love."

Rick nodded towards Leo, and added to Frank's definition, as if modifying one that was already out there were easier than searching our deeper selves for something new but potentially more satisfying.

"What about staying your whole life with someone who's crazy?"

Fortunately it did not appear Leo noticed that we were incorporating mocking of him into our debate.

"Extreme loyalty for sure," Carl allowed, "and love, which we've yet to catch the exact essence of, may indeed have been involved."

My expanding animosity towards Carl refused to allow me to participate in this momentary exercise any longer, as if we were quizzed poetry students who had yet to capture and convey the "essence" of a poem to our growingly condescending Professor's satisfaction. I decided to skip the rest of the philosophical definition game, and shift the orientation of this going nowhere inquiry back to the target I had initially intended. Again I turned directly towards Carl and with what I hoped was a piercing glare, I then asked him:

"Has anyone ever cared, or thought they cared, so much about you that they couldn't live without you?"

His silence, his catching my stare, and holding it without responding made me think that alas, unexpectedly, I'd hit on at least an aspect we'd all agree upon was crucial to love, even him. What seemed like the faintest hint of a tear welling up in his eyes made me realize that I may have, and now regrettably, nicked my shovel in the dirt of Carl on something even deeper for him.

"I used to be a College Literature Professor," he softly started. "Here in Houston." Then after a brief pause, "I had been a graduate assistant, lecturing for Intro level classes for a few years, then staying on, and teaching...at a higher level, more focused courses…in smaller groups, while doing or attempting the writing that was expected of me as a faculty member."

Carl had never revealed so many personal facts…at least not in this park setting, not to my knowledge. The group was speechless, and uniquely attentive, in some sort of combination of curiosity and respect. In another seemingly unprecedented act, he came around from his usual standing position behind the bench Frank was sitting on, and sat down on the same right sided bench. After seeming to reflect and shape his thoughts, he continued, in a tone that seemed to threaten the ushering in of some impending sadness.

"Anyway…I had a student…Anna, in my Fall English Novel Class. It was a small class, maybe only 12 or 15 students. She was only 19, shy in public but intensely reflective. We began to spend a lot of time together. We would discuss the novels we were covering in class, but even more so, talk about other books, books far from the standard curriculum that we both loved to read. She would read what I was writing, and said that she loved it…all of it. I read what she wrote, both as a Professor…like reading assignments, and as a growing confidante, reading things written outside the boundaries of the classroom."

He seemed to begin having difficulties continuing but he proceeded, albeit hesitantly, as if approaching a potentially convulsing therapeutic endeavor. Frank placed his right hand on Carl's left shoulder, imparting the fragment of missing human support necessary for going on.

"She enrolled in my Spring course, focusing on certain classic American novels of the Early 20th century…and the time we were spending together was growing. She told me, once, without my knowing how to respond, that she loved me. She wrote it far more times."

He took a deep breath, while extending his head and neck upward, arching his face temporarily towards the night, as in ritual tribute to the darkness, the keeper of potentially inappropriate relationships.

"I didn't know what love was," he offered as if responding to Anna as well as us. "All I knew of love was what I'd read in books, in poems…all my life. But, I didn't think it was a good idea for me to try to understand my feelings towards her or especially try to convey them to her…under the circumstances."

A few of us nodded, following his thoughts as his decision to carry on his tale appeared to be gaining momentum.

"Anyway…it didn't matter. Turns out, and I knew this already of course, that her father was on The Board of Trustees. Word somehow got around to him, implying the inappropriate relationship of his little girl with one of her teachers. Without any exploration of potentially uncomfortable details, the Department Chairman, with the support of The Board, strongly encouraged my resignation… immediate resignation."

A few eyes widened, with brows lifted in unison, evident even in the moonlight, and expressing our surprise at the level of punishment imparted to our friend, our Park companion.

"As per other implied conditions…and maybe because I thought this was the wisest solution as well…I never spoke to Anna again…never answered her… heart-felt letters."

It would have appeared that this sad story was over from Carl's point of view, as he rubbed both palms along their corresponding legs while straightening his back up a bit, and taking an accompanying deep breath.

"What ever happened to her, do you know?" Rick, perhaps in lawyer mind set, finally broke the brief following silence.

Carl responded, with his face towards the ground, but in a voice just sufficient for all to hear, "She committed suicide that next summer."

None of us knew what to say. What could we say? We sat there, first shocked, then saddened, then in the state of absence tending towards utter disconnect, the feeling we always try so hard to avoid in our daily lives, which Carl had brought up from the depths and implanted on our consciousnesses. I had opened a can of worms that now I wish I'd never even taken out of the pantry. It didn't matter whether Carl had admitted to us his loving her in return. It was clear that this had condemned him to his self-imposed book lined monastic solitude and its sanity- preserving protection, never to open his fragile self to such potential danger again.

Finally, maybe as a Pavlovian utterance deeply ingrained from so many counseling sessions he'd likely endured on the very subject in the lifetime ebb and flow of his condition, but equally in the inappropriateness that only mental illness and/or its medications could allow, Leo pronounced to the group, "You shouldn't commit suicide."

In a sheer, maybe equally reflexive black response, the kind I'd always imagined him capable of (just based largely on unwarranted impressions possibly), but now which I understood the complete unforgiving hole from which it justifiably issued, Carl lashed back "You shouldn't go insane either."

I'm not sure that Leo even registered that he was referring directly to him.

I just got up and turned to walk away, saying, as if in a cautionary statement to myself or anyone else in the cosmos that may be hopefully capable of truly absorbing it and acting to make a difference, "Maybe neither."

As I walked away, I could hear in the fading background, Leo asking "What got into his britches?"

And Rick's response, "I think he's going home to make a phone call to someone he can't live without."

...

After I had exited the park and made it halfway down the block, I thought I could see Carl again turning his head heaven-ward, his face extending as high as he could stretch it, bent at almost 90 % to his neck, where his bulging Adam's Apple made a haunting and seemingly hopeless silhouette against the full moon, like the dark image of a witch flying by, and in the silent depths of my soul, our collective unconscious as some of my colleagues might describe it, I thought I heard him howl: the howl of the damned, the howl of the irreversible, the howl of despair. I paused, putting my face in my hands, letting a small fraction of the possible and deserved tears come, the tears for every mistake, every faulty move of all men, from all time, which we somehow seem to share. And I silently joined Carl in his howl, his primitive but hopeless outcry to eternity, turning it inward to far greater effect than waking the neighborhood.

XV

- *Seattle; Late June, 1994*

Was it Aristotle, Harry Truman, or the inventor of Ex-Lax® who first proclaimed time to "shit or get off the pot?"

I was in Seattle over the weekend as requested by Kim and as desperately yearned for by me, but not without some sense of dread. It was essentially a year since Kim and I had physically separated to pursue a temporary diversion in what had seemingly developed into a poorly defined long term plan. I had arrogantly assumed that she would join me in Houston, given the presumed nature of my position and the theoretically mutually decided short term deal of her initial arrangement. Maybe both of us realized that her job, given her obvious skill and talent level, could evolve into an equally long term job if desired. For sanity and at least temporary marriage salvaging, this hadn't been majorly brought up, or at least not discussed in any battleground details at the time of the climax of our unrest; a process which I now realize had been evolving over many months, if not longer, before we went in kind of our separated ways last June. Maybe I knew it then, but in some default auto-protection mode I ignored it at the time, expecting that as always my forever on and never derailed rationality would win in the end. There would be heavy conversations this weekend. They were inevitable. They were lurking in the background of our initial kisses and hugs, like an upcoming trial while out on bail, like trying to relax on a Saturday evening when you knew you had a big test on Monday, and you would have to be "cramming" all the next day, and both the upcoming torturous study session and the dread of the test itself were occasionally creeping into your thoughts, putting a not too infrequent damper on the fun you were trying to have in the meantime.

But as always, or maybe almost always, when Kim and I were together, something else took over. Despite the years of familiarity and that most of the last one had been spent together only relatively sparsely, we just always seemed to evolve into being together, having fun, enjoying each other's company, and pretty soon forgetting about everything else. Clearly, whether consciously or otherwise, we had both decided to put the heavy conversations on hold, and shortly after my arrival Friday afternoon, we were sitting outside on the waterfront, watching the ferry to Bainbridge Island and all the other gentle and occasional chaotic movements of the water on an absolutely glorious sunny, clear day, and eating "flights" of oysters with crisp white wine at a perfect location at a place called Elliot's.

I was fascinated to learn that there were so many different types of oysters, with supposedly unique and characteristic taste profiles, kind of like wines in fact. I couldn't quite decipher initially if they were indeed all different species, or if many were of the same species and named instead for where they lived and were harvested from, with different water areas supposedly imparting different flavors, sort of like wine appellations and "terroir," I guess.

Not knowing a damn thing about what any of them may taste like, but wanting to try lots of different ones to see if there really were detectable differences and to begin investigating which we may like best, I largely ordered them based on how much I liked their names, or particularly, what sort of sexual or other stupid comments I could make based on those names. For example, I told Kim that, "I'd certainly like to put my Bald Point in your Totten Inlet."

She played along, with responses, such as "Are you sure you don't want my Eld Inlet, instead?"

"No, I'm tired of the same Eld Inlet. I need some variety."

And, of course, I had to order some Olympic Miyagi's, so I could make really stupid Karate Kid references that our waiter didn't quite understand. Kim quickly got fed up with that to the point of telling me that if I didn't shut up with the Miyagi thing, I'd have to wax off all by myself later....

But, there can't possibly be a better name than Hama Hama, and for at least a week or two, I used this as my preferred Oyster name metaphor for all things resembling sexual interactions. We certainly also deferred in part to our waiter's suggestions, along with Kim's already gained experience during the various power lunches, after-work gatherings, and client dinners, all of which reminded me further of our apparent or actual separate lives. But rather than being a sensitive weenie about the latter, I opted to really try to detect the subtle and sometimes not so subtle flavor differences and the seemingly bizarrely described taste characteristics that our waiter discussed and that we could read on the menus matching the currently available mollusk collection. As a land based Central/South Texan, I could probably do a better job describing differences in steak cuts. Oysters were whatever came out of the Gulf, the varying sizes (and occasionally funky tastes) of which we probably subconsciously ascribed to mutating effects of all the refineries. We often buried the funky tastes with ridiculously ice-cold beers at Captain Bennies on Main Street south of the Texas Medical Center.

However, I could appreciate differences in salinity (it reminded me of issues of differences in laboratory buffers, not that I often helped myself to a swig during any experiments), and I'd eaten enough salads to appreciate the bizarreness of a "cucumber aftertaste." But, come on, how many times have I eaten seaweed, to make a truly valid comparison? I suppose there were many who had, intentionally or accidentally, in these parts. It was reminiscent of the often ungraspable components of a snooty wine tasting description. I don't think I'd ever eaten a currant, not sure I could even recognize one, yet that didn't seem too exotic. Fig paste was not a staple in my past (not even sure the inside of a Fig Newton, cookies I didn't particularly like, would qualify, as more likely generated by mysterious natural and artificial flavors), and I know for a scientific fact that I'd never eaten granite; and if I'd ever had tar, it was as a child, equivalent to eating paint or glue, none of which I remembered the flavor aspects of.

We had a very nice early evening, but after walking around the waterfront a bit, the dreaded serious talk, the inevitable heavy talk, the debates on our current and future life that did, after all, very much need to be addressed, began during a late light supper. Too intense for public display, crests got dampened only after a few heads at adjacent tables turned, not reaching complete and irreversible embarrassment stage, as all married couples know this degree is within the acceptable range when exerting the right to have personal talk anywhere. True couples don't usually exceed this to the level of human common area explosion (although the threshold can be alcohol lowered), knowing that no matter what, the date (sometimes unfortunately) can't just end when you at least temporarily cohabitate.

Despite a non-officially announced but mutually executed temporary cease fire during the seemingly much longer than usual drive back to Kim's apartment, it picked up again during the immediate change into pajamas, tooth brushing, face washing activities that suggested no chance of inserting a brief respite for usual romance of the physically separated. Oysters are supposed to be aphrodisiacs, but sometimes the potential biologic effects of even unknown compounds can't overcome their psychological vetoes. Sometimes there just aren't enough oysters…no Hama Hama.

…

Marital Cold Wars can survive a night of heated argument, especially when there's not been a critical heinous act committed by one or both, and which was way outside the acceptable boundaries; that is, especially when it's just another gradual dose of the under surface tensions. Husband and wife can sleep, as in the physical state of slowed mental activity interspersed with REM, together in the same bed after such occurrences, the degree of which is still under the sofa or hotel threshold. There are even different levels of acceptable touching during the night: from the middle of the night "I'm sorry" sudden passionate kissing and feverish, typically missionary style sex (allowing for healing soft kissing and comments); to holding, an acknowledgement of solidarity without spoken words; to slight hand overlap and foot touching; all the way to instantaneous reflexive withdraw of any portion of the accidentally contacted partner in even glancing brushes. This night was somewhere between the middle and low end of the spectrum, and I lay there for several hours thinking about the things I had thought about on the plane, edges of which were shadowed in tonight's heated discussions, but from which I hoped we would both still hold back and not completely allow ourselves to cave.

And then just a couple hours after I'd finally been physiologically conquered into a mentally and emotionally exhausted sleep, the phone rang at a ridiculous time in the morning. I assumed it was for Kim. No one would be calling me while I was on "vacation," at a phone number that nobody had, even at just Pacific early time.

Knowing that it could in no way have anything to do with me, and not suspecting anything suspicious related to a call for Kim, I logically and now without challenge nodded back off.

"It's for you," Kim surrealistically indicated while gently rubbing me on my shoulder, as I'd turned my back to her to secure at least a few hours more of sleep.

"You're kidding," I barely heard myself say, but stirring adequately and turning slightly to weakly grasp the phone in that sort of on-call jerk-reflex mode.

"Jeff…it's Carl…," I barely heard from the other end..

Carl…Carl?…Park Carl?…How the fuck did he know I was naked…and was in bed?…I didn't even have sex, I transcendentally thought while trying to shake the night, the dreams, the distance out of my head.

"I'm sorry to call you so early…" he vaguely continued.

I wasn't yet in response or even concrete perception mode, so there was a long pause, after which Carl finally added after clearing his throat: "Curtis is dead…I thought you might like to know."

"Dead…," I paused for a long time. "How is that possible?" I then added in stupid M.D. fashion, as if I couldn't possibly be out of town if one of the patients I was seeing, even if just on a consulting basis, was peri-terminal.

Carl didn't respond, as if adding the obvious response that he had terminal AIDS would be acknowledging the unpleasantness of my acute insanity.

I rescued him (maybe both of us) by quickly adding, "I mean…where did they find him…what happened?"

"His friend Ramón found him…at his place. He called the police, and then he saw my number and a few others, I guess. He called me. I was actually over there when the police and the ambulance were there," Carl continued in report like fashion.

"I see," I responded, for lack of anything more insightful in my current state. Kim was now looking at me, perplexed and concerned.

"I thought you might want to know," Carl had now warmed up, but still cautiously proceeded, and as if answering an obvious but still unasked question, he added, "I got your number…Kim's number you left…finally…from someone at the Neurology Department….I finally convinced them that you would want to know directly…personally…about this patient."

There was a pause. Kim graciously handed me a cup of coffee.

"Good job," again for want of anything more insightful…perhaps in admiration and appreciation of what I imagined could have been a fair amount of red-tape Carl had to overcome in order to track me down. And then in more professional speak, as I discerned might be appropriate for such an occasion, I inquired,

"What about his family?" (none of whom I'd ever even spoken to during the many months I'd been involved in his care).

"We're still trying to get a hold of them," he responded. Then after a few transition comments, we hung up.

…

Why had Ramón gone to Curtis's house (I thought they had broken up eons ago)? Why did Curtis have Carl's phone number so readily available? Why had Carl felt compelled to alert me to Curtis's passing while I was on vacation?.... These were just some of the more mundane questions passing through my mind as I sipped my coffee and watched Kim finish getting dressed.

Then my first more caffeinated thought, filtering through my human self-preserving head, was that I had to get back…get back to Houston right away. I even started trying to recall flight schedules that I had scrolled through a few times before.

Curtis was partly my patient. I had helped take care of him. I had failed him. And, I had "illegally" or at least "unethically" given him an investigational glutamate receptor antagonist to try to help him with the progressing mental aspects of his condition that were freaking him out the most, amongst the so many horrors of his rapidly deteriorating physical state.

The drug didn't hurt him, of course; who knows if it helped. It would always be hard to tell in any individual patient, and he wasn't actually enrolled in the trial anyway, so we weren't even monitoring his status as closely, or as thoroughly, or as frequently as we were for formally participating patients.

Then after I woke up even more, I had accelerated panic. Curtis died in his own house. The coroner and/or police may investigate. What if they found the bottle of tablets I had given him – a non-FDA approved drug given by a physician outside of any currently defined clinical indication and not part of a properly executed clinical trial enrollment? What could the implications be for me?

I needed to get back. How could I control anything: the health of my patients, the progress of my research, covering my ass, etc., if I wasn't there physically? Then, more rationally, as I accepted a refill of my coffee from my beautiful wife, who appeared to have slept better than I had, I reminded myself of several key facts related to the least truly significant aspect of my worries.

The bottle wasn't labeled and the pills I gave to Curtis were not inscribed in any way; they would not be identifiable on mere visual inspection, not even on intense inspection. AIDS patients typically had dozens of "over the counter" remedies, homeopathic potions, extracts from weird named plants, roots, and substances from all parts of the planet - late-20th century "snake oil" equivalents, none of them scientifically proven to be beneficial, ordered and purchased and consumed out of the frustration and despair of having essentially no discernibly better options.

Besides maybe one or two bottles of established drugs, such as AZT or Bactrim, for example, there would be in his medicine cabinet or out on his kitchen counter or who knows where, bottles of pills, tablets, capsules, and syrups and jars of strangely colored maybe foul smelling liquids and powders that may or may not be labeled with strange names and promising unjustified descriptions. Curtis had advanced AIDS; it would be known or quickly deciphered by anyone assigned to the task of confirming his inevitable death. No one would care about any bottles of open or unopened medicines or remedies. Unless there was an open and emptied bottle that could have contained hundreds of benzodiazepines, such as Valium, or other potentially suitable suicide weapons, his death would be ruled as something like "respiratory distress and/or cardiac arrest secondary to dehydration complicating advanced AIDS/HIV infection." There'd likely be no real autopsy at the M.E.'s office given this commonly observed death mechanism and related scenarios, no toxicology analysis showing some "weird" uncertain HPLC peaks, one potentially corresponding to the parent compound or a metabolite of our investigational drug interspersed with potentially hundreds of complex chemicals contained within exotic plants promised by the charlatans or barely hopeful optimists alike as AIDS cures or at least "quality of life" enhancers.

And in this case, maybe like so many sad others, there'd be no family, no angry father or disheartened mother banging their fists on the walls, not understanding how this could happen to their dear, beloved son at such a young age. No ill-founded law suits would be inquired about, or initiated by some sort of ambulance chasing Rick analogue, or out of mere frustration of a family's "WHY?" There were no mysteries here regarding the death event itself, only the potentially unacknowledged thousands of deeper mysteries regarding how to do anything towards preventing, or at least reducing it, for the millions of similar potentially evolving victims of the future.

And wasn't this why I really needed to get back? Wasn't I doing important work? Wasn't my small individual contribution a crucial part of the growingly massive global effort? Wasn't I a cog in one of many wheels in the vast machine? How many more Curtis's were out there, increasing every day? Wasn't this what I do? Wasn't this who I was?

...

After hanging up the phone and then collecting or diffusing my thoughts, I peed, rinsed my face, and came into the small living room. Kim looked up from where she was sitting on the end of the sofa, setting a book down on her lap, a fairly neutral expression on her face anticipating my telling her who from Houston would have called me on her home phone and for what presumably significant reason.

I hesitated briefly, unintentionally, as I stared at her. She did look a little tired, after all, not so much physically, as perhaps emotionally. Too often lately, I think we'd both been wearing the faces and showing the demeanors of two individuals that despite caring were now twelve months into an already trying intended six month physical separation. We were trying to make somehow occasionally mutual (as married life is designed to be) into two almost mutually exclusive existences, with few if any overlapping events and characters.

Without adequately formal "What are we doing?" or "Where are we going?" conversations since Kim had decided she needed to spend substantially longer in Seattle than the six months we had initially discussed, it seemed that despite the usual getting along quite well together, there were increasing moody phases (longer than brief and passing) on both our parts, maybe subconsciously punishing the other for our current dangerous predicament. Last night the broaching of the topic of now extending even more time past the sort of agreed upon subsequent consecutive three month extensions seemed to have brought things to a necessary pivot point. Would our loves allow one of us to swallow our pride and/or make what would seem like almost insurmountable modifications to our current career plans and jobs to enable us to truly be together again? Would our frustrations, our potentially growing resentments, selfishness, foolishness, foolish indiscretions propel one of us out of the orbit of what should on all levels be a love, a commitment, and a respect that should be enough, enough to let this one be one of those that actually lives up to its stated vows, despite their issuance at a stage of a relationship that neither party has any idea of what the future truly holds, without an inexhaustible supply of foreknowledge on what types of stressors, from the mundane to the spectacular, they will have to survive and adjust to if the marriage is to endure?

I truly wondered if Kim had these exact or closely related thoughts.

My apparent delay as I pondered these things and analyzed the features of Kim's face must have increased her concern that whatever phone conversation could instill such hesitancy into me could in fact be something grave.

She had gotten up and walked over to me and taken my hands in her hands. Her squeeze and the look she cast up to me seemed intended to express something like, "It's O.K. Tell me. What is it?" without having to speak a word.

"My patient, Curtis, died," I finally uttered, focusing on just one of the things that was gnawing through my chest into my vertebral column.

Kim may have been a bit relieved. She knew about Curtis, of course, and she knew how sick he had become. I'd shared these tidbits with her a few times in our exchanges on the foreign characters from each of our local stories, and this likely seemed less severe and unexpected than something within the range of what she may have been dreading in light of my projected somberness after the abrupt phone call.

"I'm sorry. He was your friend," she said, as if clarifying his status or my reaction.

We stood there in silence for a few glorifying moments, holding each other. Despite the subtle unfamiliarities occasionally arising in the overall trivial elements of new hair styles, new clothes, new perfumes manifesting in a strange foreignness on our reunions, there was something so fundamentally right in our being together like this, I just wanted to stay here, in this symbiotic posture for awhile. I think I needed comforting for far more than my friend's death. I needed at least the effort we can all throw in from time to time to fill gaps that maybe can never be truly filled; the deficits that can only be bolstered against, to keep us going in a manner that makes it all bearable. If I really thought about it (which I think I had been lately), most of the time I was driven by forces I didn't bother to analyze, that just seemed inherent. Questioning them, comparing them to anything that could be more pleasant on a day to day basis but incompatible with such a fundamental drive, an essence, could be dis-raveling in a manner that makes what happened to Leo seem frighteningly plausible. All I knew was right then, this hug, this body, this mate, this comfort, this company seemed essential.

After a much longer than usual embrace that must have conveyed to Kim my combination of need, sorrow for last night, for last year, sorrow for Curtis, for all things I couldn't fix the way I wanted, she conveyed her sensitivity, the understanding only a true partner can, with the look she gave me as we finally parted.

"Do you need to go home?" she respectively inquired, causing me to internally grimace again at the notion of a "home" without her.

"No," I said. "Surely that part of my life can exist without me for a few more days…or I've done a bad job of putting a lab together," as if the impossibility of the latter somehow emphasized that I could stay. "I'm going to stay until at least Wednesday…maybe all week…if that's O.K. with you."

Kim softly smiled, reflecting without words that despite last night, and what still might have to transpire over the next few days, that that was quite alright by her…maybe even an unexpected, un-Jeffian surprise.

"Plus," I now continued, still holding her hands in mine, "I have a bunch of interviews in the Neurology and Neurosciences Department at University of Washington on Tuesday, and a couple in Immunology on Wednesday."

Her surprise made it all the way up to the sparkle in those big brown eyes, which I missed and was glad to see again, despite the massive professional turmoil any still difficult to conceive of consequences such interviewing could potentially cost me.

"Get the fuck out of here," she exuded with the left upward lip curl that I also missed too much to keep going on in a fashion not to keep it around more…somehow, someway.

"Yeah, and I figured that after whatever happens on Tuesday and Wednesday, especially if it's promising, there'd be some further possible meetings, lab and facility visits, and such on Thursday and even Friday," I further exposed my plans.

"You can stay as long as you want," Kim smiled, "but I won't be here Wednesday evening or Thursday."

I tried not to be irritated, assuming it was related to her seemingly expanding job duties.

"I'll be in Houston," she then surprised me with. "I have a job interview."

I didn't know quite how to respond. I was pleased, for sure, and I wanted to be optimistic, even before I knew the details. But the implications were more important than the specifics.

Without waiting for a possibly expected jubilation on my part, she continued, "I assume I can stay at your place?"

As my mind climbed back towards objective reality, I recalled that the inside of my little rented bungalow was not in the state I usually (or, maybe always) tried to get it to if I knew that Kim was coming.

"Our place," I corrected, "but it may be…um…a little messy."

"That's O.K. I just need a place to sleep and to shower, and it's actually pretty conveniently located for where I need to be Friday morning. I promise I won't hold the condition of the house against you."

I wasn't sure how to take the last sentence. For some reason, I couldn't tell if Kim was just teasing. Perhaps it was the new way she looked…our time apart. But I think she was partly kidding while at the same time delivering a portion of something deeper.

She then told me some of the details regarding the possible job. The firm's offices were located at Westheimer and Loop 610, just about 5-10 miles or so on non-highway routes from the little bungalow. She even added that we could live in either Bellaire (conveniently located to both the Med Center and the Galleria area her theoretical office would be at, and less expensive than the West University neighborhood more immediately surrounding the good sides of the Med Center) or maybe the Memorial Park area, slightly to the north and right inside the Loop from the Galleria. Both areas had nice neighborhoods, convenient shops, restaurants, and outdoor recreational opportunities, such as parks, etc.

Listening, I felt strange. I felt as if I were a traveler being treated with growing comfort when I'd been preparing for harsh conditions; like someone who'd found an unexpected oasis when on the verge of losing his mind wandering in the desert.

Kim went on to describe the anticipated nature of the job, objectively, with any excitement seemingly derived primarily from the fact that it would allow us to be together, rather than from the job itself. However, it did indeed seem like a very good match, and it seemed to provide a lot of potential for advancement. She had even brought up the possibility with the firm she was interviewing with of at least temporarily consulting with Edith's firm and GeoDyne, and they seemed receptive or at least open minded toward it. Everything sounded very promising. Yet, I wondered to myself. If Kim were single, if I weren't involved, would she be looking at a job like this? It would at least initially pay a little less than what she was currently getting in Seattle. But, of course, living in Houston is much cheaper…and in this case, there was another consideration, and maintaining one household would obviously be cheaper than the current situation.

Great, then, I tried to remember that I should be thinking. No way Kim wouldn't get any available job she interviewed for. And, at worst, she had clearly started the process of re-locating her work and career. Even if this one didn't work out as ideally as may be desired at this stage, she could at least do it for awhile, or if she didn't get it, we could easily survive without her working for awhile, as she continued to look while we were reunited in Houston…as initially planned…so long ago.

But, in the state of what I could only perceive vaguely as potential uncertainty, which I'd been walking around with seemingly more and more of late, I decided it may be best…best for all…maybe even good for me…to experiment with the notion that I just may not know everything. I may NOT have had a perfect plan. How would I actually know without experiencing other possibilities? Things were rolling for me at Baylor, and the Clinic was a great source for HIV-positive patients to enroll in the trial. But the University of Washington was a world-class medical center, a great institution of research, and has a large number of diverse teaching hospitals. Seattle was a pretty cool place. Maybe I could arrange to have sun imported.

From my side, it was out. Despite all the angst that even the thought of trying to move my efforts to another program at this stage had caused me over the past several days, it felt better to say it, and to say it with meaning it.

Kim had seemingly been raised to another plane, a plane of female emotion that must parallel some sort of appreciation for romance, of commitment, that men still only vaguely get glimpses of, in moments of divinely drifted down enlightenment.

The finishing touches of our at least one-week plan included the irony of me staying at her apartment in Seattle and her staying at my house in Houston, until the weekend. She then suggested that I simply fly home and we spend the weekend back together, and she could fly from Houston back to Seattle Sunday night. Logical, I suppose. But, without forethought, I suggested that maybe we should meet for the weekend on something akin to "neutral" ground, and recommended a "romantic" weekend in San Francisco, reasonably "half-way" between our two current cities, and a place of some pretty wonderful memories. She thought it was perfect, and we instantly rattled off various choices of possible hotels and wonderful restaurants we could indulge in to go over the results of our various options for the future. By the way she hugged me, longer and tighter than ever before, and the way I hugged her back, I thought that no matter what, the life planning conference in San Francisco would have a different outcome this time. "I'm hungry," she said, as if eating were somehow crucial to keeping this momentum growing.

As she turned to walk towards the little kitchen, I found myself staring at her incredible rear...as so many zillions of times before. It was still too early in any sort of cease-fire to think of it more crudely as "ass."

"How do you want your eggs?" she offered over her shoulder.

"Unless sucking them off your breasts is on the menu," I may have prematurely responded, "I guess the usual way."

As if at least agreeing to re-enter the peace talks...enthusiastically, she said, "O.K. Let's start off with over-easy then...and we'll go from there."

In Search of Mrs. Pearson - Glossary

ADC (AIDS dementia complex) – a constellation of symptoms and signs of CNS (see entry) abnormalities that can be seen with HIV infection, typically in late disease; includes impairments in cognition and motor abnormalities; progressive, serious; distinct from pathologic abnormalities due to opportunistic infections or AIDS associated tumors involving the brain

antigen (antigen presentation) – a biomolecule, typically a protein or chemically modified protein, that elicits an immune response

ascites (see also cirrhosis) – the clinical condition in which there is prominent accumulation of fluid in the peritoneal cavity, the space in which most of the abdominal organs are located

astrocytes – the most abundant cells in the brain; have important supportive function for maintaining proper neuron function, including in maintaining the protein- and other biochemical- containing intercellular matrix

attending (attending physician) – in teaching hospitals, the senior physician on a medical service, who is responsible for supervising the actions and care plan of the resident(s), intern(s), and students

autoimmune (autoimmune diseases) – the process (and consequent disease conditions) wherein the body's immune system, responsible for eliminating/controlling various types of infections, basically "attacks" one's own cells and tissues; examples include systemic lupus erythematosus (SLE, "lupus"),rheumatoid arthritis (RA), scleroderma, and Sjogren's disease

autonomic innervation (e.g., of GI tract) – refers to the portion of the nervous system that regulates non-voluntary processes, including that of organs and in the skin

"awake, alert, and oriented x 3" – a standard shorthand or abbreviated way for stating normal results of that part of a routine physical examination that addresses consciousness and whether a patient is "with it"; oriented x 3 refers to person, place, and time

AZT – abbreviation (derived from its chemical formula 3'-azido-2',2'-dideoxythymidine) for the anti-HIV drug with trade name Zidovudine; the first licensed anti-HIV drug, which works by inhibiting the HIV enzyme reverse transcriptase (as do many of the subsequent anti-HIV drugs)

Bactrim – trade name for drug formulation consisting of the combination of the two antibiotics trimethoprim and sulfamethoxazole (also called cotrimoxazole); both drugs work against infections (e.g., bacterial infections) by inhibiting folic acid metabolism (necessary for DNA synthesis) within the invading microorganism (similar to long established sulfonamide or "sulfur" antibiotics); following the recognition of the clinical entity of AIDS, Bactrim quickly emerged as the drug of choice for treatment and then for prophylaxis against *Pneumocystis carinii* pneumonia (PCP; see separate glossary entry)

beta blockers – a class of drugs that blocks one type of receptor within the sympathetic part of the autonomic system (see entry above); beta blockers have been used extensively in the treatment of cardiovascular disease over the last three decades

betadine solution – trade name of Purdue Pharma's brand of 10 % povidone-iodine (PVPI) solution used as a topical anti-septic, including for surgery preparation; has very characteristic brown staining color

bioassay – a research tool or approach in which the "reporting system" is derived from a living organism, subjected to manipulations and in which effects or their treatment modulation can be fairly reproducibly observed and aspects quantitated

blood brain barrier – a physiologic system by which the vasculature providing blood to the brain is modified (compared to that of other tissues/organs) in a manner preventing entry of macromolecules and many foreign chemicals into the brain

brachial plexus – a complex branching and anastomosing collection of nerve trunks located deep to the axilla or armpit; derived from nerve roots exiting the cervical (in the neck) spinal cord; the nerves exiting the brachial plexus extend variously down the arm to innervate movement of specific muscle groups and sensory input from corresponding portions of skin and soft tissue

cachectic (adjective form of cachexia) – refers to a generalized wasting state; can occur in advanced cancer patients; can occur during the course of HIV-infection, including a "wasting disease" seen widely with infection in African men and women; commonly seen in terminal AIDS patients in the U.S. as well

CD4 (CD4 cell) – a complex protein molecule expressed on the surface of an important subset of T-lymphocytes, thus designated as CD4 positive or T4 lymphocytes (see entry); CD4 + T-cells are the major cell target for viral invasion and destruction in HIV infection, which is initiated by virus binding to the CD4 protein; CD4+ (expressing) T-cells are particularly important in regulating the body's immunologic responses against infectious disease causing microorganisms

cell saver – an instrument occasionally used during a surgical procedure (e.g., for severe trauma) in which blood loss is so heavy and ongoing that transfusion becomes impractical; the suctioned operative field (blood, tissue fragments, irrigating solution, etc.) enters via a tube and is processed (including filtering) and the product returned to the patient intravenously

cerebrum (cerebral) – the top most and largest part of the brain; that portion most recently developed in evolution and largest in humans; divided into right and left hemispheres and anatomically distinct lobes associated with different advanced functions

cirrhosis (cirrhotic) – end-stage, irreversible scarring of the liver, which can result from a variety of chronic injurious processes such as alcoholic liver disease, viral hepatitis (hepatitis B or C infection), toxins, and inherited genetic abnormalities in various metabolic pathways; cases without identified initiating cause are "cryptogenic cirrhosis"; associated with a variety of clinical abnormalities due to reduced liver function and increased pressure within the portal vascular circulation (see entry); treated with supportive care, but fatal without treatment by liver transplantation

CNS (central nervous system) – the part of the nervous system composed of the brain (and its supporting tissues/structures) and the spinal cord; distinguished from the peripheral nervous system, composed of the nerves (and their surrounding linings) that exit the spinal cord and extend in progressive branching to all body parts; diseases of the nervous system can characteristically involve the CNS, the peripheral nervous system, or both, patterns of which can be delineated by clinical and laboratory examinations

coagulating proteins – a complex series of enzymatic proteins, which circulate in the blood stream maintained in an inactivated state; different mechanisms activate two initially different coagulation cascades, ultimately resulting in formation of a fibrin (protein) thrombus (clot); primarily synthesized in the liver, can be impaired in liver disease; notorious for giving medical students memorization nightmares

COPD – chronic obstructive pulmonary disease; lung disease primarily associated with long-term, heavy cigarette smoking; individual patients typically show features of either emphysema (thin patients, "pink puffers", who have destruction of the walls of the alveoli, the distal air sacs for oxygen exchange to blood), or chronic bronchitis ("blue bloaters", in which inflammation involving airways and increased mucus production leads to impaired air flow within the bronchi, associated with coughing)

CSF (cerebrospinal fluid) – a typically clear thin fluid that circulates within cavities of the brain (ventricles) and around the outer surface of the brain between the thin meninges (membrane like tissue that covers the brain) and underneath the dense dural tissue that encloses the brain and spinal cord; a sample of CSF can be obtained by lumbar-puncture ("spinal tap") (see entry below)

CT (CAT) Scan – computed tomography or computer-assisted tomography; lower dose x-ray-derived images are acquired and software analyzed to yield high resolution diagnostic images that can detect lesions (tumors or other abnormal masses) less than a cm in diameter; routinely aided by use of contrast agents, radio-opaque materials injected intravenously; CT scans of the brain in HIV infected/AIDS patients are useful for detecting possible mass lesions, such as infections (e.g., toxoplasmosis, with characteristic "ring-enhancing" image on CT with contrast) and CNS lymphomas, both markedly increased in AIDS patients

cyclic AMP – a biochemical molecule belonging to a diverse group of "signal transduction" mediators that regulate a variety of processes within cells; when certain molecules (e.g., hormones) bind to the surface of a cell via a specific receptor (like an anchoring molecule) that utilizes this signal-coupling process, rearrangements of that receptor and its coupling to other proteins activate biochemical processes that result in formation of intracellular cAMP; increased cAMP can have stimulatory or inhibitory effects on the overall process being considered; cAMP within a cell is rapidly broken down (within seconds) by an enzyme known as cAMP phosphodiesterase

cytokines – a group of proteins secreted by a variety of cells, particularly activated lymphocytes and macrophages (see entry); modulate the functions of other cells by binding to specific receptor proteins on their surface; examples include various interleukins, interferons, colony-stimulating factors, and tumor necrosis factors; effects include amplifying immune responses and killing viral infected cells; may contribute to neuronal cell injury and death in ADC (see entry)

dementia – a clinical condition characterized by impaired cognitive and intellectual function and failing memory; the most common etiology is that of Alzheimer's disease; also a component of ADC (see entry)

demyelinating (demyelinating diseases) – a process in which the outer coating (myelin) of nerves is compromised by destruction or altered maintenance; demyelination compromising nerve function can be seen due to a variety of primary and secondary disease processes; produces abnormal results on nerve conduction velocity tests (see entry)

distal – an adjective used in medical language to indicate an object or process that is situated away from the point of reference, such as origin or attachment; e.g., the hand is distal to the shoulder, the rectum is distal to the sigmoid colon, etc.; compare to proximal (see entry)

dystonic (in "ego" sense) – in perhaps more standard clinical pathology usage, dystonia refers to abnormal muscle tone; in this particular implied psychological sense, it can refer to ideological content that does not "sit well" with the current ego structure

EKG – abbreviation for electrocardiogram, the procedure of monitoring the electrical activity of the heart by the placement of electrodes on the skin surface; most typical is the 12-lead EKG, in which standardized placement of the leads provides for different orientation of recorded signals, allowing for optimized detection (and even indicating locations) of a range of possible abnormality-causing lesions; diagnosis is based on pattern of signal abnormality

ELISA - enzyme-linked immunosorbent assay (ELISA); a common technique used in laboratory diagnostics and research, particularly for detecting and quantifying a protein of interest; ELISA quickly became the technique of choice for screening for HIV infection by detecting antibodies characteristically generated in HIV-infected individuals; a positive result would be confirmed by Western blot (see entry)

EMG (electromyogram) – a diagnostic procedure performed by a neurologist to help distinguish between diseases of muscle (myopathies), nerves (neuropathies), or neuromuscular junctions (e.g., as in myasthenia gravis); needle electrodes are inserted into muscles and electrical potentials recorded; EMG patterns are displayed on an oscilloscope screen; myopathies and neuropathies have characteristic abnormal patterns; typically performed at same time with nerve conduction velocity (NCV) tests (see entry)

encephalopathy (see also hepatic encephalopathy) – a clinical syndrome characterized by disturbances in consciousness and behavior; can result from a large number of conditions affecting the brain, such as various metabolic abnormalities

endocarditis (bacterial endocarditis) – infection (mostly bacterial) of the heart valves; patients (typically older) with abnormal valves (as may be seen in rheumatic heart disease; see entry) are predisposed; in younger patients and in the setting of normal heart valves, the condition is most commonly seen in intravenous (I.V.) drug abusers (due to use of non-sterile needles); requires prompt diagnosis and treatment, traditionally (including in period of novel) with long term I.V. antibiotics

enterocytes – the absorptive lining cells of the intestine; absorb nutrient molecules (e.g., amino acids and sugars) that have been broken down by enzymes (gastric and pancreatic) from larger dietary molecules (e.g., proteins and starches); certain characteristic opportunistic pathogens in HIV infection and AIDS bind to or live within enterocytes, potentially causing clinical symptoms such as diarrhea

ER – Emergency Room; can be further classified according to Trauma Center status, number I being the most complete (what the ER of the Houston county hospital in novel is); ERs with class I Trauma Centers are qualified for all traumas and the most severe emergencies, including by having neuro- and orthopedic- surgeons on call "in house" (see entry)

esophageal varices (see also cirrhosis) – dilated vessels in the wall (towards the interior or luminal aspect) of the lowest part of the esophagus, near the esophagogastric junction (where the esophagus empties into the stomach); this is a site in which the normal blood vascular system forms anastomoses (connecting channels) with the usually much lower pressure portal system (see entry); when portal pressures are increased ("portal hypertension" as in cirrhosis of the liver; see entry), these anastomotic sites can dilate; such varices are at markedly increased risk for rupturing, which can cause a catastrophic and fatal upper gastrointestinal bleeding episode

externship – a typically upper level (i.e., fourth year) medical student clinical rotation of one or more months, in which one functions basically at the level of an intern M.D. (first year resident) in terms of clinical responsibility; often performed at another institution at which the student is highly interested in for undergoing his internship/residency training

facies – the general clinical term for relevant facial appearance, specifics of which may be characteristic of certain disorders or severity of some disorders; e.g., a depressed person may exhibit "sad facies"

fellow – in the clinical setting, someone undergoing further subspecialty training past completion of residency training; of variable numbers of year duration depending on field; for example, someone may be undertaking Gastroenterology (G.I.) or Cardiology subspecialty training, as a G.I. or Cardiology fellow, after completing an Internal Medicine residency of three years, in order to be a Gastroenterologist or Cardiologist, respectively

focal (CNS) signs (focality) – a sign on physical examination (e.g., localized weakness or reduced sensation) that suggests the presence of a pathologic process that involves only a part of the brain (that is, a "focus"); causes may include damage due to a stroke, a tumor, or infection; the nature of the abnormal exam finding may suggest the site of brain involvement

gait – clinical term referring to the pattern of walking, and in which certain patterns of abnormality may be associated with specific disorders or locations of lesions within the neuromuscular system; gait abnormalities can be observed in things as common as a herniated disc (of the lumbar spine) and can be seen in ADC (see entry)

GCRC – General Clinical Research Center; a shared in hospital or clinic facility with a small number of beds (e.g., maybe 8-12) and expert nursing care, in which can be conducted clinical research

gel electrophoresis (including two dimensional gel electrophoresis) – a commonly employed research and clinical diagnostic technique, especially as coupled with subsequent specific detection steps; proteins are separated on the basis of size (molecular weight) during passage through a suitable substrate or matrix under the control of a regulated electrical field; subsequent detection of a specific protein may be accomplished by transfer of gel-resolved proteins to a suitable membrane and incubation with a specific antibody, as in a Western blot (see entry); two dimensional gels provide greater resolution by applying separation in two vs. one dimension and are particularly useful in research discovery work

glutamine receptor antagonists – a class of experimental (at time of novel) and subsequently clinically incorporated drugs that block the effect of the amino acid neurotransmitter glutamine at the site of synapse between two neurons; represented a rational approach to possible amelioration of the pathology and clinical manifestations in ADC (see entry)

Gram stain (Gram positive or Gram negative bacteria) – a slide staining technique for examining bacteria by use of high power routine light microscopy; based upon cell wall composition, bacteria may stain either positively ("gram-positive") or not stain ("gram-negative"); in combination with the shape of the individual bacteria, the staining properties allow for classification in ways useful for organism characterization in context of the clinical presentation

"**grumper**" (as in "grumper-reading") – slang for bowel movement, or "number 2"

gumma (referenced in somewhat facetiousness to a pimple or zit) – the characteristic pathologic lesion in more advanced stages of syphilis infection (more common in the eras before anti-microbial agents effective against syphilis were available); of note, syphilis infection complicating HIV infection is common, leading to an increase in the incidence of syphilis following the beginning of the AIDS pandemic; usually confined to genital (primary) syphilis and easily treated effectively

gynecomastia – clinical syndrome and associated characteristic pathology of male breast enlargement, typically bilateral; due to hyperplasia (cell proliferation and gland enlargement) of the typically small/rudimentary breast tissue present in males; can be seen in association with a variety of clinical scenarios, including sex chromosomal abnormalities and in cirrhosis of the liver (context utilized herein; see entry), in which the diseased liver is not capable of inactivating circulating estrogens, leading to increased levels and stimulation of breast tissue

H2-blockers – a class of drugs that block a subset of histamine receptors, used primarily to treat conditions related to gastric acid production including ulcers, gastritis and reflux-esophagitis (heartburn); histamine released locally in the stomach acts on a subset of gastric cells (parietal cells) by binding to protein receptors of the H2 class on the cell surface to stimulate acid production; familiar agents include cimetidine (Tagamet), ranitidine (Zantac), and famotidine (Pepcid)

hematopoiesis – the process of production and maturation of blood cells within the bone marrow, including lineages that become the mature red blood cells, platelets, neutrophils, monocytes, and certain types of lymphocytes; very complex process involving a variety of growth factors and disorders of which can result in a variety of clinical disorders from anemias to leukemias

hemostat – a surgical instrument used for a variety of purposes, but including the clamping of blood vessels during surgical operations, to which their name is related; can be straight or curve tipped; have found widespread use, from first aid kits to removing fish hooks

hepatic encephalopathy – encephalopathy(see entry) related to dysfunction of the liver (hence "hepatic"); can be acute or chronic, with various and fluctuating neurologic symptoms including confusion that can be progressively severe, accompanied by lethargy and eventually coma; most commonly occurs in settings where there is severe hepatocellular dysfunction, as in cirrhosis (see entry); toxic substances (derived from intestinal absorption) are not removed in the sick liver; nitrogenous substances, such as ammonia, and amino acid derivatives are implicated

histoplasmosis – infection due to a fungus that causes characteristic, primarily pulmonary disease syndromes in humans; the responsible organism is *Histoplasma capsulatum*, which is widespread, and particularly densely present in the Ohio and Tennessee River Valleys; most infection in immune-competent humans is asymptomatic; in contrast, in immunosuppressed patients, and particularly advanced HIV infection/AIDS, this common organism is a leading cause of so-called "opportunistic infections", serious infectious diseases caused by widespread and generally harmless organisms

H. pylori – a bacterium that has importantly been identified as etiologic in gastric inflammation (gastritis); can alter gastric functioning leading to acid hyper-secretion and hence peptic ulcer disease, including the common duodenal ulcer (involving first part of small intestine, immediately after the stomach); can be treated medically; changes with chronic infection implicated in development of gastric carcinoma and lymphoma

hydroxylation (as in metabolism of vitamin D) – chemical or biochemical process in which hydroxyl (-OH) groups are added to other molecules; in living organisms, a variety of relatively specific enzymes catalyze these reactions, such as in drug metabolism occurring in the liver; successive hydroxylations at specific sites on the vitamin D molecule are catalyzed in the liver and kidney, with the subsequent dihydroxy-form undergoing final activation in the skin under the influence of U.V. light

hyperchylomicronemia (hyperlipidemia) – a condition in which chylomicrons are increased in the bloodstream; the most severe form is genetic and classified as type I hyperlipidemia; chylomicrons are the first form in which absorbed lipids, including cholesterol, enter the portal vein system after intestinal cell processing; normally cleared quickly in the liver in a process leading to other cholesterol transport forms, such as VLDL and LDL (which can be elevated in other genetic or lifestyle influenced conditions); the relatively large size of chylomicrons is partly responsible for some characteristic symptoms, such as pancreatitis and joint abnormalities, due to lodging in small blood vessels

immunopathology – a broad sub-discipline within pathology or a category of techniques and approaches used in pathology in which either the subject is particularly the immune system and/or immunologic techniques are used to supplement older techniques in the pathology laboratory; examples may include the likes of identifying specific types of auto-antibodies in auto-immune diseases such as systemic lupus erythematosus or using specific antibodies to detect normal or abnormal proteins in tissue sections

immunosuppressant drugs – medications of different chemical classes that work through different mechanisms to suppress the body's own immune system; used in the treatment of autoimmune diseases (see entry) and for the prevention and treatment of organ transplant rejection; patients managed with such drugs are at markedly increased risk for developing infections, including by organisms that are not pathogenic under normal circumstances ("opportunistic infections"), similar to those whose immune systems are compromised by certain genetic diseases (primary immunodeficiencies) or HIV infection/AIDS

"in house" (as in "in house call" or a patient being "in house") – refers to being in the hospital (hospital assuming the designation of "house", not inappropriately given the number of hours that interns and residents, particularly, put in there); corresponding to the designation of interns and residents as "house officers"

intercostal space – the soft tissue space between adjacent ribs, wherein course blood vessels and nerves in close proximity to the bone, as well as being occupied by skeletal muscle; number designated (e.g., "third intercostal space") according to the rib number above the space; such sites may represent appropriate levels for not only designating injury but also for referring to a targeted area in certain procedures, such as for thoracentesis (inserting a needle to drain fluid for therapeutic purposes and/or diagnostic analysis by tests on the fluid obtained) or insertion of a chest tube (to remain in place for an indicated duration of time)

Institutional Review Board (IRB) – a committee within an institution, such as a medical school or hospital, which is responsible for reviewing proposed research protocols according to standards designed to protect patients' rights

ischemic bowel disease – a condition in which arterial vascular supply to the intestines is inadequate, leading to potentially progressively more severe injury, from pain and bloody stools to extensive bowel wall damage and death; etiology is most commonly related to atherosclerotic disease of the arteries originating from the aorta and branching to the respective segments of bowel

in vitro – (Latin for "in glass") general term referring to experimental processes that do not involve intact living systems; for example, experiments in the lab that utilize cultures of isolated cells

IP – intra-peritoneal; a route by which some drugs are delivered directly into the peritoneal space (of the abdominal cavity) for absorption and potential reservoir effects; not commonly used; the space is equivalent to that which is utilized in peritoneal dialysis

isoniazid-resistant TB – the description for strains of *Mycobacterium tuberculosis* (causative agent in tuberculosis disease or TB) that have developed resistance to the commonly utilized anti-TB drug isoniazid; the inherent immune system processes that contain the difficult to kill *M. tuberculosis* bacilli involve T4 lymphocytes (the cells infected by HIV) and stimulation of monocyte/macrophage cells to from so-called granulomas that basically "wall-off" to contain the infection; as these processes are markedly compromised in HIV infection/AIDS, there has been a resurgence of TB since the beginning of the HIV pandemic; infections in this setting typically involve much larger numbers of bacilli than in immunocompetent hosts; this has facilitated the emergence, expansion, and spread of isoniazid-resistant TB, complicating therapeutic strategies

IV – intravenous; a route in which dissolved drugs and fluids can be administered, either into a smaller peripheral vein (as of back of hand, wrist, arm) or into a larger central vein (e.g., neck region), allowing for faster, higher volume delivery, including nutrition supplements and for more prolonged periods

Kaposi's sarcoma (KS) – a malignancy of blood vessel cells, that occurs with markedly increased frequency in patients with advanced HIV infection (AIDS); an AIDS defining illness from the earliest days of disease classification, this was one of the clustered disease processes in young males that led to the identification and characterization of AIDS; KS appears to be more common in AIDS patients with homosexuality (anal receptive intercourse) as risk factor for HIV infection

Krebs cycle - (also known as the tricarboxylic acid cycle) a complex biochemical metabolic pathway of aerobic respiration that takes place in the mitochondria of cells (the so-called "powerhouses" of the cell, located in the cytoplasm); produces energy from breakdown products of fatty acid and sugar metabolism in the form of ATP molecules (see cAMP entry) and CO_2 (carbon dioxide); involves ten enzymatic reactions, the enzymes for which, products of which, and co-factors or other aspects of which are notorious memorization targets for medical students and other students of biochemistry

lesion – a non-specific designation for a discernible abnormality (by naked eye or palpation on physical examination or radiologic imaging) within or upon any site (e.g., skin, deep soft tissue, muscle, bone, organ) and which upon pathology examination may correspond to a benign process (benign neoplasm or reactive conditions, such as inflammation) or a malignant process (e.g., "cancerous lesion"); the generic word allows medical professionals to speak towards a process being evaluated (e.g., "there's a lesion in the proximal tibia on x-ray," or "he has multiple skin lesions on his chest"); basically a grown-up/professional equivalent of the childhood term "boo-boo"

Level I trauma unit (or center)–designation referring to the highest level of care and expertise available for trauma cases within an emergency center (i.e., of a hospital); Level I trauma centers have a full range of specialists and equipment available 24 hours a day; required to have a certain number of surgeons, emergency physicians and anesthesiologists on duty 24 hours a day at the hospital, as well as prompt availability of care in varying specialties, such as neurosurgery, orthopedic surgery, and plastic surgery (e.g., on call for hand and facial injuries)

limbic (limbic system) - refers to a set of brain structures composed of regions of cortex and sub-cortex, along the inner border of the cortex; essentially "deep" to, and regarded as having evolved prior to, the neocortex, which is so prominent in humans; includes brain structures such as the thalamus, hypothalamus, limbic cortex, and amygdala, which are implicated in a variety of functions, including long term memory, behavior, and particularly emotions

loading dose – an initial dose employed for the administration of some drugs (depending upon the drug's pharmacokinetic characteristics) in order to achieve a therapeutic level more rapidly than would be achieved by just beginning with the subsequently employed maintenance dosing regimen

lumbar puncture – (LP; colloquially known as a "spinal tap") a medical procedure in which a sample of cerebrospinal fluid (CSF; see entry) is obtained; a spinal needle (with an open caliber outer sheath containing a central stylet) is inserted in the midline between two adjacent lumbar vertebrae (e.g., L4 and L5, or L3 and L4); the stylet is removed and fluid begins to drain from the in place metal bore; serial tubes are collected and sent to appropriate laboratory divisions for more specialized testing (in addition to fairly standard protein, glucose, and cell count determinations) depending upon the differential diagnosis (e.g., cytology to rule out malignant cells; microbiology for culture or other techniques to detect possible infectious agents)

lymphoma – a malignant neoplasm (or proliferation) of variously differentiated lymphocytes; can originate from bone marrow derived B-lymphocytes or thymus-derived T-lymphocytes; the malignant neoplasms variously re-capitulate these cells' normal differentiation phenotypes; this forms the basis for classifying these malignancies (along with cell size, morphology, and often specific molecular genetic alterations), which have variously severe prognoses and differential responses to defined chemotherapy protocols; lymphomas typically present as enlarged lymph nodes, and can be focal or disseminated (with higher stages), as well as involve organs (e.g., liver, spleen, stomach) or other tissues (e.g., skin, bone) in part depending on the type of lymphoma; some can cause an increase in corresponding abnormal lymphocytes in the blood stream, the latter being the characteristic presenting feature of leukemias

CNS lymphoma is a form of such a malignant neoplasm primarily or exclusively involving the brain, most commonly seen as a large B-cell lymphoma; CNS B-cell lymphomas occur with markedly increased incidence in patients with AIDS; in AIDS patients, lymphoma including as CNS lymphoma, can be associated with Epstein-Barr virus (EBV) infection of the involved cells; CNS lymphoma in HIV may be diagnosed by imaging; it carries a grave prognosis (superimposed on already advanced HIV infection), requiring aggressive therapy

macrophages – cells within a variety of tissues, derived from circulating bone marrow generated monocytes (see entry); function in the ingestion and destruction of foreign debris, necrotic tissue, and invading microorganisms, including in the processing and presentation of antigens (see entry) to lymphocytes in generation of specific immune responses

"med stud" – slang abbreviation for "medical student"

Mental Status Exam / Mini Mental Status Exam (MMSE) – refers in general to the assessment of the cognitive function of a patient, which can be accomplished easily at the bedside (e.g., in hospital) or in clinic or physician office; consists of reasonably uniform questions to assess orientation (person, place, time), long and short term memory, ability to process general information (converse, understand), perform simple calculations, grasp abstract ideas, name objects, perform imaginary tasks to assess coordination of motion, and process and express written and spoken language

metabolized (as in drug metabolism/elimination) – the process of altering the chemical form of a molecule in order to facilitate its elimination from the body; involves processes such as oxidative hydroxylation (performed by a group of related enzymes predominantly within the liver) or conjugation (addition) of specific small molecules

monocytes – (see also macrophages) bone marrow derived white blood cells (~ 2-10 % of circulating white blood cells) that appear to function primarily as precursors for macrophages, when under response of different stimuli they enter tissues and further differentiate; monocyte/macrophages are CD4-positive (see entry), though the CD4 molecule on their surface is expressed at lower density than on CD4-positive T-lymphocytes (T4 lymphocytes; see entry); as the binding protein (receptor) for the HIV virus, HIV binding to and infection of circulating monocytes may serve as a portal for entry (analogized to a "Trojan horse") of the virus into the brain

MRI (Magnetic Resonance Imaging) scan – a method of non-invasive imaging utilizing a static magnetic field and radio frequency waves that has grown in use over the last few decades, including replacing CT scan (see entry) as the radiology method of choice for many applications; particularly useful for brain and spinal cord imaging; resolution is determined in part by magnet strength (size), and can also be augmented by use of the paramagnetic contrast agent gadolinium (by prior injection, similar in principal to CT contrast enhancing materials); it is particularly well suited for detecting possible white matter lesions within the CNS (see entry for neurons)

myelopathy – primary disease of the spinal cord (i.e., the white matter or nerve tracts that run through the spinal cord, such as descending motor pathways and ascending sensory pathways), with symptoms depending upon the nerve tracts involved and the level of the lesion; approximately 20 % of AIDS patients have a clinical myelopathy, with involvement of motor systems (producing gait abnormalities; see entry) or sensory pathways (with ataxia, or clumsy movement of limbs, or tingling in extremities); most patients with spinal cord involvement have some degree of dementia, such that the pathophysiology is likely related to that of ADC (see entry)

myoglobin – a major protein in muscle, which like hemoglobin in red blood cells, contains iron (Fe 2+ or 3+) as a prosthetic group (bound within the molecule in a biochemically precise way) to which oxygen binds (as with hemoglobin, for blood oxygenation and tissue delivery); functions in oxidative regulation of muscle function; muscle injury can release myoglobin into the blood stream, and large amounts (as with so-called rhabdomyolysis seen with massive muscle injury) can cause kidney damage

myopathy – primary disorder of skeletal muscle, presenting primarily with muscle weakness; diagnosis especially involves electromyography (EMG) and nerve conduction velocity (NCV) testing (see entries), with confirmatory muscle biopsy; in patients with HIV infection, a primary myopathy may be present, ranging from asymptomatic elevation of the muscle enzyme CPK in the serum (indicative of injury), myalgia (pain or muscle ache), marked elevation of CPK after exercise, to proximal muscle weakness (with muscle damage and inflammatory infiltration on biopsy)

NCV (Nerve Conduction Velocity) study – electrical based diagnostic testing typically performed in association with EMG (see entry) in the work up of disorders of neuromuscular function; stimulation of major peripheral nerves (e.g., in the arms or legs) at different points along the length is performed with electrical probes in association with monitoring of the expected muscular contraction response, allowing for determination of the velocity of the impulse along the nerve; useful for defining primary pathology within the nervous system (e.g., spinal cord or peripheral nerves, as in neuropathies; see entry) in contrast to the muscles (e.g., in myopathy; see entry) or neuromuscular junction

neurons – functional cells of the nervous system, located within the brain and spinal cord, with cellular morphology and molecular correlates of function varying depending upon location; in the brain, primarily located within the so-called "gray matter" (denser and darker due to greater cell density) as opposed to "white matter" that consists primarily of nerve fibers, the extensions from the cell body (where the nucleus is) that carry nerve signals; neuronal function is carefully regulated by supporting cells (such as astrocytes and glial cells) and tissue matrices, including by contact and soluble mediators; abnormalities in these systems rather than direct infection of neurons is thought to be involved in HIV infection-associated cognitive and motor abnormalities

neuropathy – primary disease of peripheral nerves (and/or autonomic nerves, which regulate organ function), which can lead to motor and/or sensory abnormalities; symptoms may include muscular weakness, decreased sensation, or tingling, in part depending upon the specific underlying etiology; etiologies include immunologic response to viral infection, rare hereditary disorders, toxins (including certain drugs and particularly ethanol abuse), and systemic metabolic disorders (particularly diabetes mellitus); EMG/NCV studies (see entry) are particularly important in establishing the diagnosis; nerve biopsy and/or other laboratory procedures may be indicated to ascertain the specific etiologic condition

NIH - National Institutes of Health; a federal agency of the U.S. Dept. of Health and Human Services; the primary agency by which the U.S. government financially supports biomedical research, through currently 27 separate institutes (e.g., National Cancer Institute or NCI, National Institute of Allergy and Infectious Disease or NIAID); the top research funding mechanism in the U.S. (~25-30 % of total research support; ~$25 billion dollars/year)

Organic Brain Syndrome – a general term, used particularly in the setting of psychiatry and neuropsychiatry, as indicating decreased mental function that is due to a medical disease rather than a primary psychiatric illness (such as depression or schizophrenia); some causes include hypoxia (inadequate blood oxygen levels due to various conditions) or hypercapnia (excessive carbon dioxide in blood) such as due to inadequate ventilation, cardiac arrhythmias, stroke, Alzheimer's disease, multiple sclerosis, metabolic abnormalities including thyroid disorders, alcohol withdrawal, sepsis, and meningitis

pathophysiology – basically, the mechanisms of diseases; the abnormal molecular, cellular, organ and systemic processes by which are caused specific diseases and disorders; in HIV-infection, the pathophysiology involves viral infection, primarily of CD4 (T4) helper lymphocytes; results in destruction of such cells as well as abnormal regulation of normal immune function, leading to the characteristic increase in secondary infectious and neoplastic disorders

phenothiazines (phenothiazine neuroleptics) - a class of anti-psychotic medications (also sometimes referred to as neuroleptics, related to the neurological and motor effects), which share a common chemical structure of a three ring phenothiazine nucleus; the major use is in the treatment of schizophrenia; chlorpromazine (trade name: Thorazine) is one of the oldest agents, extensively used in past; newer agents with other chemical structures may have preferable side effect profiles or utility in some subtypes of patients; all are capable (to various degrees) of resulting in notorious neuromuscular side effects (referred to as "extrapyramidal symptoms", or EPS), including fairly acute onset dystonia (slow or spastic contractions leading to involuntary movements) and delayed onset of tardive dyskinesia (see entry)

pimped (as in a medical student getting "pimped" on rounds) – slang designation for the process in which medical students are asked questions by higher ranking physicians, most commonly while visiting successive patients for which the medical team is responsible on its so-called "rounds"; if attending (see entry) rounds, interns and residents may be quizzed as well; if rounding with just interns and residents, usually more informal and less gut wrenching; questions are routinely prompted by specific patient clinical features or pathophysiologic processes and/or treatment options of involved disease states, but in essence nothing is off limits; there are classic pimp questions in various medical specialties, advanced knowledge of which is highly recommended; can also occur in other settings, such as being "pimped" by the attending surgeon while assisting during an operation; the consequence of wrong answers may vary from bland disregard to dismantling; the consequence of correct answers may vary from bland disregard to praise; depending on time spent with attending physician, performance may be a major factor in student evaluation (grade)

Pneumocystis carinii **pneumonia (PCP)** – a common opportunistic infection occurring in patients with advanced HIV/AIDS; one of the initial diseases noted in young homosexual males that lead to characterization of the disease AIDS; in patients with HIV infection, PCP is an AIDS defining illness; *Pneumocystis* infects the lining cells of the air sacs (alveoli) of the lung, causing dyspnea (shortness of breath), fever, and non-productive cough, with progressively severe pneumonia that is highly fatal if untreated; acquired/spread via the respiratory route; characteristic X-ray changes are commonly but not always present; diagnosis is made by identifying the characteristic organism (with any of multiple tissue slide staining techniques) either on induced sputum, or most efficiently on bronchiolar alveolar lavage (BAL) fluid obtained at the time of endoscopic examination of the airways into the lungs; the preferred treatment is with the antibiotic combination of trimethoprim-sulfamethoxazole TMP-SMX (or Bactrim; see entry); because of the markedly high incidence of this infection in patients with advanced HIV/AIDS, those with CD4 count < 200/ul (AIDS defining level in later classification schemes) should receive prophylaxis with TMP-SMX

pentamidine – an antibiotic that is as effective against PCP (see entry), but more toxic, compared to the more frequently used combination of TMP/SMX (see Bactrim entry); for patients not able to tolerate TMP/SMX (e.g., due to hypersensitivity/drug allergy), it provides an alternative for both the treatment of acute infection in moderate to severe PCP (in which it is given by the I.V. route; see entry) and for prophylaxis against PCP in indicated patients (see PCP entry), in which it is given by monthly inhalation

phylum (as in modified form, "phylogenically superior") – in biology, the phylum is a taxonomic rank (i.e., in the hierarchical classification system) below kingdom and above class; in botany, the term division is the same; the Animal Kingdom contains approximately 35 phyla; whereas the Plant Kingdom contains 12 divisions; both humans and dogs are in the Phylum Chordata (animals with notochords) and in the class Mammalia, with humans in the Primate Order and dogs being in the Carnivore Order; "phylogenetically superior" is hence a slang reference to being a more advanced life form (which clearly depends upon criteria, such as intelligence vs. olfactory ability or intra-species decency)

PML (progressive multifocal leukoencephalopathy) – a severe neurological disease that occurs in the setting of immunocompromise that has markedly increased in incidence following the emergence of the HIV/AIDS pandemic; the disease affects white matter in the CNS (areas of myelin-encased nerve fibers, rather than gray matter in which neuron cells are concentrated) in a multifocal fashion; caused by the infection of astrocyte and oligodendrocyte brain cells (which maintain and produce myelin) by a virus identified as JC papovavirus, a DNA-type virus (similar to the kind that causes measles); seen in advanced stages of HIV infection, patients commonly present with visual impairment and/or impaired mental function (confusion, dementia) and commonly have or develop motor abnormalities; MRI scans show multiple irregular white matter lesions (see entry) and is more sensitive than CT scan; the prognosis is grim

portal circulation - a general term denoting the circulation of blood through larger vessels from the capillaries of one organ to those of another; in routine clinical physiology, applied primarily to the passage of blood from the gastrointestinal tract (as well as the spleen and pancreas) through the portal vein to the liver; the portal venous system carries blood from large portions (from lower portion of the esophagus to the upper part of the anal canal) of the gastrointestinal tract to the liver, such that substances absorbed from much of the intestines travel first to the liver for processing before draining into the systemic circulation, continuing to the heart; (see Cirrhosis entry)

proximal - an adjective used in medical language to indicate an object that is situated closer to the reference point, such as a point of origin or attachment; e.g., the knee is proximal to the foot, the ascending colon is proximal to the descending colon and rectum; the duodenum (first part of small intestine) is proximal to the jejunum (second part of small intestine); can be used to describe the location of a lesion (see entry); compare to distal (see entry)

reflux (gastric reflux) – the abnormal passage of acidic gastric contents back up into the esophagus, manifested as the familiar "heartburn"; modern treatment includes proton-pump inhibitors to lower gastric acid, as well as reducing contributing factors

renal tubules – portions of the so-called nephron, or the functioning unit of the kidney; the glomeruli are the filtration system of the nephron from which the filtrate enters into an associated renal tubule; the tubule is composed of distinct segments lined with corresponding unique cellular types that function in a variety of processes, such as ion and water transport prior to the filtrate entering collecting ducts and passing into urine

resident (resident physician) – a physician in training and hence "in residence" at the teaching hospital(s); different medical specialties require different lengths of residency training; a first year resident is the same as the intern level; residency typically begins in July, in keeping with medical school graduation and enrollment calendars; resident level status is commonly designated by year of training, such as a "second year resident" or PGY-2 (post-graduate year 2); on clinical rotations, medical students primarily serve under the direction of an upper level resident, though they may spend substantial time doing "grunt work" with interns or lower level residents

rheumatic heart disease – chronic rheumatic heart disease is a possible long term (i.e., decades until symptoms develop) consequence of rheumatic fever, an acute complication that sometimes follows streptococcal infection (i.e., "strep throat"); in some such cases, the heart valves can be inflamed and then damaged by scarring following the inflammation; particularly involves the mitral valve (between the left atrium, where oxygenated blood returns from the lungs, and the left ventricle) and sometimes in association with involvement and scarring of the aortic valve (between the pumping left ventricle and the aorta); valve disease with scarring can also predispose to later valve infection (endocarditis) by other microorganisms having transient blood stream access

ribosomes – the cellular organelle (macromolecular complex within a cell's cytoplasm) at which proteins are made; composition includes characteristic RNA molecules (ribosomal or rRNA); at the ribosomes, the mRNA (which encodes the DNA-carried sequence for a specific gene) is matched to so-called transfer RNA molecules (tRNA); specific amino acids (the individual building blocks of proteins) bound to corresponding specific tRNAs are assembled in a linear sequence at the ribosomes where the mRNA and tRNA associate

Study Section – a committee (any of a large number of specifically designated ones matching the grant administrative process) that reviews NIH grants; commonly meeting at the NIH in Bethesda following grant reviews by individual members, in order to further discuss and score grant applications for possible funding; typically formed of experts in a given field, including relevant NIH grant recipients, as well as NIH affiliated researchers and administrative staff

T4 lymphocytes – a class of T-lymphocytes characterized by expression of the so-called CD4 antigen; these are the lymphocytes that are primarily and directly infected by the HIV virus, that actually binds to the CD4 molecule on the cell surface via proteins that are expressed on the surface of the virus (in the viral envelope); viral infection can lead to cell destruction, which is the rationale for monitoring CD4 cell levels following HIV infection; a count of < 500/ul constitutes one definition of AIDS

tardive dyskinesia – a long term neurological side effect that can develop in patients undergoing chronic treatment with anti-psychotic medications, such as phenothiazines (see entry); can manifest as involuntary slow abnormal movement of head, trunk and limbs and perioral movements such as tongue darting and facial grimacing; risk varies by specific drug agent and increases with duration of treatment; severity can be from mild to incapacitating

TB syringe – a 1 cc (relatively small and skinny) syringe, typically attached to a small gauge (thin) needle (e.g., 25- or even smaller 27-gauge); traditionally used for making a subcutaneous injection, as in TB testing (seeing if prior exposure to TB); useful in some other clinical or research applications as well

Toxoplasmosis (CNS Toxoplasmosis) – clinical disease due to active infection with the parasite *Toxoplasma gondii*, which is markedly increased in patients with advanced HIV disease/AIDS and in which CNS involvement is most frequent and most consequential; infection with *T. gondii* is actually quite common, but is usually asymptomatic in persons with an intact immune system; in patients with AIDS, CNS toxoplasmosis usually takes the form of multiple discreet lesions in the brain (typically < 2 cm); patients may present with impaired mental function with or without focal signs (see entry), such as localized weakness, localized sensation abnormalities, movement disorders, vision or speech abnormalities; with appropriate clinical features, radiographic examination of the brain can be strongly suggestive, with multiple so-called "ring-enhancing" lesions present on CT scan with contrast (see entry)

UCSF – University of California at San Francisco, a leading clinical and basic science research medical center and top tier medical school, with main campus located in the Parnassus Heights section of San Francisco.

UIL – University Interscholastic League; an organization created by The University of Texas at Austin to provide leadership and guidance for extracurricular activities in the form of interschool competitions, at the high school, junior high school, and elementary school levels; UIL sponsors district, regional, and state tournaments in athletic, music, drama, and academic contests

Vacutainer– Becton-Dickenson's trademarked name for a device used to facilitate venipuncture (e.g., in arm) for blood collection; tube (empty cylindrical)-shaped clear plastic (typically green) that allows for insertion of separate specialized needles at the narrow opening end that will face the patient's vessel site and for insertion of appropriate rubber stopper tubes that fit into at the wide (full width) opening at the other end; such vacutainers are commonly carried around in the white medical coat pockets of medical students who have to collect blood by themselves (in addition to scheduled blood draws by phlebotomists of the hospital lab)

vagus nerve - the tenth cranial nerve (one on each side); originates in the medulla oblongata of the brain stem, descends down through the base of the skull (via the jugular foramen); supplies nerve fibers to the pharynx, larynx, trachea, lungs, heart, esophagus, and the intestinal tract as far as the transverse colon; paired as anterior and posterior at the level of the stomach, where branches extend to innervate gastric function, including acid secretion; also brings sensory information back to the brain from the ear, tongue, pharynx, and larynx

Western blot – a laboratory technique utilized extensively in research and in some clinical applications allowing for the specific identification (detection, or with some modifications, quantitation) of targeted proteins of interest; proteins are first extracted and then separated by gel electrophoresis (see entry) followed by techniques for antibody-based specific detection; this technique became incorporated into the diagnosis of HIV infection very shortly after the causative agent was identified, being used to detect a patient's possible antibodies (which are proteins) to the HIV virus with high specificity; has been standardly used to confirm the positive results noted in a screening ELISA test (see entry)

Acknowledgments and Credits

Thanks to my brother Colonel Steven R. Shappell for reading early first draft fragments (began way before my diagnosis, with which this book is specificaly unrelated), encouraging me to continue when visiting approximately just one month after my ALS diagnosis, and reading the final draft, during which while complimenting with much high praise, he found despite all the previous eyes four additional minor typos (which I hope we've corrected herein - military rigidity remains safely in place). Thanks to Katy Rigler for reading and making editorial suggestions on the finished first draft and for her support of my writing in general. A special huge thanks to my sister Sally Kilpatrick for reading, making editorial suggestions, and helping with incorporating all of the various suggested comments, including reining in some of the more horrendous run-on sentences while still helping maintain the casual narrative style, even respecting the occasional neologism and the nonconventional creation of adverbs. In a language that doesn't always have the right form or specific sentiment of a word, modifiers sometimes ascend to the rule from their hiding place as the exception.

Thanks to Natalie and staff at Little Mombo Camp, Botswana, for creating such a great atmosphere and specifically feeding me so well when writing rather than going on morning safari, as I pictured myself as some sort of pseudo Hemingway figure scribbling prose on the sunny decks with the most incredible background including organisms appropriately not all that interested in my activities. Likewise thanks to the staff at Kings Pool in the Okavango Delta who along with adjacent elephants playing in the water also provided a dream background for a little more a.m. writing. Closer to home, I should likewise thank the staff of the Lake Austin Spa Resort for creating the casual atmosphere where a man can sit in a robe after various activities and write without feeling uncomfortable while spouses participate in other stereotypically more female activities, and to all of these for verifying that I did actually take an occasional vacation back when I was still working fulltime as a Physician-Scientist.

Thanks to Blair Shamel and Dr. Harry Rittenhouse for reading the novel and making useful suggestions regarding the glossary and to Blair for specific comments regarding details of San Diego and the surrounding area. Thanks to Dr. Scott Lucia for specific comments related to aspects of the NIH in Bethesda and surrounding areas. Thanks to Dr. Simon Hayward for suggestions and comments related to San Francisco medical facilities and surrounding areas.

From the deepest levels of my heart, I thank each and every patient that I may have only briefly to extensively encountered during my medical training and practice. It is a privilege to work hard in general and an honor to serve in every form of patient care, something that I have come to appreciate from a different angle after April 2009. With more gratitude, admiration, and respect than I can adequately express, I thank all of the various house staff and attending physicians that I interacted with in whatever fashion and was taught by during my medical training. Various segments of variously recalled aspects of those patient and teacher encounters naturally surfaced in the setting of writing this book, and the narrative no doubt falls within the general claim that most writing is in some way autobiographical. However, the only individuals designated by name are not personally encountered and are used in a strictly fictional sense for historical setting purposes. In unnamed or fictitiously named characters, any superficial resemblance to real individuals is not specifically targeted and can only be another manifestation of the deep respect and gratitude with which I regard all past components of my medical experience.

A special thanks to Linda Apple for capturing within her cover painting the sometimes unexpected quaintness that can be found in the middle of even the largest of cities and the subtle psychological potential conveyed by the empty park bench as the setting of unexpected camaraderie. Thanks to Travis Scott Lee Shappell for incorporating a few good and ignoring the several bad suggestions while displaying his architecture-associated graphics art design skills in generating the cover. Thanks to Scott Baber at Hekasa Publishing for laying out the book design and accomplishing the other acts that allow a novel to manifest as an actual book (as well as the form that still seems to magically show up on a wireless connected e-reader.)

Finally, thanks to my wife Heidi for unceasing attempts towards normalcy despite the husband character she was fated with and for the undeserved support she has shown me during these last several particularly demanding years. It was specifically within the early years (which are often some of the best, of course) in which I read a particular 1995 article outside at her condo pool (where I often studied during the final phase of residency and fellowship training) that was on cell-cell interactions in the possible pathogenesis of HIV-related neurological disorders, at which point I decided to incorporate this sort of pathophysiology into a hypothetical future novel as presented herein. (Reasonably, I did not want to default to a more career-related prostate cancer research setting, and I felt reasonably comfortable with the science aspects having studied molecular mechanisms of cell-cell interactions in my Ph.D. work). Perhaps somewhat ironically then, with an idea tracing back to 1995 and a novel started perhaps six or seven years later, I would not have imagined at either of those time points that I myself would eventually be taking a drug somewhat similar to the receptor blocker that was the focus of the completely fictional clinical trial within the novel, in this case for ALS, beginning in 2009. For all patients and their doctors and researchers and their families, keep fighting and may you know peace sometime before or at the end.

References

AIDS – arts timeline, from Artery: The AIDS – Arts Forum. Accessed online, 8/18/2004; http://www.artistswithaids.org/artery/AIDS/AIDS.html

Atkins, Robert and Sokolowski, Tom. *From Media to Metaphor*. Independent Curators Incorporated, New York; 1992.

Baker, Rob. *The Art of AIDS: From Stigma to Conscience*. Continuum International Publishing Group; 2000.

de Young Museum: http://deyoung.famsf.org/about/history-de-young-museum; http://deyoung.famsf.org/blog/when-earth-shakes-come-de-young;   http://

www.americanheritage.com/content/museums?page=2; http://www.sfgate. com/bayarea/place/article/15-seconds-that-changed-San-Francisco-The-Loma-2641747.php#ixzz2P5vnqJJa

Grover, Jan Zita. "Public Art on AIDS: On the Road With Art Against AIDS", in *Leap In the Dark. AIDS, Art & Contemporary Cultures*, ed. by Allan Klusaček and Ken Morrison. Véhicule Press, Montreal, Quebec; 1992.

Harrison, T. R. and Wilson, J. D. *Harrison's Principles of Internal Medicine*. New York, McGraw-Hill, Health Profession Division; 1991.

James, John S. (ATN) San Francisco AIDS Conference and Related Events: Issues and Update. AIDS Treatment News No. 102 – May 4, 1990. Accessed online, 8/18/2004; http://www.aegis.com/pubs/1990/ATN 10201.html

Kasper, Dennis L.; Braunwald, Eugene; Hauser, Stephen; Longo, Dan; Jameson, J. Larry; Fauci, Anthony S. *Harrison's Principles of Internal Medicine 16th Edition*. New York, McGraw-Hill, Health Profession Division; 2005.

Klein, George. "AIDS", in *Pietà*, MIT Press; 1992 (first published in Swedish, as *Pietà*, Albert Bonniers Förlag AB, Stockholm; 1989).

Klusacek, Allan (Editor) and Morrison, Ken (Editor). *A Leap in the Dark: AIDS, Art & Contemporary Cultures*. Véhicule Press; 1992.

Lipton, Stuart A. and Gendelman, Howard E. Dementia Associated with the Acquired Immunodeficiency Syndrome. N Engl J Med. 332:934-940, 1995.

Mentored Clinical Scientist Development Award (Parent K08) (Postdoctoral Individuals / New Independent Researchers): http://www.nhlbi.nih.gov/funding/ training/redbook/newrek08.htm

Nash, G. and Said, J. W. *Pathology of AIDS and HIV Infection*. Philadelphia, Saunders; 1992.

Price, Richard W. AIDS Dementia Complex. HIV InSite Knowledge Base Chapter. Accessed online 8/21/2004; http://hivinsite.ucsf.InSite?page= kb-04&doc=kb-04-01-03

Spoor, Rob. Art (and History) on Trial: Historic Murals of Rincon Center. http://www.sfcityguides.org/public_guidelines.html?article=197&submitted=TRUE&srch_text=&submitted2=&topic=The%20Arts

Star of India: http://www.sdmaritime.org/star-of-india/

Stein, Mark A. Panel Sounds Warning on AIDS in S.F.—Medicine: The mayor's task force says the city must double spending to fight the disease. 'We require disaster relief in order to cope,' it warns. Los Angeles Times-Thursday, January 11, 1990. Accessed online, 8/18/2004; http://www.aegis.com/news/lt/1990/LT900106.html

UIL: http://www.uiltexas.org/about

Vaucher, Andrea R. *Muses from Chaos and Ash: AIDS, Artists, And Art.* Grove Pr; 1993.

CPSIA information can be obtained at www.ICGtesting.com
Printed in the USA
LVOW08*0236170813

348153LV00002B/6/P